"D........ ....S!"

The crowd in the Temple yelled with an insane passion.

"Who is Satan?" Ngen cried.

They roared back. "The false God, Spider! Death to Spider! Death to Romanans! Jihad! Jihad! Jihad!"

It went on for so long Darwin, Susan, and Reesh became inured to Ngen's message of hatred and destruction. And finally it was over. The huge holo of Ngen flickered out. The side doors opened. Darwin kept his eyes on the first worshipers up. They were the ones who had been aware. Dazed now, they staggered toward the light while the others remained, heads down.

"Don't move," Darwin ordered on a hunch.

"What? What is it?" Susan's gaze flickered around the room.

Two techs were working a panel at either side of the door.

"Let's get out of here," Reesh was fidgeting.

"No!" Darwin tried to keep his voice low. "Move and we're all dead! I know now what this place is! It all makes sense. God, what a monster Ngen—"

Then the voice boomed out. "We know you are here. I see you hiding in the midst of the holy! Stand and be recognized—*Agents of Satan!*" The priest on the pulpit pointed right at Darwin Pike's little group.

Pandemonium broke loose. . .

THE WEB OF SPIDER

W. MICHAEL GEAR

DAW BOOKS, INC.
DONALD A. WOLLHEIM, PUBLISHER

1633 Broadway, New York, NY 10019

Copyright © 1989 by W. Michael Gear.

All Rights Reserved.

Cover art by Sanjulian.

DAW Book Collectors No. 786

First Printing, July 1989

1 2 3 4 5 6 7 8 9

PRINTED IN THE U.S.A.

TO UNCLE JOE GIESICK
FOR ALL THE STORIES TOLD
OF ELK AND DOGS AND GOLD
AND FOR WARMTH IN TIMES OF COLD

ACKNOWLEDGMENTS

This book would not be possible in this form were it not for my wife, Kathleen O'Neal Gear—a world-class author in her own right. Kathy's constant proofing, criticisms, and perceptive insights can't be underrated. Her expertise in comparative religion helped hone the ideas presented here. Katherine Cook and Katherine Perry, of Mission, Texas, read the text for technical errors. To Sheila Gilbert—my outstanding editor at DAW books—I offer a special appreciation. Her salient and thoughtful comments regarding the manuscript were top notch, invaluable, and penetrating—as usual.

Thank you all.

PROLOGUE

Varta Station: Lenin Sector.

The beginnings of Varta Station date to the late Soviet period just prior to the Confederate revolution. Originally established as a navigational outpost and exploration supply base, the station industries proliferated from ³He, alabandite, and carlsbergite recovery, to include zero g pharmaceuticals, graphite fibers, silicon carbide cables and foam steel, gallium arsenide microelectrics and ceramic industries, and later, as the station expanded, agriculture through bioengineering. Current census estimates place the population at 7.56 million.

In silence, he read, totally absorbed, heedless of the faint whispering of Varta Station that drifted down around him from the atmosphere ducting. Recessed lighting displayed pale, featureless walls; the half-million credits worth of holo projection devices they hid, dormant. Opulence—the kind few men could even dream of—surrounded the occupant: ignored.

A thin man, his skin reflected brown, honeyed tones in the muted light cast by the walls and ceiling. Body limp, he lay, floating, cuddling the monitor as his quick dark eyes scanned the flashing lines of text. The headset circlet—resting on his brow like a tiara—glinted with the slight movement of his head. Occasionally, a flicker of expression betrayed itself in the quiver of a thin lip, a narrowing of the heavy-lidded eyes.

"Fascinating," the man whispered to himself, raising a long narrow-boned hand to stroke at his firm jaw. Eyes glued to the monitor, he resettled himself, the fine Arcturian fabrics of his loose clothing billowing in the zero g of the antigrav. Tilting his head back, he stared down his flat nose, the hollows of his cheeks shadowed by the soft green light of the monitor. Unlike the flamboyant station folk, his hair had been cropped close to his skull. A high forehead rose above intelligent eyes. Delicate fingers rasped hollowly on the sparse wisps of beard gracing cheek and chin.

He didn't turn as the door slipped open with a subdued hiss. Illumination increased as the room sensors detected movement.

"Still reading?" the fat man called, breaking the reader's concentration as he stepped through.

The newcomer wheezed slightly as he walked, panting from the exertion. A thin film of perspiration shone from his bald head. Multiple chins dived into the expensive fabric at his throat. The fingers of his pudgy, death-white hands glittered, circled in lighted rings. A nervous trait, they wiggled as if possessed by a life of their own. He wore a violet and pink swirl of monosatin that flickered internally and billowed about his rotund body in a caress as he ambled forward.

"Fascinating, Pallas. Absolutely fascinating." The thin brown man straightened easily, stretching, rubbing his hands together in an almost sensual manner as he pried his attention from the monitor.

The fat man gestured with a pudgy hand, smiling uneasily as he padded across the luxurious svee moss carpeting and tapped a dispenser button with a sausagelike finger. The bejeweled light rings clicked softly off each other and splashed bands of orange and green across the wall console as he reached for a stemmed crystal glass that had filled with amber liquor.

"I don't understand it." Pallas turned, raising the bourbon to his fleshy nose to sniff, then sip. His lips smacked an approval which didn't reach the tight fat pads under his eyelids. A slight frown lined his blanched round face, a disturbed squint to his small blue eyes. "What's hidden in those records? History? The stuff of dusty old professors in sterile classrooms in University? Not your kind of—"

"The lessons of the past," the thin man corrected. He cocked his dark head, black eyes pinning Pallas. "Consider, my friend, over the past three hundred years, the Directorate has excised so much of our species' past. Cut it out of the collective memory. Thrown it away. Discarded. Lost."

He touched the monitor thoughtfully, tracing the square of light with a lean finger. "I, too, didn't understand how much they'd taken."

Pallas pursed his fat lips, rounded shoulders lifting to a shrug. "So a man in defeat goes to old books? I wouldn't . . . well, it's not like you. I thought you were a man of . . . of . . ."

"Yes?"

"Action, Ngen. A doer. Not a reader of musty old—"

"The secrets of the past almost handed me the Director-ate." Ngen Van Chow neatly flipped himself over the side of the antigrav, velvet clad feet sinking into the svee moss as he landed. He stood for a moment, lost in thought, before nervous energy got the best of him. He began pacing, hands knotting behind his back, a deep frown lining his high brow as he absently chewed his upper lip.

"And what secrets do you pry into?" Pallas indicated the monitor, ripples of light moving down his arm as he ges-tured. "In the dust of dead men's thoughts, what mysteries do you find, eh?"

"The most powerful of all," Ngen replied, an awed tone in his voice. "Religion."

Pallas started, hesitating a second before he snorted a laugh. "Religion? Do I hear you right? You call foolish superstitions a secret? How can mystical nonsense be a . . . a powerful—"

Ngen stopped cold, wheeling to face Pallas Mikros. "You weren't there! *You* didn't see! Those Romanans . . . bar-barians, with their future-seeing Prophets—"

"Oh, come! Surely you don't believe they actually know the future!" Pallas lifted a sweat-shiny lip in a sneer.

Ngen bit off his next remark, eyes narrowing as he stroked his chin. Calmly he answered, "No. But what I believe, and what the Sirians were led to believe, are two very dif-ferent things. They swallowed it—all of it. Took this Spider into their very hearts, drank it as if it were fine wine. This superstition—as you call it—ripped Sirius right out of my very fingers. These barbarians . . . and their Spider God . . . turned me into a laughing stock. *Me!* You understand?"

He swallowed hard, turning away, a vein throbbing vi-brantly along his temple. "Pallas, you didn't see the power of it. You don't know the potentials."

Pallas Mikros cocked his head skeptically, watching as Ngen walked to the opaque white wall and waved his arm. White vanished in an awesome display of stars shotgunned across the black veil of the universe.

"Out there," Ngen whispered passionately, "all of humanity lies trembling. Our reality has shifted, changed. Everything they believed inviolate . . . truth, if you will . . . has become so much sand shifting under their feet. Instability, uncertainty, anxiety over the future . . . fear. *Think,* Pallas! Think of fear! Think of how it grips the imagination, winds 'through a man's dreams. Eats away at his equilibrium. Each and every one of the trillions of humans out there. They're all afraid. Afraid because I beat the Patrol! *Beat them!* And the people know. The Romanans are loose. Warriors . . . men who kill other human beings in savage ways. The Directorate lies impotent. The big-headed freak caretakers of humanity can no longer even care for themselves. Nothing is predictable anymore. Chaos hovers over thoughts and dreams, creeping down the subconscious because reality changed.''

''But I don't see how silly superstition like religion can—''

''When men and governments fail, who do the ignorant trust?''

''I . . . well . . .''

''God, Pallas. God.''

Pallas shook his head slowly back and forth as Ngen Van Chow smiled wickedly.

''Go ahead and doubt. But I've seen. I intend on manipulating that blind trust. That's been my obsession. That power—and how to wield it, old friend. I've mapped the way to touch each of those fearing millions—to answer their need. And with it, I *will* control the Directorate.''

Pallas lifted a thin eyebrow, petulant lips pursed skeptically.

Ngen laughed and changed the subject. ''So, did you take my data? Run it through your illegal networks?''

Pallas filled his lungs and tossed off the last of the fine bourbon. ''I did. I found your planet. Place called Bazaar.''

''And?''

''Bazaar,'' Pallas continued, ''fits the criteria you supplied. You wanted religious fanatics . . . you got them. The original colonists—Bazaar was a Soviet Gulag planet—were Moslem extremists who'd been irritating the Kremlin. Subsequently, the Soviets deported radical Christians and intractably Orthodox Jews. Anyone who balked at domination by the World Soviet on religious grounds. Bazaar got the ones from the Middle East area of Earth. A Soviet joke. Drop them on that worthless ball of dust and let them murder each other. Six thousand years of hatred all bottled up on that planet." Mikros smiled. "You could have hardly done better yourself, Ngen."

"And they've never advanced?"

Pallas spread his hands. "Any time one group begins to show superiority, the other two overcome their dislike long enough to destroy the threat. The result is a planet in total stagnation, impervious to outside influences. For all intents and purposes, the Directorate washed its hands of Bazaar two centuries ago. The religious elders obstructed any effort at Directorate education to keep the voices from the Gi-net from diluting the Word of God. You see, the idea is that—"

Ngen raised a hand. "I think, Pallas, that I understand the concept better than you. Ignorant, you say?"

"Almost totally." Pallas' chins quivered as he nodded. "Only religious elders read—and then only the Holy Books."

Ngen smiled as he slapped his sides in approbation. "Bazaar, hmm? Indeed, Bazaar refers to a marketplace and the coin of exchange shall be the hearts of men. The final commodity traded? The Directorate!

"Ignorant fanatics, you say? They couldn't be better for my plans if they had rings in their noses!"

CHAPTER I

Arcturus: Directorate capital.

Established 2101 by the Victorious Confederacy under Brotherhood guidelines, the red star was chosen as the new capital since it lay outside any previously administered Soviet Sector. From its neutral location, the original Council Station expanded, industry and service industries following until the awesome station depleted the solar system. Now the largest population center in human space, the census records over ten billion people in orbiting stations in the Arcturian system.

Director? The call sifted through multitudes of thought. Skor Robinson shifted in the zero g of the Gi-net control room. The umbilical life support system that provided nourishment and eliminated wastes twisted behind him like some weird thick-bodied serpent. He blinked into the blue haze, seeking a boundary beyond visual perception. Endless blue echoed infinity. Delicate fingers of exhaustion stroked the frayed edges of his thoughts.

Tired. We're all so tired. Life support provided a flush of oxygen to stifle the yawn tickling the back of his throat. Skor turned a portion of his giant mind to the inquiry.

Yes, Assistant Director Roque?

I have just received a most disturbing communication from the head of Arcturian security. The disembodied voice formed in Skor's mind, transmitted through the labyrinth of Gi-net to be implanted in his brain via the huge headset helmet he wore. He'd never seen An Roque—or his other counterpart, Semri Navtov—in the flesh. He knew them only through their thoughts—as he had since his coddled childhood in the crèche.

A disturbing communication? Skor suffered a tingle of premonition. A shiver—so long absent from his atrophied body—elevated his pulse and attention. *Yes, go on.*

A comm technician, one Suki Yamasaki, has disappeared from Security Archives. She . . . well, there is no trace. With our resources, monitoring, and security, this is most irregular. I can't . . . excuse me for a moment.

Silence.

Skor's anxiety rose. So much had happened during the last years. A randomly intercepted radio signal had led to the discovery of a lost colony of humans—the barbarian Romanans. An expedition had been sent under Dr. Leeta Dobra. Despite Skor's orders, a Patrol battleship, the *Bullet*, had committed treason, failing to exterminate the wild Romanans when they proved dangerous. Who could have expected the discovery of men who saw the future? *Bullet*'s officers and crew had turned against him, against the civilization of the Directorate. Patrol had fired on Patrol. The Dobra broadcast—sent illegally into placid Directorate society—had germinated the long dormant curiosity of human beings about their fellows; humanity had begun to question. An entire planet, Sirius, had rebelled against Directorate authority during the ensuing chaos. Only an alliance with the Romanans had stopped the fiend, Ngen Van Chow, and quelled further rebellion. Barely. And at what price? Now

Romanans traveled Directorate space in starships armed and shielded with Van Chow's technology. Those same ships had savaged antique Patrol ships of the Line. In response, Skor Robinson and his fellow Directors stretched the Sirian-decimated Patrol between too many star systems and free stations. Exhausted, with too few resources, they strained to maintain some sort of equilibrium in a civilization that staggered, bursting at the seams. Human beings everywhere waited, wanted, seeking something. Even through the sterile binary of the Gi-net, anticipation pulsed—tangible.

Now, a year after the debacle on Sirius had been brought to a close, even insensitive An Roque hesitated, unable to complete a report without stopping to ameliorate the effects of some minor disaster on a planet light-years distant. Humanity simmered and steamed, waiting to erupt.

Roque? Skor asked again.

Excuse me, Director. A riot on Trypec Station. I was reporting on the disappearance of Suki Yamasaki. The woman monitored maintenance in Security Archives. Her absence three weeks ago caused her supervisor to file a notice. With our preoccupation elsewhere, I assumed it to be a simple missing persons report. The matter was not brought to my attention again until Yamasaki's replacement conducted a routine cleaning and molecular examination of the contents of the microfilters in Security Archives. She found human skin cells, body oil traces, and flakes abraded from human hair.

Skor interrupted, *In scanning the specs for limited access computer rooms, I note that monitors should have picked up increased CO_2 and H_2O from respiration.*

Correct, Roque agreed. *In this case, the monitors had been overridden from the outside. Tampering with Security systems requires immediate behavioral modification of the—*

What does this mean? Skor demanded. *Security lies within* your *expertise.*

A pause of several seconds added to Skor's unease. Monitoring Roque's vital signs, he noted elevated stress. Arterial pressure increased, blood glucose flooded, cellular metabolism elevated. Stress—once foreign to their systems—had become routine.

"We're falling apart," Skor whispered out loud. He blinked weary eyes and sighed—a most human reaction.

Pardon me, Roque accessed through the system. *I needed a moment to conduct some statistical analyses.*

"Liar," Skor whispered, blanking his thoughts from the system. "You're becoming human, Roque. Becoming as fallible as the rest of us. And now, of all times, we can't afford a single mistake. If only the Romanan Prophet, Chester Armijo Garcia, were here. If only he'd tell . . ."

We have identified some of the skin particles as those of Suki Yamasaki. The other individual remains unidentified. We continue to run analysis on the DNA. The problems are self-evident given a registered gene bank of some thirty-four trillion, five hundred billion—

I understand the numbers, Assistant Director. Skor considered for a moment, monitoring Roque's wildly fluctuating vital signs. *What data were stored in the section of Security Archives under Suki Yamasaki's responsibility?*

Roque's metabolism skyrocketed as he reported, *Brotherhood data. We've screened it already. You received the report immediately after the Sirian blasters had been observed—*

I'm aware of that report. Skor accessed the information, everything they had on Brotherhood technology. He correlated the data to the tags and file names available to Yamasaki. *Computer codes. No other Brotherhood technical information could have been accessed by Yamasaki.*

What could she do with ancient comm codes? How could she possibly compromise our *systems?*

Skor frowned. *In review of our comm security, no codes are translatable. The intruder only retrieved an historical oddity. A curio of no value. In running permutations, I find no probability that the codes accessed could affect any of our systems. It would be analogous to loading ancient internally combustible cartridges into a blaster.*

A correlation established itself in Skor's complex mind. "Call it intuition," he whispered, stifling his dread. Tripping Roque's net, he issued orders to Security Identification Division.

Instantaneously, Roque's fluctuations spiked. Skor quickly overrode the Assistant Director's control over his biological monitors and added a tranquilizing agent to his bloodstream, buffering norepinepherines, lowering system tone. The indicators stabilized. Now what had Roque found?

What else, Assistant Director? Skor waited; Roque's system continued to oscillate despite his adjustments.

I have just received . . . a second report. Security reports that in their detailed investigation of the room, they have discovered a device. I am reviewing the details now, Director.

Roque's system exploded. Skor caught him just short of shock, administering a complete treatment to the Assistant Director's bloodstream, slowing his heart. Deftly, he plucked control of Roque's net away before instability could be reflected into the myriad systems under the Assistant Director's control. Having no choice, Roque lapsed into unconsciousness under Robinson's close scrutiny.

"What has happened to us? How can this be? We weren't trained for this. How can we take this? Our minds and bodies have been tailored for logical action—not for passion. And the people call us freaks? We, who have given so much? We can't take this much longer. Damn it, we're not like ordinary men!"

Calm yourself. Skor blinked, the steady thump of his heart reassuring as he took a deep breath to settle his overwhelmed mind.

Assistant Director Semri Navtov, report. Skor waited, knowing Navtov had taken a long overdue rest period. Even Directors, with their genetically enlarged brains, needed sleep. In the meantime he studied the information Security sent from the violated Security Archives computer.

Director? Navtov queried.

Skor shunted records of the entire incident into Navtov's net, at the same time, monitoring his associate's response, anticipating the bodily crises. Navtov's irritation flowed into interest which grew into fear. Directors didn't handle fear—such a novel reaction—with any competence.

Control yourself, Assistant Director. You can see what actions I had to take with An Roque, Skor admonished. *I can't afford wild swings of emotion. I need rational evaluation and assessments to understand the implications of this intrusion and to determine and implement a policy to counter any instability generated by the release or utilization of this knowledge.*

Navtov's system stabilized with Robinson's biochemical assistance. *I cannot help but assume this is directed toward introducing further Brotherhood technology into the system. Is this Romanan intervention?*

I don't know. They have an interest in Brotherhood technology. You are aware that a Romanan ship has requested port rights at Frontier. Whether there is a Brotherhood connection is unknown. Skor paused, utilizing most of his mind for a moment to restructure the planting schedule for Range. *No, were Romanans interested in the Security Archives, they would have come and asked. They don't sneak—that approach requires a more sophisticated . . . A moment, Director. The report is coming in from ID.* Skor processed the data and stopped cold. Fright ate into his mind as the name of Yamasaki's accomplice appeared. He could feel his system slowing as Navtov undertook to limit his reaction. *Thank you, Assistant Director. How far have we fallen that our ability to govern hinges on monitoring each other— damping emotions we were never designed to handle?*

Times are perilous, Navtov returned. *You just learned something?*

Skor paused a moment to war with his physical self, controlling his quivering limbs. *Assistant Director, the device located in the computer room is not of Directorate manufacture. Rather, it is something beyond our technological abilities. Speculation is rampant as to the device's origin and nature. The singular salient observation at this time appears to be that the device is both a monitor and transmitter which works on subatomic principles which defy our physics.*

Can we ascertain the destination of the transmission? Navtov asked, accessing the data, seeking a way to interpret the incomprehensible design of the device.

Skor ran permutations through tech systems, analyzing theoretical capabilities of subatomic transductive iota-rega generation. *Negative.* Skor's body threatened to betray him again as he groped for stability. *If the engineering programs I have tapped are correct, that tiny device employs the whole of Arcturus as the transmitting dish. Given the size and power pack—*

Impossible! Our theoretical physics indicate no such device could utilize a torus the size of Arcturus. The energy to generate that—

It exists, Skor reminded. His heart fluttered as his incredible mind reeled at the implications. "Condemned to be free. You told me that once, Prophet. Your Spider's universe is a frightening place." He steeled himself as confirmation of his intuitive guess came through. Skor closed his eyes. "What if I can't take this? What if I'm not strong enough? If Roque or Navtov breaks?" He swallowed hard, plunging ahead.

We're being monitored, Navtov, monitored by someone

employing a technology we can't conceive of. Let us hope the intruder who invaded the Security Archives is not the individual who planted the transmitter. If so, we are in terrible danger.

Navtov asked, *And that intruder?*

Ngen Van Chow.

Navtov remained silent, only metabolic monitors wavering.

"Who?" Skor whispered to himself. "Who watches? And from where? And what do they know of Van Chow? Of the Romanans?" Only the needs of humanity begged for his attention. He shifted responsibility of Roque's net to Navtov. If only he could sleep for a couple of hours, dream for a while in some safer reality.

"Who watches?" he whispered absently as he shunted an emergency shipment of foam steel to Skylar Station to repair an accidental meteor strike.

"Who?"

Bazaar: Ambrose Sector.

Bazaar is one of the older Gulag planets dating to 2066 of the Soviet era. Barely habitable, the planet would have suffered the same fate as Mars had the planetary mass not supported a more lively CO_2 cycle. Still the resultant greenhouse effect and lack of H_2O in the system make Bazaar a windy, arid place. The few concentrations of standing water are brackish, heavy in salts, alkaloids, and gypsums—totally unfit to drink until distilled. Nevertheless, early terraforming did make the planet habitable. Currently, genetically adapted terrestrial plants support nomadic pastoral peoples. In Soviet eyes, the planet made a perfect prison for Middle East radicals in the twenty-first century.

Pallas Mikros pulled absently at one of the folds of his chin as he watched the holo. A group of haughty, wary men dressed in billowing desert robes walked down the Temple nave. The bodyguards, like nervous ferrets, fingered heavy blasters, waiting, ready. A priest scuttled forward, hands together in a blessing gesture of prayer. The newcomers slowed, disdain on their faces.

The Temple itself had originally been the high mosque. Now the pools had been filled in. Two-meter-thick, heavy columns brooded along each of the stone walls, squat under

the weight of the arching wide dome spanning above. Once
the sounding resonator of pleading prayers to Allah, the
dome had been painted in geometric designs, dulled now,
hidden by streaks of soot and obscured where plaster had
cracked and fallen. Even here, Bazaar's dust wafted along
the wear-polished buff of the stone floor.

"So, he's finally come to see for himself. Superb," Pallas
whispered under his breath. Tiara came to stand behind him,
resting her long slim hands on his shoulders. He could feel
her firm breasts pushed against his back as she watched.
Despite his fascination with the holo, Pallas couldn't help
reaching back to stroke the curve of her magnificent hips.

"What's this?" Tiara's sultry voice caressed his ear.

"Shaik Ahmed Hussein," Pallas explained. "One of the
hold-out Shi'a leaders. Lives back in the desert. He and his
tribe make their living looking for jewels. Occasionally doing a little mining while they starve their goats to death.
He's one of the powerful ones—a Mullah. According to rumor, Allah speaks to him from the desert wind. Mohammed
writes across the sky in lightning. Supposedly, only Ahmed
Hussein can read it."

Tiara laughed, a tinkling sound.

Pallas smiled. "Silly? Of course. But he's one of the
hawks. I'm told by our spies that he came here to destroy
us. To preach a crusade of Holy War—jihad they call it—to
wipe us out."

Always the temptress, Tiara wound herself around the
bulk of Pallas for a closer look. "You know, with a bath,
he might be most attractive."

Pallas cocked his head, studying the image in the holo
monitor. He could appreciate Tiara's attraction. An unhum-
bled vibrancy surrounded the man—something elementally
male, untamed. Ahmed Hussein, burnoose flowing around
him, walked like a tiger. His features, partially masked by
the kaffiyeh, reminded Pallas of a wolf, long, lean, keen.
The face was striking, well-formed, the thin brown nose
balanced by a neatly trimmed black beard. Those black eyes
gleamed with power, with fanaticism.

"And yet he's come to us," Pallas mused. The monitor
recorded the events. Hussein accepting the gift of water,
standing proudly before the Sanctuary.

He approached a priest and crossed his arms. In a commanding, disdainful voice, he uttered, "I have come to see
this . . . *miracle* of Deus." Behind him, his retinue smirked

and shifted on booted feet, humor reflected in their gleaming raptorian eyes.

The priest bowed and inclined his head to the Sanctuary.

"Now," Pallas whispered, clenching a chubby fist, rings sparkling as they clicked. "Now we've got him."

Tiara settled her chin on his shoulder, waves of silky black hair tumbling down over his arm. "Always the same?"

Pallas shrugged, watching Ahmed Hussein stroll arrogantly into the Sanctuary, bodyguards staring thoughtfully around as they fingered blasters and knives. The curtain dropped behind them. The small room measured no more than five meters across—barely enough to hold Hussein's party. Long buff-colored curtains of fine Arcturian fabric lined the walls. A single stone stele rose at the rear of the room. To this, Hussein turned his attention.

"Now we hit them with stun," Pallas whispered. At his word, Hussein and his entourage collapsed to the floor. Immediately, the curtains rose at the sides, techs swarming in. The top of the stele lifted, swinging out to present an ordinary medical psych unit. Techs positioned the Mullah, lowering the boxy psych to fit securely around the skull.

"And Hussein leaves touched by the hand of God?" Tiara traced the side of Pallas' face with cool slim fingers.

"Indeed. The Word of Deus is whispered in his ear . . . and burned into the very synapses of his brain." Pallas flicked the screen off, turning to enfold Tiara in thick arms, to press her against his massive belly and stare into her sea-green eyes. "He'll only remember the bliss of Deus, the light of exulted joy, and harmony with God. His men will remember him rising, carried into a shaft of golden light while they cowered, deafened by the voice of Deus. Technology to overlay ignorant superstition. Brilliant. I never thought it would work so well."

She shook her head, spilling her incredible hair over his hands, head tilted slightly, dropping thick eyelashes to tease him. "What are we doing here? Pallas, let's go back to Varta . . . back to someplace clean where we can talk to people who—"

"Hush." He smiled at her, dropping his hands to grope her firm buttocks. "For the moment, I'm fascinated by this. I think I'm beginning to see what Ngen has in mind. Already our power is growing, sweeping across this waste of a planet like one of their dust storms."

Tiara wet her rich lips with a pink tongue, narrowing her

eyes to slits. "And you trust Ngen? What's that room he's building in the bottom of the Temple? The one with all the beds, hmm? Going to run prostitution as a sideline to God?"

Pallas considered it for a moment. "Might not be a bad idea. But no, I don't know what Ngen intends down there. How he entertains himself is no concern of mine."

"But why *here?*" She broke away, turning to the thick one-way glass of the window. "Look out there! Where's the horizon, Pallas? All you can see is blowing dust, red-brown billowing clouds of it. And they call this a city? Blessed neutronium, those hovels they live in are made of dirt and rock. They throw their garbage in the streets for the dogs and goats to eat. They urinate on the walls, for God's sake! Step outside and the air's so dry your nose bleeds, your skin cracks and feels like the cursed sandstone underfoot."

As they watched, lightning flared across the dusty heavens, streaking the skies in white violet through the ionized dust.

"And the people?" Tiara shook her head. "Pallas, I've seen breeding cattle in the stations that were smarter than this . . . this rabble! Why here? What is this place? I want to go back."

He reached for her, turning her to face him, running his heavy fingers down her body, stroking, caressing. "We're here for the future, precious pet. On Varta Station, someday, I would have to run. No, now look at me. You know how it is. I'm a smuggler. I'm a vendor of stolen merchandise, an arms broker, a dealer in illegal human flesh for that matter, hmm?" He kissed her slender hand, running his thumb over the soft palm.

"For the moment, the Directorate is staggered. The Patrol is stunned. You have no idea how the Romanans and the Sirian rebellion unsettled things. But the Patrol will be back—and they won't be nice anymore. Me, I see a brilliance in Ngen Van Chow, an insightful genius everyone has discounted. They'll regret that one of—"

"He lost at Sirius," she reminded tartly. "Pallas, don't let him blind you. Don't let him suck you up into this mad scheme of his. What you can do on this shitpile of a planet and what you can do by psyching—"

He sighed heavily. "Sucker me? Me? Pallas Mikros?" He laughed, genuinely amused. "No, my dear. To sucker me takes more than Ngen. I haven't lived this long in the shadow of the Directorate by being stupid. Nor would I be alive today with my brain unfried had I been a fool. Ngen has showed me an opportunity. Where once I enjoyed a delightful apartment in Varta Station, I would become the owner, you hear, *owner* of a world.''

She lifted her chin. ''Grandiose. And you think Ngen will let you have all this? You want this world? This Bazaar? Full of blowing dust and sheep-screwing louts. They don't even bathe here, Pallas. They stink. They squat to leave feces in the street. *In the street!!*''

''Water's at a premium.''

''They don't read. They don't speak Standard. They kill each other in the back alleys—fighting over the same God because they were dumb enough to give it three different names!''

''And that's what we shall exploit,'' Pallas rubbed his hands together, causing the rings on his fingers to dance light over his face. ''And Hussein will be leaving within minutes to tell the desert tribes that Deus is the true God, come to save his children and bring them together.''

''It's psych,'' Tiara answered. ''Changes in behavior like that are a tip-off. Someone will spot that one of these days and your goat runners will come slit your throat.''

''Not on this planet, dear Tiara. We chose well. What do these dolts know of psych? When the Directorate couldn't control them, they left them alone. Their science—where it exists—is rudimentary. They can't conceive of psych. The only Directorate interest here is—''

''A prize of a planet.'' She crossed her arms before her. ''And what will you call yourself? Lord of Dust?''

''I won't stop here, Tiara, my gem. Perhaps I will call myself Lord of Earth? Master of New Maine? Ruler of Indus? This is only a beginning.''

She looked bored. ''I want to go home, Pallas. I want luxury again.''

He steepled his fingers before his chin. ''Tell me, pet. Do you love me?''

She watched him warily. ''In a fashion. You treat me very well. I like being a rich man's woman. I pay you back very well, too, Pallas.'' Her body undulated suggestively. ''In all the Directorate, you might find a handful of women with my talents to please a man.''

He cupped one of her full breasts and pulled her close. ''Money is power, Tiara. Stay with me. Endure this. Who knows, perhaps one day I will give you a planet, too.''

She leaned close, nibbling the lobe of his ear, whispering, "I can be patient . . . for a while."

CHAPTER II

Aboard *Bullet*, Geosynchronous (GEO) orbit above World: Beyond Far Side Sector.

First discovered as a result of a GCI-intercepted radio transmission on 9/1/2782, World is a colony of humans beyond Directorate control. Originally deportees from the World Soviet, ancestral Romanans seized their ship, the Nicholai Romanan, *and spaced to World. The exact records of their journey and subsequent survival are not available in Directorate files. Following discovery by the Directorate, World and its inhabitants have disrupted and dominated Directorate politics. As a result of the illegal Dobra Broadcast and the Sirian rebellion, Romanans have gained political power within Directorate space. The results of this cannot currently be understood.*

Admiral Damen Ree scratched the back of his head and settled himself in the command chair. The resilient padding automatically contoured itself to his body. The last of the arrivals slipped through the hatch, finding their places along the long table and checking in with comm through their headsets. Ree nodded to a private who poured out glasses of fine sherry, reaching to set them on the table as officers and staff settled in the contour chairs, bending over their personal comm units, occasionally gazing up at the overhead monitors.

Filling his lungs and ordering his thoughts, Damen Ree glanced around the war room. The single long table bustled with his officers and staff. Around them, monitors and screens studded the white walls. Overhead, comm units displayed ship's stats as officers read *Bullet*'s condition. Aides hurried back and forth amid the growing murmur as voices rose to compete over the hubbub.

The Admiral let his eyes search each of the faces. Major

Rita Sarsa—red hair pulled back in Romanan braids—stared thoughtfully into the distance. A frown traced lines in her forehead, lips pinched slightly. Subtly aware, she cocked her head, feeling his scrutiny. Her green eyes rested coolly on his, radiating intelligence and challenge. Her pale skin seemed to glow through the freckles. Success—and the stability Iron Eyes had brought to her tumultuous life—suited her, Ree decided, watching her finger the coups at her belt. She returned his wink.

Her husband, John Smith Iron Eyes, War Chief of the Romanans, sat to her right. A muscular man, he could dominate a room without saying a word. His black eyes, like hot magnets, seemed to draw a man's soul out where it could be weighed and evaluated. John had single-handedly killed one of the Romanan bears with only a knife—a fact Ree accepted with difficulty. Iron Eyes spoke earnestly to the man on his right.

Major Neal Iverson, blond, tall, the poster picture of a serviceman, listened attentively to Iron Eyes. Iverson, ever a model of efficiency, had become Ree's perfect second in command. Always unflappable, Neal seemed to be made of iron. Images of Sirius, of the calming influence of Neal's voice stuck in his thoughts. Would any of them have lived had it not been for Neal? How many times had he spotted boarders before the others, calling the crew to action as the Sirians attempted to storm the disabled *Bullet?* A warm glow built under Ree's heart.

Major Glick sat across the table, headset pulled down tight over his bony square head. Eyes closed, arms crossed on his chest, Ree could guarantee the Major was coordinating and overseeing more of the modifications to the ship. He'd remain that way until the meeting started.

Then there were the others. Captains Mishima and Max Wan Ki, Lieutenant Anthony, all of whom had stuck with *Bullet,* stuck with him through the insanity of the last few years.

The last figure in the room perplexed Ree—and most likely everyone else. Chester Armijo Garcia was a Romanan holy man. They called him Prophet, or Old One, even though he was a young man. Perhaps no more than thirty, his serene brown eyes made him seem ancient. Those eyes saw things a normal person couldn't.

Chester sat quietly, a slight figure of a man, his flat, round face lit by a perpetual smile, unassuming, gentle. Chester never hurried, never seemed flustered, and never—God forbid—demonstrated emotion beyond light amusement. Through it all, that damned serenity seemed to flow from the man and ooze out, infecting those around him. Even Iron Eyes refused to look the Prophet in the face. Partly it stemmed from cultural tradition; but sane people got nervous whenever a Prophet appeared in their midst. How could a man who could see your death—the many futures which might be—be treated with equanimity?

"I thought it would be a good idea to have a few minutes to ourselves before the conference," Ree began, sipping his sherry and gathering his thoughts.

Sarsa leaned on her elbows, eyes measuring. "Do you know what they want?"

Ree tightened his chin muscles. "No, but they might be after technical information. I know the Patrol wants those Fujiki Amplifiers for the blasters."

"We don't give them away," Iron Eyes didn't need to raise his voice.

"No, we don't," Ree agreed. "With the amplifiers, *Bullet* is invincible."

"We're still rebuilding, Admiral," Iverson added. "It's been almost a year since we got shot up off Sirius. It may take as much as six months to complete all the work we've started. Uh, well, there's a possibility we could still be working a year from now if Giorj doesn't get back. He's the only one who really understands his design concepts. Glick tries, but . . ." He ended with a shrug.

Major Glick nodded. "We need Giorj back."

Ree grunted in assent. Hell, he knew all that.

"Maybe they heard about the expedition to Frontier?" Rita suggested, leaning back. Her expression darkened, one hand shifting to the hilt of her fighting knife.

"It's a scientific expedition and Romanan ships have port rights on any Directorate world," Ree reminded. "If the Grand Master objected, he was told to contact us first. He gave his word. They take that sort of thing very seriously."

"You know what potentials lie in those old computers," Neal reminded. "There's a lot at stake here, Damen. What Giorj finds might be enough to destroy what little balance remains in the Directorate."

Ree nodded, half to himself. "If anyone but us understood that. At the same time, that gold mine has been open to the Directorate ever since they chased the Brotherhood out two hundred years ago.''

Sarsa motioned wearily. ''But they hadn't just suffered a revolution the likes of Sirius. The Patrol had never been defeated before. Everyone knows Ngen stumbled onto Brotherhood technology. Their damn blasters tore half the fleet to scrap off Sirius. Toby and the rest might be involved. And, by Spider, we can't forget Yaisha Mendez has no reason to love us.''

''Will the remains of the Patrol always try and cut each other's throats?'' Neal wondered.

Silence stretched as each individual settled in thought. All that is, but Chester; he simply sat and hummed to himself, seeing something far away. The only movement came from brown fingers interlacing themselves over his ragged leather shirt.

''Communication from Arcturus,'' the comm announced.

''I guess this is it,'' Ree tensed in his seat. ''Put it on.''

As expected, Director Skor Robinson's face formed next to that of his two associates, An Roque and Semri Navtov. Awesome, monstrous, the sight left Ree queasy. The Directors' skulls had to have been three feet across, looking like big, flesh-colored balloons with a face caricature pimpled on the bottom. Those giant brains interfaced directly with the Gi-net computers which directed human commerce and information. The latter remained the only resource they could truly control now that the Directorate was falling apart.

''Director,'' Ree greeted, bowing slightly. Something caught in the back of his mind. Some difference in their tight faces. Pale . . . yes, that was it. A harried look, features pinched, the telltale lines of too much stress, too little sleep, etched at the corners of their dwarfed eyes.

Chester smiled warmly and Skor's eyes froze as he picked out the Prophet's visage.

''You have come to test my free will, Prophet?'' Skor asked in his scratchy, little-used voice, ignoring the others in the room.

''A cusp is coming up,'' Chester said, expression bland. ''Mine?''

''We shall see, Director,'' Chester replied, voice soft.

Robinson turned his attention to Ree. ''The other Patrol Colonels would attend.''

Ree waved a hand showing he didn't much care one way or the other. People squirmed in chairs, straightening.

Indeed, Ree thought to himself, *something important has happened. What? Where is the trap this time? Why does he need the Colonels? Who's pushing the program? Mendez? The rest of the cutthroats? Careful, Damen, they'll gut you and leave you out to dry in a split second.*

The conference room seemed suddenly crowded as the holographic projections formed, backgrounds oddly interweaving. Before him, assembled into one conference, were the most powerful humans in the galaxy: the combined command of the Patrol and Directorate. Seeing a dark-skinned face, a warmth stirred under Ree's heart. He let himself wink at Maya ben Ahmad. She'd backed him in those last horrible moments off Sirius. Now a twinkle shone in the eye of the commander of *Victory*—a promise of what might have been had circumstances been different.

Maya's rich black skin contrasted with the white background. Her eyes gleamed, animated with spirit and intelligence. Her forehead rose smooth and firm above her graceful brows. Firm cheekbones supported the straight lines of her nose, flaring into broad nostrils that accented full lips. Only the hard lines of command etched the corners of her mouth. Her full, curly black hair hung in thick ringlets over broad shoulders.

Reluctantly, Ree tore his eyes away.

Toby Kuryaken of the *Miliken,* her silver-blonde ponytail over one shoulder had appeared to Maya's right. She and Yaisha Mendez of *Toreon* had been with him over Sirius when *Bullet* was shot up. They'd been ready to blow *Bullet* to junk on Skor's orders. Even now, a grim reluctance steeled their expressions as they stared across the room at Ree. Yaisha's hatred burned like a thing alive.

The other Patrol colonels were there, too. White-bearded, aging Ben Mason of the *Gregory;* delicate, Oriental Tabi Mikasu of *Kamikazi;* the cunning, young, beautiful black tigress, Amelia Ngurnguru of *Amazon;* the sleepy-eyed, balding, cadaverous Claude Devaulier of *Uhuru;* and pale-skinned, black-bearded Peter Petrushka of *Ganges.* The entire strength of the Patrol and Directorate—all that stood between a rotting civilization and who knew what?

For the moment, they waited, bodies stiff. Traitor. Pirate. Renegade. Their eyes branded. The silent set of hard lips shouted. Taut muscles condemned. They hated him—and all of *Bullet*'s remaining crew. Slowly, each unforgiving set of eyes measured the others present, stopping at Iron Eyes, Sarsa, and Chester. Executioners, they had judged.

A prickle of premonition shivered the hairs of Ree's neck. Sarsa's fists knotted, tendons standing out under freckled skin. Iron Eyes stared at the Patrol commanders, eyes slitted—a predator crouched to spring. Neal's jaw muscles bunched under smooth skin.

Ree shot a quick glance Chester's way. The Prophet met each person's eyes, nodding, unflappable, humming peacefully to himself. Even now he could see multiple realities—like looking up a tree and seeing the different futures as branches which spread before. Each branch was a choice—a cusp which would determine the future. Only Chester couldn't tell which of the multitude of leaves would be the final destination. It was said that Spider guarded free will jealously.

Chester noticed Ree and asked pleasantly, "Have you ever heard Vivaldi's *Four Seasons?* Such beautiful music. The tones and melodies will lift you, carry you like the wind. It stirs the soul. Most enjoyable."

"No," Ree said easily, aware the tension had cracked. He enjoyed the incredulous looks. The antagonistic colonels had lost their balance, attention now on what they considered to be a madman. Ree swallowed his laughter, used to Prophets and the things important to them.

Chester lapsed into his reverie, tapping fingers to the music in his head.

"Shall we come to order?" Maya suggested, leaning back and stuffing tobacco into her mouth. She worked the chew around until it was juicing and spit into an unseen spittoon.

"Yes," Skor's stiff voice agreed. He fixed his bright blue, piglike eyes on Damen Ree. "Admiral—if we should call you that—"

"It *was* your promotion."

"—we have a serious problem to discuss with you."

Ree nodded his willingness to hear. True, *Bullet* had declared its independence from the Directorate. He was, nevertheless, the admiral of the Romanan fleet, and though it was composed of but three ships, their armament was nothing to sneeze at.

Robinson continued, "It has become apparent in the last few months that the system of trade, government, and social stability which has preceded us for generations is becoming unmanageable.''

Ree interrupted, ''I believe the term Doctor Leeta Dobra would have used is 'Social Evolution,' Director.'' *And something else is horribly wrong, Skor. You don't yank this many Line officers away from duty for a chat on domestic policy.*

Skor studied him like a lion might a mouse. ''Call it what you will. Certain facts remain, however. One is that those of us assembled control 83.671 percent of the manipulatable power in human space. That power makes up only 0.000015 percent of the total resources of human civilization given manufacturing, production, human resources, and some three hundred seventy-two thousand, two hundred and six other correlated variables which can be statistically quantified for our purposes.

''The result is that changes in social behavior are slowly eroding this power base. In the event our combined power falls below 62.1467 percent, we predict a complete inability to direct the course of human development. The results would be chaos and no effort on our part could recover control.''

''A rather skewed power pyramid, don't you think?'' Ree asked, ignoring the hostility around them.

''But functional,'' Robinson reminded. ''Second, significant variables have evolved which we cannot satisfactorily quantify. In the past one year and five months, Romanan religion has spread rapidly through the Sirian systems and into University. The effect is considered negative and deleterious to the overall economic stability and social health of the species. Similarly, Spider cults have spontaneously appeared among disaffected young throughout Directorate holdings. Productivity of those following the teaching that God is Spider, has dropped off by three percent.''

Ree didn't look impressed. Other eyes had turned to Chester who, oblivious, was humming something from Brahms.

''At the same time, your Romanans are creating considerable sociocultural disruption. Parents find themselves unable to deal with discipline. Children ask questions which cause distress.'' Robinson tried to frown. The effort obviously hurt the atrophied muscles in his face. ''They have become obsessed with warrior cults which in turn have led to irregularities in social behavior.''

"Not our problem, Director."

"Now see here, Damen," Yaisha Mendez leaned forward in her command chair. Eyes glittering she raised a pointing finger. "You and your rabble spawned this, you can damn well—"

"Thank you, Colonel," Skor's voice, though soft, stopped her cold. "Emotion and condemnation will advance nothing here."

From her strangled look, Yaisha might have just swallowed a live frog.

Ree fought a smile. The Romanans had been sprung on an unsuspecting galaxy. The fact that Prophets could see the future played havoc with accepted physics. The established Judeo-Christian-Moslem traditions were crying, "Devil Worship," while the Hindus shrugged in "I-told-you-so" manners, and the Buddhists nodded happily and asked when the last blade of grass would achieve Nirvana.

Among the adolescents, knife feuds had become the vogue and civil authorities were recoiling under a wave of coup collecting, stolen aircars, and raids that emulated what the youngsters saw on the holos. The ripples from the contact with the lost colony of Romanans were still washing onto distant shores.

Ree studied Roque's mask of a face. The Assistant Director's eyes betrayed fear. *And it's not just a bunch of kids playing Romanan, either. No, something deeper is at work here. What do they know that's pushed Roque to the edge?*

Robinson cleared his throat. "Third, we do not understand another new religion." Ree looked up, suddenly curious. "It has formed on the planet Bazaar. While it is small, the messianic nature, coupled with the spread of Romanan religion, has us somewhat baffled. We are at a loss to explain it."

"Tell me about it," Ree said, and leaned forward, interest stirred. *Is this it? Another religion? Could* that *be scaring them all witless?*

"We know little," An Roque spoke. "A new messiah has proclaimed himself on Bazaar. This individual has allegedly performed miracles among the poor and is preaching a new galaxy for those who will follow in the footsteps of Mohammed, Jesus, and Abraham."

"Bazaar has a mixed population," Maya ben Ahmad muttered, frowning as she accessed her comm. "Christians,

Jews, and Moslems all slammed in there together with limited resources. Mostly, they fight each other—each faction trying to kill the others off.''

"They're no longer fighting." Ben Mason pulled at his long, white beard. "Bazaar's in our Sector. We never really worried about it. Little chance of them causing trouble because they were so poor. No space capabilities. But they've taken over the Directorate consulate—and the orbiting station. Now they're broadcasting. Wish we knew where they got the transductor. Anyhow, they've touched a raw nerve. Cults have mysteriously sprung up throughout the Sector. Whoever brought in the transductor is sending people to other planets. Looks pretty well organized.''

"You trace the manifests? Who authorized the travel?" Toby wanted to know.

"That's just it." Mason spread his hands, uneasy. "No trace. This isn't spontaneous.''

"That's about as far as you can get from Romanan space," Ree mused. "Coincidence?''

"Why now?" An Roque demanded, unaccustomed voice almost screeching as he tried to control the intonation.

John Smith Iron Eyes spoke then, granite-carved face holding their attention. "Your civilization has become a spiritual wasteland. Suddenly, with new information at hand, they are seeking to revitalize themselves. They see Romanans as exciting, having truth, Spider, and future sight. They clutch at our beliefs, hoping Spider will bring them salvation. They perceive their society as being sick and wish to install new values or revive dead ones from a long gone day.''

Mendez cursed under her breath, lips curled in a sneer. Petrushka bit back a caustic remark. Ree caught a glance of Sarsa's restraining hand as she calmed the bristling Iron Eyes. The War Chief glared at Mendez as he stiffened and gripped the handle of his fighting knife.

Robinson's attention fastened on Iron Eyes. "Then Romanans are behind this cult on Bazaar?" At Iron Eyes' curt negation, he demanded, "Then how do you know so much of Directorate psychology, barbarian?''

The muscles rippled along Iron Eyes' jaw, but the War Chief's words came easily, "Study the anthropology texts. You might think the principles limited to ancient tribes and long gone cultures, but I suggest you look to your own. Any People would wish to make themselves strong again. I predict nativistic movements among most of the ethnic planets. There will be revitalization efforts among others. Your People are seeking, Director. They feel desperately lost, cast loose from what always anchored them. They will grasp at anything now that their reality is changing.''

"Why?" Yaisha demanded angrily. "Civilization has changed before.''

Iron Eyes gave her a measuring appraisal. He smiled wickedly, watching her reaction. "Never before has a civilization realized it was made of sheep—and suddenly desired to become wolves again. In the past, such a situation never had time to develop because the wolves came in from the outside . . . and destroyed them.''

"You insolent, ignorant—''

"I am only honest," Iron Eyes corrected. "Or have you forgotten Sirius where you hung in the sky—powerless.''

Iron Eyes waited, arms crossed, implacable while Yaisha's red face blanched.

"Easy," Mikasu muttered through clamped lips. "We'll get ours. One day.''

"One day," Yaisha repeated despite gritted teeth, challenging Iron Eyes.

"But that is illogical!" Semri Navtov snapped, heedless of the singing tension. "Why would intelligent men give up order for chaos and uncertainty? I can perceive no rational being accepting irrationality to guide his life. To do so is . . . is . . . *irrational!*''

"Religion, any religion, is idle superstition," Robinson agreed. "A method of self-delusion. A means of placating forces their ignorance can't integrate into a reality of balanced physical laws or concepts. A wild appeal to some parental mandala which will assume the role called God. A mere childish fantasy—''

Chester looked up, calm eyes on Skor Robinson. "You do not understand the nature of true religion, Director. Nor do you understand Spider—the being you call God.''

Attention shifted again. Robinson's lips quivered and a red tinge crept over his pinched features. He'd faced the Prophet before and, despite his incredible brain, had always been befuddled.

"When the Directorate began to erode," Ree changed the subject, "the people had their surrogate of psych control taken away. The existence of the Romanans—who practiced what they preached—along with the Sirian rebellion, cracked and unhinged an entire pan-galactic reality.''

Chester smiled. ''Exactly. We are seeing the very beginnings of a significant social upheaval. The way of Spider is loosed. What will He catch in His web?''

''Controlled ignorance will make it worse,'' Rita added bitterly. ''Bazaar is an excellent example.''

''Ignorance how?'' Maya propped herself on an elbow, head cocked.

''Thanks to all those years that Skor and his friends have been controlling access to education, censoring the news, shipping food to reinforce proper behavior, and most of all, controlling society by enforcing psych adjustments on deviants, they've succeeded in developing a population of human sheep.

''If you look back in history, any government could control its people so long as they didn't have the ability to think! The agent of control was called heresy—be it political, religious or, in our case, economic. The lesson? A people who can't question or examine their beliefs never have more than faith. When that faith is shattered, they have no ability to restructure their lives. They grasp desperately for anything which promises relief.''

''And the Patrol suffered a severe setback at Sirius. Our mystique is broken,'' Amelia Ngurnguru interjected softly. ''The Directorate is no longer thought of as invincible.'' She raised her eyes and looked around the room, twining dark fingers in her kinky black hair. ''The outward reactions were minimal. What are the deep-seated realities? Can our psychologists tell us?''

''Rotten hell, you aren't agreeing with *her?*'' Yaisha sputtered. ''She's a . . . a barbarous traitor!''

''Yaisha,'' Maya warned. ''Watch it.''

''I doubt your psych people can tell you much,'' Rita muttered, throwing a quick, murderous glance at Mendez. ''Today, psychology consists of adjustment procedures. I doubt if we even have anyone who knows the theory well enough to monitor the population and predict reactions. It's been done on an individual level for too long.

''The sociologists have slowly but surely been weeded out. After all, the Directorate couldn't entertain people who examined their society. Anthropology was allowed to survive because the study of extinct primitives did not threaten the Directorate.''

"Must they always blame us?" Navtov asked under his breath. Mendez growled something about "pirate scum."

Maya ben Ahmad snorted, glaring at Mendez, who glared back. A crafty smile curled Maya's lips. "So, our perfect system has harvested a tornado in the end, hey?"

"So it would seem," Ree agreed.

"It is illogical. We will control communications better," Robinson decided. "With proper reinforcement, the population will behave. I remember a suggestion of dismantling transduction receivers. Perhaps—"

"And cripple commerce?" Navtov blinked curiously, obviously feeding information into Skor's headset. "Consider the permutations, Director."

Skor's mouth worked absently and he sighed. "I . . . yes, your point is well taken."

Worried glances flickered back and forth among the Patrol commanders.

Ree was shaking his head. "It's out of control, Director. How many illegal transduction messages have you received over the last twenty-four hours?"

Robinson hardly even hesitated as he tapped the Gi-net system. "Four hundred and seventy thousand."

"You're too late." Ree shrugged. "They found an entire universe out there to talk to."

"How were we to know?" An Roque cried. "How were we to understand the meaning of illegal transmissions? In a properly functioning society, such actions are totally illogical! Humans are not driven by random impulses; they must follow the track of reason. Provided with rational solutions, they will take that course of action."

"As they did during the Sirian situation?" Maya countered. "Remember the reaction you got when you broadcast gigabits of data concerning Van Chow's revolution? You alienated half the galaxy."

Navtov's mouth worked soundlessly as he groped to verbalize his thoughts.

"And on Bazaar," Rita murmured, "a seed has fallen on fertile fields."

"Plowed, fertilized, and furrowed by Directorate policies," Neal added.

Maya snorted and spit a brown streak into her spittoon. "After the Sirius debacle, I wonder what this religion will bring. You say they preach Holy War, Ben?"

He nodded, still pulling his beard as he studied Rita Sarsa

with open dislike. "According to the broadcasts we've received, they claim the Directors are Satanic figures, subverting the will of God and the souls of men. Their messiah claims to be a sliver of fire sent by God to unify Judaism, Christianity, and Islam into a sword of truth and salvation. He's very clever at weaving the Tanach, Bible, and Koran into one self-reinforcing document."

"And support is growing?" Ree asked.

Mason nodded again. It hurt him to talk to Ree. "On Bazaar, it's beginning to look like you're unified . . . or you're dead. They've established a theocracy."

"And this messiah? You know who he is?"

"We're working on that. All communication regarding the messiah is monitored. We can't get information from the planet. Probably some desert nomad in need of psych."

Skor turned his massive head, blue eyes boring into Ree's. "So you see, revolution again. That's why I called this meeting. We will take steps to control it. Give me your word in the meantime that your Romanans will not contribute to social disturbance."

"We won't." Ree turned to Chester. "Well, old friend, what do you see? Should we be concerned or not?"

Chester smiled easily and cocked his head. "There are many cusps yet to come, Damen. Spider watches. Depending on the cusps, humanity may be snuffed dead. As you might say, a botched experiment. Another way, humanity may embrace a golden age the likes of which it's never imagined. The choices remain. What would you do, Damen?"

Tabi Mikasu snickered. Iron Eyes tensed, thick muscles knotting beneath his war shirt. Rita's restraining hand lay openly on his shoulder now.

Mendez shook her head, raising her eyes. "Quaint shamanism. What's next, rattling bones? Looking in chicken guts."

"Enough," Skor ordered, bending his bulbous head to observe the colonel. Mendez's jaw tightened, but she lowered her eyes.

Ree frowned, propping his chin in a callused plam. *I'm still missing some bit of information they're not telling. The Directors are plainly frightened. The Patrol command is jumpy. Someone isn't telling everything.*

"Can you see anything, Old One?" Iron Eyes asked. "How should we be thinking?"

Chester parted his hands, face beaming. "On this hand,"

he opened his fingers, "there are worlds burned to cinders in the name of Deus, the Father God. Stations and planets are burned in the name of Spider. If other choices are made," he flexed his other hand, "there are happy worlds, children who laugh and giggle, hopes, and spirit quests. And, of course," he wove his fingers together, "there are mixtures of the two paths. As always, the cusps will decide . . . and he who exercises prudence and intelligence can alleviate the suffering."

Chester smiled. "Those who would war for Deus understand nothing of Spider. They are souls of ignorance and must bear great pain."

"So what do we do?" Colonel Petrushka demanded, slamming a fist on the table. "Listen to this . . . this savage dreamer? Do the Directors make policy based on the ravings of a barbarian charlatan?"

"Enough, Colonel," Skor ordered.

Chester smiled into Petrushka's hostile, demanding face and shrugged. "What is your free will, Colonel? Spider—or God, if you will—grants you the power to choose. I will not take that choice from you. Who am I to alter the way of Spider?" He ended with a respectful nod and Petrushka turned blue with rage. Unaffected, Chester closed his eyes, humming to himself again.

"Worlds burned off?" Tabi Mikasu cried incredulously. "Delusions of a dreamer? What could this ignorant Romanan know of—"

"He sees the future," Ree insisted.

Sidelong glances illustrated Patrol feelings.

Skor exhaled loudly through his nose. "He sees the future. You may disbelieve if you wish. Nevertheless, events in the past have proved the Romanans' value in times of trial. We may all need to work together."

Roque's face flushed, and Skor hesitated, undoubtedly under a mental barrage by the Assistant Director. Icy expressions graced Patrol faces, unspoken skepticism shaking their resolve.

Be careful, Skor. For the first time, they're afraid you've lost your grip. Normal people fear your kind anyway. Don't let them think you're over the edge. If the Patrol deserts you, you're dead in the water. All human space will unwind then.

Ree cleared his throat to redirect their thoughts. "Ladies and gentlemen, as the Directors reminded us, we control considerable power.'' He paused, thinking rapidly. ''Let's keep in mind that what we fight isn't a traditional enemy. We can't employ battle tactics or firepower to any advantage against this type of foe.''

Damen,'' Colonel Yaisha Mendez responded scornfully. ''We have the old Brotherhood blasters we obtained on Sirius. What could possibly stand before us?''

''The human mind, Colonel.'' Ree's eyes hardened. ''The same thing that scotched me when I went to the Romanan planet. *Bullet* was defeated by a group of fanatical tribesmen who believed in a God they called Spider—and men like Chester who saw a different reality. *Bullet* had no weapon to defend against that.''

Hostile and disbelieving eyes stared back. Only Maya ben Ahmad nodded. Toby fingered her chin, not liking it, but agreeing nevertheless. Veterans of Sirius, they'd seen what the Romanans did there.

''Your people are a plague, Damen,'' Yaisha insisted.

''I think,'' An Roque said in his weak voice, ''that this time, the Directorate can handle its problems without Romanan involvement.''

Again, with the exception of Maya, heads nodded in agreement. One by one, the holos faded.

Skor Robinson, mouth pursed, eyes glittering; Toby Kuryaken, hesitant, reserved; and Maya ben Ahmad, concerned, remained.

''Damen,'' Maya began, steely eyes on Ree. ''Toby and I have talked about it; we think we're in for a real tough time. Would you be willing to accept an alliance with us? Would your Romanans accept that?''

''I suppose you want a Prophet, too?''

''Don't mock us, Ree.'' Toby's thin cheeks puffed out. ''I still owe you one for Sirius. I wasn't there. Had I been, my guns would have taken you apart. Yaisha Mendez and her people are still fuming. They hate you more than they fear the future. Me, I'm willing to cut my losses where I can. Understand?''

Ree nodded, gaze shifting to where Skor Robinson waited, evidently unconcerned that his Patrol dickered with rebels.

''As to your Prophet, Damen, not yet.'' Maya shook her head. ''But we'd like port rights at World. I think we may need them.''

''I would speak for port rights for Patrol,'' Iron Eyes said. ''While the Old One will not speak to influence our decisions, I believe there's wisdom in mending old fences. I've seen Sirius. I know how the People of the Directorate can be led. Sheep? Not a bad analogy, but I see them more as domestic dogs. And dogs, I would point out, can bite back. But Colonel, I remind you of one thing. When you come to us, do not mock our Prophets . . . or our beliefs. We will respect you and your people. Grant us equal consideration.''

Toby stroked her chin, eyes narrowed. "I . . . very well, War Chief. We'll meet that demand . . . if it comes to that."

"Planets burned off," Neal Iverson whispered, shaking his head. He looked up in disbelief. "That much death and destruction in the name of God?"

"There are many cusps yet to be decided," Chester said cryptically. "Free will is the legacy of existence."

"Unlike my counterparts, I am worried, Prophet." Skor lifted his underdeveloped chin. "I cannot like my Patrol forging new political alliances, but I fear what may be. I fear your visions. These are dangerous times."

"What are you hiding, Skor?" Ree shifted to one side, chewing his lip thoughtfully. "There's more to this."

Skor blinked, a nervous tic in his cheek. "Nothing which needs to concern you. You have your responsibilities, I have mine. I would only keep my options open." Blue eyes turned to Chester. "You have taught me well, Prophet. See what I have learned."

"Damn it, be careful, Director. You're not used to the cutthroat style of Patrol politics. You shook them just now. Rattled their faith in your abilities to lead. Among Patrol Colonels, that could be political dynamite."

"I am touched at your concern, Admiral."

"Yeah, so am I. We may not be friends, Director, but we're not necessarily enemies either."

"I will remember your words." The holo flickered out.

For a long moment silence filled the room. Colonel Kuryaken pulled at the lobe of her ear, thoughtful eyes on Ree. Maya spit loudly, the spittoon echoing metallically. Stone-faced officers sat around the table.

"Damn! What's he hiding?" Ree demanded. "We need an expert on religion. But who?"

CHAPTER III

Frontier: Sol Sector.

Frontier was one of the original Soviet Gulag worlds. The first colonies of the Brotherhood were landed in 2078 during the first exiles. The Gulag program provided a great many advantages to the World Soviet. Because of the deportations, economic colonies could be developed, worlds and nebulae exploited, and exotic goods could be shoveled into the constantly straining Soviet economy. At the same time, deviants and troublemakers could be exported, their energies dedicated to taming alien environments rather than sabotaging the benefits of the world worker's paradise through sedition and violence.

The knock brought him wide awake from a half-sleep. With a warrior's reaction, Friday Garcia Yellow Legs rolled off the cot, balanced on the balls of his feet, his wicked fighting knife reassuring in his grip.

"Yes?"

The latch on the ancient steelwood door lifted and a shaft of light spilled onto the stone floor as Giorj Hambrei leaned in. "Friday? You awake?"

"Yep." Friday padded across the room, touching the switch that turned on the lights. He blinked owlishly at Giorj. "I feel like I'm buried in here. Like it's a cave, you know. Can't breathe. The air's all stuffy. Not like a war trail ought to be. Not like being in a ship either. The place creaks like it's alive or something. Spooky."

Giorj lifted a bony shoulder. "I think I've got it. Just came to me in a dream. The sequence, I mean. I know how to break in."

Tall and thin, Giorj Hambrei dressed in the spare, gray, form-fitting clothing normal for working professionals. A belt clung to his gaunt waist despite the burden of pocket comms, diagnostic scanners, and assorted tools. A gray man, colorless, the sight of him always sent a chill up Friday's spine. His face appeared oddly expressionless, totally

38

uninhabited by emotion. His complexion was albino white, his eyes possessed a washed-out look, almost dead. Like a corpse, skin hung lifelessly following the angles of bone beneath. Sparse mousy hair didn't hide the outline of his skull. Narrow colorless lips added to the effect, belying the brilliance of the brightest engineer in all of human space.

Friday yawned, stretching, smacking wide lips as he worked to swallow the bitter taste sleep left in his mouth. He took a quick look at the reflective glass and grimaced, pulling his gnomish face into a wrinkled snarl. Next to the engineer, the comparison could be thought ludicrous. Friday couldn't have been more Giorj's opposite.

Short, and squat, the top of Friday's head barely came to the bottom of a normal man's breastbone. What he lacked in height, he made up for in muscle. Unlike the engineer's translucent skin, Friday had been burned practically black by the fierce rays of World's sun. Over his broad muscle-packed shoulders, he wore tanned hide clothing, the stylistic design of a spider on the chest. Gleaming black braids fell to either side of his face, the legacy of his ancient Amerindian ancestors. A belt of human hair—coups—snugged around his waist. The flat features of his face had been spun capriciously around broad cheekbones, a generous mouth, strong jaw, and a nose broken too many times: a face made for laughter. Now, only a ghost of the old smile remained, its phantom image modified by the creased lines of sorrow.

And Giorj thought he had the answer? A dash of hope leaped inside Friday's chest.

"Great! Let's get in, pipe the stuff to the ship upstairs, and get the hell off this ball of rock!" Friday slipped the heavy fighting knife into his belt and checked his blaster's charge. Giorj moved aside as he passed the heavy door into the dormitory hall.

They walked in silence for a moment before Giorj drew a deep breath and asked, "Why did you come?"

Friday lifted a slab of shoulder, looking over and up at the engineer. "Major Sarsa and the War Chief asked. I guess the idea was Admiral Ree's first." He shrugged it off, hedging. "They needed me to snow the Grand Master."

"And Susan didn't have anything to do with it?"

Friday blinked, heart jerking in his breast. "I . . . it was just duty and . . . You don't buy that, huh? Okay. Yeah. She had everything to do with it."

How could I say that? What's wrong with me? Just be-

cause Susan's forgotten I'm alive doesn't mean I've gotta spill my guts to just anyone. And why him? WHY?

Giorj nodded soberly, thin neck pulsing as he swallowed. "You know, it's not you. What Ngen did to her . . ."

"I'll kill him someday," Friday added after a long pause to get his screaming mind under control. "Can't believe he's vanished without a trace. Destroyed Sirius, killed all those people, did to Susan what . . . what he did, and we can't find him." Friday smacked a gnarled fist into a callused palm.

"Listen," Giorj began. "About Susan and me. I . . . well, there was an accident when I was younger. The radiation . . ."

Friday looked up at the taller man, oddly touched. A confession for a confession? "I know," he supplied softly. "I'm not without my sources. Major Sarsa, well, she takes care of me."

Giorj's lips twitched. "Susan doesn't fear me, you see. I can't . . . can't . . ."

"You're safe," Friday finished, the deep-soul agony welling.

As if he felt the pain, Giorj turned, concern apparent. "Does it bother you? To be my bodyguard, I mean. To be responsible for the man who lives with the woman you love?"

Friday smiled faintly, starting down the steps that led to the comm center far below. "I'm Spider's tool, Engineer. Just like you. I'm here because I made a decision a long time ago on a mountain on World. You know about our visions . . . the praying we do, the fasting to bring ourselves closer to God. Spider's spirit-helper came as a dot of light and asked me what I wanted most. I told him I wanted to spread the word of Spider through the stars."

Friday sighed before adding, "At the time, the vision asked if I would sacrifice what I loved best. Thinking it meant my life, I said yes."

"You've spread the word, Friday," Giorj reminded. "Your face, and the speech you made on Sirius, are known all over the galaxy, you know. Of all the Romanans, maybe only the War Chief John Smith Iron Eyes is known more than you."

"So I spread the word of Spider." Friday raised his war-hardened hands in futility. "And it cost me Susan. I have fulfilled my destiny, Giorj. Spider works in strange ways. I

. . . I don't know. I feel useless, tired, you know? I can't laugh like I did before Sirius . . . before Susan . . .''

"But you still serve. The Galactic Grand Master wouldn't have let us come despite Directorate orders if you hadn't been here to tell him about Spider and the Prophets. But that's immaterial. Why, Friday? Why believe in a God who treats you like this?"

"Because we're not here to be happy. A man who lives in constant bliss ceases to question. He stagnates. We're here to learn, to fill our souls until Spider calls us back. The core of my body," he jammed a stubby thumb into his chest, "isn't Friday Garcia Yellow Legs. It's a bit of Spider called the soul. The body's only a husk, disposable. What I have learned, that's the eternal part. The part I send back to Spider."

"And your love for Susan?"

Friday winced, frustration and grief rushing up from deep inside. Her voice came drifting up from his memory. *"Friday, it's not you. Understand? It's me . . . my fault. I can't . . . can't be with you. After Sirius, after what happened, I . . . I just . . . just . . . Look, go away. Live your life and forget me. Pretend I don't even exist. What we had is gone. Forever. Dead and buried back on Sirius with . . . with Hans. Now, leave me alone. I'm no good for you, Friday. Go away. Go . . . away."*

And he'd left.

He'd never forget the fear-glazed look she'd given him. Any time she'd even seen him, her body had tensed, muscles locked. The worst had been the hell in her eyes: loathing and hurt, mixed—an inner mayhem let loose. The very sight of him seemed to shred any peace she might have had. Ngen had done that in his chamber of horrors. He'd broken her—destroyed the only woman Friday had ever loved.

The image of a bloodstained bed, of a retractable psych machine, prodded Friday's painful memories. He shivered, feeling Susan's horror-ridden eyes staring at him out of the darkness. How had Ngen. . . .

No, no more. Don't torture yourself over it.

Deftly, he changed the subject, knowing Hambrei's one exploitable weakness. "So, you broke the comm lock, huh? Funny ain't it? I can't even fix a broken aircar I stole from Sirius. Okay, tell me, how do you break into a Brotherhood computer?"

Friday Garcia Yellow Legs tried to keep his attention on

Giorj's droning voice. The long dimly-lit stairway leveled out into a murky shadowed hallway. Like a cave, the gray stone walls dimpled with shadows, dark and somber. The air came damp to the nostrils, pungent with dust, musty, reeking of age and a more prosperous era long vanished. The place hadn't always been like this. Only one out of every five of the old Brotherhood light panels had been left in place—the others pirated in past eons to who knows where.

The smoothly polished floor under his boots undulated slightly, pitted, grooved, and worn with time. Friday realized with a start that the stones were individually fitted. He stopped and bent down, fingering the aged granite.

"What is it?"

"The floor," Friday looked up, amazed. "It's all stone!"

"Oh, for heaven's sake!" Giorj slapped a hand against his thigh in frustration and shook his head. "Of course it's stone. People have been building with stone for years. In limited economies, it's cheap. Like wood and dirt. What's the big deal?"

"Think of the age," Friday whispered, ignoring his pale companion. "They say this place is six hundred years old." Friday bit his lip as he stood. "They were fitting these stones when my ancestors were landing on World."

Frontier had been one of the first Gulag planets of the old World Soviet. The Brotherhood had been dumped here, left to apply their philosophy to taming a world, fighting the bull-bears and the terrible climate instead of corrupting more docile citizens of the Soviet into reflecting on Soviet policy.

Giorj's voice was pinched. "Now, if you don't mind, let's deal with that relic of a computer, get the information, and get out of here! You can play archaeologist some other time."

The fish eyes studied Friday, unyielding, expressionless.

"Don't engineers get brilliant ideas in the middle of the day?" Friday grumbled as he yawned and trotted to catch up.

"I couldn't sleep either," Giorj admitted, long legs eating the distance.

"At least we can get it over with. Get back to World. I keep dreaming of home. I don't know, maybe I'll pack up a couple of horses, take a long trip. Go see that other ocean Iron Eyes went to that time. Live in the mountains, maybe."

"Get eaten by a bear, maybe," Giorj's spectral voice added.

"I don't fit any more," Friday mumbled, eyes searching the shadows left by pillars of rock. "Maybe being eaten by a bear wouldn't be half bad. I hear it's quick. That huge sucker grabs you and you're up in the air and plopped in that acidy mouth. No muss, no fuss. A week later, you're just a pile of brown smelly stuff in the bayonet grass."

"Fix your aircar," Giorj suggested. "You'd like machinery if you ever began to understand it. Clean. Logical. Everything elegant in the way it works in harmony with other parts."

"Uh-huh. I fix it, it breaks. Harmony? That aircar's more like black magic—a curse. I have nightmares about it. Remember the time it left me a week's walk from the Settlements? Me? Keep it running? That thing's a nightmare when I see it awake! To finally have it floating off the ground! It was pure bliss." Friday twisted his lips into a sneer of disgust. "Damn thing'll never fly, and I know it. Thank God for horses!"

Friday had insisted on fixing the broken vehicle himself. It didn't matter that Giorj was the finest engineer within light-years. It had become a matter of honor. Friday had come a long way for a man who, only two years ago, won fame as the most outstanding horse thief in his Spider tribe.

"And I might be able to break the entire system wide open!" Giorj breathed. "Think. The wealth of the Brotherhood at my fingertips!"

"Praise the name of Spider," Friday muttered. "Patch it through and tell Susan to have the shuttle on the way. This place gives me the jitters. I'd rather face a Romanan bear with a dinky little knife any day." He looked around from under lowered brows. "I bet there's ghosts in these halls."

"Ghosts?" Giorj chuckled. "If there are, they can't intrude into the physical world. The dynamics of matter preclude . . ."

Friday let it fade into a drone. He didn't understand the words Giorj used anyway.

Friday kept his trot, matching the long, vibrant stride of the engineer. If Giorj had broken the safeguards, they could set up a transfer and tap the banks right into the ship Susan held in orbit overhead. Day after day of frustration had passed as Giorj tried one trick after another to access the system. Through it all the Grand Master who guarded the place calmly assured them the secrets of the ancient Brotherhood were well guarded, but they could try. Others had, to no avail.

"They left it," the old man cackled, voice loud in Friday's memory. "Left it here until humans came to their senses again! A wealth, that's what. A wealth of knowledge. Ha! And this was the *old* comm. The sentient ones—computers that thought for themselves—they took with them. Now, there, boy, was a treasure trove! The data here? Humph! The dregs. Dregs, I tell you, but better than anything the Directorate and the pumpkin heads have!

"Oh, you go right ahead, try to access that data. Others have—and failed. Humankind's not ready for this kind of knowledge yet! No one smart enough to get in, huh? But one day, yes, one day, someone sharp will break in. By the Divine Architect of the Universe, I swear, on that day they'll see the mistake they made when they ran the Brotherhood out of human space. Mark my words, boy! Mark them!"

Friday turned his attention to stones again. Old, so incredibly old. And the Brotherhood? What sort of mysteries had been theirs that even Giorj, brilliant as he was could be baffled by a comm unit the Brotherhood considered obsolete and left behind? What sort of people had they been to wield such power only to have—

He almost pulled Giorj's arm out of its socket as he jerked the engineer back. He managed to clamp a strong brown hand over Giorj's mouth as he motioned for silence. Friday dropped to his hands and knees and sniffed at the spots on the stone.

Giorj knelt beside him. "What?" he whispered.

"Blood." Friday barely mouthed the word as he pulled his blaster. The dark hallway had been eerie to start with; now the blackness ebbed down around them, sinister. Friday fought a cold shiver as he wondered if the haunted places on Earth would affect him this way.

"The guard?" Giorj suggested as Friday nodded and trailed the blood into a darkened niche off to one side. The Romanan-made boots could barely be seen in the shadowy light. Friday bent down and ran competent fingers over the body.

"Not more than an hour at most. He was killed with a laser. Cut the spinal chord. Nice job, real clean." His senses sharpened in the old combat wariness. Ears probing for sound, Friday carefully searched the shadows, aware for the first time of Giorj's peculiar odor.

"It's Peter Reesh. Computer room guard." Friday stood carefully, bending to peer down the gloomy hallway.

"The computer room?" Giorj whispered. "Who? Who could . . ."

"They want what we want!" Friday bit off a curse, ghosting down the hall.

Friday drifted across the floor, leather-clad feet silent on the ancient stones. The Romanans were that way. Until three years ago, they had been warriors, raiders, thieves, and stock raisers. Now they were fighting their way into the Directorate, learning to deal with the technology of star travel and stirring the politics of the stagnant social system. Even here, in the guts of one of the oldest and most civilized planets, a hunter could be an asset.

Giorj followed as quietly as he could, unsure as he dogged Friday's skulking advance.

Friday reached the door where the guard should have stood. Made of stainless steel, the huge portal contrasted oddly with the archaic stone and wood-arched hallway. Friday sniffed carefully about the hinges and handle. He spotted the wires and pointed as Giorj caught up.

"Good thing you didn't touch it," Giorj muttered.

"Sirius taught us well," Friday reminded grimly.

Hambrei reached into a pocket and pulled out a coiled strip of conductor. "We'll have to hope he doesn't have any other surprises. When I short the system, you go in. I'll cover your back."

Friday's eyes gleamed. "No way. Give me five minutes. By that time, you should be down the hall and in touch with the ship. Susan needs to know about this. Get me some more men for backup, too. Reesh and his crew, all right? Sirian vets."

"But I'm here, Friday. There's no sense wasting time while I—"

"Damn it, man!" Friday hissed passionately. "We need you! You're our only engineer. The only one, hear? You know what we're up against. I risk you, and I risk my People . . . all of World."

Giorj cocked his head slightly, considered it for a half second, and nodded. He slipped the conductor in place, slapped Friday on the shoulder, and left on the run.

Friday faded back into the now welcome shadows and

waited, slowly counting the seconds in his mind. A fist tightened around his intestines, the runny feeling of fear tickling the base of his spine. Premonition hovered just overhead in the blackness.

Who waited behind that door? Who knew of the Brotherhood secrets? No, it wouldn't be the Patrol. They'd just come and try to crack the system like anyone else. No this was someone . . . A tugging thought tried to surface from the depths of his mind. He never finished it.

The steel door moved, a shaft of light falling across the worn floor. Something rattled metallically over stone. Friday threw himself flat. A blinding explosion knocked him back.

How had they known? Some remote sensor? Maybe Giorj had tripped a switch when he nullified the booby trap?

"Now or never." Friday blinked and stumbled forward, face partially shielded by his arm. The blaster rested reassuringly in his knotted fist. He jumped through the doorway and jerked aside instinctively as a blaster bolt shot a violet lance crackling and sparkling through the boiling smoke.

Just like Sirius. The reflexes had returned.

Friday rolled and came to rest on his belly, the IR sight of his weapon sweeping the room. He could make out a figure hunched over the computer. He needed no more. A battered brown finger triggered the blaster. Friday grimaced as he watched his shot hit home. The woman jerked spasmodically as her back exploded in chunks of fried blood and bone.

A woman? Oh, no! Not a woman. Even after the ones on Sirius, I can't . . . Friday swallowed, frozen with horror. That second lost, triggered by Romanan custom, became final.

Movement at the edge of his vision started Friday swinging the blaster, scrambling forward to—

His body cartwheeled crazily through the air and slammed down on the shivering floor. Dazed, he groped for the lost blaster while the computer showered a fountain of fire, smoke, and debris. Shocked, he stared in fascination as lights flashed in the guts of the system and darkened as the mechanical brain died.

An ominous silence descended on the room.

"So," a soft voice said with resignation. "With that . . . it's all gone."

Friday blinked to clear his fuzzy sight and looked up into

the smoke. A man approached from the side, blaster leveled on him. Friday tried to speak, only to cough. A strange tingling began to throb pins and needles below his waist—an all too familiar feeling he forced himself to disbelieve.

"A Romanan," the cultured voice continued. "I should have known. Well, I didn't get everything, but perhaps I got enough. I wish you hadn't killed my tech. She'd been studying Brotherhood computers for a long time. I hate losses like that. When I hit you, your blaster bolt took out the whole panel—reflex, you see—and detonated the explosives we'd planted. Everything is gone now, Romanan. The wisdom of the ages vanished with your last shot."

His vision shimmered. That voice! He'd heard it before. If only his mind hadn't clogged in a haze of jangled nerves. He gulped a breath, the whirling room slipping in and out of focus. Concentrating, he managed to reach forward with one arm and pull himself around. Horrified, he looked down to see his legs had been blown off. Severed arteries pumped jets of crimson.

A frightened cry choked in his throat.

"Yes, you'll die now," the soft voice continued, almost cooing. "The meds can't help you. Die in agony for me, will you?"

Friday looked up as a heavy boot smashed his face. Pain and lights blasted through his staggering senses. Through tears, the shadowy figure of the man slipped away into the smoke and fire.

The voice! Yes, of course. Like a horrible dream, it all came back.

"Got to tell them. Got to."

He pulled himself forward and reached down, fingers seeking along his belt for what he knew was there. The hilt slipped through numb fingers. Battling for seconds, he reached down, fingers dipping in his blood. Jaw clamped, he traced letters on the gritty rock.

The tingling where his legs had been was growing fainter and he wondered what that meant as he fought to control trembling fingers. To move became so difficult. His eyesight kept fading.

"Susan, I . . . oh, Susan." His breath caught. "Sorry you'll be the one to . . ."

He tried to look at his work. He couldn't lift his head. His hand didn't respond.

He looked up into the darkening room and blinked. A

robed man, face hidden in a flowing hood, seemed to float through the battered door. In the shimmers, he drifted over to the huge computer, checked the damage, and sighed. On silent feet he approached Friday and leaned over, placing a cool hand on his forehead. The features remained hidden in shadow as the man studied Friday's scrawled writing. Yellow Legs blinked again and looked up. The hooded one vanished in the twisting smoke—if he'd ever existed.

"Seeing things," Friday mouthed. "I'm . . . dying. Spider, I . . ."

The smoke had to be thicker now; the whole room had turned gray—darker . . . darker. An acrid smell of smoke burned the insides of his nose. The crackle of the flames grew in volume to encompass the world.

Friday felt his soul lift and he rose among floating dreams to seek Spider.

CHAPTER IV

Bullet's **bridge, in orbit over World.**

"Transduction from Captain Andojar, Major," Tony called from his comm station. "We've got antenna lock and refinement. She's a long way off, but it's refining."

The bridge hummed; various officers bent over their duties, monitoring the huge ship. Rita Sarsa sat in the instrument-cluttered command chair at the rear, the entire arc of monitors hanging from the curve of white ceiling panels easily visible. Comm and operations consoles hovered within a fingertip's reach behind the rotating chair. To one side, the navigational comm lay empty, the headset hanging, ready for use on the reclining seat.

"Run it." Rita swiveled the command chair to face the image forming in the holo. A raven-haired young woman stared out at her. A striking beauty, men stopped to stare after her. The copper-toned skin of her ancestors graced finely molded facial features. A straight nose and full red lips accented the hollows of her cheeks. Only her eyes shattered the illusion. Strained and red, a curious fear burned behind them, giving her a fevered look.

Rita tensed. *My God! What the hell happened? Relapse? Last time it almost destroyed her. Not again, damn it. Was it Friday? He do something to her? Set her off somehow? So help me, if he did . . . I'll break both his short legs off at the . . .*

The woman spoke, voice at the tensile limits, "Captain Susan Smith Andojar reporting, Major."

"What's wrong, Susan?" Rita had risen half out of her chair.

Susan took a deep breath, trying to calm herself. "Someone blew up the Brotherhood computer room on Frontier. The entire system of banks has been destroyed. The intruders evidently murdered the guard and mined the unit. We don't know all the details. Giorj is still working on it. The Galactic Grand Master demands an explanation—blames us for it."

Rita settled back into the command chair, a knot in her throat. Damn it, it had been a simple assignment. A proving of Susan's abilities. No risk. How could it have gone so wrong? Her mind raced to piece together all the ramifications. That computer bank supposedly held the engineering knowledge of the long vanished Brotherhood. Knowledge which had allowed them to build sentient ships, knowledge which had led humanity to unsurpassed heights during the age of the Confederacy.

"Is there any chance something can be saved?" Rita asked, measuring the brittleness in Susan's eyes. *What are you hiding, Susan? I know you too well. You're fragmenting inside. Eyes glazing. Just like before. Don't . . . don't do this to me!*

"No," Susan whispered unsteadily. "Giorj says the destruction was complete." She hesitated, facial muscles jumping as she fought for control.

"What is it, Susan?"

"F-Friday Garcia Yellow Legs is d-dead."

Friday? Dead? Damn it, no! Not Friday. Rita drowned the sudden ache within. Susan took precedence. *Careful now. Play this cool. One wrong word and she'll shatter into little sharp shards. God! Why did I let her go out alone?*

Rita kept her eyes leveled on Susan. "Any other casualties?" Once before, Andojar had almost broken. She'd been on the verge of insanity until the Prophet, Chester, had pulled her back. Since that time, Susan had risen through the ranks, tackling every challenge with her keen mind and unquenchable drive to succeed.

"Do you have any idea who did it?" Rita demanded, facial muscles going tight. Who could she put in charge if Susan began to break? Moshe? Could he handle her if she resisted? Did something crazy?

Susan nodded, the strain around her eyes giving her face a starved look. "We received a message that a group calling itself 'Fatherhood of God' did it in retaliation for the Brotherhood's Satan worship." Susan seemed to hesitate; terror shot bright sparks in her eyes.

"We've heard of them," Rita nodded. "Susan? What's the rest of it? Don't jack around with me. I know you too well."

The young woman swallowed hard, warfare raging within as she sought control. Her mouth moved soundlessly for several seconds before, "F-Friday didn't d-die immediately. It t-took him perhaps a minute to b-bleed to death. In that time, he . . . he wrote a . . . a word." She stopped, eyes glazing. "God, Rita! *HE WROTE IT IN HIS OWN BLOOD!*"

"Susan? *Damn it, Susan!*" Rita was on her feet, fingers digging into the comm panel. Andojar had begun to shiver uncontrollably.

"Moshe?" Rita thundered. "Moshe? Are you there?"

The captain, expression pinched, appeared behind Susan. White-faced, he waited, eyes on Andojar as she trembled on the verge of hysteria.

"No," Susan croaked, raising a hand in warning. "I-I'm all right. It's just . . . just . . ."

"What word?" Rita demanded, brooking no delay. *Do I relieve her? She's falling apart. Moshe could step in, take over now.*

Susan clenched her fists until they white-knuckled. Anger, frustration, and shame contorted her beautiful face into a savage visage. "The word," she rasped, "was *Ngen!*"

Rita swallowed, nodding, feeling her heart pounding against her ribs.

"Susan," she said calmly. "Are you all right?"

The young woman bent her head, hiding her face behind the wealth of glistening raven hair. She nodded briefly and looked up, dark eyes tortured. "I feel like . . . like my guts have been ripped out. I feel sullied, trashed, and degraded

. . . but I'll make it. That bastard almost destroyed me once. I swear, never again!''

Rita nodded, eyes locked with Moshe Rashid's. He met her glance, knowing, and retreated out of view.

Guts ripped out? Yeah, you ought to feel that. And Friday's dead? Do you mourn, Susan? Do you mourn the man who would have given his very soul for you? Jesus! What the hell do we keep living this shit for?

"We'll want Friday's remains for the burial platform," Rita said slowly, evaluative stare on Susan. Yes, she seemed to be pulling herself together.

"The shuttle will bring them up shortly. Giorj is expected aboard too. He's due in an hour."

Rita cocked her head, forcing herself to ignore the burning sting of Friday's death. "If it turns out that in Giorj's opinion there's nothing to save from the computer, proceed at once to University Station. We've been in contact with Doctor Emmanuel Chem there. He's to provide you with an anthropologist to transport to World. In the meantime, have Giorj prepare a complete report." *And damn you, don't break on me, Susan. I bucked Ree and Iron Eyes to get you that command!*

"Yes, Major." Susan nodded slowly, a flicker of defiance in the set of her tense frame.

"You want to go after him, don't you?" Rita asked softly.

Susan's expression hardened, the muscles around her mouth quivering, eyes pools of hatred. Answer enough.

"Spider teaches us patience, Susan." She lowered her voice. "Don't muff this, kid. Stick it out and I'll get you first chance at Ngen. I swear on my honor."

The young woman considered before nodding. "I won't let you down, Major. I . . . I just . . ." Susan bit off the words. "I know my duty." She straightened and snapped out a salute.

Rita returned the salute and turned off the screen, flopping back into the command chair to stare at the empty monitor.

"Shit!" She puffed her cheeks as she exhaled violently.

Friday? Dead? A pain twisted that vulnerable private place within. Another kind, decent human light, gone, forever taken from her. A bit of her spirit darkened and died, as so much of it had before. She shook her head. The sawed-off little warrior had been the strength of an entire combat team during the Sirian fighting. His ribald jokes had kept the

Romanans from letting their nightmare fear of space combat affect the attack on the Sirian ships. Friday had been Susan's first lover. He had fought knife feud for her honor.

Her eyes found the effigy Leeta Dobra had drawn so long ago on the overhead bridge panels. "Spider, you're a damn bastard God. You know that?"

It wasn't too late, she could still order Moshe to take command. He was doing the piloting anyway.

Friday's dead. Friday . . . Friday, why did it have to . . . No, don't think about it. Kill the pain. It's nothing new. The problem is Ngen now. You want to do something for Friday? Think about getting Ngen.

Rita drew a cup of coffee and considered. If Ngen was at the bottom of this Father of God religious fanaticism, things would be a lot more dangerous than any of them expected. They all knew from past experience just how brilliant Ngen could be when it came to social manipulation. He had kept the Sirians fighting when their planet lay in ruins around them—and Sirian hope lay crushed and mangled under a Romanan boot heel.

She shuddered at the memory of the tapes a Patrol tech had found in Ngen's flagship, the *Hiram Dastar*. Ngen had recorded his methodology into some sort of depraved archives as he methodically abused, raped, and psychologically destroyed his female captives. He'd degraded a Sirian First Citizen and a Patrol Colonel into whimpering animals. He'd almost crushed Susan Smith Andojar, too—broken her will and spirit. Had she not been so strong—had Chester not been so brilliant—they could never have brought her back.

Rita didn't realize she'd crumpled the cup in her hand until the pain of the scalding coffee blasted through her anger.

Bazaar: Capital city of the planet by the same name.

Bazaar is a substandard city under every established Directorate criterion. Deficiencies in structural engineering, sanitation, power transmission, utilities, comm reception, emergency facilities, and pollution control abound. The people could be thought of as primitives living in squalor. Such conditions haven't existed since twenty-first century Earth.

* * *

Zekial Lichud struggled against the EM restraints that bound him in the blackness. Beyond belief, he'd been trapped so easily. Shame burned deep in his wiry gut. Nine of the elders had sent a message. *Come. Come to David's. We are only nine. With you we have minyan.* And Zekial, rabbi that he was, hadn't been able to turn down the call from the wilderness. Not with so much of the old way eroding beneath their feet like the sand of the deep desert in a violent wind.

So they had taken him. Shot his bodyguards down from behind, sullied his honor, and violated the ancient law. Disgrace. Disgrace upon disgrace.

For long hours now, he'd been lying in the dark. They'd placed him in some sort of box. From the sensations, they'd transported him in an aircar before the crate was carried into a structure and deposited on a plasteel bench of some sort. No matter how he kicked and banged, he'd been ignored.

Eternity loomed. His bladder filled, pained him, and finally released in defiance. The only sound came from his protesting stomach.

Feet scuffed beyond the muffling walls of the crate. The lid squeaked. Strong arms lifted him, the hoodwink and gag keeping him disoriented. The pressure of the dirty cloth against his tongue prevented Zekial from swallowing. Saliva leaked around the corners of the saturated cloth to trickle down his cheeks.

The worst, however, proved to be the fear of what would come. His body flexed in their arms as they carried him. Booted feet grated on sandy stone. From the jouncing and the way they handled him, they climbed steps of some sort. A door opened. Even through the blankets he could feel the humidity of the place. No Bazaaran dwelling, this.

"In here," a voice called in Standard. Standard? *Deus! The cursed Fathers! Heretic filth! Spit-licking vermin! Perverters of the Laws of Abraham and Isaac!*

They dropped him without warning. Lights blasted behind his eyes as his head smacked the floor. A ringing droned in his ears as tears blurred the blackness. Harsh hands ripped the hoodwink away. Zekial blinked the shimmering out of his eyes, a growing ache in his head from being dropped. He smelled of urine and sweat and fear.

"Ah," a smooth voice called. "The last one? The final leader of the resistance?"

Zekial twisted his head, searching the room despite the pain the bright light caused his eyes. Some sort of tower? Overhead, an unfamiliar boxy piece of equipment hung from the eight-sided domed ceiling, hovering over what looked like a pedestaled table. Examining room? Opulent off-world furniture surrounded him. Fathers, that curious lackluster look in their eyes, stood somberly around, staring at him with the mindless revulsion of their kind. Mindless? A wisp of an idea shadowed his thoughts only to vanish as fear possessed him.

The gag loosened and he spit it out, grateful to move his tongue again, despising the taste left behind.

"Zekial Lichud," a grossly fat man said happily as he walked into the range of Zekial's vision. "The last hold-out."

"Such a surprise!" a new voice cooed.

Zekial closed his eyes. The false messiah! Knotting the muscles of his jaws, he ground his teeth. Tears spawned by anger and impotence crept past tightly pressed eyelids. His nose was running. Could the God of his fathers have left him so? Had his faith been for nothing? The servant of YVEH, had he failed so miserably?

"Come, my friend," the messiah called gently. "Don't do this to yourself. I've not come to harm you, but to release you from the bondage of the ages. I am here with the word of Deus. I am the unifier."

"*You are Satan!*" Zekial growled hoarsely.

Laughter broke out around him.

"It's true," Zekial continued. "Look into the eyes of those your hand touches. Part of their soul dies, false prophet. A spark leaves them! They become as clay. Unable to think, to know the Laws of Moses, of Abraham."

The man who called himself messiah grabbed a handful of Zekial's hair and wrenched his head sideways—something he never could have done unless Zekial had lost his yarmulke. A yawning emptiness welled under his heart. His grandfather had given him the yarmulke: a gift from the old man's deathbed. As if under a broken keystone, despair avalanched down around him.

Now he looked into the messiah's hard eyes.

"Someone murdered five of the Fathers as they spread the Word of Deus on *Shabbat*. I was off planet. Pallas, here, fortunately, took matters into his own hands."

"I killed them gladly, you filthy servant of Satan! To

shame the *Shabbat* like that! To walk boldly into our synagogue and shout your lies . . . Yes, we killed them. I'm proud of that, *you filth.*"

The false messiah smiled easily. "I will take great pleasure in converting you, Zekial. You've gone out of your way to—"

"Convert me? To your polluted Godless religion? *Never!*" And he laughed at the very idea of it. Death would be easy now that hope had fled.

"Ngen, let's get it over with." The fat man, Pallas, stifled a yawn. "It's been a long day. Preparations for your arrival have occupied me since before dawn. Tiara is waiting. She's planned something special for me tonight. For the Arcturian cloak I had you bring. She adores it—and wishes to express her gratitude."

The false messiah loosened his grip in Zekial's hair and stood, looking down at the rabbi, a curious detachment in his eyes. "You treat her too well, Pallas. She's only a woman."

"An expert woman," he corrected. "As much a genius at what she does, as you are in your profession."

"Genius? Hmm. I suppose we were successful. I got most of the data, Pallas. I couldn't understand a lot of it. We'll need help. The best we can find. Ah, if only Giorj hadn't . . . but that's long past. How are conversions?"

Pallas spread his fat-swollen hands; a Babylonian's ransom of jewelry flashed, confirming Zekial's suspicions of Satanic influence.

"One at a time," Pallas sighed. "Slow, but sure. We're making headway. Many come now who haven't been treated. With Zekial converted, the others will flock to us. Your power and truth will be undeniable. The Jewish resistance—"

"Never!" Zekial hissed under his breath. "The God of Israel is my God. You are filth, despicable, evil filth."

The false messiah smiled down at him. "Many called me that at first. Ahmed Hussein, Reverend Jacobs, Abdul Muhammed, Elias Arhat, and others. Doesn't that strike you as a sign of my power—that they came to me?"

It did. Zekial's mouth went dry. "My faith will keep me. The Laws of my fathers are stronger than yours, evil one."

"You got his family?"

Zekial stiffened involuntarily. He cringed as the evil one noticed and laughed softly.

''His daughter is very beautiful,'' Pallas added. ''Were it not for my Tiara . . . Ah, well.''

''And his wife?''

''Terrible thing these Jews do. Shave their women's heads. Curious, isn't it, that they go to such lengths to make them undesirable?''

The false messiah chuckled. ''Very well, go to your Tiara, good Pallas. Let's see how much sleep her 'genius' lets you get tonight.''

Pallas left, swaying from side to side as he waddled away, a look of hungry anticipation in his eyes.

To one of the Fathers, the false messiah added, ''Bring me Zekial's daughter.''

''*No!* Leave Lishia out of this! She's a good girl! Please. My business is none of hers! Hear me? *Leave her be!*'' The heart began to tear in his chest as he pleaded to deaf ears.

The door opened; Zekial froze, muscles locked rigidly.

''Papa?''

He bit his tongue to stifle his outcry. ''Not my daughter,'' he whispered. ''She's only sixteen. She's an innocent. Take me. Do what you will. But leave her. Leave her be.''

The false messiah walked around, beckoning to the girl. She came timidly, downcast. At the fear in her eyes, Zekial's spirit collapsed.

''A beauty,'' the false messiah admitted. ''I'm impressed, Zekial.'' He motioned to the two Fathers who stood to either side. ''Take her clothing off.''

''*No!*'' Zekial cried, his scream a shriek.

Unable to watch, he turned his head. The sobs of his daughter pierced his ears like burning knives. The tearing of fabric mirrored that of his soul.

''Make him look,'' the messiah ordered. Rough hands jerked Zekial's head around. Fingers pulled his eyelids up, taping them so he couldn't blink, couldn't shut out the sight. Lishia shivered on the table, trying to hide herself. Terrified, her teeth clattered as Ngen stepped out of his robes.

''Blessed Lord YVEH, smite these abominations. Unleash your wrath, oh, Lord God.'' God had to have some reason for this, didn't he?''

They forced Lishia down, screaming, kicking, and fighting. Tears flooded Zekial's eyes. When he'd cried himself out, his daughter lay on the table, the curious instrument on her head. Her young body undulated suggestively under the stimulus of the machine.

"Zekial," the messiah soothed. "You stood in my way at every turn. You have single-handedly caused me more trouble than anyone else on this planet. Tomorrow you will walk the streets of Bazaar and call the masses to my Temple. You will close your synagogue and come to worship the Word of Deus. You will be one of the greatest of the Fathers. Fanatical, undying in your loyalty."

"Never . . . as I . . . swear," Zekial rasped.

"But first, I want you to see my power. Not that you'll remember, unfortunately—but you need to see, to learn what it is to cross Ngen Van Chow. The psych machine on your daughter's head implants thoughts. Makes a different reality. You see, the machine is already teaching her the proper responses to my caresses, placing new behaviors in different parts of the brain." Ngen gestured. "Like my Fathers, you see."

"No," he sagged, head still held by the Fathers who watched expressionlessly.

"Yes, Zekial." Ngen cradled his chin in his palm "In your Lishia's case, however, I won't make behavioral changes. I'll leave her sense of values untouched. She'll remember every detail of this night. What woman wouldn't want to remember her first joyous coupling? But what should I have her remember? Hmm? What would be suitable . . . Ah! Of course!

"Perhaps her memories will be of her father making love to her wondrous body? Perfectly fitting! You look ghastly, Zekial. Don't worry. Physically, I shall possess her, and I am quite expert at this. You'll only take her virginity in her mind—stimulate her to that first shattering climax. I assure you, she'll never forget this final gift from her father."

Zekial screamed, fighting, struggling against the iron arms that held him. He shrieked himself hoarse as Ngen climbed onto the table and lowered himself to caress her trembling body.

Zekial Lichud walked in a blissful dream. Around him, men and women nodded and spoke warmly in greeting. At the steps of the synagogue, Zekial turned, throwing the doors wide to crash loudly against the hewn rock walls. People had stopped on the street.

A curiously detached horror twisted the very heart in his body. Some disembodied anxiety, a wrongness, drifted like a feather through his head. The hot tears running down his face tickled as they ran into his beard. More people crowded around the steps, watching warily.

"Rabbi? What do you do?" Itzak called up. "What has happened?"

Shivering with uncontrollable spasms, Zekial blinked down at the people he'd known all his life. To speak took the greatest effort—as if he battled something deep within that he couldn't remember. "I . . . I have committed the greatest of sins! I have . . . have raped my own daughter!"

People gasped, stepping back.

"I . . . It was Satan who possessed me." Curiously, he looked down at his hands. They shook so hard he had to knot them. Yes, it *had* been Satan. "And . . . and when I had finished, my d-daughter ran to the Temple of Deus. I-I ran after her. There, inside the . . . the Temple, she hid in the Sanctuary. I-I followed, and she was borne up into the sky on a golden rod of light and . . . and eternal bliss filled me. You hear?"

"Raped Lishia?" Itzak was shaking his head in disbelief. "Zekial, you're not well. I can't . . . can't believe . . ."

The words were coming easier now. Some final horror had given way deep in his mind. He let himself flow with the message of Deus. "Deus, the Father, came to me. Came to *me* who had sinned against his very daughter! You hear? Deus lifted me! An abomination! Washed clean my sin! I have atoned in the eyes of Deus!"

Itzak cocked his head uncomfortably. "I don't believe this, Zekial. I don't believe you. What of everything you've taught? What of the principles you claimed you'd die for? What of the Law? Of the Talmud and Tanach? Do you just turn your back on the ways of our fathers? Our people?"

"They are the way to Deus," Zekial replied. "Only men—like you and I—have misread the Word of Deus. To do otherwise is sin, my people. As I have opened the doors of the synagogue to Deus, so have I illuminated the insides of my heart. Come, come with me to worship Deus."

Itzak, arms crossed, stood to one side as Zekial descended the stairs.

Most of the others followed, though, as he strode purposely down the dusty street. At the sight of the Father's Temple, some hesitation came on him. Vague disquiet stirred in the depths of his subconscious. Thoughts of the bliss of Deus soon dispelled the anxiety. A fleeting thing, it never troubled him again.

CHAPTER V

Arcturus: Dock 27, University Station.

*University Station remains the only official institution of
higher education within Directorate space. While various
stations and planets have been urged to specialize in manufacturing under Directorate policies, University remains
the source of Directorate brain power. Scholarship to University is necessary for admittance into many Directorate
professions and must be approved by station or planet
supervisors with subsequent authorization by one of the Directors.*

"Thrust, zero point one seven six." Susan Smith Andojar corrected her deceleration, mind locked on the data
comm fed through her headset. "Yaw right, point six degree."

"Acknowledged," Moshe's disembodied voice confirmed. "Lock is seventeen meters, sixteen, fifteen . . ."

"Cut thrust, point zero zero six. Cut thrust point zero
seven. Cut thrust point one."

"Dead stop."

Susan glanced at the monitors. "University tractors extended." A faint clang sounded. "Matched and grappled."

"Confirmed. University Station sends their compliments
and regards. Power down to one half."

Susan filled her lungs and exhaled. "Acknowledged.
Power down initiated. Reactor damped." She pushed back
in the command chair, aware of an aching knot in her shoulders. With one long finger, she poked under the golden circlet of her headset, wiping at the perspiration.

Moshe rose from his chair, eyes on the endless banks of
readouts. He turned and nodded, a faint smile on his lips.
"Couldn't have done better myself."

A faint flutter stirred in her chest. "Thank you, Captain.
Put Bullwing Reesh in charge of security. Giorj is to be
accompanied at all times by a squad. At least two of them
ought to be marines. Shore leave must consist of no more

than four to a party . . . and at least one marine must accompany each group of Romanans. I want no incidents. We're here to pick up the anthropologist and fill requisitions from World—and nothing more.''

Moshe nodded. ''After what happened on Frontier, I don't think you need to worry. We're all . . . well, still pretty upset about what happened. Everyone will be on guard here.''

Susan nodded, the dead feeling eating away the satisfaction of a perfect docking. Frontier, just another of the growing list of soul-searing memories. She turned, scanning the spotless bridge, seeing the weapons officer shutting down most of his boards.

''Commander?''

Susan turned back, one eyebrow lifted. Moshe made a small gesture. ''What about you? I mean, are you going to see the sights? University has a couple of great restaurants and some bars that will knock your socks off. I could—''

''Thank you, Moshe, but I think I'll pass.'' She ducked through the hatch to avoid the reservation she knew would grow in his eyes.

''Damn,'' she muttered under her breath. ''Rita, you've got them all jumpy. I'm okay, damn it. In control.'' Her heart beat soddenly against her ribs. The pain tried to well up from where she'd buried it. A horrible image of Friday's blasted, charred body whirled in her memory. The glassy horror in his dead eyes stung her very soul.

She knotted her fists, slumping suddenly against a bulkhead. A bitter burning of tears throbbed behind her eyes. ''Not now,'' she hissed to herself, swallowing the grief, pushing on toward her cabin. She slapped the hatch with a callused hand and wilted against the wall. A trembling finger punched the dispenser. Eyes closed, she cradled the coffee cup in her hands, sniffing the hot fragrance.

''Get it together, damn it.'' She sipped the hot brew, feeling her tongue burn, enjoying the pain of it. ''One hurt to cover another.''

Susan shivered, forcing herself to breathe deeply. ''Damn you, Spider, can't I ever have a moment's peace?''

Comm announced, ''Engineer Hambrei.''

''Giorj?''

''Here, Susan.'' His gray face formed on the monitor. ''I've got all the specs I need. I'm on my way out now. I've put access codes into the system if you need me, but there's a whole squad here. They say you ordered them to—''

"Yes, Giorj. And they will. If anything happened to you, I'd—''

"Now, Susan, don't overreact to—''

She stiffened, a cold chill in her soul. "And if someone got you like they got Friday? You're important to us, Giorj." *Important to* me, *damn you. If anything happened, how could I go on? How could I face it?*

As if he read her distress, he smiled slightly. "As you wish, Susan.'' He paused. "See you later.''

"And don't get so cursed wrapped up in your studies you forget where you are!'' she shouted at his back as he started down a long winding lock.

"We'll remind him,'' a young Romanan called as Giorj's bodyguards followed on his heels, anxious for the adventure of University Station.

Susan grumbled to herself and cut the connection. She tossed off the last of the coffee and turned to the comm. Settling herself, she fought against the urge to cry, to let go and wallow in her misery. Giorj wouldn't be back until they spaced for World. He'd forget she even existed as he probed the best minds he could find in University for technical advice. The yawning gulf under her heart widened.

"Blessed Spider, Susan, pull yourself together. You've made it this far.'' In a dark recess of her mind, Ngen's voice cooed.

She tensed, muscles rippling, eyes squeezed closed. Unconsciously, her fingers wrapped around the heavy leather grip of the long fighting knife she'd taken so long ago from her uncle's dead body. Reassured, she pulled the heavy blade from her belt and laid it on the comm table.

Single-mindedly, she opened the file Admiral Ree had sent and began processing orders through the Arcturian net. Approval from Director Skor Robinson's office appeared with startling rapidity.

Credit sifted on the monitor, showing debits from the Romanan accounts, accounts built from toron sales off World and from profits tagged to the Romanans from the Sirian GNP. Too quickly, it was over.

"Commander?''

"Yes, Moshe.''

"I have ten applicants requesting transportation to *Bullet*.

They're the people Ree has offered positions to. Recently graduated techs looking for a Patrol job.''

"Have Reesh put them in the Deck C barracks when they arrive.''

"Acknowledged.''

Friday's voice drifted up from the mists of memory, *Susan, I'll love you forever. I gave you up for Spider. I know that now. I see Spider's hand in this. I just . . . just didn't recognize it would hurt so much.*

"Friday, Friday, you don't understand. It wasn't you. I . . . I loved you, Friday. I just couldn't . . . Ngen did it—used psych. Made me think it was you when he raped me. Can't you understand? The horror of it . . . To love you and hate you . . . that's what Ngen did to me. Used your memory, used your love against me, Friday. That's what that bastard did. Now, all I've got is guilt . . . and pain. Always pain.''

She closed her eyes and sniffed. "Damn you, Spider. Why are you doing this to me? What in hell do you want next?''

Comm beeped and she looked up, running rough thumbs across her tear-blurred eyes. A file had been inserted in the comm access.

Darwin Pike, Ph.D., it noted, had been selected for the Romanan position of religious anthropologist.

Susan scanned the vitae. Pike came from Earth—someplace called the Alaskan Free State. She studied the holo of him, seeing a pale-faced young man with weathered features. Kind eyes stared out of an even face. His jaw looked strong, and a wry humor set his lips at an angle.

"Great,'' Susan, mused. "Another Directorate fop. Damn it, Ngen's loose. Friday's dead. Some weird cult is stirring up the other side of space. The Patrol is coming apart so fast it's popping rivets. Humanity is on the rocks, and I have to nursemaid a soft, spoiled Directorate sheep like you, huh?''

She shook her head slowly. "Well, Dr. Darwin Pike, let's see how long it takes for reality to wipe that silly smirk off your overprotected face.''

She saved the file angrily before standing and pacing her small quarters. "Something's coming, Spider. I can feel it. You're not done with me. Friday . . .'' grief staggered her, "Oh, Friday. First Hans . . . then you. I hurt.''

And Ngen waited . . . out there . . . somewhere.

* * *

Darwin Pike slipped another armful of his cherished possessions into the plasteel trunk he affectionately called his "war bag." The only remaining links to his heritage hung on the wall. He reached up and unhooked the old Targus blaster that had been his grandfather's and gently placed it in the trunk where it would be protected by clothing.

The antique survival knife was last. He could barely make out the manufacturer's stamp on the polished, scarred blade. The faint words, "Randall Made," could only be seen when the blade was held up to catch the light just so. He had no idea as to the age of the trinket; it had been recovered from a wrecked twentieth century aircraft his great-grandfather had looted in the polar ice back on Earth.

Hands on hips, he made one last inspection of the room. Nothing remained to mark it as his. Curious, all those long hours of occupancy and only plain white walls remained. The room continued—as bare of Darwin Pike as it had been the day he moved in. God, did they have to construct everything in space out of white materials?

He sighed and rubbed his jaw. "Farewell, University."

Hell, he'd never been a good academician anyway. Of medium height, his frame went to the muscular side—legacy of his youth in the Terran wilderness. A hunter by nature, how had he ever ended up here? When he looked in a mirror, a modal Caucasoid stared back out of evenly spaced blue eyes. Compared to the station folk, he looked squatty, compact. Absently, he fingered his thin nose and realized he needed to shave again. When he let his beard grow, it came out almost black compared to his sandy brown hair.

He snapped the buckles closed on the war bag and looked around the little room for anything he'd missed. The door chimed and announced Chem's arrival.

"Come on in." Darwin called, dropping into the chair.

Doctor Emmanuel Chem, head of the Department of Anthropology, shambled in—a tall awkward old man whose bushy brows framed a lined face. Tiny blood vessels, too close to the skin, traced intricately around his bulbous nose. He'd originally been in charge of the Romanan expedition—returning allegedly for health reasons. At the same time, persistent whispers of other reasons floated through the hallowed halls of University. The older members of the faculty claimed Chem had never been the same after he'd gone to World.

"Have a seat," Pike waved at the now bare room.

"I say, I brought along a bottle of exquisite scotch," Chem began, clearing his throat with a ragged growl.

Darwin pulled two glasses from the dispenser as Chem poured.

"How do you feel, old man? I'm terribly sorry to drag you away like this . . . but you know you're the only one."

Darwin laughed. "Honestly, I feel like I'm twenty-eight going on one hundred, Emmanuel. Harried, you know? So damn much to do in so little time before the grant ran out. Oh, sure, I'd like to get my studies completed. The resources here are fantastic! But . . . can I confide in you?" Darwin smiled easily, running fingers through his light-brown hair.

"But, of course, good man!"

"This station is driving me nuts!" Darwin exclaimed, jumping to his feet. Chem looked mildly appalled. Darwin laughed. "Look, you were born on a station, Doctor. I wasn't. I've come a long way from Glenlen. That's a little place about one hundred fifty miles from Ankrage. I don't fit Arcturus. My world is the Alaskan Free State. Things are so different here. Why, there's no outdoors! I grew up hunting and fishing and doing real archaeology! You know that the Inuit and Aleut still cherish their ancient values. That's what got me into anthropology in the first place."

Chem chuckled. "I knew you were unhappy here, Doctor Pike." He looked up sheepishly. "If I might be honest, I chose you for this project specifically for your vigorous constitution."

"Not just the fact that I was running out of money?" Darwin knocked back his scotch and handed the glass to Chem to refill. "There are people on the faculty who'd kill to get my place," he muttered. "I'm *not* a Romanan expert."

Chem shrugged. "They don't want a Romanan expert. Bella Vola and Marty Bruk are still on Atlantis, er, excuse me. They call it World." Chem ruined the Romanan pronunciation.

"So they get a generic class I anthropologist, certified to be conversant in cultural peculiarities and in acceptable health. May we see his teeth, please?" Darwin took a breath. "If you had to send me anywhere, why didn't you send me home? Maybe I could drum up some more Inuit cultural grant money? Besides, I miss the hunting and fishing. Never thought I'd yearn for the Gulf of Alaska in the spring—but then I guess insanity's endemic in my family.''

Chem waved impatiently. "Look, Doctor. Outside of the fact you signed the contract to get an extension of research time, consider it a favor to the department. You know how precious the Romanans are. Why, we have a gold mine of information that comes in each day from the research station there. At the same time, you know how politically powerful Iron Eyes and his bunch are. Ever since they pulled the Directorate's fat out of the fire at Sirius, they get anything they want. This time, they want an anthropologist to study religion—so they get you.''

". . . And you get a superb consultant's fee to keep the budget fat. Tina Alleeta is the religious expert. How come she's—''

"She's also station bred. She's got spindly bones like mine.'' The watery blue eyes looked amused. "Romanans demand someone a little more, shall we say, rough and tumble? An Alaskan should just fit the bill.''

Pike looked glumly across at Chem. "And I signed that damned contract. Ah, well, you've only got your hooks into me for a year. After that I can come back and finish my work. It'll be a break—relief from white walls!''

Chem smiled wickedly. "Knowing Romanans, I'm sure it will.''

A servo robot entered and inquired what was to go. Pike pointed at his trunks and the machine scooped them up, turned quickly, and fled down the corridor.

"Come,'' Chem finished his scotch and stood, "and let me walk you to the spaceport.''

Darwin Pike didn't look back as he palmed the door plate. "I hate white.''

His father had worked at Glenlen at the control station that constantly adjusted the huge space mirrors which kept the glaciation from continuing to grow. Earth was heading into another ice age—a fact that had become apparent as far back as the late twentieth century when the climate began gyrating and the Great Salt Lake yearned to turn itself into Lake Bonneville again. Now, men like his father played a delicate balancing act to keep solar radiation focused at just the right intensity on the ice sheets.

Darwin had spent his youth digging for artifacts, hunting moose, bear, and caribou, and fishing for the giant salmon. He had lived in the forest, sneaking through the muskeg,

cursing mosquitoes, and leaping lithely among the black
spruce with his Inuit friends. The life had filled him out and
left him with a streak of the barbaric and an insatiable curiosity about the past.

As always, the docking area had been placed in zero g
along the spin axis of University Station. Darwin Pike could
look out at the strands of Arcturus which orbited around the
star. The largest city in the galaxy, Arcturus looked like
threads of silver wire stretching out of sight. The effect
might be compared to the rings of Saturn—only the threads
consisted of huge hollow tubes, spinning endlessly, housing
an incredible city. Arcturus—the heart and soul of Galactic
humanity.

Darwin took long enough to stare out an observation bubble. Brilliant lights flooded the scene, contrasting to the
black of space and the reddish shadows cast by the giant
sun. What looked to be a standard GCI docked at the hatch,
umbilical lines running from the gray, pitted outer wall of
University to the smeared white of the ship's hull. Numerous blisters—nonstandard to a GCI—curved around the an-
tenna-fuzzed hull to be obscured by a transduction dish.
Additionally, a huge spider effigy had been painted on the
side of the ship.

He turned back from the smudged port and watched the
servo haul his trunks into the yawning mouth of the lock.
Service techs trotted back and forth, gray suits flexing as
they made notations on portable comms. A low frequency
whine permeated everything and the air smelled sharp here,
cold, bearing the trace of deep space in its metallic odor.
Security personnel chatted in low tones to one side, eyes
going uneasily to the heavy lock. Not much could be seen
beyond the bend of the access tunnel—just the damnable
white of the curved walls.

"Well, this is it, I suppose." Chem took his hand. "If
you have any serious trouble, or if you just can't make a go
of it, call me." This time, the concern in the watery eyes
looked sincere.

"Thank you, Doctor."

"Doctor Darwin Pike?" a crisp voice called out.

"Here." Darwin turned, stepping uneasily in the artificial gravity of the lock. The man who'd called studied a
comm and looked up. Darkly complected, a guess of Middle Eastern ancestry could be made from his phenotype.

"I'm Captain Moshe Rashid. Pilot for the *Spider's Trea-*

sure. I give you Commander Andojar's compliments. If you would follow me.'' The captain saluted.

The inside of the ship—to Darwin's dismay—gleamed eternal white. On the bulkheads, though, numerous effigies of spiders in all forms had been scrawled—the effect that of undisciplined children gone mad with marking pens. Having lived with the Inuit, it didn't bother him. Spiders were part of nature.

Captain Rashid led him down vacant corridors to a small cabin that measured no more than six meters by four. His trunks had already arrived and been clamped to the floor.

''You're Romanan?''

Moshe shook his head. ''From Levant originally. You'll know the true Romanans when you see one. They all carry knives in their belts. They keep their hair in braids, too. I don't carry a knife in places like University. It's too easy to get hauled off to psych before they know who you are.''

''Why a knife?'' Pike asked, wishing he'd paid more attention to the Romanan ethnographies.

''Means you're a warrior,'' Rashid said as he left.

And so it proved. After they had left University and were accelerating for the jump, two men approached talking animatedly in a language Pike didn't understand. At sight of him, they eyed him curiously, nodded with reservation, and passed. They wore leather clothing like something out of an anthropology text. The sleeves and fronts of the shirts had been painstakingly decorated in gaudy colors. Spider effigies covered each chest. Tattered fringe—some of it obviously used to patch rents—swished as they walked in their wiry, easy stride. Long braids of glistening black hair swayed behind their backs. The faces hadn't been rude or coarse; rather, Romanans proved to be handsome people. Only the oversized wicked-looking knives on their belts and the multicolored tufts of hair dangling from one man's vest stood out as barbaric.

Darwin reentered his cabin and went about unpacking.

With three hours to dinner, Pike asked his way to the gym and dialed the gravity up to 1.5. Jogging and lifting weights, he didn't notice the girl at first. She had engaged the combat robot in a duel behind a partition.

Pike saw her, stopped, and looked again. When he did, he almost dropped the heavy lift bar.

She literally danced as she punched, kicked, and chopped at the robot. Except for the battering the robot received, her

actions could have been finely choreographed ballet, such
fluidity and grace did her blinding movements betray. Further, she was an expert at hand-to-hand combat, dark hair
flying behind her as she pirouetted and slammed the robot
to the mat again. Darwin pulled his jaw up, straightened
his shirt, and went over to watch.

She might have been taller, he couldn't tell. Such judgments could be biased when a body looked as perfectly pro-
portioned as hers. Her lithe figure rippled with muscle as
she arched, the robot feinting past her.

Jumping high, she smashed the robot's neck with a blow
that would have decapitated a man and jumped back, ready
for a follow-up. Darwin clapped his appreciation and the
girl whirled, facing him, ready for combat. A sparkling vibrancy burned her black eyes, illuminating them with a spirited vitality that lured him.

"Excellent!" Darwin called happily, noting for the first
time just how attractive she was. Something tingled in his
chest as he tried to shift his stare. A slight flush of embar-
rassment tugged at his composure. Only he knew if he
looked away, it would be right at those superbly firm breasts
molded so spectacularly by the body armor she wore—or at
her flat, muscular belly where it cradled between the enticing swell of her hips. No, eyes were safe. She couldn't kill
him for ogling her eyes.

She relaxed slightly and studied him. "Thank you. Do
you know combat?"

"I, uh . . . no." He laughed, trying to break the log-jam
of his sudden frustration. "I guess that's a little beyond my
field. But I mean . . . well, you looked marvelous just then.
I . . . I admire an expert when I see one. And you're that.
An expert, I mean." Panic tried to choke him. *She's just a
pretty woman, you dolt! Relax!* His heart stilled a little.

"You seem fit," she said, looking him over. "I suppose
you could learn. You must be Darwin Pike, the anthropologist."

"That I am. My pleasure . . . uh?" He cocked his head
and she smiled, faintly amused.

"Susan."

"My pleasure, Susan," he amended. "I meant what I
said, you're very good at combat. Have you been in the
Patrol for long?"

She laughed and shook her head. "I'm Romanan."

"Oh," Darwin retreated, surprised. "I thought Romanan

women didn't go to space." Then he remembered a female had even fought against the Sirians.

"Things are changing. I thought those reports Bella and Marty have been sending back would have told you all about the cultural innovations on World."

He let himself drown in those dark eyes. "I must admit, I haven't been too keen on Romanan ethnography. I suppose I should change that." Those eyes fascinated him, cloaked with some mystery, guarded, obscuring some vulnerability.

"I thought everyone at University was absorbed by us primitives," she challenged, a wry smile on her full lips.

"My interest lies in the grander scale of social interaction. Um, like what occurs when humans have to adapt an entire society to a changed environment. Acculturation, if you're familiar with the technitalk. That's the—"

"Yes, I'm aware of that, Dr. Pike. I read your transcript and vitae very carefully." Her eyes were guarded now.

Darwin showed his surprise. "You did?"

She nodded, hands on hips. "Ours is a suspicious and wary race, Doctor. Our first meeting with Directorate civilization almost ended in our destruction. We suffered fifty percent casualties on Sirius before we took the planet. We do nothing by half measures—including military intelligence."

"Military . . ." Darwin realized he was walking with her toward the showers. Annoyed with himself, he repeated, "Military intelligence?" trying to keep the confusion out of his voice. *Military intelligence? What the hell is going on here? Chem, damn you, what did you get me into?*

"I'll leave that for Admiral Ree and John Smith Iron Eyes," she said simply.

Darwin smiled, desperate to take the offensive. "Understand that I'm not familiar with your customs—and don't wish to offer any insult—but would you mind sharing a drink with me? If you have a husband or male friend, you may also bring him. Doctor Chem left me an excellent scotch and I would like to gain an inside understanding of how I should behave." . . . *And what the hell I am doing screwing around with military intelligence—no matter whose it is!*

She paused for a moment and thought while Pike held his breath. He'd taken a hell of a chance, he knew, playing on his supposed ignorance. Her husband—if she had one—could kill him.

"I'll meet you in your quarters in fifteen minutes," she decided.

"Excellent," Darwin grinned, feeling himself flush with success. He still didn't know if she had a man in her life, but it had been so long since he'd seen, let alone talked to, such a beautiful and attractive woman. Then, too, that element of guarded mystery and presence intrigued him.

Military intelligence?

As he showered, he considered her, running the entire meeting through his mind, seeking to forget the effect she had on his concentration. An odd mixture of brassy toughness overlay some deep vulnerability. He couldn't put his finger on what made him think the woman he'd seen pound the combat robot to pulp could possibly need protection, but his subconscious had been stirred by just such a desire.

Frowning, he followed the despicably white corridors back to his room. She was called Susan—a member of Romanan military intelligence. As he palmed the hatch and entered his little cabin, comm announced that Commander Andojar requested his presence at supper that evening. He forwarded a message stating he would be delighted, and broke out the scotch, setting the old blaster and the battered Randall knife on the dresser.

He studied how he looked, growled at himself for being vain, and set some of the hunting pictures up on the hooks. He gazed at his favorite. In the holo he stood proudly—one foot braced picturesquely on a lightning-riven stump—next to a twelve-foot Alaskan brown bear that had collapsed over a tangle of deadfall. The bow and arrows he gripped so tightly had been carefully crafted by hand—the old way. Spirit had been sung into the wood and sinew and glue. Soul had been breathed into the very grain of the weapon. Shield Downey stood on the other side of the bear, his wide Inuit face split by a smile that exposed straight white teeth. The photo touched a yearning warmth deep inside as he savored the sweetness of the memory.

"Hatch," comm informed him.

"Enter."

Susan passed the thick white door as it snicked back, and looked around, darting black eyes missing nothing.

"I'm not exactly settled yet," Darwin told her easily, aware his heart was making an irregular nuisance of itself. He bit his tongue to slow himself down. Cripes! Nervous!

But then it had been a long time since his wife . . . A sting, unblunted over the years, haunted him.

Heedless, Susan had picked up the antique Randall and pulled it from the plasteel scabbard. "Very old," she said. "You keep a good edge on it. Where's it from?"

He told the story of his great-grandfather. "So you see," he grinned, handing her the scotch, "my infatuation with anthropology is inherited."

"You should wear it." She pointed to the long fighting knife that hung on her belt and turned her attention to the holographs. "I've never seen animals like these. Fascinating. From old Earth, too?"

"That's moose. That's caribou. This one is elk. And this one here is a record bear." A glow of pride filled him. "I killed it with an arrow. Made it myself, and Shield Downey blessed it and made me sweat for four days before the hunt."

She listened intently and shook her head. "But it's so small!"

"*Small!*" he shouted. "My God, woman! He stood twelve feet tall! I didn't even have a blaster for backup! Shield and I sat in a tree for two hours until he died!"

Her eyes were on him again, measuring, evaluating. "They must be fierce for their size. On World, we, too, have bears. Ours are much larger with two tails and suction disks which they use to seize prey. Their mouths are full of acid which dissolves their victims. We used cannons to kill them, or rifles, before we had blasters."

Darwin felt himself stiffen. Killing the bear had been the single greatest achievement in his life. The bear represented more than his Ph.D. An obsession, he'd hunted the bear for years in one way or another. When his turn came to try himself under Inuit law, he'd been ready. He and Shield had prayed to the old Inuit Gods, to Raven and the Big Giant. They'd made the weapons, sweated, attended to all the rituals, calling on bear's soul. Alone, armed only with their wits and primitive weapons, they'd walked into the wild lands, splashed across the muskeg, battled through the willows and tripped over the wormwood to claw through the berry bushes. And they'd found the bear. Another week of hunting—and being hunted—passed before Darwin got his shot, driving an arrow into bear's side. Bear almost killed them before they reached safety. Only Shield's courage saved Darwin's life that day. Shield, brave Shield, baited the bear—actually reached out of a tottering black spruce to slap the animal on the back, distracting it while Pike climbed out of reach.

Susan smiled as she settled herself into the chair and Darwin felt himself grow cold. She knew she had riled him, humiliated him. To hell with this woman who seemed so damned superior. He bit his tongue, wishing she would leave.

"You should wear the knife. It is accepted among our People . . . unlike yours," Susan said easily, as if nothing had happened. "Do not let the men tease you about its length."

He slipped the knife onto his belt and fought to control his anger, happy at the familiar weight on his waist. He'd skinned a lot of game with the blade. It had been his favorite tool in camp and on the hunt.

"I would suggest, too, that you pick up as much Romanan as possible. It will definitely be an asset. In the meantime, orders have been given that you are not to be harassed by any of the crew or the warriors. They know you're different and unused to our customs." She laced her fingers together, still studying him.

"You seem to know an awful lot."

"I get by."

By the Gods! he thundered to himself. Was she made of ice? Did she have none of the common decency shared by the rest of humanity? It was almost as if she were toying with him.

"I was going to ask the commander, but how soon will we reach World?"

"Five weeks ship's time." She didn't even hesitate although a strange amusement could be read in her eyes. "That should give a man with your abilities sufficient time to pick up all the background material you'll need."

His reaction to her physical beauty softened the anger. If anything, that understanding threw him into an almost fever pitch of irritation. Damn male gonads anyway! Could he pry anything out of her?

"You mentioned military intelligence. Dr. Chem said nothing about that. In fact, I find it highly irregular. I'm an anthropologist . . . not a general. I didn't sign on to play cloak and dagger. I'm a social scientist. Perhaps I'd better call Commander Andojar and demand a line back to University. I have serious research I could be attending to." His voice sounded cold. Maybe he didn't care anymore.

She paused before she spoke. "You know, Doctor, you live in a very soft society. As a people, you haven't faced survival in a very long time. You've come to expect luxuries which are impractical. We, on the other hand, have been scratching out an existence against the bears and each other, competing for limited resources. We can't afford luxury, not even that of sending you back to your precious studies."

"I'm not sure you understand my—"

"We need you, Doctor. Much of humanity needs you. I don't have all the information, but I assure you, Admiral Ree, Iron Eyes, and the Prophets have been considering options. You are one. A Romanan conquest of humanity is another."

"I . . . *Conquest?*" Darwin thundered incredulously. "You must be out of your mind! The Patrol would—"

"The *Patrol* would do nothing. They couldn't even stand against untried Sirian rebels. Seriously, how would they stop Romanan wolves?"

"My God, you're talking about an entire—"

She waved it away. "That's meaningless anyway. The point is, the Prophets see a dire threat to us unless certain cusps are decided in our favor. That entails free will so we don't know how it will end. Therefore, we're stacking up options which might guarantee success one way or another. That's where you come in." She laced her fingers together, head cocked, waiting.

"Comm. I would like to talk to Commander Andojar."

"The Commander will be unavailable until supper, Doctor," comm intoned.

"Who else can authorize communications to University?"

"Captain Rashid, with the approval of the Commander."

Darwin's anger built. "Damned bureaucracy!"

"Consider it a test," she said, the dark pools of her eyes sucking him in. "Perhaps you're being pulled to see how far you can stretch before you break, Doctor. Very few are ever truly tested." Her eyes hardened. "Have you ever faced death, Doctor Pike?"

Off guard again, his emotions became a confusion of anger, helplessness, frustration—and this damnable woman still exerted a pull on his masculinity. What the hell, Shield would have mocked him. He laughed, gulped his scotch—forgotten in his hand—and flopped into the small bunk.

"Yes. More than once. I've been lost in Alaska. I've

tracked wounded bears into the brush. I've faced starvation
. . . and freezing to death.''

"You're different than we expected,'' she mused. "You
must've had a tough time at University.'' She was curious
now, drawing him on.

"Yeah, they didn't really understand me.'' He poured
more scotch and refilled hers. "Thought I was a heartless
monster because I used to kill what I ate. Wasn't any way
to make them understand the link between a hunter and the
hunted. They couldn't comprehend how your respect for an
animal grows when you track it for days, learning its habits.
They had no reference point for how your own soul cries
when you take the responsibility for killing another creature.

"They couldn't conceive the nature of the Inuit either. I
gave them lecture after lecture, talking about Raven, and
sweat baths, and curing dances. They spouted back theories
of community integration, shamanism and cultural innovation—missing the whole point of Inuit reality. That's when
I started dealing with sweeping cultural changes.'' He
frowned at the amber liquid in his glass.

"And now you rail at being abducted by hunters?'' The
classic lips curled into a half-hearted smile.

"Maybe it's Raven,'' he muttered, thinking of the Inuit
spirit.

"Maybe it's Spider.''

The hostility slowly drained away. All the conflicting
emotions had tied themselves into a senseless knot easier to
ignore than decipher. And Susan? A whole different facet
of her personality had been exposed. For minutes they sat
there, each lost in their own thoughts. As he watched, a
shadow of sorrow began creeping across her face. The expressionless veil reformed as if magic. What pain did she
hide so well behind that competent exterior?

"I have to go,'' she said softly, as if aware of his scrutiny.
The coldly professional smile bent her lips again. "I hope
you enjoy your meal. I hear Commander Andojar sets a
wonderful table.''

"You won't be there?''

Her smile shrouded secrets. "Oh, we'll run into each
other again.''

Pike stood easily, wondering what to say or do with this
confusing woman. Part of him wanted to invite her back
while a different voice screamed a frantic "no'' and ached

to mentally teleport her to the far ends of the universe. Maybe all spies were like that? He shivered. What a grisly life that would be.

"I sincerely doubt it," he smiled genially, trying to still the roiled thoughts. "I'll discuss my situation with the Commander tonight. He'll get me clearance to cancel my stay among your People."

When she smiled, he thought his heart would melt. "You seem very sure of yourself, Doctor. Would you perhaps make me a small wager?"

Small? "Of course."

"My fighting knife for your, what did you call it, 'bear' holo?" She cocked her head, eyes taunting.

"A couple of credits, perhaps. The bear . . ." Frost settled in her expression. He hated himself for doing it, but slowly he nodded. "All right. The bear, Susan. I don't know what I'll do with your knife at University. Classroom exhibit maybe." He give her a malicious glint. "Your commander won't want an unwilling passenger."

"We shall see. Like I told you, Doctor, we can't always be masters of our destinies." She smiled in victory. Turning on a shapely leg, she palmed the lock plate. Before he could answer, the hatch was whispering shut behind the whirl of lustrous hair.

Darwin Pike stood, mute, watching the white panel which had passed that angel's body from his view. So she was beautiful? What of it? Why did she seem to capture his soul? Shaking his head, he began unpacking, thinking of what he'd tell Commander Andojar. That done, he pulled Vola's *The Romanans: A Study in Culture Contact* from his locker and began thumbing through the pages.

Somewhere in Vola's report, he'd become totally engrossed. He almost missed the supper call. Pike let himself whistle as he swung down the companionway, conscious of the Randall on his belt. Aware no one even noticed it although the Romanans seemed to be sizing him up.

Susan's fighting knife would provide a lot of amusement when he got back home. He could see the Downeys and the Lees and some others ringing a late winter fire, telling jokes and stories while he demonstrated the Romanan fighting knife and told how easily he'd gotten it from a lady warrior.

He found the mess and ducked through the hatch. He spotted Captain Rashid, asked for the Commander's table, and learned he'd found it. Rashid wore a belt of hair which Darwin realized was made of coups—human scalps taken in combat. Curious, he studied it furtively, recalling Vola's descriptions. Romanans were black-haired. Rashid's belt consisted of black, brown, red, and blond hair. Sirian, Pike realized with a start. He swallowed dryly, feeling his heart pound. So entranced had he become, he failed to note the arrival of the Commander.

Everyone snapped to attention while Commander Andojar was announced and Darwin turned, a smile on his face. He began to introduce himself to . . . *Susan!*

"I'll collect my bear tomorrow at your leisure, Doctor," her melodious voice insisted.

Any trace of appetite vanished.

CHAPTER VI

Bazaar: Temple Square.

"Deus! Deus! Deus!" The swelling cry seemed to shake the very foundations of the building. Ngen Van Chow raised his arms to the sullen lightning-streaked skies and the cry came again, thundering off the walls that hemmed the huge, open square before him. More than a kilometer long by 300 meters wide, it stretched, lined on all sides by a mud-plastered stone wall with overhangs decorated in muslim arches. Once this had been the marketplace of Bazaar. Now, it served as the only space large enough to hold Ngen's masses. Along the walls, boxy black speakers projected his words, while above him, on the roof of the Administration building, a large holo projector recreated his passionate expression.

They stank! He could smell the unwashed bodies below him. The square reeked of packed humanity, dust, and moldy clothing. Ngen fought the nausea which almost overwhelmed him every time he addressed the throngs. Heat rolled off them, lifting the odor up to his position. There, the wind wafted it into his face like a soft slap. Was this why the Christians had built the ceilings of the cathedrals so high?

Not one single foot of the packed square remained bare. Below him a sea of speckled color washed, tides of humanity polka-dotted by solemn faces, staring up at him in religious ecstasy. Ngen reached for the sere sky and the cry came again, *"Deus!"*, a roll of sound ripped from a thousand throats. Even from where he stood, reeling from the stink of them, Ngen could feel the power flowing from the crowd and electrifying him. When they screamed their devotion to God, they seemed invincible.

"Deus has come to me!" Ngen shrilled, raising his hands to the thunderous roll of voices. "He has come to *me!*" A boom of voices followed. "He has said to me, 'See the evil done by the foul Lord Satan! See Jew split from Christian and Moslem! See how Satan has twisted the words of Abraham, Jesus, and Mohammed!"

The roll of sound thundered below him like huge breakers off an angry coast. The sound crashed against the building on which he stood, shivering the edifice. For Ngen had brewed exactly such a storm from his endless human ocean.

"And Deus said, 'Satan has turned Brother against Brother! Did not Jesus preach the law of Abraham? Did not Mohammed preach the law of Abraham? Did not Satan divide and kill us by rending the sacred words of our prophets? With each stroke of the sword, Moslem killed Jew— and damned his own soul! With each shot did Christian slay Moslem—and in turn damn his own soul! Who reaps this feast of souls . . . slain and slayer?' "

"Satan!" The crowd boomed back.

"Aye!" Ngen shouted, raising a clenched fist over his head. "Satan, the damned, has set one against the other and dimmed the voice of Deus! Who, I ask you, do the Jews believe in?"

"YVEH, the Father!"

"Who do the Christians believe in?" Ngen demanded, supplicant.

"God, the Father!"

"Who do Moslems believe in?" Ngen shouted.

"Allah, the Father!"

"Who is YVEH? Who is God? Who is Allah?" Ngen howled.

"DEUS! DEUS! DEUS!" The volume increased until earth, structures and sky reverberated from the din.

He raised his hands again. "My brothers, Jews, Christians, and Moslems, I call all of you to my breast. Eat with me! Drink with me! Feel my flesh! See my body! I am as you!''

They thundered agreement, a roll of sound.

''But Deus has come to me! Deus can come to any of you!'' They roared in a frenzy of excitement, milling and swaying back and forth, eyes glazing as they feasted on his words.

''Satan is loose, my Brothers! He feeds on the souls of our friends and families. We are of the body of Deus . . . and they are of the body of Satan! Satan's lies are the Directorate! Satan and the false Spider God are one! Satan lives by lies—but where do you and I find truth?''

''DEUS! DEUS! DEUS!'' The wave of sound threatened to sweep him from the roof.

''How do we bring the Fatherhood of God to the Galaxy?''

''Death to the Romanans! Death to the Directorate! Jihad! Holy War! Crusade!'' Their anger mounted in time with pulsing raised fists.

Ngen dropped to his knees, hands clenched above his head, veins standing from his straining arms. In a posture of supplication, his face glowed with the power of his communion. The masses rent the air with a final overwhelming explosion of sound. Ngen could see the foremost writhing on the ground, tongues lolling out as they gibbered nonsensically. Others jerked in trances, spastic limbs flailing their ecstasy. The fevered eyes that remained on him were bright with the fever of Deus!

The hooded figure—an anomaly—caught Ngen's attention. He stood quietly off to one side, a curiously empty space around him. The hooded one moved slowly through the crowd, a way parting automatically for him as he passed. Face hidden in shadow, Ngen couldn't tell if it was man or woman. Oddly the figure didn't seem to bob, as if walking, but instead, appeared to float.

Ngen raised his arms again, bringing forth a deafening shout. The hooded one moved heedlessly through the crowd. Some mystic from deep in the deserts of Bazaar? Ngen drew another surge of power from the crowd, but when he looked back, the hooded figure had mysteriously disappeared. Where? No portal emptied on that side of the square. Though he searched as he preached, he could find no trace of the oddly-robed individual.

They kept him there for hours, screaming hoarsely until

night fell and Ngen could escape. Physically exhausted, he reached his well-guarded quarters and showered the reeking smell of human filth from his hot body.

Once, in the beginning, they had made him vomit. In the sudden silence that followed, he looked up and told them he was purging Satan from his soul. They had howled their delight and—to his amazement—vomited in their own turn!

"Very good," Pallas sat at the comm console as Ngen stepped out, a tingle of rejuvenation in his limbs. "You've packed the Temple. I estimate only fifteen percent of the attendees have been psyched. The rest were rolling along on your charisma alone."

Ngen rubbed the back of his neck as he padded over to the dispenser and punched up a whiskey, the dry air caressing his naked skin. His quarters were lavish for Bazaar; not the palatial surroundings he'd enjoyed on Sirius or Varta Station, but bearable. The furnishings reflected the spare reality of life on this planet, the walls made of hewn and squared native stone. Even the comm terminal Pallas used had come secondhand from Directorate surplus. Thick wool rugs, dyed a rusty red from native clays, padded the gritty floors. The whiskey came from a local manufacturer—each batch differing in color, bitterness, and proof. He downed it in one long gulp, refilled it, and settled on a scarred buff antigrav recliner, rubbing a hand along the skin of his leg. Revolution—on Bazaar at least—required sacrifice. A good place to start; who'd want it? Ngen reordered his thoughts.

"That's for now. How long will they keep going on a high like this, Pallas? What happens when they start to come down? Humans are creatures of short attention spans. They tire quickly—even of the novelty of emotion."

"We can always treat more. Six new machines are coming within the week. Expensive toys, Ngen. Medical psych machines don't come cheap."

"And the technicians from Gonian? You got them, too?"

Pallas lifted his hands and fluttered his fingers to create a dazzling display of multicolored lights. "My people got them. All of them. Best psych engineers in the business. They know the machines and the theory. Most had no interest in the enticement we offered. They came . . . well, with reluctance—but they'll work. Amazing what a blaster to the head will do." He smacked his rubbery lips. "I'm sure the Directorate is puzzling over their mysterious disappearance. Sira handled it most adroitly."

"And perhaps they can decipher the Brotherhood data." Ngen sipped his whiskey, thoughts on his followers. "That's the answer, Pallas. A society molded to our needs. I've been wrong, you know."

Pallas turned, grunting as he fought his huge bulk. "Wrong?" The grav chair whined under his weight, compensators straining.

Ngen nodded. "They don't deserve a new way. No, I've watched them. Unwashed, human flotsam, that's what they are. Despicable creatures. The more they love me, the more I despise them for their fawning adulation."

And he did despise them. Yet at the same time, when he stood above them, the sensation was like an orchestrated dance to bring them to a fever pitch and string their minds into absolute bliss. Indeed, power came from that—power greater than that held by generals—power greater than the Directorate's.

They called him Messiah. When he walked the streets, they slunk back, out of his way, fearing to have the eye of Deus fall upon their unworthy souls.

Pallas waited, pulling uneasily at his hanging chins.

"Most humans, my old friend, aren't worthy." Ngen cocked his head. "Consider Sirius. I stood before them, offering to bring a new light, a new age of learning, science, and freedom. They turned on me. Put their heads right back in the Directorate noose. Here, I've come to build a society—and what do I find? Fawning masses. No initiative. They fall all over themselves . . . and not to serve any God. No, they want to serve me. Me! Not the slightest understanding of the message."

"I thought that's what you wanted?"

"I'd hoped for more. A challenge . . . a rivalry between them and me. A game of wits over the nature of their God. I thought they'd be . . . well, they could care less about the reality. Only the emotion is important to them. The short-term gratification. Mindless vermin."

"And is God important to you, Ngen?"

He smiled sourly and tilted the glass to his lips. "There are times, standing there, looking down into their awed faces, that I think I'm the only one worthy to be God. Maybe—considering the sum intelligence of those worshiping humans out there—I am."

"I don't see—"

"Don't you? They clamor for God . . . and I'm the surrogate. That simpering rabble howls to throw themselves at my feet, to cheat themselves . . . and in doing so, their God, too.''

Pallas rubbed a chubby hand over his sweaty face, shaking his head slowly.

"You've seen them. They themselves are proof that God doesn't exist . . . or doesn't care.''

"Oh?''

Ngen snorted, tipping the glass up for the last drop. "Indeed. Any God with self-respect would have exterminated them for the vermin they are millennia ago.''

Pallas considered, shrugged, and changed the subject. "Tiara is beginning to make trouble. She wants to travel. She's come to the conclusion that Arcturus is the place for her now.''

Ngen studied Pallas from the corner of slitted eyes. "And?''

"I haven't decided. I think—all things considered—that your 'Deus' revelation is succeeding better than I ever dreamed. No matter what you think of the masses. I hate missing . . . I mean, I'm willing to gamble on getting a piece of the Directorate all my own. A planet . . . a nice planet.''

"You realize that . . . well, Tiara can't leave us. She knows too much. Her weakness is money—and power. If the wrong people should hear of what we're doing here. . . .''

Pallas sighed sadly. "I watched the tape you made of Lishia and Zekial. Incredibly diabolical of you, Ngen. Me, I'd hate to lose Tiara. Her skills, you see. She can work around my fat, keep me in ecstasy for hours on end. A talent like that shouldn't be wasted idly.''

Ngen nodded soberly, thoughts retreating to the past, to the Romanan girl who—unlike the sheep on Bazaar—had been worthy of his skill. "I think, old friend, there is a way you can keep your beauty. Keep her most compliant—and without losing a bit of that extraordinary talent.''

"Would you like to attend to the chore, Ngen? You have a certain magic when it comes to psych programming.''

A giddy excitement warmed him. "With pleasure. With most definite pleasure.'' Ngen jumped to his feet, stretching. "Nothing like the thought of challenge to refresh.''

"Do let me know how Lishia's doing. I hear you've almost driven her mad.'' Struggling to rise, Pallas studied

Ngen's naked body critically. "Getting a bit of a belly, too, Ngen. Emulating me? Or is this just an experiment to see if Bazaarans will grovel before a fat god?"

After Pallas left, Ngen palmed the latch to his private sanctuary and admired the beds, placed in a long row. Some of the women gazed at him dull-eyed. They were the broken ones. Lishia turned hating eyes on him and glanced away. Some just wept miserably. The last two, doe-eyed girls with bodies ripe to be plucked, stared at him with worship on their beaming faces.

Ngen chose, feeling his maleness come to life, and smiled as he drew close. "Now, my beauties," he crooned. "I shall teach you the pleasure of Godhood!" By his art, he could break any woman to a whimpering hulk. The new maidens sighed. To still the rapture in their eyes he taught them how to scream first.

CHAPTER VII

Arcturus: Directorate Headquarters.

A single fact sent the portion of Skor's brain devoted to monitoring the Bazaaran situation into panic. A holo of the messiah had been obtained.

The cold rush of tingling nerves left him unable to think, to deal with the multifactorial problems of humanity. Even though the radiation contamination cleanup on Illych's Planet demanded instant attention, the people there would have to wait.

Skor took a deep breath and blew it out, staring into the endless blue of his control room. The psych techs had chosen that color based on the deep tests. Blue touched the depths of his subconscious. Endless shimmering blue soothed some resistant human need in his psyche which even the genetic engineers couldn't overcome. A safe womb in which he would forever float—for his body couldn't withstand any sort of gravity. His huge head would snap the spindly neck beneath it. His heart would fail against the strain. Skor would live forever in his blue reality, the monitoring machines cooling the blood that fed his marvelous brain.

But no one had anticipated the effects of fear—or of contact with the Prophet, Chester Armijo Garcia. Robinson recalled his first encounter with Chester. "They call us freaks, pumpkin heads, balloon brains. Directors aren't human. We can't afford to be. We're responsible for too much. We can't afford humanity, Prophet. We simply cannot. So much for your concept of soul—we're damned."

Over the last years, he'd come to understand the ludicrous actions taken by ordinary men. They had a purpose—diffusing atavistic emotions. They had no safe blue wombs within which to spend their existences.

He scanned the information again. No doubt of it. Security ID had employed a fractal program to fill in a shadowy holo of the Bazaaran messiah: Ngen Van Chow.

Skor blinked, gathering his wits. "We have him. Now, if I coordinate this correctly, he won't know we're on to him."

He accessed the system, checking the location of *Gregory*. He shuttled an order to Colonel Ben Mason, rerouting *Gregory's* patrol. Telemetry showed no other ships in Bazaaran orbit.

Assistant Directors? Skor received their confirmations, slipping them bits of information. "Got to feed this slowly. Can't afford shock. Damn it, why didn't they teach us emotions? Why did they leave our lives so sterile?"

Ngen? Roque queried, putting it together on his own. Skor sent him an image of the fractaled ID.

I propose immediate interdiction. Navtov supplied, sending implementing procedures almost immediately. One part of Skor's mind began evaluating and critiquing the plan.

Certain Bazaaran exports are required for the Zion industrial workers. With feelings as high as they are there, we can't interrupt the flow of wool, drycotton, or flax from Bazaar. To do so will precipitate riots which may be more detrimental in the long term than Ngen preaching to rabble on a sterile world. Roque supplied figures to back the assertion. Statistically, no doubt remained. Zion needed the imports for worker stability.

Skor considered before adding, *I have rerouted* Gregory's *patrol. The best projections I can make indicate that* Gregory *will arrive over Bazaar within six weeks Standard. At that time, I shall order Mason to drop his full complement of marines to arrest the criminal Ngen Van Chow. In the meantime, raw materials are being rerouted from Far Side where drycotton and wool are in slight oversupply. Within six months, we should be able to eliminate Bazaar entirely without commercial repercussions on Zion.*

You haven't informed Mason of the messiah's identity? Roque asked.

Skor chose his words carefully. *We have no proof that Ngen Van Chow didn't place the listening device in our Security comm. We do know that he didn't place any such item in the primary Gi-net. I took great pains to cover our identification procedures when we utilized the fractal program. Perhaps—and I admit I'm gambling—we will have a better chance of capturing him if he believes we're ignorant of his true identity. Interdiction will be consistent with our attempts to stifle his irritating religion. In the event we offered no response, Van Chow would become suspicious and perhaps escape again. No, Assistant Directors, interdiction is completely within normal policy parameters.*

And the Romanans? Navtov inquired. *You know how badly they want him.*

I do, Skor replied. *And if we control something they want, we have a credit to barter for something in the future. I don't like Romanans. They are a source of social disturbance within our space. Nevertheless, we no longer have the option of bottling them up in their system. A significant percentage of Directorate citizens are enamored with Romanans and Romanan ways. Their Spider god has piqued the interest and imagination of too many for comfort. Rather than have them as enemies, I suggest we work syncretically to integrate and dilute their social effect.* Skor submitted a statistical model for his Assistant Directors' inspection. *It may be the only way to salvage some semblance of control in the end.*

Have we fallen so far? You talk in terms of defeat. Roque responded in rebuttal. *I have run simulations of a simple military operation to irradiate the Romanan world. Plausible deniability is built into the strategy. Scenario: A primitive people have obtained technology beyond their understanding. We cannot be responsible if they allowed an antimatter reaction to go beyond their containment skill.* Skor's unit received the preliminary feasibility study.

And their Prophets? Skor couldn't help but respond, returning the entire study with veto.

I still have not convinced myself they can see the future.

To read quantum wave effects lies beyond the abilities of the human brain. I—

I believe they see the future. Skor chopped him off. *Furthermore, I am the Director. I suggest you consider the words of the Prophet, Chester Armijo Garcia. I suggest you review the records of those situations which have defied our projections over the last several years. Do you note a statistical trend in our errors? Garcia—and Ree, for that matter—continually remind us that we're missing the human element. I, for one, would learn that lesson. Both World and Sirius burn too freshly in my memory.*

I agree with the Director, Navtov submitted. *In running permutations and probabilities, I find little evidence the Romanans would bear us ill—despite our past policies toward them. They could easily be persuaded to adapt their customary raiding behaviors to Directorate worlds should they perceive continued antagonism on our part. They already exhibit limited respect for Directorate citizens whom they consider little more than mindless domestic stock. (Note— Terminology employed: sheep. Genus, Ovis; species, aries.) I approve the syncretic assimilation program of Director Robinson. Through such, I anticipate we can maintain an ameliorating effect on sociocultural turmoil. Yes, Director, we are talking in terms of a problem beyond our control. Let us employ rational standards to contain the sociocultural damage they might inflict on civilization. A little, to quote the pirate, Damen Ree, is better than nothing.*

We have not *heard the last of the Romanan problem,* Roque predicted. . . . *And the criminal Van Chow is loose— beyond our grasp for at least six weeks.*

Six weeks. So much could happen in six weeks. Skor fought the desire to contact Damen Ree. What would the renegade do? Precipitate some random act to disable all Skor's carefully prepared plans? No, leave the Romanans out of it for the moment. Besides, a Patrol containment of the Deus religion—and Ngen Van Chow—would restore a severely fractured Patrol reputation, build confidence in a reeling military, bolster morale. Involving Romanans, or Ree, might simply escalate the problem.

Krankov City, Mystery: Ambrose Sector.

Named as a result of the constant cloud cover and continual precipitation, Mystery is a swamp world with a high oxygen-CO_2 atmosphere. While much of the planet suffers from tectonic vulcanism, the high-silicate shield volcanoes are mostly confined to deep sea trenches. Settlement developed slowly. A lush, hot, marshy planet, Mystery is the original source of svee moss, the material from which expensive live carpet is derived. Krankov City began as an outpost built on pilings sunk to bedrock. A protective environment was necessary to inhibit fungi. Currently, population figures are sketchy but estimated at fifteen million.

"The time has come to feed our souls!" The youth stood on one of the hydroponics pumps, staring out over the faces which ringed him. Most had been passing on their way home from work, stopping for the entertainment of a Spider cult youth. Now they stood around, smiling uneasily at each other, watching the skinny kid with his fake coups, a converted moss harvester's knife on his belt. The brown cloth shirt hanging from the kid's bony chest sported a curiously drawn spider on the front.

"First came the Dobra broadcast! Remember? Remember the fight over World? The Directorate wanted to kill them all! Genocide! Hear me? Is that our legacy? Thank Spider for the courage of Leeta Dobra! She prevailed. And lo!" He turned, slowly, index finger raised. "What should happen?"

"Sirius!" Someone grunted from the crowd.

"Sirius!" the youth affirmed. "You look at me. All of you, and tell me that wasn't a sign . . . the dawn of a new age. Now, I stand before you, one young man. But I don't stand alone! No, I have something," he thumped his thin breast, "Here . . . inside, I have God. My soul and Spider are one. I—"

"Blaspheming heresy!"

The youth stopped, mouth half open. He blinked, seeking out the man who pushed his way through the crowd.

"You can call it what you will." The youth crossed his arms, head back.

The challenger rushed forward, a muscular man in his middle years. Before the kid could react, he'd reached up, snaring the youth by the ankle and, toppling him, sent the youth sprawling.

"Spider? Satan! That's right," the man growled, looking around at the uneasy people. "You've heard the broadcasts . . . heard the Messiah from Bazaar! Who do you believe? This . . . this dirt!" He kicked the kid in the butt, sprawling him face first. "So you see Spider." The big man shook his head. "Go . . . go home all of you. Deus is coming."

The stunned youth managed to get his feet under him. Blood streaked from his nose.

From the outskirts of the crowd, two more men closed in, grabbing the bewildered youth by the arms.

"Hey! What are . . ."

"Shut up." They hustled him back into the shadows of the heavy pipes.

News reports the next morning made note of the beaten body found behind the hydroponics pumps. The boy's neck had been broken, his features so badly damaged that ID had to be made from DNA. Above the body a spider had been drawn and crossed out in the boy's blood, and to the side of that, an ominous note claiming, "SPIDER IS SATAN!!! DEUS IS COMING!"

Administration building: Bazaar.

"Do you realize just how vulnerable we are?"

"I do. It bothers me to be in a hole like this. Directorate interdiction bothers me even more. They—"

"The fact they took so long to act had me nervous, Pallas."

Ngen chewed his lip, a nervous affliction of his. "Had they done nothing—"

"But interdiction *is* serious, Ngen. They're going to send the Patrol now. You know that. Patrol always follows interdiction. Think about all the times—"

"Exactly!" Ngen smacked a fist into his palm. "Consider, Pallas, we've been broadcasting. Cults have developed on other planets. Our agents are laying the groundwork for us on Arpeggio. There are only two explanations for their lack of response. Either the situation is worse than we know out there and they're bogged down with problems, or they know more than we think and are laying a trap."

They walked slowly down a long vaulted hallway in the main administration complex—once the seat of what smattering of Directorate government existed on Bazaar. Now the white-washed halls rustled with the passage of Fathers in cowls, yarmulke, or kaffiyeh. Some bowed or touched their heads. Others walked by mindlessly, a vacancy behind their eyes. Sand gritted underfoot and Ngen grimaced at a stained spot where a man had urinated on the wall.

Pallas shivered. "Ngen, I've trusted you. I've done a lot for you, but I don't care to face the—"

"Hush," Ngen soothed, a loose smile on his lips as he thought. "Despite the interdiction, they're sending the regular GCI. They demand the textile shipment be shuttled up to the station as usual. Perhaps we're a little ahead of schedule, but some risks must be taken—and, to be truthful, I'm surprised we got this far."

"Your techs are making progress, too. With the input of the Gonian engineers, they've made some astounding breakthroughs. Were it not for the logistics of bringing in high-tech comm and . . . But you know about that. Manufacturing sensitive equipment in a dust bowl is no simple matter." Pallas laced his fingers behind his back. "Nevertheless, they've demonstrated remarkable progress with the unified psych field. I can't understand exactly, but it does something with cytoskeletal proteins in the brain neurons. I'm not much for brain microanatomy, but they've found a wide field which affects a microtubule-associated protein, MAP they call it. They're in the process of refining it now."

"And how soon do they think it will be on line?"

Pallas looked at him skeptically. "Maybe a couple of days if they can get the hyperconductor they need."

"Strip it out of the old Directorate Consulate building."

"Um . . . Well, there's a trade-off. Seems like what you gain in the wide field, you lose in fine discrimination within the brain."

Ngen looked at him from the corner of his eye. "Is this a problem?"

Pallas wet his fleshy lips, fingers twittering in a flickering light display. "Well . . . using the wide field, you can only overlay in a gross fashion while most of the brain—especially the frontal lobe—is blanked. Your people . . . Um, they . . . you might say . . . they become like robots."

Ngen nodded, continuing down the long hall. An ever present odor of dust, of ionized air, filled the place. They didn't filter the atmosphere here. "We're not interested in producing innovative individuals, old friend. I pursued that route once before on Sirius. This time, I want obedience. I take it I'll get that?''

Pallas shifted uneasily, waddling along with effort now, a fine beading of sweat on his pale brow. ''You'll get it, Ngen. From the masses at least.'' He didn't look happy.

''And Tiara, my friend? You approve of the adjustment I made?''

The subtle cues of apprehension disappeared as a satisfied smile replaced them. ''Indeed. She's most ardent now—like in the early days. If I'd only . . . I mean, I didn't understand. About the power of psych, you see. She . . . well, almost drives me to exhaustion. No, past exhaustion. Insatiable, you know?''

Ngen nodded. *Yes, my old friend. I know. One of my better attempts at behavioral modification. How curious the human mind? You waddle in bliss, ecstatic at being milked by a muscular vagina as an athletic whore contorts around you. Me, I find no fulfillment in mere physical pleasure. But to look down and see the horror in their eyes as their bodies turn against them? To see a mind tearing, a personality shredding under my manipulations, ah, what heights that drives me to.*

''Yes, Pallas, I'm happy to provide you with your perfect woman.'' *And you'll stay with me. Reward . . . and threat. Oh, I know, Pallas, old friend. I monitor you. I know how often you pull up the Zekial tape to stare in fascinated horror. Yes, you've received the subliminal cues. You know I'd do that to you without the slightest hesitation. Dear old friend, you're no longer your own man. Your heart—your very soul, is mine.*

The fat man nodded eagerly to himself, enjoying some memory of Tiara. ''Yes, most happy, Ngen. Most happy.''

''Keep me informed as to progress. I'll want the retooling at the wool storage warehouse completed within the next two weeks. We'll need to be in production sooner than expected.''

''I'll see to it,'' Pallas agreed as they stopped before a scarred wooden door. ''In the meantime, Sira Velkner is bringing in a second shipment of blasters we looted from a Patrol warehouse. Good stuff, the charges are less than a year old—probably produced specifically for the Sirian uprising.''

''Then I may have done myself some service in that disaster after all,'' Ngen added dryly. ''Good, see to distribution. We'll need them by this time tomorrow night. I'll inform the 'Chosen' inside,'' he jerked his head toward the door, "that Deus calls.''

Pallas nodded as Ngen entered the big room. Once a library, his Holy Crusade had pitched the books into a raging fire during a frenzy of religious zeal. The populace had roared louder than the fire that greedily devoured the few paper items remaining. Melting sizzling tapes had made a stink only Satan could have appreciated. His power had been assured that night. The final sources of knowledge had been destroyed. The few mosques, synagogues, and cathedrals left had been searched—all records obliterated On Bazaar, Ngen controlled access to ideas.

Now, the spacious round room served as his meeting place. Once a beautiful room surrounded by high vaulted windows accented with Christian-style frescoes, dust had coated everything. Here, even the open casements and arid breeze didn't dissipate the odor of unwashed bodies. On a world where water meant more than life, bathing had evaporated from the culture long ago.

A hush fell over the room as he entered. The Fathers waited, keen black eyes on him. A couple whispered mongrel Hebrew mixing with bastardized Arabic. They stood, the thirty most powerful religious leaders on the planet. Faint traces of the psych machine could be read in the zeal burning in some of those dark eyes. For others, the promise of power had been enough. Fanatics one way or another, each had been picked—or "converted" for their abilities or power. Ngen smiled at the shock troops of the Messiah.

A round table of sorts had been built and Ngen took his place at its head, all eyes turning in his direction. The glow in Zekial Lichud's eyes pleased him most particularly. With a single motion, Ngen had them kneeling.

"In the name of Deus," he said softly, and dropped to his knees. They muttered along with him as he led the assemblage in a long-winded prayer.

"My Brothers," he greeted, throwing them a beneficent smile. "I believe we are ready to take the blinding light of Deus into the galaxy. Just now, I've heard the hallowed voice of Deus." He raised his eyes to the brightly lit dome overhead. They all muttered an "Amen" as he held his pose.

Dirty, unwashed, their eyes seemed to gleam with a crazed passion. A warm satisfaction filled him. *They want me! They live to serve ME! I have found my place. Soon . . . soon all the Directorate shall look up to Ngen Van Chow—the whore's son, the dock rat—and humanity shall worship like these stinking vermin. I shall become humanity!*

Ngen savored the rush of power then continued, "If you will place your souls in the service of Deus, we *will* smite Satan and drive him from the galaxy! The time is *now,* Brethren!"

They began to chant and he had to quiet them.

"A GCI will arrive in our orbit tomorrow. Satan has caused the Directorate to interdict this planet. Yes, my Brothers, *they fear us now!*

"Oh, they plan well. Satan always does. Remember that. Satan will eat at you, try and erode your will through subtle ways. And now? Now we get supplies so we don't starve . . . and we send out crates of flax and wood for the traditional textile industries of Zion. As the lion may walk with the lamb, so shall the soldiers of Deus hide in the crates of the fruit of their labors!"

They shouted again as he waited for their zeal to subside. "When we are aboard, Brothers, the Sword of Deus shall sever his children from the tyranny of the Directorate and the foul master Satan. We shall take that CGI, and with it, embark on the road to the stars.

"I've heard from our brethren among the stars. They're ready to strike at the hour Deus has demanded. When they do, we shall bring the light of Deus into the galaxy and Satan will be exposed!"

Fists raised to the roof, as they chanted, goading themselves to frenzy. He had the stupid fools primed now, the perfect fodder to fling a searing torch into the pustulant body of the Directorate. The time had come.

"Deus! Deus! Deus!" The haunting cry resounded in the old library. Written in three languages, the sign which said "QUIET" still hung over the door.

Arpeggio: The fringes of Ambrose Sector.

Arpeggio has one of the most colorful of histories. Founded sometime in the early Confederate era as a pirate stronghold, Arpeggio existed for almost seventy years in secrecy. As the power of Arpeggian pirates grew exponentially, so did their political and military clout. Perpetually at war

*with the Confederate Council and Patrol, the Arpeggian
Houses nevertheless formed a crucial alliance with the Sirian power cartels, eventually leading to a rise in influence
which led to the final expulsion of the Brotherhood from
Confederate space. Subsequently, Arpeggio discovered that
respectability carried its own traps which led to the decline.*

"Torkild, I'll see you now." The old man bent over the
desk, a thick hand rubbing the back of his neck—a gesture
of weary acceptance.

The office—walls glittering with heirlooms, displays, and
mementos—made opulent use of space. Airy and light, a
man could spend long hours here. The ceilings imparted a
feeling of freedom, high and vaulted, supported by translucent nacre walls that rose in graceful arches, drawing one's
gaze upward toward the stars which had nurtured Arpeggio's pirate lords in the early days. Underfoot, the carpet
slowly shaded through the visible spectrum, reflecting off
the walls in ever changing patterns.

Behind the old man, a holo of Directorate space moved
against a background of distant galaxies. The grand Alhar
desk had been forged of silver in some long forgotten place
far beyond Arpeggio's star. Tarnished now with eons of use,
the delicate filigree shone where papers, clothing, and flesh
had polished the rich metal. The House of Alhar had stolen
the desk hundreds of years past. It continued to serve the
descendants of the original thief—a monument to the glorious days of Arpeggio.

Torkild Alhar stepped athletically through the doorway,
immaculate in his cobalt-blue uniform cut in Arpeggian
fashion with gold filigree on shoulders and sleeves. The buttons, studded with jewels, glimmered colorfully in the light.
A young, blond Adonis, he stood straight to face his father.
"Sir."

The old man sighed. "You broke his neck, Torkild. By
the time they got him to med, the brain damage couldn't be
reversed. They . . . let him go." Afid Alhar coughed into
a silk handkerchief. "Kinder that way, I suppose."

Torkild's lips twitched under his straight nose, a controlled glint of satisfaction in his steely gray eyes.

"Damn it! Don't you understand? You're the brightest
student in the academy! Your marks excel those of your instructors! You're the best chance Alhar has had for a captaincy in generations—and now . . . now *this!"*

"Sir, he insulted M'Klea. He tried to seduce her. When I challenged him about it . . . he called her a slut. In public." The clipped tones conveyed confidence. Torkild's face remained like a mask.

Afid groaned under his breath, looking up from beneath gray bushy eyebrows. "Arpeggian honor. Boy, you'd better understand that in the eyes of the Directorate, our 'honor' is murder anywhere else in this godforsaken space. The Directorate has no interest in our culture. Hear, boy? They have no interest in our morality. Now, I'll do my best to cover this up—but the cost might be too great. We're not the power we once . . . But you know. I think . . . well, your chance to actually go to Arcturus, study there . . ."

"Father," Torkild leaned forward, hands out. "He tried to seduce M'Klea. I . . . I don't know. He might even have kissed her. You know how young women are. Their passions, once released, might take them to . . . to extremes. He wanted to bed her! Understand, father? Wanted to . . . to . . ." Torkild swallowed hard and turned. "Then . . . then, when I confronted him, he called her a slut. Before witnesses, father. What other choice did I have?"

Afid worked his mouth, trying to rid himself of the sour taste. "Torkild, did it ever occur to you that M'Klea uses you? Hush, don't interrupt. I want you to think about it. Ever since she was tiny, you've doted on her. I could . . . almost think it unnatural. Now, she's grown to such a beauty. Yes, she won the pageant . . . the most beautiful woman on Arpeggio. She has a taunting quality—and she knows it. I think, Torkild, that she's smarter than any of us know. I also wonder at her motives. I think she set that boy up. Knew exactly what would come of—"

"Father?" Torkild gasped, bending over the desk, shocked to bluntness. "Is this my sister—your *daughter* . . . you speak of so? I . . . I can't . . ."

"Torkild, don't let your love for her blind you. She's not what you believe. You see her as she was . . . a delightful child. You worship her as something delicate, a living doll. One of these days, you must see her as a person, a human being like—"

"Not as some *tart!*"

"No, indeed. I've been talking to some of the other Houses. I'm trying to get her married, Torkild. Considering this last unfortunate incident, the chances . . . What's wrong?"

His jaw clamped, the corners of his tight mouth working. "Married? She's too young! Just an innocent—"

"She's a woman. Or hadn't you noticed? And this ability of hers to manipulate people has me at wits—"

"But she . . . she . . ."

"Torkild, you must let her go. Don't look at me that way. Yes, I love her, too. But she's a woman. And . . . and even though she's my own daughter, she's got a mean streak. And she enjoys using you. Beware of her, Torkild. Don't let your affection blind you to—"

"I refuse to hear this from you." He stood proud, muscles tense. "My sister is a most precious—"

"She'll cut your throat one of these days, son. Think, boy! In the glory days, a brother *had* to guard his sister. You know the kind of world we had. Sometimes men couldn't control themselves. To deal with it, we established the custom of brothers taking responsibility for their . . Torkild? *Torkild!*"

Torkild Alhar didn't wait to hear. Shaking his head, he stamped out of the room, red-faced, jaws clamped.

Afid raised a weary hand to his forehead and sighed.

CHAPTER VIII

Krankov City, Mystery: Directorate Administration building.

The office consisted of a square room twenty by thirty meters, comm terminals hanging from each of the graphite walls, displayed the commerce of the planet in the numbers and charts which monitored Mysterian industry. Assistant Supervisors bent over their terminals, coordinating the entire needs of the world.

Dong Jenkins Cheng smiled briefly as he entered the room, nodding to those who looked up. At his office door in the back, Louise Andropovich waited, gray hair pulled back, a serious look on her pinched features.

"Good morning, Louise. Trouble?" He cocked his head,

a slight irritation in his stomach. Too much fat in the diet. Fried squid always elicited that response.

"Indeed."

"Well, let me get my wits and we'll solve it. Your daughter got in last night?"

"She did." She followed him in, waiting as he walked to the dispenser to punch a cup of tea from the spigot.

He crossed, picking up his headset, placing it on his brow and lifting the screen from his one window. "Clarise is all right?"

Louise flushed slightly, lowering her eyes. "Better. You know, we can't thank you enough. She returned last night on the transport. If you hadn't gone out on a limb for us . . . well, she'd never have made it to University. She's a bioengineer now." The shy smile that occasionally touched Louise's lips lingered. "And she didn't come alone. She has a husband now. Nice boy—also a bioengineer. Anyway, they'll be in later today looking for a work assignment. And Dong?"

He sipped his tea. "Yes?"

"She's going to have a baby in four months. Fil and I are so happy. We're . . . well, you can imagine."

"Indeed I can. With all that, what put that horrible look on your face a moment ago?"

Her eyes dropped. "Another riot this morning. The Deus faction evidently rounded up the Spider leaders. The bodies were left hanging, quite dead, with notes."

Dong winced rubbing his forehead. "This . . . this isn't good. We . . . we'll have to send a full report. Transduction to the Director. It will reflect on all of us." He ground his teeth, feeling his stomach turn. "What? What can we do?"

Louise lifted a shoulder. "I . . . I don't know. The note said that this morning would be the coming of atonement. That the hand of Deus would be felt all across the planet."

"Anything concrete?"

"Only that we'd know by 10:00." She looked up at the chronometer. "A minute and a half. I'd begun to fear you'd—"

An alarm went off in the outer office. Dong hurried, staring out at the pandemonium as his assistants stiffened, working frantically.

"What? What is it?"

Jorge lifted his head. "Someone has just destroyed the transduction dish. We've recorded explosions in major facilities all over the planet. Every Directorate building in the—''

Beneath his feet, the floor jumped. Dong hardly felt it as the walls exploded in gouts of flame.

In the tumbled walls, the rescuers found only fragments of bodies amid the wreckage of comm terminals. As they worked, a muscular middle-aged man stood on the corner by the wreckage.

''Deus has come! Death to the Satan of the Directorate! Prepare yourselves for the coming of the Messiah!''

Stunned, people stopped, listening to the man, taking the literature he handed them.

Aboard *Spider's Treasure:* Mid jump: Arcturus/World.

Darwin Pike couldn't sleep. The language tapes had been threading their way through his brain for the last three nights as he picked up Romanan via sleep stim. Learning by electronic stimulation couldn't be easier. Subjects that once had taken years of hard study could be imparted within days. The brain, though, paid a price by suddenly having lots of facts on tap—but often no framework within which to fit it all. Pike wondered if it didn't affect personality, too. After sleep stim, he always thought he'd become someone else— a stranger in his familiar mind.

Pulling himself to his feet, the light automatically brightened. He pulled on an old pair of trousers and a shirt and palmed the hatch. One fist knotted about the hilt of the Randall as he walked the corridors. A soft vibrant hum permeated the decks, a thrill of the power of the mighty matter-antimatter reactors that powered the vessel through the light jump. From the oblong light panels overhead to the subtle vibrations in the walls, the ship lived around him. Stylized spiders had been carefully drawn on hatches or pieces of equipment. The Romanan means of distinguishing ''Thou'' from ''it.'' Effigies of Power, the symbol of their God surrounded him as firmly as the graphsteel bulkheads.

Ships didn't really have night or day. They ran full-time with one third of the crew on duty at any given moment. He let his feet take him where they would.

He couldn't make up his mind about Commander Andojar. Every time they met—be it supper, or over some duty— he ended up intellectually squared off and trading punches.

She never failed to infuriate him to the very limits of his patience.

"She's a damned wolverine," he growled to himself. And her love life? The ludicrous thought left him laughing. He could see Susan and the object of her affections approaching each other like two porcupines!

In his own mind, he called her the Iron Lady. She ran the ship with a steel fist, and once he had witnessed her chewing on a poor Romanan's butt: most sobering. Further, she had taken more scalps in the Sirian revolt than any other Romanan. Her men spoke of her with awe and admiration tingeing their voices. He could see it in their eyes; they'd kill for her.

For the first time, Darwin Pike had to admit to being completely intimidated by a woman eight years younger and ninety pounds lighter. Perhaps something besides sleep stim kept him up nights. To ameliorate the situation, Darwin made up lies about his manhood as he tried to soothe his bruised ego.

The absolute worst of it all proved to be his incredible infatuation with the woman. She filled his erotic dreams most ardently. He spent what little free time he had wondering what she was really like—hoping she had a warm interior under that tough, chain-mail manner. Most of all, he periodically caught glimpses of the pain which was so superbly hidden under that powerful mask; he couldn't help but puzzle over the wound she concealed.

Susan had become an obsession.

He rounded the corner of a corridor to see the object of his thoughts enter a hatch at the end of the companionway and grinned sourly. If he couldn't sleep, maybe one of her tongue lashings would make him feel normal again. Besides, there *had* to be a way of getting his bear holo back.

He found the right hatch and palmed it. The door slid open and he stepped quietly in. She stood at the far end of the room, the sound of his entrance covered by the grating of the pallet that slid out of the wall. A wisp of condensation rose in faint tracery as cold metal met warm air.

Darwin swallowed at the gruesome sight of the mangled corpse. The remains of a man lay on the slab. Muscular, broad of chest, and strong-armed, the Romanan features couldn't be mistaken. That now-pale face showed laugh lines around the eyes and mouth, although the slitted eyelids couldn't hide the mask of death—of the horror that had possessed him in that final moment.

Both legs had been blown off just below the hips. The femurs protruded in splintered fragments through flesh roasted brown in places, and washed out pink in others. Obviously the blast hadn't cauterized well enough to stem the flow of blood from the big femoral arteries.

Susan reached out to one of the still hands and held it in her own, stroking it. Slowly, carefully, she bent over and kissed the cold flesh, shoulders rising and falling in stifled sobs. The trace of a tear, like a faceted jewel in the light, twinkled on her cheek.

"Oh, Friday. I loved you so. After what Ngen . . . did to . . . I just couldn't be with you. In my mind, Friday, he . . . he. . . . My dear beloved, forgive me. Blessed Spider, forgive me."

Darwin quietly palmed the hatch and stepped out before she could notice him. The words echoed hollowly in his mind. He didn't sleep any better afterward.

Habber's Star: MKA-6 complex, L4, Ambrose Sector.

Habber's Star consists of a small asteroid mining colony processing chondrite asteroids for manganese, aluminum, silicon, sulfur, iron, gallium, germanium, arsenide, indium, and nickel. A small mobile colony consisting of a single station, MKA-6 has been mining the Habber's system for roughly thirty years now. Population has maintained at roughly 420 individuals.

Colonel Ben Mason pulled at his beard as *Gregory* slowed and lowered her shielding. MKA-6 mining station looked like it always did, except the huge lasers weren't blasting molten vapor out of the accumulated asteroids. The giant rocks waited motionlessly in the magnetic net which contained them. The long spindly field generators which funneled the vapors into the processing plant hung motionless, powerless, oddly pathetic against the black of space. Behind *Gregory,* the faint K class primary known as Habber's Star cast rouge shadows over the mining station.

Crimson light, like blood, played eerily over the gantries. A GCI floated at the end of a tentacle lock, grapples keeping it in place. A Type III yacht could barely be seen around the curve of the domestic dome. Scanners showed antimatter generation in both the station and ship. Other than that, the emergency beacon which brought them here despite schedules continued to squeal.

Stations were always getting in trouble. Or did it just boil down to the fact that his job entailed answering those distress calls? Did it only seem like things were falling apart with greater frequency these days? Mason and his crew had been shuttling constantly since the Romanan outbreak and the illegal Dobra broadcast. To Ben Mason's eyes, humanity waited, anxious, ready for trouble. He and his crew had run out of energy trying to keep the pot from boiling over.

An AT moved out from *Gregory*'s locks, cleared with the control sail, and vectored to settle at a side lock below the midline of the station.

A monitor flashed to life among the array of panels cluttering the bridge screens. A Patrol marine stared out from a similarly cluttered AT's bridge. "Docked, sir. I've got a man on the other side who's practically crazy with relief."

"Captain Lallemand, find out what happened. We don't have a lot of time to fool with this. The Director wants us over Bazaar . . . and yesterday wouldn't be too soon. Fix their problem—whatever it is—and get back here."

"Yes, sir."

Mason was left staring at an empty monitor.

"Everyone's weird these days," he muttered. "Comm officer."

"Sir?"

"According to the records, MKA-6 has burned out the powerleads three different times in the last seven years. Makeshift repairs probably got them again. Damn, when are people gonna realize we're not a mobile parts store? Can't they get it through their hard goddamn skulls to conduct a little preventive maintenance?"

"Sir?' Lallemand's voice came through. "Looks like burned out powerlead."

"No joke?"

"They just need a couple of meters of number thirty and they can splice in and be back on line. Can we accommodate? The project director here, uh, Tav Ohashi, says he's got to load that GCI or everything gets fouled up."

Mason nodded. "I'll have engineering open shuttle lock . . . That the only shuttle they got? That great big one?"

Lallemand turned to talk to someone before answering,

"Yes, sir. That and a personal yacht. The guy here says the yacht's not available."

"Then they can dock at shuttle bay three. Only one big enough to handle that thing. Get the powerlead on board and get back here."

"Yes, sir." Lallemand hesitated and lowered his voice. "Weird, sir. It's like they're half asleep here. Ohashi is really strange—like drugged. Kind of . . . well, you know, stupid. Not all there." He pointed to his head meaningfully.

"Not all there? Hell, everyone's getting strange. Too many hours, probably. Just get back here. We're overdue, remember?"

Lallemand nodded and Mason turned, unaware the monitor snapped off immediately behind him.

"Shuttle bay three?" the comm officer asked. "Pretty close to sensitive parts of the ship. Regulations—"

"What do a bunch of asteroid miners know of Patrol ships of the line? So we detail security personnel to load the powerlead. One to run the antigrav in, another to keep an eye on things. Besides, that's the only bay that can handle that thing. Wonder where they got a shuttle that big, anyway?"

The comm officer started to say something and shrugged.

The Colonel drew a cup of coffee from the use-polished dispenser. Looking around the bridge, he grunted, satisfied with the stat boards, and settled into the command chair. "More routine. I feel like nursemaid to half the galaxy. No wonder we got our butts kicked at Sirius. We're a roving hardware store, hospital, and handyman service. Just the thing to keep a crack outfit like the Patrol ever vigilant. You think anyone sleeps better knowing we can fix the plumbing?"

The comm officer chuckled absently.

Ben Mason didn't wait to watch the shuttle dock. Instead, he turned himself to the daily reports. Corporal Stephensen had been placed on report again for belting Arnson in the mouth. Lieutenant Skia applied for transfer to Arcturus. Reason given: Father with terminal illness. Ben rubbed his cheeks. "Should I let him—"

The blaring of security klaxons brought him bolt upright.

He looked up in time to see two impossible lances of violet blaster light snap into existence as the docked GCI opened fire. "Where'd they get blasters?" Mason bellowed.

"GCI's don't carry blasters!" *Gregory* trembled under the concussion of direct hits. Then the power went dead.

Geosynchronous orbit over World: Beyond Far Side Sector.

Bleary-eyed, Darwin Pike unstrapped from the shuttle seat and tried to remember the last two weeks of his kaleidoscopic life. Mostly he'd lived in his bunk, plastered flat by what felt like a thousand tons crashing down on his chest.

A most annoying odor drifted up from his unwashed body. *Spider's Treasure* had come through the jump and received a message from *Bullet*. They had made the two week deceleration at almost forty gs, pushing the compensating grav plates to the limit and causing more than a little distortion. If any of the old Patrol personnel thought they'd seen tough duty before, Susan Smith Andojar showed them just how far their personal limits could be stretched—and how far beyond she could strain them.

The shuttle lights flickered as it plugged into another grid. A faint thump sounded somewhere and the gentle noise of the atmosphere plant dimmed. The deck plating below the zero-stick carpeting thudded under the load of many feet. A lock clacked and hissed behind him.

Darwin stood and stretched, relief flooding his system. Romanans, haggard looking, pulled packs from retainers and walked toward the lock. Susan ducked through the bridge hatch and motioned.

Darwin followed, weaving slightly as he rubbed the stubble on his cheek. Under the g stress, no one had eaten much solid food. Pills and occasional sips of water would stay down. Anything more substantial came boiling back up in a hurry. With the gravity, it proved almost impossible to clean up.

The air in the shuttle smelled of plastics, graphitics, and artificial fabrics. Susan cocked her head, a wealth of raven black falling over her shoulder.

"You all right?"

"Must be the constant travel," he mumbled. "Where in hell are we now? All I got was an order to grab notes and follow the private. I didn't expect to leave the ship so soon. Christ, the gravity just got back to normal. Uh, can I get a shower and—"

"Later." She spun on her heel, padding down the aisle.

''For the moment, the Admiral wants you in conference . . . asap.''

She waited at the lock, making sure he got through the zero g section. Even with her help, he almost fell on his face crossing those few centimeters of weightlessness. The sensation was that of being pulled three different ways at once.

''And this is?'' He looked past armed marines down endless corridors of white.

''Bullet.''

Darwin had never even seen combat armor before this trip. It followed that he lived in it for nine days straight, the amount of time it took them to reach World on that horrible trip. He enjoyed the sensation of stripping the hard stuff off and handing it to the private. *Did I really survive the experience?* He shot a quick glance at Susan. She still appeared fresh, cheeks rosy. *Inhuman bitch.*

They walked no more than thirty meters to a lift. Looking closely, the walls seemed a bit irregular—as if they'd been pasted up in recent construction. In places, plating gleamed, suspiciously new. Inside, Darwin leaned gratefully against the paneling and tried to catch his breath. The valise he carried seemed to weigh a ton. He tried to close his eyes and pull himself together, but the hatch hissed open and Susan was leaving him behind with her easy dogtrot.

Reeling, Pike followed down more corridor—some looking a bit battered—and through a security hatch guarded by a Romanan with a blaster. Darwin blinked his way into bright lights.

''Admiral, may I present Dr. Darwin Pike. Dr. Pike, this is Admiral Damen Ree.'' Susan stepped back.

A medium-sized muscular man shook Pike's hand. Maybe in his fifties, Damen Ree carried himself easily. No nonsense eyes measured him from either side of a stubby nose. Life had used the craggy features of the Admiral's face poorly. The strong jaw jutted out in defiance, lines of command graven into his cocky features. A compact arm gestured.

''Dr. Pike, this is the War Chief, John Smith Iron Eyes.''

Darwin's hand disappeared in the grip of a heavy-muscled, dark-skinned man wearing Romanan hide clothing. Most of Iron Eyes' belt glistened with black hair. Sharp black eyes peered out around a long flat nose. Flared zygomas gave the face a flat look despite the generous mouth.

Long black braids framed his features. Like being face-to-face with a wolf, he decided. Pike had heard of Iron Eyes—the man who'd helped Leeta Dobra save the Romanans. He'd just met the War Chief who'd ravaged Sirius and beaten the planet to its knees.

"Major Rita Sarsa, my third in command," Ree introduced, indicating a redheaded woman. Under other circumstances, Pike might have looked twice. Now, the cool green eyes took his measure, challenging, almost deadly. Her pale skin didn't hide the ghosts of freckles. Fine bone structure gave her chiseled features. She, too, carried herself well, balanced and lithe, a most attractive woman were it not for her hard eyes—eyes that had seen too much of the tough side of life.

Maybe all the women around Romanans are that way. Magnificent specimens of female perfection—all armed with knives and ready to shred a man before he can even smile innocently!

"Major Neal Iverson," Ree continued. Darwin shook hands, feeling at ease for the first time. Compared with the others, Iverson just looked like a veteran officer, tall and blond, a competent manner about him. The perfect career man—not a predator like the rest. Hell, no wonder Susan seemed so tough. Look at her playmates!

Practically shoving Darwin into a chair, Ree accessed comm through the headset circling his close-cropped skull. They all wore headsets—even Iron Eyes, and it left him looking slightly like some fantasy book warrior.

A star map blinked into existence. "Here's what happened," Ree began. He bounced on his toes, hands clasped behind him. "Our last communications with—"

"Excuse me, sir," Darwin blinked owlishly to clear the ache out of his eyes. "Could I have a cup of coffee? The trip in was a little trying. I can hardly think."

Ree cocked his head, mouth hard, then waved it away in irritation. "I'm sorry. I suppose it was. You look a little ragged. Forgive me."

At a gesture, a private standing in the background punched the dispenser and handed Pike a steaming cup of black liquid.

Ree waited while Darwin got his coffee and gratefully slugged back a mouthful of the hot brew, burning his tongue and the roof of his mouth. Between the pain and caffeine, he perked up. Pegging the last of his coffee, he drew a deep breath. "All right, Admiral, I'm fit for another week at least."

Ree nodded and five stars lit up on the map. "This is Bazaar and the systems nearest to it. Notice they include Ryan, Trist, and Habber's Star. Almost two weeks ago, Bazaar managed to seize a GCI from the Bazaaran transshipment station. At the same time Directorate buildings, government houses, and comm centers on the surrounding systems were destroyed by explosives. Ngen—"

Susan gasped. "Ngen? He's . . ."

"The Bazaaran Messiah," Rita supplied.

Susan's color drained as she stiffened, a glittering in her eyes.

Ngen? Ngen Van Chow? Like the one she was talking to Friday's corpse about? Is that what just scared her so? Who is this Ngen, anyway, that he can get a reaction like that out of the Iron Lady?

Ree continued, "Communications centers—including holo stations, and some key transduction centers—they spared, overrunning them instead with armed commandos. Those stations are now preaching holy war. Ngen announced Satan—namely the Directorate—was being driven from among the faithful. His purges started immediately. We've had no further word from the five systems. We do know they have at least seven ships now . . . and maybe a Patrol ship of the Line, the *Gregory*. The Directorate has received no word of her since the takeover.

"Now," Ree crossed his arms, bullet head tilted back, "we know what Ngen can do with captured ships. He's got access to a lot of classified Brotherhood technology. How much, we don't—"

"Brotherhood technology?" Pike squinted. "Like in the historic records?"

Ree cocked his head. "Just like that. The same sort of . . . never mind. For the moment that's not your concern. We want your anthropological insight."

Darwin leaned back, thinking. "I read your preliminary assessment. Major Sarsa was very astute regarding the situation. As far as I can tell from my statistical manipulations, this Fatherhood religion should sweep the Directorate like wildfire. Every sociocultural factor is right for a religious movement."

"We know," Iron Eyes said easily. "What is your assessment of the religion's impact on us? How will it affect my people? Should we be worried?''

"Anytime Ngen's involved, you'd damn well better be worried," Rita growled, flashing Susan a look.

Pike didn't miss the subtle communication between them. Andojar had stiffened, some of the color draining from her face. Mulling that over, Darwin realized Ree and Iron Eyes had riveted their attention on him. To gain time he steepled his fingers authoritatively.

"Let me give you some background information before I plunge into that." Darwin gathered his scattered thoughts. "We accept that any revitalization movement which involves religion goes through five phases. First, they move from steady state—as in the Directorate before the Romanan discovery. Second, comes a period of individual stress where people begin to wonder what's wrong with their lives and why their needs aren't being met. The third is a period of cultural distortion. Just what we've seen happen in the last two years—kicked off, of course, by the Romanan presence and the Patrol defeat over Sirius. Fourth, a strategy of revitalization is implemented . . . what we see manifested in this Deus religious craze. Finally, a steady state develops again when all the shouting is over. A new order has been established—and not always a better order, I might add.''

"Just like that? Patterned change?" Iron Eyes frowned, doodling with a pen. "Like a machine performs some—"

"No, the process isn't cast in stone. Remember, we're dealing with human behavior and that's a plastic adaptation to change. Several strategies can be employed to modify the sequence. In this case the movement is messianic. The savior, avatar, prophet—whatever you want to call him—directs the return to mazeway. When you've got that aspect—"

"Return to *what?*"

"I'm sorry." Darwin smiled an apology. "Mazeway is the mental image we have of the idea, concepts, practices, artifacts, behaviors, and environments which create our world. We all see them as a maze, and the means by which we manipulate and move through them is the way . . . hence, mazeway. The mazeway becomes suspect in the individual stress period I mentioned earlier. Something's wrong. A person's needs aren't being met. Enough deprivation to bother him deeply. Obviously, he tries to change his approach and build a new mazeway which will allow him to deal with the world around him. In this case, your Ngen has provided a solution prepackaged. Messiahs tend to do that.''

"All right," Iron Eyes nodded. "We follow you, go on.''

"In this particular case, our messiah is promising a Golden Age just around the corner. This serves two purposes for Van Chow. He has an established scapegoat—the Directorate—on which to pin blame for the loss of mazeway. Second, he has a unifying threat in the Romanans whereby that Golden Age might be unjustly ripped away from the people. The Romanan threat is strengthened by the realization that your mazeway is so vastly different from theirs. If you win, they'll lose their reality . . . and the future will become something different and frightening. You can see the appeal to a civilization which has been safe, secure, and spoon-fed for so many years.''

"So Ngen must destroy us?" Iron Eyes mused. "Eliminate the threat so the promised Golden Age arrives on schedule. That's what we needed to know." His hard eyes shifted in Rita's direction.

A crooked smile bent the redhead's lips. "Spider's after us again, John. The bastard never promised it'd be easy.''

Ree looked puzzled. "Do these things always go full circle?''

Darwin shook his head. "No, they don't. They can be short-circuited at any point along the way. The direction can be changed by a loss of faith in the messiah's message . . . or by a more powerful messiah arriving on the scene. The people can be wiped out by disease or war. A technological breakthrough can alleviate the needs of the people, redefine the mazeway, if you will. A thousand things can change in a normal system.''

"Is this a normal system?" Rita Sarsa chewed the end of her stylus, green eyes frosty.

Darwin shrugged. "I don't know. I don't have enough information on Ngen Van Chow to tell. Too much depends on his motives . . . and how adept he is at keeping his followers whipped up to a fever pitch.''

"He led the revolt at Sirius," Damen Ree reminded. "He kept them fighting when their planet was charred rubble.''

Darwin leaned back in the chair, miserably weary. Each muscle felt unhooked and limp. "I won't say it's hopeless, but you must understand that Ngen . . . if he's as brilliant as you say . . . can counter any move we make. So long as his disciples see change and improvement, they'll continue to follow. We can provide rational appeals for calm, but jihads are supported by emotion, not logic.''

Iron Eyes shifted uneasily. "We have Prophets. Maybe we can substitute? Use a Prophet to supplant him?''

"If they'll help," Rita added coolly. "Prophets don't like meddling with politics.''

Ree returned to his map. "Since we first heard of the takeover, the following systems have been swept up." Three more lights blinked. Acts of sabotage have taken place on the following worlds." A series of lights flickered, including Sol system.

Pike pointed, wiggling his finger. "He's moving very fast. He must have an excellent logistical ability. The coordination is incredible. I mean, consider what it takes to expand at that rate? You think it's just him? Alone? To organize—''

"He's that brilliant," Ree observed dryly. He leaned on the edge of the table. "Doctor, we want you to give us some ammunition so we can stop him. If he carries through with his threat to overwhelm the Directorate, Ngen and his people can squash us by their very numbers.''

Darwin fingered the stubble on his chin and squinted at the shining lights on the map. "First and foremost, I'll need to understand their entire philosophy. When the flaws can be determined, we'll have some idea of where to start picking and prodding. Using their logic against them we can—''

"What do you mean? Flaws?" Susan's brown eyes probed his.

He blinked at the gritty feeling in his eyes. "Any religion has logical flaws built into it. Since Ngen has elected to utilize a Judeo-Christian-Islamic approach, it'll be a little easier to demonstrate them. He already has a major contradiction in his good-evil relationship. If Deus is omnipotent, like Ngen says, Satan can only exist at Deus' will . . . otherwise Deus isn't all powerful. You see? Logical inconsistency. You can't have it both ways. If we could find a way to put the logical inconsistency into an emotional framework . . .''

He could see her digesting his words, light lines tracing into her brow. *Finally! You see, girl, I can be taken seriously.*

"That sounds pretty shaky." Rita glared at her stylus before looking up at Darwin. "Such a simple thing? *That* can be used against Ngen?''

Darwin yawned. "Any religion is based upon assumptions. One of the keys to Ngen's is that God, YVEH, and Allah are all one and the same. Study of the Tanach, Bible, and Koran produces obvious differences of interpretation. Since the religions were syncretically derived—meaning they wanted to include a little of everyone's pet beliefs to sell their package—contradictions riddle the holy books. Those, in turn, led to centuries of terribly bloody warfare, genocide, and every kind of horror perpetrated in the name of a benevolent Deity.''

Ree fingered his chin. "If someone like Chester will help, so much the better. After all, the idea of future sight worked for us on Sirius. Would you antagonize someone who can see 'your' future?"

"How do your Prophets react to that?"

"Playing upon belief in Spider for military benefit amuses them. To Prophets, such actions have no founding in Truth. They claim what will be will be.'' Rita screwed up her lips. "They say Ngen cannot change the nature of God with his religion. What is ultimately real isn't subject to human whim.''

"Any chance Spider will get mad and kick Ngen's ass?" Neal Iverson asked. "Maybe all those lies will get a reaction out of the old boy.''

"Men have been lying, killing, and extorting in the name of God for millennia.'' Darwin studied the man. "Nobody ever won a war based on what he beseeched God to do. Someone once said God sides with whoever has the most blasters. God doesn't care what humans call him—or how he's worshiped, for that matter.''

Ree continued to gaze at the star map. "Providing his revolution gains ground in an exponential manner, Ngen will be knocking on the doors of our Sector within a year and a half. That figure doesn't account for him having to stabilize his holdings after the Fathers take control. He'll need to put together logistics in his back country. No matter how you look at it, he needs a support system to figure out resource redistribution.''

"That means taking over Arcturus, lock, stock, and barrel.'' Rita tapped her stylus on the plasteel tabletop. "He's got to. Once he has Arcturus, the Directorate falls. *Urbs et orbis.*''

Ree turned to Darwin. "What would the effect be if one of his home worlds—say Bazaar—got raided one fine day? Any value in that? Can it be turned in our favor?"

"That depends on how it's carried out." Pike frowned.
"If you hit them in a way that bruises their pie-in-the-sky
anticipations, the impact could be devastating. The thing to
avoid is creating martyrs in the name of Deus."

"War tends to escalate." Susan remained expressionless.
"After the first shot is fired, you can't go back. Fate takes
over. Sanity fades away like a puddle in the hot sun."

A shiver ran down Pike's spine, but he continued, "Look
to your history. Human behavior in these situations remains
pretty much stable over time. Study the terrorist politics that
dominated Earth in the late twentieth century. When the
western governments began publicly executing Islamic ter-
rorists by smothering them in bacon grease, the wind went
out of terrorist sails real quick. They died in a state of pollution which Allah simply could not accept. They believed
their souls were lost."

"Does Ngen's revolution have any weaknesses you can
see, Doctor?" Ree turned skeptical eyes his way.

"Sure does. A very basic one. He has to better their lot
some way or another. If he doesn't, they'll suffer additional
loss of mazeway. Now, if that happens, the faithful will
react against him just as emotionally as they're reacting
against the Directorate. Think of it as . . . I mean, you see,
the problem with being a messiah is that unless the promises
are met—or you get lucky enough to be martyred—your own
converts inevitably tear you apart. No one likes a lying messiah."

"But they're being bilked," Neal cried.

Pike spread his hands. "So you think humans dislike being bilked over their religion? Big deal. Most religions bilk
the followers anyway. They get away with it because the
people can't believe it's happening under God's nose. He's
watching all this, right? It's the oldest con around."

"How soon should we move?" Ree paced, head down in
thought, hands still clasped behind him.

"Don't go too fast," Darwin advised. "The more ground
he gains, the tougher his administration will become. At the
same time, fear of his jihad will spread to other systems.
The threatened populations will be nervous—ready to jump
in any direction. If we play our cards right, we can turn
them against Ngen."

"I thought you weren't into cloak and dagger," Susan
crossed her arms, a shapely eyebrow lifted.

Darwin smiled lamely. "I'm not. I consider this the ultimate challenge to applied anthropology."

"Didn't Leeta Dobra say that once?" Ree asked, talking to himself.

Iron Eyes nodded wearily. "She did."

"I'd give my right arm for some preliminary data concerning his programs and strategies on those planets," Darwin said aloud, lost in speculation. "Might give us a clue about where to work a lever into the mortar of his religion. Once you pry a couple of bricks out of the wall, the whole thing wobbles."

"That can be arranged," Ree said suddenly. "I'd been thinking the same thing. I want a military reconnaissance of what Ngen has to fight with. In the event we're up against *Gregory,* I want to know. So far intelligence is pretty damn spotty. I get the feeling that even Skor's at a loss, and damn it, if he's overextended, who knows what might happen?"

"We also don't know what Ngen got out of Frontier when he blew up the Brotherhood computer there." Susan shook her head slowly, stung by a private memory. "If you will all recall, he gave us a terrible surprise on Sirius."

Silence stretched.

Iron Eyes knotted a scarred block of fist. "We must not forget *our* advantages. We have one thing Ngen hasn't counted on. A resource he can't even begin to conceive. We have the Prophets." Heads nodded.

"I don't know if I buy the idea about Prophets seeing the future, but we can get definite PR boost from them. They ought to sell well. Holy men usually do. Maybe do a couple of spots with them looking mystic or something."

The look Iron Eyes gave him did anything but reassure. In a voice like a knife edge, the War Chief said, "I'll take your ignorance into consideration."

Pike tried not to squirm under the heat of those black eyes.

"Let's call an end to this, people," Ree added from the side. "Dr. Pike has been informative . . . and I think he'll be an asset for our side."

Iron Eyes looked down to where his powerful dark fingers gripped the table's side. "Perhaps."

"We've got a lot to consider. Neal, see to accommodations for Dr. Pike. Susan, I'd like a debriefing at your first opportunity." Ree palmed the hatch to disappear down the corridor, face a study of worry.

Pike could feel Iron Eyes' stare burning a hole in his back as he left the room. A giddy feeling of mortality fluttered in his stomach.

As a private led Darwin Pike to his new cabin on *Bullet,* he tried to put it all in perspective—only to realize the whole thing had to be crazy. No one had ever asked a dingbat anthropologist to single-handedly defuse a religious movement—let alone one on a galactic scale! They were all stark raving nuts. No wonder Susan rotated a little off center.

His war bag had already been delivered. This cabin proved to be larger—with a full access comm. He thanked the private and flopped on the bed, heedless of the smell of stale sweat that clung to him.

CHAPTER IX

GEO orbit, Transshipment Station, Arpeggio.

The huge Patrol ship of the Line filled the monitors. "What I'd give to space on a vessel like that," Torkild Alhar breathed.

"One day, brother, perhaps you will." M'Klea tilted her head to a coquettish angle and smiled wistfully. "I wonder who this Messiah is? He commands a Patrol battleship. A most powerful man." She sighed audibly, aware of the looks the guards gave her. She narrowed the lids of her deep blue eyes and flipped the wealth of her pale gold hair over her shoulder.

All things considered, the room they had to wait in could barely be claimed as decent. Scuff marks marred the tiles underfoot. Through the years, a coating of filth had built up on the walls. The seats had been stained so many times the original colors were difficult to perceive. Even the air carried a rank tang. Hardly the place for M'Klea to be.

"The Patrol isn't high on my list," Torkild snorted. "Rejected my application. Can you imagine? Soldiers themselves, they turned *me* down for violence?"

"Ah, Torkild, just because you kept me from . . . from . . ."

He smiled and placed strong fingers under her chin, lifting so he could look into those incredible eyes. "A matter of honor, dear sister. So long as I live, no man will so much as cast his eyes upon you except in utmost respect. Our ancestors stole only the finest beauties from human space. It's in our blood to cherish our women—and you, blessed flower, are the finest of Arpeggio."

She smiled up at him shyly, the corners of her mouth quivering with delight. "You're the best brother in all of space, Torkild. The best."

A man stepped out into the waiting room. "Torkild Alhar?"

"Good luck," M'Klea cried, reaching up to hug him. "I know you'll do fine. I just know it. And when you get a command, you'll take me to the stars. To Arcturus where everyone can see me."

He laughed and smiled down at her. "I'll do fine. Now, don't you worry. The Messiah needs spacers. Where else but Arpeggio would he come? And I'm the best."

M'Klea blew him a kiss and watched as he walked proudly for the door. She turned, aware of the two bodyguards who waited, arms crossed. She gave them her best smile, getting exactly the reaction she wanted.

"Feel like a rotted slave," she whispered to herself. "Cattle have more freedom." In a rustle of burgundy skirts crafted from the finest Arcturian fabrics, she settled herself disdainfully against a cleaner looking spot on the wall and pulled a pocket comm from her jeweled pouch. Slim fingers pressed the news-tab stud. The Messiah's dark features formed on the small holo. M'Klea turned up the volume, listening again to the announcement.

"Citizens of Arpeggio, I know you've heard of our arrival in your skies. The Directorate has frightened you for no reason. I come not as an enemy, but as a friend. That I come in a Patrol battleship is but another sign of my strength. You've been lied to for so long, the truth will be strange to your ears.

"A new life has come to humanity—and it is the way of *Deus,* of the Fatherhood. Here, among you, I come to establish Temples, institutions of learning. Through the shared voice of God, we will all become closer, true brothers in a wondrous new future. Mankind has been stifled, virtually incarcerated on planets and stations. What you read, what you see, what you do, how you think, is controlled by the Directorate—by those huge-headed freaks who never want, whose *every* need is met. What can *they* know of you? How can those pampered, egotistical freaks understand the hunger within each of you? How can they understand your longings, your desires for a better life? Deus knows! Deus hears! Come, my people of Arpeggio! Allow me to build a Temple, to spread my word among you! I come to free you, to restore the glory that was Arpeggio in those fabled years so long ago!

"In proof, I am taking applications for fine young men and women to serve on my fleets. You need not convert. You need only be willing to work for decent pay. You need only desire to see beyond the farthest star—to see your family fed and your accounts swelling with credits. Send me your best. Send me your brightest. Accept the hand of Deus and raise yourselves to the stars. A golden age has dawned for humanity with the overthrow of the Directorate and the crumbling tyranny of the Patrol. See the rays of prosperity shining through the heavens. Deus is come!"

M'Klea ran delicate fingers down her smooth throat as she studied the Messiah. A passion burned in his dark eyes, the likes of which she'd never seen. Fascinated, she studied his face, wondering if she could bend him to her will like every other man she'd ever met—excluding, of course, her father. Even through the tiny screen, he appeared to challenge her. Challenge? Indeed, even as he challenged the Directorate itself. She slitted her eyes. Torkild would receive a position in the Messiah's fleet. Of that, she had no doubt. The House of Alhar had few rivals in power or influence. Prior to gaining any Arpeggian influence, the old families would be courted. The Messiah would come to M'Klea. And when he did, she'd be sure to suitably impress him. Handling Torkild, however, might be a bit of a problem—but then, she had always managed Torkild's jealousies, hadn't she?

M'Klea smiled to herself. "And my bondage is over, brother. No one is craftier than M'Klea. You will see, brother. You *will* see."

Krankov City, Mystery: Soccerplex arena.

The crowd hollered, voices raised as the Messiah's face filled the huge holos at each end.

"The new way is come! Look to your souls, my people, look to your souls. Deus is the savior, the true God. Indeed,

I have heard his voice, come to free you from the ignorance and bondage of Satan.''

Sira Velkner nodded to himself. Killing off the Spider gangs had been a simple matter. Setting the explosives to decapitate the Directorate came as old hat to a man of his many talents. Now, as he looked down over the swelling crowds filling the stadium, the entire project awed him. Indeed, how lucky that Pallas Mikros had allowed him in on the ground floor. But then, he'd always provided excellent service for Pallas . . . and been paid well.

''Deus! Deus! Deus! the thunderous cry rose, bouncing off the very weather dome that capped the city so high overhead. Ngen's bowed face faded, leaving the crowd silent, struck with the awe of his holy presence. Damnation! What a speaker Van Chow was!

''Wait!'' A voice called out through the speakers. ''Citizens. Listen to me!''

Sira turned where he stood in the observation booth, looking down at the announcer's platform, seeing a single man on the stage.

''You know me,'' the speaker raised his hands. ''I'm Johnathan Hart, your retired Supervisor. And I know that face . . . that man who calls himself Messiah!''

Sira straightened, suddenly uneasy.

''I tell you,'' Hart cried passionately, ''that face filled the holos crossing my desk for every day of my supervision until my retirement. Let's not allow what happened to Sirius to befall us here.''

Triple cursed! Hart knew Ngen? Sira backed away, taking the lift to the ground floor. He moved quickly, ducking into the long dark tunnel that led under the main stands, booted feet echoing hollowly on the graphsteel.

''I tell you the man you'd call Messiah is a criminal! I tell you that first he ruined Sirius, and now he's coming to ruin you. That man . . . that Messiah is Ngen Van Chow! That's why he sabotaged the Directorate here. You think about it. You think!''

Johnathan Hart stood, feet braced, looking out over the growing roar of the crowd.

''Mister Hart?'' Sira called, motioning. ''If you'd spare me a minute? I have some information on Ngen Van Chow which you might need.''

Hart stared at him, uneasy.

"Quickly," Sira hissed. "My informant won't wait. He's already afraid."

Hart's lips worked in his fleshy face. "I . . . all right. But make it quick. We've got to stop this. Kill it before it gets out of hand."

"Then hurry," Sira agreed fervently.

"Citizens!" Hart addressed the loudspeaker. "I have some fresh information. If you will excuse me for just a moment." He stepped down, feet clanging on the stairway. Sira motioned, practically running back into the tunnel.

"Yes? What? Who?" Hart asked, blinking in the dark.

"I bring you greetings from Ngen Van Chow, Supervisor. He wants you to know we can't afford your big mouth. For the moment, our plans are too sensitive."

"You . . ." Hart froze, staring at the ugly blaster in Velkner's hands.

"Me. If you'll come along? You can do it alive or dead."

"Never . . . not for Van Chow or any of his lackeys. Shoot here and now."

"If you wish." Sira triggered the weapon.

Bullet in GEO orbit over World.

"Doctor Pike?" An oddly emotionless voice pried into his dreams.

Darwin managed to crank an eye open. "Mffffzzzat?"

"Doctor Pike, I'm sorry to bother you. I need some idea of your requirements for surveillance gear," the flat voice insisted. The hatch light blinked indicating Hambrei stood just outside.

"Come in, engineer."

Darwin pulled himself upright, fighting sleep from his muzzy system. He managed to focus on the pale engineer's face as he stepped through the whispering hatch. Giorj Habrei's odd colorless eyes could have belonged to a corpse. Darwin ran his tongue—when had he burned it?—over the fur grown on his teeth overnight, and groped a cup of coffee out of the dispenser. Every joint in his body felt unhinged. Gravity flux from Susan's mad deceleration from light speed.

"Surveillance?" he managed, trying to pull himself together.

"I understand you wish to investigate the worlds currently under Ngen's rule. Plans are being made for the construction of a recon probe which will orbit the star systems in question and ascertain the potential for landing a small party to conduct covert operations and gain intelligence. Several options are currently under consideration depending on the final accepted method of implementation. Until that decision is finalized, I must anticipate all design parameters.''

"Now, why didn't I think of that?" Darwin ran a hand over his face and winced.

"I would like to know what sort of equipment you will require for your investigations."

Darwin blinked hard, mind staggering. "Uh, I'm kind of new at this. What kind of equipment have you got?"

"Standard Patrol issue sensors, or, if you desire, I can produce specialized pieces which will meet outstanding circumstances.''

Didn't the man's expression ever change? And *this* was the character who lived with Susan? Darwin tried to make sense of it—and came up totally blank.

"You had breakfast yet?" Pike asked on the way to the head.

"It would be time for lunch, Doctor," Giorj called through the door.

"Right, well . . . lunch?" Darwin stepped into the shower, punched the water on, and sighed as the force field squeegeed the water and stale sweat off. Partly alive, he groped around for his clothing.

"No, I haven't. I thought I would see you first." Giorj watched Pike's circumambulation of the cabin.

"Well, if you don't have plans, you can tell me over a meal what the sensors will do and I'll let you know if I think they'll work. Considering my ignorance, that might be the best, don't you think?" Darwin scowled at himself in the mirror and made faces as he plopped a sterilizing pill in his mouth to kill the plaque.

"As you wish, Doctor. But please be aware that I have a rigorous schedule to maintain."

"Uh . . . sure. I understand." He smiled uneasily at Giorj. The engineer could have been a machine. No, android. That was the right word. Darwin palmed the hatch and gestured. "After . . . after you."

Throughout the meal, Giorj talked about the abilities of the sensors.

"So for all intents and purposes, I could hear a mouse sneeze from an altitude of two hundred kilometers?"

"Assuming you wish to investigate rodents. I imagine size wouldn't be much trouble. The remote control linkages, however, might be severely limited by the logistics and maneuverability. Mice tend to occupy places where the difficulties of monitoring can be readily understood. Now, we're verging on the edge of microminiaturization for long distance surveillance. The problem, of course, is how the mice will react to the probe. You see, the parameters of the sending unit might create microwaves which will disturb the natural behavior of the mice. Otherwise, I can't guarantee clean reception."

"Uh . . . yeah. I . . . well, yeah." Pike nodded, mouth half open. "Well, I was just using that as an example, you understand. I . . ."

Hambrei stared at him.

Darwin took a deep breath. "I think you had it pegged the first time." He smiled superficially, nerves painting a queasiness around the base of his spine. "The remote microphones and drone holo recorders will be fine, Giorj. More than sufficient. Can't . . . can't think of anything I need more for my first spy trip." *And now what do I say? He is human . . . isn't he?*

Giorj nodded, chewing slowly on his steak.

"So, tell me, how do you and Susan manage such diverse careers?" He pasted his most genial smile on—knowing he sounded inane.

"Susan and I do what we must."

"That's all?"

"Is there more?" Giorj stared at him from flat eyes.

"I mean . . . well, you care for each other, but . . ." Darwin swallowed, throat going dry. "Well, I was . . . you know . . . she's a different sort of . . ."

Giorj watched expressionlessly.

"Never mind. I'd better be getting back to work." Panic made for miserable retreats. "Overslept as it is. Um, you be sure and . . . and call me if you need more . . . more information on monitoring devices."

Darwin got up, smiled into the blank gray face again, and tried to walk out with at least a shred of decorum.

In the hall, he muttered, "Where this side of hell did *she* find *HIM!*"

Streaking through the skies over World above the Settlements.

Susan Smith Andojar rotated the thrusters, blasting reaction forward as she banked in a twenty g turn, swinging
wide over the Bear Mountains. Tradition dictated a War
Chief attend to this task. It *had* been her command. He *had*
been her lover. The duty doubled, painful, terrible for all
the needs of the People.

*Friday . . . Friday, how did it come to this? Why can't I
forgive myself? Why doesn't the grief ever diminish? Why
did we have to end like this?*

With iron control, she blocked the memories that clung
to the corners of her mind—images of her and Friday Garcia
Yellow Legs climbing upward through the ragged, weathered red granite below. Images of his knowing eyes as she'd
descended the steep path, returning from her first vision, a
medicine song filling her with promise. Carefully, she de-
nied the pain, ignored the burden of the container strapped
down in the crash webbing against the weapons bulkhead
behind her. Instead, she funneled her concentration into the
gyrating AT, shedding V over the mountains that stung her
heart, circling back toward the Settlements at an altitude of
twenty-five kilometers.

"Ground Control, this is AT22, descending to glide
path."

"AT22, acknowledged. You're on descent. The pattern is
clear. Request you use vector one three zero. Repeat, one
three zero. Smith clan is moving cattle and would appreciate
avoiding knife feuds over stampeded stock."

"Acknowledged," she answered, a slight smile curving
her lips. Cattle and shrieking, howling ATs didn't mix. So,
her People were changing. They used air traffic control now.
ATs tended to send livestock through polewood fences.

She banked out over the sea, sweeping low over the blue-
silver waves. Descending, the altimeter flashed an endless
stream of numbers as she leveled out a klick over the waves.
Feathering the throttles back, she dropped air speed to
500 kph, the AT shivering slightly in the lumpy air as she
approached the beach at 130°.

Concentrating, she brought the AT whistling in, the familiar sight of the wrecked *Nicholai Romanan* warming
something in her heart. Despite it all, this was home. After
all those ages of bears and Raiders, the Romanans came

from space again. This time, on their own—not as refugees of the World Soviet.

She settled to one side of the dusty square. They'd marked the place for ATs now. A bubble-dome for ground crews had been constructed. Lasers guided her in. She settled without the slightest jolt and powered down as Ground Control read out figures.

Taking a deep breath, she shut the system down and puffed out her cheeks. The familiar pull of World hugged her. She'd come back, back to the place that bore her. Here she'd sucked the milk of survival from her mother's breast. Her planet had molded her, shaped her. And she'd survived— and succeeded.

"Perfect," Ki called. "Couldn't have done better myself. I don't see any reason why you can't be rated Grade Two. I'll send the confirmation through to Major Iverson."

"Thanks, Ki." She smiled at him as she stood from the command chair. Ki grinned, flat face lighting. A small man, his shoulders packed beefy muscle. He kept his hair close-cropped on his skull. A red spider had been stenciled on his uniform. A different spark began to grow in his brown eyes—one she couldn't allow him to develop. *Escape. Now!* Quickly she stripped off the headset and passed the hatch.

The white box waited. One emotional upset to another— a continuation of reality. Fear . . . or pain, her guiding lights. The box beckoned

Steeling herself, she unfastened the straps, an aching hollow yawning within. For a moment, her fingers hesitated on the wide graphsteel buckles. She swallowed, and pulled them loose.

"Want an antigrav?"

She didn't look back to where Ki stood in the hatch between the weapons pods. She shook her head quickly.

"Look, if you want to talk, you'll know where to find—"

"Thanks, Ki. Not now. Maybe when . . . well, not for a while."

"I understand." He moved away, the sound of his fatigues receding as he went forward.

She bit her lip to still her trembling jaw. Under her breath, she whispered, "You can't understand, Ki. No one can."

Dry-eyed, she lifted the lid, a puff of condensed vapor drifting cold over her skin. She swallowed hard again, forcing herself to look. "Wish it was me instead. Damn it, I . . . I . . . Why couldn't it be me?"

Planting her feet, she braced herself and lifted Friday's icy corpse. Heedless of the chill seeping from his stiff flesh, she turned, shifting his weight to her back, bent under the burden. Awkward and off balance, she palmed the hatch release. The assault ramp dropped to a whine of mechanics and thumped solidly on the packed soil. Susan walked down into the bright light of World.

The smells of Settlement hung full and familiar in her nostrils, marred slightly by the stink of the AT's cooling thrusters. The yellow ground underfoot supported several resistant blades of trampled grass, clutching to life as did her People. The warm wind caressed her, tickling long strands of hair along her cheek. Home. A warmth to fight the chill of Friday's corpse eating into her back.

"Home, Friday. I brought you home. Back to everything you helped me escape. Who'd know I'd come to love you so—or that it would end this way?"

Another of the endless memories struggled to weave itself through her mind. Crystal clear, she recalled that day in Rita's quarters. A desperate day. She stood before Friday, feeling his warm hands on her skin, the longing love in his tender kiss. He waited, ready to fight knife feud for her honor, placing his life at risk for her. His eyes sparkled again in her mind as he looked up into her very soul. And she'd given herself to him, pulled his manhood deep within in that most ardent expression of love. Her body had throbbed, warm, rushing, filled with Friday and love. Now the wispy ghost of her virginity clung to his frozen flesh, a tattered shawl for this man—this first of all lovers.

An aircar approached, a grinning Romanan youth at the controls. The joy faded as he slowed, seeing what she carried. He nodded respectfully, helping her place the body in the rear seat.

"I guess you want to go to the platform, Commander Andojar?"

Susan stared at him, eyes narrowed, seeing the fullness of his youth. Youth? He couldn't be a year or more younger than she—and ages upon endless ages behind.

She stopped herself from snapping, drawing a deep breath, "Haven't your elders been teaching you? If not, you're in trouble, boy. No, we go to Mama Yellow Legs' house. Only when she's had time to weep, and clean her son's body, do we go to the platform."

The youth swallowed. "I . . . I . . . . thought maybe he

was your . . . your husband. I'm sorry, Susan Smith Andojar.''

She nodded and slipped into the seat next to him. ''It's
all right. An honest mistake.'' Only she felt dead inside, as
dead as Friday Garcia Yellow Legs in the back seat. And
she'd continue to feel that way, even after she'd placed his
body on the platform, after she'd left Friday for the People
to see. Another hero home from the stars.

Bullet in GEO orbit over World.

Rita Sarsa found him engrossed in some research as she
passed the hatch to his quarters. Pike looked up, leaving
the text on screen as he took the series of figures she handed
him.

Rita dropped into the seat he indicated and studied him
as he scanned the flimsies.

*What is it about him I don't trust? He's not crafty, mean,
or callous . . . just . . . What? Innocent? Since when is
innocent untrustworthy?*

''I'd say he's going to solidify his position on Arpeggio.''

Rita leaned back to stare at the tiles overhead, mildly
aware of his eyes. She entertained a wry humor concerning
men and the way they looked at her. The gleam in Pike's
eye came from interest and appreciation. Damn fool.

''I'd agree with you, Doctor—only for military reasons.
Arpeggio has a better industrial base. They can reoutfit his
fleet, provide logistical support and maintenance for high
tech equipment.''

Pike managed to quell his appraisal of her physical assets
and turn his mind to the problem at hand. A stir of irritation
growled in her gut. Not untrustworthy—untried. That was
it. Pike lacked that essential security of identity. He didn't
know who he was . . . what he wanted. And until he found
it—if he ever did—he'd have to be watched.

''I'd say it would be a step in the right direction.'' Pike
leaned back, propping an elbow on the comm. ''He'll need
to refine his message, too. Arpeggio will allow him to experiment, see what works and what doesn't. He hesitated.
''No way a Patrol ship of the line could get in and blast
Gregory before he refits?''

Rita shook her head. ''That's the Director's decision. We
don't know what he's decided. For some reason, we're not
in Skor's close circle of confidants.''

"I suppose not." Frown lines marked Pike's brow.

"Anything else?" Rita stood, turning for the door.

Pike hesitated.

"Yes, Doctor?"

"Who was Friday? How was he killed?"

Where in hell had *that* come from? "That's an interesting question. Friday Garcia Yellow Legs was one hell of a warrior. He served as one of my squad leaders in the Sirian fighting. We promoted him to second in command of the Romanan forces—John's right hand in the last days of the pacification. In fact, if you'll take the trouble to look up the Sirian surrender document, you'll find his signature there as the Romanan witness. He was one of the first Romanans to risk his life to keep the Directorate from exterminating World. He was a very close, very dear friend."

"A lot of people around here speak highly of him." Darwin paused in an effort to find the right words. "Then there's Giorj. Quite an interesting character. Had a professor like him once. Completely opposite of what I understand Friday was like. How'd they get along?"

An amused smile curled Rita's lips and she chuckled softly. So that was it. "Interested in Susan, huh?"

Darwin blushed and muttered lamely, "I was simply curious."

"One bit of advice, Doctor Pike." She held his gaze, overpowering his sudden defiance. "You don't have the foggiest idea who Susan is . . . or what she's been through. You seem like a nice kid, so I'll give you a break. You're a little green, Pike. You're sharp . . . and you're a hotshot, but I don't think you know what kind of stuff you're made of. Until you find out you're tougher than toron, Susan would eat you up and spit you out in little pieces."

"I've had a few lumps, Major," Darwin attempted to make it sound easy.

"Maybe," Rita shrugged. "We don't know your limits though, do we?"

To his credit, Pike met her deadly stare.

"No, I guess we don't," he gritted back.

Long after she was gone, Darwin Pike tried to figure out why he felt so inadequate. He almost looked forward to landing on World. The way he felt, maybe he'd just go out and strangle one of those Romanan goddamned bears. That would at least get him a new picture!

CHAPTER X

Aboard the captured Patrol ship *Gregory* rechristened the *Deus:* in GEO orbit over Arpeggio.

Ngen reclined in his quarters, staring up at a holo where a man studied a comm terminal. Behind the fellow stretched a room of bustling comm techs staring into monitors, communicating through their headsets.

"We've loaded the technical data from your private vessel, Messiah." The tech looked back at the schematics flickering across his monitor. "Looks like a perfect take. I've got engineering working on the weapons as we speak. A lot of them are baffled. This stuff, well, it's light-years ahead of what we're used to. I don't know if we'll ever be able to grasp some of it."

"Just begin with the basics." Ngen chewed at his lip, conscious of his sweaty hands. "For the moment, the weapons systems are first priority."

The tech nodded and looked up a little nervously. "The Fathers . . . well, the ones you sent us. They, uh, know what we're talking about. They do just fine when you show them a design. But they're . . ."

"Yes?"

The tech raised his hands helplessly. "They're not all there, you know? They don't anticipate problems. Don't act like . . . like real people."

"Different cultures are that way. Do you think the people on Bazaar would see you the same as another Arpeggian would?"

A helpless look filled the tech's eyes. "Uh, no, I guess not, Messiah. But—"

"I'll expect a progress report every day. Time is of the essence." Ngen cut the connection, sighing. "They're becoming more concerned about the Fathers." He looked across the spacious quarters, brooding. One entire wall filled with a holo of Arpeggio where it spun, real time, below the vast bulk of the ship.

"We kept the psych to a minimum with the Patrol techs."

Pallas wiggled his light-jeweled fingers, idly watching the flickers of color trace across the plush paneling of Ngen's quarters. "Nevertheless, the wide field works better than I could have expected. They obey and perform any job you give them. Fascinating. Modifications on your ships are . . . are almost inhumanly quick."

"A new order." Ngen smiled as he lifted a glass of Arcturian brandy. "I think I'll have this room turned into my private palace, hmm? An access through that bulkhead will lead to my private recreation—and I'm hoping to find many new challenges for my abilities. The Directorate lies open before us."

Pallas sighed, accepting the glass Ngen handed him. "And you think you'll be ready for the Patrol when they arrive?"

Ngen smirked as he settled into a plush command chair. "Oh, I've slowed them considerably. Amazing what a little sabotage can do to wilt the resolve of the Patrol. Your agents blow up a transductor on Santa del Cielo, and the Directors panic. Do they send the fleet after us? Or is the prudent move to maintain a presence in the skies of a troubled planet where a Directorate official has been assassinated? You know, I like this game—and so far I've kept them paralyzed. I've bought my time precisely, manipulating their confusion to my benefit. Oh, I assure you, they've lost."

Pallas smiled weakly. "We have a small corner of space, Ngen. It's a big Directorate out there."

Ngen shrugged, sipping his Star Mist. "Young Alhar surprises me. I watched him in the exercises. I think he's a genius when it comes to command. I'm thinking of giving him *Gabriel* as soon as the conversions are completed."

Pallas tilted his head back, staring at Ngen from half-lidded eyes. "He may be talented, but he's also Arpeggian. Beware, Ngen. They have a tradition of—"

Ngen waved a sultry hand. "There are many traditions, my friend. There is only one Deus, and His voice is the Messiah. Traditions, like the Patrol . . . like so much of the useless baggage left us by the Directorate, will fall like chaff. And, in the end, there's always the psych. You've seen. The Temple is being built on Arpeggian soil. Another shall follow, and then another. The changes will be small at first—only a convert here and there—but they will be the important ones. Heads of the old Houses—like Alhar, political leaders, influential people. The masses will follow. Trust me.''

Pallas laughed to himself. ''Indeed, I do. You know, I thought you were a madman when you came to me after losing Sirius. I . . . No, don't look at me like that. What would you have thought? Hmm? But now, Ngen, I'm convinced of your genius.''

Ngen studied him from the corner of his eye. ''And ambitious? Seeking more for yourself?''

Pallas twiddled his rings in a blazing display. ''Always . . . but not in the manner you might worry about. Me, I'm a simple man. No, when it's all finished, I want a planet. Maybe Earth, maybe Jewel, or one of the better ones. That, and, of course, all the finest courtesans in space. You know the kind.''

''You're a hedonist, Pallas. That's the ancient word for it. A slave to pleasure.''

''Give me that, Ngen, and I want no more. You rule as you wish. Give me my planet . . . and my girls, and you needn't worry.''

''You weren't always this way.'' Ngen held the glass up to study the amber fluid.

''What I did to survive in the Directorate, and what I'd do in a perfect society are two different things. No, I'm tired of scrambling. I paid my dues, kept my skin despite the best efforts of the Directorate. Because I was good at it doesn't mean I liked it. I would simply rest.''

Ngen smacked his knee. ''Then rest you shall, but for the moment, it will have to be on Bazaar. I need someone to supervise the manufacturing there. Ah! Don't wince like that. Consider it an installment on a better planet. Unless we arm and supply our Fathers, we'll lose even this.''

''Bazaar,'' Pallas sighed. ''Very well. After all, it's only for a little while.''

''And I need a man with your skill and insight to solve any problems which develop. We're building a system, after all. Things will go wrong. Unfortunately, that's how we learn. Perfect the implementation for me. Besides, don't worry, you've got the psych.''

Pallas lifted his fat-puffy hands, full cheeks contorted in a resigned grin. ''And I have my Tiara. Life could be worse.''

Ngen cocked his head. ''Ah, the sacrifices of war. Did you happen to see Torkild's sister at the reception her father gave? There's a chance, Pallas, that she's the most beautiful woman in the galaxy. She oozes sexuality when she walks. Half the men there were panting—with one eye on Torkild, however. They fear him—and lust after her."

Pallas's lips twitched. "You understand Arpeggian honor, Ngen?"

"She seemed very bright. Of all the women there, only she didn't fawn. Do you know how delightful that was? She just looked at me—a sort of challenge. And such an incredible beauty."

"Ngen, I remind you . . ."

"Yes, yes. But a God must look where he will."

Bullet in GEO over World.

After a solid week of scouring Jewish, Christian, and Moslem holy books, Darwin Pike found time to escape to the gym. He palmed the hatch and stepped through. The long room appeared empty. The slight chill in the air invigorated him. A large spider effigy dominated one of the white walls—the art work superb. Weight bars and various exercise machines lined the wall opposite. Cushioned matting overlay a grav-sensor grid which would break a hard fall.

The combat robot stood by itself in one corner. Pike grinned and walked over to the lone machine, looking it up and down. Human in shape, he prodded it, amazed that skull, ribs and the other bones felt right. The density modeled that of human flesh. He inspected the setting on the machine and instructed the computer to use the first step novice program.

Then he squared off.

Reality gyrated.

Darwin shook his head and blinked up at the ceiling while the robot recovered and stood waiting. The pain in his side didn't seem terminal, so he stood up and tried to hit the robot in the mouth.

This time he had to pull his face out of the mat. From the feel, his nose hadn't been broken. While he dabbed at the blood, he made sure the robot controls were indeed set for the lowest function.

"If finesse doesn't do it . . . use brawn." He ducked his head, reached out, and rushed it full tilt. When he quit bouncing, the ceiling filled his blurry vision again.

Wincing, he pulled himself up and flexed his muscles.

Nothing seemed broken. Hell, he'd carried an entire moose hind quarter fifteen miles out of the muskeg! He was healthy and strong!

Angry, he attacked the robot with a flying leap, managed to bull one arm around it, and land a glancing fist along the left ribs before the machine exploded in a frenzy and he slammed into the mat again.

Gasping for breath, his stunned body tried to catalog all the pain. He pulled his way to his feet, glaring hatred at the combat robot. He tried sneaking up on it.

The ceiling of the gym, he figured, didn't deserve prolonged scrutiny. No, his arm hadn't been pulled out of place. The room spun a little as he stood up. He walked toward the robot slowly, leaping high into the air at the last moment and kicking viciously. He scored! Then the robot whirled, caught his foot, and smashed him to the mat again.

He wasted a good minute coughing before he fought his way to his feet. The warm feeling came from the blood dripping out of his nose. Trying to catch his breath, the huge spider caught his eye. The thing seemed to stare at him, watching, mocking, entertained; it fed his irritation.

Then he went berserk.

Darwin Pike, Alaskan hunter, noted anthropologist, couldn't be sure if his eyeballs hurt when they moved. Through jangled nerves, such discriminations as isolating an individual agony could only be accomplished with difficulty. When he got the scoreboard into bleary focus, he could see the robot had twenty-three; Pike had four. Blessed gods, he could still feel his toes. The damn machine hadn't broken his spine after all!

He wiped at the blood dripping from his nose and fought his way to his feet again, growling rage at the robot. The loud ringing in his ears annoyed him. He tried to smash the machine with an elbow and experienced a brief gratification when the machine staggered. He barely got a fist back before it caught him up and piled him into the mat again.

"Gotcha first, damn it!" he grunted, waiting for the lights to quit sparkling behind his eyes.

"First doesn't always win the day," a familiar contralto called. Darwin moaned, wishing he could crawl under the mat. He forced his broken neck to turn and assured himself Susan Smith Andojar indeed leaned against the wall, arms crossed. How much had she seen?

Wearily, he pulled himself into a sitting position and took

another swipe at his swollen nose. He tried to kill her dead with his stare. It didn't work. Instead she walked over and pulled a towel from the wall.

"Quite a score," she said, bending down to help him clean his face with the damp cloth.

"There's a first time for everything." He tried unsuccessfully to stifle a cough.

She hesitated, dark eyes searching his. "You've never had any instruction in . . . I see. In that case, you didn't do all that badly. You know, you're lucky to be conscious. That's a military machine. It's designed to handle advanced attack when students have reached the stage where they can kill each other."

"Oh!" Did he always sound dumb? "You made it look so . . . so easy."

At his compliment, her expression yielded by a fraction. "How long have you been after that thing?"

"The way I hurt . . . twenty years." Darwin felt to make sure his jaw hadn't been disarticulated.

"Stand up." She offered a hand.

He tried not to wince, but couldn't be sure he succeeded.

"In the first place, put your feet so, and squat like this. Weight balanced so." Step by step she showed him how to stand. Then she led him through several easy basics and he was allowed the opportunity of throwing her by the end of the session.

"How long till I can kill that robot?" He jammed a thumb over his shoulder, throwing the inoffensive machine a dark stare.

"Considering what I saw of your first assault . . ." She paused, thinking. "Maybe a year or two." Her eyes twinkled and the laughter bubbled naturally.

Darwin fingered his ribs and cringed. He shook his head. "You must think I'm a complete idiot."

Her serious look pricked a deep-seated vulnerability.

"No," she said easily, crossing her arms and scuffing the mat with a toe. "You're just out of your element. Things are different here, and on World. You don't understand this reality. Romanans see the universe differently than Directorate—"

"I'm an anthropologist," he retorted. "We're supposed to be able to understand different realities."

Her eyes flashed for a second. "Understanding isn't a matter of mental gymnastics, Doctor. It's a common experience of worldview, shared perceptions. You're not going to understand Romanans until you've lived with them. Ask Marty Bruk when we planet. Ask Bella Vola, or S. Montaldo. I've read the textbooks your Dr. Chem wrote—they're superficial at best.''

He started to sigh; a stitch of pain stifled it. ''Like me trying to tell the faculty who the Inuit really are. All right, Commander, I'm out of my element. I'm doing the best I can . . . and I'll be damned if your machine—or your Romanans—are going to get the best of me.''

A softness crept into her voice. ''In the event you're serious, Doctor, you'll do just fine. But I'll warn you now, Spider tends to extract a terrible price from those he chooses for his purposes. If you're willing to pay so much, you'll earn everyone's respect—and kill the robot, too. Only, beware. When you ask something of Spider, you never know what you'll pay. And those who ask and can't deliver, Spider breaks . . . and casts aside. Understand?''

For one electric moment, he could glimpse her soul, staggering.

As quickly, it passed. She clapped him on the shoulder and smiled a wistful reassurance before walking toward the shower. He stood, stunned, then the notion crept in around the edges that she'd treated him as an equal for the first time.

The slow smile curling his lips stopped cold as he looked at the huge spider on the wall. It seemed to hang, now, as predatory as any of the Romanans, ready to spring. A keen anticipation animated the gleaming black eyes, a hungry look. Pike swallowed dryly, the tingle of premonition climbing his spine on a thousand icy feet.

''It's just a painting,'' he muttered.

Santa del Cielo: Ambrose Sector.

Santa del Cielo was established by the Soviets as a Gulag planet. Hot, wet, its diminutive continents covered by curious nonsentient plant/animal species, the place originally received shipments of South and Central American radicals interested in destabilizing Soviet influence in the always volatile region. Subsequent to the clearing of land and planetary exploration, deposits of metals, fissionables, and the extreme fertility of the soil led to a dramatic rise in colonization and development. Currently, Santa del Cielo is the manufacturing brilliance in Ambrose Sector, its exports of-

ten rivaling those of Arcturus. Population is estimated at 6.5 billion.

Dimetry Shastakovich studied the faces around him. The meeting room felt tense, crowded, the very air pensive and thick to the nostrils. Settled around the table before him, his four Assistant Supervisors waited, some fingering taza cups nervously, others staring up at the tan gywood panels overhead. The air conditioning hummed in the background, the picture-hung walls depicting the planet's settlement seemed brooding, the colors darker, appearing aged and worn.

Antonio de Garza cleared his throat. "The people will listen to you, Dimetry. They trust you. It's been this way now for a long time. You've stood up for them. Fought for them. They know it. They know you. Now they're scared. We've had riots in the streets, Fathers killing the Spider youth gangs. Open warfare. The time is now."

"I agree," Silencio Marcos added, tapping his finger-nails on the hard surface of the table. His black bushy eye-brows rose high, wrinkling his forehead. "We've had too many riots. Where is the Patrol? There are rumors that the Fathers have taken *Gregory*. I see control crumbling. We're not a backwater like Mystery or Bazaar. We must act now."

Maria Antessa leaned forward, fists clenched. "Claim control, Dimetry. Now, before the Fathers can intensify their campaign against us. You must. The people will listen. You're the one strong voice who can stop this religious mania. If . . . if you don't, what will happen?"

Dimetry sighed and stood, pulling at his earlobe. Limbs leaden, he paced, hands clasped behind him as his feet sank in the deep carpet. "Very well. I will address the people tomorrow night."

The electromagnetic rifle balanced easily on the steel retainer as Winston Zimbuti squinted down the IR sight, aware of the two polished rails extending out almost two meters. Where he crouched in the blackness of the Cultural Events building roof, the air clung, hot, wet, stale. Zimbuti shifted slightly on the ceiling hanger, pawing at the sweat beading on his brow.

So the Supervisor had done it. Rumor claimed he'd take control of the planet tonight, outlawing the Fathers in his speech. Winston licked his lips and placed his sweaty cheek against the rifle stock, feeling the hum of the charge pack.

Far below him, Dimetry Shastakovich stepped out to a fanfare, holo pickups rolling in close as the Supervisor raised his hands. The rehearsed audience stood in a thunder of applause while the Cielan anthem stroked up.

Winston took a breath and let it out slowly, the hero of the people filling his sight aperture. Through the magnification, Zimbuti looked full into Shastakovich's eyes, seeing the man's soul, pressed, harried, worried. For that brief second, reality stilled. The barest pressure of Zimbuti's finger, perhaps a heart flutter, closed the circuit. The magnetic pulse shot down the rails, accelerating the projectile it pulled behind to four thousand meters per second. The 5 mm bullet caught Shastakovich full in the chest as he opened his mouth to speak, arms raised to the people of Santa del Cielo.

Winston Zimbuti was running along the roof, jumping to the door of the waiting aircar even as the explosives detonated, blowing his EM rifle to fragments.

"Well?" the driver asked as they rose, accelerating for the space port.

"I was paid, wasn't I?" Zimbuti looked over at the coordinator for Deus. "Do you seriously think anyone else could fill his shoes?"

GEO orbit above World.

Chester Armijo Garcia hummed under his breath as he smiled and bowed slightly to the stunned guard. Without a care, he passed the gaping marine and walked down the long white corridor from the shuttle lock. Time washed all around him, rolling through, over, and on all sides. He looked up at the right monitor and smiled warmly.

"Hello, Damen. I'm on the way to your quarters." No more needed to be said. Admiral Ree would be there. After all, it would be the future and, for now, free will would play no part—though the Admiral didn't know that. Prophets didn't worry much about the future. No purpose could be served fretting about the inevitable. Resisting the irresistible only wore a human out—and without purpose at that. Better to let the inexorable be, and watch, and learn, and nourish the soul with that knowledge. Only by passively watching the choices of the cusps could the fragile human mind cope.

Chester sighed as the shining lift door opened before him and he stepped in. "Damen Ree's deck please." The door closed. "Magic," he told himself. Seeing the future had become second nature. On the other hand, lifts that could transport his physical being through so imposing an artifact as *Bullet* daunted him.

The hatch slid open half a kilometer from where he'd started. So quick! And no sensation of motion. "Magic."

He walked down the long white corridor, ignoring the visions floating just behind his eyes, allowing them to play out as if no more than a daydream. Far below, on the planet, a young man would cry in fear this night, tortured by dreams of a future beyond his comprehension. His cusp lay near, swelling the paths of the future into a complex knot that blurred in Chester's mind, the fuzzy reality of the cusp—Spider's legacy to men. How would the young man choose? Suffering stretched beyond the various extensions Chester could see.

He stopped before Ree's door, knowing without looking that the Admiral trotted down the hall behind him. Ree's first words played through his mind.

"No, Damen, no emergency exists. Nothing is wrong. Only a simple transduction from the Director. He wishes to talk to me."

Damen Ree, puffing slightly, nodded and palmed the lock plate to his private quarters.

"Good to see you again, Chester." Ree led him in, turning to comm. "We've got a message coming in from Arcturus, patch it through to my quarters immediately."

Ree turned, eyes curious as always.

"Thank you, Damen. Scotch will be delightful," Chester anticipated and settled himself in the antigrav—more magic—and watched as Ree performed the moves of the vision. Two realities, future and present, only out of phase with each other, one passing in the mind—then again in life.

"Haven't seen you for a while. What's kept you busy, Chester?" Ree smiled easily, warmly. "You've found some new music?"

"Opera. Fascinating. But that answer misleads the intent of your question. I spent the last month with the horses." A happy flush filled him at the memory. "I stayed with a herd up at the foot of the mountains. I needed the change. I won't have much time in the future for such simple pleasures."

"Horses?"

Chester raised a hand. "I'll save you the time of . . . as you say, beating around the bush. Horses are beautiful creatures, Damen. Not so complicated as men, but no less possessed of their own concerns, fears, and pettiness. To watch them run with their manes and hooves flying in the sun is poetry for the soul. Perhaps no animal has the fluidity of horses in motion. Spider meant for humans to enjoy such grace for its own sake. Beauty is the balm of the soul—a treat as delightful as a massage to the physical body.

"At the same time, a Prophet needs a break from the constant preoccupations humans have with their problems. Horses, obsessed by their own needs, true, make fewer demands. They don't fill the future with so much anticipated tribulation. To a horse, life is 'now' oriented. Refreshing for one with my . . . proclivity? Mares are the best. Mares enjoy life more than stallions. The sweetest grasses, the clearest cool water, flies, socializing—and sometimes an insistent foal—dominate a mare's major concerns. Can you call that a bad life?

"To be human, I believe, is to be a born complicator of nature and behavior—a trait of that frontal brain lobe Marty Bruk is so fond of discussing. Humanity enjoys a preoccupation with making trouble for itself. No human could be more miserable than to be placed in utopia. Imagine perfect surroundings with no threats and every need met. Indeed, such a place would drive a human totally insane with the need to wreck it somehow. The more incredibly complex and complicated and sophisticated the trouble, the better. I think people do it for entertainment."

Ree laughed. "And which do you prefer, Chester? People or horses?"

Chester spread his hands, sighing openly. "Horses are by far the more refreshing and honest, Damen. Humans, on the other hand, fascinate and constantly pique my curiosity. Humans are bothered by the most *peculiar* things. And how could a species which produced Mozart, produce Ngen Van Chow?"

Ree spread his hands, face blank.

"There is no answer to that, Damen. Each is simply another gleaming facet of the human condition. The variety of facets is as variable as humanity itself. Encompassing."

Ree ruminated on that, looking up suddenly.

"How do you do it? Actually see the future? I mean,

you've told me about visions. Do they run all the time? Like some holo or play? And how do you tell time?'' Ree settled himself across from Chester under a display of Romanan rifles and fighting knives from *Bullet*'s early days on World.

Chester touched the tips of his fingers together. ''What were you doing at the moment you heard that your father was dead?''

Ree scrunched his blocky features, thinking. ''I was in my room at University. Feet propped up, with a monitor on my lap. I had an exam the next day. Stochastic mechanics and quantum gravity. My roomy, Felix, came in . . . that kind of strained look on his face, the one he got when something was wrong. 'Uh, Damen, he said, 'look, I think you'd better read this.' And he handed me the flimsy.''

''As you can see the past at a traumatic moment, so do I see the future, just like that. Events in your memory telescope into the past—the process just reverses for the future. The time frame is the same, an indefinite before and after . . . events in sequence until they disappear in a maze of possibilities.'' Chester cocked his head, considering the various ways of communicating the idea to Ree, finding the best one. ''When I look to the future, it's just like remembering the past. You can think back to breakfast this morning. I can think forward to dinner tonight—the same way. How many breakfasts can you remember? A week's worth? More than that becomes a blur, meaningless. The important events, however, your father's death, the battle over World— those you see clearly. You know which came first. The future looks the same way to a Prophet—only more so since the cusps will lead to only one branch. Like looking up a tree trunk. Which leaf will be the final destination of the journey?''

''I always have trouble with that. Sure, I can accept seeing the future like imagining memories. Humans do that all the time. Daydream of what might be. It still boggles my mind.''

Chester smiled. ''Indeed. Close your eyes, Damen. That's it. Lean back in the chair, and relax. Imagine Neal Iverson walking down a long corridor. See the corridor in your mind? Good. He's walking, walking. Ahead is a T intersection. One way leads to the shuttle bay lock. The other leads to an AT lock. You don't know which is which. Now, there's a gap. A fuzziness, if you will. Neal is walking into a lock.

Imagine him checking the stat boards that monitor the lock. Can you see him closing the lock to the AT?''

"Yes.''

"Now change. Can you see him closing the main hatch to the shuttle?''

"Yes.''

"Did he go right or left at the T intersection?''

"I . . . I don't know. Which one leads where? You didn't tell me that.''

"Nor does Spider tell me which way a cusp will go.''

Ree opened his eyes. "So, it's like imagination? Like thinking things up?''

A bittersweet longing filled his breast as he shook his head. "No, Damen, it's real. That's the only difference, the quality I can't get you to experience with Neal in the corridor. Suppose now, that if Neal takes the shuttle, he'll die. Irreversible. You can see his death, his screams as a blaster from space blows him apart. What do you do now? Tell him? Of course you would . . . only you wouldn't in the end. The responsibility would suck you up. The power of the future would draw you on because you couldn't stand the pain. You'd fall deeper and deeper, each coming horror and pain too much to bear. So you try and fix it, change the future. And you're drawn deeper, and deeper, until in the end, you've lost yourself. You can't get back to Damen Ree . . . to *this* present.'' Chester spread his hands. "I fear words will never express the terrible impact of the reality. To survive is to disassociate—and accept reality as it happens. At times, it tears your soul.''

Ree stared at his scotch. "I have a vivid imagination. I'll trust you for it.'' He grunted softly. "I don't envy you, Chester.''

Chester blinked, a harmony within. "I have learned to accept, to allow Spider his will—and his way. I am happy, Damen. More, I am content with myself. How many can claim that? And I watch and learn and always try to understand.''

"Better you than me. I'm not sure I could take it.''

"We all do what Spider wills us. Now, the time has come to visit with Skor.''

As he spoke, Ree stiffened, receiving a message from his comm headset. More magic. To think a simple circlet of metal could implant words in a man's mind!

The holo flickered to life, the familiar monstrous visage

of the Director filling the screen. And speaking of magic, how did they get a living three-dimensional image out of a flat screen like that? And over such incomprehensible distance, too!

"Greetings, Director," Chester heard the words rolling out.

"You are there? I thought I would have to—"

"Why should I make you call twice? I would save you the time. To do so didn't meddle with the future. No cusps were compromised."

Skor blinked. "And the Admiral?"

"I called him. I needed a private transduction monitor. His was easily available. You don't desire too many to know you would speak with me. Besides, considering your needs, Damen—a student in his own right—will get as much out of this conversation as you will."

Skor's dwarfed mouth worked, blue eyes glittering. "I have no idea why I put up with your insolence, Prophet. Perhaps I only wished to reaffirm how irksome your nature is."

"Was it not within your power to replay the tapes of my visit to Arcturus? You could have satisfied yourself at less expense, could you not?"

"Do you goad me?"

"Do I have a reason to goad you?"

"You are a . . ." Skor stopped cold, face working under the bulbous helmet covering his swollen cranium. "I would like to discuss the situation within the Directorate."

"What would you learn?" A deep melancholy stirred in Chester, a vision forming in his mind. So much pain and horror lurked along the paths Skor Robinson must follow. Sorrow lay heavy within Chester's breast.

"Ngen Van Chow leaves me baffled. I and my colleagues are tired, physically exhausted and mentally fatigued. Our efforts are strained, Prophet. No matter that we rarely sleep, the harder we try, the more our control falters. Humanity is losing cohesion like a gas in vacuum. What do I do?"

Chester laced his fingers over his stomach, the strains of Bizet's *Carmen* drifting through his mind, reflecting the bittersweet of suffering. "I cannot tell you what to do, Director. To do so would compromise free will—drive me to madness. I can tell you what you seek of me—though you will not admit it."

"And that is, Prophet?"

"Simply to talk . . . to know that you are not alone in the universe. You feel alienated—cut off from the very humanity you struggle so bravely and futilely to save."

Skor blinked again, the tiny mouth working. "And I . . . You are most presumptuous, Prophet."

Chester smiled warmly, a gentle sympathy expanding in his chest. "Yes, Director, you *are* a brave hero. In another era your role would be portrayed as great drama . . . and great tragedy. I can do no more than offer my appreciation as a single individual for your struggle and sacrifice. No human may truly speak more honestly."

Skor's face pinched, poorly controlled. "Why do you say this? You know I ordered your death more than once. You know I would have destroyed your Romanans—and the traitorous Patrol who backed you. Why would you call me hero? Your action is totally without rationality or logic. I have been your enemy, your nemesis."

"And now you have learned what it means to struggle." Chester smiled. "You have learned to displace yourself, Director. You have learned pain and fear and despair and hope and all the other emotions humans share. In your infancy of dealing with them, you've come to *feel* for your fellows. For that, I applaud you. You have something to send back to Spider upon your death."

"Your religion means nothing to me."

"If you say so, Director. Nevertheless, you have come to doubt your atheism. Perhaps you have discovered more about yourself—and Spider—than you feel comfortable knowing."

Skor stared at him. "You are a major source of irritation, Prophet."

"That which irritates teaches, Director."

"You are a foul abomination, Prophet."

"As you wish."

"Van Chow has taken *Gregory*. Acts of sabotage abound. I must keep Patrol ships over troubled worlds to reassure the people that they're safe—or to intimidate as the case may be. Our position has become untenable. If we move against Van Chow, humanity is unsupervised. If we hesitate to deal with him, he grows stronger. What can I do, Prophet? How can I win?"

Chester smiled. "You would have me risk insanity to guide you?"

"I seek advice."

"Do you?"

"Teach me."

"What would you learn?"

"How to deal with Van Chow and avoid social disturbance."

"Is social disturbance bad?"

"It is chaos!"

"And chaos is bad?"

"Of course. Lack of order is detrimental. Chaos stirs discontent. Discontent spawns violence. Violence and suffering are wrapped within each other."

"Then you have answered your own question, have you not?"

"But Van Chow is a criminal!"

"Does he think so? Do others think him a criminal?"

"You defend him? He is a vile disrupter of social order."

"Is that bad?"

"You argue in circles, Prophet!"

"I only seek your answer, Director. I do not argue."

"I repeat, you are a vile abomination. Humankind would have been served had I disposed of you when I had the chance."

"I would return if you sincerely wish to kill me. In the event you truly believe mankind—and Spider—is served by my death, I submit myself willingly."

Ree made a choking sound.

Skor stared, the tiny hole of his mouth falling open. "You are mad, Prophet."

Chester smiled pleasantly. "Am I?"

Ree cleared his throat as Skor's face reddened. "Van Chow has *Gregory?*"

"He does."

"I don't suppose he's forgotten how to build those blasters."

"It would seem most improbable since he had two on his personal yacht."

"We're most interested in sharing information—"

"That is not propitious at this time. Feeling among the Patrol is weighted against you—as is that of my counterparts. Some prefer Van Chow, who is a—"

"Idiots."

"—known factor, rather than Romanan savages who might cut their hair off barbarously."

"Are you taking any action against Van Chow?"

Skor blinked. "As much as I can. For the moment, sabotage and its prevention have engaged the entire resources of the Patrol. We face a serious shortage of ships and matériel. As soon as we can stabilize, I'll order the fleet against *Gregory*."

"You've got to move now." Damen leaned forward, smacking a fist into his palm. "We'll support you with *Bullet*. Get him before he establishes a broad enough base to—"

"And if, by removing our presence, every disillusioned province rises as Sirius did? What then, Admiral? Which strategy seems preferable? One front? Or thousands? Which offers the greatest chance for victory? Which the greatest for defeat? Van Chow can always be negotiated with if nothing else—but Directorate-wide revolution?"

"Chester?" Ree looked across the cabin.

"Which do you suggest, Admiral?"

"Van Chow, now. Am I right?"

Chester smiled. "That will depend on the cusps, Admiral."

Ree raised his hands and let them drop in disgust. "Prophets," he muttered under his breath.

"We share an opinion for once, Admiral." Skor turned his gaze to Chester. "If I negotiate with Van Chow, will he keep his word?"

Ree made a strangled noise as Chester replied, "Does he have a reason to, Director? Would you trust one man? Or all of humanity? The individual? Or the mass? You must decide based on your own understanding of humanity and its needs."

"He'll cut your throat!" Ree gestured passionately. "He's . . . *he's a butcher!*"

"A most emotional display, Admiral." Skor studied him somberly before switching to Chester. "Thank you, Prophet, I think you've helped." The holo went dead.

Ree had jumped to his feet, a fist raised at the blank monitor. "You stupid, imbecilic . . ."

"His decision is made." Chester felt the changes, a different branch of the future sliding inexorably toward him.

Ree's color drained. "Blessed Spider, Ngen'll . . . Damn. *DAMN!*"

Chester smiled, standing to place a restraining hand on Ree's arm. "Please, Damen. Your cusp will come."

"What did he want? Why call here?"

Chester's beneficent smile widened. "To talk to me. You see, I'm his only friend. The only person in the entire Directorate who treats him as a human being. Ah! I know what you're going to say. No, it doesn't bother me that he calls me an abomination. Damen, you must understand, he has no social skills."

Ree stopped, a finger half lifted in protest. "By Spider, he doesn't, does he?"

Chester sipped the last of the scotch, placing the empty glass on the counter. "Thank you, Damen. I appreciate your allowing me the use of your quarters and transductor. Your scotch proved most enjoyable. Now I'll be on my way. Again—"

"Hold it." Ree rose, blocking the Prophet. "You called me a student earlier. You knew how this would turn out—or had a good idea. You can gain access to a transductor anywhere—and in private. Why did you want me here?"

Chester patted Ree's arm as he walked past and bit his lip, trying to place his palm the right way on the lock. The hatch didn't slide open.

"If I simply told you, Damen, how well would you learn the lesson?"

Ree rubbed the back of his neck. "You know, over the years, I've come to realize that you do very little that doesn't have layer upon layer of meaning, Chester. You accomplished a lot here today that I can't even perceive yet. I think, though, that you wanted me to see Skor—and that talk about social skills and horses wasn't empty."

"You are very astute, Damen. How does this door work?" Strains of Bach began whirling in his head.

Ree slapped the lock plate, the hatch hissing open.

Chester stepped into the corridor still staring at the lock plate. "Magic."

CHAPTER XI

Settlement, World: Beyond Far Side Sector.

Settlement is the original landing spot of the Soviet transport, Nicholai Romanan. *The wreckage of the ship—never meant for planeting—still lies to the side of the village square. While development has accompanied the rising fortunes of World and its wild inhabitants, traditionally minded people remain in their drafty shelters built of hide and wood. Currently, however, younger warriors are more desirous of modern housing, importing domes from their share of the Sirian economy. Sanitation, however, still relies on a local omnivore, the green harvester, which eats organic waste.*

Not even a jar marred touchdown.

Darwin fiddled for a couple of seconds before he figured out the quick-release from the cushioned seat and stood up. Military shuttles had limited observation ports. Sure the comm monitors showed a planet out there, but damn it, a monitor could show anything.

His pulse leaped, excitement causing him to fumble as fingers turned clumsy in the rush to undo his war bag from the kit storage above his seat. A new gravity tugged at him, heavier than *Bullet*'s. Real gravity. Planet gravity.

The ramp dropped and Darwin stepped out into bright morning sunshine, wincing at the strains and pains of his healing muscles. *Damned combat robot!* World stretched before him, a real gravity well of a planet. How like Earth.

Carefully, he knelt, running his fingers over the smooth silty soil. Yellow-brown in color, curiously formed pods stippled the surface between mashed grasses. Reverently, he rubbed the fine stuff between his fingers, feeling the texture.

Overhead, a vault of turquoise—deeper green in color than Earth's sky—stretched to a bank of white clouds that packed up along the peaks to the east.

"Goddamn," he whispered. "I'm really on another planet." He stood, scuttling the silly idea of kissing the ground. "I'd look real stupid. Susan would probably be watching, or something."

He sniffed the scented breeze blowing in from the sea to the west; the air—alive and free—filled his nostrils, humid, pungent with dust, a tang of smoke, a fragrance of cut vegetation and alfalfa—yes, alfalfa, the Earth kind, growing green and lush in a specially fenced pasture to one side of the spaceport. Otherwise, the native grasses? Sure looked like it, but then parallel evolution cropped up everywhere. Some forms naturally developed in gravity wells. He bent to finger a particularly spiky patch and cursed as a leaf neatly sliced his finger open.

Darwin scowled, searched his memory, and chuckled. "Figures, the first thing I grab on World is bayonet grass!"

He turned in the direction a lumbering freight carryall had gone, following the fence line toward the low buildings. An animal scent brought a smile to his lips. The bite of horse sweat mingled with that of manure. The sun warmed his face and hands. Around him, colors, movement, the feel of the wind—all brought him home—a link to Alaska, to Earth, to life in a *free* environment.

"I feel home," he mumbled under his breath, comparing the bite of the hot sun to that of Earth's. A little hotter, a little brighter, it left him squinting a bit more, the midday colors more washed-out. "My first new planet." Stations didn't count. Everyone made it to a station sometime or other in their lives. Stations were everywhere, artificial environments were old hat.

Darwin lifted his hands, dancing in a tight circle, whooping aloud. "And it ain't painted *WHITE!*" He cackled with glee, jumping up and down, laughing maniacally—and froze in place, realizing a wizened little woman leading a cow up the road had stopped, black eyes squinting warily out from beneath a threadbare red scarf. One hand crept to the old woman's knife, her undershot jaw working as she mumbled something.

Pike caught his breath, nodding amiably, hurrying past nervously as the old woman backed away, taloned fingers still wrapped around the knife hilt. He could make out her mumbled, "Crazy star man. Goofy . . . all of them. Insane. Touched in the head like . . ."

The old woman stepped around to watch him, shaking her head, the cow standing placidly at the end of the lead rope. He continued—albeit less exuberantly—eager for new sights and sounds. He fingered his nose and flinched at the sting of healing tissues. The swelling had receded from his sensitive beak so at least he looked almost normal again. The bruises on his ribs would fade, too. Hell with them, he had a whole planet to explore!

The village looked like the holos he'd seen. He noticed a similarity between the prehistoric Inuit shelters he'd excavated and Romanan huts. Each measured five to six meters—longer than Inuit shelters, granted. Excavated maybe seventy centimeters into the ground, a roof of poles covered by hides stretched across in a dome. Smoke rose from an occasional smoke hole. Incongruously, number three powerlead crisscrossed the grass, disappearing into the hide walls. Music and comm programming penetrated out of the thin walls along with laughter, talk, and sometimes argument. Horses shared corrals with aircars. Well, where else would you put one? Everywhere, a curious mixture of primitive and modern had been pasted haphazardly into a working whole. New graphitic domes rose here and there among the shelters—out of place. From what Darwin could see, the division between dome and shelter depended on age. The young lived in domes—the elderly in traditional housing.

The wreck of the old Soviet transport, the *Nicholai Romanan,* drew his attention. He turned his steps there. What an archaeological treasure! He ran his hands down the rusted sides of the ship and wondered if anyone had attempted excavations around it or inside. So much dirt had been tracked in over the ages, untold antiquities might be buried within.

He turned and spotted a long, low, wooden platform about which people gathered. Two boys trotted past, beating a herd of baaing sheep ahead of them. As he neared the platform, he recognized the body people pointed to as they talked in hushed tones: Friday Garcia Yellow Legs. The wounds looked worse in the light of day, exposed to the stares of the mourners and the flies that circled overhead. The drying flesh had turned black, splintered bone garish.

Darwin stopped short and swallowed. How . . . barbaric. Something inside tried to flip over. The queasiness built as disturbed flies rose in a column.

"You Darwin Pike?" a voice asked in Standard.

Darwin turned and took in the young man who approached, a lazy smile on mobile lips. No Romanan this, light brown Caucasoid eyes inspected him from under tumbled brunette hair. A full beard ringed the features of his face—a straight nose, fleshy cheeks. A medium frame didn't support much in the way of muscles. His light skin indicated someone who worked indoors but got enough sun for a light tan. He didn't have the look of Patrol either. The man wore Romanan skins, and a long fighting knife hung at his belt.

"Yes, I'm Pike." He couldn't help but look back at the scaffold. Revulsion churned over the macabre display. Yellow Legs deserved more than this—to be a spectacle.

"Sure is tough about Friday. That's a real loss for all of us. Guess he'd learned what he needed to. Spider yanked his web and Friday went. I'll miss him. Had some good times."

The man offered a hand. "I'm Marty Bruk. I've got an aircar waiting. We'll fly you out to the research station if you wish. If not, I've arranged quarters for you here, although they're a little primitive. No running water, no inside toilet, and I don't think there's any electricity. I suppose coming from University, you'll want more civilized—"

"You knew Friday?" Darwin asked, unable to pull his eyes away.

"Sure, he was quite a character. He and I . . . well, we got along pretty good before he went to Sirius. Didn't see much of him afterward, but then, Sirius made a lot of changes around here."

"How do you feel about this? Laying him out like . . . like . . ."

Bruk's wide mouth tightened. "It's Romanan, Doctor. Just their way. Like some of the weird rites on the stations. You get used to it . . . come to appreciate it, in fact. Think of it as . . . as not hiding from the dead. You look at Friday there, and it's difficult to maintain any quaint illusions about life or death. That's the way of Spider. You don't hide from reality. Deal with it instead. Learn about it. Life isn't any sacred grail. It's real, tough, wonderful, and temporary—so you'd better make the best of it . . . and don't kid yourself."

"I guess there's a kind of elegant simplicity in that. Romanans seem full of such things. They have a bar around here? Let's go get a drink and you can tell me about Friday. Maybe fill me in on some things—like Romanans, and how I learn to live with them."

The tavern couldn't be considered a Romanan institution. Rather, the sign on the door claimed it had been in business for the last year. Rifles, pictures of Romanan bears, coups, and scenes from the fighting on Sirius covered the graphite fiber walls. Chairs and tables consisted of hand-hewn pole-wood covered by dry-shrunk rawhide.

Romanan whiskey jolted him with an experience worth writing home about. Crude, bitter, and, for all Darwin could tell, aged for at least three weeks, it could be likened to carbon tetrachloride.

"So, how's University? The department still in one piece? Chem still enshrined as department head emeritus?"

"Not much has changed. I've only been there a little over a year. Chem drafted me for this because of a loophole in my research contract. So far as University is concerned, there is no anthropology unless it's Romanan anthropology."

Bruk laughed, twirling his glass on the hard hide of the tabletop. "We've made a lot of progress here. The genetics are fascinating—especially the brain imaging the Prophets do. Different morphology, but then, I'm sure you've seen the REMCAT data."

"How about the Prophets? What's the real truth about this Spider religion of theirs?"

The crow's-feet around Bruk's eyes deepened. "I'm supposed to be an objective observer, an unbiased recorder of this culture."

"So?"

"So, I get the runnies every time a Prophet looks at me sideways. Dr. Pike, I've seen them . . . no, proved, that they see the future. You can flip through the notes and double-check my work. As to Spider, well . . . if there's a god, it's Spider. Maybe I've been here too long. The reviews of my articles coming out of University indicate a suspicion that I'm going native, but I've satisfied myself—and Spider for that matter."

Pike sniffed and suffered another swallow of Romanan rotgut. "They didn't like what I told them about Raven either."

"The Inuit spirit-helper?"

"Uh-huh. I guess you just had to be there. Inuit and Romanans are a lot alike—and a million kilometers apart."

Bruk nodded. "You've done vision quest?"

"Yep."

"You might fit in here, Doctor—if you live long enough. World is hard on anthropologists. Uses them up real fast."

"How about Friday?"

Bruk began to talk, relating story after story about the short hero. Pike learned the man had been a noted horse thief, an occupation worth coup. A war chief during the early, troubled days of the Directorate exploration and fighting on World, Friday's status grew as a veteran of the Sirius fighting. Some still thought him a buffoon. His exploits with a recalcitrant aircar were legend.

"How was he mixed up with Susan Andojar?" Darwin asked, the whiskey warming him, making him less cautious.

Bruk turned knowing eyes on Pike. "Susan, huh? That's some package. Nice to enjoy in safe male fantasies. I'd steer clear of her though. She's trouble."

"Oh?"

Bruk squinted into the distance. "I don't mind wasting my time watching that gorgeous female protoplasm. I'll do a little dreaming about her, too—so long as Bella doesn't suspect. But beyond that," he shook his head, "she's one strange lady. Something happened to her on Sirius. I guess Rita, Iron Eyes, and Giorj know, but they don't talk about it. She was pretty weird when she got back. Hacked a lot of good warriors up in knife feud. I know a bit about the human mind and I'm not afraid to tell you, she was at the point of crack-up. Severe psychoses, you understand?"

"Any idea why?"

"Nope, only that it was traumatic."

"But she is good to look at."

"Got that right."

"So tell me about these Romanan bears." Darwin gestured toward the holo on the wall and signaled for two more whiskeys.

Bruk screwed his face into a grimace. "Pretty nasty beasts. The young men still go out and try and kill one to make coup. Since the raiding here has toned down, that's big stuff nowadays. Personally, you wouldn't get me within miles of them."

"How big are they?" Darwin asked mildly.

"Stand about fifteen feet at the shoulder. Of course, they can reach twice that high with those suction disks. I'd say the big ones get to be forty feet long. You might find one—"

"Forty feet! So they did kill them with cannons!"

"Oh, yeah. Until they managed to cast the cannons, the bears almost wiped out the colony. Of course, Iron Eyes killed one with a knife, but that was a medicine ceremony. Bear is part of his spirit world."

"Think a person could kill one with a bow?"

Bruk was shaking his head emphatically. "Positively, no way. Iron Eyes killing one with his knife was a fluke. That was Spider's will. As it is, they lose one out of every five youngsters who goes out to kill a bear with a rifle. I don't think there's a way to drive an arrow deep enough to hit the brain—and you need terminal energy to shock the animal.''

Pike nodded, wondering.

''Hey, Bruk!''

Marty turned. Pike watched an old man hobble through the door on crutches. His right leg stopped just above the knee, his trousers carefully tailored to fit the stump. A wicked light gleamed in the beady black eyes that glared out like jewels from the patterned creases of his face.

''Good to see you, Bill.'' Marty shook hands as the old man positioned himself in a three-point stance, a happy grin exposing toothless jaws.

''Hey, you ain't been by in a long time. You quit sticking all them little metal sticks in people? You marry that Bela Vola and settle down to raise kids and cows like a real man?''

Bruk laughed. ''Me? No, I'm still sticking monitors into people. I just got tired of you messing up my data. Here, Bill Reesh Garcia, meet Darwin Pike. He's from University, too.''

Pike shook the old man's hand, the ancient skin warm against his; thick calluses still padded the gnarled fingers. ''My pleasure.''

''You a friend of Doc's?''

''Leeta Dobra's,'' Bruk supplied at the blank look on Pike's face.

Darwin smiled. ''No, I'm afraid I never met the woman. Um, I was working out of her office for a while though. I'm here to work with Admiral Ree and Iron Eyes.''

''Hayaaa!'' the old man breathed. ''You a big war chief, eh?''

Pike grinned at the devilish twinkle in the old man's eyes. ''Nope, I'm just another anthropologist like Bruk here. I like sticking folks with monitors, too.''

The old man's face broke into a happy smile. ''Yeah, you're okay, Doc Pike. Hey, you come out to my place tonight, eh? Had a calf die. Rock leech got it. I cut the leg off before the leech could get way inside—but the calf died anyway. You know, couldn't stop the blood. He bled out real good. Good tender meat, huh? That's what I come to town for. Gonna throw a party. You come.''

Bruk looked at Pike and shrugged. ''You interested?''

''Wouldn't miss it for the world.''

Bill Reesh's habitation at the foot of the Bear Mountains.

Sparks, like a million fire sprites, danced upward in a spiral from a polewood fire. Grizzled faces of the old men reflected in the light. Women shuffled in the background, long Romanan knives gleaming in the yellow light as they sliced thick steaks from the carcass that rotated over a deep pit. Bright-eyed children took turns cranking the spit, singing a game, and taking time out to clap each other's hands in the process. Laughter and the irregular bubble of talk soothed something deep within Darwin Pike's soul. He looked up to trace the irregular patterns of the stars. Polewood smoke clogged his nose, an exotic incense. A piece of his soul had come to rest, soothed by the strangeness of these people, of this world so different—yet so similar to his.

"I feel like I'm home," Pike admitted.

"You like it, huh?" old Bill poked him in the side, balanced on his crutches. "Most star men, they come, stand around all formal like, smiling funny, you know? Like they don't know what to do with themselves. You, you come, eat like a man, get all greasy, and just smile happy like. Where you from?"

"Alaska. Last wild place on Earth. I used to love nights like this. We'd roast fish, or maybe a caribou. Last time, it was a bear that Downey's cousin killed."

"Hey? Don't joke old Bill Reesh Garcia. Man can't eat a bear."

"On Earth you can."

"You killed a bear?" One of the other men grunted, knees popping as he got to his feet. The hushed voices of the old men around the fire had stilled, hawkish faces turned Pike's way, eyes like obsidian in the flickering light.

"Earth bears aren't anything like Romanan bears. But yes, I did. With an arrow. You know what that is? Yes, like your children play with."

"I got bear trouble now," Bill Reesh growled. "That and rock leeches. Never seen so many rock leeches. Lost five calves already. Then that damn bear comes out from the mountains. Hangs out up in them canyons someplace."

"Figured someone would have gone up and shot him by now," Bruk said thoughtfully from the side.

"Too many getting ready for this damn war." Bill Reesh lifted his hands. "What's a bear, huh? What's a bad bear when everyone talks of Ngen and what he's doing in the stars? No, the kids all got stars in their heads now. The War Chief's got 'em all up in the stars—learning to be warriors. My cousin, Bull Wing Reesh, he's supposed to come down with an aircar. Maybe we'll fly up there in the canyons, see if we can find this bear. If I don't, damn bear'll eat most of my stock in the next year. You know bears. Then I got nothing. Got to go starve on my clan's good will. Can't do that. Hell, I'll get him myself first—one leg and all.''

"Don't you do nothing foolish, Bill. That bear, he catch you up there all crippled, he'll finish what that Santos bullet started years ago. You call us, we'll help. Maybe somebody can get a shot into him.''

Bruk winced. "None of you ought to be up there running around. Not a one of you is under fifty.''

"Hey, I'm forty-eight, Bruk,'' a thin man hollered from the side. "What you think, huh? We're all dead?''

"And you've got arthritis so bad Mary has to pull you out of bed every morning, too,'' Bruk reminded, waggling a finger.

"She probably has to pull him *into* bed, too, huh?'' Bill cried, smacking horny hands as he leaned on has crutches.

"I'd take a crack at your bear,'' Pike called. "I've killed Earth bear before, Romanan bears couldn't be that much—''

"Whoa!'' Marty was on his feet, hands out. "Forget it, Darwin. Leave well enough alone. You don't know—''

"Hey,'' Bill waved his hands. "Let Doc Pike talk, huh? He's killed bear, he says. That's coup, Bruk. How many bear you killed?''

Marty swallowed his next outburst, seeing the censure in the old man's eyes. "Listen . . . Darwin may have killed bear on Earth. That's coup. But it's not right to get a man killed because he doesn't understand the danger of fooling with—''

"Relax,'' Darwin said softly, gesturing to Marty. "Take it easy, I'm not some station type, Marty. I've lived off what I could stalk and kill with my bow. I've survived out in the muskeg for days.'' He turned to Reesh. "You say Bull Wing is coming out with an aircar? I'd like to go. What do you use to kill bear with? Blasters?''

An old man hunched over and hissed in disgust. "Man ought to kill bear with a rifle. There's coup in that. Blaster don't show no respect for the bear. Bear has power, spirit power. You hear that, Doc Pike? You know what that means?

Huh? Spider made us to have honor. Where's honor in using a blaster on a bear?''

In the sudden silence, Darwin realized every eye had turned to him. Only the polewood fire crackled and snapped, sparks dancing to a life of their own against the black sky. One of the three moons had just risen over the granite crags of the Bear Mountains.

"In my land, the Inuit have made it law that only the bow—or sometimes a rifle—can be used to kill the animals. Without it, the Inuit believe the spirit of caribou, of bear and moose and elk, would leave Earth forever. The great totem, Raven, told this to the holy men a long time ago after the Inuit had almost died out after the Soviet unification. It's been that way since. I've prayed in the old ways. I would use a rifle and do bear honor."

"Pike?" Marty cried. "You're outta your—"

"Hey, I've got five days. Ree told me I could have them, no strings attached. Besides, Bull Wing Reesh will be there with an aircar. He'll pull me out if there's any trouble. I won't let anything happen." He took Bruk by the arm, pulling him out of earshot of the old men. "And besides, Marty, how would you feel if Bill, or Ray, or one of the others here got killed by that damn bear? Look at them, they're losing their stock. Look in their eyes. You know they'll try and tackle that animal. If any of them were fit enough, they'd be up in *Bullet* training with Iron Eyes."

"I got a real bad feeling about this," Bruk grumbled. "Maybe I ought to call the Admiral. When he said no strings, he didn't know you were going to go fooling with any bear. I told you, World is tough on anthropologists who don't—"

"I've been there before, Marty," Pike looked him in the eyes. "Trust me."

CHAPTER XII

Aboard *Deus* in GEO orbit over Arpeggio.

Ngen steepled long supple fingers as he leaned back in the command chair on the rechristened *Deus*. Around him, the bridge curved in a white arc, his officers busy with the ship stats. In the transduction monitor, Admiral Kimianjui cocked his head, aged black skin giving him a shrunken appearance.

"The Directors," Kimianjui continued, "have given me discretionary powers in this matter. I have considerable latitude to bargain if you'll simply tell me what you wish—and cease your depredations of Directorate citizens."

Ngen nodded soberly to himself. "I am not committing depredations on Directorate citizens, Admiral. I'm sure Satan's agents would wish that people everywhere believed that, but I am a simple man of God following—"

"A man of God in a Patrol battleship," Kimianjui reminded. "We're aware of your potential, Messiah. Still, we're willing to negotiate. The Directors will allow you to remain in the sytems you've captured. We wish a cessation of hostilities. In exchange, we shan't retaliate for your piracy of our vessel. You may rule your systems and we will rule ours. Warfare between us would achieve no aim except our mutual destruction. Surely you can see this."

Ngen chewed his lip, lost in thought. "You will allow me to discuss this with my staff?"

"Most assuredly."

Ngen bowed to the monitor. "Then I shall be happy to pursue this discussion again. I will place a transmission through to your headquarters in the next day or so, depending on how soon I can coordinate with my advisors. I shall be in touch with you no later than three days Arcturian time. Is that satisfactory?"

"Most satisfactory. Good day, sir."

The monitor flickered off.

Ngen leaped from the command chair, exploding with a wild whoop, a triumphant fist held high. "I've got them! Blessed Deus, I've got the damned pumpkin heads running!"

Sira Velkner looked up from the comm. "Running, Messiah?"

Ngen hopped and pirouetted across the bridge, aware of his officers and their open interest. "Damned right, running! The balloon-headed freaks are suing for peace! They want a reprieve! Ignorant stupid bastards. Who do they think I am? Some bumpkin to be placated until they suppress the unrest I've stirred? Do they think I'd give them a moment's rest?"

"Then you'll turn him down?" Sira asked, curiosity reflected in his thin face.

Ngen smiled. "Most definitely not, Sira. No, I'll accept eagerly, and in doing so, give us time."

"Time?"

Ngen laughed, smacking a fist into his palm. "Time to destroy some more of their transductors. Time to refit *Deus* with the new shielding. Time to retool more production into those Brotherhood blasters. Time to train our crews. Time to unlock more secrets from that Brotherhood data from Frontier and turn it into a force not even the pumpkin heads can imagine! Indeed, Sira, we have time for revolution now. We can consolidate our strength—and when we rush outward from Arpeggio, no one will stand against us!"

Bear Mountains, World.

The Bear Mountains consist of a highly asymmetrical overthrust anticline. While younger shales, sandstones, and algalitic chert strata are found in the upper levels, the core of the mountains is a 3.8 billion-year-old red-pink granite. Grabens and faulting have dropped younger rock along the steep western exposure of the range. The dip is roughly ten degrees on the eastern slope with a strike of N85°E.

Darwin Pike wondered about the nature of human stupidity as he scrambled up the rocky cliff face. The raging bear—bear *hell,* the thing looked more like a dragon—climbed below him, pulling its vast bulk over the rocks. His Romanan guide—safe in the aircar overhead—circled, trying to find a way to get down past the fierce winds that ripped through the canyon.

Around him, reddish granite rose in exfoliated knobs and twists leading up to the sedimentary rock above. Cracked and tumbled, dendritic patterned drainages had inscribed the stone, leading down to a flat valley bottom thick with mellonbush, knifebush and the curious star-burst polewood trees. The opposite wall rose no more than two hundred meters to the north, rough, weathered, and eroded under the resistant cap of calcium-rich yellow sandstones.

Daring the vortex, Bull Wing Reesh attempted to make a landing and missed smashing himself into the rocks of the canyon wall by inches in the eddies of the updrafts.

"Get out of here!" Darwin shouted, motioning Reesh

clear. "I'll climb out! Don't risk yourself!" He gasped a ragged breath into his searing lungs and scrambled higher, wishing for a blaster.

Sweat traced down his cheeks in jagged streaks, dropping into the three-day beard and trickling down his neck. Romanan summer scorched from a blasting sun, dry as splinter-cracked bone. The rocks radiated a staggering heat which the blast of hot wind then used to suck his body dry.

Darwin looked back as a huge suction disk planted itself on the ledge he'd just climbed over. Panicked, he leaped for a handhold and scrambled up higher, the rifle swinging madly on his back. Rock ate into his torn flesh. Panting, he searched for another purchase. The gun was useless now. The brass cartridge had split and stuck in the chamber. He couldn't reload.

Almost frantic with fear, Pike caught a toehold and scrambled up the cliff face. He jammed fists of bloody flesh into a long crack, muscling himself up by brute strength. In the process, he tore the nails off three fingers. A fiery ache burned in his chest as he gasped for breath. Muscles spasmed in exhaustion. How long could he keep going like this?

Inexorably, the wounded bear pulled itself up behind him. The suction disks gave the animal enough purchase to lever its stubby legs into holes in the rock. Then came the second disk and the bear lumbered higher, propped awkwardly by its tree-trunk legs on the unstable boulder detritus.

I jerked the shot. I lost it. My fault . . . my fault . . . Damn, what happened to me? The size of it, coming so fast, the tentacles reaching up to— And I jerked the shot . . . panicked.

Pike flopped over one last faulted shelf of rock.

End of the line. Sheer wall, unbroken by so much as a crack, stretched up to the aqua sky. He'd made it as high as he could without technical equipment or a jetpack. Cornered, he pulled the rifle from his back. Dead gun—live club.

Lungs seared, he couldn't gasp enough breath. A wooden raspiness filled his dry throat. *God, but for a drink to still the thirst!* Looking around frantically, he took store. The head-sized rocks felt rough and gritty as he grabbed them up, muscles straining, and pitched them down at the bear. The animal moaned in its odd way as the rocks pattered ineffectually off thick hide. Braced, it searched for another purchase.

"Ugly bastard!" Darwin muttered, looking at the creature. So huge, it might have been two brontosaurs stuck together like perverted Siamese twins—this one had to be fifteen meters in length. Two fat tails balanced out the two tentacles and suction disks. The mouth consisted of a fleshy slit between the tentacle bases. Beady eyes rested on rubbery stalks rising on each side of the waving masses of flesh. For the moment all six stubby legs pumped desperately in the loose scree, trying to propel the bulk up the rocky talus.

The beast began to slide sideways and Darwin allowed himself a brief moment of prayer. When it seemed inevitable the bear was going to plunge down the slope, it got traction and levered itself another half-body length up the slope. A tentacle began to extend its disk into his last sanctuary.

Darwin huddled, eyes locked with the bear's. He stared into the black depthless eye, feeling something twist in his soul. A question, a pulling, a feeling of eternity, that eye drew him.

"No," Darwin croaked through his swollen throat. "You killed Bill's cattle. If not me, someone else. You'd have killed old Bill. Understand? Damn it, we're alike you and me. Predators, you hear?"

The black eye held him, knowing, angry, feeding on his very fear. Pike ground his teeth, bloody fingers knotting painfully into the rock as sweat trickled and he clamped his hot eyes closed, forcing himself to blank out the sight of the bear. Only he could feel it, somehow tied to his very soul—an umbilical draining his life away, eating at his resistance. The power of the bear buffeted at his stunned mind, tangible, impossibly real.

"Damn you! *What are you?*" he screamed at the animal, panic triggering anger in some atavistic survival response.

Pike's heart jackhammered against his ribs. The reality of death grayed the brilliant day. He choked on his dry tongue as he attempted to swallow and cursed himself for having left his grandfather's blaster in the Settlements. All he had was a rifle to club with, and the Randall knife—trinket and heirloom—against this monster from a psychotic nightmare.

The suction disk smashed down. Darwin threw himself

aside, a whimper breaking his dry throat. The rubbery purple flesh missed by millimeters, slapping the rock. The disk, a meter across, molded itself to the rock and contracted, forming a perfect seal. He bashed the butt of the rifle down with all his might. The disk could have been rubber for all the effect he had.

The bear's flesh gave off a faint nauseous odor—like rotting seal meat in the sun. Darwin wrinkled his nose and smashed again and again with the rifle butt, frantic, unwilling to cower. The suction disk appeared nerveless.

The second disk pulled loose from the ledge below and began rising in his direction.

Fear whimpers stuck in his throat as he ripped the ancient Randall from his scabbard and hacked at the spongy flesh, slashing violently as adrenaline flooded fear-charged muscles.

A viscous, black fluid oozed out around the cuts and the stink gagged him. A shrill squeal rose from below. More than sound, it battered at his gibbering mind, causing him to physically flinch.

"Live, Pike. *Survive, damn you!*" he gritted, finding some stubborn sense of self-identity and clinging to it.

Forcing himself to concentrate, he worked the Randall deep into the meat and began circling the tentacle. The flesh around the cut began quivering and jerking in a macabre way, causing Darwin to shiver insanely as he sawed.

Where the hell was that second sucker?

From the corner of his eye, he could see the disk shooting in his direction. He threw all his weight on the blade, sawing frantically as cut arteries spurted the black fluid over his hands, arms, and face. The stink, like sulfuric fumes, ate into his sinuses, unbearable, Tears blinded him. He swallowed the vomit as his stomach spasmed.

Flesh stretched, black-smeared tissues parting before his eyes. The tentaacle parted with an elastic snap, almost breaking Darwin's wrist and slapping him against the rock with the relieved tension. The knife clattered, ripped from his fingers.

Sobbing in fear, he scrambled for the Randall where it lay at the edge of the precipice and peered down, lungs heaving. The bear perched awkwardly, the one tentacle flailing for balance as the huge bulk wavered. The severed member looked like a cut fire hose, twisting back and forth through the air, spraying foamy black fluid on the impervious reddish rock.

Darwin's breath ripped his lungs in trembling spasms. Willing his shaking legs to function, he tumbled down the slope until he found a boulder that seemed unbalanced. Shoulder behind it, he pushed, groaned, and shouted, feeling the stone bite harshly into his shoulder. The muscles in his legs quivered with the strain. The rock grated, moved, and finally slid, falling clear of the slope to bounce with a crack, cascading smaller rocks and boiling dust. It hit again and landed on the stubby legs of the bear.

Fear and rage blasted through Darwin's unstable mind. He hunched under the sheer brutality of it.

The creature screamed and fell, skidding down the rubble to the bottom of the slope. Darwin watched, seeing the tails, tentacles and legs waving feebly. After retrieving the rifle, he almost killed himself getting down the disturbed detritus. When he reached the colluvium, trembling legs barely supported him, ready to buckle.

Bull Wing Reesh could be seen, flying his aircar up the canyon. Leery of the remaining tentacle, Darwin approached the huge animal. "You and me," he mouthed hoarsely, "the same. Hunters. Shared spirits . . . even from different worlds. But what kind of . . . *thing* are you?"

"Why didn't you shoot him again?" Reesh demanded, jumping from the aircar and walking up casually, dust kicking up from his stained boots.

"Here, see if you can get that case out." He handed the weapon back to its owner, nerves rattling like a buzzer as the animal's pain and fear twined with his own.

Humming to himself, Reesh jacked open the breech and eyeballed the chamber. "Head separation."

"Head . . . separation?" Meaningless words in a whirl of conflicting thoughts and emotions . . . his and the bear's.

Reesh muttered to himself and, grumbling, walked back to the aircar.

Despite his cotton-dry mouth, Darwin walked over to the dying beast. "What . . . are you? How do you call to me?"

The bear responded by weakly lifting the remaining disk off the ground and sending it futilely in his direction.

"Still trying?" He sensed something of what it must have been like to be a Romanan before the cannons were cast. These had been the beasts which molded the spirits and souls of the People.

Reesh approached, gravel crunching underfoot, rifle fixed. He handed it back and motioned at the dying monster.

The voice came spinning from nowhere, filling his mind. *Be strong this time. Be worthy, for once, man who failed me. See if you can stand this time. See if you can hold your ground despite your fear.*

Darwin winced, refusing to believe. "Crazy. It's the heat. That's what. Just the heat . . . and thirst. Exertion does things like that. Out of shape. That's it. Overextended and out of shape." The rifle wavered as he settled the sights where he knew the brain should be. He said a quick prayer for the animal's soul and triggered the heavy single-shot.

The boom of the gun echoed around the canyon walls as the bear tensed, stiffened, and relaxed forever. Darwin stared, the rifle lowering in his hands. As if the bullet had blown it, an empty spot appeared in his soul. Something in the universe dimmed and flickered out.

Hands . . . pulling . . . pulling his arms.

"Pike! Damn it, you all right?" Bull Wing Reesh's voice cut through the vertigo.

"F-Fine." Darwin blinked. "Wh—What happened?"

"Beats me. You shot the bear . . . and fell flat on your face screaming something I couldn't understand." Reesh cocked his head. "You sure you're okay?"

"Heat . . . must be the heat. Dehydrated, you know?" *And why can't I believe that?*

Reesh fiddled with the camera, tongue stuck out the side of his mouth. Darwin laid the rifle on the ground. His holo showed a man with a grim, black-spattered face, holding only an antique knife.

Bull Wing Reesh's hunting camp in the Bear Mountains.

Bull Wing Reesh situated his base camp at the foot of the Bear Mountains. Darwin relaxed where he lay next to the fire. A plasti-heal covered his battered hands, disinfectant and anesthetic seeping into the inflamed tissues. Reesh was humming to himself as he cleaned the gun and inspected the cracks in the stock where Darwin had used it for a club.

"Guess I'll have to make another stock. Then again, maybe it's worth it. For a fight like that, sure. Thought he had you a couple of times. Magnificent! You showed courage. Spider gave you strength and wisdom. Lucky I thought to get it on holo.''

"I was scared to death." Darwin declared, unable to break his melancholy.

"I said nothing about fear," Reesh's voice came softly in the night. The polewood fire crackled and snapped, sparks twisting upward to the two moons casting divergent shadows over the knifebush-dotted hills around them.

"Fear goes with us throughout our lives. Fear makes us strong. I've never been so scared in all my life as I was with Susan Smith Andojar on Sirius. We lived in terror for every beat of our hearts. Pretty rough times. War, the way it's played in the Directorate, is one moment of fright after another. Here, on World, war got played—you know, like a game. Sure, you could get killed playing, but a man didn't live his terror. It didn't pump in his veins like acid. We didn't have any Spider-cursed violet light appearing in the sky to blow us to pieces at any second.''

"So you fought with Susan?" Darwin worked his hands, feeling the plasti-heal flex. "Was it fear that made her the way she is today? Is that what she's hiding so well?"

The bear talked to me. Face it. It was real!

Reesh carefully wiped dust from the barrel of his rifle and shook his head as he leaned the long gun against the knifebush. "Susan has her fears like any of the rest of us." He settled himself near the fire and pulled a pipe from a pouch. Taking an ember from the fire, he lit it and puffed until he had it going. "No, Susan doesn't need to hide her fear. She hides her scars, Doctor Pike.''

"Scars?"

Reesh shrugged. "She loved two men on Sirius. One was Hans Yeager, a marine on *Bullet*. The other was Friday Garcia Yellow Legs, the legendary Spider War Chief. I knew them both. Fought beside them. Got scared with them. Drank, pissed, and shit with them. Good men, both of them. To know them did me honor. And they became the best of friends themselves—even if they loved the same woman.

"We were closing on Angla, the Guard making one last push, when the Sirian battleship blasted our patrol. Orbital bombardment, they call it. We dived for cover. Friday saved some of us, but the group with Hans got cooked. Susan changed . . . was different after that, you now? She didn't talk much, but killed Sirians wherever she could find them.

She did other things, too.'' He paused, lost in thought, before he added, ''She mutilated them—cut them like we'd cut a calf. Took their manhood.''

Darwin stared into the fire.

''Then, one night, we were dropped in the city of Helg. We killed and counted coup while we destroyed their comm and transport and blew up their power transmission. On a raid, Susan got captured. The Sirians took her up to the ship Ngen Van Chow commanded. You may guess what happened to her. No one says . . . but you may guess.

''I was there after she was rescued. She seemed like someone else. That was when she and Giorj moved in together. Friday took it hard—but he was too good a man to hold a grudge. He still loved her very much so he became Giorj's friend. Together, with one of the Prophets, they made her well again, fixed her mind somehow.''

Reesh pulled at his pipe and looked over at Darwin's creased brow. ''Those are the scars she hides. A mind can be fixed, I suppose, but I don't think it ever forgets. Now, Friday is dead, too. We've heard, Doctor. Ngen Van Chow killed him—just like he killed Hans with his blaster. He's still loose out there,'' Reesh pointed with his pipestem toward the stars, ''and he ruined everything in Susan's life—even degrading her soul.''

Darwin nodded, remembering her mourning Friday Yellow Legs in the middle of the night. Alone. Where no one would see. And Ngen had become a messiah, leading a crazed jihad. Ngen still scared Susan—and Ree, and Iron Eyes and Rita. Pike swallowed. A lesson lay in that.

He couldn't stand it any longer. ''Reesh, be honest with me. Bears, uh . . . do they have any . . . any psychic powers? I mean has anyone ever talked about it? Maybe stories about . . . about . . .''

''Bears having power?'' Reesh sucked at his pipe. ''Yes, Dr. Pike. On World, we believe bears have power. That they test men for their own reasons.''

Darwin swallowed, trying to make sense of it. ''I . . . I felt the bear today. I . . . I panicked. Pulled that first shot. And the bear . . . Damn it, it's crazy! Like it knew what I was thinking! I sound like a lunatic again.''

Reesh's stern face sombered. ''On World, we believe that men and bears and harvesters are all one. Part of Spider. Why men and animals are different is Spider's doing . . . and who am I to know Spider's purpose? We each do our part. You, me, the bear, all our souls are part of Spider. Same with horses and dogs and cattle and sheep and maybe even flies. All part of Spider's web, Doctor.'' He cocked his head. ''What did bear want of you?''

Darwin let his gaze drift with the rising sparks. ''I . . . Courage I think. I don't . . . it isn't clear.''

Reesh nodded thoughtfully and pointed with his pipestem to emphasize his words. ''This is a different planet, Doctor. Here, we are Spider's. If you would learn of yourself and what bear wanted, you must be willing to seek, to ask Spider. Do you want to know? Are you willing to find out?''

''I . . .'' Susan's words echoed through his mind. *When you ask something of Spider, you never know what you'll pay. And those who ask and can't deliver, Spider breaks . . . and casts aside. Understand?*

''Yes,'' he added lamely, heart pounding.

''Then you must purify yourself. Follow the path of the People up—''

The voice from the dark took them both by surprise. ''Do not move, Spider filth. Rifles are aimed at your hearts. We *will* kill you!''

Reesh sank down and said softly, ''Do as they say. I think they are Santos raiders. If they are, be ready. We'll have to kill them.'' Darwin gawked his disbelief as Reesh called, ''We won't move.''

Two men entered the light of the fire in skirmish crouches, rifles held low. One ripped Reesh's rifle from the knifebush and back away, weapon centered on Bull's broad chest.

''Where's your rifle?'' a barrel-chested Santos demanded of Darwin.

''I don't have a rifle. I'm an anthropologist.'' Pike spread his hands.

A third man entered the sphere of the fire. ''Stand up slowly. Hand over your knives. You have no horses? Only the aircar?''

''What good are horses?'' Reesh asked, getting slowly to his feet. In Standard, he told Pike, ''When I hand my knife over, kill the man closest to you.''

The big leader sneered, bending to shout in Reesh's face, ''You're *not* Romanan! You're one who went to kill the Sirrians. They were as sheep, eh? See us, Spider trash? We're *still* Santos! We haven't been weakened by aircars and blasters. We're still strong and cunning! The Spiders are *nothing*

now that they've taken to the stars. You've lost your strength
. . . no longer a challenge for the Santos!''

Reesh shrugged, unbuckling his knife belt. "Perhaps. I
would surrender my knife to the leader of Santos.'' He
stepped back from the rifle, offering the sheathed blade.

"Less than harvesters! *Cowards!* Your testicles are living
rot! Your courage is powerful as sheep dung.'' The Santos
spit full in Reesh's face. "There is no honor left in the Spiders! You are less than a woman. I piss upon your—''

He never had a chance to finish. Reesh—electric motion—leaped in the air and broke the man's neck with a
lightning kick. He landed, balanced, blade magically bared,
and spun on his heel, lashing into the Santos next to him.

Darwin had been busy swallowing his fear, running his
tongue around his dry mouth. His hand went to the Randall.
It came as instinct that he dropped into the stance he'd been
practicing with Susan. His opponent swung his rifle to fire
at Reesh. Darwin acted on impulse, knocking it out of the
way as the weapon discharged. Then the Romanan charged
him, bellowing rage.

Darwin backpedaled and ducked a vicious butt stroke.
The rifle hissed through his hair. His highly-educated brains
would have been all over camp. Before the man could recover, Darwin jabbed with the knife, the sensation the same
as poking the keen edge into a bowl of spaghetti; he'd expected more resistance.

The Santos grunted, eyes growing big in the flickering
light of the fire. Darwin froze, knowing he'd killed the man.
Only the Santos' surprise turned into a snarl as he stumbled
back, pulling free, drawing his own blade. Darwin stood in
shock, failing to believe the man wouldn't quit.

Howling his rage, the Santos charged and Darwin willed
himself to retreat, falling over the body of the dead Santos
chief, rolling out of the way as forty centimeters of Romanan fighting knife sliced at his head.

Halfway to his feet, he felt the Romanan blade slip into
the soft flesh just over the hipbone. Pike turned against the
blade, pushing close and jabbing. The Santos grunted as
Darwin pulled up in a gutting stroke, sawing the blade
through the warrior. Hot blood rushed over his hand, racing
down his forearm. Ropy intestines slid eerily over his skin.
A hot explosion of breath on his cheek ended as the Randall
sliced the diaphragm. The Santos pushed away violently,

grabbing at his spewing belly. He staggered and fell, blowing the rest of his guts out the long, irregular wound.

Darwin looked down at the huge Romanan knife sticking out of his own abdomen. Queerly, he could feel the chill of the steel clear through him.

"My God!" Darwin whispered. "I'm going to die!" The Randall clattered from nerveless fingers. He couldn't take his eyes off the hideous sight of the Romanan knife. Blade and handle sticky with his blood, it shone in the licking, yellow firelight.

Reesh calmly continued carving the coups off the other two men.

"I'm dying," Darwin called, voice verging on failure. The gaping wound began to sting like someone had poured alcohol into a deep scratch.

Reesh stood and squinted in the firelight. He trotted over and inspected the wound. "Not enough blood to have cut that trunk artery," he muttered to Darwin's absolute horror. "I'd say we've got three or four hours before you're critical. I wouldn't pull that knife out if I were you, might make you bleed like a stuck sheep!"

Darwin couldn't make the words come. Was Bull Wing Reesh so callous? So . . . He struggled to keep the world in focus as it spun and began turning gray. He remembered screaming out in terror as he felt himself falling into the blackness.

CHAPTER XIII

Bullet in GEO orbit over World

Rita Sarsa turned as John passed the hatch. Seeing the look on his face, she sighed, lifting the headset from her brow and blinking as the comm went dead.

"So, how's it going?"

A dry laugh got by his lips as he shook his head and punched the dispenser for a carbonated drink. "We would have been better off to have followed in old Smith's footsteps and junked that damn radio years ago. He told us, 'Keep the computers and radios and sending devices, and the Sobyets will follow us here to World.' That's the legacy of Smith clan. He broke the machines. And what did we do? Kept that Spider-cursed radio to keep track of bears and Raiders. That's how the Directorate found us."

She stood, easing the kinks out of her back and walked over to rub his shoulders. "Okay, so you should have smashed the radio and kept stealing each other's horses and women down there. Fine. I'd be trying to cut Antonia Reary's throat so I could get in line to cut Damen's and get control of *Bullet*. Leeta would be a nice pleasant psyched anthropology professor living with Jeffray on Arcturus. Wonderful."

A wry smile curled his broad lips. "Well, maybe we could have sent just a small radio signal through, huh?"

She laughed at the light in his eyes. "What happened?"

He flopped muscular shoulders in a shrug and sat on the edge of the bed. "The usual—training warriors for space duty. Today we got the new men—er, excuse me, people. Got to call them people. The five new women would want to swear knife feud. I told you Susan would be trouble when she went to space. She sets a hell of an example."

"So? She made it, didn't she?" Rita crossed her arms, one foot insolently forward. "Not only did she make it, she did it beyond anyone's expectations. She overcame difficulties that would have broken a man—and you damn well know it!"

He lifted his hands in defeat. "Yes . . . yes, she did. And, to be honest, I'm glad. If I'd known all the trouble you and Leeta were going to turn out being, I'd have left you with the Santos way back when."

"And killed Philip and World through your own stubbornness. Remember, Philip told me about the vision. You knew what you were getting into."

"Loud-mouthed no-good cousin of mine. Never knew when to shut up and . . ." He looked up. "Hey! You just fell in love with him. He was *born* my cousin."

Despite the brief sting, she chuckled and sat down next to him, letting him take her hand and caress it. "So the new people are driving you nuts?"

Iron Eyes winced, a hopeless desperation in his eyes. "Was I that stupid when I first . . ." He caught the look in her eyes. "Okay, maybe I was."

"You all were," she reminded. "I thought Damen would lose his mind in the beginning."

"You made the difference, you know. Every man, woman, and child down there owes you . . . and Leeta. An entire world lives because of you." He leaned over and kissed her reverently.

Rita's arms crept up around his neck. She pulled him close, refusing to release him, kissing him harder.

"It's the middle of the watch," he finally managed.

"Uh-huh," she breathed. "So?"

He turned and called, "Comm?"

"Yes."

"This is the War Chief. Major Sarsa and I aren't to be disturbed. Under *any* circumstances. Understood?"

"Acknowledged."

Decks 7 & 8, Section 22: Aboard *Bullet* in GEO orbit over World.

Damen Ree craned his neck to watch, his critical eye on the techs as they placed antigrav jacks. "Easy there, Corporal. You don't have more than a couple millimeters clearance from that compressor mount. Any vibration will make shredded junk out of that centrifugal turbine in there."

The huge strut rose up out of the mess. Were it not in the process of rebuilding, Damen would have winced. The job of surgery on *Bullet* continued, a complete reengineering.

"Yes, sir." The corporal studied the bulky mount, moved his jack and checked the alignment with his laser gauge. "That ought to be it."

The hole they'd cut ran down at an angle, the two-meter-thick strut hanging, balanced, waiting to dart into the guts of the ship. Below, through the cut, the layers of *Bullet* lay exposed, like cells in a plant, vulnerable, naked to view. Powerlead, piping, duct work, and plumbing, all rerouted in angles and curves of white.

Ree accessed comm. "Giorj? I think we've got the last jack placed. We're ready when you are."

"One moment, Admiral."

Ree waited while the corporal checked and rechecked his jacks. A scarred Romanan in a radiation suit climbed up from the inspection crawlway in the cooling induction—like a worm from a huge white fruit—and looked up, shaking his head.

Ree could accept that. Like some giant arrow, the huge

graphsteel support lay waiting for the gravitic flux which
would slide it into place through seven different decks.
Above them, stars blinked beyond the atmosphere sealing
where gantries held the far end of the huge structural support. Around him, *Bullet's* very guts lay exposed as if a
surgeon had sliced her open. Piles of plating could be seen
stacked like cards, waiting to be reassembled back into
walls, decks, and supports.

Ree turned to see Giorj Hambrei round the corner to the
campanionway.

The gray man cocked his head and nodded. "The props
are placed below. I am satisfied. Let me check this end
personally."

"Right. I think the corporal's done a pretty decent job."
Ree turned to the Romanan who'd flopped the loose helmet
back on his radiation suit and scowled at a scintillometer
readout. "What have you got, warrior?"

The Romanan shrugged. "If what Major Glick told me
is right, I think there's a deficiency in the number three
coolant induction line. I don't know, maybe a crack or
something under the strake spine."

Ree ran his tongue over front teeth, trying to remember
the specs. "Could be. Poor old *Bullet's* been blasted, compressed and decompressed so many times, it's a wonder she
doesn't fall apart at the seams. Get through to Glick. Have
him send a tech up here pronto. We've got the tunnel exposed, let's get it done now, before we have to cut all this
shielding and bulkhead out of the way again."

The Romanan nodded and turned to the comm.

Giorj peered intently into his laser optic transit. "Looks
fine, Admiral."

"All right, Giorj, take her slow."

The washed-out engineer nodded, moving to a portable
control panel and checking the relays.

Ree turned to the comm. "Everybody clear. We're moving the support. Stay out of the way, people."

The Sirian would make *Bullet* stronger, adding a support
which, in turn, could extend the gravitation grid through the
ship's midsection, allowing another five gs of acceleration.
Lip pinched between his teeth, Ree held his breath as Giorj
began manipulating the ship's gravity. The giant structural
support began to creep into the guts of the ship.

"Looks good," Giorj added from the side, eyes never
straying from the instruments.

"Ought to," Ree grumbled. "You were the one who burned out this section if you'll recall."

"I had hoped I'd be able to make just this modification."

Ree rose onto his toes. *Yeah, for Ngen, Giorj. Thank Spider you came over to our side!*

"Admiral Ree?" Comm interrupted his thoughts.

"Yes."

"We have a message from the planet. Doctor Darwin Pike has been injured. He is currently stable, but incapacitated."

"What the hell happened?"

"Evidently a brush with Santos raiders during a bear hunt."

Ree stopped cold, an icy disbelief gripping him. "During a bear . . . *He WHAT?* That goddamn idiot anthropologist, just wait till I get his butt in my . . . Get me Major Sarsa!"

"For the moment, she doesn't wish to be disturbed."

Ree caught himself on the verge of bellowing. What the hell, Rita probably had a good reason. He changed his mind. "Get me Commander Andojar. Damn it, she brought him here. *She* can keep him out of trouble."

"Yes, sir."

Hospital: outskirts of the Settlements, World.

Darwin Pike couldn't move. The worst part: he could feel *things* wiggling inside him and it scared him queasy.

"Set his threshold a little lower," a professional sounding voice penetrated the layers of his mind. Warmth drifted up to wrap around him, leaving nothing but the memory.

Which memory? The Romanan fighting knife sticking out of his flesh? Or the bear, lying broken and dying on the rocky bottom of a pink canyon in the Bear Mountains? The bear. The bear . . . watching, even now, the little stalk-supported eyes . . .

Yes, the bear. He could *feel* the animal watching him. Feel the soul, drifting like the warmth around him. Whispers, whispers from the bear, *"Are you worthy. Are you worthy of my soul, man?"* In soft, sibilant hissings from loose, dragon lips, the words rocked him, leaving him to wonder.

"I don't . . . understand. Worthy?"

"Spirits call," the whispering voice probed him. *"The bears call, the Santos calls. Do you kill without honor, man*

*of the stars? Do you always panic and run? Did your Raven
teach you so poorly?''*

"Raven? My spirit-helper? What's he . . . I just . . .''

Darwin tried to escape, to move away from the voice that
pelted him like spring rain. He tried to push it out of his
mind. The whispering remained, surrounding him softly.

Suddenly angry, he shouted, "Look at my soul, bear!
Look at the sorrow. Look at the hole I made in it when I
killed you!''

"Easy!'' another voice—commanding—intruded from
outside. A firm hand lay cool on his forehead. Darwin pried
sticky eyelids open and blinked away the fuzziness. A
woman stood over him, critical eyes on his. Above her a
domed graphite fiber roof supported lights, powerlead, and
atmosphere ducting. Standard med units—some occupied—
huddled like cocoons on all sides.

"Wh . . . Where am I?'' Darwin managed to croak.

"Settlement Hospital. You're plugged into a med unit.
You can't move. If you do, the unit will automatically put
you down again. Attitude is a big factor in how soon—''

"How long?''

"We'll have you for another three days. Then you'll be
transported up to the *Treasure* or maybe *Bullet*. Some pretty
important people—''

"You're Patrol?'' Darwin moved his tongue in a stale
mouth, wishing he could have a drink of water.

She shook her head. "Sirian. I got raped and carted off—
excuse me, married—to one of these barbarians. I guess
you'd say I'm bride price for my world. It's not that bad.
Turns out he didn't like me much . . . and he has four other
Romanan wives anyway. He leaves me alone and I leave
him alone. Being the top certified medical specialist on
World, I run the clinic and it pays very well.''

"Uh, you don't hold a grudge, do you?''

She dropped the corners of her mouth in a frown. "Depends on what a patient does to piss me off. I suppose you
could push me and find out just what a nasty bitch I—''

"I'm good! I'm *real* good.''

"Uh-huh.''

At that she left. He rolled his eyes in relief since it seemed
the only expression he had and, to his surprise, caught sight
of two holos: One of him and the dead Romanan bear. The
other—the one that drew his gaze—that of two smiling men,
one a young Darwin, foot propped on a lightning-blasted

stump, the other a laughing Inuit, and between them sprawled a huge Alaskan brown bear.

Darwin let himself drift off to sleep; but the echo of the whispers rustled in his ear.

Are you worthy, man? This isn't Raven's land—that's behind you. Are you worthy of bear . . . of his power? How does your soul measure up, man? Are you worthy of a Santos? A bear? . . . Or Spider? The words rocked him in the gentle waters of a dream.

He stared again into the passionate eyes of the Santos, felt the blood rushing and gushing, beating on his flesh as the Randall cut upward. Intestines, like writhing snakes, entwined around his arm, slithering powerfully up, reaching for his throat, constricting, strangling his very soul.

I killed a man. I looked him straight in the eyes and cut the guts right out of him. The knowledge obsessed him when he woke up. He looked at his right hand, tanned, clean skin. The memory of that hot blood pumping out, the feel of the Santos' intestines rolling over his flesh—memory and dream, rolled into one: forever.

"What are you worth, man?" He could hear the bear's voice in the soft hiss of the machinery. For long hours he stared up at the dome overhead, wondering.

Reesh showed up later and brought him a leather pouch. "Good to see you up! You scared me pretty bad out there. Couldn't understand why you'd fall over from a silly little scratch like that."

"Who were those men?" Pike asked, repositioning his head.

Reesh shrugged and looked down. "Not all Romanans are happy with the way things are now. Spider has given us the stars. Some of the Santos joined with us to take the path beyond our world. They've begun to pray more and more to Spider. The other Santos—and some Spiders, too—have moved back into the hills, keeping the old ways, raiding each other for horses and women. Several months ago, some tried to raid the Settlements. Rifles can't match blasters with IR sights. We, too, must change."

"It doesn't seem right somehow," Darwin said softly, lost in his thoughts. "They were killed over nothing."

Reesh cocked his head. "They would have taken *our* coup. Somehow, I can't see that as nothing, eh?" He lifted a hand to his hair. "Keep in mind, Darwin Pike, this is a different place. The rules here are different. I think there's something weak inside you. That, my friend, is a luxury you can't afford among Romanans. If you learn nothing else among us, learn honor, pride, and courage. In the end, your soul belongs to Spider—not to you. Spider never promised you a long or easy life, Alaskan.''

"Guess not." Darwin looked up into those burning eyes and swallowed. He was starting to believe it. Things happened too fast on World. *What* am *I worth?*

Darwin opened the pouch, drew out something furry, and froze in horror. The scalp from the dead Santos. Revulsion twisted his gut. His fingers felt unclean where they touched the foul thing. He tensed to fling it away—and stopped, aware of the fierce glow in Bull's eyes.

"It's yours, Doctor . . . from the man you killed. Wear it with pride, for you took it the old way. You're a warrior now. Romanans will look at you with respect. You've become a man of the People, Darwin Pike. You are a worthy man."

The whisper echoed in his subconscious. *Worthy?*

Darwin ran his fingers over the hair, remembering his dream, ill at ease—as if something remained that he really had to do. He was being called to from another place. Straining, he wished he could hear the words.

Deus en route to Santa del Cielo.

"Torkild!" Ngen ordered into the comm pickup. He enjoyed the sensation of the stars before the monitors. The bridge of the big Patrol ship curved around him, a protective womb of white, his officers available at a spin of the command chair. At long last, he controlled power, true power, the kind which would leave so many stars like rubble under his heel. Through the headset, he could feel the awesome forces at his command. Godlike, he commanded this mighty artifact of destruction—and Ngen Van Chow wanted more.

"Messiah," Torkild Alhar, bowed as his image formed. Behind him, the bridge of *Gabriel* appeared.

"What is your progress concerning the independent stations, Captain?" Ngen inspected Torkild's appearance. A lean, blond man, he seemed to be born to a uniform and command. Those blue eyes glittered with resourcefulness. Women might have thought him dashing; falling easily for a man as handsome as his sister was beautiful. And M'Klea never strayed far from Ngen's thoughts. The memory of the challenge in those violet-blue eyes couldn't be forgotten. And she would come to him. Not like the others—to be broken for the joy of raping her soul from her body—but as a partner.

I'm becoming lonely. All these years, now, and finally, I have come to understand myself. Only, I must ask, is she worthy of Ngen Van Chow? Capable of standing beside me instead of acting like a fawning slut, spreading her legs to power like Mikros' Tiara? Can she stand my radiance—or must I break and discard her in the end?

Torkild's words brought him back.

"We have delivered ultimatums throughout the three Mayan systems, Messiah. We didn't get satisfactory responses, so we shot up one of the lesser manufacturing stations—nothing more than an inhabited asteroid—while the others watched. We have the entire colony moving toward Bazaar at this moment. Each of the stations understands their total capacity will be geared for production to feed and supply the planet."

"Excellent work. Why didn't you report?"

The look on Torkild's face reflected mild amusement. "With all due respect, Messiah, I didn't think you wanted to be bothered with the details of a flawlessly implemented operation. Had there been trouble, I would have notified you immediately."

"And have you found engineers to meet the criteria I outlined? Ngen tensed, absently chewing his lip. So much would hinge on finding men to decipher the Brotherhood diagrams. Enough could be discerned to tempt. If only the damn Romanan hadn't killed Suki—or blown up the computer before she milked it dry. Not all of the physics made sense yet. Too many bits of data were missing. The skeleton of a concept lay hidden in the incredible gravitational physics of the Brotherhood. If only he could fill in the pieces. If only Giorj hadn't gone with the Romanans!

Torkild couldn't hide his predatory look of pleasure. "I have two men who might be of service, Messiah. I will transfer them at first opportunity."

"Carry on, Captain. Your next assignment will be to take *Gabriel* into Zionist space and redirect their orbiting industry. You may have to offer some persuasion . . . as you did in the Mayan systems. If they present you with problems, burn the area around their precious temple. They keep Joseph Smith's bones in it. I wager they'll capitulate rather than lose their Mormon shrine. Reroute their GCI capacity to our sphere of control. If you catch sight of the Patrol ship of the Line *Uhuru*, run. You have more legs than they. You can't take them . . . and I don't want to lose you or your ship. At the same time Sira Velkner will take *Michael* into Gulag Sector and make similar arrangements among the stations there; that will spread *Uhuru* rather thin.''

"I understand then that we're no longer attempting to perpetuate the fraud of peace with the Directorate?''

"You might understand that—but very unofficially, Captain. I believe I can stall the Directorate for a while longer yet. Claim a mistake has been made or some other fantasy to slow their responses. For the moment, I think they'd prefer to delude themselves than face the truth.''

"Very well, Messiah. I understand perfectly. In the event I can further the 'fantasy' I'll do so. At the same time, those who cannot transmit information concerning our actions, can't contradict our official policy.''

"Your intelligence pleases me, Captain. Carry on.'' The screen went dead.

Ngen accessed a map of the galaxy. So little of the whole consisted of human space. And even the Directorate's size boggled the mind. For the present, the Patrol would be off guard, shuttling madly from planet to planet as *Gregory* had been. The Directors thought they had a nonagression agreement. How long before they massed to hit him from strength?

Ngen fought the urge to open a channel to Cheng, Zimbuti, and Raskolnikovski: too risky. Somehow, the Patrol might be able to anticipate his strategy if they caught an undecipherable code being beamed through their space. His rapidly converted GCIs remained too poorly armed to fight Patrol ships.

"I need an expanded industrial base—and Arpeggio can't handle it. No, it's got to be brought in, or captured from outside. Bit by bit, we'll update. Then I'll crush the Patrol—and space will be mine.''

Ngen drew a cup of coffee and scowled up at the screen. His advance ships were jumping into the far reaches of Patrol control to create a diversion. The Patrol couldn't mass forces if their worlds and stations suffered random raids. Public outcry for protection would cripple the Patrol's ability to move against him. Ngen had to keep them pinned down while his propaganda laid the groundwork in New

Maine and in Gulag Sector. Ambrose Sector would follow along with Zion and Mystery. Holy war was spreading; how long until it leaped through the galaxy of its own volition?

Ngen caught himself chewing his lip again. He sipped his coffee and looked out over the stars. Great men never had time to plan. Rommel, Joseph ben Aron, Rastinkov, Shmirenski, all had been under pressure and brilliant! The axiom was to make more than enough out of what was at hand.

Ngen checked the transduction monitor and smiled gratefully. At this very moment—spurred by his agents—crowds milled in the streets of Desseret, New Jerusalem, even Arcturus. Food production moved on its way to his hungry masses where they trained to become infantry on Bazaar.

"If only I had a way to transport them." He gripped fingers into a fist.

Every moment of every day, unseen hands planted and exploded terrorist bombs in stations and cities across human space. The Directorate couldn't help but catch a few of his fanatics. They took them, psyched them, and turned them loose again. If he caught them again, he'd just re-psych them and throw them back into the fray.

Ngen let his heart warm at the thought. The raid on the Brotherhood computers may have gone sour, but the psych info had more than paid for itself. Ngen laughed. No one had ever thought of psyching so many people at once. Even those freak-headed moralist bastards who ran the Directorate would have been appalled by a concept so alien to their genetically mutated reality. No one but Ngen Van Chow would have thought of so audacious a project.

Sheer genius. He didn't need to keep the lavish promises he made to the cheering masses once the people were psyched. He would move the food systems and manufacturing along right behind the front of his jihad. All he had to do was keep the population happy until they went to worship and got their brains reprogrammed. After that, subsistence feeding and full time production would be their lot. The Temple would keep them happy, psych leaving them the illusion of joy and prosperity.

Ngen clapped his hands. A man ran up from where he stood at the back of the bridge. Some of the Arpeggians looked over and winked at each other. "Yes, Messiah!" The man almost slobbered all over himself.

"Fetch me roast lamb from the mess," Ngen ordered imperiously. Sure, he could have had it in less than a second from the ship's dispensers, but this was much more emotionally satisfying.

"Yes, Messiah!" The man bobbed his head and left at a run, face beaming with the glory of Deus.

Under the spell of the psych, they'd kill with the same soul-satisfied look on their stupid faces. Things were progressing superbly. Perhaps another six months and he would be on Arcturus. Then all he had to do was deal with the Romanans.

Aboard *Daniel*: Freehold Station: Sirian Sector.

Captain Pietre Raskolnikovski couldn't help but feel nervous as he watched the station blow apart. He'd been born on Arpeggio, but he had spent time on the orbiting power stations that circled his home world. He knew the kind of men and women who lived in the structure his blasters had just gutted.

Crystallized gases, soil, dead humans and animals, tangled bits of equipment, and prefab walls continued to spew out of the decompressing rupture, leaving a spiral trail against the background dusting of stars. How many people, he wondered, eighty thousand? More?

He drew a deep breath and bit back a curse. "The will of Deus. We all must do our part. What, after all, are a few lives compared to the works of God? Satan shall perish from the universe." He turned to the crew, seeing the somber looks they threw at the screen.

"Difficult, isn't it?"

They nodded, bewilderment apparent on their shocked faces.

"I remind you, we're the Glory of Deus. If these dead bring humanity to His fold, they will ride through heaven on golden lances of fire, eternally praised. A soldier of God must be willing to accept a great responsibility. Are there any of you who doubt?"

One by one, they met his eyes, a determination of will hardening their expressions.

"Yes, the Messiah chose well. He is proud of you. Very well, enough of the station, set course for Reinland. Tell the weapons section to prepare the warheads. The godless shall pay! The work of Deus is our work."

"To Deus," they echoed, each bending over his duty station.

Raskolnikovski settled back into the command chair, stroking his thin, pointed beard. In his mind, he'd never forget the dead who spiraled out of the blasted station. The price of human freedom and salvation never came without pain and sacrifice. He, Raskolnikovski, must bear his burdens despite the unease of his own conscience. His work was indeed that of Deus. He brought the light of God to humanity. Deus, in His infinite wisdom, would care for the innocent dead along the way.

Minsk Station: Gulag Sector.

Minsk Station orbits DCC-917A III, fourth planet of the Minsk system. The station is only ninety-five Arcturian Standard years in age, having been an original terraforming project over the developing planet. Currently, Minsk produces atmospheric ozone which is injected in the planetary atmosphere. At the same time, CO_2 production is increasing the greenhouse effect and rudimentary terrestrial plant forms have been released on the planet's surface. Station population consists of four thousand seven hundred people of whom two hundred live on the planet in one research station, rotating shifts once every three months. The rest of the population is engaged in hydrocarbon production used in dye making.

Feela Metz waited by the recirculation compressor. Arms crossed, feet braced, she propped herself against the curve of the head-high piping, staring down along the curving hallway. Felix couldn't have forgotten. He just couldn't.

Angrily, she took a deep breath and walked off toward the Complex Supervisor's office. Maybe something had happened? What? The office didn't need to coordinate the planetary personnel shuttle for another six days.

She trotted along in the 0.6 gravities of the station rim and took the lift to the spindle. Around her, the station hummed, the warm sound of security she'd grown up with. Home, haven, her world. And soon she and Felix would augment it with their official marriage.

Young, giddy, she gripped her fingers before her swelling breast and closed her eyes, imagining the way it would be. Together, they'd get a larger apartment—one worthy of Felix's position. And who knew? Within another ten years, old Wan Bang would die and someone would move up the Supervisory ladder. Why not Felix? He was the brightest.

The lift stopped, Feela shuffling down the hall in the zero g. One day Minsk would be rich, with an entire planet to ship from. When that day arrived, they could afford artificial gravity. Of course, she'd never set foot on the planet. Too much g down there. Only the study team went down—and they had to live in the high g balls hung out beyond the rim.

She stopped at the Supervisor's office, suddenly leery. After all, what if Felix had some extra duty? Should she even poke her nose in? Might get him in trouble—or worse if he'd already gotten in trouble.

She frowned and chewed her lip for a moment before palming the lock plate. The hatch slid back.

No one waited in the outer office. Feela walked past the reception desk, a curious nervousness charging her thin limbs. Peeking around the corner of the Supervisor's room, she saw them waiting, staring at a dot on the comm.

Felix bent over the comm. "Attention, approaching ship. You are in violation of velocity regulations in the Minsk system. Repeat, you are in violation of velocity. Bear away. Repeat. Bear away!"

Feela stepped in, hearing muttered curses. Felix, with the usual sensitivity he shared with her, looked up, catching her eye, his face tense.

"I don't understand." Supervisor Bang pulled himself up to his full height. "Don't they know how much radiation they'll bombard us with at that speed? Don't they understand? We . . . we'll report this. The Directorate will know about this. The Patrol will know."

"Out of control GCI?" Tap Darney wondered, stroking his long chin.

Felix shook his head. "It would respond. No, this is manned. Wait, what's that?" He pointed to the magnified telemetry. Violet lights, like threads wavered into life, reaching for Minsk.

"My god!" Bang staggered back in shock. "They're . . . That's blaster fire. He's shooting at—"

The station rocked suddenly, comm demanding instant attention.

As quickly, it passed. Lights flickering and going out. the floor shuddered and shook beneath them, half the comm units dead.

Felix found her hand in the dim glow.

"What?" she whispered. "What happened?"

Felix pulled her close, hugging her tightly. A distant roar could be heard. Somewhere beyond the office door, someone cried out, afraid, lonely in the dark.

"We're decompressing. Feela . . . we're going to die. Whoever that was, they've killed us . . . killed the entire station."

"But the . . ." She shook her head, a different giddiness filling her. Oxygen tension was decreasing. She could feel it. Anyone station bred knew the signs.

Shivering, she clung to him, closing her eyes and burying her head against his chest to cry.

CHAPTER XIV

Reinland: Sirian Sector.

Reinland was first colonized in 2112 when Soviet deportees were landed on the northern continent of Svensk. Subsequently, additional deportees, dissidents, and counterrevolutionaries were dropped along the shores of the continent. One of the few worthwhile gestures of the Soviet in those days came from the minimal effort to place peoples in environments similar to that of their terrestrial origins. Reinland drew Yahgans from South America as well as Lapps, Scandinavians, Chukchi, and Aleut.

Milt Yranh felt the concussion in the tunnel. The lift hesitated, lights flickering to emergency, and continued to rise.

Not that he worried; things like that happened in the mines. Only he knew something had gone terribly wrong when the lift stopped short of the headstock.

Milt yanked the door open, putting all his brawn into it. The whole mill sounded quiet. A curious smell met his sniffing nostrils. Through cracks and holes, he pieced together that the main building had collapsed. Squeezing his thick chest through the gap, he pulled himself up, crawling along on his belly until he could wiggle through a rent in the wall.

Rain—muddy rain at that—swirled down around him from tortured clouds that roiled and rose. Beyond the horizon, a brilliant flash seared the clouds, leaving Milt blinking at the afterimages.

"What the . . . ." He turned, looking around, staring in disbelief at the flattened mining complex around him. Walls, like cardboard flats, stacked over equipment. Smoke rose crackling from inside some of the structures. Nuri Aktarimi staggered around, tears running from his red blistered face, clawing at his eyes.

"What happened, Nuri?" He caught the man, grabbing him by the shoulder, whipping him around.

Nuri's mouth opened, only whimpers coming out.

"Nuri?" Milt swallowed, staring. Just like radiation sickness. The skin tone, the sightless, running eyes. What could have gone up? The power plant? Impossible!

"Turita!" he cried. He turned, running, vaulting the rubble blasted around the complex. None of the aircars worked. "EMP," he muttered, slamming a fist into the dash. "Gotta go on foot."

To the south, fires raged up through the trees while grit fell from the skies, rain twining down off and on, sometimes in big drops, sometimes in small.

Everywhere he looked, the sight proved the same. Buildings flattened, anything flammable on fire.

The edge of the city shocked him. Structures, flattened, stretched away, reeling wounded staggered about the overturned aircars, poking through wreckage, clothing streaked and tattered.

Milt knew; he understood before he ran panting up to the twisted burning junk pile that had been his building. Across four hundred square meters, the entire tower had fallen. Here and there, structural spines poked up through the graphite walls. A searing heat had scorched the bright colors from one side, the other crushed beneath the very weight of the building.

They found him there three days later, head bowed, kneeling, hands clenched before him.

"Hey . . . hey, pal. You better get to the main shelter. You been out here? You've got a triple dose of radiation by now."

Milt blinked, looking up, aware his skin had begun to flake, the dry heaves no stranger anymore. He blinked at the men in suits looking down from the battery run aircar.

He pointed. "My wife. My son. My daughter. My mother. My father. They're there. You see? They're there."

"Lost his mind," one of the men muttered, staring over the flattened wreckage.

"Forget him. It's getting colder. Come on, let's look for the ones we can still save."

Milt lowered his head, hardly aware of the passing of the aircar.

Holo transmission to *Bullet*'s bridge in GEO over World.

"It's not good, Damen." Maya ben Ahmad shook her head, a sour expression pursing her dark lips. "They hit ten stations. Just flew by and blew them out of space. There's a half-million people dead. Then they dropped fission bombs from orbit over Reinland. Hell, why didn't they just use antimatter and get it over with!"

Admiral Ree raised his arms in a gesture of helplessness. "Maybe they didn't have the antimatter to spare—which says something about their strength. The other possibility is they didn't want something too final. Fission bombs leave a lot of cleanup and absorb substantial resources treating casualties."

Colonel ben Ahmad nodded. "Or both at the same time, Damen. They have limited combat resources and they want our hands tied. They don't want us to get into their systems, so they make sure our Sectors are screaming for protection."

"And what does Ngen say? I thought Skor was going to dicker for some sort of treaty. Something like: You don't shoot at us, we don't shoot at you."

Maya made a rude noise. "That scum-sucking Sirian bastard was on the horn to Kimianjui before we even had word of atrocities claiming he'd been raided, too. Claimed that the mysterious 'pirates' who hit him were Romanans using *his* name as a cover for their raids. I guess . . . well, some Patrol colonels are buying it. Skor scuttled as much as he could." Maya's eyebrows cocked and she pulled at her kinky hair. "What's with that old bird? He turning human in his old age? Getting sense?"

Ree lifted a shoulder. "For what it's worth, we didn't raid anybody. *Bullet* and *Spider's Treasure* are here. Sirian ship-fitters are still working on the conversion and redesign of *Coup* over Sirius. Hell, you know that. It's your jurisdiction."

"I feel trapped—like that bastard is one step ahead of us. It's frustrating, Damen. Like a catastrophe is just waiting out there . . . ready to—"

"Get out now. What have you got to lose? We need you, Maya. It's a chance. You're already stretched too thin to be everywhere at once. It's impossible for us to patrol all of space with only eight ships left. Unlike Skor, I think maybe we ought to let the people take care of themselves. It's their turn to learn responsibility. They ought to be thinking in terms of taking something back to Spider besides mindless sit-com holos and that phony drama pap they get from Ginet distribution."

Maya slumped wearily. "Maybe so, Damen." She rubbed her eyes with nervous fingers before looking up. Her classic African features lined with an ironic smile. "You know what I think about duty and orders. I won't leave my post. That is, not until it's obvious I'm fighting a losing battle. I've got to at least try. Maybe save a couple of lives for your Spider, hmm?"

"Don't wait too long, Maya."

A brief radiance illuminated her worried eyes, the hard lines of her mouth softening. "You really care, don't you, Damen? Never thought it would matter. Command is a wretched life. But when it's all said and done, maybe we're human after all. The galaxy would be a dimmer place without you."

"And without you, too, Maya. I mean it. Don't push your luck. If things fall apart, push *Victory* for World. You've got a place here. *We* want you. I . . . I want you."

"Haven't we had this discussion before?"

"Times change. Nothing is stable anymore. Do what you need to—but don't risk yourself."

She fingered her chin, flaring her nostrils as she studied him through lowered lashes. "No one but another commander would understand. That's what keeps me going, you know. You're there, a couple hundred light-years away, but you understand. I don't . . . don't feel so alone with all this coming apart under me."

Ree nodded, wishing she weren't just a holo image.

"Blast! I'm getting maudlin, Damen. Back to business. All right, maybe I'm fighting a holding action . . . waiting for a miracle. If they get too close, I'll run. Hang it, Damen. There are over a billion people in this Sector alone who depend on me for protection. I can't just waltz out of here now!''

"But I can waltz anywhere I want to go," Ree reminded. "Will you send me those fast transports? I want the fastest you've got.''

Maya grinned. "You'll have them in orbit within days. I've already gone ahead and authorized three of the best for Romanan use. I did it under the board without reporting changes in routing to the Directorate. I think, but I can't prove it, that Kimianjui knows what's afoot. He's hated having to deal with that puss-licking Van Chow. FTs don't have much in the way of shielding, but they're all legs. You'll have to arm them with whatever is available.''

"Tygee Station is in our sphere of influence. We've had them manufacturing for us for over a year now." Ree smiled. "That, dearest old friend, is privileged information. Just know we're not poor, defenseless tribesmen cowering while Ngen Van Chow decides our fate.''

"Romanans are as defenseless as Silurian sand cobras!'' Maya spat. "Still, I'm glad to know I have a loaded blaster covering my backside.''

"What does *Miliken* say these days? Have you and Toby done any talking?''

The Colonel nodded. "Unlike the rest, we remember Sirius. We'll be headed for your back door if things get sticky. We've agreed to treason, Damen. I think it comes from rubbing elbows with scoundrels. You can relax. If it all falls apart, you'll have a fleet of Line ships to back you. We might want some trades though. Your technology for our services.''

"You want Fujiki-amplified blasters," Ree rubbed his chin and considered. "Maya, you've got Romanans in your crew on *Victory*. I can trust you—you've earned it, damn it. I'll give Fujiki blasters to *Victory*. When you become a Spider ship, there ought to be an advantage like longer teeth, thicker shields, and faster legs. You'll also have the option of recruiting Romanan marines. I'll make that trade.

"But the others?'' Ree paced uneasily. "Yaisha and Toby would have cut our throats off Sirius. The other colonels would as soon blast *Bullet* and World as they would Ngen. I don't know. We'll have to see.''

"I can live with that." Maya hesitated. "Do you think it will do us any good if things go that far? If the remains of the Patrol can only escape to World? How do you figure a

few tattered remnants can stand against Ngen after he gets
entrenched?''

Ree twirled his coffee cup on the arm of his command
chair. He peered at the doodles idly before he met her eyes.
''One way or the other, we'll make it, Maya. If we can hold
them, we'll do it. I don't brag when I say *Bullet* is the
toughest ship in the Directorate. If we can't stop them all,
we'll at least be able to blast our way out and escape.'' He
waved a hand in the direction of unexplored space. ''We've
filled considerably less than a corner of the galaxy. Lots of
room out there. New places to live. Things to discover.

''The Brotherhood disappeared when it was apparent they
were no longer wanted. We might do the same if our time
has come.'' Ree cocked his head. ''I think you might want
to consider keeping the best brains in your Sector handy in
case you need to evacuate them. The same thing goes for
priceless art work, libraries, technical manuals, anything
you think might be irreplaceable.''

''Spider's blood, you're serious, aren't you?'' She
blinked, a pained look in her eyes as she considered.

Ree played with his coffee cup as he thought. ''Spider
helps those who think for themselves. Let's just say Ngen
had more under his hat than we expected last time we tangled. This time, I'm expecting him to be even more tricky
and difficult to take. I'm not walking into a confrontation
with him as blithely ignorant as I did last time.'' A pause.
''And it's a religious war.''

''So, if it's over God, it's just bloodier. Doesn't mean—''

''Don't get me wrong, I'm not whipped yet,'' Ree smiled.
''I'll bet my chips with Spider, one way or another.''

''You really believe that, don't you?''

''Let's put it like this, Spider's brought me this far. I've
lived with the Prophets and seen them do some incredible
things. I've heard the arguments and listened to the philosophy. I think they have most of the bases covered. The Romanan beliefs don't demand anything from a man besides
knowledge, honesty, and courage. I can accept my soul be-
longing to whatever God is.''

Maya had crossed her arms. ''And do you think your
Spider can stand up to Ngen's Deus?''

''Let's say—for the moment—that Spider is truly God.
Does it matter what Ngen preaches? Like Chester says, you
can call a fish a bird all you want. No matter how much
faith you have or how firmly you believe in your mind that

fins look like wings, you'll never get the fish to fly. A fish will be a fish and a bird will be a bird. The true nature of Spider, God, or whatever you call it, won't change in response to our beliefs. Ultimate reality is. Plain and simple.

"Besides, according to the Romanans, the fate of humanity is meaningless. The important thing is knowledge to—"

"I don't feel meaningless," Maya growled. "I don't think those billions of people feel that way either. They're scared. Everything's going sour after all these centuries of—"

"Then they can damn well accept responsibility—not some fairy tale. Isn't that a matter of maturity, Maya? It's a nice nursery blanket for frightened, insecure people to think they have a friendly, warm God just over the horizon. So long as you believe that, you needn't ever grow up. Instead, you can propel yourself through life living in an eternal childhood."

She propped her chin on a palm and considered. "They've had a Directorate blanket for a long time."

"The real universe isn't like that, Colonel. The only Truth I'm sure about is responsibility. I don't know about God like the Prophets do. I haven't experienced Spider in this incarnation. They say my soul is part of God. So be it. However, I do know that so long as I accept responsibility for my actions, I'm taking the best possible care of that soul, or God, or whatever. Rebuttal?"

"Doesn't that make you feel lonely?" Maya asked, lacing her long fingers together.

"Not at all. If you accept that your soul is part of Deity—and if you accept that Deity is the only constant and eternal quality in the universe, it's rather reassuring."

Maya snorted a grunt of amusement. "Sounds like you Romanans have all the answers. People with all the answers make me nervous. I'll bet things get a little touchier when they start preaching to each other. Seems religion always gets hung up on dogma . . . and one bunch wants to argue truth with another."

"I've never heard a Prophet argue." Ree shook his head. "The only Romanans who seem to have trouble are the Santos. They have too much Christian baggage left over from their Mexican ancestry. Built in contradiction, Pike says. The Spiders were Native Americans. They never had a written tradition to get them all balled up. Experience remained the essence of the religion, so it's simpler; no hokey rules about what to eat or what to say or who does what."

"Let's hope Spider can kick Deus' butt!" Maya grunted, shifting in her command chair. "Hell, I've already got their damn spider drawings all over the ship. Ben wears one on his armor. My second in command. A Patrol major! He's a convert. All that from a couple dozen Romanans aboard." She leveled a finger. "You did that when you put them on my ship."

Ree gave her a big grin. "Stick with me, Colonel, I'll get you out of this one way or another." He poked at the spider drawn on his breast. "If you can't beat 'em. . . ."

A silence stretched between them. Maya's lips bubbled with laughter, a genuine delight in her eyes. "You remember when I said you were too good for Robinson and the Directorate?"

"Yes."

"I meant that. I don't know, maybe when this is all over . . ."

"That a proposition?"

"Sure," she said dryly, eyes challenging.

"You'd have to give up *Victory.*"

"Hell!" She snorted. "Just like a man. Ah, you'd be too much of a pain in the ass, Damen. You'd want to run your ship—and mine."

"We made our choices too long ago, I'm afraid." Ree played with his cup and looked up from under lowered brows.

"Yes, we did. And it's been a damn fine career," Maya agreed. "Well, you'll bury me knowing I asked."

"And you'll shoot my body out the hatch one of these days knowing I would have accepted." For a moment their eyes held before he added, "Thanks for the FTs. I'll try and send them back in one piece."

"I'll keep you informed, Damen." She settled back in her chair, the shine of moisture in her eyes. "Give my best to Rita and Iverson. Hope we don't see you soon."

Then the screen was blank.

Time for Ree to take matters into his own hands. Ngen had begun raiding. How long before he hit World? Bless her heart, Maya had cut him not the two he'd requested, but three of the fast transports. With only four at her disposal, she was laying groundwork to cut and run. Ngen's jihad worried Maya ben Ahmad. That didn't surprise him. Outside of her obnoxious preoccupation with the letter of an order, Ree couldn't name a more perceptive commander.

And if worry was eating at Maya's gut, things had to be looking pretty grim in Directorate space.

AT Dock 13: AT Deck *Bullet*: GEO orbit over World.

Susan locked down the controls, watching the compensators as the AT powered down. Comm chattered in her ear as the Tactics Control officer carried on a desultory conversation with Moshe's assault exercises on the northern continent. Everyone seemed to be training all the time.

"Lock down." Grapples shivered the sleek craft.

She double-checked the system, seeing that AT22 had indeed been shut down and plugged into *Bullet*'s grid. Slapping the quick release, she wiggled her hips out of the command chair and walked back through the hatch, the lock swinging open as she approached. A tech smiled and waved on the way to attend to some maintenance duty.

Stepping inside *Bullet*'s white corridors, Susan accessed the ship's comm, finding only a staff meeting on her schedule for the next morning. Tired, she detoured to a section where the deck plating was torn up, swearing techs doing something with powerlead and plumbing. No, this had to be major. Whole sections of bulkhead had been sliced away. The last of the new structural supports? One never had the same experience twice crossing *Bullet* these days. The ship she'd known on the way to Sirius had been completely rebuilt under Giorj's gentle guidance. She wondered if even Ree knew his beloved vessel these days.

"Section ten, C Deck," she called as she entered a vacant lift. She leaned against the wall, blinking at the tiredness in her eyes. How long since she'd had a night off? And Giorj would be there to hold her, to prove another warm human existed outside of imagination. Outside of the insidious dreams Ngen had laced into her subconscious to eat at her peace like acid.

The door slid to the side and she headed down the familiar white corridor to palm the hatch and enter, expecting to see Giorj. Empty. The hatch slid shut behind her—a finality in the locking click. She grumbled under her breath and punched the dispenser for a glass of lemonade, stripping her suit off and kicking it into the corner despite the guilt at doing so.

She accessed comm, Giorj's face forming on the monitor. "Hi. I'm home. You coming sometime soon?"

Giorj's pale face betrayed his own exhaustion. "In a while, Susan. For the moment, we've got a technical problem with the grav plates. The quadrupole formation generators are acting up. Some irregularity—probably software. The result is a deviation in the stress-energy tensor waves which skews the angular momentum and energy of the gravity waves we're producing. For the moment, we've got to integrate those fluctuations. It's a complicated matter of balancing the slow motion formalisms in relation to the perturbation formalisms of the internal gravitational field generation in the new structural member. Otherwise you get what might be considered microgravitational heterodyne."

"Giorj," Susan sighed, "what does that mean?"

"Um, until we balance the system, people tend to get sick to their stomachs because of the flux. Affects all the nerves which interpret motion or orientation. Inner ear, etc. The med techs are irritated at the number of complaints. Lots of headaches, that sort of thing. Comm is also affected and we'll end up with metal fatigue in most of the ship. A potential spin-off might be loss of artificial gravity during high g acceleration. Need I elaborate?"

Susan ground her teeth with frustration. "No. I understand. We lose the grav plates for as much as a couple of nanoseconds and we're flat mush against the nearest bulkhead—or through it as the case might be."

They stared at each other, an awkward silence stretching. "The anthropologist is all right?"

"Yeah, crazy idiot. Ree appointed me babysitter. For the moment, he's out cold in a med unit on the planet. I'll check on him after the meeting tomorrow." She pursed her lips. "He's not a bad sort, just, well, trying too hard, you know? He doesn't sit still long enough to relax. He's . . . young. Does that make sense? Like he never knows when to sit back and simply exist."

"Yet you like him."

She considered it. "I guess I do. He's safe, unlike most men. I don't need to worry about him getting ideas. So far he's too insecure with himself to be a threat. He's innocent . . . not a predator." She cocked her head. "I can be alone with him in a room and not . . . not start shaking. Ngen's voice doesn't whisper in my ear like it would if he were a stronger . . . no, wrong word. Pike's strong, just . . . You can't take him as a serious threat. He's vulnerable."

Giorj shook his head, expression blank. "You know, machinery is much cleaner. Humans make no sense. They have so many incomprehensible quirks. But machines are elegant, Susan, working within easily definable parameters. I dislike dealing with men, they have no absolutes. They live in total behavioral chaos.''

She stared at him, a growing loneliness within. Her excitement drained. ''You're not going to come back tonight, are you?''

Giorj tilted his head, frowning as he thought. ''I'm not sure. It depends on whether we get a break. Sometimes Minkowski values are difficult to control inside a reduced field like a grav plate. The hard part here is the expansion ratio leading to deviations in the metric coefficients. We get that ironed out, and we can calibrate the systems, program for macro-stress variables, and have everything under control.''

''Giorj?'' A hollow desperation spawned under her heart. ''Can't you let it go? Just this once? It's been weeks since you and I had a night alone. The dreams have come back. Ngen's . . . becoming too real again. He's out there. I . . . I need you tonight. I need you to hold me—be there when the nightmares come. Please, Giorj.''

For a brief instant, his expressionless face looked pained. ''I promise, Susan. I'll try. We're working hard on this. As soon as we get this structural member integrated and work out the glitches in the gravity, I'll take a day or two and we'll go—''

''You said that when we got back from Frontier. Remember? There's another structural member going in just aft of AT Lock 22, isn't there?''

He nodded. ''That's scheduled next. It shouldn't be near the trouble. Each one goes in easier. We've worked out a lot of the variables with the preceding—''

''Is it so impossible? By Spider, you've trained half those techs, can't they—''

''Susan, I'm right here. A comm call away. Sleep. We'll get time. I promise. Right now, balancing this system has to take precedence.''

She nodded, knowing defeat, and cut the connection. With insensitive fingers, she lifted the headset from her brow and racked it, staring dry-eyed into the distance. The longing emptiness expanded, encompassing her soul. Closing her eyes, she leaned her head back, thick tumbles of shining hair spilling softly down her bare back. Fists gripped at her sides, she ground her teeth at the futility of it.

"Why am I so alone? Ngen, rot your guts in your body, why did you do this to me? Why did you foul my life? Why? *Why, DAMN YOU!"*

She fought the desire to cry, throwing herself on the empty bed, curling into a fetal ball.

A faint whisper stirred from a corner of the room, imaginary but no less powerful for it: *"Dearest Susan, don't fight me. I've come to teach you pleasure . . . pleasure . . ."*

She screamed softly, shivering, huddling into the corner, finally unable to stop the sobs.

Tactical Situation room: *Bullet* in GEO orbit over World.

Ree considered the information coming in through comm. "And the modifications? If we have to space, how soon can we? Worse, if World gets hit, can we fight with half the ship torn up? I need some sort of time line in case of an emergency, because Ngen could be on the way here as we speak."

I hate staff meetings. God, why are we here? Nothing seems to be happening . . . and Ngen's out there. Blessed Spider, what I'd give for just one night's sleep. Susan blinked, eyes gritty as she tried to stifle a yawn.

Major Glick twitched his lips, bending over a portable monitor, figures flashing across the screen. "Another week at the most, Admiral. Giorj is accomplishing the humanly impossible as it is. We've got a couple of gravity problems with the new supports—but I think a week.

Ree barely noticed Susan stiffen in her seat. "How're the new recruits doing?"

Iron Eyes winced. "Like new recruits. Zero g training is like . . . well, I'd rather train a horse to stand on his head."

Ree grinned wryly. "Want to work on gravity with Giorj?"

Iron Eyes shot him a deadly look. "The answer is a flat no. I'm still having problems dealing with gravity as a form of radiation. If I can't get through Laplace effect, how do you expect me to contribute to Giorj's work?"

"You have my every confidence in your ability to deal with the recruits. In the meantime, I'll send you a couple of lieutenants. I think we're going to be needing a lot of people in the next year or so. Can you put out the word? Will we have any trouble filling slots if we need a thousand warriors or so?''

Iron Eyes straightened. ''A thousand . . . Most are lined up waiting as it is. Maybe the Old Ones have said something? Something's happened. What?''

''Ngen is raiding without restraint. So far, the Directorate is a greater threat than we are. Almost a billion people are dead—maybe more. Maya's intelligence was still coming in. Ngen's Holy War is accelerating. We may not have as much time as I thought. You'll also need to coordinate with Chester, see what you can put together for Spider broadcasts.''

''Ngen's raiding?'' Rita leaned on an elbow. ''A billion dead? So quickly? Blessed Spider, it's Sirius all over again.''

Ree gave her a hard squint, turning to Susan. ''How's Pike doing?''

Susan settled herself with a cup of coffee and looked up. ''He's alive. The med has him in recovery now, bowels resected, and both septic and chemical peritonitis under control. According to Bull Wing Reesh, Pike even made coup with that tiny knife of his. He'll be out of med within two weeks.''

Ree pushed an angry breath past his teeth. ''Damn him! We wanted him for his brain, not his . . . Can he travel?''

''He has a belly wound,'' Susan said with a shrug. ''According to that Sirian doctor, he should heal nicely.''

''Then he can heal on the way to Bazaar. I want him where he can get a firsthand look at what's happening there.'' Ree turned his attention to Rita. ''Major, you'll take three ships and proceed immediately to Bazaar. Maya has seen fit to send us three FTs. Blasters and shield generators are waiting and will be loaded and installed during flight.''

He accessed the stored files Maya had sent. Images formed on the overhead monitors of what looked like ripped, twisted tin cans. ''I wanted you to have some idea of what we're up against. Those are some of Maya's stations.'' Another image formed of a planet's surface. ''That's Reinland after the Fathers flew by. Maya says similar raids are occurring all over the Directorate. The strategy here is to tie up the Patrol and to give Ngen more time to solidify his base of operation.''

''I take it we can do as we please to their systems?'' Neal asked. ''Use his own strategy against him?''

"That's right," Ree looked from face to face. "I want them pushed back on the defensive so the Patrol has more breathing space. Take along a party of marines for each ship. You'll each be able to carry two ATs. Take care of them, they'll be the only means to get your people up and down. FTs don't have planeting capabilities."

"Supply ships aren't very big." Rita remarked. "They're mostly reactor."

"Correct," Ree agreed. "I've had Giorj going over the specs in his alleged spare time. He agrees that we can mount only four big Fujiki blasters per FT. More would tie up reaction power and cut out either marines or an AT. It's a compromise, but the best we can come up with. Keep in mind, Ngen is converting GCIs again—and he's evidently utilizing Arpeggian crews. You won't have much shielding. Your only advantage is having the fastest ships in the galaxy and those Fujiki blasters just might carve a hole in his Brotherhood augmented shielding—unless of course, he learned something from the computer on Frontier."

"Hit and run," Susan said with a wicked grin. "I think we can accomplish that, Admiral."

"Your duty will be a little different, Captain Andojar. Your first responsibility will be to keep that fool anthropologist alive and to obtain intelligence regarding Bazaar, Mystery, and—if possible—Arpeggio while Rita and Neal keep the Fathers off your back. Is that understood?"

Susan's face flushed hot. *Shepherd that soft idiot around while Rita and Iverson steal the glory?* "Respectfully, sir, I have enough combat experience to . . ."

"If you can't do the job, Captain, I'm sure Moshe Rashid can. I want you specifically because you *have* more ground experience than any of my other officers." Ree bent over her, controlled fire in his voice. "This war will not be won by raids. It will be won by intelligence—and thoughtful strategy."

Susan swallowed reflexively, mind racing. "Yes, sir, I understand perfectly, sir. We don't want a repeat of the Sirian disaster. You've got to have an accurate assessment of Ngen's strengths and weaknesses before strategy and tactics can be derived which will allow for his defeat."

"No heroics." Ree paused. "I know you'd like a crack at Ngen, Susan. We'll get him for you—but I want to get him smart, not stupid."

"No heroics, Admiral. I'll get the anthropologist in and out."

"Excellent," Ree nodded, turning his attention to all of them. "The other thing we can't afford is subspace transduction communication between Bazaar and here. There's too much space between. No matter how tight a beam is focused—and FTs are restricted that way—someone might pick it up. You're on your own out there. I leave it up to your discretion to determine when you have enough information to return with a report. Of course, we've got some latitude in that, too. If Ngen's people are on to your true mission, there's no point in keeping quiet. How do I stress this? *Use your heads.* And remember, you can't count on the Patrol out there. They're as likely to shoot at you as Ngen."

"Great!" Rita's lips curled distastefully as she met Iron Eyes' frown.'

"Why not take *Bullet* and bull our way through?" Iverson asked.

"Because we don't know what he obtained from those Brotherhood files before Friday caught him. We think *Bullet* is the most powerful ship in space, but after Ngen had access to those files, I don't want to risk her. I also don't want to space until we've got her tip-top. I think you can all remember what happened on Sirius when *Bullet* wasn't one hundred percent.

"On the other hand, if we leave World defenseless, Ngen could do to us what he did to Reinland. It's a gamble no matter what we choose. If he's got some magic technology, and shows up here, all's lost. On the other hand, you might all be leaving on a suicide voyage yourselves. But then," Ree smiled tightly, "Spider never gave us any promises," did he?"

"Have marines been assigned?" Neal asked.

"No, you can fill your own complements. I think you'll find enough volunteers. Keep your options open out there, so select people who can pilot. You may get a chance to capture a couple of GCIs. We can use anything which will space, mount armament, or transport. Tygee Station has been running at full production for the last three months and they've got a pile up on the docks awaiting transport to World. We don't have many carriers. I've redirected a couple of stations their way, too. At the same time, our Sirian interests have been alerted and the industrial complex is manufacturing combat armor, blasters, and components.''

"So we're in pretty good shape?"

"Our 'shape' depends on too many variables," Ree admitted, sticking his battered, stained cup in the dispenser and punching the coffee button. "I've tried to pump Chester about what he sees. He says too many cusps need to be decided and, after all, what difference does it make in the end? Prophets infuriate me. Any questions?" He looked around.

"How about Iron Eyes?" Rita asked.

"John'll be staying here."

"Why?" Rita asked, eyes frosting. "If anyone can appreciate Ngen's—"

"Because I'm *not* about to risk all my top echelon on the Fathers." Ree had that same half-angry look on his face as he turned his gaze on Major Sarsa. "I want Iron Eyes here so we can try and tack some sort of game plan together. Do you know of a better strike tactician than the War Chief, Major?"

"Shhhh!" John Smith Iron Eyes put a finger to his lips, taking up Sarsa's hand. "I think someone needs to keep Damen on his toes. He doesn't have a raider's heart or soul."

Rita gave him a bitter smile, flashing her attention back to Ree. "No, I don't know anyone better, Admiral. No more questions."

Rita didn't like it. For the first time since Sirius, since the tragedy of Philip's death, Sarsa wouldn't have him with her. She'd feel the loss. *Like I should have felt for Friday,* Susan thought bitterly, a constriction in her chest. The nightmare in the hidden places of her mind stirred and sent icy tendrils through her brain.

"As further details come in, I'll keep you updated," Ree was saying. "That's all for now."

Susan stood and started to leave. "Captain Andojar," Ree called. "A minute, please?"

Susan turned.

"Until you're ready to go, keep an eye on that damn fool, will you?"

"Yes, sir," Susan agreed, feeling her heart sink. "I'll need to spend some time on the mountain though, sir. I'll need to speak with my spirit-helper."

Ree nodded, a softness shading the hard lines of his mouth. "I understand. Well, find a . . . a baby-sitter for him someplace. Just keep him out of trouble. Bear hunting, for God's sake? Why'n hell'd he do that?''

CHAPTER XV

Chaca Garcia Yellow Legs' barn: Settlement, World.

Patan Andojar Garcia sat alone in the darkness, taking comfort from the sound of the horses moving in the corral before him. He sat on the poles in the dark and looked up at the stars overhead, so like crystals of snow that had been cast across the blackness.

No more than eighteen, he'd always been a gangly boy possessed by dreams. His eyes appeared large amid the angular bones of his face. Like a knife, his thin nose dominated his face. The curve of his lips betrayed a sensitive nature unused to the rigors of raiding and space. The youngest son, the odd one, Patan had cared for the cattle and the horses, happy in the back country. Free to live with his dreams—and the curious visions that had haunted his sleep.

Now, the dreams had turned against him, familiar friends gone amok.

He took a deep breath and rubbed his eyes, as if the paltry movement of a thumb and forefinger could stifle the images in his brain. He hadn't eaten for days. He couldn't. Patan forced himself to stay awake during the long nights. Bone weary, he suffered, physically and mentally exhausted. When the pictures which formed in his mind were particularly bad, he'd take himself out beyond the Settlements—beyond the herds of cattle and the bored guards—and scream into the darkness, seeking to drive the sights from his mind.

He fingered the fighting knife at his belt. It might be the final answer. All he needed to do was pull the long, cool steel from his belt, center the point in the notch under his ribs, and pull in and upward. Afterward, in Spider's peace, the visions would no longer spin out of the edges of his mind to torment him.

The image possessed him; he saw himself pulling the knife from his belt. And living the dream, his muscles obeyed the vision. The melding of vision and reality stunned him. The feel of the leather handle merged from vision to actuality—as if time blurred, telescoped. In the dream, he pulled open his shirt. Patan felt his fingers undoing the bone laces. He felt the cool, sharp point of steel against his hot skin, tickling him as the weight of the knife rested under his heart.

Dream, so powerful, so rich, dictated reality. He was about to die.

Patan felt himself tense, balancing carefully, hands gripping the leather tightly to make sure the knife wouldn't slip at the last moment. His dream state jerked as he drove the knife deeply into his body, the steel foreign and cold inside him, a slight stinging accompanying his thrust. Hot blood pumped from the sliced heart membrane. He experienced no fear, no pain, only a drifting euphoria.

Patan tensed himself, feeling his grip on the firm leather just as in the dream. He took a breath, as he had in the image and closed his eyes to savor the feeling of his own death, longing for the euphoria.

"You see," said a gentle voice in the dark, "it is not so hard. Men drive themselves away from that doorway all their lives."

Patan opened his eyes. He had not heard this voice in the dream. "Who . . . who are you? Are you another . . . another dream?"

"I am not. You called to me and I came," the serene voice soothed Patan's ragged nerves.

"I called no one, spirit. I am not seeking a vision. I have too many already." Patan kept the point of the knife dimpling the hollow under his chest. Not a muscle quivered.

"I am not a spirit. I am as real as you," the voice was warm. A form emerged from the darkness and easily climbed up on the corral beside Patan. The youth could feel the poles under him creaking with the man's weight.

"Wh . . . Who are you?"

"I am Chester Armijo Garcia. Some men call me Prophet." The soft voice sighed like the wind.

"You are not in the visions." Patan whispered to himself.

"I am not in your visions. Tell me what you see. It's unclear in my mind, clouded by your fear, made hazy by the coming of your cusp—your free will."

"I see my death," Patan said hoarsely. "I know all men must die. But I see my death so many ways. I have died of old age, rotting with disease. I have died of terrible torture

in places that are not of this world. I have died in the middle
of space, my body bursting, blood rushing from my lungs
and no air around me. And most horrible of all, I . . . I've
died lost in my . . . lost . . .'' He cried out, *"Oh, Spider,
no! Not that way."*

The man waited patiently.

Patan gathered his thoughts, fighting the horror of that
vision of insane death. "I mean, I've died a thousand ways.
I can't stand to die in my mind anymore."

"Why do you not stop the images?" Chester asked,
clasping his hands in his lap.

Patan lowered the knife and shrugged, the wicked blade
gleaming in the faint light of the stars and the third moon.
"I can't help myself. Something in my mind, you know—it
drives me to see. As terrible as the visions are, not to know
is even more terrible."

"Would you be a Prophet?"

"A Prophet? Me? A . . . I'm a poor man." Patan stiffened at the words. "My father died . . . and my mother has
nothing. I am not a . . . a Prophet, just a . . ."

"Each death you see is real. Each may happen depending
on how cusps are decided. If I had not spoken, you would
now be lying in the corral, your soul floating back to Spider
while your blood soaked the manure.

"You only see death because your fear limits your vision.
If you choose to see, you *will* see. If you choose to kill your
fear . . . and if you are strong enough to let go of your
concept of Patan Andojar Garcia, you can experience the
totality of the visions. You see, the great truth is that you
cannot remain Patan. Tonight, you must lose that false self
and become one with time and Spider. That is your cusp,
your decision. However you choose, Patan will end tonight,
here, in this corral. Spider has chosen you, young friend."

Patan closed his eyes. He'd feared this moment. He shuddered; obsession with the visions vying with his fear as it
had since he'd turned fifteen. One way or the other, he *had*
to have peace.

Like the double vision he'd experienced when he fell off
his horse, he could see himself blurring, one Patan dead
and bleeding on the ground, the other walking away to the
future with Chester. Perhaps the dreams might be happy
again with this man who seemed to understand. Might that
be the path of Spider?

"The dreams . . . I miss the dreams. What must I do to become a Prophet? I would see."

"Come, we will go into the mountains and I will teach you to let loose your fear. I will teach you that Patan Andojar Garcia is no more." Chester's voice carried warmth and invitation, a cloak against the terror in Patan's mind.

The knife lay forgotten on the ground just outside the horse corral.

Settlement plaza in front of the *Nicholai Romanan*: World.

The old days still lived deep in Susan's memories. She remembered the fate which would have been hers had not Rita Sarsa taken her under her wing and given her a chance at the stars. Now, as she walked across the square from her AT, Susan carried herself erect, head back. Here, in this square, she'd slunk like some furtive animal, wary of the eyes of others, fearing her uncle and his kin.

No one paid her any extra attention, but she knew they watched. Some of the young girls nodded to themselves and returned to their studies. The older men and women waited until she'd passed out of sight before shaking their heads, lamenting the day women went into space and wondering at Spider's purpose.

For those who had spoken too loud there had always been knife feud. Susan had a collection of eight Romanan coups. The feeling of that shining hair running through her fingers brought a grim smile to her lips.

The hospital clashed with the buff and dun-colored background. An artifact of Sirius, it stood shining, made of foamed metal and graphite, a sharp contrast to the hide, timber, and stone of the older Romanan structures. Susan paused at the door, shook her head, and entered.

Pike lay propped up, studying figures on a viewer, the middle part of his body digested by the white, irregular shape of the med unit. His incredibly pale feet stuck out the other end, toes wiggling nervously. Susan walked over and checked his condition on the monitor. All the tissue had knit and was now mending, filling out at the cellular level as specific electrical currents, polymerases, and radiation were applied to the damaged organs.

She took a breath of resignation and went over to where he read so avidly. A long Romanan knife lay on the antigrav next to him. She picked it up casually, testing the balance and edge as he started. She noted the Santos etchings on the blade and chuckled, "Souvenir? Or did you decide you needed a larger knife after the Santos carved you up?" She tried to keep her boredom from reflecting in her voice. Why did his eyes have to light up like that?

"I'm glad you dropped by." He gestured at the med unit. "I'd like to practice combat, but as you can see, it would be difficult. I'm behind in lessons. If I learn more . . . I might save my ass next time."

"Our schedule is moved back a couple of days. We're taking a different ship. The Patrol is sending something faster. I think you'll be out of here about the time we space." She settled herself on the edge of the antigrav, swinging a foot back and forth.

"Who were those Santos characters? Why the devil did they jump us like that?" Darwin demanded. "It was a tough enough day dealing with that bear!"

She shrugged. "The Santos are undergoing a stressful period. Their religion is in decline. The Spiders have political control. No new Prophets have arisen among them for the last couple of years and their world is changing. Some are desperate. You're the anthropologist, tell me about desperation. What do warriors do when they see their way of life dying around them?"

"Revitalization movements. Ghost dances. Nativistic things."

Susan waved toward the eastern wall. "They've been holding dances to Haysoos back in the mountains. I hear that at the dance last year, they nailed four men to crosses, one for each holy day. Never have they crucified so many."

She looked up at the new bear photo. Reesh said Darwin should have been killed. He had given the bear an extraordinary fight. Actually cut the suction disk off with his toy knife and killed the animal after it had driven him up a cliff. The story continued making the rounds in the tight-knit community, always growing in scope. Pike was becoming a local hero.

"They nailed four men to the crosses? Blessed gods, that must be excruciating. It must give them a much higher social status."

Susan's voice was dry. "I'll say. It usually takes about three days for them to die. That's pretty high status all right."

"Die?"

"Is there a higher sacrifice a man can make for his people? It *is* their belief that Haysoos was killed in just such a manner so their ancestors would live in perpetual freedom."

"Nativistic revitalization," Darwin muttered. "They're trying to placate their spirit world. Trying desperately to work their way back into God's favor." Frown lines deepened in his forehead. "Any other changes? Suicides? Drinking? Drug use?"

"How'd you know? There've been a lot of drunken Santos roaming around. I don't know about suicide—except there have been reports of raiding parties who attack larger groups of Spiders and claim they are immune to blaster bolts. None have lived to perpetuate the tradition. Then, too, the Santos are fighting among themselves—those who join the clans and go to space are hated and despised by the hill people. They used to be the most numerous Romanans, now they keep killing themselves off."

"Disease has increased among them, too?"

"Very good, Doctor. But how—"

"We've imported foreign microfauna that's having a field day among the traditionalists." He looked up. "What you see happening to the Santos would have been the fate of your people had not one critical factor intervened."

She gave him a disgusted look, lips wrinkling. Her People, turned into trash like the Hill Santos? Impossible.

"Oh, yes," Darwin seemed so assured. "They would have gone the same route. There's no golden rule which says negative acculturation can be whipped by character or strength of personality. The reason the Spiders are surviving is because of the Prophets . . . and the external political situation. You have something the rest of humanity critically needs."

"Explain."

Darwin's face lit. "The Prophets allow for syncretism." At her puzzled look he added, "That's the ability to absorb outside influences, behaviors, technology, or whatever, by integrating it into your own social structure without causing stress to the culture as a whole."

"We have our own ways of—"

"When you were taking off for Sirius, your Prophet, Garcia, was ameliorating the official line of the Directorate. During the first days of Patrol contact, your Old Ones explained to the people exactly how the changes would affect them. Thus you can decide what comes into your society and how fast change is allowed by accepting only those elements you desire and discarding the rest because the Prophets can guide you and explain the ramifications."

"And you say the Directorate needs us?"

"Of course." Darwin reached out to absently finger the Santos knife. "The Directorate is ripe for a fall. A gigantic power vacuum is developing. The population as a whole no longer has the skills it needs to survive in a competing economic structure. For too long, they've been stagnant."

She laughed. "We call them sheep."

"Sheep? Perhaps. But I'd choose cattle myself. Directorate control was completely artificial. A masterpiece of socially directed propaganda—control imposed upon people's beliefs, totally orchestrated and maintained as a self-perpetuated myth, and backed up by psych for the completely recalcitrant deviants who couldn't be indoctrinated."

She crossed her arms in reservation. "Humans can't be led by the nose like that if they still have honor or—"

"Of course they can! Any time education is controlled, people are controlled. Here's the proof. From the standpoint of anthropology, political science and economics, the galaxy is a wide open resource base. There should be no competition for resources such as toron, metals, or energy. But there is. The Directorate artificially imposed that shortage. It didn't occur overnight, of course; it took three hundred years to reach the stage it's reached now. The key was ever increasing control over education and communication. Call it the seeding of a lie. And the lie grew and became reality."

"So Robinson and his cronies trained them to be sheep," Susan agreed. "They still have heads. They could have thought their way out of the snare."

Darwin shook his head vigorously. "You can only think that way if you know you're in a snare in the first place. They didn't know until Doctor Dobra broadcast the existence of the Romanans to the entire galaxy despite Directorate control. She upset the system and it began collapsing internally within weeks."

"Then why is . . . is Ngen becoming so powerful?"

"Remember that power vacuum? It has become apparent to most people that Directorate control is in name only.

They're starting to ask just where real authority lies. One of the answers is in the ultimate, God—Deus, if you will. They're lost and scared, seeking security as they look out at a suddenly hostile universe.

"The criminals, strong men, egotistical leaders and other powerful figures, are finding people will cling to anything they care to preach. We're entering a period of severe trials and violence. Humanity is undergoing a period of culture shock worse than the Santos are. What we see in the Santos loss of mazeway is a pittance compared to what's about to be loosed in the galaxy. You see, the shock is wearing off. People will demand protection and stability now. The only question is the price they are willing to pay for it."

His words made her shiver and she unconsciously rubbed her hands along her arms. Visions of Sirius twined in her head, the horrors, the terror in the eyes of cowering people. Bodies, mangled bits of human flesh exploding under the impact of blaster bolts.

"Fools," she whispered. "They'll never know what the hell they've unleashed until it sweeps them up. Blessed Spider, once it starts, it doesn't stop until random holocaust blasts so much blood and intestine around the original cause is buried from sight in misery and wretched horror. Only when they've suffered to the point they forgot what the war was about, will they quit. I've seen it, Pike. I was . . . was part of it."

"Hey, don't worry. We'll figure something out. As quickly as Ngen is spreading out from Bazaar, Spider is spreading out from World and Sirius. They are both solutions, one benevolent, the other possibly evil."

"You said the Directorate is in a power vacuum." At his nod, she continued, "If the Patrol can't stand against us, perhaps the smartest thing for the People's protection is to take as much territory as possible to create a buffer zone."

Darwin shrugged. "That would make sense . . . if you're willing to pay the price."

"What price?"

"That of being a conqueror. He who conquerors is in turn ruled by what he has taken. On the other hand, your empire is already limited . . . the clock counting down again—just like years ago in the Confederacy. When men realize there's no crime in free speech, when they learn brains are for thinking, they'll be beyond anyone's control. Once more, you'll find yourself in an open system, attempting to govern something ungovernable. Trying—if you will—to ride fence on a fenceless universe.''

''That would be acceptable.''

''What?'' Darwin asked, eyes showing mystification.

Susan smiled at him, satisfied. ''Perhaps I was wrong about you, Doctor.''

Darwin seemed to perk up, an irritating anticipation in his eyes. ''Wrong how?''

''I was extremely disappointed when Admiral Ree sent me down to—as you would say—ride fence on you and keep you out of trouble.'' Darwin's look of hope crumbled. ''I'm beginning to see why the Admiral is concerned about your health.''

At his long sigh, Susan gave him a quick smile and added, ''Not even a thanks for sending your holo back?''

He looked up guardedly, steel in his voice. ''I do appreciate that. It leaves me in your debt.''

She tried to shrug it off. The damn thing had been in the way in her cabin. She had had no use for it other than competition. When she heard he'd been wounded, she'd sent it back.

''No, no debt,'' she said amiably.

''So you're a baby-sitter?'' A burning anger possessed him. ''The Admiral feels he needs someone to keep track of his precious anthropologist.''

''It isn't that bad,'' Susan began, the lie brittle between her teeth. ''We're only concerned that—''

''Concerned? *Concerned, hell!*'' he shouted. ''Damn you all, I'm a human being. I just didn't happen to be born Romanan! I'm not a child who needs baby-sitting! How does a man earn your respect? What do I have to do? Move worlds with my finger? Around you, I feel like a bumbling five-year-old! I get condescending treatment from Major Sarsa. I get condescending treatment from Doctor Bruk! And I sure as hell get a double dose from you!''

The monitors on the med unit jumped high enough to trigger the circuit which promptly put Darwin Pike to sleep.

Guilt edged color into her face as she stared down at him. Even in the enforced sleep of the med unit, anger molded the corners of his eyes, the set of his lips.

''I'm sorry, Doctor.'' Maybe next time it would be different.

Susan was checking to see if he'd done any damage to himself when a med tech came at the run.

"What happened?" the man asked, checking the tissue strength readouts.

Susan took a deep breath. "I guess he's mad at all of us."

"Seemed like a nice guy to me."

Susan fought an uneasy feeling in her chest. "Yes, I suppose he is. You know, maybe that's his problem."

Hospital: The Settlements, World.

The Santos whispered in Darwin's ear, a keen fire in his black, gleaming eyes. The bear stood out in the plain before him, beckoning, seeking to draw him on. As if heard through water, their words muddled and reverberated, unintelligible through the invisible barriers. Darwin tried desperately to understand, grasping a corner of the concept only to lose it, the purpose ever elusive. An unknown urge shaped in his mind. Wind teased his back, the grasses of World bending, as the gale tried to blow him forward. He tried to pursue the bear as it moved toward the mountains on six remarkably agile legs. The Santos' laugh faded in the wind, spirited toward the far upthrust rock. The answer . . . the answer lay out there . . . somewhere. Looking down, Darwin gasped, seeing his feet growing into the red-brown dirt, grass rustling dry and brown around his ankles. Again and again, he struggled to move, kicking, battling to break free of the binding soil that imprisoned him.

CHAPTER XVI

When Darwin opened his eyes, he yawned and looked around for his baby-sitter. This time it was Marty Bruk.

"How's the guard?"

"I'm not a guard!" Bruk said. "I'm doing penance for setting up the trip with Reesh. Maybe I came to apologize for getting you into this mess."

"Not good enough. I can see what's on your mind, Doctor. You're already fretting about the time you're losing from your research."

Bruk shrugged. "Susan's up in the hills. She took off

yesterday. Reesh wanted to go pray, too. I said I'd cover since everyone's out there.'' He waved toward the east and the mountains that rose along the horizon.

A haunting urge stirred Darwin's unconscious. His dreams twisted lightly through his memory, pulling him east—as if something strange awaited him there.

''How's the monitor look?''

''Says you're knit. If it was up to me, I'd spring you. Some of the collagen is still realigning . . . but folks pull more tissue than that with a bad case of gas.''

''Hell, go back to your lab, Marty. I'm not going anywhere.''

''The Captain said—''

''You just told me she was out in the hills!'' Darwin grimaced. ''I know you're almost at the breakthrough that will let you code those Romanan brain genetics. Get out of here; you're holding up the progress of science.''

''The Admiral'd have my ass!''

''Look, go find a comm and give him a call.'' Darwin gestured in annoyance. ''It'd drive me nuts to have to sit around and watch a hairy Alaskan look like a hot dog in a bun.''

''Well, maybe. If the Admiral says . . . Sure, I'll go give him a call.'' Bruk shrugged and left, a faint light of hope kindled in his expression.

Darwin cast a quick look around the hospital. The meds were all congregating over a unit at the end of the hall—some kid who'd been kicked by a horse was giving them trouble.

Darwin pulled himself up, moving slowly to keep from triggering the unit's warning system. He hummed to himself, concentrating on keeping his heartbeat slow. If he weren't so long of limb, he'd never have made it. Med units weren't necessarily designed to prevent escapes, but that didn't make getting out easy, either. Darwin switched off the unit.

He rolled the pallet out and swung to his feet, naked as a neonate. One hand snaked up his clothing as he tiptoed behind a dressing screen and pulled on the one-piece suit. He had a jolly scar the unit had been busy eliminating, but what the hell, what was another scar here or there? Scooping up the rest of his belongings, including the Romanan knife and the coup Reesh had brought him, he sneaked to the door—fearing cries of alarm—and slipped out into the twilight.

He belted on his knives and the coup and struck out for the east. He'd perpetrated a nasty con on Marty Bruk, but it was only a fair return for everyone treating him like baggage.

"I'm a human, not just a library of anthropological theory or a walking encyclopedia. And damn it, Admiral, you and Susan better just damn well start realizing that!"

The evening breeze tantalized him as it, too, headed east toward those beckoning mountains.

"So, I'm free. How am I supposed to get there?"

It was a standard Sirian aircar. It sat inside a flimsy Romanan shed, where a horse had once been stabled. Like most things Romanan, the key stuck out of the slot. Someone had scratched the operating codes into the dash with a sharp implement—probably a knife point. The last thing a Romanan worried about was the theft of anything but horses and women—and that had finally begun to change. Darwin checked the charge, backed the car out, and sent himself sailing silently toward the east.

What would have been a full week of walking turned into a thirty minute flight. He slid down into a cool canyon, letting the aircar prowl its way up the twists and turns of the drainage, enjoying the light of the three moons which made the night no blacker than a darkly clouded day.

The flicker of a fire caused him to slow. Darwin eased the aircar to the ground and studied the place. Firelight reflected off the ceiling of a large, dark cave. He could see two horses staring at him from where they'd been grazing at the mouth of the shelter.

Darwin shrugged to himself and sent the aircar up the slope, letting it come to rest at the dripline. The small fire crackled in a slab-lined pit, unattended as far as he could tell. He looked around, half expecting Santos to appear out of the rocks, hand ready on the accelerator should danger appear. No one emerged.

"Hello!"

Nothing. No answer. The horses watched, whickering slightly. The saddles and packs bore familiar colors. A spider had been carefully drawn on one of the parfleches. Relieved, he shut the engine off.

Darwin stepped out of the vehicle and walked over to the flames. A little pot steamed at the edge of the coals. Squatting, he reached his hands out and enjoyed the warmth, memories shifting to another time, another place, where round, smiling, brown faces laughed and sang as they joked and told the old stories at the edge of the polar ice pack.

"I could have killed you long ago," a guttural Romanan voice called.

"I suppose." Darwin agreed. "I'm Darwin Pike, an off-worlder. If you wish, I'll leave. If you won't let me leave, I suppose I can always swear knife feud and take my chances. Isn't it said among your people that no man lives forever?"

"Spider has his own ways," the voice returned. "And to be honest, right now, I'm wondering what his purpose is in bringing you here." John Smith Iron Eyes stepped out from behind the rocks.

"Oh, no!" Darwin moaned, closed his eyes, and shook his head wearily. He looked up to see the blaster in the War Chief's big gnarled hand. "Well, hell, it was a good try."

To his surprise, Iron Eyes holstered the blaster and squatted down next to him. "Aren't you supposed to be stuck in a med unit?"

"God, yes, I had to con Bruk to get him out of my sight. Don't be too hard on him. It really wasn't his fault. I don't think it would have occurred to him that anyone might have escaped a med unit."

Iron Eyes chuckled. "Why'd you want to escape?" The War Chief pulled two slabs of jerky from his pack, dropping them into water boiling at the edge of the flames. Leaning back, his black eyes studied Darwin, a grim smile on his lips.

"I feel like one of your Romanan cows. Damn it, I'm a piece of flesh trotted out to render an opinion and trotted back into its field to graze when my work is done."

"You're also in trouble all the time. Let's see, almost killed by the combat machine in *Spider's Treasure,* almost eaten by a mad bear, stuck in the guts by a renegade Santos, loose in backcountry with a mediocre aircar, walking up to strange fires ready to swear knife feud and take your chances."

Pike sat quietly, looking down at his hands.

Iron Eyes laughed. "I've always had a soft heart for fools, Doctor. You must understand, you're a highly valued man among us. Some almost think you gifted by Spider." Iron

Eyes pointed up at a blackened drawing painted on the ceiling.

"Either I'm part of the team or I'm not." Darwin studied the effigy over his head. "What is this place?"

"I'll make you part of the team. This place is Gessali Camp. It's been used by my People for many centuries. Probably since the *Nicholai Romanan* landed here six hundred years ago."

The War Chief hesitated. "I almost died here once after a fight with the Santos. I have a scar," he pointed to his chest, "here, where a bullet caught me. Leeta kept me alive with her skill. Now I come here to be alone—to seek an understanding of myself. And to be with Spider. I put all the aspects of my life in perspective here . . . and wonder about the way men, and nature, and events work out. And I can share my speculations and observations with Leeta here in the silence and solitude."

"You loved her?" Darwin asked, hiding his mouth-watering sniff at the boiling jerky.

Iron Eyes nodded to himself, a private smile reflected inside. "We never had our time together. She was just one of many taken from my life. The path to and from Gessali Camp is one of tears, Doctor. At the same time, it is one of rapture. That's why I come to this place . . . to find that balance between suffering and bliss." His keen eyes met Darwin's. "Why do you?"

"I . . . don't know."

"I think you do. If you don't talk to me, tell me what lines your face with trouble, I can't help you. Perhaps, Doctor, you, too, are here for balance of some sort?"

Pike gestured futilely. "It'll sound foolish to you, but I had dreams. The bear I killed kept calling. Then that Santos I had to kill was always behind me, pushing. Among the people I used to live with on Earth—the Inuit—we believed that Raven made a link between man and the realm of souls. That belief followed me here, I guess." He looked up, expecting ridicule, seeing only acceptance as Iron Eyes nodded.

"I told you I was wondering at Spider's purpose. Bear sent you to me. Spider wants you for some special purpose, Doctor."

"What do you mean?"

"Bear is my spirit-helper . . . my power. In Romanan, we call it medicine. Leeta told me that name is very old for my People. A term of power and antiquity. See, Leeta always fills my thoughts here. I think a part of her is here—that it waits to be with me on these occasions until Spider can take us both back together. But I've lost my story. Once, Bear let me take his life to give me spirit power to take Spider to the stars. You're important, Doctor. Spider has sent you to me. Tell me of your dreams in detail.''

Darwin's mouth went dry. ''During the bear hunt I . . . I heard the bear. Not in words . . . I mean, not spoken words. Like some sort of link formed when I looked in the bear's eyes. Thought it would kill me to kill it. Then afterward, I'd never felt so lonely, so empty. And the bear and the Santos both come in dreams. The bear always tries to beckon toward the mountains. The Santos and the bear whisper, asking if I'm worthy. I don't understand, but I just felt I had to go to the mountains. So I'm here. I just picked a canyon by chance and stopped when I saw your fire.''

''You need to make medicine.'' Iron Eyes rubbed powerful hands together. His hard eyes seemed to bore into Pike. ''Do you believe in Spider, man of the stars?''

Pike shrugged. ''There are many gods including Raven and the Great Giant. Those spirit-helpers gave me a bear on another world. I spent too long with the Inuit not to believe in their God and the spirit-helpers. I don't know Spider.''

Iron Eyes set the jerky away from the fire, making Darwin's stomach yearn.

''You've been in the med unit. Your time is now. Follow me. You won't need that.'' He pointed at the steaming meat.

''My time is . . .'' Darwin stood uncertainly, looking at the food with desire. Sighing in resignation, he followed Iron Eyes into the dark. Surely, it wouldn't be long before he was wolfing the stew. *Well, if this is some sort of test, damn it, I'll pass it. I'm tired of having Romanans acting so damn superior. Anything the War Chief wants, he'll get. Or, by this Spider of theirs, I'll die trying!*

Then they started to climb. So, it wouldn't be the short outing Darwin had hoped for. He was panting and wheezing with effort as he pulled himself up the sheer walls of rock. Two of the moons slid behind the horizon as the War Chief seemed to scale the rocks like a human spider. Pike scrambled along behind, feeling his strength waning. Going so long without real food, living off the med machine, had robbed his system. The long days of electro-stim had kept the tone of his muscles, but the effect didn't reproduce this kind of stress. Sweat beaded on his brow, his fingers were bleeding—again.

The third moon was sinking into the ocean to the west when Darwin pulled his aching body over the last knob of rock to look up at the sky. He thought of the jerky, now undoubtedly stone cold.

"You will stay here, Doctor Pike. This is where the bear called you to. This is where the Santos meant you to come."

"The bear I can understand. But why the Santos?"

"I myself had to ask the blessing of the first man I killed in knife feud," Iron Eyes said softly. "You're here to make medicine if you can. That's why you came to me. Spider sent you here to pray—to seek a vision as a warrior of the People. It is the nature of things."

"What do I do?"

"Stay and pray. Eat no food. Drink no drink. Think only of Spider . . . and what you would have yourself become. You are the guardian of Spider—how would you treat a part of God? What would you do to be worthy?" Iron Eyes lifted a muscled arm, pointing high into the night sky. "Look to the stars where we will walk. What would you have for them?"

Darwin looked up at the vastness of space. When he finally looked back, the War Chief had vanished with the night breeze.

Eat no food? Drink no drink? For how long? Darwin relaxed on the rock. The War Chief would come back when enough time had passed. Surely he would—like in Inuit vision quests. This test he would pass.

His dreams settled peacefully over him that night. The sun blazed high overhead when he awoke. His healing wound felt tender. The view took his breath: spectacular. Wryly, he decided there were worse places to suffer starvation and thirst. Far off, at the edge of the foothills, he could see the tiny dot that was one of the Romanan bears. The sight calmed him and he started reviewing his life for want of anything else to do. The War Chief took time off to seek balance. Maybe that would be worthy of bear.

So went the first day, his body fevered for lack of water, stomach rasping emptily. That night he shivered and shook with the cold. How long before Iron Eyes came to get him? How long before Susan or Major Sarsa dropped from the sky to scold him and make him feel inferior for running away? Why was this happening to him? Would Iron Eyes back him up? Or had he become the butt of some supreme Romanan joke?

As if he could see into the War Chief's eyes, he remembered the grim seriousness of the climb. In the firelight at Gessali Camp, he'd seen the solemn expression on the Romanan's face. No, it was no joke.

Inuit shamans went out on the ice to learn the ways of the other world. Like the Inuit Old Ones, Darwin, too, quested for vision. He'd known that, he thought. Way down deep, the anthropologist had been peeled back and raw soul lay exposed. At University, they hadn't understood what he tried to tell them about the Inuit. Did he now understand what World was trying to teach him about Romanans?

Through the next day, body growing ever more numb, he wondered what he wanted to learn. The place where he'd been wounded itched and burned. Had he torn something in the long climb up the rocks?

It had grown dark after the third long day had finally passed. He relived the terror when he'd scrambled up the ledge, the bear reaching for him with those terrible suction disks. He tried to swallow in his dry throat, thinking of the fear and how he'd almost frozen. The bear would have killed him then. The bear would have had his soul. Would he have bothered the bear's dreams?

"No, man," bear's voice called from behind. Darwin didn't need to turn—he could feel the animal.

"You know reality, don't you," Darwin whispered through his dry, cracked lips.

"I am not at war with myself, man. I am one with all around me. Spider is, and I am, and we are. That is so hard for men. They do not know that I and you and it are one. You fight to maintain distance between Darwin Pike and Spider. You would make your soul into something different. You cling to illusions of life and make living sacred while God is not. You feast your mind and starve your soul. The universe is not made to divide; it is made to unite."

"But I am me!" Darwin cried. "I am a being. I exist."

"Do you? For what purpose? How do you know?"

"Because I say so. I feel . . . experience. I know myself!"

"You know nothing. Perhaps I should have killed you. You learn very poorly. You are too proud of your knowledge and unable to accept your ignorance, vain man. Maybe I shall kill you now?"

Darwin could feel the tentacle reaching out, the suction disk hovering over his head. He looked up at a black blot obscuring the stars and shivered, feeling his life hanging by a thread. His fingers plucked at the belt, pulling the ancient Randall loose, calmly aware of death and no longer afraid.

"Come on, damn you!" Darwin croaked from his dry throat. "I'm tired of waiting. Do it! Here, take my soul. Take this part of Spider back!" He looked up at the blackness, almost eager to feel the parting of body and soul. The black dot began to shrink. "What's wrong? Where are you—"

"You learn. You may live long enough to learn the rest. You have taken a first step. Discard the value you place on life. Set yourself free of your preoccupation with yourself. Set yourself free of Darwin Pike . . . free of life." The words faded into the whispering of the wind. Had they been real? Darwin shook from exhaustion and chill.

He fought to keep himself aware. His soul had become a slippery thing. He fought to retain the fragile identity of Darwin Pike, feeling wretched. He was lying on his stomach, cheek against the cold, gritty surface of the rock. The sun burned warm on the other side of his face.

"I'm not winning," he told himself, listening to his voice rattle in his wooden throat. "Let myself go. Let Darwin Pike go. Be like the bear." He willed himself out of his body. "Let Pike go. Let life go. Let life slip away . . . away . . . like wind over the grass."

"It's not so hard to die," a familiar voice agreed from above. Darwin had trouble fighting his eyelids open. The Santos sat on the rocks, knees drawn tight against his chest, black eyes intent on Darwin's red, burning ones.

"No," Darwin gasped through stiff, cracked lips. "Death is not hard at all."

"You seem to worship death while you fear it, Alaskan." The Santos looked out over the vast space, toward the ocean to the west. "You took great pride in your ability to deal death—but you fear it for yourself. You saw your death in mine. You stopped that first thrust short of killing me. You were only lucky, you know. I should have had your life instead. A lucky accident that one so weak as yourself should have killed me." The Santos cocked his head. "Are you worthy? Are you strong enough?"

"I'm not weak! I'm Alaskan! I'm proud of my strength. I've faced blizzards and bears. I'm strong."

"You've never faced true suffering. You've never faced yourself when you have *nothing left to lose!*" The Santos shouted angrily, knotting a passionate fist. "What do *you* know of misery, of thirst, or of pain? When has your soul been torn out of your body? When have you wished you could cry, while all you love is dead in your arms? Oh, your body is not soft—but your mind is. You don't know the laws of God!"

"I'm strong. St . . . strong."

"You have an untried soul—a spoiled soul. If you died today, Spider would send it back to you."

"I want to be strong! I want to be strong. I want to . . . to . . ." Darwin lost his thought.

"Strength comes at a cost, Alaskan." The Santos looked up at the glaring sky. "Out there is a whole species of men. You, Alaskan, are a pillar of strength compared to them. Take them strength . . . but take it to them in blood! Make *them* strong!

"Do you know how a knife is forged? A smith fashions his blade in fire with a hammer. When the steel is right, and glows with spirit, the iron is hammered to shape. While the keen steel still burns, it is plunged into cold oil and heated again before the fire is quenched in aged leather to impart spirit. Then the blade is ground and polished and given its final edge."

"A man is a knife?" Darwin tried to focus on the hazy figure.

"When the forging is done, the knife is tested, Alaskan. No matter what the experience or cunning of the blade-smith, do you know what happens if the metal is of poor quality or flawed?"

The Santos pulled his long blade from Darwin's belt and ran a thumb along the edge. He held it in one hand, the other gripping the point. "The knife snaps under pressure!" the Santos gritted, jaw muscles cramped.

Brown fingers strained, tendons rising from the thews of his forearms. He bent the knife, steel quivering with the stress. Metal began to sing as the blade bent almost double. A metallic crack shook the rock as Darwin watched the blade snap in two.

Horror left him weak, shivering as he tried to find words.

"That may be the fate of humanity. Perhaps you can do something about it." The Santos peered curiously at the broken blade. "We will see how well we forge humanity—

and you, Darwin Pike.'' With that, he cast the two pieces of knife to clatter to the rock.

Shivering, Darwin looked up from the broken steel. The Santos disappeared into the crystal air as if he'd never been.

Darwin blinked, trying to clear his vision. It seemed to shimmer in the bright sun. He pulled himself into a ball, hugging himself tightly about the middle, trying to force the memory from his mind. Numbly, he fought to bring the world back into focus.

His consciousness centered around breathing as he sucked air into his chest, felt it expand, and pushed it out again. Like the first breath of a newborn, he reveled in the experience. He ran his hands up and down his legs, feeling the living flesh, enjoying the sensation of life. He opened his eyes and looked out over the vista, seeing color, feeling the breeze, even enjoying the wanting and deprivation of thirst and hunger.

Getting to his feet, his muscles pulled tautly through his hot body; and throwing his head back and his arms out, he enjoyed the sensation of life pumping through him.

His time on the mountain was over. He'd faced the compelling urge. The War Chief had seen more clearly than he.

Pike took one last look around. Something caught the sun and reflected—a bright shaft of blinding light. He squinted at the painful glare and shaded his eyes with his hand. Leaning over, he picked up the Romanan knife. Hot metal seared his fingers. The blade had been snapped right through the middle.

CHAPTER XVII

Bridge of *Spider's Revenge*: GEO orbit over World.

Susan Smith Andojar sipped from the bitter tea—a brew of knifebush root and mellonbush stem which had been a Romanan staple for generations. Under her hard eyes the AT slipped into the belly of her ship. A deadly aerodynamic dart, it filled the monitor. The stubby wings gleamed whitely in the light of World's sun, stark against the night curve of the planet below. Despite the innocuous look of the weapons blisters above the gimballed fusion reactors, she'd seen them turned loose on Sirius. Flares of reaction sparked blue-white as the AT lifted into the cargo recesses.

Susan puffed her cheeks, exhaling. The timing had been close. Worse, Pike's escape had enraged the Admiral to the point of exploding. Red-faced, Ree had bawled Bruk out the first time to vent his frustration and anger—then a second just for good measure . . . and because he had no one else available to yell at.

Susan smiled humorlessly. It *had* been clever of Pike to dodge the med unit. True, it didn't demonstrate good discipline, but the furor had provided her with some enjoyment. So no damage had been done in the end. Bruk had taken the heat aimed at her. And the last person to rebuke her for praying in the mountains would have been Damen Ree. A warrior needed that time, that moment to seek.

And why didn't my spirit-helper come to me? In this time of greatest need, why didn't Spider send me reassurance? Is it me? Am I all right? What did I do wrong? The dreams are— "No, Susan," she told herself sternly. "Don't even think of it." But a constriction tightened around her heart.

She spun in the command chair, reading the monitors. The bridge—large enough for only three people—felt cramped after the *Spider's Treasure*. Glowing monitors lined the upper panels curving into the ceiling. The cathodes cast an eerie glow over the consoles, shading the inevitable white in soft pastel colors. Some monitors displayed World; others detailed the reactor status, course calculations, and operations clearances.

Moshe Rashid leaned back in his command chair, head pillowed in the cushioning, eyes closed as he ran figures through comm and helm by means of his headset. The navigator, Sig Marggaff, fed information into the navcomm, buried in his computations for jump.

A light blinked from engineering, matter-antimatter reaction stabilizing. The ship awaited only her order to space. Technically, the vessel was PSA1-775, or P-Patrol, S-Supply, A-Arcturus Base, 1-Victory assignment. As of her arrival—some two days past—the Romanans recommissioned her as *Spider's Revenge*.

"AT docked, Captain," José Grita White Eagle said through comm.

"Lock down."

Under her feet the FT trembled as grapples clamped the AT in place.

"Acknowledged."

Susan accessed a channel to *Bullet*. "We're ready to go, Admiral. The last AT is locked down and our systems are check and double-check. All green. We have Doctor Pike aboard and equipment for modifications stowed."

Ree's angular face formed on the screen next to Rita's, Iverson's features flickered to life a moment later.

The Admiral listened absently to something on his bridge and nodded before looking at Susan. "Very good, Captain. Chew that damn fool's butt for me. Tell him I'll settle with him when you get back. You might also inform him that if he's lucky . . . the Fathers will get him first!"

Susan nodded grimly, wondering what she'd say to Pike. He seemed inoffensive enough. Besides, he did have a complaint. After his outburst, she'd given it a lot of thought. Maybe they had treated him a little rough—expected too much. After all, he was only an average Directorate sort.

"Major Sarsa," Ree continued. "It's officially your command. I wish you Spider's luck and speed. You've been briefed and we've given you the best we have. I know what the coming months will be like. People, I just want you to know I appreciate you—all of World owes you. Do us all a big favor. Take care out there. Come back alive."

Sarsa spoke, "Thank you, Admiral. We'll do our best, sir." To Susan and Neal, she added, "You all have course information. Comm will give you acceleration, constant for thirty-five g pending completion of structural and technical modifications."

"Acknowledged," Susan responded, feeling a slight sensation of acceleration until the grav plates compensated.

"I hope Spider rides with you," Ree added, tone changing. "We'll be here, waiting. Be careful."

"Wish we had a Prophet," Iverson's voice came through the system.

"Couldn't find Chester," Ree offered. "He disappeared into the hills. The four old men don't go to space. Sorry, you're on your own. Any last questions? No? Very well, people. Again, good luck."

The screen went dead.

"Captain?" José's face formed. "You might want to come aft. We have an extra passenger who came up with the last AT."

Susan bit off an interrogative. The concern on José's face spoke for itself. What had that damn Pike done this time? Brought a woman to keep him company? Is *that* where he'd been for five days?

"Be right there." Susan glowered into the pickup. "Have Mr. Pike and his . . . 'passenger' present in the mess." Temper flared as she hurried down the narrow corridors of the cramped *Revenge*.

On the way, she growled, "This is too much! We're headed out on a combat mission, destination the middle of Ngen's space. I've got limited provisions aboard—barely enough for three months. Another mouth cuts my options that much more; not to mention where I'm supposed to put Pike's wench. I'll kill him. I'll . . . I'll . . ."

If it caused her to delay and off-load, she'd be a day behind the others, forced to install blasters and shielding at forty g. As it was, the safety factor at thirty-five would be pushed to the limit. If a grav plate happened to be deactivated at the wrong time, the rest of the system could compensate. At forty g? Who knew? At that gravity, they'd scrape crew remains off bulkheads with razor blades.

She entered the mess ready to explode. Pike waited at the end of the long table, an odd expression on his face: hollower, with a curious detachment in his eyes. So maybe he did know just how much trouble he'd caused?

The second figure wasn't a woman. Susan stopped, head cocked as she inspected a lean man—no, more like a boy, perhaps twenty, if that, although she couldn't tell. Worn hide clothing hung off an emaciated frame. Dirt had mixed with grease, leaving the leather shiny in places. Long black hair hung in two braids, bits of grass and twigs still sticking in the whole. Clan colors had faded along the frayed sleeves but looked like Andojar and Garcia. A faint spider could be made out on his shirt breast. The knife scabbard on his belt flapped, empty. For the moment, his eyes were closed and he seemed absorbed in something else.

"All right, Pike! Who the hell is this?" She stormed forward, on the verge of breaking his damned neck. "We don't have room to bunk this man . . . and we don't have time to off-load him. What the *hell* were you thinking of anyway? Where the hell have you been? Ree's about apoplectic, and—by Spider—he's going to be a pussycat compared to what I'm tempted to do to you. You wanted to be treated with respect as I recall. Well you've got to damn well act worthy in the first place!''

She stopped short, hands on hips, practically nose to nose. But a different Pike met her glare. Jaw muscles rippled and bunched under his bronzed skin. This Darwin Pike didn't suddenly crumble as he had in the past.

Pike took a breath—only the other man spoke first. ''I believe the Doctor acted in the only manner his cusp allowed. To find Spider . . . and to find soul . . . are the single most important accomplishments in any human being's life, Captain.''

Susan spun and looked into those knowing eyes, choking on her words. ''By Spider,'' she whispered, the corners of her mouth tightening. ''Who *are* you?''

''I am called Patan Andojar Garcia,'' he said evenly, bowing slightly. ''I am pleased to make your acquaintance, Captain. You now have the answer to all of your questions and may resume what you believe to be your duties. This is all still very new to me, please, excuse me.'' He closed his eyes again and seemed to nod off as he sagged to the mess bench.

Susan swallowed, body frozen in mid-movement.

''I was with the War Chief,'' Darwin's voice intruded on her confusion. ''Bear and the Santos called. I . . . I guess your Spider wouldn't let me rest. That's why I left. I assume you understand these things.''

Susan nodded absently, unable to tear her stare from the Prophet.

''Iron Eyes brought me back to the Settlements. This man,'' Pike pointed, ''and somebody called Chester Armijo Garcia were there. Chester spoke to Iron Eyes and this man just walked into the AT. Bull Wing Reesh was there. He waved the guard down, looking real scared.''

No wonder there had been no advance warning. No one meddled with a Prophet. They went where they pleased—when they pleased.

Susan forced herself to breathe and settled lightly into one of the chairs. The Prophet didn't move as she mumbled, ''Why us? Prophets don't just . . . I mean it's . . . Blessed Spider, *what's going to happen to us out there?*''

''You might want this.'' Darwin handed her a cup of coffee and she tore her gaze away to look up at the anthropologist.

''Did he say anything?''

"No," Pike said easily, settling himself next to her.
Silence stretched.

Pike pulled part of a broken knife from his belt. "I've
seen many things in my life and dealt with many odd phenomena. Home, in Alaska, I trained myself for a vision
quest. I saw Raven. He interceded with bear so I could take
his life. But here, on World, your bear spoke to me as I
killed him—and after. The Santos I . . . killed. He broke
his knife. I've never had a vision break a physical object
like this." Awed, he ran sensitive fingers over the rough
fracture.

"The soul of the Santos I killed said I'd be tested like the
knife. He said I'll be forged—and if the material isn't strong
enough, I'll . . ." His eyes returned to the piece in his hand.

Susan shivered despite herself. "I was . . . tested like
that once, Doctor." Her voice strained as she tried to stifle
memories of Ngen Van Chow's voice, of his lean body.

"You didn't break."

"Maybe I . . . Damn. I . . . don't really know, Doctor.
Cracks, brittle places . . . If he said the right thing. Looked
at me just so. I'd . . . I'd . . ."

Her eyes shifted to the Prophet. Patan continued to breathe
easily, oblivious. Chester had saved her once with help from
Giorj and Friday. Her heart missed a beat. Friday? Oh, God.

What the hell are you doing? she screamed to herself.
*What are you telling this . . . this stranger? Get control,
damn it. Get a hold of yourself before you do something
you'll regret forever. He's a man . . . and men use things
against you!*

Panicked, she shook herself and gulped the coffee. "I'm
needed on the bridge." She shot to her feet, powered by
adrenaline. "I'm sorry for my harsh words. I didn't understand where you had been . . . or why."

He nodded. "I thought some pretty mean things myself.
Forgive me."

Her attempt at an ameliorating smile ended up as a quiver
of lips. "Yes, well, make the Prophet comfortable."

"Can I do anything else? Perhaps help with the weapons
or something? There's some refitting to be done, isn't there?
I used to be pretty good with machinery."

She turned, hand on the hatch, nervously aware of the
Prophet sitting so calmly. "I'll see what we need to have
done."

* * *

Directorate Station: Arcturus.

Skor floated, curled in a fetal ball. Data continued to pour in, staggering him with the horror of it all. Disaster upon disaster: only by numbing his mind could he cope, curling tighter and tighter as the immensity of it overwhelmed him. But for the expanding flow of data, he would have panicked—cried out in terror at the images recorded by relief ships and survivors. The casualty lists grew.

Eyes closed, all his genetically altered faculties geared to the problem, he struggled to ease the needs of the devastated populations dependent on his resources. Medical relief teams and disaster assistance squads disintegrated under his orders. Where once a cohesive group of skilled personnel would have been dispatched to an accident, a single individual was now routed through a patchwork of GCI nets; the gamble being that a single person, armed with Directorate authority, could handle an impossible situation. At the same time, he employed a psych backup to install a profound belief in the tech's ability to do so. Only Skor had no more teams to disperse, or GCIs to dispatch, or emergency sheltering, or food, or survival kits to release.

How did this happen? Navtov continued to demand through the system each time the frantic calls flooding the strained Gi-net slackened slightly. *How? How? HOW?*

"Because I trusted Ngen," Skor whispered audibly to himself, a brief flash of Damen Ree's face triggering a soul-stabbing of guilt.

I have another report, Roque's input intruded. *Svilensk Station has been destroyed. Emergency beacons are flashing throughout the system. My resources are depleted. I need immediate relief. The lives of the survivors are—*

We have no more relief to send. Skor suffered an unusual dryness in his throat as he made a final scan of their shipping. *We have just reached saturation, Assistant Directors. The diversion of any more shipping will precipitate riots as a shortage of food and raw materials for manufacturing accumulates on critical worlds. Such would play even further into Ngen's hands. Already transshipment points are filling with surplus. The diversion of more transport will starve—*

I MUST have shipping! People are dying as we speak. My . . . my responsibility . . . I must have relief for Svilensk! I MUST HAVE RELIEF! I MUST HAVE . . . HAVE . . . Roque's biomonitors flared dangerously.

Roque? Not now! We can't afford to lose you at this . . . Roque? The monitors peaked, Roque's system panicking.

Skor shivered where he floated, carefully monitoring his own response as he reported to Navtov. *I have sedated the Assistant Director.* Skor closed his eyes, physical pain in his own tense body. *He's at the point of collapse.*

I understand and concur. Navtov hesitated in order to reroute clogged circuits on his net. *Director, I've been manipulating my own metabolism. Be aware that I have added point zero seven percent stress inhibitor to my bloodstream. My judgment in some matters may be suspect. Yet to do otherwise is to risk Roque's unpredictable reaction.*

I understand and note your actions. When possible, I shall double-check your decisions. From the exhaustion curves reflected by Roque's biological indicators, I shall let him sleep for now. In addition to the shock he just experienced, his entire body is strained.

What do we do, Director? What of Svilensk Station's survivors? Thousands of people—

—Will have to survive on their own initiative for the moment. Skor grimaced into the endless blue light of his control room. Images of humans freezing, slowly suffocating in survival pods, or absorbing too much radiation whirled in his mind. Too much! He shut it out, checking the system.

Survive? These are humans, Director! Our responsibility is to keep each of them alive, no matter what the cost to—

Watch yourself, Navtov. Despite your tranquilizer, your system monitors are indicating irregularities. Remain calm. Control yourself. You can't afford Roque's—

We are FAILING, Director! How can this happen? What is happening to us?

Skor tripped the system, overloading the Gi-net in one stunning instant—a neurological slap to Navtov's brain.

The Assistant Director scrambled, reflexive reaction coming into play.

Navtov, you've got to control your own body. I can't take the time to monitor you and Roque anymore. Do you understand? You must be responsible for yourself.

I . . . I . . . Understood. A pause in the system. *What happened to us, Director? Why are we unable to meet this crisis? We are killing ourselves, and we can't save civilization. How did this happen?*

Skor blinked into the endless blue, aware of the frantic appeals for help and relief jamming the transduction nets.

The Gi-net was saturated, attempting to route the millions of calls to the attention of the Directors.

Skor closed his mind to the clamoring of humanity and lifted thin fingers to rub his aching eyes. Aloud, he whispered, "It happened because I made a mistake, Navtov." A flash of Damen Ree's impassioned face filled his huge mind. "I trusted Ngen Van Chow."

To Navtov, he sent, *No matter how it happened, Assistant Director, we are responsible. All you, or I, or Roque can do is the best we can. People will die, but we only have so many ships, so many options. For the moment, you are directed to save the greatest number of lives possible with the limited means at hand. The others will simply be the price we pay.*

He swallowed hard. "Only how long until we break ourselves, Semri? Where are our limits?"

Skor sighed in a most human fashion, grinding his fragile fingers into his burning eyes as he bent back to the impossible task of attempting to salvage something of human civilization.

"Hang on. We've got to hang on, Navtov. Without us, it all falls apart."

Aboard *Spider's Revenge* accelerating toward jump.

Susan immersed herself in supervising the installation of the blasters and shielding generators. She ordered half the ship depressurized while techs cut bulkheads and rerouted powerleads. Almost weaving from exhaustion, she wished Giorj hadn't been ordered to stay on *Bullet*. Her men were good enough, but Giorj would have been able to improvise in half the time.

"And I'm lying to myself. I'm . . . scared. Scared of being alone in my cabin."

She sighed as she made her way back to her cramped quarters. Even with a shipyard, it would have taken a month to do what her struggling crew was attempting in two weeks. She entered her cabin, folded up the bed so she could get to the shower, and luxuriated in the hot water. For a moment, she considered returning to the bridge, blinking against fatigue. Her physical body cried for sleep. In trepidation, she lowered the bunk and lay down.

She hadn't been asleep for fifteen minutes when the nightmare came twisting its way up from the depths of her brain.

Ngen stood before her, leering as he played his whip over her quivering body. Gasping, sweating with fear, she lived through every eternal second as Ngen cooed and murmured in her mind.

"*Pleasure, my dove,*" his smooth voice repeated over and over. "*Let me teach you pleasure!*" She screamed, bolting upright, cabin lights brightening around her.

She caught her breath, a fist knotted at the base of her throat. Cold sweat ran down her fevered body as she shivered. Frantically, she searched the cabin. Her eyes rested on the place where Giorj should have been reaching up to hold her. The narrow cot didn't even hold his memory.

Susan drew a cup of coffee and settled back in the corner of the bunk. She hunched to rest her chin on her knee, shining hair falling around her in a dark curtain. The dull ache in her heart didn't mask the horror of the nightmare.

"Giorj? Where are you? He's . . . he's out there. And I'm . . . I'm getting closer and closer . . ."

She shuddered, alone with the numbing memories—the nightmare that had been real. No one waited to take the horrifying uncertainties from her, to cast them away. She sat there, sleepless, alone with a ship of strangers, herself, and the despicable phantom of Ngen Van Chow.

Alone.

Could she tell anyone? Share the fear? Maybe with Moshe? She'd known him for so long. Would he hold her? Banish the phantom? Vigorously, she shook her head. He wasn't safe. He'd want more . . . more than she could ever give to a man again—not after what Ngen had done to her.

Giorj was safe. He'd been effectively neutered by a radiation accident while modifying one of Ngen's smuggling vessels. That portion of his brain which controlled the male reactions had been burned out years ago. He could hold her; and she need never fear. Any other man would shatter that delicate trust she so desperately craved.

She killed the coffee and leaned her head back, hearing the vibrations—a ship's constant. A mild knocking could be heard through the bulkhead. Somewhere, someone fought to string a powerlead past resisting metal.

How could she feel so lonely accompanied constantly by fear? She sat—afraid and sleepless. The long, empty hours passed.

* * *

Patan Andojar Garcia struggled for survival. His mind groped to comprehend, still unaccustomed to the rush of events tumbling down on him—like the torrent of a waterfall. So much information! It filled his head, rushing through his life. He would pick one future and watch it unfold, only to have a cusp decided and the whole picture change while thousands of other visions crowded, spun, and danced like insane wraiths to scatter his concentration like so much chaff.

Patan forced himself into a state of calm and tried to relax. Chester had said it would take time to divest himself of the confusing emotions that constantly clouded the visions. How long? Patan cleared his mind again, seeking to release himself, to let the future spin its tendrils and wind together into a present which would flow through him and into the past.

But the reality around him intruded; the constant pounding and moving about in the ship rattled his concentration and left him feebly trying to grasp the changes when a cusp half the galaxy away changed everything. Free will intruding was bad enough, but the pounding? The rise and fall in gravity? Patan reeled, physically sick at the confusion.

How in the thunderous name of Spider had Chester ever taken time enough to read so many of the classics? Patan's fear rose to choke him. "What if . . . if I don't have the ability to control the visions? Prophets go mad. They let themselves be sucked into the future to see more and more of what might be and less and less of what was. Spider . . . don't let that happen to me."

As he spoke, the vision twisted and whirled—a memory of what would be. A pathetic undernourished shadow of Patan Andojar Garcia crouched, wilted, eyes rolled back in his head. He heard himself scream, a ululation of piercing terror, soul-searing in its despair.

Patan blinked, wretchedly frightened of the images, alternately advancing and retreating as his mind tried to make a truce with the rivers of future rolling endlessly toward him.

Somewhere between brilliance and blackness, in the hope and despair, in the fear and confidence, lay a path that led easily through the myriads of tangled cusps and unfolding flowing events. If only Patan Andojar Garcia could find that thin trace before he was sucked up forever . . . or driven from the lure by unspeakable horrors.

Did Truth shadow itself in all that maze?

Appearing as a man asleep, Patan fought a valiant battle for sanity and understanding, face creased by an ever-present pain, hands resting on his lap, eyes closed so he could better concentrate on the vastness unfolding in his mind. Only his heart betrayed the fear, beat by steady beat. The blood sugars dwindled in his starving body, fat reserves exhausted.

"We're going to be short." José Grita White Eagle bit off a curse as he eyeballed the section of powerlead that filled half the corridor. "We ought to run this straight up from the reactor."

Darwin Pike dragged a grimy hand over his forehead to catch the dripping sweat trickling down toward his eyes. "That means we'd have to cut a hole in the reactor room wall three bulkheads back, unpack all the food supplies, shuffle the weapons and body armor into the ATs, and—worst of all—pull the ten meters of this stuff we've already laid and patch all the holes we've cut."

White Eagle chewed the inside of his cheek before pulling his laser rule from a stuffed pocket and shooting the end of the powerlead and the blaster carriage that bulged inside a newly constructed blister in the *Revenge*'s skin.

"Fifteen centimeters too short." He shrugged. "Yeah, that's what it means—unless you can stretch powerlead."

Pike clamped his hands on his hips and exhaled audibly. "You know, if I live long enough to get back to University, I'm gonna break Emmanual Chem's ancient neck in five different places."

Darwin started horsing the heavy powerlead back toward the hole in the bulkhead he'd just pulled the thick, slippery cable through.

The only advantage of working so hard was not having time to dwell on the mind-twisting vision which had been his companion since his spirit quest. He could also ignore the haggard fatigue he saw in Susan's eyes every time they met in the narrow companionways. He shook his head, throwing all his weight against the powerlead and gaining at least three centimeters. What obsessed him so? That she was one of five women aboard—and undoubtedly the most beautiful? Or was he really stuck on the girl?

"C'mon, Pike!" White Eagle hollered. "We've got to have that baby hooked up in less than thirty hours. That's jump time remember? The Captain's gonna be real upset if we have the reactor off-line while she's trying to pop outside of real space!"

Pike cleared his mind of Susan, and fate, and dead Santos warriors, and heaved with all his might.

Ten hours later—so tired he could hardly stagger down the narrow corridors—Darwin made his way to the shower and washed. He dragged clean clothes over his aching body and tried to decide if he wanted to sleep or fill the vacuous cavity under his ribs. Stomach won.

The crew ate at odd hours, grabbing a bite whenever they could as the work progressed or hands collapsed from over-exertion. He had the mess all to himself. Darwin settled the headset on his brow and programmed himself a reasonable repast. Yawning, he stretched and found a corner, thankful for the privacy. Intent only on his tray he allowed his mouth a chance to water before picking up a utensil. He turned then and froze. Visibly shaken, Susan huddled over the dispenser, dark skin curiously pale. She clutched a cup of coffee, desperately trying to get it to her lips without spilling it. Drips of the brown liquid spotted the deck, streaking her fingers.

Darwin set the cup down and grabbed her shoulders, feeling her shuddering muscles. Coffee went everywhere as she started. She looked up at him, angered by his boldness, exhaustion dull in her eyes.

"My God, what happened to you?" he asked softly, trying to see past her sudden defiance.

"I'm f–fine, Doctor. L–let me go."

"You're not fine. I'd say you're about a half-step from a complete collapse."

"I'll . . . I'll b-be fine. *Leave me alone!*" she exploded. "I can't stay here. If some of the crew . . . Let me go!"

He nodded and grabbed up his tray and her coffee. White Eagle and the Patrol engineer emerged from the aft companionway talking to each other about the powerleads.

"Sure, Captain," Darwin said jovially. "I'll take a look at those figures. Let me get your tray, too." He smiled easily, shrugged at White Eagle, and griped, "No rest for the weary, José." Then he was pushing her out of the mess, heading for her cabin.

When the hatch slid shut behind her, she collapsed on the bunk, tremors wringing her body. She closed her eyes, taking a deep breath.

"Clean this place often?" Darwin asked, noting that the floor was gleaming in the bright light. Everything had been polished. The room corners were spotless. Nervous energy?

"Thank you," she said wearily, looking up from red-rimmed eyes. "I just . . . just got the shakes all of a sudden. I couldn't stop. I was headed for the bridge and thought a cup of coffee would help. It's worked in the past."

"Right, caffeine rush. Just the thing for jittery nerves. You're past that now, Captain. You need sleep."

"I've been busy. There's too much to—"

"Is it grief? Are you still feeling the loss of Friday's death? Don't . . . *Hey!*"

She was on her feet suddenly, poised, body arched to attack.

"Don't you *ever* mention his name to me again!" A crazy glare glittered in her black eyes—she teetered on the verge.

Darwin nodded slowly, backing up a step. He waited, remembering the bear reaching for him out of the darkness. *Careful, Darwin. She's about to come unhinged and dump your guts all over the floor. Be cool. Be easy, and be smart. If she shatters, it will be into a million shards.*

Using all his nerve, he said evenly, "I'm sorry I never got to know him. My life will be poorer for that."

She hesitated for a moment. The rage in the dark eyes changed, wavering from deadly to resigned. She seemed to sag, then slowly let herself down onto the bed, head tilting into her hands. "You're either an incredible fool . . . or half Prophet," she announced, voice grating like gravel on wood. "I almost killed you just now."

"I know. The fear of dying isn't as bad as it was. It's almost preferable to the fear of what's coming. I hope it isn't as terrible as the hell you keep fighting."

She leaned back, long hair falling loosely over her shoulders to gleam in the light. Darwin watched the pulse racing in her neck. The tremble hadn't left her fingers. Only her eyes were the worst—driven, haunted, crazed.

"Pike, don't push your luck. Not now. I'm about fried. I've got the jitters, and the last thing I need is your concern.

Now, I thanked you for covering for me just now. I appreciate it, and I'll take care of myself. Thank you. That's the door right there behind you.''

"You want to tell me why you can't sleep? I've been working all kinds of odd hours and I hear you over the comm, always on duty. There's something eating at you way down deep inside. From your reaction just now, Friday's only part of it.''

"You don't learn, do you?'' She studied him carefully. "I have a definite urge to kill you. It would be a lot easier than putting up with a pain in the ass like you. Make me feel better.''

"Would it? Not really . . . at least, not in the end. You'd just be putting off the obvious. What would have happened if Captain Rashid had seen you shaking like that? You lost control in there . . . and it panicked you. You ought to be in med right now, under sedation. Your command would be suspect. Perhaps it already is. Captain, too many people know you're fighting something.''

Her laugh was more like a snort. "God damn you, Pike. You like trouble, don't you? No wonder you're such a god-cursed irritation. You don't have any sense. Damn it, just because I can't sleep without bad dreams you don't. . . . It's the . . . the nightmare of it . . . comes back every time I . . . shut my eyes. And I . . . I . . .'' Her fists twisted the fabric of her uniform. She looked up suddenly, realizing what she had just said, eyes glazing. "I . . .''

Careful. This is the edge right here. She's balancing on the knife edge of disaster. "Happens to me, too,'' he lied. "Sleep stim helps.''

"Not . . . not when you're the C–Captain. Sleep stim . . . slows reaction time for the first hour after you awake.''

"Look,'' he waved with irritation. "Maybe it would help if I sat here for a while and ate my supper. You lie down and get some shut-eye. I'm the last person in the world who's going to jump on you when you're least expecting it. For one thing, I don't do that. For another . . . you'd kill me so quick my soul would be back with Spider before my body hit the floor! Right?''

"I'll be fine,'' she insisted stubbornly. The crazed look had begun to fade from her eyes, replaced by a soul-trying exhaustion. "God, what's happening to me?''

"It might help to know someone was close. Someone

safe. I'd imagine that's made a difference before.'' Direct hit; he could see it in her eyes. "It might mean your command, Susan. You're too good to lose it over something like this.''

She laughed uneasily, hands rubbing jerkily on her uniform. "All right, Doctor. I'm not sure it'll work, but I'll try. I'm desperate enough to even take the advice of a lunatic Terran.''

"Thanks for the vote of confidence,'' he muttered, diving into his dinner.

"And you're right. I'd kill you if you ever tried to . . . to . . . Never mind.'' She leaned back, periodically forcing herself to check on him.

He finished his food, and took down her headset. Thoughtfully, he ran a finger down the smooth metal, glancing over to see her chest rising and falling. The deep shadows of worry had softened with sleep, leaving her soft, vulnerable looking, beautiful. Pike tapped the headset, absorbed by this latest facet of Susan Smith Andojar.

This particular headset graced her fair brow? He studied it, aware she'd never see him for all the warriors around. Mildly, and with regret, he dropped the instrument over his head, feeling the familiar warming. He accessed a tech manual and began reading with interest, trying to understand just what it was he'd been doing with the blasters.

He lasted maybe all of five minutes, eyes getting heavier and heavier. He looked over to see Susan sound asleep. Smiling to himself, he shut down the comm, kicked his feet up over the table, and let himself drift off, a warm feeling of satisfaction deep within.

The muffled cry woke him. Struggling to sit up, he practically fell from the chair, no feeling left in his legs. She twisted and kicked on the bed, face contorted in some dream terror.

"Susan? Susan! It's a dream. Damn it, wake up!'' He hobbled up, using the corner of the tray to prod her in the side. Catlike, she whirled, battering the tray into the wall, blinking owlishly as she recovered.

"You're all right, just that nightmare of yours.'' He smiled sheepishly. "I only used the tray because I thought you might break my neck.''

"Pike?'' voice sleep-thick, she looked up and blinked.

"That's me." He bent to pick up the tray and gasped. Circulation pounded in his legs, pins and needles tingling.

"You all right?"

"Legs went to sleep. Now, lie down. I'm still here. Go back to sleep. You're safe."

She flopped over, mumbling to herself, curling up. "Thank you, Giorj," she sighed, oblivious.

Pike opened his mouth, a hot retort on his lips, only to whisper softly, "Sleep, Susan. Just sleep."

When Darwin awoke five hours later, legs gimped up again from the awkward position, she still slept. He suffered through the circulation pains again before getting to his feet. On the monitor, he left a note:

Greetings: Looked like you were sleeping pretty sound. I'll take the chance that your problem doesn't recur. If there is a flare-up, give me a call.

Repairman

To his surprise, he didn't see her again for almost three days. When he did, he was working in the midst of a group of marines and techs. He appeared half-installed into a bulkhead himself, trying to hold powerlead over his head, sweat dripping down his nose.

He did get enough of a glance to see she looked partially rested, if not one hundred percent. She caught his eye for a brief instant and nodded, startling him with a cautious wink.

Darwin's heart bumped, a slow smile spreading as she walked off toward the bridge.

CHAPTER XVIII

Aboard *Spider's Revenge*: Light jump.

They made the jump on schedule. To Darwin's dismay, work didn't slack off. Rather, he spent endless hours at the never ending job of rebuilding equipment, refinishing odd contraptions that had been cobbled together by the engineers and their innovative techs. Now that the *Revenge* could function in the capacity of a warship, she needed to meet specifications for damage control, repair, and maintenance. Darwin began to learn code specs for Patrol vessels.

"You know, you got a regular talent for figuring out machines," White Eagle told him as he bent over a section of grav plate they'd cut and spliced. He pulled the SIMS goggles down and pressed the activating switch. "I still get baffled by the damn things. A year ago, someone told me hydrogen was a gas. I thought gas came from eating too much. Now I'm looking for a hydrogen contaminant? And what? If I find it, I sputter it and anneal it so the grav plates work and we don't get spattered and flattened ourselves!"

Darwin wiped a greasy hand over his coveralls, bending down to settle a compressor bearing in its race. "Comes from the times I used to help my father. He orchestrated a lot of climate control back on Earth. I guess I grew up with machinery. And you learn a lot about how to fix stuff when your life depends on it. Aircar breaks down out on the pack ice, and you'd better repair it or you don't get home alive. As you can see, I fixed all mine."

"You didn't get gravitational theory out there on any ice," the Patrol tech reminded.

Pike smiled gnomishly. "Nope, that came from sleep synch."

"Sleep synch?" The tech rubbed the back of his neck. "I'm not working you hard enough."

"What can I say? I'm a born student!" *And I don't know what the hell Spider has in store for me either, pal. Knowledge is power—and survival.*

Pike ran the sonic welder around the compressor casing.

"And that's that. I'm taking five. If there's any trouble on the run-up on this," he tapped the compressor with the welder, "I'll pull it apart first thing next shift."

He found the Prophet asleep on the deck. He looked at the hollow-cheeked youth, seeing his eyes wiggling in REM state, and carefully picked him up. That's when he discovered the Prophet had wasted to skin and bones. Checking his pulse, Darwin frowned and carried the stick figure to med.

"You know anything about Prophets?"

The med tech, a corporal, stopped, looking around uneasily. "Hey, don't let a Romanan hear you say something like that. They get real nervous about Prophets."

"They'll get a little more nervous if we let Patan die. Check him out. I don't think he's eaten for days—maybe weeks."

"Help me slide him in here." She lifted the lid on a med unit, assisting Darwin as he laid the Prophet out and snugged him down. As the lid lowered, monitors jumped to life.

"Blessed Spider, starvation!" The corporal looked up, mystified. "What's with him? Even if he never used a dispenser, all he had to do was ask."

Darwin shrugged. "I've heard Prophets are kinda strange. Maybe he's fasting for some reason? Maybe we shouldn't be feeding him."

The tech shook her head, studying the brain scan. "Goddamn, what Bruk says is true. Look at the activity. He should be completely overloaded. Marty reported the same syndrome from his observations of Chester. I wonder if . . . You've had developmental anatomy, haven't you? Think back to the brain growth curves. You know how up until about age two, the entire brain is involved in the learning and problem solving process? Maybe that's what we've got here. He's learning to use his brain. I think we're all right. I'd bet he's just too carried away with the visions."

"So what happens?"

The tech sucked on the end of her stylus as she ran program after program through comm. Finally, she nodded, stopping at a report. She skimmed the text, grunting occasionally. "Yeah, I think this is it.

"From the report, it looks like he's in what Bruk calls an orientation phase. He's still learning to use his powers. Either he'll come out of it having learned to deal with future distortion . . . or he'll shut down completely, living so far in the future he can't get back. Furthermore, if Bruk's right, he won't even *want* to come back.''

"Can't we do something?"

"Sure," the tech said sourly. "Wait. That's about it. I do know the last thing you want to do is try and psych a Prophet. Something goes real wrong if you do. In fact, only about a third of the Romanans are susceptible to psyching, another third aren't affected at all by the process, and the last third, well, that gets real spooky."

"Spooky how?"

The tech looked at him soberly, clipping her stylus to the portable comm with finality. "Their minds overload in a way you can't imagine in your worst nightmares. They go completely berserk. You get a psychotic that literally rips his body apart from the inside out. The stuff nightmares are made of.''

So Darwin stopped off every chance he got to check on the scarecrow holy man. The Prophet stabilized in the med's protection and care, not losing, not gaining, brain activity at a fevered pitch.

Pike didn't know exactly when it happened, but somewhere amid all the work, he became one of the crew. Bull Wing Reesh and José Grita White Eagle accepted him as one of their own.

"What happens when we get back to World?" Darwin asked once during a rest period.

"I'm going to stay put for a while," Reesh said firmly. "I have five kids to raise. I'm tired of hopping about the stars. A man should have time to raise his children."

White Eagle shook his head. "He'll never make it as a home sitter. When the call of the War Chief goes out, he'll take up the knife."

"No," Reesh smiled slightly. "I can miss a few such trips. After Sirius, I learned my soul could get called back to Spider any time. So far as I'm concerned, much can be learned for Spider's benefit by watching sons grow tall and daughters grow pretty. Do you have a wife anywhere, Darwin?''

"Once." He let his mind slip back to that long gone day. "She was the sister of my good friend, Shield Downey. She and her mother died in the Gulf of Alaska. Freak accident. Their turboboat's comm misread a navigational signal and crossed into a solar transmission beam. The beams are used to warm arctic waters for plankton production. They were cooked immediately.''

''I hope Spider kept her soul.''

''It doesn't matter,'' Darwin said stoically. ''It was a long time ago. Shield killed himself in an aircar accident a couple of years later. I guess I lost most of my friends through some sort of mishap or another. When you're young though, the pain isn't as deep or as lasting. I hadn't seen Shield for almost a year. I was at University by then, too deeply involved in my studies to take the time to mourn.''

''Death comes to us all,'' White Eagle reminded.

Bull smiled. ''That's his cue to put us all back to work.''

Darwin laughed and picked up the molding tool he'd been using. He hadn't felt part of a group since the old days on the Bering Sea.

They dropped out of the jump four weeks from Bazaar. The trip in was made at ever decreasing speed to avoid tripping deep space detectors.

Darwin watched Rita Sarsa and Neal Iverson head their ships off and slowly shrink into the blackness.

''There they go,'' White Eagle mumbled to himself. ''We're all alone now. They'll hit Arpeggio and Mystery, trying to draw Ngen's attention in case anything goes wrong with our mission. Let's just hope no warships are guarding Bazaar, huh?''

''Three little ships,'' Darwin said to himself. ''In all my life, I never figured I'd ever be in the middle of a war.''

On the bridge, Susan Smith Andojar watched as the antennae and sensors began to sweep the surrounding space. Three hours later, Sig Marggaff nodded to Susan and put the transmissions on comm. Susan sat back while the computer sorted out most of the noise.

''I've got a message from just off Arpeggio,'' Sig cried at last.

''Run it.''

An image formed on the main monitor of a man wearing a gold-laced kaffiyeh.

Susan jerked, fear-frozen in her seat. She closed her eyes, gripping the arms of the chair while that familiar, smooth voice talked about Deus, and the evil of Satan in the Directorate.

''Just . . . record it,'' Susan choked, struggling to keep her wits. ''I'll be in my quarters if anything comes in. Call me if there's an alert.''

She made it out of the bridge on shaking legs. Desperate, a cry stifled at the base of her throat, she stumbled against the wall, weaving, fortunately passing no one.

Susan slapped the hatch, tumbling into her cabin, propping herself in the corner as her mind staggered, images of Ngen almost overwhelming, his voice cooing out of the air around her. She bent double, hands clenched to her ears to keep the soft strains of his voice away.

"You've got to deal with it," she gritted through chattering teeth. "He's out there. You're getting closer and closer to him. He can't hurt you. He doesn't even know you're alive."

Believe that. You've got to. You're in enemy space. Any contact can destroy you. The Captain has to be capable, calm, collected. Every life on the ship—maybe even on World—depends on your wits and abilities. She tensed, Ngen's leering face taunting in her memory.

Susan tried to calm herself—tried to remember Chester Armijo Garcia and the things he had told her that day when he'd broken her out of her half-psychotic obsession. No matter how she tried, the only words in her mind were Ngen's.

Half-hysterical, she picked up her headset, running the delicate piece of equipment over her fingers. "If there is a flare-up, give me a call," he'd written. After all, he was harmless—an inoffensive Terran who had strange ideas about himself.

"Sweet Susan . . . before this week is done, I will hear you call for me . . . no longer will you deny me the opportunity to bring you bliss . . . bliss . . ."

"DAMN YOU, NGEN!" she screamed, fists clenched, the sobs breaking loose to drown her.

"Susan, delight will be yours . . . you will call for me . . . call for . . ."

"NO!" Struggling, she pulled the headset over her sweating brow, fighting the quivers and sobs.

"Doctor Darwin Pike to the Captain's quarters." Committed, she shivered and lifted the headset, tossing it to the bunk. What now? She could still just ask him a couple routine questions and send him on his way. Her hand was trembling. No good, he'd see it immediately.

"Better . . . better than Ngen. Better than the memories."

She waited, half curled on the bed. He'd brought her sleep. After that, she'd kept a close monitor on him. Never once had he hinted at her weakness. He'd never even made a cryptic remark to any of the warriors. Even so, how far could she trust him?

"Hatch. Doctor Pike," comm intoned.

"En—enter."

He stepped in, smudged, an ultrasonic molding hammer hanging out of his pocket.

"Sit down," she muttered, working her mouth to fight the dryness.

His quick eyes were on her as he let himself down into the chair. "You've been crying."

She closed her eyes. "I just need someone to talk to."

"We all heard that a transmission from Ngen had been picked up." Darwin inspected the backs of his dirty hands. "Look, Susan, I know Ngen is at the bottom of what's bothering you." He stuck his hands in the ionizer next to the small bath and looked at her. "What can I do to help?"

She shook her head. "I don't know." It was insane! Why hadn't she insisted on Giorj coming along? He knew! He had been there! Giorj was safe!

"We've got the blaster leads almost finished up. I'm almost able to understand what goes where and why things don't work now. That is an incredible improvement for a dumb professor."

She waved him on. "Please, talk. Just keep taking so I . . . I can think." As he droned on, her thoughts settled. Ngen hung there at the edge, held back for the moment while she gathered her strength, nurtured the ability to resist.

Pike talked for an hour, rambling on about the ship, about what he thought of Bull Wing Reesh, José Grita White Eagle, and the Prophet he visited every time he went off duty.

At length she laughed nervously and held up a hand. "Enough, Doctor." She frowned thoughtfully at the foot of the bed. "You know, it's funny. I lived through some of the toughest fighting on Sirius. Saw things that . . . Well, I'm here beyond all the odds, Doctor. I dealt with Sirian captivity . . . and I lived through what . . . what Ngen Van Chow did to me. But what really bothers me is I wonder if I actually survived it—or if I'm always going to be teetering in the bottom of my mind?" She mashed hard palms into her red-rimmed eyes, grinding out the frustration.

He cocked his head, waiting.

"Damn him!" She rubbed the back of her neck. "I've got to live with it . . . but he used psych. Understand? I

. . . Spider curse it, I don't know if I'm fit for command, Pike. What if . . . if I lose it? Have to face him. I could . . . could kill us all. I broke, you see. Broke under his . . . his . . ." She swallowed hard, throat constricting. "Why didn't you tell anyone? You know how close I am to falling apart. Why?"

He shrugged. "I don't know a better commander. You're the best I've seen." He frowned, steepling his fingers. "Damned if I know why, but I trust you. If anyone can get us in and out, you'll do it. Despite Ngen."

"Trust? A terrible burden, Doctor. So very few are worthy. And I'm not one, remember that. You get your ass caught, and I'm gone."

He nodded. "I suppose. You've got the ship to worry about. My life isn't important. Getting the data and intelligence back to Ree is. I accept that."

She closed her eyes and took a deep breath. "And Ngen is out there, sending transduction messages to make me cringe. Spider, what do I do if . . . if . . ."

"I don't know. Want to run his transmission again and see how it affects you? We can always shut it off. I think it's worth seeing if you can handle it." He inspected his nails and looked up, his expression neutral. "Most problems can be licked if you tackle them a little at a time."

"Comm, access that file we just picked up from Van Chow." Her voice held the tone of authority. She flinched as Ngen's passionate features formed on the holo. She shivered as his soothing, purring voice filled the room.

"He has a very polished delivery. His charisma carries him though the flaws in his argument," Darwin speculated. He shot a quick look at Susan. "What do you think?"

Think! Fight. Answer Pike's questions. Concentrate. A test. That's what it is, a test to see if you can think.

"I . . . I think . . . M-More than that. He . . . he's a master at appealing to emotions. He m-missed his calling by not being a holo star. I think he could play any part right up to Director . . . and . . . and do it so well you'd think he'd spent all his life at it."

"I think," Darwin mused, "that his is the greatest criminal mind since Hitler's or maybe that Soviet general, Rostokiev, who masterminded the deportations in the twenty-first century. You know Ngen better than anyone. Where, if anywhere, does he have a vulnerability?"

Did she dare tell? She fought her reaction as she remembered the only time she'd hurt Ngen Van Chow. "He . . . he's very j-jealous about his masculinity. Thinks he's . . . he's . . ."

"Hmm," Darwin didn't miss a beat. He didn't even seem to notice her hesitation as she felt herself begin to shake again. "Susan, if you can, put your mind to work on it. Perhaps we might be able to think of a way to exploit that weakness to our advantage."

God, no! Never! Think about his . . . Please, Spider, no!

The holo came to its end and the screen went blank. Teeth gritted, she relaxed her clenched fingers and took a deep breath.

"Was it as bad as you thought?"

"I guess I lived," she managed, voice husky. "That's something, isn't it?"

"A first step. Now, while you've got no choice, get back to the bridge and run Ngen again. That's where you might have to deal with him. Push your success." He winked at her and was on his feet.

"Wait! T-Tonight . . . well . . . would you mind coming back when I'm off duty? I'm afraid . . . sleep might . . ."

"Sure, no problem." He made it sound so easy. "I'm going to bring something to cushion my legs though. After that table ate them last time, I couldn't walk for three days." Then he was gone.

Susan watched the white of the hatch slide shut. Everything was fine for the moment. How long would it last, though, before he wanted what she could not give? Susan closed her eyes, breathed deep and stood up, forcing herself to the bridge and Ngen's foul face.

Administrative Center: city of Bazaar, Bazaar.

"The problem comes from the psych." Pallas thoughtfully bit into a fat peach, the juices running down the side of his mouth. He wiped at it, multicolored rings sparkling. Behind him the administrative office echoed Bazaaran austerity. Buff walls still bore ghostly traces of drably-colored Christian murals, now mostly covered by comm panels and monitor screens. Powerlead had been strung here and there, stapled to the wall in a series of black ropes leading to the roof above.

"And that is?" Ngen said from the bridge of *Deus* de-

tailed in the holo. Compared to the dingy earth-tones of
Bazaar, the bridge seemed clean, light.

Pallas frowned, swallowing his mouthful of fruit. "It
works too well. I fear that we've been too drastic with the
field effect. Those few untreated individuals left have run
for the deep desert. As to their potential threat, well, it's
hard to say at this moment. Suffice it to say, I've imported
most of my contacts from other worlds for security personnel. I hadn't—"

"What of the natural converts?" Ngen cocked his head,
eyes narrowing.

"I'm afraid they lost ardor when they saw the effects of
the Temple psych. Most joined with the refugees in the deep
desert."

"And the situation? How badly do you think the manufacturing is compromised? You know how important—"

"Please, Ngen," Pallas waved it away, "we're not about
to be compromised by any rabble creeping out of the desert
in the midst of a sandstorm. In the first place, they can't
appeal to the average citizen's sense of justice or patrio-
tism—that's been effectively negated by the field psych. Nor
can they cripple our manufacturing capabilities or supply
lines. The logistics are protected and monitored. The security I've imported simply restricts their ability to carry
out irritating sabotage. We've had none so far, but I like to
plan ahead for—"

"Then why did you call me? I can't see where the problem—"

"It's the psych, Ngen. It's too good. I have to—"

"What do you mean, 'too good'? Pallas, what's the problem? You're supposed to work these things out, debug the
program."

"You can't!" Pallas pulled himself up slightly, the peach
waving in his pudgy fist, a drip running down the sagging
fat of his pale arm. "Ngen, let me finish. The psych works
too well. The people walk through the Temple and get
treated, converted, whatever we're calling it now. Of necessity, the program is balanced to affect the greatest number of individual brain types. Like any other human
characteristic, the brain more or less fits a normal distribution curve. A bell-shape curve, they call it. The Gonian
psych techs have refined the field to deal with the vast majority of people—the middle of the bell-shaped curve."

"Which is what percentage of the population?"

"About eighty-six percent for our psych applications. Outstanding, considering the range of human variation, metabolic influences, the diversity of brain morphology, and a host of other variables. The two tails of the curve are wasted, meaning simply that some take a partial psych, the others go nuts—completely erased. We dispose of the failures most efficiently."

"Then I still don't see the problem."

Pallas shook his head vigorously. "Ngen, the problem is a lack of initiative. Please, consider this. For Bazaar, and the kind of work we're doing here, it isn't much of a bother. Oh, I've had to bring in security personnel from my personal Directorate-wide network. They don't mind. Women, drugs, and booze are free for them—and they're paid better than ever before. They'll become bored in a while and I'll have to draw in some favors for more qualified people—but in the meantime, I've set the Gonian psych team to the problem *you're* going to face very soon."

Ngen's expression tightened. "And what will *my* problem be?"

"You'll have to screen your applicants, Ngen. You see, after they walk through the field psych, they can't think— um, anticipate and innovate. Displacement is gone—wiped clean. You're going to have to earmark those individuals with superior skills, con them, blackmail them, or tailor each episode of psych to their particular brains as the Directorate did with single deviants. Otherwise, you get robots who perform their task, but don't have sense to come in out of the dust unless it's programmed into them. Do you see?"

Pallas sucked his peach, slurping at the juice while he watched Ngen's lip slip back and forth between his teeth.

Ngen nodded, a deep frown incising his forehead. "I'll have armies of devoted blaster fodder—and no field commanders capable of using them to implement strategy. Yes, I see. And you say you've detailed the Gonians to solving that problem?"

"Overtime, I'm afraid." Pallas took another bite of his peach. "Thank you for sending the agricultural stations. I fear I'll gain so much weight I won't be able to move but for antigrav."

"Have they been able to expand upon the Brotherhood data? That solved the wide field psych to begin with. Can they refine it? Lessen the wide field effect?"

Pallas nodded, licking his sticky lips. "At the expense of that eighty-six percent. The weaker the field, the fewer people affected. We also have trouble with the children. Young brains seem particularly susceptible."

Ngen waved it away with a flick of his wrist. "We can waste a generation. So long as they can breed, we'll always have humans."

"Very well. I suggest you experiment on your own on Arpeggio and Mystery. Watch out, though. The unaffected ones can draw some surprising conclusions about what happened to them. You might get a nasty kickback."

"What of your Tiara? Doesn't she burn any of your calories off anymore?" Ngen smiled as he rubbed his long hands together.

Pallas sighed and snapped his fingers. Tiara walked forward, standing, expressionless. "In a sense, Ngen, she brought the entire problem into focus. You see, she went to Temple one night when I was working. I fear that her skills have been turned into the simple ability to copulate. Alas, even had I the desire, my girth won't allow it. I've taken the liberty of importing another girl, but I fear it will be a month or more before she arrives from Arcturus—perhaps longer. Directorate space is in terrible turmoil—even for contraband runners."

"I'm truly sorry. I'd send you a couple of women, but none have the requisite skills of so great a courtesan as Tiara." Ngen paused. "You're sure nothing can be done to recover her mental faculties?"

Pallas lowered his head, fat face sad. "You give up something to get that eighty-six percent, Ngen. One of the prices of compromise is irreversible brain programming. Tiara can now be trained for task specific behaviors. Currently she knows how to make blasters. If I ran a different program, she could run the machines which manufacture combat armor, or space suits, or what have you. But that intuitive use of her magnificent body? No, old friend. I'm afraid that glorious imagination is gone—forever. She's a simple uninspired female body now."

"I'll try and find you a talented woman, Pallas. Only next time I send you a specialist, do keep her out of the Temple. In the meantime, I'll check the Directorate records for initiative and military or supervisory predisposition. Those I'll have my techs psych individually. Who knows, maybe the answer will come from your research."

Pallas shifted his bulk on the antigrav, grunting in the process as his fat wiggled. "And I'll let you know what the Gonians come up with. In the meantime, be aware that your command structure must be given special priority."

Ngen's face lit with an inner glow. "You're a most precious resource, Pallas. When this is over, I promise you'll have your planet. Any planet you choose. I reward loyalty well."

The holo faded to leave Pallas staring at the empty receiver. He took another bite of the peach and frowned, satisfied only with the limited pleasure of Tiara's hands on his body. She could still answer that command—but it didn't provide the bursting ecstasy the old Tiara had.

Aboard *Spider's Revenge* decelerating into Bazaaran space.

Darwin Pike studied the scanner thoughtfully as *Spider's Revenge* coasted easily through space, reactor damped, power at a bare minimum. Gravity varied through the ship, all efforts bent to concealing their presence from long-range scanning.

For days they'd been dropping toward Bazaar from the high side on an eccentric orbit, Susan tapering acceleration as they came closer and closer to sensor range. Moshe reclined in his control chair, eyes closed as he balanced the power of the remote sensors, playing a game of field intensities, trying to keep the stations in orbit around Bazaar from detecting their snooping.

Susan studied the same monitors Pike did, hoping she might see something he missed, fighting boredom as the meaningless scenes of lusterless towns, drab fields, and dull rocky landscape flashed past. Some screens monitored specific Bazaaran cities while others watched dingy factories and one locked constantly on a large temple whenever it was visible during the planet's rotation.

Darwin pushed himself back in the control chair and stretched, a deep frown on his face. "I don't understand."

Susan looked up.

Pike flipped through various files. "Watch this. I'm having comm tag all the repeat customers at the temple." Figures flashed on the screen.

"We'll take four different days." The screen split into four images. "Now we eliminate everyone who only went

to the temple once.'' Half of the dots disappeared. ''Now
we'll remove the people who only went twice.'' Nothing
happened. ''Three times.'' No changes occurred on the
monitor. He looked up, curiosity in his frown-wrinkled features. ''The people left on the monitor are all four timers.
None of the people who went once came back for a second
or third time. Why? Five hundred and twenty-eight went all
four times; not one of them missed a meeting. Why?''

''Statistical error based on sample size? What's your N?''

''About a thousand.'' Darwin responded dryly. ''Do you
know the statistical odds against what we've seen? Our expected and observed are staggeringly different. Run a Chi-
square and see if we have a meaningful—''

''I don't need to. Through the roof!''

''Now, watch this.'' Darwin began accessing different
programs. ''I want you to pay attention to the activity in the
streets. With the exception of prayer hours, notice the
amount of activity.''

View after view came on the screen, stayed for thirty
seconds, and flashed off. ''I've taken these over the last four
days since we came into viewing range, taking a holo at half
hour intervals with comm monitor full time.''

''I don't see any change,'' Susan told him, baffled by his
concern. ''It all looks normal to me. One shot doesn't seem
any different from another.''

Pike had a glint in his eyes. ''That's exactly my point. In
any regular society I know of, behavior is patterned. At
certain hours of the day—like immediately after work—the
density increases on the street. At other times, the streets
ought to be deserted—folks at home sleeping, right? Study
the scenes at night. Activity remains constant. Then here's
another anomaly to consider. Locations we call 'Central
Places' pick up clots of people who talk together, exchange
information, and socialize. Maybe it's a market? Or a place
where clothes are washed? A square, perhaps? Where do
you see that behavior on Bazaar? The only pattern here is
monotony.''

Susan interjected. ''Ships don't work that way. We run
twenty-four hours a day.''

Pike shook his head, an absent expression on his face.
''There are five Central Places here in the ship. The mess
for one, reactor for another, crew bunking area, bridge, and
blaster and shielding stations.''

He had a valid point when she thought about it. Crew met

there to talk even when they were off duty. Stories were told, bets made, desultory talk, flirting, you name it. Her eyes went back to the flipping scenes. The rise of activity began as the sun rose, plateauing within a half hour, and beginning to dwindle an hour after sunset. "It's almost as if they weren't people," she remarked to herself.

"Yeah," Pike agreed. "That's been crossing my mind, too. None of the behavior is what we associate with being human. All humans need food, water, shelter, and some sort of outside stimulus. Watch the big antigrav. As it winds through the streets, it drops a package of supplies at each door. A man or woman comes out and gets it, then goes back inside. It's almost like an insect society—only this seems logistically perfect. No milling. No lost effort."

Susan got a cup of coffee from the dispenser. "What does it all mean?"

"I haven't got the foggiest notion. It's just not right! They're little robots down there. I'd give my firstborn son to see inside that temple! Why do only certain ones go back time after time and others only once? Why is there no Central Place? What happened to social activity? Why don't they act *human?*"

"Maybe it has something to do with what Ngen got out of the Brotherhood computers."

"Was the Brotherhood ever into hive mentality? I heard they did some strange things." Pike's eyes showed an odd flicker of interest.

"They weren't as bad as the legends would have you believe. Actually, they were good friends with the Patrol. The Sirians and Arpeggians along with some pirate factions were behind them leaving Directorate space."

"I don't know why Ngen is complaining. If that's his model society, he's one up on the Directorate." Pike hesitated. "I've got to go down there. I have to see what they're like up close. I need to get into that temple and see what happens in their houses."

Susan winced. That meant leaving the safety of the ship. Pike had changed from the green, easygoing, carefree scholar who'd boarded at Arcturus, but did he understand the risks? In the ship, she could run and fight. What about on the ground? Ground action put her that much closer to Ngen Van Chow's grasp. His voice hovered at the edge of her consciousness, whispering.

* * *

Susan cornered him later, finding him in the mess sharing a cup of coffee with Sig Marggaff. Sig politely said something discreet and left.

Susan hesitated, tapping her fingers, trying to think of words which would lessen the effect of what she wanted to say. Finally, she began with, "You know how dangerous it will be down there."

He nodded, expression softened. "Yeah, I have a pretty good idea. Still, I don't worry too much. I've been taking the language tapes at night. Standard on Bazaar has evolved quite a bit, but I'm up on the slang. Dressed in mufti, I can pass as a local."

"I don't like risking my only anthropologist. Not considering what Ree will do if I come back without you."

"That your only reason?" He raised an eyebrow, anticipation widening his eyes.

"To cop a phrase from the War Chief, I like to win. You've already seen more on Bazaar than Moshe, White Eagle, and Reesh put together." *And why in hell am I so nervous all of a sudden. What in hell did he mean, "the only reason?"*

"I'll be all right down there. Drop me off from an AT, I'll do my nosing around, then meet you at the pickup point." He shrugged. "It's as simple as that."

"Are you positive you can't get what you need from high orbit? Didn't you talk to Giorj about equipment?" She felt her temper rising exponentially.

"Yes. From what he told me, I thought the standard stuff was fine. It is. The problem is that a remote drone would stand out like an Arcturian whore down there. It's an insubstantial thing, Susan. I need . . . well, to scratch around under the skin. Understand? I can't interact with a man through a machine, can't determine how his psychological profile differs from the norm if I don't have him where I can observe him in his natural setting.

"Then, too, I need to find out what goes on inside that temple. We've run the scans—inconclusive, right? With the ship's equipment, we'll be able to hear when we get closer. But me getting inside provides an opportunity to pick up an intuitive grasp of how he sells his Deus. The other odd thing is the amount of power that building draws. IR gives some interesting readings and there are a lot of electrons being shed around it." He smiled easily. "I'm sorry, Susan, but

I'm intrigued. I can't solve the problem until I expand our baseline data.''

"You're not going alone. I'm taking a team to back you up." Damn him, did he have to be right?

"I appreciate that, Captain, but there's no need to risk a whole party. It would make it much more difficult for me to—"

"Overruled. Do you know why Admiral Ree gave me command of this aspect of the mission?" Her eyebrows raised questioningly. "It was because I was the best he had on the ground in Sirius. If anyone can get you in and get you out, it's me, Reesh, and the rest. Maybe you've noticed the number of Sirian vets who've shipped with me? There's a reason. I just . . . just wish we still had Friday, too.''

"We're not going into combat," Darwin protested. "This is a simple . . . What's wrong?"

Susan sighed and studied him carefully. "I hope not, Doctor. Sure, you're probably . . . No. It's Ngen at work here. If we do end up in a fight, we're in real bad trouble. But if that necessity does arise, wouldn't you want the very best in the galaxy trying to get you out?''

Pike waved at the holo on the screen. The dusty looking ball of Bazaar twirled half in shadow, surrounded by a wreath of shining silver.

"See the gleaming ring around the planet? We didn't expect so many stations. There's three times the number there should be . . . and tugs are pulling them away day by day. Since we came within visual range, the number of deliveries being made by the stations has dropped ten percent. Whatever is going on is slowing down. The stations are being launched toward Mystery. They won't be looking too hard at Bazaar. I'll bet Ngen thinks it's a closed book . . . and I damned well want to know why. I'll bet the Admiral wants to know why, too. I won't be in any danger.''

"This is still my command," she reminded. "We're going with you. I'll worry about the unexpected, Doctor. You're not a warrior—or do you want me to remind you what an ignorant Santos did to your bowels?—you're a different type of fighting knife for my People and I intend on using you well.'' With that she stood, bowed slightly, and left.

Fighting knife? Why had she used that analogy? Darwin sat thoughtfully as he sipped his coffee, fingers on the broken Romanan blade in his belt.

CHAPTER XIX

House Alhar: Kapital, Arpeggio.

"I don't like him," Afid affirmed as the huge battleship reflected on the holo. He shook his head, listening to the news clip recounting the conversion of Deeter Station to the jihad of Deus. "Of course they converted. Facing a Patrol ship of the Line, you'd convert, too."

Afid pushed back in his chair, the news holo flickering off and fading in the gold-trimmed viewer. He sighed, pouring a splash of rich red-brown brandy into a cut crystal globe. He swirled the liquor, staring up at her from under lowered brows, lips pursed in irritation.

"Father, you just dislike the Messiah calling here." M'Klea smiled evenly, forcing herself to look demure. "I would think you'd be honored that he has become one of my friends. You, of all people, should recognize the benefits which our House might fall heir to."

A careful choice of words. Did he catch them? No? Dear father, you've never been a match for me.

Afid swiveled in his chair, knowing eyes on his daughter. "Girl, he took Torkild to space—put this family back where it belongs. Stations are appearing in our orbit, that's true. But I don't trust him. And what's with these Temples? What happens there? I don't understand. Some of my oldest friends have been to his Temple and converted." Afid's ancient brow furrowed. "They're not as sharp anymore. You know what I mean? Lost some . . . some . . ." He shook his head, baffled. "I don't trust him. Not in the long run. I don't like you talking with him."

M'Klea turned it over in her keen mind as she paced slowly across the thick carpeting. She stopped to finger one of her father's Confederate vases—a choice piece of Chouhoutien manufacture. Priceless. She traced the curve of the vessel, a true masterpiece.

Yes, the converts did lose something. Several of her friends had converted—silly things. They had lost even their half-wits after going the Temple, babbling dreamily about Deus and the Messiah. And now a new Temple was rising within a block of Alhar House. Would its worshipers be a bit less than bright? She placed a fingernail in the groove between her incisors, studying the deep glossy colors of the vase.

"Father?" She turned on her heel, rich laserlit skirts rustling and shimmering colors as she moved, swaying her hips just so to augment the effect. "Were I you, I'd go to Temple and find out just what this conversion is all about. I know you dislike the Messiah calling here. Why don't you go see what his religion really involves? Then, if you still disapprove, I'll cease to accept his calls—even if he is my brother's commander—and even if he does command such a powerful warship."

Afid started, studying her distrustfully. "M'Klea, your suggestion that I go would normally be enough of a warning to stay away from such a place. Unlike your brother, I know you for the deceitful—"

"Father!" she cried, raising her hands to hide her face. "How could you say such a—"

Afid slapped the table where his brandy sat. "Oh, come, M'Klea, don't play the brainless beauty with me. You're a cunning, intelligent young woman. And you scare hell out of me most of the time." He looked away, a weariness in his sagging expression. For a moment, she could almost feel sorry for him as he rubbed his age-freckled hands together, gaze fixing on the holo behind his huge silver desk.

She turned away, head lowered and cocked to the light, allowing it to shimmer to greatest effect in her hair.

"Then don't go to Temple. I shall continue to take the Messiah's calls in that event." She sounded cold—and knew it.

Afid looked up, a twitch at the corner of his mouth. "I suppose you will, M'Klea. Oh, very well. For all the good it will do. Yes, yes, indeed, I shall go to this Temple. I'll sit in the back row and observe. Nothing more, you understand. No communion or whatever they do. No food or drink. Just observe. Then, if I don't like what I see, you're to take no more calls from the Messiah." He paused, waiting for her explosion. "And M'Klea, this is still Arpeggio. When a father denies his daughter a caller—even a man like this Messiah—it will become family law. Not even *you* will disobey."

She lifted her chin, turning to her best profile. "I'll accept that. I think you'll approve of his works, father."

Afid studied her, a distant look in his eyes as if he inspected some specimen instead of his daughter. "And M'Klea, if you disobey me about the Messiah, I shall inform your brother. I think you know what that means?"

She nodded, a cold shiver in her breast. Torkild could be handled, but it would have to be done very carefully—or from a position of power. Lips pinched between her teeth she nodded, seeing no give in the old man's eyes. If what she suspected about the Temple was true, her father might be eliminated as a serious threat to her ambitions. And if what Ngen Van Chow hinted at could be counted on, she'd have the power to deal with Torkild.

"I'll wait for your decision after you've attended the Temple, father," she assured, slightly curious as to why she felt no remorse. But then, the laws of nature had always provided that the young supplant their parents.

Elliptical orbit over Bazaar.

An AT, Pike found, had been refined into a most remarkable war machine. At a little more than one hundred meters in length, its capabilities included providing devastating blaster cover with its four, Fujiki-modified, medium blasters. The nose had been designed to pierce the sides of enemy shipping, disgorging marines inside the punctured vessel. And while it didn't have interstellar capabilities, it carried limited shielding and armor. Three hundred assault troops could be transported in addition to the regular crew. With its sophisticated sensors and electronics, the AT could elude simpler detection devices. Bazaar didn't have many to start with.

Pike watched with curiosity as part of the crew—bundled in the loose, flowing garb of Bazaar—took positions in the crash webbing. It would be a long trip in, following in the sensor shadow of one of the returning tugs.

Pike bit his lip as he wondered about that. Why had the stations been sent to Bazaar in the first place? Why were they being sent to Mystery now? Mostly, stations consisted of self-sufficient cans—contained environments growing their own food and manufacturing enough for their needs with a surplus to market. Stations utilized highly refined fusion reaction to manufacture basic elements and mined asteroids or gas clouds for additional raw materials to augment what they received in trade through the Directorate.

He watched the long, lean shape of *Spider's Revenge* slip aft to dwindle in size to a tiny speck—then vanish in the myriad of white stars. Gravity began to decrease as they neared the vector used by the tugs. Thankfully, Darwin Pike didn't have to experience that frantic lurch of senses which always caused his stomach to empty in a most undignified manner.

"I still wish you hadn't decided on this." Susan stared at him, a hardness in the set of her lips. The burnoose gave her an exotic appearance, the loose robes hiding the promise of her perfect body—all the more provocative for it.

"I think if we can discover what's happening on Bazaar, it will reveal Van Chow's strategy." Pike hung in the crash webbing like a bug in a web. *Spider's?* he wondered.

She didn't say anything, lost for the moment in her own thoughts.

"How are you doing?" Darwin asked in a low voice, seeing they were alone for the moment.

She glanced up, eyes alert, before she smiled wistfully. "I still have the dreams; I just try and cope. Between you and me, Doctor, I'm scared stiff to go down there. I don't like being vulnerable. If he gets us in space, we're all dead. On the ground, too many variables outside my control affect capture."

"You're looking better," he said with a wicked grin. "Your skin is glowing again. Your hair shines . . . and there's spirit back in your eyes."

Her eyes widened slightly as she studied him. His heart jumped, drawn into those deep, dark pools, partially seeing the eddies and currents of her conflicting emotions. He saw a wall of harsh resolve forming, covering some other deeply-seated vulnerability.

"Let's stick to business, Doctor."

He could see anger, frustration, and mistrust building as her posture stiffened. "Hey, I'm sorry. Remember me, Doctor Darwin Pike? I'm the fellow who's on your side. Don't do this to a friend."

"Excuse me, Doctor Pike." He could hear the regret in her voice. "I'd better check the reactor status. I'm neglecting my duties."

"Wait," he called, putting a hand lightly on her shoulder. "Don't go. The remark wasn't meant to be forward. I was just happy to see your health is better. Never think I would use my knowledge as a lever against you.''

When she turned back, the strength and resolve in her eyes startled him. ''I thank you for your concern, Doctor. Further, your resolve never to move against me proves your intelligence surpasses my expectations.'' She kicked lightly away and sailed artfully down the companionway.

Shocked, Darwin swallowed a protest and watched her go, caught flat-footed by the harsh tone of voice. What had he said? What had he done? She had no right to treat him like that! He'd gone out of his way to be her friend, to try and help her. Even if she'd never be interested in him as a lover, he deserved better than what she'd given him. Didn't she understand that certain levels of intimacy came with friendship?

Worst of all, her rebuke hurt. It shook him to the roots that a woman he had come to care so much for could be so cruel to him. Resentment dropped to the middle of his belly and festered.

''If that's her gratitude, then damn her. She's worse than those poor bastards on Bazaar. Susan, you're a wretched robot!'' *And I'm a patsy for her failings.*

When they finally came down to planet, Darwin was sure he was about to die, seeing his fiery end coming second by second as the AT twisted its way into a deep, rocky gorge. The walls seemed to flash past the monitors by bare millimeters while wild g forces threw his suddenly vulnerable body first one way then another.

When motion ceased, Darwin let his mind catalog his body. Everything seemed to be there. Only then did he realize he'd closed his eyes through the last horrible minutes.

''Bloody hell.''

''What did you expect?'' Bull Wing Reesh called from behind him. ''Did you think they'd drop you in the middle of the town square? This is the best place we could find to hide this baby on the whole planet!''

''About the only place,'' White Eagle agreed.

''I suppose I'll have to survive it all over again, getting out of here,'' Pike groaned.

''If you're lucky,'' Reesh slapped his shoulder as Darwin stepped down onto gravity-firm deck plates.

''Why is that lucky?'' Darwin asked, making sure his trembling legs didn't betray him.

"'Cause we'll still be alive then," Reesh chuckled.

"Uh-huh." He wondered if Susan had even trembled seeing the walls rushing up to meet them. Had she faltered inside, seeing a quick death as the AT smashed into those forbidding walls of rock?

"Quite a trip," White Eagle grinned. "I knew she wouldn't let us down."

"She who?" Pike's breathing finally came back to normal.

"Why, the Captain, of course. You don't think she'd let just any of us fly this thing into a nightmare like this, do you? It takes someone with guts of iron to pilot through a hole like this." White Eagle shook his head, eyes gleaming with admiration.

Pike bit his lip, anger building as he remembered the shaking wreck who'd been about to dribble coffee all down her front not so long ago. What would her loyal crew say if they knew how close her mind teetered to the edge? He turned to tell them—to get back at the woman he'd done so much for and who'd then turned around and figuratively spit in his face!

"Let's go!" Reesh pushed him ahead. "This's your show, Doc. Shake a leg. Let's get the aircar out and get this over with."

The cold night air smacked him in the face as he trotted down the ramp, feeling a little light on his feet in the 0.8 gravity of Bazaar. The air sucked his skin dry, humidity so low his nose ached. Under his boots yet another planet's sand crunched lightly.

Bazaar was a poor world. Hot during the day and bitterly cold at night, wracked by electrical storms and blowing dust, it had limited water and even fewer mineral resources. Over the years, the population had adapted to the lower oxygen tension and the higher concentrations of nitrogen. Some terraforming had taken place and more children lived to adulthood.

At Reesh's motion, he hopped into the aircar, settling himself down in his robes to keep warm, then looking up at the dark night sky. Only the brightest of the stars showed through the dust that always stirred in Bazaar's thin air. He sniffed, the dry cold eating into his nose. The air bore the scent of dust.

"Calm night," Reesh added from the side, gesturing up. "Normally, it's pitch black from blowing dust."

"Wonder what kind of silicosis morbidity they have here? Must be an interesting adaptation through the years. Lungs like leather."

Another person trotted out of the AT and leaped lightly into the seat. He didn't need to look closely to recognize Susan. Through the long days, he'd carefully cataloged her characteristics. Before, he'd always held his breath, longingly watching her, hoping for what might be. Now his bile rose and he wished she'd just stay on her damned AT and dream of her pallid engineer.

The aircar rose silently and they climbed their way out of the narrow defile. White Eagle hadn't lied. Only dumb luck would reveal the AT's location.

"Praise be to Spider." Reesh grinned wickedly. "They don't have a warship in orbit like that time on Sirius!"

"Doctor," Susan asked, voice flat, "how do you want to come in?"

"Drop me at the edge of town. It should be sunrise in about a half hour. I can go from there." His voice grew hoarse as the reality of what was happening began to sink in. Intellectual curiosity might be one thing, but he was about to venture into Ngen Van Chow's personal domain. At that particular instant, the awful, lonely truth of foreign intelligence became Pike's intimate companion. Susan skimmed the aircar in between two low buildings Pike identified as storage sheds.

Stiffly, he stepped out of the aircar, dusty gravel grating below his boots. Muffled shapes gathered around him in the dusk. He heard Susan order White Eagle to stay and guard the car. "Doctor, Reesh, let's go."

Darwin led the way out into the narrow street. Reesh's hand on his shoulder brought him to a quivering stop.

"Not so fast," Bull said easily. "From those tapes we made, none of them walks much past a shuffle."

"Yeah," Darwin breathed, stilling his heart. "Right. Don't you guys think you'd better stay with the aircar. No sense in all of us sticking our necks out."

"We go together, Doctor," Susan's sibilant voice returned.

"It's your command." In his heart, no real opposition developed to having an armed Romanan escort.

The sun reddened in the east as they made their way past the crude, square, stone and compacted-earth dwellings. Inside, hushed voices could be heard. Occasionally, a child cried out. Only chickens, goats, dogs, and cats saw them pass. Darwin couldn't help feeling like he'd stepped back into Earth's past. Only the solar towers, comm antennas, and the muffled shrill of a lifting shuttle compromised the effect.

Darwin tried to absorb the feel of the place, the soul of this outskirt of the capital city of Bazaar. The morning breeze bore animal scents, the dank odor of human wastes, the smell of spicy food cooking. Dust had drifted along the edges of the squat earth-colored houses. Bits of metal junk, occasional animal bones and rags had been kicked to the side of the narrow path which passed between the houses.

A muffled figure, robes pulled tight, rounded a corner and came toward them. Darwin found himself slowing down until Reesh pushed him ahead.

"Salaam, Deus is Lord," the man whispered.

"Salaam, Deus is Lord," Darwin repeated, finding his voice. "My Brother," he said. "You are out early. Where do you go in the name of Deus?"

"I go to my place, Brother." The fellow tried to move past.

"What place is that?" Darwin asked, curiosity rising to vie with fear.

"We all have our place in Deus," the man replied, becoming anxious over being delayed.

"Go with Deus," Darwin said, stepping to one side.

The native hardly looked at them, almost hurrying to be off. From under his kaffiyeh, Darwin watched him go.

"Weird."

"He didn't seem right," Reesh muttered.

"No," Darwin said, "he didn't. I wasn't sure, but his eyes seemed oddly lifeless."

Minutes later Darwin hurried to follow a man who was making his way in the early morning light. "Salaam, Deus is Lord. Is there a place where a weary traveler might find a bite to eat?"

The man turned. "Salaam, Deus is Lord. Have you no place, Brother?" The man's eyes were only mildly interested, something preoccupying his thoughts.

"I have but just arrived," Darwin told him amiably. "I and my companions would quell our hunger." He bowed slightly.

"Deus will give you a place." The man's voice was toneless. "Go to the Temple and your place will be found." He bowed and walked on.

Darwin followed several hundred feet behind. The man made his way to a big structure, supposedly a wool storage warehouse. Keeping back, out of sight, he led Reesh and Susan to a window and with the corner of his mufti, wiped the pane until he could see in.

"By Spider's Prophet," Bull breathed.

A long line of machinery whirred and clattered in the early morning silence. The entire room bristled with bulky blue-black machines working along conveyers—robotic assembly lines. Even from where Darwin stood, he could make out the items being rolled past by antigravs: military-style hand blasters.

"Wool warehouse?" Darwin asked. "Keep an eye on the door. I'm going in there."

"What for?" Susan demanded.

"That man, he didn't seem to be a weapons manufacturer. There wasn't enough savvy in his eyes. It won't take long. I want to verify a hunch." At that, he left them, hurrying to the door, Susan's growled protest in his ears.

Swallowing nervously, Pike entered. The office area still smelled mustily of wool. Dust lay a half-inch deep on the gouged, old plasteel desk. Darwin followed the path worn in the dust to the back door and stepped through. He could see ten men monitoring equipment. At the last, the man he'd followed was taking the place of another. The relieved man bowed and walked easily toward Pike.

"Salaam, Deus is Lord," Darwin greeted. The man "salaamed" and passed, apparently unconcerned. Darwin—heart battering his ribs—approached the first man. "This is my place in Deus," he announced, voice half-toned.

"Salaam. You are too early to take my place." His half-aware eyes drifted back to the monitor. Darwin watched graphs and technical specs flash across the screen. Periodically, a flawed casting would pass the monitor and the man would signal the unit. A robot out on the floor would retrieve a piece and drop it into a return bin.

"You do good work." Darwin watched the man for reaction. "Have you worked here long?"

"This is Deus. Deus is Lord."

"What do you make here?"

"This is my place."

"Do you have another place?" Darwin tried to be friendly.

"There is no other place except in Deus." The man turned toward Darwin. "You said this was your place?"

"My place is in Deus," Darwin agreed, thinking, trying to keep in character yet draw a response.

"Then you know. There is no more reason to talk." At that, he turned back to his work and nothing Darwin did could regain his attention.

A different man, big and hairy with a full beard, entered and started walking down the line, ignoring Pike. Darwin almost ran to catch him. The bearded one stopped at a position. "You are relieved," he told the operator.

The operator left without a word.

"You are relieved," Darwin told the bearded man who had assumed the headset.

The big man cocked his head. "This is my place."

"This is my place," Darwin interjected. "You are relieved."

The big man handed over the headset, frowned, and started to walk away only to return and nonchalantly inform Pike, "You are relieved." Darwin had placed the headset on his brow, and begun rejecting blaster parts randomly.

"You are relieved," the big man repeated, a curious frustration creasing his blunt features. "You are relieved." An urgency built in his voice.

"You are too early to take my place."

"This is my place." The Bazaaran was trying desperately to think, face contorting.

"Your place is in Deus," Darwin corrected.

"I am of Deus. This is my place."

"If this is your place, why am I here?" Darwin watched his opponent struggling to make sense of the situation.

"You are relieved," the man tried again, mind returning to a course of action which should have worked. Thereafter, anything Darwin said drew a rejoinder of, "You are relieved."

Darwin let the man have his monitor and left quietly. He stepped out the main door and walked around to the alley, lost in thought. As he turned the corner an aircar slid past, drawing his attention. Three armed men dropped lightly to the ground, talking among themselves as they opened the door he'd just left.

Susan pushed past him, a blaster in her hand.

W. Michael Gear

"They must have a monitor in there somewhere," she hissed. "Let's get out of here."

Realizing how close he'd come to capture, he followed on Susan's heels until they had covered several blocks.

"What'd you learn?"

"They don't *think!* I don't understand it, but they can't solve simple problems like who's going to work when." He pounded a fist into his palm. "They didn't even ask 'Who sent you here?' They didn't even know they were making blasters. All they could talk about was their place."

Susan shook her head. "They're crazy—mindless. One of them walked past us while you were inside. We just said salaam and he ignored us, as if we weren't there. What . . . I mean, how do they . . . Spider's bones, it's spooky."

"Those guards who showed up weren't salaaming," Bull Wing Reesh reminded.

"So there's a superstructure watching over the whole system," Susan deduced. "They may suspect we're here . . . if those security guards arrived because of Pike's presence in the blaster plant."

"Seems so," Reesh growled, eyes indicating an aircar with more police descending on them. "Never thought I'd say it, but I wish this was Sirius. I knew the rules there. Look dumb."

"Eyes ahead," Susan whispered. "Don't even look at them."

Darwin fought his fear, feeling his bowels loosen.

The words were harsh: "In the name of Deus, *halt!*" Darwin looked up to see four men bailing out of the aircar. Susan had turned, facing them, bowing deeply, her easy greeting of "Salaam" sounding unfeigned.

"Three of you together, eh?" One of the burly police asked suspiciously. "Wouldn't have just come from the sheep plant, would you?"

Susan straightened. Reesh and Darwin had drawn up on either side, hands clasped before them. "Deus is Lord," Darwin tried to keep the tension out of his voice.

"Lord, my ass," another of the police spat as he stepped forward, reaching out to pull Susan's kaffiyeh to one side. "My, you're a beauty. Maybe you'll come with us before we take you to Temple." He was laughing so hard, he missed the sudden berserk look on Susan's face. Her fingers seemed to shoot through the man's very throat.

Eyes and tongue bulging from their sockets, the guard

pitched to the ground, hesitating only as Susan kicked his sternum in and hammered his now limp head hard enough to audibly snap his neck.

Reesh was plunging his fighting knife into a second man while Susan grappled with the third for his blaster. Darwin, heart pounding, knees weak, stepped sideways and slid the Randall between the fourth man's ribs, hacking sideways in an intercostal cut, opening the slit wider as he met the man's eyes and stared deeply into a soul drowning in fear and disbelief.

Darwin staggered back, the nightmare of the man's death engraved forever upon his memory, bloody knife forgotten in his straining grip. Hot blood pumped from the severed aorta as the man twisted away, falling limply.

"No coups! That'd be a signature." Susan turned to run.

Reesh grabbed Pike and hustled him into a narrow gap between buildings. Darwin couldn't forget that look of abject terror. The man's pleading, bone-rattling fright would be his forever.

"Where to?" Reesh asked, unaffected. "Back to the ship? They'll be crawling all over us in about ten minutes."

"The . . . the Temple," Darwin's voice almost cracked as he spoke. He *had* to know more. It was imperative now. That life had to be worth something. Besides, if he went back now, he'd never have the nerve to try anything like this again. Some essence inside would die. A strength came swelling up from his gut.

Reesh's jaw dropped. "You're out of your raving lunatic mind if you—"

"*We've got to!*" Pike met their skeptical looks. "The answer's there and . . . and they'd never look in their midst for fugitives. They'll think we're radicals running for cover. They'd look along escape routes first. Not toward the center."

A muscle in Reesh's cheek twitched. He looked at Susan. "Well?"

"To the Temple," she decided, a tightness in her expression. "But you'd better be right, Doctor. It'll take a half hour to get the AT here to get us out. All surprise will be blown—if we live that long."

Darwin nodded, granting a sigh of relief. "One at a time, though." He looked down to see only tiny spots of blood had stained his mufti. The rest had run down his arm, making the inside of the garment sleeve tacky and cold.

They split up, walking one behind the other, almost thirty seconds apart, which left Darwin feeling dazed and alone. He stilled his heart, thinking about the changes which had occurred in him. He felt different, a strangeness creeping through his veins, adrenaline surging along his limbs. Not since Alaska had he enjoyed the thrill of living—and then not with the vitality he now experienced.

To either side of the broad avenue he walked down, the buildings sat squat and dusty. They'd entered the business district. Only it didn't reflect the vigor, the presence, of a commercial center. The street left him with an impression of shabbiness, the windows streaked and dim. Here and there, sastrugi had formed in the miniature sief dunes that blew out around the corners of the grim faceless structures. Overhead, streamers of dust-laden clouds twirled darkly with the blood red of Bazaar's sun. Like the tortured clouds, Darwin marched forward.

He shivered, knowing they walked into the lion's den; in his mind he called upon the bear and the Santos, whose soul he had sent back to Spider. He'd killed two men now—taken their warm, living bodies and sliced them open with his knife, leaving them violated and bloody: a thought to dwell on. Who was he becoming?

At the main Temple gate a line formed. Darwin crowded up behind Susan, knowing Reesh did the same behind him. He experienced a momentary touch of comfort, feeling his bodyguards packed around him.

With relief, he remembered how quickly and cleanly Susan had killed her antagonist. He couldn't even remember the sequence of her moves, but the body had thudded lifeless to the ground. So quick, so clean.

They shuffled in past the large doors. Darwin looked around the inside of the huge building. Once it had been a mosque, now the pools were filled in. Along with those in front of him, he knelt on the hard floor, feeling Susan's warm body next to his while Bull Wing Reesh's muscular form covered his right. Copying the behavior of the others, Darwin began bobbing his head while he mumbled prayers over and over.

He caught sight of an odd figure in the shadows the columns cast against the wall. The individual seemed to be waiting, observing. It wore a loose hooded robe, but in a fashion very different from the Bazaarans'. In the shadow of the hood, the face couldn't be seen, the features shrouded in darkness. The figure seemed almost to float as it walked behind the huge round pillars that supported the roof.

Darwin sensed purpose in the being's actions that defied the dull-eyed norm he'd observed and come to expect in Bazaar. The spectral figure continued slowly along the wall, stopping periodically and looking out over the masses who wailed prayers. Darwin tensed as the hood turned in his direction—and stopped.

Fear tingling his spine, Darwin ducked his head in the slow bob of the pious and whispered a mumbled prayer of his own, hoping he hadn't given himself away.

Seconds passed before the unusual figure turned and disappeared in the shadows. His breath pressed anxiously at his chest, and he let it out suddenly, bringing his mind back to the people around him.

"Notice anything?" he asked in hushed Romanan.

"They stink," Susan gritted.

"There aren't as many people. The numbers are down. Not only that, but there are some here and there who are looking around with sentience in their eyes. They're uneasy from the looks of things—downright scared."

She began looking around. "You're right. What does it mean, Doctor? We've hauled you a long way to get the answers."

A man climbed into the pulpit and raised his hands in benediction. "Deus!" The thundering cry caught them by surprise. "Deus! Deus! Deus!" Then they sang and after that, the sermon began. Darwin felt Susan shrivel beside him as a huge holo formed in the back of the Temple.

They stared into Ngen Van Chow's fiery eyes. Beside him, Susan began to shiver. Carefully, he slid a hand behind her and pulled her close. He shot a quick glance into her blazing eyes and whispered, "Easy. It's only a holo."

The muscles along her jaws rippled as if she were vowing to kill him first chance she got. Darwin allowed himself to shrug mentally. If she didn't, Ngen's goons would.

"Get your hand off me!" she hissed back, voice a dagger of meaning. He chuckled and turned his attention to the congregation.

". . . and the foul Lord Satan is among us. He has placed his wretched hand on mankind and rotted the very stars. How do we clean this corruption from the universe?"

"Deus! Deus! Deus!" the crowd roared. Some were on

their feet now, dancing and cavorting. Others fell on the rough stone, kicking, writhing with an insane passion.

"Who is Satan?" Ngen cried.

They roared back, "The false God, Spider! Death to Spider! Death to Romanans! Jihad! Jihad! Jihad!"

Each of his companions had gone rigid. Staring sideways, he could see glittering hatred welling up in Reesh as his hand clutched a blaster beneath the mufti. On Susan's face a look of total revulsion, desperation, and blinding hatred molded her features.

"Easy," Darwin whispered. "There will be time later."

It lasted so long they became inured, but Darwin noted the odd change which overcame those few frightened glances among the congregation. Gradually, they were becoming wound up in the occasion—but that didn't explain the human wreckage he'd seen in the factory.

"Take the message with you. Bless you all. Deus be with you." Ngen finished, a look of holy rapture on his impassioned face. The huge holo flickered out. A somber babble of voices arose around them, coupled with the soft rustling of garments as people stood.

The side doors opened. Darwin kept his eyes on the first worshipers up. They were those who had been aware. Dazed now, they staggered toward the light while the others remained, heads down.

"Don't move," Darwin ordered on a hunch.

"What? What is it?" Susan's gaze flickered around the room, a raptor seeking prey.

Two techs were working a panel at either side of the door. "Of course!"

"Let's get out of here." Reesh was fidgeting.

"No!" Darwin tried to keep his voice low. "Move and we're all dead! I know now what this place is! It all makes sense. God, what a monster Ngen—"

Then the voice boomed out. "We know you are here. I see you hiding in the midst of the holy! Stand and be recognized—*Agents of Satan!*" The priest on the pulpit pointed right at Darwin Pike's little group.

Pandemonium broke loose.

CHAPTER XX

Bridge aboard *Gabriel* during deep space resupply: Gulag Sector.

Torkild frowned at the ship displayed on his screens and pulled pensively at his golden beard, fingers absently twirling strands of hair. The *Deus* had just arrived from Santa del Cielo. Slipping alongside, *Deus* matched velocity to transfer weapons, food, and materials to *Gabriel* prior to Torkild's next mission.

The sight of the huge ship pleased and bothered him at the same time. Why did a Sirian have to hold sway over so much of Arpeggio? Granted, Ngen had brought prosperity, returning Arpeggians to space, and arming them. For the first time in three hundred years, Arpeggian crews spaced in ships armed with Arpeggian-made blasters—based on a design provided by a Sirian. The thought rankled.

Torkild braced his chin on a propped arm and shifted his glance to the monitor which tracked *Deus*' shuttle—a stub-winged thing that inched across the intervening space. Bruno, the comm tech, muttered softly into the system, coordinating with the shuttle as it closed.

A slight shiver shook the ship as the shuttle grappled.

"Clumsy moron," Torkild hissed. "Can't the Messiah find competent pilots? Bruno? Have a damage report sent up immediately and see that supplies are stowed. I want our best technical team to uncrate and see to installing those blasters—assuming the idiot shuttle pilot didn't damage them."

"Yes, sir."

Torkild pinched the bridge of his nose in an attempt to stifle the slight headache behind his eyes. He grunted in irritation, leaning back in the command chair and stretching.

Uneasy, he inspected the holo of *Deus*. "Well, perhaps we shouldn't complain. We're getting the first guns produced by Arpeggian industry in three hundred years—and a flagship brought them to us. A curious manner of upgrading combat capabilities—piece by piece. Why not let us go home for a refit?''

"Captain," Bruno reminded, "our factories produced aircars, industrial vacuums, compressors—''

"Yes, I know, upgrading industry isn't done overnight. It's, well, shoddy. And being done by a Sirian.''

"That bothers all of us. We're all Arpeggian, Captain. We feel the unease. Honor and pride . . . still, the Messiah's kept his word.''

Torkild sniffed and nodded. He had. The blasters and supplies had arrived.

Bruno tapped a security approval on Torkild's order and shifted, reaching for a cup of coffee. "Our people are on the job. Heinar is in command of the transfer." Bruno cocked his head, staring at *Deus* where she rested several klicks away.

Torkild nodded. "Excellent. He supervised tug maintenance, didn't he? No matter that the Messiah's a Sirian, we're armed and in space again, Bruno. Not just running tugs either. Consider this rendezvous. Meeting us halfway, at velocity, to minimize the time we spend shedding delta V. We'll be off to raid Cyclops system within hours—no time wasted.''

Bruno tossed off his coffee and clicked the cup against the comm frame. "And a wonder of navigational abilities to match so quickly. They must have incredible equipment in that ship. A factor for us to keep in mind when we finally engage the Patrol in combat.''

Torkild squinted up at the *Deus,* goaded to consideration. "Bruno, you may have just saved our lives. A most astute observation." And Bruno was nothing more than Houseless riffraff with no social standing! "I'll be giving that knowledge every attention. And to think, I'd considered standing and fighting, our guns against theirs. Romantic suicide.''

Bruno smiled at the compliment and bent back to his system, taking some communication.

"Call, Captain," Bruno informed, turning, a black eyebrow lifted. "Your sister requests you speak to her.''

"Put it on," Torkild said, a warm grin softening his hard features.

Bruno discreetly dropped a full comm helmet over his skull to provide Torkild privacy.

Indeed, a very good officer. With a fleet of such, I could place Arpeggio at the top of Directorate power—where she should have been three hundred years ago had not the decline allowed the Sirians to institute the Directors. Perhaps, with the right . . .

M'Klea's ravishing features filled the holo screen. She smiled—a thing of light and wonder. Long golden hair shimmered in a pile from the top of her head. Torkild gazed, tracing the familiar lines of her face, those blue eyes, firm jawline, and almost translucent skin. Arpeggian breeding proved out in the end.

"Ah, M'Klea. What pleasure this is! Why have you called? Nothing is wrong with mother or father, or the rest of the family?" He felt his face pinching. "For you to make so expensive a transduction—"

"No, dear brother. Everyone is hale of body . . . and soul." Her face lit with excitement. "They have just completed a Temple to Deus in the square. It reminded me of you, so I thought I'd call and find out how you are." Her eyes twinkled.

"And father let you spend the credits? I find it hard to—"

She narrowed her eyes and lifted her chin mischievously. "Shhh! You can't tell, Torkild. Father . . . well, he's out, you see. So's mother. They won't know I did it until the statements come in . . . and then it will be too late. It—"

"M'Klea!" Torkild started half out of the command chair only to sink back as her eyes twinkled. "Well, I suppose that were you not the most beautiful—"

"Enough of me! How are you, Torkild? We hear such splendid things about you and your *Gabriel*. The whole planet knows your name. It seems that every other day we hear of your daring exploits. Some say you're the greatest captain since the days of the Confederacy."

"We have no complaints." Fondness almost made him maudlin. "When you're the captain, you can't even complain about the food."

"I miss you." Her delicate features bent into a frown. "I have, however, had the pleasure of meeting your Messiah, Ngen Van Chow. A most remarkable man." She let herself sigh. "I'm trying to finagle an invitation to come see you. He said he might let me come and visit if I could stay away from Temple that long. Why would he say that, I wonder?" She cocked her head slightly, expectant, as if he might be party to some private knowledge.

"How should I know?" Torkild spread his hands. Another thought darkened his joy for a brief instant. Why did

Van Chow wish to grant M'Klea favors? A flash of hot rage tugged at Torkild's thoughts before he banished it. Surely, the great Messiah knew the importance of virtue among old Arpeggian families. Quick to rape, they guarded their daughters with blood passion.

"He was no doubt ravished by your great beauty, dear sister," Torkild said with his best smile. "But I wouldn't—"

"I thought him very dashing and attractive, brother. "Do you think I could become an empress at his side? Can you see me so? Sitting in power over all the Directorate?"

Torkild laughed despite the cold chill settling in his stomach. "I always told you, no man was good enough for you unless he was half god." He *had* said that. He'd even proved it more than once to swains who'd sought to compromise her chastity. And he'd continue to prove it until the day he died—unless, of course, he found a man worthy of her. But the Messiah? He simply couldn't imagine the holy vessel of M'Klea's body possessed by the man. Something about him . . . well, it was unthinkable anyway—a young woman's silly fantasy.

M'Klea cocked her head. "Half god? Ngen Van Chow is, dear brother."

Uncertainty tightened the base of his throat. "Sister," he warned, hoping she'd see his displeasure. "The Messiah is a great man. He meets many women. I know that none are as beautiful as you, but he has great things on his mind. You will not be disappointed if he fails to call you? You're young yet. These things . . . well, they seem to be the universe when an older man simply makes a casual remark."

"I know that," she teased. "Still, isn't an emperor every woman's dream? Imagine if he really found me attractive, Torkild? As empress, I could provide you with many things, brother. Not just a command, but a governorship—perhaps command of the entire fleet? The possibilities are endless if you'd think about them—and you will, won't you? For me? For your M'Klea?"

"Yes," his voice came huskily.

"Did you know that we've been receiving so many wonderful things? So many stations fill the sky at night now that the whole heavens shine. We have more food than you could imagine. The merchants are either screaming because they can no longer market older, expensive goods, or they're hawking anything imaginable for dirt cheap. No matter, they're making credits hand over fist. Manufacturers are screaming for help. People are scurrying like mad insects, working all hours of the day. I tell you the social schedule is almost dead! Everyone is so busy. Why, there's no time for parties anymore! I never would have believed Arpeggio would again become the queen of all planets. I'm so proud of you, Torkild. You and your brave crew are making it this way for us.''

He smiled again, the happy mood restored. ''For you, my little angel, I would conquer the universe!''

''And that, nasty brother of mine, is exactly what you're doing for me.'' Her voice held a note of pique. ''If *only* you had let me come with you.''

''A warship is no place for such as you, flower of the heavens.'' He gave her a big wink.

''Romanan and Patrol women fly in ships,'' she pouted. ''We've seen their pictures though. The Messiah has broadcast all kinds of information about the Patrol. But their women? They're fat, like pigs. Further, they provide the most disgusting sexual favors for the men. I swear they service—''

''*M'Klea!*'' he lashed out, surging up from the command chair. She giggled happily at the reaction she'd goaded from him. Angrily, he raised his hands and brought them down on the chair. ''A woman of your . . . How could *you?* Blessed Gods, sister! If I weren't twenty light-years away, I'd paddle you so you wouldn't sit for a week!'' He thundered, ''You are a lady! *Act like one!*''

''I'm through with you this time, brother,'' she smiled, in satisfaction. ''We all send our love and wish we could be with you.'' She blew him a kiss and the screen went blank.

He stared at it, listening to the sound his teeth made as they ground uneasily. He couldn't help but shift his attention to the holo where *Deus* floated in the blackness. Torkild shook his head. No, not Ngen Van Chow, it was all nonsense of M'Klea's imagining.

Temple of Deus: city of Bazaar, Bazaar.

As the booming voice echoed in the great mosque, Susan leaped to her feet, blaster out and leveled. Frantically, she searched for the closest exit. The techs were turning from the boards, scanning the room, finding her, Darwin, and Bull Wing Reesh as they jumped to their feet.

"This way!" Susan ordered, hopping over bowing, praying Bazaarans.

"No!" Darwin screamed, grabbing her. "Out the way we came in! It's the *only* way. The doors are a death trap! That's how they've done all this! The side doors—"

A man reached for her. Pike's bigger bulk physically dragged her back. As one, the worshipers on the floor rose and stared at them.

"We've got to get out of here. This way. Hurry, damn it!" Pike was pulling her through the crowd to the wall, Reesh backing to cover them, blaster held menacingly low.

"Who is Satan?" The priest on the pulpit demanded, his voice like a knife in the sudden silence.

"*Spider! Spider! Spider!*" the congregation roared.

"Death to Spider! Death to the Directorate!" The priest shouted, pointing at Susan's group with both hands.

"*Death! Death! Death!*" the hollow-eyed crowd yelled, fists raised and beating in unison to the chant. They came surging forward, a shouting human tide of rasping robes, pattering feet, and grasping hands. Susan turned—back to the wall—and snapped a shot at the priest. She came close; the bolt hit the pulpit railing, blasting it into fragments, sending the man running, frightened and splinter-pricked, through a small door.

Then she turned her blaster on the surging crowd of robed fanatics spilling down on them in a crushing wave of shaking fists, howling voices, and impassioned eyes.

Three crackling threads of blaster fire laced the packed bodies. Like exploding melons, limbs, chests, and heads burst as frail human bodies absorbed the charged particles. Reality became a chaos of spattered blood, viscera, and death. For a second, the line held—but the sheer power of the three guns backed the mob away, touching some remaining thread of preservation in the mindless horde.

Darwin settled himself and centered the sights on the doorway, his bolt hitting the control panel, sending the techs diving for cover as metal shards and ceramic fragments detonated.

The few individuals still standing in the portal screamed horribly, grabbing and hammering at their heads before they dropped, kicking spasmodically, to the ground. A brilliant flash shot fire and smoke out from the panels. Somewhere in the depths of the Temple violent shorts of electricity crackled and popped angrily. An alarm shrilled in the chaos.

Susan had time to catch the ghastly grimace on Pike's face as he turned his bolt on a second door. It, too, exploded with the same effect, killing those within its grasp in a most horrible manner.

"*Kill them!*" a voice ordered from the crowd and the mass surged forward again.

"This way!" Susan began pushing along the wall. She could hear Reesh and Darwin whispering to each other as they followed.

"Do you understand what Ngen is doing?" Darwin cried, voice strained in terror. "*Do you understand?*" He grabbed her by the arm and turned her. She looked into the eyes of a man pushed to the limits.

"I understand," she whispered huskily, breaking his grip to lace a group of worshipers with violet energy bolts. They died, screaming as they fell, bodies hideously maimed.

"You've got to get the information to Admiral Ree and the Directorate. Promise me you will!" Pike screeched at her. "*Promise! Promise . . .*"

"Yes, damn it, *I will!*" she gritted, "Now *shoot,* damn you! Keep them back!" She spun on her heel and blew a man in half. In the process, she didn't see Darwin and Reesh begin their howling charge into the midst of the Fathers, shooting, kicking, screaming.

"*No!*" Susan ordered, too late to stop them.

To her amazement, Pike whirled on his feet, hollering, "*Duck!*" She threw herself flat, spurred by reflex, as his blaster pointed her way—and blew a hole through the wall several meters away from her.

Stung by the flying mortar, half-blinded by the dust, she could see him waving her through.

"We'll be right behind you!" Darwin yelled. "Cover the outside!"

Susan sprinted for the opening, gratified to see daylight filtering through the hole—ripples of light in the swirling dust. She leaped through, tripped on the rocks, and rolled free, coming to a combat stance, blaster ready. She found only a vacant alley.

A second explosion followed the first, masonry falling to block the hole completely. She stared, disbelieving. *Pike had shut off his retreat!* It didn't make any sense, he'd just condemned himself and Reesh to death! "*Stupid son of a . . .*" She ran for the front of the building, seeing armed guards bailing out of their aircars en masse. Other ground transports came flying, dust billowing from the ground effect. From all sides they shot in, disgorging security personnel. Pike had guessed this would happen. Of course, the damned fools had set themselves up! That's why Pike had questioned her so about understanding Ngen's operation. He and Reesh were still in there, buying time for her to escape.

"Damn him. *Damn him!*" Susan's battle-fear melded into anger. The damned anthropologist had outthought her. He'd been planning the whole thing, recognizing immediately what the side doors had to mean and why the techs were monitoring the controls.

A growing sense of guilt and inadequacy filled her reeling thoughts. It had been *her* job! Pike had covered for her again, having a plan, making a way out, while she was drowning in self-centered emotion over a hologram! Never since that day when Ngen had degraded and broken her had she felt less worthy of living.

She bit her lip and began running for White Eagle and the aircar, trying to make sense of bumbling Darwin Pike—wrenched that he would die now. At the same time, she mentally abused herself, not liking the reflection in her mind.

Administration building: city of Bazaar, Bazaar.

More than a little irritated, Pallas Mikros turned to the comm in his office. "You have them?"

"We have two cornered in the Temple, Lord Governor," a dark-complected guard told him. "We'll be able to kill them as soon as we can get controlling blaster points."

"No!" Pallas ordered, slamming a fat fist onto the table; lances of light shot from his rings. "I want them alive. We need to know who they are. Indeed, if they're even Bazaaran. We've got to know what they're here to do. Can you understand why that would be important, Corporal?"

The man nodded, sprinting from the screen and bellowing out orders. Pallas focused a monitor on the inside of the Temple, employing a security pickup hanging from the top of the dome. He could see the incredible carnage wrought by the intruders. Tossed corpses piled in jumbles. Flopped limbs blown off bodies leaked red onto the stone floor. Eyes stared sightlessly up into the monitor. Gray-blue strings of intestine lay strung over the entire pile as did brain matter and chunks of pulverized meat.

The mob of worshipers milled around in the process of being regrouped by shouting security personnel. The Fathers advanced under command, sent toward the corner where the two intruders had taken refuge, partially shielded by the huge stone columns.

Pallas could see some of the security forces bringing in a riot stun gun. Praise be to Deus. The thing had been crated, ready for shipment to Arpeggio. He'd held it back on impulse. A blaster bolt leaped at the ceiling, blowing a hole in the old roof, showering the worshipers with bricks, mortar, and dust. The advance stopped while Pallas' monitor image jumped and bucked.

A second blaster bolt shot up, followed by more erupting masonry. Pallas struggled to his feet, fascinated as their scheme became obvious. The damn fools were trying to bring the roof down! From where they were, shielded by the columns, they might even survive.

"Pull that gun back!" Pallas shrilled. "Get back! Get out . . . out from under the dome!"

He could see the riot gun swivel. A blue net of energy lanced out and shimmered the corner of the temple as a final violet streak touched the ceiling. Horrified, Pallas watched as the pickup for his monitor dove into the scrambling masses on the floor. He blinked at the silent impact and stared at a featureless gray screen.

He accessed a different channel. "Get the two men with blasters," he told the officer in charge of the outside perimeter. "They're behind the left side columns. The team inside stunned them before the roof fell. They're no longer dangerous . . . and they might even have lived."

Pallas settled himself in his chair again. Who were these maniacs? He shook his head. From the image he'd watched, one had tried to blow a hole in the wall. The third had dived for it and the first had killed the escapee as that individual was at the brink of safety. Or had that other person gotten out?

Pallas shook his head. It didn't matter. One man loose out there wouldn't go far. "Put a full-time guard on the spaceport," Pallas ordered, pouring himself a glass of wine. "Further, I want twenty-four hour patrols throughout the city. Anyone out after curfew and without a place will be immediately apprehended. Those who resist will be executed."

A corporal snapped a salute and Pallas shut the monitor

down. He sipped the wine and sighed. Things had finally become interesting when Bazaar couldn't be considered anything but a closed book. Under his control, the population had long since lost any ability to become a threat. The desert rebels—so pitifully few—couldn't motivate the bulk of the population—not without psych control. Bazaar had been tamed. Pallas chuckled to himself. And now they made a feeble gesture? Too little, too late.

Mystery had begun to fall, Temples rising across most of the planet. Pallas would apply his skills to the more sophisticated population there upon full automation of Bazaar. Those final administrative and logistic problems were ironing out. An administrator of lesser talents than Pallas' already had taken up the Bazaaran reins.

A face formed on his monitor. "We have them, sir. They're both alive, and bound in EM restraints."

Pallas smiled. "Superb. Bring them to my interrogation quarters." He stood, Tiara, like a puppy, rising to follow on his heels. At first her mindless presence had annoyed him, sparking memories of what she'd once been. The looks, however, that his security wolves threw her way, more than assuaged his irritation. No matter what, she still dazzled with that sexy body of hers.

30 k west of Bazaar in the Neenegev.

She didn't talk to White Eagle as the car raced across the dunes and scrub bushes, cresting rocky ridges to dive into wind-scavenged valleys. Even the bucking aircar didn't penetrate the fuming anger—the feeling of frustrated defeat.

The narrow gorge almost flipped them over as White Eagle fought against the torturous buffeting winds that whipped out of the gaping maw of rock. Carefully, he crept forward, grains of sand chattering off the front of the aircar.

Hot, dry wind sought to rip her off her feet as she jumped down, bending forward, helping stabilize the aircar as they waited for the ramp to drop on the AT.

Inside, the closing hatch shut off that wind-wailing universe. Only the gritty sand in her hair and clothing remained. And the memory of Darwin Pike.

"What's the word?" she asked, moving forward.

The pilot looked up. "We've got tight beam from Moshe. He's monitoring their communications. They've got Reesh and Pike. They're alive."

Susan swallowed hard, fingers digging into the back of the command chair. "Blessed Spider. That means they're Ngen's prisoners."

"Orders are to remain covert," the pilot reminded.

Susan bit her lip, eyes clamped shut. Numbly, she nodded. "I . . . I told Pike we'd . . . we'd leave him behind if . . ." She gritted her teeth. "Damn it! *He knew the risks!*"

Administration building: city of Bazaar, Bazaar.

The prisoners were conscious by the time Pallas waddled his bulk into the little room. Here he'd watched Ngen break Zekial Lichud into a quivering pile of tear-stained meat before psyching the man, thereby snapping the back of the Jewish resistance. Now the room and the victims were his. Pallas studied the eight eggshell-white walls bending out of the roof where two round globes for comm centered overhead. The psych machine, so artfully used by Ngen, rested to one side.

The guards had stripped them, of course, searching every possible hiding place on their bodies, using remote scan to make certain no bombs had been implanted in their flesh.

The first prisoner struggled fiercely, a bronzed fellow whose skin rippled over cords of muscle. Violent dark eyes glared out from under a shock of black hair that hung in long braids. The second looked miserably beaten, pale skin and light brown eyes somehow vulnerable compared to the caged wolf his partner seemed to be.

Good. Make the strong one cry out and the weak one would talk.

"Who are you?" Pallas asked easily, checking the EM restraints where they bound the victims to the pallets. He motioned the guards out of the room, satisfied there would be no possibility of escape. Tiara started forward, eyes on the men. Irritated, Pallas pulled her back.

"No answer? Well, we thought we had eliminated any cells of resistance on the planet. Our methods are very good. You can tell me. Make it easier. I'll know in the end anyway, but it still might be more, shall we say, friendly?"

Neither man spoke, nor had he expected them to.

Turning to the tray which held their weapons Pallas lifted a blaster and inspected it. "Of course, Patrol equipment. But how did you get here? I know for a fact that you don't have a battleship up there in orbit. Rode in on one of the tugs?'' He raised an eyebrow as he looked at the dark-haired one.

The man spit at him.

Pallas sighed. ''I'd really hoped you would be more co-operative.'' He chuckled his amusement. ''It doesn't make any difference, you know.'' He placed a headset on his brow and accessed the psych program. The boxy looking assembly floated over from its place in the corner and settled at the head of the pallet. Pallas almost could have wished it had been more difficult. With bored displeasure, he initiated the psych treatment, the machine energizing, reaching into the man's—

The bloodcurdling scream shocked him so badly he didn't think to stop the program. Instead, Pallas Mikros gaped at the man jerking and spasming in the iron grip of the EM restraints. Muscles slid and rolled under the skin, some knotting into bulging balls where they had pulled themselves in two from the seizures. Urine and feces were shot across the room as organs convulsed in his gut.

But the man's face gripped his appalled attention. The eyes started from the skull—rolled this way and that as the facial muscles contorted. The soul wrenching screams froze Pallas' blood in his veins and he shuddered as the man bit his tongue off, part of the bloody muscle hanging down the side of his twitching cheek by a sliver of unserverd tissue. Blood began dripping from the man's lips as he chewed out the inside of his mouth, oblivious to the pain.

Physically sick, Pallas tore his eyes away from the horrid scene, canceling the program. The form on the table relaxed, stone dead.

In the seconds it took Pallas to calm his pounding heart, he looked at the second captive. The man's face had twisted into a mask of disbelieving terror as he stared, glaze-eyed, at the contorted corpse. Even Tiara appeared fascinated, perhaps touched by some deep-seated fear.

''Most amazing,'' Pallas heard himself say.

The captive looked up, pupils dilated, labored breath wracking his body. He stared sightlessly at Pallas before his fear-bright attention shifted back to the horrible remains on the pallet.

Pallas accessed the guard. ''Remove this . . . and conduct an autopsy. I want to know what they've done to render this result to psyching.'' The guard entered—stopped as he tried to swallow his horror—shot a frightened glance at Pallas, and was trembling by the time he had the body out the door.

Pallas began to wring his hands as if the colored sparkles of light would wash them clean of the foul mess that had been his first captive. Speculatively, he looked at Darwin. "So they made you psych proof?" This time he laughed unsteadily. "I suppose I shall have to make other arrangements. What is your name?"

"D-D-Darwin Pike," the captive managed after several attempts.

"I see," Pallas accessed comm. He had no records of a Darwin Pike. "Who sent you here, Mr. Pike?"

No answer.

"How did you get here, Mr. Pike?"

No answer.

Pallas walked over and hit Pike hard under the ribs. "That is the first step, Mr. Pike. A very dainty first step compared to what is coming. Do you understand? You see, without psych, interrogation becomes a challenge. I must make you miserable. When your misery becomes unbearable, you'll talk. It's an old process, mostly forgotten since the advent of psych. But you know, I've studied. Fascinating what pain will drive a human to do."

Pike nodded and looked up. His eyes studied the ceiling for a second and his gaze froze there, locked. A curious strength seemed to flood into him and he was suddenly able to look at Pallas without fear. Mikros looked up—saw nothing but the ceiling and comm globes—and happily pulled a device from under the pallet. The compact machine might have been a scepter.

Pallas laughed as he let the globe roll down Darwin Pike's naked body. The man's screams were almost as horrible as the first captive's had been.

"Now, Mr. Pike. Why are you here? Who sent you?"

No answer.

Tiara leaned forward at his screams, lips parted, a dull gleam in her eye as she approached and began fondling Pike's genitals.

The man writhed, trying to wiggle away from her prodding fingers.

"Not now, Tiara," Pallas ordered. He cocked his head toward Pike. "She's been trained, you see. A naked male body . . . well, you can understand what she thinks." He hesitated. "But perhaps, Mr. Pike, if you cooperated? She's most desirable. Look at her body, the ultimate in sensuality, don't you agree?"

Pike's jaws clamped as he looked away.

Pallas sniffed, "Very well." He checked the tools available, and considered his options. By the time he turned back, Tiara had stripped herself and resumed fondling the prisoner. Pike jerked and grunted, face pained.

"I said, *not now!*" He waved her back, irritated. "Damn what the psych did to her. You'd never know that she once . . . That's pointless, I suppose. Mr. Pike, you will now begin answering my questions."

Pallas pressed an electrical prod up Pike's anus and released the charge. The scream proved most gratifying.

CHAPTER XXI

Administration building: city of Bazaar, Bazaar.

Comm called out softly. Pallas wiped the sweat from his fleshy features and looked up. Ngen Van Chow's face formed on the wall screen.

"Greetings in Deus, Governor." Van Chow's silky voice filled the room. "I understand the Patrol has finally become interested in Bazaar? You have two of their agents?"

Pike had been gasping for breath, now he looked over at the monitor, groaning.

"We have only one prisoner, Messiah. Unfortunately, I tried to psych the other. He died most horribly . . . and I didn't want this one to go the same route." Pallas bowed. "He will talk. It is only a matter of time. I must admit, however, his stamina surprises me."

"There were weapons?"

Pallas showed him the blasters, then lifted the knives. Ngen nodded. "No wonder the one went mad. You have Romanans, Governor." Ngen frowned as he thought. "Romanans? Not Patrol? A most incredible catch you've made. The implications . . . Well, we'll worry about that in the future. For now, let me make some suggestions . . ."

An hour passed, with Pallas marveling at the Messiah's

impressive skills. Van Chow seemed to know just where the human body was the most frail. "The result of my, let's say, 'experiments' on women. Part of the process of severing their minds from their bodies. As I did most adroitly with Lishia."

Pike's head turned, cold sweat dripping down his face. He looked with undisguised hatred and loathing at the Messiah.

"All he does is stare at the ceiling and scream, Messiah," Pallas admitted, toweling the sweat from his face and neck, feeling it running down between his shoulders.

Tiara waited, lips parted slightly, eyes on Pike's sweaty body. Damn her, she practically panted to be at him.

Ngen's thin face contorted and demonic light began to glow in his eyes. "Too bad there isn't a friend or lover he could watch. Another's pain always breaks a man before his own . . . but this should bring him to talk. You see, Pallas, there is another area of human weakness besides the body."

Pike closed his eyes, breathing deeply.

Van Chow cocked his head. "You say your Tiara is wasted? Good. Use the psych. Instruct her to follow your orders explicitly."

Pallas hesitated, then turned to access the program.

Pike stared anxiously, eyes glazed with pain and suffering, as Tiara stepped out from the machine. His chest shone with pooled sweat. His bladder and rectum had emptied shamelessly, long ago. Misery seemed to ebb and flow in the husk of his body.

"Now take the scalpel," Ngen began. "Cut off his little toe . . . either one."

Pike barely trembled as Pallas severed the digit. "Now, feed the toe to Tiara. Make sure—

"*Ngen!*" Pallas gasped, head tilted in disbelief. "Feed the . . . To Tiara? You can't . . ."

Ngen steepled his fingers, eyes narrowed. "Pallas, consider your options. You work for me. You've done so since the beginning. Don't cross me now."

"But Tiara has been . . . my . . ."

"Do you remember Zekial?" An eyebrow lifted. "There are several lessons in what happened to Zekial." He spoke very slowly, very deliberately, "I enjoy prompt obedience from *all* my people."

Pallas fought the constriction in his dry throat, swallowing loudly.

Ngen continued as if nothing had happened. "Make sure Pike watches as his flesh is devoured before his eyes."

Pike screamed his horror as Pallas handed the rubbery piece of meat and bone to Tiara who stood mutely, eyes completely lifeless.

"Tiara . . . eat it," he said woodenly.

Pallas shivered at the sound of the bones cracking under her teeth. Impossible. He remembered the times her mouth had met his in a passionate kiss, how she'd used it so . . . He shook himself.

Pike howled as Pallas glued his eyelids up and locked his head in place with an EM restraint.

"Now another toe," Ngen Van Chow's cooing voice ordered.

Pallas worked his tongue over dry lips.

Van Chow turned his attention to Pike. "Come, Mr. Pike. You can tell us how you got to Bazaar. We're really not your enemies. You, my friend, can end this terrible nightmare. Simply talk to us. Is there a need for such resistance on your part? Surely you can see there is no resisting the hand of God? Deus is taking the universe under his sway. Do you defy God?"

Pike's eyes flickered, shifting to look up—as if that would help, Tiara stood immediately beside him. Van Chow's calming voice droned on as Pallas periodically cut another toe. Each time, he cauterized the stump with a searing iron lest Pike slowly bleed to death.

"No!" Pike continued between soul-twisting shrieks. *"Oh my God, no!"*

"His sanity is leaving," Van Chow said simply. "I'm really not sure we can get anything out of him. Most unusual. When he starts to babble, hit him again with the pain."

"That was his last toe. Shall I begin cutting off fingers?" Pallas asked, sweat beading on his nose and under his cheeks to trickle into the folds of his chins. Despite his care, blood had begun to obscure the lights of his rings.

Ngen thought for a second and shook his head. "Try stripping his legs. Cut out a piece of meat several centimeters in width and feed it to Tiara. Perhaps that will erode his resistance."

Pike emitted a strained, insane whimper as the blade slid down his calf. His glazed eyes danced with disbelief as Pallas lifted the long strip of skin and muscle. Then he jerked rigid as the wand cauterized the bleeding tissue. Pallas checked the vital signs, brain activity, and nodded to himself before handing the strip to Tiara.

"Eat," he commanded, watching with a horrid fascination as Tiara began to chew on the strip of flesh, a dribble of blood tracing the smooth line of her throat to slip down around the marvelous swell of her perfect breasts.

"Come, my dear friend," Ngen soothed, a sad pleading in his voice. "This need not continue. Is it worth a few words on your part? Tell me, what is making you fight so for such a small reward? Will your friends ever know your bravery? Will they ever reward you for proving yourself so much better than they? They would have sold you out long ago. Where are they now, Darwin Pike? Do they even care that you're here, feeling what you're feeling? No, of course not. They're half a galaxy away, laughing at your predicament. Talk to me . . . be my friend."

Pallas shook his head, Ngen's soft tones reaching into his tired spirit. He caught himself whispering that he'd say anything, only to force himself back to the terrible reality of the situation. Amazed, he looked at Pike and wondered how the man could possibly resist.

Tears streaked gleaming paths down Pike's face as Pallas continued the torture. The Governor fought the growing queasiness in his stomach and drew a breath of cool air. He was tougher than this. How could Pike resist when he, Pallas Mikros, interrogator, was crumbling from the stress? Was this Pike inhuman? Didn't he feel, didn't the sight of his flesh . . . Pallas shivered.

"Darwin," the soothing voice crooned as Van Chow's face loomed in the room, "don't you want to go back to your home world in one piece? There must be a woman there waiting for your—" Pike flinched and Ngen grinned, his voice dropping to a gentle murmur. "Yes, a woman, a Romanan woman, who would welcome you with warm, soft arms. A woman with black hair and deep, passionate eyes."

Van Chow paused, eyes closed as if remembering. "A woman with silky skin. Feel it, Darwin? Feel it warm against yours? Think of her, Darwin. Think of her and how much you would like to be with her—to hold her next to you and enjoy her love." A hesitation, then, "A woman like Tiara."

Pike mewed piteously, twisting, face agonized.

"I must leave for a moment, Messiah," Pallas said huskily. He had to get away from the suggestive voice. He had to have air. Blindly, he stumbled for the door, leaving Pike to deal with the Messiah by himself. Tiara continued to chew on the last strip of meat, her stomach bulging suggestively.

Closing the door behind him, Pallas Mikros slumped wearily against it, for the moment not caring about the staring guard. He panted for breath, sucking the cool, untainted air into his lungs. Nothing in all his long life had ever shaken him like this. He let his bulk sink to the floor, almost shivering as the cool breeze drifted down the hallway and the dry air evaporated the rivulets of sweat from his fat neck and shirt.

Eyes closed, he reviewed his life for the first time. Why in the name of hell wouldn't Pike break? Damn the man! Pallas feared *he* might give out before Pike finally recanted and talked. Where did the man pull such resistance from? He just stared up at the ceiling and got his courage back!

Pallas sat up, suddenly alert. What *was* on the ceiling? He pulled himself to his feet and opened the door. The stench hit him with a humid fist, almost gagging him, reminding him of the horrors of the room.

Bulling his way in, he studied Pike, the dried-out, glassy eyes like pools of terror as Ngen continued to chip away at his resistance. Pallas looked up where Darwin occasionally shot a quick glance. The two dark globes of the comm unit sat side by side, one larger than the other, the eight lines of the walls coming down like spindly, thin legs. Nothing there!

Pallas turned back and studied Pike, frowning. The solution to breaking him floated somewhere just past his consciousness. "Another strip of flesh, if you please, Governor." Van Chow sounded distressed over having to order it.

Pallas picked up the scalpel and returned to his work. When the floor suddenly shook slightly, Pallas stopped cutting.

Then, feeling no more tremors, he began another stroke as Pike twisted a gruesome shriek past tortured vocal chords. The eerie sound grated on his ears and slivered its way into his soul.

A banging rumble sounded in the distance and the building shook again.

"What was that?" Ngen Van Chow asked.

"It is nothing, Messiah. You know how the dust rises in the air when the winds blow. The currents lift and the dust is ionized from the friction of conflicting air. When the positive and negative ionization builds up, we get lightning. We had a storm predicted for this evening. It has arrived and the thunder will become louder.

The building trembled again. Ngen's voice returned to its soothing monotone. "Come, Pike, who is God?"

The man whispered, fever-burning eyes staring up at the ceiling.

"Who?" Pallas bent down, trying to catch the cracking voice, worried at the tremors of terror which spasmodically shook the man's failing body.

"Spider," the feeble whisper told him.

Pallas stepped back and looked up at the ceiling. It all clicked. "Of course!"

"What, Governor?" Ngen asked gently.

"The room is designed so he sees a spider form in the way the comm globes and the walls come together. It's like we're standing underneath a huge spider!"

Pallas moved to access the psych unit and brought it to hover over Pike's field of vision, blocking the ceiling from sight.

"Now, Messiah, he will break," Pallas decided, feeling the floor shiver again as a loud crack of lightning emphasized his words.

"No!" Pike cried out, trying desperately to see, throwing his body against the EM restraints—the spider effigy blocked by the hovering psych unit. He screamed—a wailing howl that grated on Mikros' nerves. Pallas picked up the knife and positioned himself over the shredded, bloody mass which had once been a leg. Pike whimpered, sobs shaking his trembling frame.

"Cut his testicle off," Ngen ordered. "Be careful, those veins and arteries . . . Well, you know."

Pallas trembled. With Pike sobbing in horror and twisting under him, he made a mess of the cutting. Pike's squeals of mindless panic ruined his concentration. Pallas straightened with the pink-white globe of tissue.

Ngen gestured toward Tiara.

Pallas felt his stomach lurch, Pike's mindless gibbering like fingernails on slate to his reeling mind. He handed the warm organ to Tiara, whispering, "E-Eat."

"Think, Pike. *Think!*" Ngen's soft voice crept into Pallas' horrified senses. "Remember your Romanan girl, so like Tiara. Look at the majesty of her body. Look at her, slowing eating your resistance, Darwin. That's what they do, you know. Destroy you, devour who you are. Come, talk to me. Be my friend and I'll destroy the Romanan woman who emasculates you so. Think of the times she's hurt you. Even your Spider has left, fled. You're alone with us now. Let us help you. Help me, Darwin. Join with me. Let's end the suffering. Let's . . ."

"I . . . I . . ." Pike choked through the wretched sobs. "S-Susan?" He began shaking, mumbling under his breath. "Said she'd leave . . . leave . . ."

"Got him!" Ngen whispered to himself.

The lightning cracked loudly and the building shook dangerously. "My, that was close!" Pallas laughed nervously. Thoughts of Tiara's mouth, of the way she—

At that instant, Tiara, stomach overfilled, vomited profusely. Pallas stared—tried to stifle his own heaving gut—and vomited in turn all over Pike.

"Pallas! Of all the stupid . . ." Van Chow snapped harshly over the comm. "Damn you, Pallas, we had him! It may take hours to build him to that point again."

The room seemed to shake as the thunder boomed again, only this time Pallas thought he heard men yelling over his pumping stomach.

"Spider! I *can't* see you!" ripped from Pike's throat. "Reesh, come back to me! Make me strong, bear. Don't let me fail!" His mind-cracking cries shattered Pallas' weakened constitution as he stumbled back.

The governor shook his head, staring at Tiara where she stood waiting, ribbons of dried blood running down her body, streaking down muscular legs. "I have . . . have to leave," he muttered, wiping at his mouth, tasting the bile of vomit, wondering if he'd ever be able to eat again.

"Stay put!" Ngen ordered.

Pallas careened for the door and pulled it open in time to see the guard disappear in a blinding flash, a severed arm spiraling past Pallas' face to splat into the wall as the body exploded.

Weaving, he leaned against the door, Ngen Van Chow shouting behind him, Pike screaming hideously.

Trying to make sense of the world, he saw a young woman—long black hair in a flying tangle about her head—

lead a group of shouting, combat-armored men down the narrow corridor. She stuck a blaster under his chin.

"Pike? *Where is he?*" Her fierce eyes cowed him—broke the last of his resistance.

"Th–There," he managed hoarsely, pointing.

She caught the smell then, face twisting as she darted past his fat bulk. Pallas stumbled through the door, seeing her stop, staring at Ngen's face in the comm.

"Susan!" Ngen's voice cooed. "How delightful to—"

She looked away—caught sight of Pike—and shot a hot look back. *"Bastard! Sirian FILTH!"*

"I ruined him for you. But come . . . come to me. I long to fill your wondrous body with—" The Messiah's smile of anticipation was still on his face as she blew the monitor off the wall and staggered back, visibly shaken, features paling as she fought for control.

"Spider?" Pike cried weakly, trying to turn his head as the Romanans burst through the door, faces churning with disgust as they slowed, taking in the room.

The warrior woman forced herself up, trembling, and canceled the EM restraints from the wall controls. Pike's abused body dropped weakly. She caught him, repelled by the bloody mess, her face pinching at the sight of his butchered crotch.

"Get the AT here, *fast!*" Then she turned to Pallas. "Where's Reesh?"

"He died," Pallas heard himself say. "He went crazy under psych!"

Pallas didn't see the Romanan strike, but Tiara's head rolled across the floor, eyes still dull, mouth streaked with more than dried blood as the jugulars emptied. Her headless body flopped loosely to the side.

He was crying then. He was still crying as a knife slid into his fat paunch, stinging through his fat to be followed by a hot burning of severed intestines. He was crying as they carved off his scalp and left him for dead. His last memories were of the whistle of a Patrol AT and the now recognizable crackle of heavy duty blasters milliseconds before the subsequent explosions rocked the very foundations of the world.

He saw the hooded figure enter and look slowly around the room. Pallas cowered on the floor, half-blinded where the blood ran from his searing scalp into his eyes. The figure seemed to float over him, the face shadowed by the large hood. He heard no sound as the hooded being silently passed.

Pallas Mikros looked up at the ceiling, life gone, and stared at the huge spider that stood over him.

Susan led her raiders back down the halls of the administration building, shocked by the whimpering wreckage that had been Darwin Pike. At the same time, her body pulsed, vigorously alive—soaring on the crest of rage which sustained her. Oh, how delicious that moment had been when she blew Ngen's surprised face into fragments! *The first step on the road back, you Sirian filth! By Spider, I swear, Ngen, I'm coming for you now. I'm coming, and I'm going to win.*

She looked down at the tape in her hand. After her time as Ngen's captive, she'd expected it—retrieved it, and blown the comm to junk. Now she slipped the tape into her pouch, suddenly reminded of Rita Sarsa in another time. A mad flash of guilt ate at her. So much had begun to come clear now. How had they managed to put up with her for so long—trust her so far?

The AT approached, whistling its way across the low flat roofs of the dun-colored buildings. Like an avenging lance it roared out of the swirling dust, bright blasters lacing destruction into anything which looked like a reasonable target. In the blood-red light of sunset, whole structures erupted in dirt, rock, and graphite vortices as the violet lances gutted the city. Two more of her teams came at a trot, randomly blasting buildings, tossing sonic grenades into power terminals and dragging occasional booty behind. Fresh coups hung here and there on belts—not the number she'd expected, but then, who'd find honor in slaughtering walking dead?

The AT set down deftly, raising a squall of boiling dust. "Get Pike on board," she ordered, trying to shield his wounds from the blowing dirt. "He's the first priority." As the ramp slapped the red-brown dust, they were running him up and into the heart of the deadly white ship.

"Close it up," Susan hollered, waving her crews in through the blasting dust and stink whipped by the reaction jets. "We don't know how much time we've got. Ngen knows we're here; let's move!"

She counted heads as they scrambled up the ramp. Satisfied no one would be left behind, Susan jumped lithely up the ramp and slapped the hatch. The ramp slid shut behind her as she wove past milling warriors. The lights dimmed as the heavy blasters drew power. She paused long enough to see Pike's bloody flesh encased in a med unit before hurrying toward the bridge.

Marines racked blasters in a clatter of efficiency, already strapping into the crash webbing as the grav plates fought to counter acceleration as the AT shot up, headed for orbit.

Susan slipped her blaster into its holster as she passed the bridge hatch and dropped into the command chair.

"Fire control!" she hollered, pulling her headset over her brow. "On the way out, we're hitting everything within range."

"Acknowledged."

She opened a line to *Spider's Revenge*. "Moshe, what have you got in the way of incoming traffic?"

"Susan," Moshe's face formed on the screen. "We have three tugs coming in after releasing stations." He looked up at something out of her field of vision. "Um, additionally, we're tracking four stations being towed out by tugs."

"Can you punch those stations on the way in to get us? For our part, we'll make an orbit to pick up velocity and smash everything in reach before following their vector out."

"We can do it, Captain." Moshe nodded, a ghost smile on his grim lips. "I guess we're taking the blinders off?"

"Yes," she admitted wearily. "There's no going back now."

Moshe caught her meaning, nodding before the holo flicked off.

"Fire control." Susan turned her head to another monitor, "We have one pass. Let's set a record. Engineering, give me one-hundred-and-ten percent. We're going for broke!"

An affirmative flashed on the screen. As they rose from the planet, brilliant blaster bolts lashed out of the AT, stitching the big spinning cans. The stations ruptured, blowing out dirt, atmosphere, machinery, animals, men, and vegetation as they decompressed.

Susan pulled a cup of coffee, eyes glued to the screens. She checked each shot, individual monitors following blaster bolts on line of sight. The round sides of the stations buckled, collapsed, and died in puffs of fogging atmosphere and crystallizing, freezing moisture. Fires flared momentarily until the jetting oxygen was exhausted. One station died in a blinding flash of light as its reactor overloaded. Debris, cartwheeling steel plate, dust, and frozen liquids belched from fractured structures, a path of pinwheeling desolation behind the AT.

"Most of them aren't hostile," White Eagle muttered. "They were just manufacturing and food production for the planet."

"That's right. That bother you?"

White Eagle shrugged, lowering his eyes.

"Not a warrior's honor, huh? No, maybe not, José. This is something grimmer, more important. We're striking a major blow against Ngen's industrial base. It wouldn't surprise me if they weren't all mindless robots . . . like down there." She indicated the planet. "He's leaving an army of psyched people behind him. Unless we hit hard and fast, we can't win. You think of it, José. It's them—or us."

José Grita White Eagle nodded, swallowing hard, grim eyes on the death the AT unleashed on the defenseless stations. "I looked in their eyes, Susan. What I saw was an abomination in the eyes of Spider. Men without souls. You know?"

She reached out, gripped him by the shoulder, and shook him in shared camaraderie.

"Moshe," Susan accessed *Revenge* again. "I'm sending all the information we have, including pictures and interviews with some of the human garbage we saw down there. The Admiral needs this posthaste."

"Very good, Captain, we're receiving and storing. As soon as I can refine the dish, we'll be sending it out. That should be . . . Hang on. I have the Admiral on my circuits. I'm patching you through."

"Not a bad job of dish refining," she mumbled dryly, waiting as long seconds ticked by.

Damen Ree's craggy face—unshaven and bleary-eyed—filled Susan's monitor. He nodded, yawning from interrupted sleep. "Go ahead, Captain. I'm keeping an eye on both screens. I take it everything has broken open?"

"Yes, sir. We burst in on a subspace transduction between Ngen and the governor of Bazaar. Van Chow recognized me immediately."

"Report, Captain." Ree's voice sounded like gravel.

Susan filled him in on all the details. "You see, Admiral, he has no rear supply lines to stabilize politically. All that stuff that Pike told us about a Messiah? He's changed the formula. All he has to do is sell them, get them into a Temple, and they're his: mind-wiped. He's turning his people into human machines governed by psych. All those temples he's building are no doubt processing centers to manufacture more workers. Government on Bazaar consisted of one administration center for the whole planet. Everything else is watched by comm. We captured most of their programs in the administration center. We'll sort them out and pass them on."

Ree paused, blinking his eyes. "So the farther he goes, the greater his resource base gets, and the more the Directorate's is limited."

"Sir? You know what he'll . . . Well, have you thought about the military force he can create? If Ngen can obtain enough ships to carry his people, who can stand in his way? He could literally drown us in bodies. How long can we last if the odds are one hundred thousand to one? Right now, he's investing manpower in manufacturing. When he's built his supply base, he'll psych the workers; then the men who build the blasters and uniforms will shoot and wear them."

"What's Pike's evaluation of this?"

"I don't know, sir," she hesitated. "He's in med. Ngen had him for just about six hours. They did some terrible things. We'll give you a report as soon as he's stable."

"Well, at least he's alive." A pause. "And tell me, Captain, how did you let him get captured?" Those steely eyes ate into hers.

Susan stared back, a warm flush in her gut. "He and Reesh decided to be heroic. They were covering an escape hole and closed it off from the other side. I guess they figured if they couldn't get through, neither could the Fathers. I . . . well, I suppose it worked, although I'm not sure Pike will like the price he and Bull Wing Reesh paid." She pursed her lips, tilting her head to stare defiantly. "Pike was right, Admiral. We *had* to see inside the Temple. Looking back, I can honestly say his capture was my fault. I'll take that responsibility. But, Admiral, you wouldn't be getting this data if not for his guts and resourcefulness."

A slight flicker of a smile tugged at his tight lips, a spark of understanding in his eyes. "So he won't stay an anthropologist, eh? Wants to be a warrior? Damn him, nothing but trouble. Well, if you need to sit on him—chain him to a desk, you've—"

"I think Spider has pulled him into his web, Admiral. It . . . uh, has been known to happen before."

Ree's eyes glittered at the challenge. "If you're referring to me, you're on the verge of insubordination, Captain. I'll consider the stressful situation you're in and make allowances. Now, get yourself out of there and come home. By the time you arrive, I think we'll have something put together. We may have some Patrol help coming and Spider alone knows what the Directorate is doing."

"Yes, sir, we'll push for home as soon as we rendezvous with Moshe." The monitor went blank as Ree switched off. She settled herself into her command chair, conscious of the terrible fatigue seeping through each limb as her battle-hype faded. How many hours since she'd slept?

The grim looks on the faces of the Patrol personnel reminded her of the terrible price her blasters were extracting from the stations. In her one orbit of Bazaar, she could have killed as many people as in the entire Sirian conflict. Hopefully, those deaths were not in vain. Perhaps the spiraling bodies that now blew through vacuum bought the rest of humanity time enough to mount a defense against Ngen Van Chow and the meaningless existence he represented.

Hours later, a hollow-eyed Susan Smith Andojar nosed her AT into its concave berth in the hull of *Spider's Revenge*. She supervised the transportation of Darwin Pike—encased in a med unit—to the main ship. His pale face haunted her, triggering a memory of that bloody room, the ghoulish woman with blood caked on her mouth. A grimness around the corners of his eyes reminded her of a death mask. He moaned softly, eyelids shifting in REM sleep.

As she turned away, the soft whimpers escaping his lips pained her. Steeling herself, she headed for her cabin. Showering, she dropped soddenly to her bunk and let the lights lower. There, in the blackness, she remembered the horrid dreams Ngen had given her and wondered what nightmare Pike was living.

CHAPTER XXII

Bridge of *Bullet*: GEO orbit over World.

A rough looking Patrol marine stood before a robed, blank-faced man. Behind them, a sere landscape extended into rough hills, the day oddly dingy, as if the air were polluted and gray. A squat mud-brick hovel could be seen behind the man, dull-eyed women and children watching, tattered and filthy clothing flapping in the dust-laden wind.

"What is your name?" the sergeant asked.

The fellow smiled slightly. "I am Yeshua Maheed."

"Where do you live?"

"In my house," came the dull answer.

"Where is that?"

"Where my house is."

"Where do you work?" The sergeant gave the man a threatening look.

Oblivious, the man replied, "In my place."

The questioning went on. Through the monitors, Maya ben Ahmad and Toby Kuryaken watched grimly. They'd already seen the tapes made of Bazaar, of the factories, of the mindless hordes, of the crumpled temple and the sheeplike Bazaarans who walked blindly through the raid, not even heeding the lightning of blaster fire that danced around them.

"*Jeeesus!*" Toby said grimly, throwing her ponytail of fading blonde hair over her shoulder.

"I believe we've seen enough, Damen," Maya said, voice sharp. She turned and looked at Toby. "I think this makes our decision. The very fact Romanans have this information and the Directorate doesn't shows us just how far things have disintegrated. What the hell is Skor doing on Arcturus, anyway?"

Toby Kuryaken nodded and sighed. "We have no choice. God damn it!" Her face worked, a desperation in her pained eyes. "All the years. I've given a lot to . . . to protect. To just walk away . . . it just seems . . . *Damn it!*"

"It isn't palatable for any of us," Maya added, softening

her gravel voice. "We have to look to the overall needs of humanity. I've just finished a futile pursuit across half my Sector—chasing shadows. I can't protect it—and hanging around trying to keep survivors alive isn't the job of the military. It's to stop the problem at its roots."

Toby looked at Damen Ree. "The rest of the Patrol won't help, Admiral. With Directorate agreement, they've come to the conclusion that you and the Romanans are becoming too powerful in Directorate politics. They fear that if you and your wild men are allowed to smash Ngen Van Chow, you'll be powerful enough to take over the—"

"By Spider," he cried, raising knotted fists. "They fear a half-million Romanans? When Ngen is making human robots out of an *entire* Sector of space? He's the one preaching galactic jihad! Romanans have three spindly converted GCIs. Don't they realize the danger here?"

"Damn it, Damen, you're a rogue to them. They've seen what your Romanans did to Sirius. You have an unstoppable military force and demonstrate unpredictable behavior. What could scare those ass-wipes more? They fear trading Emperior Ngen for Emperor Ree. Ngen's simply a power-mad lunatic . . . you're not. You're damn scary and damn competent. They figure they can *beat* Ngen. But you?"

"And how do you feel?" Ree asked, stiff-faced.

Toby Kuryaken gestured futility. "I've considered the matter with my crew." She looked down at her hands nervously, not really wanting to say what she had to. "More than a few of my people are alive because some silly Romanan bastard charged in where anyone with the sense of a dead dock rat would have run. My people—at least the marines—*like* Romanans, for God's sake. I've got little spiders drawn all over my ship. After Sirius, the handwriting was on the wall. The Directorate can no longer protect our Patrol Sector of space. The Patrol itself is fragmenting. *Ngen stole a ship of the line!* I'm pretty sure my people will . . . well, we'll choose to side with you, Admiral. Our Sector will, of course, follow suit. We do share a common border. We'll risk your leadership against that of the Directorate." She looked up, eyes clear, posture erect. "And after those last days off Sirius, you know what that costs me. I would have blasted *Bullet* right out of space. And you with her, Damen."

He nodded. "We can't forget that, Toby. It happened—a

reality we'll all just have to live with. How about instead of letting it become a grudge, we turn it into a lesson? What we need to learn is that humanity is too fragile for division right now. I need you—and all *Miliken's* talented professionals. You need us, the resources of World, and *Bullet*. What we'll remember from the past is that no man's individual word should dictate our shared morality.''

Toby's lips quivered. ''If that spirit reflects *Bullet's* attitude, I think my people won't debate for nearly as long. Pride can be . . . It's important to my people, Damen.''

Ree smiled. ''Come with your heads held high, Toby. Spider teaches us to respect pride and the reasons for it.''

''Damn, you going to let Spider undermine her ship like He did mine?'' Maya shook her head, staring at the overhead panels.

''Maya? Complaints? And after your own second in command has spent how many hours with the Prophet we sent to Sirius?'' Ree asked, shifting his glance.

''Leave Ben out of this,'' she growled.

''You haven't said what *Victory* will do.''

''Toby said it all.'' Her long sigh held resignation. ''Strength will determine survival. I think you're the best bet to whip Ngen. Besides, Damen, I know you. I don't think you'd make a good dictator. You have too much love for that despicable, rusted bucket of air you command. They'd make you leave *Bullet* to administer an empire. That'd kill you.''

Maya met his wry smile with an upraised eyebrow that accentuated the lines of her face, recapturing the striking beauty of her youth.

''Welcome to the ranks. Strategically, the first order of business is to take the punch out of Ngen's drive. Currently, Romanan vessels are doing just that—striking at his economic base. One of my captains has demolished Bazaaran productive ability in the manner you've just seen. Other targets are currently under study for similar raids. We're doing what we can with our limited abilities.''

Both Colonels considered him thoughtfully.

''Knew you'd be a jump ahead, Damen.'' Maya smiled. ''By Spider, that's what I needed to hear. Skor sits in Arcturus trying to cover every situation as it develops while you grab for the jugular.''

''Romanan influence, no doubt,'' Toby added noncommittally.

So, it was done. Damen Ree leaned back, thinking of his increased responsibilities. Another trillion people were now under his protection. Scared, huddled in stations and on lonely planets, staring out at the stars, wondering when Ngen's raiders might end their lives in fiery death—they counted on him!

He accessed comm. "I'm sending the schematics for the Brotherhood blasters Ngen uncovered on Sirius. You know the fire potentials firsthand. Your techs can begin modifications immediately. Confiscate all GCI transports and anything else which will space. We should have five that we, uh, commandeered out of Far Side Sector completely refitted within the week—armed and ready to go. Given the Brotherhood data obtained from *Bullet*'s deep banks, they should be considerably faster than Ngen's ships, although none of our FTs have tangled with any of his vessels yet to prove this theory. As you can guess, I'll remain a bit nervous in the meantime.

"Which reminds me. There's a possibility that Brotherhood data can be retrieved from *Miliken,* she's almost two hundred years old. She dates back to Brotherhood days. You might surprise yourself with what's been forgotten in the banks of your own ships." He smiled at the astonishment on their faces. "Where do you think we found the Fujiki Amplifier? It was in *Bullet* all the time."

"We'll check our comm thoroughly," Maya agreed dryly, irritated, as if she should have thought of that on her own.

"In the meantime," Ree told them, "I'm sending through a series of figures for you to channel to your manufacturing stations. You'll notice first thing that we've tagged certain production industries which can be converted to military functions with a minimum of retooling or assembly reorganization. If you need more data, contact Doctor S. Montaldo. He's our logistics expert."

Maya was scanning all the data Ree patched through. "Looks like you've given quite a bit of thought to this, Damen. You seemed to know we'd be coming your way."

"As you said, the handwriting was on the wall. You were our only hope. We had to plan accordingly."

"Why is the Romanan world the last ditch?" Toby wanted to know, eyes measuring.

Ree shrugged. "It's at the edge of Directorate space— hence the most easily defendable. At the same time, we need to put our staging area somewhere and—on the odd chance Ngen's people make a landing—they'll find the Romanans to be the toughest nuts to crack in the entire galaxy. Can you suggest a stronger location with a rougher group of defenders? At the same time, World has disadvantages. We don't have the ability to refit or repair battle damage. The industrial capability is zero—unless you're interested in single-shot rifles and forty-centimeter fighting knives.''

"Point well made." Toby pulled at her ear. "They can't turn our rear."

"No rear is unturnable in space warfare," Ree reminded. "That's a lesson my people have just taught Ngen."

"You think you've taken the sting out of his advance?'' Toby tapped at her chin with a stylus she'd begun making notations with.

"Susan estimates she destroyed eighty to eighty-five percent of the Bazaaran manufacturing capacity—though they were in the process of withdrawing much of it at the time. Major Sarsa has inflicted substantial damage to Mystery, seriously crippling their orbital manufacturing and Major Iverson has just completed the first military action on Arpeggio in almost three hundred years. Neal didn't have much of a chance since he was under fire from one of Ngen's ships, but he tagged a couple of manufacturing stations on the way by."

"So how do we keep them from doing the same to us?" Toby asked.

Ree hesitated, searching for the right words. "If I had the answer to that, I'd dance over right now and blow that bastard out of space. For the time being, we must hope Ngen believes he faces a united Directorate. The number of targets he now has is consequently large. His present advantage lies in his ability to defend a small resource base while he can destroy Directorate targets practically at will without fear of opposition."

"So he won't know our source of military manufacturing." Toby nodded.

"That's why one of our first priorities is to move manufacturing stations away from their current, known locations. For the time being, Ngen's resources are limited; he can't strike at everything he wants to. I'd say your best bet is to move your industry as far as you can, as quickly as you can. Sometimes you're pinned. We have to keep our last converted GCI—you knew her as *Helk*—over Sirius. Captain Breeze is in command there if you need anything."

"Move the stations?" Maya propped her head, looking up at a holo barely visible in the corner of her projection. "Easier said than done, given some of the propulsion systems. Then, too, even a crummy scanner will pull out a radio source like a station. I can tell you now that the Sybar system stations can't leave their sources of raw material. They produce metals from asteroid mining. We can't move them, but I suppose we can make them less vulnerable, compartmentalizing to reduce decompression danger and taking steps to reduce specialization."

"That's thinking," Ree agreed. "It's just a shift of mental framework. We're not trained to think in terms of overall strategy, but in terms of individual action. Iron Eyes has been priceless in changing my opinions."

"Total war," Toby said absently as her eyes strayed beyond them. "Who would have thought the Directorate would end in such a fashion? We were so civilized!"

"And now, we must learn to be barbarians," Ree said gently. "We have to become more vicious than Ngen. We have to beat him, run, or die, knowing we've left our species a nightmare existence." Ree let his eyes wander to the silent image of a Patrol sergeant trying vainly to communicate with a robe-wrapped figure whose eyes stared vacantly in spite of the happy smile on his face. Admiral Damen Ree shuddered.

Aboard *Deus*: GEO orbit over Santa del Cielo.

The holo played overhead, a black-haired Romanan girl, stripped and bound, writhed under Ngen's electronic whip.

"Yes, my dear. You've cost me. You've blasted my Bazaar—destroyed it, taken it from my resources. And Pallas? How will I ever find another with his skill at administration? His death, more than Bazaar's, stings my soul. Damn you. You Romanan bitch, damn you again and again. But you'll come to me again someday. And when you do . . ."

Ngen reclined on his pillows, eyes burning as he watched his holo-self move to cover Susan's body.

"Captain Velkner," comm informed.

Ngen straightened, ordering the holo off. "Enter."

Along one wall, a section of gold-bordered emerald inlay slid aside as the hatch opened, exposing the sterile corridor beyond. It had taken weeks to get the room refinished from dull Patrol white to opulent splendor. The walls shimmered

in gold filigree. Light sculpture and multicolored holos—
the finest from six worlds and as many major stations reflected his wealth and power. Genuine svee moss carpeted
the floor, its pungent aroma as delicate and changing as the
patterns of light. Above him, the ceiling had been entirely
holoed, a reflection of the spinning galaxy disappearing into
a seeming infinity—a symbol of his growing power.

Sira, the heartless smuggler, assassin, and thief entered,
stopping, eyes wide as he stared. Ngen delighted in the sensation. To have seen such an expression of awe on Sira's
face once in a lifetime would have been enough.

"I trust you had a good trip, Captain," Ngen's smile was
warm, belying his probing look.

"Indeed," Sira's smile showed his missing teeth as he
tried to free himself from the impact of the room. "This is
. . . is . . ."

"Spectacular, yes. I didn't ask you here to discuss archi-
tecture, Sira. What are your assessments of damage?" Ngen
leaned back against the wealth of pillows. A burning resentment festered that he had been dealt so stunning a blow.
Damn the Romanans! Had the Patrol been in charge of the
raids, they would have only struck military targets. They
wouldn't have mercilessly exterminated so many workers.

Ngen chewed his lip, knowing he'd once again underestimated the Romanans. He looked up at Velkner's sharp features, waiting.

"I think we can have all systems back to full production
within three weeks, Messiah. One thing the raids did which
benefits us is increase conversions at the Temples. We have
completed the preliminary psych on ninety-five percent of
the Trystans. We can begin to give them places. Once the
preliminary psych is made, we can modify them any way
we wish without disturbing the rest. Those increases offset
the fatalities.

"On the other hand, we have also recruited more independent stations. Psyching is occurring as rapidly as our
crews can force people through the psych gates."

"If their raids were so beneficial—"

Sira raised a hand. "They weren't. Bazaar and Mystery
are effectively dead. The disadvantage is that manufacturing
is now taking place in Moscow Sector instead of closer to
our current sphere of influence. Romanan blasters destroyed
a great deal of our production. And we are vulnerable as a
result. Currently, machines are more important than peo-

ple. If the Romanans strike the stations we've taken over in Moscow Sector, it could deal us a staggering blow. "On the other hand," Sira shrugged, "there's a whole Directorate out there to raid."

"I've ordered Cheng and Roskolnikovski to cover Arpeggio, the raid there didn't inflict much damage. As soon as you leave, I'll space *Deus* for Tryst to cover our interests there. Perhaps we can kill a couple of the raiders. For the moment, Arpeggio and Tryst are still necessary." *And she is here. Such a waste to have sent a single ship after one woman.*

Ngen nodded, sighing. It wasn't as bad as he thought. He'd been worried that the Romanans might have dealt him a crippling blow. If only he could give his religious sheep a complete psych all at once! That would cut his time for subduing a world by at least a month and close that tenuous link to Moscow Sector. And it would leave him with exactly the problem Pallas had warned about. No captains for his masses.

No, it wasn't worth risking. After a population had its first psyching, it didn't mind the placed ones who wandered around, eyes blank, families, jobs, and personalities forgotten. First psych was critical. Anything else would perpetuate revolt.

"We have to strike back at them." Ngen decided. "If only we could blast the Romanan home world! They'll have it well guarded for the moment. My sources report that *Bullet* remains in orbit and they've been testing upgraded weapons." Suddenly Ngen Van Chow laughed. The balloon heads would never believe he could be so audacious. "Sira, I want you and Torkild to hit Arcturus. Destroy their stations and blast their industry to junk! Put the fear of death into their hearts! We shall repay them for Bazaar and Mystery—and deal the Directorate a blow like it's never been dealt before! We'll strike fear into their souls, Sira—paralyze them in their beds."

A slow smile curled Sira's lips. "With greatest pleasure. We can get in and get out quickly."

"Wait." Ngen considered, drawing up a holo of the red star and the silver threads of the endless stations that surrounded it. "To destroy it would be enough. But . . ."

"Messiah?"

"Take your assault personnel and raid them. We need

brains, Sira, not just bodies. You know University? Here?''
A light flickered.

"I can find it."

"Do so. While Torkild keeps the Patrol and Arcturian
security occupied, I want you to capture the engineering
section of University. I want as many of the engineering
people, design specialists, and physicists as you can lay your
hands on. In particular, one Ten MacGuire is essential. He's
the leading expert on singularity manipulation."

"Very well, Messiah."

"That is all, Sira. I'll expect you and Captain Alhar to
proceed with all haste. The sooner we strike, the greater
our impact will be." Ngen bowed as the man left, the hatch
sliding shut behind him.

With relief, Ngen closed his eyes, thankful the station
containing the engineers had been spared in the Arpeggian
raid. The skeleton crew had just begun poring over the schematics for the mass converter. If they could figure out how
to build it, Ngen would once again have the technological
as well as psychological edge on the Romanans. Perhaps if
Sira could capture MacGuire's people. . . . If! Such a little
word, yet so frightful!

Holo communication between *Bullet* and Arcturus.

"I tell you, it's the only way! Look, Director, I'm appealing to you."

"And I am telling you that you are overreacting." Skor
blinked his little red-rimmed eyes. "Yes, Admiral Ree, I
have reviewed your data. Your spies are most adroit. At the
same time, I have studied the physical realities of the situation you say exists in Ngen's space. In all my manipulations, I cannot duplicate your figures. For Ngen to psych
one million people—only one tenth of the population of Bazaar alone, he would need seven point eight nine years with
three hundred machines running twenty-four hours a day.
Even with the kidnapped Gonian techs, such productivity—"

"I tell you, it's done through the Temples. My people
have been inside. Seen—"

"How? How is this done, Admiral? What is the physics
of a mass field psych?"

Ree hesitated, mouth working. "I . . . the man who
knows is in med at the moment. I'm not a psych expert. I

don't . . . Damn it, Director, we're losing time!'' Ree pounded his fist on a console. ''While we argue, Ngen is growing in power!''

''And your raids have contributed to the rate of conversion to his illogical religion.''

Ree raised his hands helplessly. ''Maybe, but it's better than waiting for Ngen to become invincible. We staggered his manufacturing ability. Rita blew his heavy blaster plant out of Mysterian space.''

''And eventually the people will become tired of his illogical banter and cast him down.''

''Not if they're psyched, Director!''

''And you cannot tell me how this is done, Admiral. Now, you must excuse me. The press of demands on my system continues to escalate.''

The holo flickered off.

Ree waited, red-faced, for a total of ten seconds before he bellowed his frustration at the silent holo. When he'd screamed his lungs empty, he took a deep breath, turning.

''It was a worthy try, Damen.'' Iron Eyes straightened from where he leaned against a planning table, arms crossed.

Ree blinked and rubbed his eyes. ''Damn it, it seemed like he wasn't even listening. Like he was so goddamned preoccupied with other things he never even considered what I had to say.''

Iron Eyes slapped his hands together and paced, head down thoughtfully. ''His empire is falling apart. How preoccupied would you be? It's like a stock raiser whose cattle begin to disappear one a day—and he can't stop the thefts.''

''But if he doesn't do something, his entire empire is going to be stolen.'' Ree rumbled. ''And we'll be looking right down the barrel of Ngen's blasters. And when we look behind those, there won't be any souls in the eyes of the enemies.''

Aboard *Deus* accelerating for Tryst.

Ngen leaned back amid his cushions and clapped his hands. A white-bearded man stepped from behind the Arcturian fabric hanging at the back of the room. He stood, waiting, dull-eyed despite his fit body.

''Bring me two brandies!'' Ngen snapped. Then he looked toward the hatch and watched it slide open.

She entered with a stately poise, blue eyes glittering with excitement as she moved gracefully across the floor. She stopped in the middle of the room, uncertain, seeing him reclining on the huge overstuffed pillows. Ngen bowed his head, smile gracious.

"I am most honored, Messiah." M'Klea Alhar nodded, eyes cool. "I thought your invitation but flattery on Arpeggio."

Ngen laughed heartily. "I never flatter, dear M'Klea. No one saw you leave?"

She shook her head, absorbing her surroundings with approving eyes. "I followed your instructions to the letter, Messiah. I assume you have your reasons. I accepted that."

"Please," he smiled. "Sit here, next to me." He patted the pillow. "You're audacious, my dear. I find that attractive in a woman."

She lowered herself demurely next to him, blue eyes leveled on his. He could see her pulse racing under her firm, white skin. He allowed himself the pleasure of visually devouring her, taking in the contours of her face, letting his gaze caress the curves of her breasts, the flat, firm belly which led down to the feminine V so delightfully accentuated by her dress. In Arpeggian fashion, her skirts went down to her ankles yet didn't hide the toned flesh of thighs and calves. Ngen's desire strengthened.

"I have asked you here to talk business," Ngen said as the slave entered, two brandies on his silver tray. Ngen handed one to her, noticing the poise of her long slender fingers on the glass stem. The slave disappeared behind the hanging.

"Business, Messiah?" her voice was cultured, feminine, alluring.

He paused as she delicately sipped at the corner of her brandy. Her tongue darted lightly along her full lips. Ngen nodded and she caught his movement, eyes questioning.

"What would you give to be an empress, M'Klea Alhar?" He caught the flicker in her eyes, the sudden sharpening. "What would it be worth to you to be the most powerful woman in the galaxy?"

"I don't understand?"

She was playing with him! The pools of her incredible blue eyes taunted from behind the veil of her thoughts. In all his life, no woman had ever dared him so!

"Oh, come, M'Klea." Ngen waved her protest down. "I

watched you at your father's court. You are not the image of sweetness and innocence you pretend. You are really a very brilliant young lady, versed, to be sure, at playing Arpeggian games of propriety, but cunning nonetheless.''

She stiffened. "I will not hear your insolent remarks! You speak to the House of Alhar. I am a lady . . .''

"You are nothing!" Ngen roared, seeing her jerk back from the unaccustomed violence of his outburst.

"I will have you know that on Arpeggio I could have you shot for that!" she hissed, eyes burning with stifled rage.

"Excellent!" Ngen cried, clasping his hands in anticipation. "You are all I expected . . . more. A spoiled, grasping young woman whose only goal is her own betterment. You have an unbridled spirit, my dear. I find that incredibly attractive.''

"My brother would kill you.''

To her credit, she hadn't spilled a single drop during the entire exchange. Ngen clapped his hands. The slave walked out from behind the hanging. "I present you a slave, M'Klea. He is yours, take him. He will obey any order you give him. Even unto placing his hand in fire until the meat cooks from the bone.''

She studied the blank-eyed man before turning to look at Ngen, face a blend of curiosity and controlled confusion. "Why? What is your purpose, Messiah?''

"I'm trying to find what you would pay to be empress.'' Ngen shrugged. "What would you give for unlimited power? What would you give to be my consort? What is your price?''

She looked up at the slave, stalling, considering her options. Cool and careful, Ngen studied her profile, rapt.

"Who is he?''

"May I present Colonel Ben Mason, of the Patrol ship of Line *Gregory* in which you now reside. You see, I have already given you a Patrol colonel as your personal body servant.'' Ngen waited happily for her next move.

She was appraising him with interest now. "You are serious, aren't you? You've stirred my curiosity. Why me?'' A trim eyebrow lifted, interest swirling the cerulean pools of her eyes.

He waved, an amused smile on his lips. "Silly reasons—and some not so trite. In the first place, you are one of the most perfectly beautiful women I have ever seen. Perfectly suitable to a god like me. Secondly, you are of House Alhar—the closest thing to nobility left in the galaxy with the possible exception of the monarchy on New Maine. I, Ngen Van Chow, a prostitute's son, a dock rat and a nobody, would possess a woman from the noble House of Alhar. You are audacious, willing to take a gamble—as you did the day I walked into your father's house. You are here. Proof enough. You haven't fawned at my feet yet. You have just the right amount of indignation at some of my slurs—yet you haven't let it get the best of you. No, M'Klea, from the day I saw you on Arpeggio, I hoped you might be worthy of me. You avoided the traps—like the Temple. You are as pragmatic as I am myself. Incidentally, I appreciate you sending your father to Temple. He's been most tractable for you since.''

"So you think I'm worthy of you?" A secret smile played at the corners of her lips.

"What would you give?" Ngen's expression remained bland. "You have everything I need and desire in a woman. And if my analysis of your personality is correct, you would sell your soul for what I have to offer."

Voice even, she remarked, "Torkild would kill you if he even suspected what you have just suggested."

Ngen laughed, startling her. "Of course, dear M'Klea. You do always have that option. I suspect you'd sacrifice your adoring brother on a whim should I annoy you. You see, my dear, that is precisely why I gave you the Colonel. My power is such that if you ever try anything so foolish as pitting your brother against me, you shall not only have Colonel Mason, but also your entire family as personal body servants."

She took the measure of his certainty from his expression and settled back into the cushions. This time, she didn't sip the brandy daintily. She cocked her head slightly. "And if I accept your proposal, what is mine? Arpeggio?"

"You may have a dozen worlds if you wish them. All of space will be yours to rule at my side. Yours will be the power of life and death. You may go anywhere, anytime, and do anything. Think of those primping rivals which were yours on Arpeggio. If you wished, you could smother them in jewels or drown them in the rarest perfumes." Ngen tilted his head back, waiting as his words sank in.

She was still thinking. "What couldn't I do?"

Ngen didn't hesitate. "I will make you die most horribly

if you ever take another man to bed. And you will not interfere with my women!''

She met his threat with level eyes. ''That is all?''

''That is all. What will you give for power, wealth, and
me?'' He reached over to run light fingers down the smooth
fabric clinging to her leg.

She reached over to brush his hand aside before she stood
and paced out over the svee moss, stopping to study the
remains of Colonel Mason. ''How do you do this? Turn the
colonel into such a lump of clay? Is it the same process
you're using in the Temples?''

''It is accomplished by means of a very sophisticated
psych technique. That is the strength of my power. Moscow
Sector will be mine within a month.'' He watched her
keenly. ''Arpeggio has just begun the process. That is indeed the purpose of the Temples . . . and why I'm glad you
avoided that temptation.''

She nodded slowly. ''I wondered about that. Not even
Torkild had any idea of why you said that.''

''I don't consider it desirable that my Arpeggian captains
know these things. It could cause serious trouble when I
need them most. I make sure they never return home—even
to the point of resupplying them en route to their destina-
tions. Their families are kept mildly psyched for any subspace transductions—as you no doubt noticed about your
father, Afid.''

She turned and fingered her chin pensively. ''You could
have psyched me and taken me any way you wanted. Why
give me the chance? What if I refuse? Psych?''

''No, I will let you go free. Of course, no one will ever
believe anything you say about me—and by the time you are
back on Arpeggio, it won't matter anyway. But I give you
my word you will be unaffected by psych.''

''Only so I can live with the memory of what I turned
down?''

''Your brother never understood the depths of your intelligence.''

M'Klea laughed again, truly enjoying the situation. ''All
that, for me,'' she mused, a glow of satisfaction warming
her soft skin. She took a deep breath, swelling her high
breasts.

Ngen motioned the slave away. The man left for the hang-
ings. ''I've never known another woman who interested me
the way you do. There was a Romanan once, but she was

too barbaric to understand what I could offer her. You see, I despise women. I enjoy breaking them. Do you believe me?''

She walked idly, hands behind her, lost in thought. ''Yes. I do. I respect that quality in you. You see, in a way, I did the same with young men. The more they desired me, the more I could lure them on—until I lured them into Torkild's hands. You might say it was one of the few pleasures allowed me. How do *you* do it?'' She cocked her head inquisitively, eyes challenging.

Ngen accessed his personal comm as M'Klea turned to watch, gasping slightly as an image of Ngen formed on the monitor. Below his naked body, a woman writhed and moaned. Ngen's smooth cooing voice teased, truly tender, as he brought her to a bursting height of passion.

''The piece of machinery you see on her temples is the psych machine. In this particular instance, the young woman perceived in her mind that I was her father. At the same time, the fear response is dampened by electromagnetic waves—her body responds as it naturally would. Of course, she feels the sensations uninhibited. In the process, I've become somewhat of an expert on human anatomy. No lover could give her the pleasure I do.''

When he was finished, he stood, leaving her heaving body wet with sweat as she gasped for air. M'Klea could see the horror in the woman's eyes. The wretched woman broke into tears, curling into a defenseless ball, whimpering softly to herself.

''You see,'' Ngen explained offhandedly, ''the trick is to make them despise themselves. Accept a human as being composed of mind and body. Normally, these are a unified whole, just as you or I at the present moment.

''There's an art to what you have just seen. I first degrade them by sexual possession. Nothing difficult in that, men have been doing so for millennia. The art, however, comes in constantly possessing them so they derive great pleasure from my actions. As their flesh comes to crave me, their minds recoil with a powerful hatred which is initially directed at me. However, as they find I control their physical selves—and their bodies can be trained through simple conditioned response—they turn that hatred against themselves and internalize all of their disgust and degradation. It destroys them.''

Curious at the excitement in her eyes, he showed her

scenes of numerous broken women. He quickly noticed the increase in her breathing, the proud breasts straining the fabric across her chest. A tinge of pink had begun to glow at the base of her throat. He stopped at one, a dark-haired, olive-skinned, muscular girl who glared hatefully from the screen.

"She is your only potential rival, M'Klea. You're looking at Susan Smith Andojar—the Romanan I was talking about. She's still alive, and I fear I might have to kill her before I can ever capture her again. I really don't think you'll ever need to worry. She's too passionately determined to kill me. If I ever get her again, it will only be to destroy her like the others."

M'Klea nodded. "I always wondered about men like you, Messiah. Even in the cloistered protection of Arpeggian society, we hear of such things. You don't seem near the mindless deviant we were taught to believe in. You're definitely not demented. But why show me all that?" Her lips curled wryly. "Another test? An attempt to make me run screaming?"

"Please," he waved his sincerity. "Messiah sounds rather stilted, don't you think? Call me Ngen, my dear.

"The reason I showed you my special hobby is so there would be no secrets between us. I wish our relationship to be built on communication." He smiled. "I desperately need to have someone in whom I can confide. It has taken me twenty years to find you. You will be my consort." He rose easily to his feet and kissed her lightly on the mouth.

"*If* I decide to take up your offer," she corrected, removing his hands from her shoulders and stepping away, profile toward him. "Do you know you are the first man who ever kissed me? Torkild killed the last man who tried."

"Please, I've had my people check. You're a virgin, M'Klea. I don't need your protestations."

"You are most deceitful. They said it was a security scan."

"Oh, they didn't lie. They just didn't tell all of the truth. I can take few chances. A great many would pay dearly to see me assassinated."

She looked up at the holo again.

"You have decided the price is right?" A black eyebrow arched. "Take off your clothes."

"That is forward," she told him hesitantly. "No man has seen my body since my father raised my blankets to see if his newborn child was a boy or a girl." Her blue eyes held his, heating desire as his blood pounded. He could smell her delicate scent, see her breasts rising as she breathed.

"Is the price right?" he asked huskily. "I offer you the universe if you will take off your clothes. I guarantee you, it will be a pleasurable experience. As you just observed, I have a great deal of talent with a woman's body."

Her fingers trembled as they rose to her dress. Ngen's heart skipped, blood rushing in his ears. He'd begun to sweat with anticipation. He swallowed nervously as the layers drifted to the floor in soft billows until at last she stood before him. He heard himself sigh as he let his fingers trace her body. His loosened robe dropped.

Her eyes centered on his maleness and she smiled in satisfaction. He eased her down onto the pillows, kissing her on the neck and breasts—short of breath for the first time in years. His flesh burned, her body cool against his.

"Why now?" she whispered as he parted her alabaster legs with a dark knee.

Ngen shivered as he ran his hands down her body. "My med techs gave you a complete physical, dear M'Klea, you're at the height of ovulation . . . fertile, my dear. You are more than ready to conceive my child."

She moaned as he entered her.

CHAPTER XXIII

Tactical planning room aboard *Bullet*.

"We've got to do something." Ree rubbed his eyebrows with a knobby thumb, refusing to stare at the holos Neal had sent through coded transduction. "Spider curse it, look at them! They're everywhere, in every station and planet in Ngen's back lines! Hordes, that's what. Like in the old-time Confederate novels. Hordes."

Around them, coffee cups, piled flimsies, report segments, and a litter of comm records lay stacked. One entire wall depicted a holo map of Ngen's holding, different colored lights flickering to indicate Father territory—and that suspected of falling.

Iron Eyes swallowed hard, looking into the mindless eyes of the Fathers as they charged a squad of Iversons's marines. Something in his gut twisted, some sickness of soul eating at him. "Once they killed the commander, nothing changed. Did you notice? As long as the officer gave orders, they responded superbly, adapting to the situation. He could change strategies. Now they keep coming."

"But these are *trained* soldiers, John. You can see the advance they're making on Neal's people. It's a damn Sirian battle tactic—executed flawlessly. The only thing that saved Neal's people is that they'd seen it before on Sirius, knew a counterattack that broke them. The important thing here is that they had to kill the Fathers right down to the last man. The last man! John, these people won't break at the sight of a Romanan. You've got to kill every Spider-cursed one of them!"

Iron Eyes stood, fingering his chin as he watched the holo play out until the final Father stood alone, firing. Marines called for his surrender, but he continued to shoot, deaf to their pleas. Blaster fire took him in the chest, sending his exploded body cartwheeling. Romanans in white combat armor advanced to take up the Fathers' positions along the curve of the station, dispatching the wounded, pausing to take coup. The reconnaissance continued past men and women who never looked up from their chores—working machines like machines. The dead feeling in Iron Eyes' chest expanded. How did he fight something like this? Where did a warrior find honor in facing an opponent who'd already died in all but body.

With a mental command through his headset, he reversed the holo to the fight scene, freezing the action just before the last Father had been blown apart. For a long moment Iron Eyes stared into the man's passionless eyes.

"How could Ngen . . . What sort of man is he?" Iron Eyes asked thickly. "And we thought Skor a monster? He'd never do this."

Ree continued to rub his eyebrows, unable to look up. A haggard look had come to replace the hard lines of the Admiral's face, a puffiness about the cheeks. Where he'd once walked crisply, he now pushed loose-limbed—a man driving a body that cried for rest. They all looked that way: too many hours coordinating the logistics, adapting commercial machinery and transport, trying to build a battle fleet across three disorganized Sectors of space.

The monitors in the tactical room flickered, some with figures, stats, and the other necessaries of running a ship like *Bullet,* the others with reports. The white walls of the ship mocked him, a tomb from which he'd never escape. Even the air had grown stuffy—an illusion. He knew the magic of the atmosphere plant. Only this air, no matter how treated, didn't carry the fragrance of freedom; only the reminder of endless hours of despair and plans and counter-plans to fight an enemy they didn't understand.

Iron Eyes poked his finger on the dispenser button, claiming yet another cup of coffee to jangle his already jittery nerves. He rubbed his jaw and sipped at the coffee, feeling his stomach roil at the bitter acids. Everything had gone stale. And Rita? Gone. Out there with Ngen's monsters. Alone. Beyond his protection.

"We can kill them by the hundreds," Iron Eyes decided, sprawling loose-limbed in the chair across from Ree. "Neal's people proved it. Outnumbered two to one, they didn't take a single casualty. The problem lies in the numbers Ngen can send against us, not in the quality of troops he can muster."

Ree bent his neck back and winced, face contorting against the pull of his tired muscles. "That's the scary thing. We can't train warriors fast enough—not unless we stoop to psyching people like he's doing—assuming Pike figured out how the machine in the Temple works. If Pike is sane when he comes to."

Iron Eyes stared into the black coffee, watching the rings undulate concentrically. "I . . ." A part of him felt corrupted.

"Yes?"

"Damen, I *can't* lead soldiers who've been . . . well, look at 'em!" Coffee in hand, he waved it at the holo. "Not like them. I'll send my soul to Spider first."

"I only wish I could argue with you. I really do. It would save us. Only how does a man with a conscience pay *that* kind of cost? How do you live with yourself? Huh? How?"

In the long silence that stretched, Ree chewed on his thumb. "It's the rate he's expanding at. I can't . . . Damn, how do we hit him? Slow him down? His jihad gets more powerful every day. Where did he move his manufacturing? He doesn't seem to lose momentum. Why do people keep flocking to him? It's obvious he's a monster, a . . ."

Exasperated, Ree slapped his hands on the chair arms.

"People are lost, Damen. They seek and he offers protection, a direction, security. He speaks to their empty souls—not their rational minds. his promise of stability soothes in these times of trouble."

"We've sent our reports out on open channels. All he does is claim it's propaganda—a tactic to show how low we've stooped." Ree blinked and gestured, "That dirty son of septic spit looks right into the monitor and says, 'What horrible Satan spawn could claim such of the son of God? See? See what the Great Satan of the Directorate has become? Only we shall turn their words against them. Look into my eyes and tell me the servants of Deus would commit abominations?' And more innocents flock to his damn Temples! More riots break out against us! Damn it, he's got a network of agents we're only beginning to perceive."

"I think I've found Chester. Mark Reesh says he's up in a cave in the Bear Mountains." A longing pulled at Iron Eyes. The Bear Mountains. He could almost feel the breeze on his cheek, the smell of the knifebush and bayonet grass. But now he could only see a total of four meters to the opposite wall.

Ree straightened, a spark of enthusiasm lighting his weary features for the first time. "Praise be the name of Spider! Can you talk to him? See if he'll do a series of propaganda spots for us? Maybe, just maybe, if we could fight Ngen's Deus with a Prophet, then they could see him predict the future, and . . . and who could stand against him? That's why Ngen gets a foothold. People *really* think he's a damned Messiah!"

Iron Eyes looked warily at his friend. "I get nervous with Prophets."

"I get desperate thinking about Ngen."

Iron Eyes nodded, the discontent in his soul stirring something foul. He looked up at the holo, watching the lifeless humans Ngen had left at Habber's Star. "In the eyes of Spider, they're an abomination."

"And we'll end up that way if Chester doesn't do something about it." Ree emphasized his words with a pointing finger.

Iron Eyes sighed, the dull place in his soul churning. And Rita was out there—with the likes of those? "I'll see if I can find Chester."

* * *

Aboard _Spider's Revenge_ boosting for jump to World.

"*. . . Pleasure, my sweet Susan. You can't resist pleasure as I take your body . . . use your ecstasy against you.*" Ngen's voice drifted down from the foggy black. She cowered, bracing herself against the mold-streaked plaster wall, her breath caught in her throat. The wall across from her ghosted into whirling wreaths of inky smoke. Which way? The hallway vanished in the swirling air. The rolling darkness closed in on her.

She jumped, feeling one of Ngen's hands close on her in the dark. Desperately, she attempted to kick his faceless shape away. Only the wall, which had meant security moments before, trapped her, some evil sort of EM restraint that bound her tightly as Ngen began stroking her, teasing the erotic centers of her warming body."

"No!" she screamed into the darkness. "Damn you, Ngen. *I killed you!*"

His supple fingers sent shivers down her flesh. "*You can't resist me, dearest Susan. You know that in your heart. You're coming to me . . . coming . . . Someday soon, you'll be mine again . . .*"

Frantically, she struck out, twisting, fighting the clinging walls in violent panic.

She jerked awake when she slammed into the floor. The impact of her body tripped the sensors, flooding her little cabin with light. Dumbly, she stared owl-eyed at the deck plating before her smarting nose, feeling the soft vibrations, the gentle hum of the ship. Above her, the bed had been devastated by her thrashing.

"Damn it!" She smacked a fist into hard graphsteel, struggling to catch her breath as she sat up, weblike strands of disheveled hair falling over her face in a black net. Wet with icy sweat, she stood, stumbling into the shower and palming the spray.

"Damn you, Ngen." She dressed, trying to integrate her desperate thoughts. The brief flush of victory had melted, leaving only Ngen . . . and the dreams.

The tray of food she'd been too tired to eat lay on the little table, cold, unappetizing. She drew a cup of hot coffee and began forcing cold bites past resisting lips, eating strictly to maintain her strength. The growl in her stomach eased as she finished off the tray and refilled her coffee.

The tape she'd taken from Mikros' comm lay there, no

more than an innocuous black disc. A Pandora's box of Ngen. What horror would she unleash if she watched it? What would it tell her of Pike? Did she really want to know?

After several long minutes of consideration, she picked it up. The plastic lay cool in her fingers, frightening despite its size. She hesitated again, looking at the slot for the converter. Just drop it in and . . . She bit her lip as she slid it into the comm. She sipped at her coffee, watching Pike and Reesh carried in, stripped, searched, and bound to the pallets. Pallas entered.

After several minutes she discarded her coffee and poured a stiff whiskey. Then another—and another. By the time she watched her holo-self burst in past that fat slob of a Governor, the glass was empty again; she felt sober as a Prophet.

They should have taken Pallas and fed him to a rock leech so he could die in slow, festering agony rather than by the merciful, quick thrust of a knife he'd received at the hands of Sam Iron Eyes Smith. If they'd only known what a monster he was.

Susan sucked air into her lungs, forcing her squirming mind to rerun segments of the grisly record. Brutalizing herself into listening to Ngen Van Chow's soothing, friendly voice again, she watched her soft anthropologist, so wracked by pain, resist their perverted persuasion, horrified as the human abomination slowly chewed Pike's flesh.

"Spider? Damn them, I . . ." She shook her head frantically, blinking her eyes and clenching her fists. When she looked up, the tape continued to run the same unbelievable hell. She bent close to the monitor, listening as Ngen cooed about dark-haired Romanan women. Her mouth watered with the urge to vomit.

"S-Susan?" Pike's rasping voice called.

She clamped her eyes shut, the room oddly distant. Through comm she stopped the program, gutted by the anguish in that one word.

She shivered, wondering if the best solution wouldn't be to simply adjust the med unit so he drifted off to sleep, never to wake again.

"And he called on me. Damn him. He knew the risks. He knew. And he saved me. He and Reesh while I should have been in charge. He . . ." The sour bile of shame rose from her grinding stomach, rank in the back of her throat.

She filed the tape under her personal code and stood, straightening her uniform. She frowned at the whiskey glass, wanting another bracer, deciding against it. Reluctantly, she palmed the hatch and turned down the corridor. The modifications they'd performed had left the vessel a patchwork—the gleaming Patrol white marred by irregular plates and powerlead ducting.

A construction—like my soul. Spider alone knows how the ship or I will hold up in the final test. He called on me.

Hospital consisted of a tiny room cramped against the bulge of the main reactor shielding. The roof curved down like a shell. With room for four med units, they'd crammed a fifth in for good measure. Despite the closeness, someone might live as a result. One unit held the Prophet, alive, unconscious, a pained expression on his thin, sensitive face. Three more waited vacant, spotlesss, powerlead running into the rounded shells, the monitors silent. And in the first lay Pike.

The tech nodded from where she sat, a manual in her hands, all the monitors for her patients readily visible.

Pike lay supine—a backward turtle caricature in the gleaming white carapace of the med unit. He blinked as she approached, conscious. He didn't move, face a grimly pale mask. Susan leaned against the med next to him, struggling to finally say, "How are you feeling?"

He didn't look in her direction. Only a tightening of his mouth indicated he'd heard.

"I'm sorry it took so long to put together a rescue. We worked as fast as we could. If I had to do it all over again I'd . . ."

"Don't," he said hoarsely. "No apologies necessary." Half-vacant eyes fixed absently on some point beyond the white panels overhead.

She stared at the floor through the narrow tunnel of hanging hair, arms crossed tightly, feet and legs pressed together. "We killed Pallas and that . . . that *thing*. If we'd understood at the time, we'd have saved them, made them . . ."

"It doesn't matter," he mumbled. "Not after what she . . ." He clamped his eyes shut, throat working as he swallowed. "She . . . touched my . . . Then she. . ."

She stood silently, wishing she could say something, knowing the inside view of his tortured thoughts—how he struggled to build walls in his head. The same as she had done after she escaped Van Chow's psycho-sexual horrors. Only the walls never withstood the pressure, no matter how

the mental mortar got mixed, or how cunningly the stone-
work was laid. The props would give eventually and it all
would come crashing down in rubble while the hideous gibbering memories flooded loose to destroy you.

And he called out for me! *Damn you, Ngen. Damn you
for playing with human minds. You're filth, Van Chow. A
pustule in the psyche of all humanity.*

"The reason's there," her voice was soft. "I found it
after he'd . . . he was done with me. Ngen twisted my brain
and body, too." She'd begun rubbing her hands together
nervously, the motion jerky. "You shared the horror. You
know why I . . . Giorj was there for me to talk to."

She glanced at him, uncertain, frightened by what she'd
admitted. He continued to stare soullessly at the panels.

She kept her voice calm despite the undertow of emotions. "I'm here if you need me. Call any time. The dreams
will come. I learned that it helps to just have someone close.
Remember what you did for me? I . . . I'd like to . . . Pike,
I'm here. Remember that."

She pushed upright off the med unit, waiting for him to
speak, to say anything.

He moistened his mouth, the corners of his eyes drawn
tight. "The dreams already come. They're . . . inside. Can't
. . . can't close my eyes. The psych . . . That woman . . ."
His voice broke in a choked sob and he closed his eyes, a
single tear tracing down the side of his face and into the
hair of his sideburns.

She reached out and gave his shoulder a firm squeeze.
"Call if you need me," she repeated.

Her legs moved with all the grace of lead as she made
her way around vacant units. With a nod of the head, she
motioned the tech outside. Her gut churned, the undigested
dinner like a weight, a sodden lump in her stomach.

"What's his condition?" The whole thing rattled her—
Pike's courage, her guilt, the intimate hell he suffered. And
Ngen preyed at the edges of her mind, waiting, out there
somewhere just beyond the safe walls of the ship.

The woman shrugged. "We're deferring some processes
like full electro-stim and polymerase injections until he sta-
bilizes. We'd like to let him settle down a little first before
attempting a psych adjustment."

"No!" Susan barked firmly. "That's a direct order, Corporal. They already played with a psych machine—killed
Reesh with it. Romanan reaction, the worst kind. Body tore

itself apart. Then they used that same machine to threaten Pike. You understand?''

The tech nodded soberly. "Pike's not Romanan. Any psych will—"

"Did you hear me, Corporal?"

"Yes, ma'am. I'll log your orders so there's no misunderstanding of responsibility."

Susan hesitated, eyes slitting. No, the corporal was only covering her ass. Just in case. "Further, any developments—and I do mean *any*—will be reported to me immediately."

"Yes, ma'am."

"How's his leg? How long until he walks again?" Susan's hot stare drifted toward the hatch.

The tech consulted her monitor. "He'll have regenerated most of his leg muscles within six weeks if he doesn't lapse. We've got the infection under control. He needs to spring back emotionally before we start adding chemicals to stimulate the growth nodes in the DNA. Nevertheless, the damage isn't as severe as a blaster wound for example, where bone has to be regenerated. The basic muscular structure is still there. His toes will grow at about the same rate as his calf muscles.

"His superficial burns will be healed within days. He suffered some damage to his eyes which we'll treat later; evidently they almost forced them out of their sockets. The trauma to his genitals might be a little more complicated. He doesn't know yet, but we removed the remaining testicle and are regenerating it and a clone. Internally, he's got a couple of hemorrhages of the colon, kidneys, liver, and a bruised heart. They worked him over pretty good before they started dismembering. In places, sonic nerve damage will take a while to heal.

"All in all, we could have him out of the machine in three weeks if you absolutely need him. Captain, be aware that reactivating his status that soon will cause some permanent damage. I'd like to keep him longer so all the tissue can knit properly and we can keep track of sequelae. We're going to need some therapy, too. A number of motor nerves must be regenerated and skills reacquired. In essence, he's got to learn to walk all over again. As to the pudic nerves? They ran a considerable current up through the sacral plexus. The damage . . . well, it might have gone all the way to the brain.''

"So he's not going to die?"

"Not from the torture. He isn't in critical danger from his physical wounds."

"You look reserved."

"I said from his physical wounds, Captain. What's going on in his head? Well, that's a different story. Without the psych to—"

"No way."

"Then I can't take responsibility for his recovery or mental health after that." The tech crossed her arms, head cocked.

"Six weeks," Susan mused. "Have you told him?"

"Yes, but he didn't seem to hear," the tech said uneasily.

Susan pinned the corporal with her gaze. "That man just survived something which should have left him nothing more than quivering protoplasm. You *will* keep that in mind."

"Yes, ma'am."

Susan shot a worried look in at Pike and left to take her watch on the bridge.

Deep in the Bear Mountains on World.

The click of a steel shoe on granite echoed hollowly up the rocky trail.

Chester smiled serenely. He'd enjoyed the cave—the solitude. The visitor, for all his mental turmoil, would be welcome. A bear inhabited the valley and often stopped to stare up at the lone man who perched at the cave mouth. This day, the bear had traveled higher up the grassy bottoms in search of the less skittish green harvesters that lived in the upper meadows, aware the visitor came. Bears did that for Prophets where they'd lie in wait for another man. Exactly why remained a secret of the bears.

Across the valley, creeping shadows deepened on the rounded outcrops of worn granite. Stark against the cooling sky, the rock above continued to radiate the red heat of the dying day. Fall had come, all World changing before the cold rains pelted the land. Here, so high, snow would fall soon, draining the emerald green of the grasses into golden tan.

Chester turned, bending to look down the trail.

The black mare climbed the last steps up the trail, whickering gently as she blew.

"Old One?"

"Here."

The rider stepped off, grabbing up the mare's reins in a strong right hand to lead her higher.

Chester tilted his head, smiling a warm greeting. The big man waited awkwardly, head bowed in respect. A hand blaster hung from the use-polished leather at his hip while a heavy rifle balanced by the action in his scarred left hand. The glazed leather shirt sported a dark spider design. Silky black coups lined his belt, flicking this way and that in the breeze until they almost hid the long Romanan fighting knife. The leather grips had been stained black from sweat and blood.

"War Chief, you don't need to stand like a boy caught playing in the manure. You and I, we're old friends." Chester waved a languid hand to a rock next to him. "Relax and refresh yourself. I don't want you to hesitate or act respectful. Be yourself."

Iron Eyes shifted uneasily.

"Oh, come." Chester laughed gently. "Just between the two of us, Prophets adopt mysterious ways to keep from being pestered all the time by people wanting to know what's going to happen to them.

"Here, sit. Enjoy the sunset. Beautiful, isn't it? Look at those spectacular clouds over the peaks. How many colors would you say?"

Iron Eyes ground-reined the mare and lowered himself uneasily to the rock Chester indicated. He turned nervous eyes to the western sky and squinted. "All the colors that are, I'd say, Old One."

Chester chuckled to himself, rocking back and forth on his blanket, knees tucked to his chest. "Yes, John. All the colors. Sit for a while now. Just watch the night fall . . . and listen to the quiet. There's peace here for your soul. Take this little bit of tranquillity—make it one with you. Feed your spirit for just this eternal moment. Spider knows, you may not have many more opportunities in the days ahead."

Iron Eyes shifted nervously, gazing out over the peaks. The last sentinels of the Bear Mountains guarded the way to the plains and the sea beyond. A cool breeze drifted down the canyon, a gentle touch of night tracing around them as the evening settled, graying the view across the rocky canyon wall.

Finally, in the growing darkness, Chester sighed, shuf-

fling on his blanket, lighting one of the Sirian lamps with
the press of a button. He smiled pleasantly. "Magic."

"Electricity," Iron Eyes corrected. "We've had lights in
the Ship for six hundred years."

"But that also takes a generator. I've seen the generator,
John. A big thing that hums and jumps while it runs. This
lamp is a little thing. I can carry it anywhere—and it always
works."

"The generator is just smaller, Old One."

Chester's broad face creased with a smile. "You will stop
calling me Old One." He raised a hand. "Don't protest.
It's your cusp. What you do in public is your business—but
here, tonight, and when we're alone, I'm just your cousin,
Chester."

Iron Eyes nodded, looking around the cave that gaped
behind the Prophet's blanket. Roomy and spacious, a man
could stand easily. Holo cubes, blankets, and assorted bun-
dles of grass and staples dangled on twine hung from nails
driven into the rock. The rear of the cave disappeared into
the blackness, hidden by lumpy twists of the walls. The
sand on the floor had been raked into curious, but pleasing,
geometric patterns. A firepit contained kindling and stacked
polewood sections, neatly cut by a laser. More "magic?"

"A nice place. I envy you."

Chester nodded, getting to his feet and playing the hand
laser on the kindling. Flames began crackling up. "You
needed time to yourself, John. That's why I let you ride out
here. You've been missing the opportunity to be with your
mare, to sit by the light of a fire and watch the stars come
out. It will be a delightful night. For now, the moons are
down. No clouds will obscure the stars. I've got a couple
of steaks here in this cooler. And I picked mellonbush this
morning. In this pan is Romanan tea. And coffee is here in
this pot for later, after we sit and drink scotch and talk like
in the old times.

"Too much changes too fast. For that reason, any way to
prolong the old times—to keep them fresh in the mind—is
to be pursued. Change cannot be stopped, but we must never
forget who we have been, who we are, or who we will become. Everything runs together. Past, present, future. Our
souls are the product of all those—and now I find out time
and space and perception are all expressions of the same
thing?"

Iron Eyes chuckled. "A man should know better than to

try and surprise a Prophet. I suppose you know I was pre-occupied and left Settlement without packing anything? So many things. I'm lucky I remembered my rifle."

"Worry isn't good for you, John. I know how much you've been taking on yourself—you and Ree. I know your mind, War Chief." Chester smiled. "I don't bias the future by telling you that she's alive. Nor will I lie to you and tell you she'll be safe . . . too many cusps. She's a warrior. War involves an incredible number of cusps, so many little things. All the way down to whether or not a man takes time to look down, wondering if he buttoned the fly on his pants. But then, you knew that. There's risk out there. Trials for her. In some visions, she comes home. In others? We are all in Spider's web."

Iron Eyes nodded, eyeing Chester as he placed steaks on spits over the rosy polewood fire. "No, Old—Chester—I didn't come to ask about Rita. The Admiral and I—"

"Hush, Iron Eyes." Chester smiled happily. "I know why you're here. I also know that you won't get my answer until you step into the stirrup tomorrow morning to ride back to the Settlement. Knowing that, you and I can relax and enjoy each other's company, forgetting all the problems and all the troubles we face. Like the sunset, let us enjoy this night. Such times are passing, War Chief, so they must be savored. Here, have this cup of tea."

Iron Eyes nodded, seeing the black mare standing at the edge of the firelight. "One moment. I saw a spring down there. The water is good?"

"Excellent. The grass is thick. I chase the green harvesters away to keep it that way."

He stood, walking out to uncinch the saddle and dump it with his pack. He unhooked the bridle and clipped the lead rope to her halter, leading her down to the pool under the cave. Iron Eyes tied her off where she could drink, eat, and not get too tangled in the picket rope.

The black mare flicked soft lips at his hand. Finding nothing, she butted him roughly before snuffling. He grabbed her by the neck, scratching her ears, laughing. The mare pulled loose, shaking her head, and stepping to one side to crop at the grass.

He bent his head back, sniffing the scented air of World. The Prophet knew. He'd needed this night, needed the chance to find his centering point. The Fathers had been taking too much of his soul. The constant planning and

training. The horror of those mindless eyes in the holos.
One day, he'd have to face the ghouls over a blaster. The
thought chilled him deep inside. High overhead, the familiar constellations twinkled, a brief flare marking the path of
an orbiting spacecraft accelerating. World filled him, soothing a disgruntled place within, anxiety draining with the
breath from his lungs.

For the first time in days, the tension ebbed from his tired
body. He smiled up at at the orange glow of Chester's cave
and turned his suddenly light steps up the trail, whistling a
song he'd learned on Sirius.

Dawn shot yellow beams of light down the canyon to set
the pink granite ablaze in red-orange pastels while the shadows lay in purple-blue streaks behind the exfoliated shoulders of the slopes. Knifebush stippled the hard rock, clinging
to each fracture and crack. Grass looked vibrantly light
green in the bottoms, while here and there a green harvester
paddled along on its six stubby legs, raking the vegetation
into its mouth.

Chester walked out with a last steaming cup of coffee as
Iron Eyes settled the saddle pad on the mare's back. He
lifted the saddle, dropping it just so with practiced ease.
The mare stood obediently while he snatched up the cinches
and snugged them. Then he turned to gratefully take the
coffee and look up the valley where the sun crested the backbone of the mountains.

"A cycle," Chester added humbly. "Dusk to Dawn. People lose a lot when they look beyond that simple truth."

Iron Eyes nodded wistfully. "I'm afraid so. But some of
us must make sure we can have the freedom to see even this
far. Ngen makes armies of soulless people. To me, Chester,
they're an abomination."

The Prophet nodded, lacing brown fingers over his stomach. "To Spider, they're an abomination. A violation of one
of his few laws. Of free will."

Iron Eyes cocked his head thoughtfully. Placing his foot
in the stirrup, he swung up, looking down into the Prophet's
eyes—a measure of how far he'd come the night before.
"We need you, Chester. The Admiral sent me to see if
you'd come to *Bullet*. We need you to speak to all humanity.
A Prophet has to tell the galaxy about Ngen's false Deus
and . . ."

Chester smiled as he slowly shook his head, a bittersweet

twist to his lips. "It isn't my cusp, Iron Eyes. I cannot compromise free will. Not even for humans . . . who fascinate and preoccupy me in my studies. No, you need someone stronger than me. And if he dies in the meeting of his cusp, well, then you have only yourselves. I . . . I made my choice once . . . chose the cusp which will lead me along the path I now follow."

"Chester, you don't understand the gravity of—"

A tanned hand rose. "I see all of your arguments . . . your desperation. I must do what I must. I think you understand."

Iron Eyes nodded, drinking the last of the coffee and handing the cup back with a tender smile. "As I did in the Santos camp of Big Man so long ago. I think I understand. And Chester, thank you for last night. I feel better about life today. I'd started to lose . . . Well, you know."

Chester Armijo Garcia watched the big man turn his black mare and ease her down the trail to the grassy canyon below.

Iron Eyes waved once as he kicked the mare to a trot.

Chester smiled, collecting his pots and pans and walking down to the pool to wash them. "And when you look back, War Chief, you know just how terrible our cusps really are. It is a blessing to only see the past. It hurts so much more to see the future."

CHAPTER XXIV

Hospital aboard *Spider's Revenge*.

Darwin Pike shivered and closed his eyes. As he did, the image of the psych unit formed out of the chaos in his head. As if he were back in that gruesome place, the psych hovered crystal clear in his mind. Like some perverted fungus, it expanded—a metal obscenity to blot out the protective body of Spider. To sever him from reality—from the universe he knew and understood. He fought the urge to scream, jaws clamped until his teeth hurt.

As long as he had seen that reassuring effigy of Spider

over his head, he had managed, keeping his strength, fighting back, in spite of the pain and terror.

If only he could just scream, and scream, and scream. Scream until he'd shouted it out of his system. Scream the flashbacks out of his head—out of his soul. Or maybe he could get hold of a blaster for just a second. It wouldn't take but an instant and the pain would be gone, exploded in a blinding flash, scattered into atoms along with bits of his brain and skull. He'd have silence then, the memories darkened and dispersed forever.

He blinked and drew a deep breath, trying to still the ragged bits of his consciousness that shrieked insanely. He'd lived it. The memories were just reality—out of time synch. He lived the horror—then and now.

Susan had come, her concern important. He wished he could have looked up at her and asked if he'd finally won her respect. She'd touched his shoulder, reassuring, and, for a brief moment, the lonely fear had eased. She'd treated him as human—not as a broken piece of filth. And Reesh had said she'd cut men? Cut them like coup during the Sirian fighting?

A ghastly image of the Susan-ghoul stirred, the bloody jaws working on his severed organ. A weird gibbering fear rustled in the back of his mind. Susan? Eating his flesh? No.

"But she cut men." An image formed of Susan, eyes flashing, the knife silver, darting. A keen sting in his crotch and she rose, clutching his bleeding manhood.

A rattling sounded from Pike's constricting throat.

He tried to swallow, mouth so dry his tongue stuck. The med unit was putting him down again, he could feel his body slowing. He cried out, knowing the dreams hovered just over the horizon of consciousness. He tried to cry again, but Pallas Mikros leaned over him, the scalpel gleaming in his hand. The knife dropped. He could feel it—so real. A dripping, red part of himself was lifted free. Then came the searing of the cauterizing burn, castrating his nerves right up to the base of his brain.

His dry painful eyes locked on the woman, on the raven black waves of hair shimmering down from her head, as Pallas handed her the bloody orb. Darwin tried impossibly to shut off his vision as he watched her take his living flesh into her red mouth, roll it with her tongue and bite down. Mind in tatters, the memory grew of those relentless jaws.

The jaws ground back and forth, matching the beat of his thundering heart.

"*A woman like Tiara . . .*" Ngen whispered, voice like a velvet solvent to invade the dream, permeate it.

And the face . . . the beautiful face . . . shifted slightly, the bones thinning, the cheeks going hollow. And Susan's black hair caught the light, bluish black as she chewed.

Darwin's breath caught in his throat as Ngen cooed, "*A woman with black hair and deep, passionate eyes. A woman with silky skin. Feel it, Darwin? Feel it warm against yours? Think of her, Darwin. Think of her and how much you would like to be with her—to hold her next to you and enjoy her love.*"

And Susan looked down at him, eyes empty as she reached for him, blood shining on her lips, tracing down her chin and throat.

The scream ripped his soul, tearing the lining from his throat.

Vortex whirled the vision away in grayness. Voices. A graying of reality. Visions seen through haze.

"He's all right. Just a nightmare. Wish I could use the psych. Half the ship must have heard . . ."

Darwin drifted, sinking in a misty fog. "Wish I could use the psych . . . the psych . . . the . . ." His soul twisted away, whimpering like a wraith.

"*Be my friend,*" Ngen's voice pleaded, sending tendrils through Darwin's mind. "*There is no need for this. Your friends have sold you out. They have forgotten you. The pain can stop. This terror can stop. Simply speak to me! Prove you are worthy!*"

The gentle strains wheedled, infiltrating the root of his resistance, eroding his will bit by slow bit. With no escape, the honeyed voice levered at the corners of his mind, widening the cracks in his sanity.

The sweat running down Mikros' nose twinkled in the light, stinging as it dripped into his raw, open wounds. Ngen's voice droned, tendrils through his mind. Each second spread—an eternity. Sixty eternities led to a minute which led to an hour which led to a day and that to a week, then a month and a year and lifetime and infinity.

Kaleidoscopic flashes—the screams of Bull Wing Reesh as the psych destroyed another bright piece of Spider. He looked inward to see Bull's ghost, feeling the guilt, knowing he would forever cry. He led his friend to that despicable death. The hollow wailing of Reesh's children and widows keened in an endless echo.

Only Spider protected him, hovered over him: invincible. Then came the psych and Spider . . . Spider. . . .

Out of the whirling blackness, the future surged like stygian vomit. Around him stars flickered and went dark. An eerie moaning—the death rasps of lost billions—grew on interstellar winds to vanish, a whirlpool of misery sucked into the eternal light death of oblivion. Raising his hand to block the onslaught, he looked into ghastly revelation, an endless nightmare of twisted corpses—millions upon millions with blank eyes and moving, masticating jaws. They spiraled toward him, belched on the offal of the future, thousands of talon fingers clawing at him, seeking his unprotected flesh, nails like knives hissing out of the obscurity.

Turning, he sought to run, to escape in panic—only Susan stood before him, black hair whipped out behind her in the fetid wind. He stopped, the footing suddenly slippery on a glassy surface clotted by warm blood. He shot a quick glance down—froze, fear charging hotly up his spine—and saw only the bones of his fleshless feet sliding in the gore.

Whimpering, he looked up, too late to avoid her arms. She gripped him, strong fingers sinking into his flesh, burning his blood. She leaned forward, opening her bloody mouth. He whimpered pitifully as her teeth ripped his flesh.

Eternity wrapped around him.

A different reality. Pain.

He blinked his eyes open as another med tech checked his vision with some device that flickered lights into his eyes. The private asked him meaningless questions. Sometimes he answered. Sometimes he didn't. Damn them.

When Spider had been crushed by the psych machine, so had his will. The blank-eyed ghoul had eaten part of his soul along with his flesh. Like Ngen was eating the galaxy, stealing souls from all men. So had he taken Darwin Pike's. Now Ngen's ghoul lay dead—probably rotting—taking Pike's soul to whatever hell she'd ended up in. Only everything was hell of one sort or another. Existence consisted of suffering camouflaged by an occasional brief illusion of happiness.

Susan cut men. Reesh told me that. The whole thing was true. What Ngen said . . . based in fact.

The med tech checked the monitors, nodded to himself and stepped back.

An idea: "Did they recover my personal belongings?"

"I think they got everything."

"I had an antique knife," Pike cried, suddenly desperate. "They didn't leave that, did they? My grandfather found it in an ancient wreck! It's an heirloom! I need it!"

"Hey, easy!" The tech reassured, placing his hand on Pike's shoulder. He bent down, pulling a drawer open somewhere below. Things rattled hollowly. "Yeah, here it is. See? All safe and sound. So relax. Now I want you to take a couple of deep breaths and concentrate on healing, huh? That's the important thing now. We've got to get you back together."

"Yeah, back together. Thanks," Darwin breathed, clutching the knife to his chest. The tech winked and walked off.

Pike's wary eyes followed him to the hatch. The Alaskan smiled to himself. The med unit would keep him awake for a while. While it did, he'd give the tech a chance to relax. After that? Simple. The important part was to center the blade exactly and pull down with all his power. He had to sever the spinal chord or the med unit would monitor a lowering blood level and sound the alarm.

He watched the tech walk past the door and raised the knife, staring down his arms, realizing his eyesight fuzzed the outline of his hands and the keen blade. The grip felt firm; he hardly noticed the fingers Pallas had pulled out of joint. The Randall poised like a spear over the center of his consciousness. The time had come.

"You are satisfied with what you are sending to Spider?" a soft voice asked.

Pike froze, muscles trembling. No one shouted alarm. He worked his mouth and looked up at the keen point, arms beginning to quiver with strain. He swallowed, peering quickly to the side. The Prophet watched curiously.

"To purposely send yourself to Spider is presumptuous, don't you think? You assume you know when God wants your soul. Why do you believe you know when Spider does not? Are you smarter than God, Doctor Pike?"

"I . . . I no longer wish to . . . to live."

"A Santos once wondered whether you were worthy," The Prophet's voice softened knowingly. "How about you? Do you think you're worthy?"

"You . . . you don't know," Pike whispered, feeling tears burn at the edge of his eyes. "You weren't there to . . . You can't understand!" He sniffed at the clogging in his nose.

The Prophet smiled, nodding. "Your flesh was nothing more than cells, anthropologist. Flesh grows again. How curious that you would believe your soul one with your body. The soul is part of Spider—of God. Does that mean then, that when Sam Iron Eyes counted coup on the dying courtesan, that he killed that part of Spider which you thought had been eaten? That is a lot to happen to one little piece of Spider."

"How do you know that?" Pike stared, openmouthed. "You've been unconscious for weeks! You can't . . . can't . . . That's impossible!"

"You yourself will tell me all about the thoughts, the terrible dreams. That's a vision, Darwin. I have also seen you lying there—dead, with the knife in your neck. Another way will leave you paralyzed from the neck down as the result of a damaged spinal chord. The decision is yours—your cusp—and I cannot tell you what to do. I can tell you that as soon as Susan hears you asked for your knife, she'll take it away. The med tech has not called in his report to the Captain yet. You have a little more than a minute to kill or maim yourself, depending on how strong your resolve is, and how right you can convince yourself you are. Spider stood by you once; He would not affect your decision to turn against Him now. Spider is interested in free will. It is *your* cusp. What will you do? What will you teach Spider?" Patan's voice remained warm, friendly.

Darwin looked at the knife. He stared at the Prophet. "Does it make any difference one way or the other? Will the world cease to turn? Will anyone know I'm even gone?" He paused, bitter irony on his lips. "Will the memories or the degradation ever go away? Can . . . can I forget?"

"It would be a travesty if you ever did. None of us are here to forget, Darwin Pike. You are almost out of time. Kill yourself now if you wish. If not, do nothing . . . which is a decision in itself." Patan's limpid eyes didn't waver. Instead he smiled his support—a gesture more eloquent than words.

Darwin swallowed, feeling his heart pound. The handle of the Randall lay cool and smooth in his grip. Steady it, look along the blade . . . and crash it down hard enough to shear the cervical vertebra. It would take no more. He was strong enough, the knife sharp and deadly.

How does the Prophet know so much? What did he mean? Why would it be a travesty to forget those long hours of pain, suffering, and horror? Am I turning my back on Spider?

Calmly, Darwin Pike laid the knife down on the edge of the little tray hooked to the side of the med unit.

"Ah," Patan Andojar Garcia sighed, eyes closing as he saw something inside his head. "It is still baffling, but I have learned. You, Darwin, have taught me much as I followed your path. I have learned to let time and events flow through me. Most fascinating. One does not need to know all. To try such foolishness is vanity and blinds man to Spider's purpose. The most difficult lesson to learn is that what will be . . . will be."

The tech came rushing through the hatch, face white with fear. He saw Pike and slid to a stop, visibly relieved, sweat beaded on his brow. He breathed a sigh and walked up with more decorum. "Are you all right? I caught a glimpse in the monitor. You had the knife . . ."

Pike looked up balefully. "Am I all right? No, most of my leg was hacked off and fed to a semihuman ghoul. My body feels like it's been the centerpiece at a banquet in Hell and I'm so thirsty I could drink the Gulf of Alaska. On top of that, every time I close my eyes, I relive every bloody second of it." *Every second, you hear, you inane simpleton! Right down to Susan's . . . no. You're awake, Pike. She wasn't the ghoul. Ngen made you believe that. This isn't the dream. Reesh said . . . Susan didn't do that. Ngen . . .*

At that moment, Susan slid to a stop outside the hatch and bolted into the hospital, a grim certainty in her eyes. She saw Pike in one piece and let herself draw a breath.

Pike shivered, reminding himself, "She's not the ghoul. Not the ghoul. Not the . . . *Leave it!*"

The tech had reached for the knife, stopping at Pike's order. He looked worriedly at Susan. She shook her head and jerked it toward the hatch.

"Heard you asked for your fighting knife," she said, trying to act nonchalant.

"I did." *And you're not the ghoul. No, see the difference. Different colored eyes. Susan's skin is darker. She's not the ghoul! Force yourself. Understand what Ngen did!* Only he couldn't control the dreams. Resigned, he reached to pick up the blade, feeling the cool steel.

Susan stepped forward cautiously, edging around the med units, balanced on the balls of her feet to spring. "Doctor, I'm worried about you. I remember what I felt after Ngen had his time with me. I was only trying to live long enough to kill him before I turned a blaster on myself."

Reesh wouldn't have lied. She cut men . . . like the ghoul. "Charming. Looks like you didn't get the job done."

She stiffened slightly. "No, I talked to a Prophet instead. They have curious abilities. They . . ." She looked over to where Patan Andojar Garcia observed through serene eyes, a benevolent smile on his face.

"Go away. I'll be fine. Don't worry your head about your anthropologist. I won't let Ngen take away your brain boy, at least, not in the near future. But you won't take this knife from me. Now now . . . not ever."

He looked at her, a cold hostility brewing. "I'm *tired* of being played for a fool by you, Ree, and all the rest. If Iron Eyes wants to take my knife, maybe he can. If not, I'll be dead first."

She nodded coldly. "Very well, Doctor."

Turning on her heel, she left the hospital. Darwin sank back on the pallet, drawing a deep breath.

"She wishes to help you." Patan cocked his head.

Pike felt his unit shutting him down again. He wanted to turn and tell him about how he had been so taken with Susan, how he'd been so concerned to get her out of the Father's trap on Bazaar, but his mouth had ceased working and he dropped into the world of Ngen, Pallas, and the ghoul-woman who became Susan. Fear wrapped around him, and loneliness, and ultimate violation while Reesh shrieked in the background.

Spider's Knife *decelerating from jump into Bazaaran space.*

Spider's Knife dropped out of the light jump, the stasis field generators shedding photons and charged particles in their wake to spread in the roiled burble of the magneto-gravitic tail they created in passage.

"Breakout," Rita called, checking the monitors. "Dump at forty gravities. When we close on their deep space scanners, employ random deceleration. We don't want to trip their alarm system. After Susan busted this place up, they might have decided to rearm.''

"Acknowledged."

Rita stood and stretched, staring at the back of the pilot's head where he lay in the command chair, communicating with the helm through his headset. Coming out of the light jump did that. At a fraction less than light speed, the energies they generated needed to be carefully balanced against the mass/velocity.

Rita experienced a slight shift in the gravity as the grav plates compensated for the acceleration. The monitors read normal stats across the board.

"Bud? How does the outside look?"

Mishima watched his monitors, the comm correcting for the background maelstrom generated by their bow shock. "Either we've got a glitch or it's dead out there. Hang on, I'm running a diagnostic. No glitch, Major. It's quiet as a dead mouse out there. Transduction isn't more than normal Directorate background.''

Rita picked at her incisors with a fingernail, green eyes on the monitor. As the sensors unbent mass-distorted redshifted light around them, she watched the galaxy come to life on the bridge monitors. Comm ran a security analysis, coming up clean.

"All right, I guess we can stand down. Doesn't look like they're nervous. That or Susan clipped their eyes and ears off at the roots." *So? If they've been hit, why turn off the warning system? Once slapped, twice vigilant.*

"I don't like it. Bud, put your mind to it. Try everything you can think of so long as it's passive. We scan actively, they'll have us picked off quicker than a bear on a harvester. They've got to have something, some way of defending themselves.''

A couple of hours later she followed the narrow corridors to the mess, punching up a tray. Bud Mishima ducked through after her, making his own selections.

Rita took one side of the scarred rectangular table. The mess in an FT couldn't be called more than a cubicle. One wall contained the dispensers—the FT too cramped for individual units in cabins like *Bullet* boasted. The gleaming white tray holders, the plate racks and cup slings didn't shine whitely anymore. The entire sequence of *Knife*'s inspace modification could be read from the stratigraphy of fingerprints. Brown for the ones made during the cutting and pasting, black for the machinery adaptation, gray for the cleanup, and white over the whole mess from the repainting. True, it made the mess look homey, but the time had come to clean it up. She made a note to comm. Good discipline for some of the marines.

Most of the marines continued to live and eat on the ATs where they were tucked under the *Knife*'s belly. For the main crew, however, the tiny mess had become home. The only meeting place where a cup of coffee could be shared and desultory talk exchanged.

"So you think they'll be waiting to shoot at us?" Mishima stifled a yawn, rubbing hands up and down the muscles of his hairy forearms.

Rita took a bite, chewed thoughtfully, and grunted. "I don't know. My sixth sense is up. You know, the one that lets you be real uneasy without knowing why. I just got a bad feeling when we came out of that jump—like there's something here I don't want to know. I'd run if I could. After some of the things we saw on Mystery, I'd just as soon go cuddle up in John's arms and raise cattle, horses, and kids for the rest of my life. But the Admiral wants us to check it out, see how quickly they recovered after Susan shot the hell out of them."

Bud frowned, leaning forward to shovel food into his big mouth, chewing as aggressively as he did everything else. She'd always liked Mishima. He had two means of dealing with life. Either he powered forward at full bore and damn the consequences, or he was asleep. In all the years Rita had known him, she'd never seen Bud do anything halfway.

He gestured with his fork, the frown still incising his bulldog brow. "All right, say Ngen's got a trap down there. I scanned the damned system up, down, and sideways. Bazaar should have stood out as the brightest radio source in this part of the galaxy. I got a blank. Their sun out-emits Bazaar in the low part of the EM scale—and I ran the scanner clear through the spectrum from one thousand km down to ten nm. The planet isn't completely silent, but given the geophysics, it's awful damn quiet—not much more than you'd expect from the electrical storms and a minimal human occupation."

Rita scratched behind her ear, thoughtful. "You know, if it's a trap, Ngen laid it brilliantly. And don't get me wrong, the only way Ngen functions is brilliantly. He had to have shut down the whole planet—and how would he know anyone would come back? Susan shot hell out of this place. I can't—''

''Ngen caught the Admiral's transmission? Decoded it? Beat us here? Hell, maybe he was orbiting Bazaar, checking the damage when someone out by Mystery had their ears pointed the right way to hear us?''

Rita finished her meal and shoved the tray away, leaning forward to prop her elbows on the table. She accessed comm and looked up at the monitor. ''Ki, shift our vector. Take us around the system. We can use the gravity wells of those two gas giants to dump delta V without spraying a lot of reaction around. In the meantime, it'll give us a chance to look things over before we're committed.''

''Acknowledged, Major. Preliminary estimates are that we'll lose a couple of weeks.''

She reached for her coffee, staring at the far bulkhead, sipping. ''We can live with that, Ki. Better late than blown out of space, huh? Keep your eyes peeled for bandits. Bud and I were just discussing the relative merits of an ambush in here somewhere.''

''Acknowledged, Major.''

She felt the subtle tug of the grav plates as Ki initiated a course change.

''Trouble,'' Mishima grunted. ''It's always trouble lately. How long's it been since any of us were bored?''

Rita smiled wistfully, turning the coffee cup in her hands. ''I think all that stopped a long time ago on that last Far Side patrol we made. Remember? Just before that damn GCI picked up a fragment of Romanan radio transmission?''

Mishima lifted a heavy leg to prop it on the bench. He leaned back, braced in the corner. ''Weren't you the one that went to meet the anthropologists? Didn't Ree send you off to University?''

Rita chuckled, nodding over the coffee cup propped in her hands. ''Yeah, I met Doctor Dobra there. Met that wretched nerd she was living with. Jeffray. Wow. Turns out that being a nerd wasn't his fault. Health Department had psyched him for screwing around with transduction theory. I don't know, maybe that's where it all started. They psyched the guy, Leeta got mad. I liked Leeta and covered her tracks so Health couldn't psych her before she left for World. She still had all her marbles and got in trouble with the Santos. We got to meet Romanans, fell in love, and kept the Directorate from sterilizing World. One domino knocking down another? Fate? Spider alone knows. But we're back to psyching people again—on a scale the Directorate never dreamed of! So, if we live through this go around, what's next?''

Mishima stretched to get his coffee cup under the dispenser and push the button. He almost toppled over getting the full cup back but didn't spill a drop. "You know, a lot of people would have happily blown you in two the day you led those screaming Romanans into the reactor room."

She shrugged it off. "You know, the second time I ever saw Leeta Dobra, she was about to be raped in a low-dive spacer bar on University. I was smashed—drinking Star Mist on Patrol credits. I chased the guy off and there was Dobra, lost, confused, a typical Directorate sheep. But she had spunk, so I thought, what the hell? and sat down. I remember, we had this long argument about the Directorate, how it was all stagnant and crumbling in on itself. I think I said, 'Too bad there ain't some way to turn the whole goddamn mess upside down on the pumpkin heads.' "

"You did it."

"Uh-huh." She raised an eyebrow, setting the coffee cup down. "The problem with the collapse of a civilization is that you never know where it's going." She paused. "World was a long shot to save a group of people from genocide. Then we went to Sirius and fought one hell of a tough war—but it was still a simple 'Beat them before they beat you' war." She grimaced. "Ngen would never have risen to power if we hadn't pulled attention away from Sirius with the Romanan problem. Maya would have drifted overhead with *Victory* and scuttled the revolution before it started."

"Past history," Mishima gave her an inquiring look. "So what?"

Rita smiled wearily. "So, back when Doc and I were gabbing in that bar, we'd have never guessed the kind of horror would be let loose like we saw at Mystery. I don't sleep well at night after seeing those walking ghouls."

"Yeah," Bud agreed. "I know what you mean."

"And I think the horror's only begun. I think we're going to see a lot worse. Way back in that bar, I never would have thought anything could be worse than Skor Robinson."

Wary, coasting, attention glued to the monitor, *Spider's Knife* dropped into the Bazaaran gravity well. Through it all, the planet remained eerily silent. As they closed, visual refined under the highest magnification. No evidence of other ships, no sight of *Gregory*, no transmissions were caught by the ship's sensitive antennae.

Days dragged, tension increased, and the slow wait stretched.

Iron Eyes filled her dreams. They rode together across the waving sea of grass, she on Philip's red gelding, he on his favorite black mare. Above them, the sun shimmered in yellow-white bliss. World lay before them, waiting for exploration, for them to disappear within its bounty.

With the magic of dreams, the image changed, the sky going dark as she wrapped herself in his arms, safe, enjoying the flickering light of a polewood fire. He tightened the blanket he held about her, leaning down to kiss her, dark eyes gleaming with that tender love he bestowed. The warm sensations of desire stirred as she met his lips, reaching up to pull him close, the feel of his powerful body a tonic to her tired limbs. In relief, she ran cold fingers over his dark skin, feeling the male hardness, the scars, the tension in his muscles as he warmed to her caresses. The fire crackling, she pulled him down, enjoying the rippling tone of his firm body as it pressed to her.

They began the eternal dance.

"Major Sarsa?"

Rita blinked, a deep charge in her system as she sat up, rubbing her eyes. At her movement, the lights came on in her tiny cabin. Bazaar. Deep space. Responsibility and dread in the voice over comm.

"Yes?"

"We're closing on Bazaar. If there's an ambush here, we're damned if we can find it. But Major . . ."

She was on her feet, irritated at the physical realities the dream had produced in her flushed body as she reached for her combat armor. Crap!

"What's wrong, Ki?"

"Well, we've got a pretty good visual, Major. Clear day on the planet for once, too. Remote scan's unbelievably good. But Major, you'd better come see for yourself."

At the tension in his voice, Rita yanked her armor on, declining the thought of a shower, and palmed the hatch. Ki didn't sound that way unless something had really gone wrong. She hit the corridor running.

CHAPTER XXV

Spider's Revenge **in jump between Bazaar and World.**

When Darwin swam up out of the nightmares, the Prophet's unit was empty, the heavy lid up, and Pike found himself alone in the hospital. The Corporal stood checking the monitors outside the hatch as usual. They wouldn't bring him around otherwise. Feeling miserable, Pike let himself breathe, amazed at how wonderful it could be to pull air in and out of the lungs. Such a simple process, forever taken for granted and never really felt. It was good to breathe.

"Hey!" Pike yelled, suddenly remembering the Prophet's words. "Where's the Prophet?"

"We dismissed him two days ago." The woman appeared in the hatch. He glanced down and saw his knife still lay in the tray.

"Two days ago?"

"We wake you up every three days." She leaned against the molded hatch frame, arms crossed, watching.

"Every three days?" His life drained away in sleep? "Why?"

"Dr. Pike, you heal better when you sleep. We're dumping a lot of growth stimulant into your system. We have to trick the DNA into believing it's growing fetal tissue, stimulating those gene nodes with DNA and fetal hormone, polymerase III and DFSK3. At the same time, a carefully maintained electro-stim has to be kept at just the right intensity around the regenerating tissue. You see, regeneration is playing with fire. If the system gets out of whack, you end up in a cancerous condition. You're in enough trouble without any sarcoma complications.

"Not only that, but your mental activity indicates you fret more awake than asleep. When you're dreaming, we can tell you're having bad dreams from the way you produce brain waves and from changes in blood chemistry—but we can damp the effect. When you're awake, you're not only upset, but you end up in depression. That triggers reactions from the pituitary and hypothalamus and a list of other glands. All of which lead to wild fluctuations of the blood chemistry which in turn biases the reaction of those chemicals we're injecting into your leg. See the trouble? Given the two alternatives, we'll take nightmares to depression. The lesser of two evils, you might say.'' She seemed nonplussed.

''Oh,'' Darwin muttered, noticing that his fingers flexed without pain. He could see marks on his wrists. His eyes didn't pain him any more and his vision was perfect again—the fuzziness gone. ''You've had me completely enclosed, haven't you? I can tell by the marks on my body.''

''That's right,'' she agreed. ''Your mental faculties are picking up. You're more alert. If you'd ever decide to work with us, a lot of things would be easier.''

''How long have I been here?''

''Four weeks. We've regrown most of your leg and you have cute little stubs where they cut your toes off. The nerve—''

''Seems I spend all my time in a damn med unit! I'm tires of having my life—''

Her expression hardened.

He raised his hands defensively. ''All right! Hold it! I'll be good. Don't put me down again. I'm thinking positive thoughts.''

''That's a switch,'' the tech said dryly. She came to stand close. ''How positive?''

He looked up, suddenly uncertain. ''Well, pretty positive.''

Could it be? Was that really a hint of a smile on her hard lips? Spider's blood! A crack in the iron bitch's hide!

''All right, Doctor Pike. I'll take a chance that you're not pissing around with me. Here's the real score. You're in a bit of trouble. The nerve regeneration isn't progressing along the curves we'd projected. That's another reason for keeping you down. The electrical currents we're using to try and retrain your muscles aren't pleasant to endure. You've got a lot of nerve damage. Whatever they tortured you with played havoc with the synapses, some sort of EM field that jangled your neurons. It's a form of cellular microdamage. You follow so far?''

He nodded, wary. ''I had considerable human biology—it's one of the subdisciplines of anthropology.''

''All right, because to be honest, unless you put all your heart and mind into it, you may never walk right again on your own. We can fit you up with a prosthetic nervous system for that leg if it doesn't heal, but that will mean a subcutaneous nerve net, a battery pack, and a headset forever. Now, the brain has a lot of power. You're familiar with biofeedback, psychosomatosis, and all the other brain-body relationships. Attitude will make all the difference.''

He frowned, losing that sense of balanced anger. Damn it, how could the holy med unit let him down? He hadn't considered for a moment that the machine might fail.

"Technology only takes us so far, Doctor," she added, as if reading his thoughts. "You'll help? It could make the final difference."

Pike bit his lip. The mental sand on which he stood had begun to shift again. She didn't understand—none of them did.

Are you worthy? It echoed hollowly in his head.

Susan had said she kept alive by thinking about evening the score with Ngen. A good place to start. A purpose. Ngen remained loose, making ghouls—torturing anthropologists and other real people. Maybe if they could put him back together, he could do something.

I owe Ngen Van Chow! I'll live. I'll get him. Somehow, some way. By Spider, I swear that. And he felt better, the rush of anger channeled. *And Susan isn't the ghoul, Ngen. You foul . . .*

"Would you let the Captain know I'd like to see her sometime. I'd like to know what's been happening while I was asleep. Maybe I can go back to work soon."

The tech nodded, evaluating him, trying to see if she'd penetrated the shell.

Susan showed up within a half hour. She entered the med unit, looking at him cautiously. "I hear you're doing better. The corporal said your outlook has picked up."

His face creased. "It doesn't seem like I'm really here. After what happened, I don't even know who I am or what I've become. Things get pretty mixed up. I guess I was pretty snotty. Accept my apology. I don't handle guilt very well. Or pain, for that matter."

"Neither do I. I've been kicking myself ever since Bazaar." She pursed her lips and shrugged. "You know, you saved both of our lives at the Temple that day. I owe you and Reesh. Because of what you two did, we got the information off to Admiral Ree."

"I wonder if I would have done it . . . knowing how it

would end? It was my idea. Reesh went along with it. I thought they'd just kill us. The way he died . . . I wouldn't have . . . didn't know I'd bring him to—''

She waved it away and dropped into a fold-out seat. "War doesn't work that way, Doctor. I've seen too much of it. Human beings die. Spider pulls the strands . . . and if you're on one, you go. It doesn't hinge on anything a logical mind can understand. I lost the man I . . . a good squad died because they went right and I went left. People go . . . that's all. Cusps, I guess. And every time you tear your heart out, trying to justify what happened after the fact—and you can't.''

He looked at her, wondering at this new vulnerability. "Okay. Maybe it does work that way. It still doesn't seem right.''

"It never does.'' She tilted her head, an eyebrow lifted. "After time passes you simply get used to it. What would have happened if they psyched you first? Think about it. The entire project would have been spilled to Ngen. He'd have known Rita and Neal were out there. You would have become one of his monsters and Reesh would have died the same way when they psyched him for anything you might have missed.'' Her eyes warmed. "Or what if you hadn't gotten me out? If they'd caught all three of us? How much worse off would we all be? Ngen would know the Admiral's strategy. Reesh still would have died like that. You'd be a ghoul. I'd be in EM bands—on the way back to . . . to . . .'' Fists knotted at her side as she shook her head, trying to banish the thought.

"You said you made it through by trying to get even with Ngen.'' Pike looked up. "I don't know what he did to you. To me, what happened was . . . I mean he cut me apart. Fed my . . . He . . . He . . . He . . . *Shit!*'' Pike gasped a heavy breath and pressed palms to his eyes. He could feel her hands on his arm.

"Now, can you understand why I couldn't sleep at night? That's what caught up with me in the mess that night. Knowing I was getting closer to him. Can you see what it might mean to be captured again?''

Pike nodded numbly.

He could sense her sudden hesitation. He looked up questioningly.

Lips pinched, she cocked her head to study him. Only this time, her expression caught him by surprise. Some uncertainty seemed to ebb and flow in the pools of her eyes. As if she might not want to hear the answer she sought.

"What? I know you too well. You're nervous about something."

Finally, she asked, "I've seen the tapes Pallas made. I . . . Why didn't you break?"

"You saw?" he asked aghast. "You saw what he did to me? You . . . Oh, my God!"

Her fingers wrapped around his. "Don't! Don't go soft on me now! You stood up, Pike. You beat him. I . . . I *broke* under his torture! I couldn't deal with it. Why did you beat him when I . . . I . . ." Her grip began to crush his hand.

She'd seen him completely stripped of his humanity. "S . . . Spider was with me." He clamped his teeth to stop the chattering. "Spider stood over me. Then they moved the psych in and Spider . . . I broke. You see I was broken, too." Resistance drained like water in a punctured bag.

She nodded numbly. "Ngen thought he had you. That he just didn't have time to complete the work. But I . . . I've watched. I'm not . . . not sure. You didn't break. That's the point. You fought . . . fought past when I could have. You didn't break when I'd have been crushed." A pause. "Spider works in . . . Will you tell me something else?" Her voice drifted away as she became lost in her thoughts.

He felt like wood as he met her nervous eyes.

"When . . . when Ngen mentioned a . . . a Romanan woman, you called my name."

Flashback: the dream, Tiara's features blending with Susan's. He shivered violently, cold sweat beading on his skin. *Not Susan! Not the ghoul.* "Not the . . . ghoul. It's not Susan!"

"Damn him!" Susan cursed, drawing her own conclusions from his reaction. "I'll gut that rock leech son of a bitch!"

He heard her move back, unable to look up at her. "It's . . . just a dream. He . . . I don't know. Made it . . . well . . ."

"It was a hypnotic plant, Darwin." She raised her hands, letting them fall slapping against her sides. Tears of hurt and rage crept from the corners of her dark eyes. "The man's a master at that. He did it to me. When I burst in, he looked at me through that huge holo image and started talking, and . . . and . . ." She ground her teeth so loudly he

could hear. "And it works, Doctor. He touched me deep
inside, stirred up all the filth with a word. Left me reeling."

A silence.

"Susan. Back on World, Reesh told me you cut men. Cut
them like Pallas . . . cut me." Stone-faced, he looked up.

She blanched, averting her eyes, stiffening as if to fight a
shiver.

And he knew, cold horror in his bowels. "You did. You
can't deny it—not the way . . . Why?"

The tip of her tongue ran nervously along a red lip. "Pike
. . . I . . . " She shook her head and exhaled painfully.
"It's war, Pike. People . . . I got a little crazy after Hans
got . . . Ngen's blasters caught him in Angla. Couldn't live
with the guilt, the pain, the loss. I . . . I wasn't whole then,
either. Seems like I've been crazy all my life. I don't . . .
Yes, I do know. It was weakness. The inability to rational-
ize, to understand. I'd been hurt. Everyone and everything
had to pay for that. Only I paid even more."

She looked at him, shamed and uncertain, eyes pleading.
"I'm no saint, Darwin. I . . . I'm just as lonely and frightened and miserable as you are. Yes, I cut men. And I've
borne the guilt for a long time. Had it all thrown back in
my face by Ngen. It just seems that I have to keep paying
. . . and paying."

The honesty stung him, shamed him in turn.

"What happened to Bazaar?" He struggled to change the
topic.

"I blew the hell out of it. We destroyed all the stations
in orbit and shot up the major industries we could locate on
the ground. Their power is gone, comm gone. Nothing left
except dwellings . . . and those mindless wrecks."

"They'll starve in days," Darwin said dully. "They didn't
have the resources, the survival skills. That plastic ability
to adapt had been burned out of them. Subsistence depended on comm. Ngen had been cutting back once his
psych program was almost complete. He would have returned for them when he needed soldiers."

Susan's features hardened. "Then his army is that much
closer to extinction. Once, killing that many people would
have bothered me. Before the burnoffs on Sirius, before
Hans . . . before Ngen."

"They aren't human," Darwin whispered, the vision of
the ghoul chewing his flesh making him shake. "I'd kill
them all."

"We may have to," Susan settled into the chair again, dropping her head into her hands. "From the nearest figures I can pull up, we might be outnumbered as much as a million to one, depending on how fast he spreads through the Directorate."

"Like burning out diseased forest," he muttered, a vision spinning out of his distant past. "There was a bud worm that hit the white spruce one year. By the time we burned infected forests, I wasn't sure but that it wouldn't have been better to let nature take its course."

"Did those worms steal the souls of the trees? Did they turn the trees into a man-eating cancer?"

"No."

"What other choice do we have? I received a coded message from the Admiral. We'll get no Directorate help—although two of their line ships have come over to our side. Defected, isn't that the word? In the meantime Santa del Cielo, Chouhoutien, Last Chance, and Ambrose Sector have had riots, mob rule, and established Temples. It's started there. The front of his activities is three times as large."

"Revitalization. A religious movement without competition. Only some limited activity on the part of systems close to World. There's nothing to stand in the way of the Fathers."

"There's Spider."

"Wrong kind of religion," Pike shook his head, the square box of the psych blotting out the image of Spider in his tortured mind.

"Why?"

"Using Spider for a religious movement would pall. There are too few Prophets. None would take a stand to preach the way of Spider. It isn't in their framework. Look at Patan. He almost went insane seeing too much in the future until he learned to let it flow. He said he was being vain about it." Pike knotted his fists. *But it was a chance! If only a man were enough of a fool—or hero—to take that suicidal responsibility. If a Prophet were to proselytize, the effect would be staggering. A counter messiah could take Ngen's jihad and wrap it right around the Fathers and strangle them in their own despicable fundamentalism.*

She seemed puzzled. "But Spider *is* spreading. All the little cults, the young people clamoring to come to World. Spider's all over the—"

"Sure," he nodded, glowing from his thoughts. "And,

given another hundred to two hundred years, it would probably be the major religion of the galaxy . . . were it not for
Ngen. It has too many strengths and too few weaknesses.
The fact remains that Prophets see the future. No one can
deny that, not even Ngen Van Chow.''

Susan stood and walked to the comm. She was accessing
it as Patan Andojar Garcia walked through the hatch and
went to Pike's med unit.

Susan just sighed and canceled the call.

"You are looking much better, Darwin Pike." Patan
beamed. "In answer to your question, yes. I am your madman. You no doubt wondered why I lingered so long between life and death . . . sanity and insanity? For exactly
this purpose should you decide among yourselves to employ
me as such a 'Messiah.' I dislike that tern. I dislike Prophet,
too. Verbal labels, however, do not affect much of reality,
do they?''

"If you knew, why did you just lie around?" Darwin
asked. "Why didn't you check into med yourself?''

Patan bowed, face serene. "I had more important things
to do, Doctor. It would have disturbed my concentration to
bother with physical facts. In that instance, I took no chance.
You could not leave me in the companionway. Your compassion wouldn't allow you. I knew you would carry me to
med so I saved myself the time.''

"You risk insanity, don't you?" Susan said, trying hard
to keep her eyes down as was proper.

"No," Patan told her matter-of-factly. "Risk implies a
chance—variable outcomes of a gamble. I face cold certainty. I will be forced to make decisions, to tamper with
free will. I will go insane.''

"Then *why* do it?" Darwin stumbled in confusion.

Patan laid a warm hand on Darwin's brow and placed
another on Susan's arm. "I do it for Spider. For the souls
Ngen would waste. Waste is one of the few true sins. That
and mediocrity. We are all part of the web Spider is spinning. Doctor, you just suffered horribly. You, Captain, have
lived with madness and pain. These things are as temporary
as your lives. All too soon we are drawn back and become
part of Spider. We are all molded to be the eyes and ears of
Spider. The vessels of His knowledge.''

"What do you see for us?" Susan asked. "Do we have
a chance?''

Patan smiled easily. "Anything is possible if the right

cusps are chosen. There were many chances that this moment would not have arrived. The doctor made several decisions . . . just as you did, Captain. The doctor chose to sacrifice his life that you might live: failing at the time to recognize the cusp. His feelings for you were more important than his own life. I am you. You, Captain, might have made an immediate escape—as was your duty—and not undertaken his rescue. You chose, not knowing you decided a cusp. I myself might have chosen not to have followed this course, not to die in madness. It was my cusp."

Susan had paled, staggered as she stared at Pike, mouth opening slightly.

Pike chewed on his lip. *How in hell does he stand there so cool and collected? The man knows when he's going to die! Damn it, he's a maniac! No one could calmly stare at the future—at what's coming—and just wait to be destroyed! No one!* Awed, he added humorlessly, "We'll play hell with causality."

Susan shrugged. "If we don't, there will be little left of our species."

Patan smiled. "And that is exactly where my courage comes from, Doctor. No, it isn't easy to lead myself to my own destruction. Only the alternatives are worse. And, as I reminded you, life is temporary. Only my soul is of Spider—who is eternal. If Ngen succeeds, Spider will learn a lot about boredom. But do not deceive yourselves, Spider learns from others besides men. We are not the only species. All souls belong to Spider. If we cease to serve Spider's function, we will be discarded."

"That's irritating," Pike gritted.

"It will irritate many people as we spin our web through the Directorate. I fear that Skor Robinson never learned enough from Chester Armijo Garcia. He would have saved many people much misery. But then, the cusps *are* exercises of free will. Humans must make their own way. Learning must be painful to be honest."

Darwin rubbed his nose and hesitated.

Patan nodded with a smile. "Yes, Doctor, there will be much violence, death, and suffering. There will be more than at any previous point in human history. When this is all finished, planets will be burned off, Sectors of space will be devastated. As to whether it is worth the cost, that is up to Spider."

"And you can't see the end of it?" Susan rapped a fist

absently against the med unit beside her. "You can't see if we'll win or not?"

Patan smiled benevolently. "No. Too many cusps will change too many futures—mine among them. For you, my children, I can only say you will both find bliss and misery in the coming months, but you have already decided price is no option."

Pike felt his gut sink. He swallowed with difficulty and looked into Susan's grim eyes.

Ngen waited. And with him, his army of ghouls.

CHAPTER XXVI

Tactical planning room: *Bullet* in Geo orbit over World.

"That will be all, people." Ree rose from the cluttered conference room table, nodding to the circle of faces. The techs erupted with that familiar post-meeting energy. Ree stepped back and stayed out of the way while the weapons techs cleared the conference room, babbling among themselves, joking, arguing or pensive as they thronged the hatch. They all seemed so young—even the familiar faces Damen had known for thirty years. The excitement in their eyes didn't lighten his malaise. After the last months, where did a man find optimism?

Giorj's theoretical application concepts for targeting augmentation appeared at this stage of implementation to surpass Ree's expectations. Applying fractal geometry to fire control for the faster than light Fujiki blasters would never have occurred to him. The techs would have their hands full writing the program to juggle redshift, target velocity, reaction time, vacuum clutter, and the new fractal interpretation to the comm.

Ree rubbed the back of his neck, peering at the stained dispenser. When did the gray engineer have time to be so damned brilliant?

"And to think I would have broken his neck the first time Susan brought him aboard!" Ree grunted to himself, still glaring at the dispenser. With a sigh, he punched the button that filled his cup with bittersweet Romanan tea.

"Colonel?"

Ree accessed comm to the interrogative in his mind. "Go ahead."

"*Victory* has entered confirmation of parking orbit. She has matched and is powering down. Colonel ben Ahmad is in transit via AT and will arrive in twenty minutes. AT Control has routed her through Lock 7."

"Acknowledged." Ree paused for a moment in the now quiet conference room. Maya was coming! The faint headache behind his eyes irritated him, a constant reminder of stress. Med recommended rest and relaxation. Spider take it, *when?*

Maya was on her way!

Twenty minutes? He had time to check on the progress Major Glick had made on the stasis definition rod rejuvenation. Sipping the tea, he started for the bridge, stopping in the familiar corridor. He winced at the headache. *Maya was coming!* Around him, *Bullet* hummed quietly.

He'd promised Glick he'd check with him, see if he needed anything. It wouldn't be more than . . .

"Hell with it. No, I'm taking a break." The tension behind his eyes relaxed slightly. He smiled at the white panels around him. Who would have thought the blasted burned hulk of *Bullet* would ever throb with life like this again?

He patted the white panels fondly. "Come on, old girl, I'm going to walk up there. Get the exercise. Probably be the last time to just talk, huh?"

He retraced his steps, strolling down the corridor, taking the companionway to F deck and enjoying the feel of his legs working.

"You know, old girl, Maya's not exactly your rival. Hell, I haven't really had a private talk with her since we were on Sirius. And besides, even if something did happen she'd still have to space in her ship. It'd only be a brief sort of thing. She's tied to *Victory* like I'm tied to you."

He passed a private and a marine who gave him a sideways glance. What the hell was wrong with them? Didn't they ever talk to the ship?

"Guess they don't understand, old girl. But then, they're young yet. Don't know how to think about a ship." He let his fingers run lovingly down the white paneling, feeling the slight irregularities of sonic welds where she'd been ripped and torn and patched. They shared a lot, he and his ship. Both scarred veterans.

She had been his life, his purpose since that first assignment to the Patrol. "My blood's in your deck, old girl. You and me, forever. Hell, maybe when I die I'll have them run my corpse through the converter and they can use the elements for deck plating or something, hmm? We'd be one then." He chuckled to himself, blaming his maudlin thoughts on exhaustion.

Despite the stiffness caused by too many hours on his feet, he climbed the companionway two steps at a time to the AT deck, stretching his legs as he used a distance-eating stride to make the last couple of hundred meters to Lock 7. He arrived breathing hard, heart thudding reassuringly against his ribs.

The monitor showed Maya's AT as it decelerated, the mains lancing the star-dusted background with bright yellow needles of reaction. One side of the deadly slim AT shone whitely, illuminated by World's sun—the other by soft light from the moon Romanans called Harvester. *Victory* herself filled another monitor, a bright ivory-colored biconvex obovoid, a duplicate of *Bullet,* only a century younger. The monitor masked *Victory*'s 1.5-k length, the recessed AT locks, like a string of black beads running down her upper decks.

"How long until they dock?" Ree asked of the corporal in charge of security. A lightness drifted feathery touches around his heart. Absently, he picked at a chip in the coffee cup with a nervous thumbnail.

"Make it five minutes, sir." The corporal paused, a slight frown ghosting his brows as he listened to something in his head. "Comm informs me that they had a scheduling problem. Just a slight delay."

Ree waited, tossing off the last of the tea and slipping his cup into his belt pouch. Expectation charged his muscles as he watched the AT close, hover over the lock, and settle perfectly. The grapples extended, reaching for the slim shape of the AT, embracing it and retracting, bringing the craft into the recessed bay. Something banged hollowly to be felt through deck plating and echo down the long gallery.

"Lock down."

"Acknowledged."

A slight whine grew faint as the AT powered down. From habit, Ree checked his people, seeing security alert. Ever

since Rita had taken *Bullet*'s reactor in that mad attempt to
save the Romanans, security had never been slack. Let no
one say Damen Ree didn't learn from his mistakes.

The hatch hissed softly as it pressurized. Safeties cross-
checked. The lock clicked. The heavy white hatch slid to
the side on pneumatics, the usual gassy cloud of condensation forming where space-cold metal met warm humid air.
Maya stepped into the tunnel. Her deep black skin contrasted with the surroundings, the effect adding to the power
of her presence.

"Damen!" she cried. "Good to see you." Her face wrinkled with a warm smile. Delight sparkled in her black eyes,
a hint of promise taunting.

He smiled, curiously off balance. Had she grown more
beautiful over the long absence? He froze that moment in
his mind, seeing her slim body, her black hair spilling in
ringlets over the white shoulders of her dress uniform. Her
proud posture accented her straight shoulders, the swell of
her breasts. Full hips, flat muscular belly, and firm legs
completed the image. As if she understood, a saucy smile
lingered on her lips as she walked slowly forward, her
movements those of a sand tiger. Lithe, powerful, she
stopped before him, challenge in her eyes.

"Maya. Welcome to *Bullet*. On behalf of my officers and
crew, I extend my most sincere hopes that your stay will be
both satisfying and pleasurable." He took her hands, a
happy constriction in his breast. For long moment, he stared
into her eyes.

"On behalf of my officers and crew, I extend *Victory*'s
compliments and respects. We are most pleased at being
able to enter World as allies and friends. *Victory* formally
offers her resources and skills—at your service, Admiral
Ree."

"And we most ardently accept. Our fondest gratitude to
your brave crew and noble ship. And now, if you'd be so
kind as to allow me to escort you, I believe we have some
serious negotiations to attend to." He bowed formally and
led her to the side. "There, we're off holo. So much for the
official record. How'd I do?"

"Did you say something about dinner?" she asked, cocking her head, eyes twinkling. "I haven't eaten a thing for
the last six hours. I'm salivating at the thought of chewing
graphsteel." She paused. "We are eating *alone*, aren't we?"

"Absolutely. *Bullet* has outdone itself to show you how

we traitorous barbarian swine throw a party." He took her arm in his and led her along the deck. "Tonight, I wine and dine you. Tomorrow, the Romanans are throwing something they call a barbecue. It's an ancient American word. Means outdoor cooking and party. Of course all your off-duty personnel are invited." He gave her a wicked wink. "You might say it's the final masterstroke in Spider's corruption of your crew."

She laughed, tightening her grip on his arm as she stared around the AT deck. "Looks considerably better than last time I was aboard. You threw out all the dead bodies. I can't see a single trip-wire, barricade, or blaster hole."

He waved grandiosely. "And we've got all the lights turned on." He stamped the deck. "And look. Gravity! You don't float away—or fall through to the deck below. The old girl is sound!"

Maya gave him a sloe-eyed look. "You really care for her, don't you?"

Damen nodded happily. "Yes. She's kept me alive, Maya. She's given me purpose. Everyone needs a purpose— something to commit to. From the first time I saw her, *Bullet* cast some kind of spell on me. I've killed for her, fought for her. I'd give my soul for her—but that's Spider's."

She squinted up at him, wry humor tugging at the corners of her full mouth. "You and Ben." She shook her head with resignation. "Almost took pulling rank on him to get him to stay on the bridge. He's dying to see one of your Prophets."

Ree lifted an eyebrow. "Well, we've got one living in a cave down there. Chester, the Prophet Skor had hostage for a while. I'll give Ben directions. If Chester wants to see him, he'll be there waiting. If he doesn't, Ben will find an empty cave."

"Ben's been like a kid since we dropped in on this side. You think your Prophet will see him?"

"Hey!" Ree raised his free hand. "No one second-guesses a Prophet."

They entered a lift. "My quarters." The door closed.

Maya turned to take his hands, professional expression fading. "Damen, you look tired. I don't think you looked this grayed and worn out when Ngen was trying to take *Bullet* off Sirius. You're—"

"But I'm a hell of a lot cleaner." He spread his arms, indicating his dress uniform. "See. Not a single drop of

blood. Not a streak! Enjoy it while you can. You usually
tell me what a filthy wreck I've become every time you set
foot in *Bullet.*''

She punched him playfully in the ribs. "That's not what
I meant. And every time I've ever set foot in *Bullet* before,
she's been fresh out of hard-fought combat.''

The door slid open and he led her down the corridor to
his quarters, palming the hatch. "Welcome to home.''

She entered, cataloging the neat room, stopping for a moment at the display of Romanan weapons hanging on one
wall. A large spider drawn on tanned bull hide stared back
from the opposite wall. A table set for two dominated the
center of the room, a leg of lamb roasted brown and glistening waited between two plates. Crystal goblets sparkled
in the low lights, an amber liquor casting tawny shadows
over the feast.

"Are you hungry?'' He indicated a grav seat.

She shook her head, seating herself. "If I wasn't before,
I would be now. You weren't kidding when you said feast.
What's this?'' She pointed to green stalks.

"Knifebush stem. Try it, it's kind of a cross between a
potato and a yam. One of the staples of Romanan diet.
Knifebush stem alone is a completely balanced diet.''

She lifted the crystal. "But first, to *Bullet,* and her dashing Admiral.''

"To *Victory* and her stunning Colonel,'' he countered.
The crystal chimed as the rims touched. For a long moment,
their eyes met and held.

She smiled, a softness in the normally hard set of her
face. "I missed you.''

"I've often . . . Well, I've wished things were different
between us.''

She nodded, accepting the meat he sliced so neatly with
the laser knife.

The meal disappeared, course by course.

"So that's how Romanans eat? No wonder they beat the
shit out of Sirius! They had all the damned calories!'' She
pushed back from the wreckage and sighed happily.

Ree stood and poured another glass of Arcturian scotch.
She joined him, taking the crystal from his fingers, setting
it aside to reach up and pull his head down. He kissed her
tenderly.

"It's been a long time since Sirius.''

He placed gentle hands on her shoulders, drowning in the

depths of her eyes. "Life hasn't been the same. Something's missing, Maya. I guess I . . . well, I never cared so much for a woman. It's getting tougher the older I get. It's supposed to be the other way around."

"You still want to keep that decision you made in my office on Sirius?" She cocked an eyebrow, waiting.

He filled his lungs and exhaled. "Yes . . . and no."

"I don't like the way you look, Damen. You've been running this side of the Directorate while Toby and I spaced for World. I can see it in you, Damen. Not only that, you're worried sick." Her eyes searched his. "You've lost weight. If you keep this up, you'll kill yourself."

He ran calloused fingers down her cheeks, awed by the softness of her skin, tracing the line of her jaw. "Do I have a choice? I know what he's doing out there. I've practically pleaded with Skor for some sort of assistance, some coordinated strike combining our forces and the Patrol. He's . . ." Ree shook his head. "Oh, I don't know. Distant? Fragmented? Doesn't he see . . . Can't he . . ."

Maya hugged him tightly. "He's a psychological wreck trying to run the Directorate like he always ran it. Navtov and An Roque are the same way." She ran her hands tenderly down the sides of his face. "Directors can't adapt. That was the fatal flaw bred into them."

He kissed her again, then pushed her back, a forlorn emptiness yawning within.

"What's wrong?" she asked, coming close again to place her hands on his chest. "You've got a horrible look in your eyes."

"You. You're wrong. I have the damnedest urge to just fall in love with you, Maya." He reached for her hands and kissed them. "And that scares the bloody hell out of me. I don't know if I can afford it. If I can allow myself that vulnerability. Not when it could all so easily end in disaster."

She laughed softly, throwing her head back to expose her throat. "If you're thinking *that* way, you *are* tired! We're not exactly young innocents, Damen. You're what? Fifty something? Me, I'm in my late forties . . . well preserved, maybe, but you don't get to be commander of a ship of the Line unless you can cut throats, stab backs, and stomp your opposition so far into the muck they can't ever crawl out."

"You do have a romantic way with words, Maya." He turned and pulled her down on the big padded antigrav.

She settled in the hollow of his arm, letting her fingers trace the lines of his uniform. "Always hated the damn dress uniform," she muttered. "Stiff and awkward."

"Watch it. I might not be responsible for my actions. Men under pressure do weird things."

"You know, I was miserable after you left Sirius. Remember all those delightful dinners? The conversations? I came to enjoy that, Damen. When you left . . . a light had gone out of my life. Had a goddamned hole inside you could have shot a blaster bolt through."

"There are other men who'd—"

She placed fingers to his lips. "That's not true and you know it. Sure, I could find a casual lover to perform sexual gymnastics. But a love? Not that, not while I'm in command. The old political structure is still hanging in *Victory's* skeleton. Who's trying to advance? Who would cut my throat? How could a lover use intimacy against me? Always on guard. And the people lower in the ranks aren't at ease. Too many rumors on the gun deck. No, you have to be celibate at the top—or damned uncomfortable." She kissed him. "You became my friend, Damen. Damn it, I . . . Hell, I almost made a fool out of myself the day *Bullet* spaced. Tore my heart out."

"It wasn't easy for me either." he chuckled at himself. "That last trip up I thought about renting one of those Sirian penthouses, getting some good wine, playing a little music, and trying to seduce you."

She pulled her hair back. "Well, you've got a good start on getting it done. How do you want me? Hard to get? Coy? Or hot and panting for your body?"

"I think I'll choose my time." He winked at her, massaging her shoulders through the uniform.

"Good. I'd just as soon have your mind on me instead of whatever's eating at you. You didn't used to be so distant, Damen. I'm not sure I like what all this responsibility's done to you. Spider's been dropping too much on your soul."

"Maybe. But then, it's his soul to dump on. No, things are . . . It's going to be bad. I'd say we've got six months' grace at most. After that, nothing will be safe. Ngen's expansion is almost exponential. I don't know how, but his underground is everywhere. I'd bet he extended the old black market networks he used to smuggle for. Anyhow, his posters appear. Then a couple of preachers are roaming around, shouting from the public transport platforms. Then the holos are broadcast and a riot occurs. The Directorate tries to suppress it—and fumbles the job of course, since they're too overextended. And that plays right into Ngen's perfect orchestration of public sentiment. Sure, one Temple won't hurt anything. Then there's two, four, eight, sixty-four. And the people are wandering around mindless, looking for their 'place.' And Ngen's gone to the next world."

She reached up and loosened the snap of his collar, pulling the triangular yoke off and dropping it. "Is that all you think about? Ngen?"

Ree reached out for her, reveling in the feel of her firm body under the uniform. "Been keeping fit."

She nodded, running a muscular leg down his. "You damn betcha. I'm third place in women's combat on *Victory*. Not bad for an old broad, huh? You going to answer my question? Or just stall?"

"Yes, I think of Ngen constantly. You don't know all of his history. Some of the horrors he committed on Sirius are Romanan state secrets because they'd compromise some of my people. Anything I do, even inviting you to dinner, is done in his shadow."

She filled her lungs and sighed. "He's really under your skin."

Damen sipped his drink and patted her. "Absolutely. Truth is, we fear him more than the average Directorate citizen does. We were on Sirius. Half the Romanan warriors we took with us died under his blasters. How many wars do you know of that were won at the expense of fifty percent casualties? I fought him through every deck on *Bullet*. I've seen the psych profiles on the people he had captive. And worst of all, I've seen the nightmare he's creating now out of happy sentient men, women, and children. And he'll send those mindless masses against us, Maya. The Fathers are no more than an army of ghouls. He's a twisted, diabolical genius at what he does. And he wants *us!* He has a debt to pay to *Bullet*, the Romanans, World, all of us. We took his victory away from him. Beat him against the odds and rubbed his face in it. A megalomaniacal madman like Ngen must think about what we did to him. We even stole his brain-boy engineer. I don't think Ngen has a short memory. I don't think he forgets. And that thought keeps me awake at night. That and the ghouls."

Maya lay silently in his arms, sipping the fine liquor. "I

don't underestimate him either. You didn't see the horror he spread through my Sector. Ben put together some firepower estimates. I think the figures are accurate. He's got the same design blaster he used against us off Sirius. Copied from the ones in his yacht, we guess.''

''He'll cut the Patrol to pieces.'' Ree frowned. ''And that presents me with another problem. What do I give Toby? Hand over the specs on the Fujiki blaster? Give her the quantum augmentation for shield generators? Toby would have helped Yaisha cut our throats if she hadn't been chasing Ngen after he escaped Sirius. And I should trust her? Give her the ability to hurt us again?

''Don't look so skeptical. We've pulled a lot of material out of those Brotherhood files. As *Bullet* stands now, she can defeat the entire Patrol fleet. No, I'm not bragging. I'll show you the figures. I mean what I say. Giorj went through the data and we've redesigned the old girl from stem to stern. Our shields can withstand the combined firepower of the entire Patrol. Granted, that will draw so much of our output that we couldn't power the blasters to shoot back— but then, if you can't be hit, the point is moot, isn't it?''

Her jaw dropped. ''You're not joking, are you?''

He cocked his head. ''No. And I'm still scared about what Ngen got out of the Brotherhood system on Frontier. Friday Garcia Yellow Legs stopped him before he got it all. At least we think he did. Ngen's computer expert was still at the console, shot in the back. Only I don't trust Ngen. That's why I want to consolidate our combat capabilities, obtain all the intelligence we can get, and kick the shit out of the filthy bastard. After that, we'll see if there's a chance we can smash his jihad.''

''You're killing yourself,'' she reminded, wiggling around to kiss him again. ''And I'm here now.'' Her fingers ran down the seam of his uniform, unzipping it. I'll take some of the heat you've been roasting under. You're not alone, Damen. I make a pretty good ally.''

He kissed her again, a burden lifting from his sagging shoulders. He ran his hand down her side, enjoying the swell of her hip, the firm feel of her muscular leg. The worry, the stress, stripped away with her uniform. She kissed him greedily, peeling the last of the fabric from his legs, light fingers tracing his skin. A fire he'd practically forgotten rose with his manhood as he cupped a full breast and teased the nipple.

She arched in pleasure, gripping him tightly as he explored with gentle fingers, kissing her passionately, feeling the desire build in her tensing body.

She sighed blissful satisfaction as she settled herself, guiding his stiff member to her.

He looked down into her eyes, a part of his soul at peace for the first time in far too long. She smiled up at him, moving to his rhythm, folding him in her arms, hugging him tightly to her.

For once, he could forget the soulless eyes, the mindless killers who waited and shouted and trained with blasters.

As he buried himself in all the splendors of Maya's warm embrace, the spider stared down from where it dominated the wall.

Aboard *Spider's Revenge* decelerating into the World system.

"Religion serves several purposes for social beings like humans. First and foremost, it provides reason and purpose for both life and the universe we perceive around us. As a result, we are imparted with a rational centering point—a self-definition—from which we can begin to deal with that universe. You could consider it the foundation, the baseline framework, from which explorations occur and from which we contrast our findings.

"Religion is also a sociocultural binding mechanism. It gives a society vertical and horizontal cohesion. For example, ego—as we call the individual—practices the same fundamental beliefs held by his father, his father's father, and so on up the line. And those basic beliefs will be held in turn by his son and his son's son. That's vertical integration—a binding of generations.

"Horizontal integration by religion allows ego to know that every member of his society has the same core behavioral reality. So, ego can approach others on a common ground of worldview. They share a basic spiritual framework, granting a basis of unity and understanding between families, clans, or groups of the same generation." Pike spread his hands, propped on the pallet, legs and hips still draped by the med unit. "Without religion, sacred or profane, humans can't define their place in nature or society."

Around them, the ship whispered quietly, the reactor pulsing its power through the deck. Susan reclined in the small fold-out seat where she often came to simply sit and talk. Patan sat cross-legged on a shining med unit, fingers interlaced, eyes closed. Someone, somewhere, had talked him out of his ratty old leather shirt, replacing it with a clean Patrol duty suit, the elbows and knees of which had already smudged. Patan's hair had been washed and his face glowed cleanly, a portrait of ancient wisdom overlying the reality of his youth.

Susan nodded soberly as she ran fingers through the wealth of her lustrous hair. "I never thought of it that way. You make Spider sound like a . . . a social creation."

"In a sense, organized religion—note the key word: organized—is exactly that, a sham perpetrated by a priesthood seeking social status and power. This is different from a shamanistic religion like Spider. Any time a church is established and the religion is organized, it has the power to become a political institution. In fact, most do. They can be combated by understanding the basic functions they serve at the expense of the individual. Then the dogma has to be attacked in such a way that the flaws appear to outweigh the social value."

"What happens to me on that mountain is not a social function." She pointed an unforgiving finger at him, an eyebrow cocked.

Darwin nodded soberly, fingering the broken Santos fighting knife. "No, it isn't. At the same time, a mystical experience does exist for everyone . . . if they'll spend the effort to seek it out. The presence of that experience feeds the spiritual fires—although the fuel is never palatable to organized religion. Consider all the mystics like Meister Johannes Eckhart, Mohammed, Thomas Merton, Jesus, Rabia, and the others who've bucked their religions. It's a rough road. Islam, Judaism, and Christianity are the hardest of all on their mystics. Consider Sufi persecution by Islam as an example. Or the Christian inquisitions. The religious heirarchy attempts to sell its authority and superiority in spiritual matters. When the minions begin talking fervently of their encounters with Deity, the top bosses get nervous and react, since their power and authority are jeopardized and undermined."

"It doesn't make sense," Susan frowned, furrowing her smooth forehead and shaking her head. "How can what I experienced be so perverted?"

"Not everyone wants to experience his god. Most people

accept what they're told by powerful leaders generations removed from the actual miraculous event that spawned the religion.'' Pike shrugged. ''That's one of the strengths of Spider. The Prophets live their experience every day. The warriors go and seek their own visions. A great deal of power rests in that virtue. Further, there is no dissension among the Prophets since the decline of the Santos.'' He frowned. ''Kind of like the Prophets, with their evolved brains, have broken through the logjam of human emotions and pettiness. They've attained a permanent state of nirvana. In touch with the ultimate reality.''

''Must be difficult to argue dogma when the outcome is already known,'' Susan added dryly, looking to where Patan sat listening, eyes closed, a wan smile on his lips.

''Obviously, there is no point,'' the Prophet agreed. ''Besides, Santos and Spiders do not dissent. They have different names for the ineffable—different myths to say the same thing. It matters not if Haysoos was a man and was crucified or if Spider was a beast who was nailed to the cross. The fact remains that what you call Deity provided a lesson, namely that men remember to remain free. And in doing so, take responsibility. Responsibility is knowledge through experience.''

Darwin laughed brittlely. ''I wonder what Raven thinks of my preoccupation with Spider?''

Patan's voice soothed. ''If you wish to pursue this question, Doctor, you will lead a merry chase which cannot be definitively answered. The choice is yours; however, may I pose a question?''

''Of course.''

''The reality of Deity *is,* is it not? Does it matter, therefore, what name is applied to that most ultimate of all realities?''

''So it's a meaningless preoccupation?'' Pike exhaled.

A slight nod and Patan's cheshire smile rewarded him.

''So how do we implement our religious revolution?'' Susan asked, returning to the main subject. ''If it were up to me, we'd put a blaster to every Directorate head we could find and say Spider is God, yes or no?''

''That works if you have enough blasters and a lot of time. We don't,'' Pike told her with a smile. ''Success in this venture is by exposure, rationality, personality, and Patan's ability to make miraculous predictions of the future.

We also have to be adept in countering attacks. The Fathers—among others—will criticize our assumptions.''

"What are those?'' Susan shot him a perplexed look. She propped one shapely leg on a med unit while she twirled her headset in her hand.

"First, of course, we assume Deity exists. Second, we assume men have souls. Third, we assume the soul is immortal and is part of Deity. Fourth, we assume Deity's purpose is to learn or gain experience through the souls we are apportioned. That means we have assumed Deity is not all knowing, although He is all powerful.''

"Why wouldn't Spider be all knowing?'' Susan squinted up at the panels overhead, raking a spill of black hair over her shoulder. "Spider's Spider, isn't He?''

"Good question. Okay, consider this: The Prophets tell us our souls are here to learn for Spider. If we accept Spider as all knowing, why would He require you to go through the trials of learning and experiencing? Why is free will so carefully guarded? And what is the purpose of the universe?''

Susan nodded slowly. She ran a hand down the angle of her chin, a perplexed frown on her brow. "Okay, I'll bite, Doctor. What is the purpose of the universe?''

"Spider seeks to attain ultimate perfection,'' Patan opened his eyes to slits while he smiled beneficently. "We are here to gather sensation and fact and experience that Spider may one day achieve ultimate perfection. In human terms that is an infinite quest. Is it not also a noble one?''

"Right.'' Darwin agreed happily. "Therefore, we assume Deity is also imperfect. So long as Deity remains that way, pain and suffering must be endured.''

"There will be many questions concerning good and evil.'' Patan's features expressed paternal amusement.

Susan looked her question at Pike.

He nodded. "Of course. The question of good and evil has always been a bugaboo for religions with well-defined spiritual hierarchies. Everything hinges on the nature of God. If Deity is benevolent, why is evil allowed to exist? Various branches of Buddhism accept that each is equal—a balance of reality. Spider teaches that evil comes as the result of random chance and, more especially, free will. Spider is neutral, neither good nor evil, learning by the presence of both, tempered by both, unsure the universe would be better with one and not the other, seeking further data. By our free will we make mistakes in order that Spider may not in the end.''

''The Directorate tried to remove evil from humanity and look how it worked out in the end. I wonder if it would be worth the price? The attempt of the Directorate to create universal good left them wide open for Ngen's universal evil.'' Susan reached up to pull Darwin's Randall from the tray, studying the reflection of light on the polished blade while she thought.

''Hey! You're pretty smart for a Romanan,'' Darwin teased.

She smiled wickedly and winked, twirling the knife in supple fingers.

''The key to living with good and evil,'' Patan interrupted, ''is to balance them, using them in harmony to improve the quality of experience. The system is now natural, controlled only by events which unleash one or the other, causing cycles of suffering and happiness which are in turn somewhat tempered by human perception. How often, when starving, have you remembered the joyful moments? How often when your life was filled with joy did worry over potential disaster make you miserable?''

Pike laughed. ''Yeah, the age-old human problem of not knowing when you're well off. Those who live in a Golden Age rarely appreciate . . . or even understand the reality of their good fortune. Those who live in the midst of Dark Ages are too ignorant, scrambling too hard just to survive, to be depressed. Oddly, too, Golden Ages tend to be periods of pessimism while Dark Ages are biased toward optimism.''

''I don't think Ngen's psyched ghouls are optimistic.'' Susan shivered, the knife forgotten in her fingers as she stared vacantly beyond the overhead panels, absorbed by the memories of Bazaar.

''No, they aren't,'' Darwin agreed. ''Ngen is pioneering new heights of human debasement. Culture is partly a reflection of technology, environment, and stimulus from internal and external sources. In Ngen's case, he has a technological innovation—a mass psyching system—which will enable him to enslave a population with greater efficiency.''

Susan settled back, emphasizing her points with the waving tip of the keen-edged Randall. ''From what we've seen, the effects are irreversible. A man's identity is purged, including his personality, memories, and social behaviors. He becomes more than a machine and less than human. We can't return him to who he was. We can build a new identity with time, but he'll never be whole.''

''Ngen is committing a crime against God,'' Patan said, opening his eyes and looking around. ''He is denying them free will. By doing so, he is blinding the eyes through which Spider would see. He is subverting the purpose of the soul. The Fathers feel physical pain and ecstasy, but their souls do not benefit. For that reason only will the Prophets meddle in human affairs this time. For that reason will I sacrifice myself.''

''You wouldn't become involved if Ngen weren't psyching souls?''

''Only once did Prophets go to war,'' Patan smiled. ''During the original fight between the Romanans and *Bullet*, two Spider Prophets went to space to counter the attempts of a Santos Prophet who would have changed human affairs. When the problem was corrected, they returned to World and are still there. Chester Armijo Garcia went to space, not to change the affairs of the Directorate, but to teach and perhaps to save Susan Smith Andojar as perhaps I saved Darwin Pike.''

Susan paled, stiffening. Pike realized he'd stopped breathing himself. The vision of himself holding the Randall pointed at his own throat flashed in his brain. ''Why us?''

Patan shrugged indifferently. ''Because, properly tempered and dedicated to Spider, you may serve his purposes. The assumption, of course, being that you choose the right cusps as the future branches.''

''And what of humanity?'' Darwin asked, intent on the smiling man.

''Humanity means nothing to Spider, Doctor. The Prophets do not care if human beings live or die. If the species survives, it is because it is continuing to provide Spider with knowledge. If humans die, there are others who continue to learn and serve God's purpose. We are not special, Doctor. Humans have a peculiar emotional quirk: a need to believe the universe was constructed especially for them. It is a most naive and immature perception.''

Darwin nodded, swallowing nervously, voice suddenly gone gravelly. ''How are Susan and I important?'' No man enjoyed the thought of being God's chosen. Deity was notorious for using His protégés rather thoughtlessly. Of course, if you were God, a draftee was hard put to turn you down.

"It depends on the cusps, Doctor." Patan's benevolent features didn't reassure. "It may be necessary for you and the Captain to do Spider's work where others fail in combination. Perhaps you can do what others cannot."

"Perhaps?" Susan asked, voice hesitant. She sneaked a somber look at Pike.

"That depends," Patan smiled, bowing slightly, "on whether you and the Doctor are strong enough—and, of course, the cusps dictate all events. I can see a range of reactions on your part. You may both become Ngen's mindless Fathers; or you may become saviors of humanity; or you may soon be dead; or you may never be tried. The future—as always—depends on free will. I have told you all I can without changing your ability to cope with the cusps you may be called upon to endure." Patan sat back and closed his eyes.

Susan knew enough to realize the Prophet was through with the discussion. It took Darwin longer to futilely exhaust himself on Patan's wall of silence.

CHAPTER XXVII

Aboard the *Romanan* accelerating across the Tryst system.

Major Neal Iverson squinted at the image on the monitor. They'd found *Gregory*, all right, just sitting there. Wide open. He ran his tongue over his lips and considered the odds. The Admiral wanted him back to World asap. Here, on the other hand, lay a tempting chance at Ngen's captured flagship.

Iverson cataloged the faces of his officers where they sat around the small bridge. He couldn't mistake the glint in their eyes as they studied the target. *Gregory* had him outgunned by five hundred to one. Still, all it took was a simple vector correction, and he'd run the supply ship right down *Gregory*'s throat at light speed. The battleship rested in standard orbit over Tryst. She was probably at leisure watch, most of the gun crews off duty.

Iverson hesitated, squinting. He couldn't call the Admiral. The decision lay squarely on his shoulders. His eyes went to his bridge crew. They looked eagerly at him. A couple of thumbs went up. Nakai chewed his lip, eyes slitted at the image on the monitor.

"Let's take her," Neal decided. He had four Fujiki blasters, an amplified front shield, and with a 0.99 C run, they'd be within range for less than thirty seconds. Their mass, shields, and targeting sensors would give them away five minutes before maximum range. Perfect! Hardly long enough for *Gregory's* crew to react.

"Alert status!" Neal ordered. "All personnel, prepare for combat. Blaster crews and damage control to your positions. Marines, man your ATs just in case." Neal watched his hand-picked crew function like a perfect machine. Not a move was wasted as his small ship prepared to tackle the impossible. The vector shift took fifteen minutes as they boosted at forty-five gs for Tryst and *Gregory.*

"They've got us on sensors," Jacob Anson called out as the sensors unscrambled the red-shifted confusion of bent light. "Our mass must have tripped a deep space sensor with transduction capabilities. They're moving their eyes in our direction."

Neal glanced at the chronometer. Seven minutes to contact. Could they scramble so quickly? He doubted it. Ngen couldn't keep blaster crews on constant alert. They were human. Weapons techs got bored. Morale dropped. People got sloppy unless they had time for amusement. Just standing there, watching a blaster, ranked right up there with watching a rock age.

"Weapons test," Iverson ordered, watching his brilliant blasters sparking through the sky. Incredible. They were bouncing off light speed and the Fujiki blasters leaped out ahead of them—the physics people still hadn't figured that one out. Some quantum wave effect?

"Range in three minutes," Neal called. His blasters gave him the edge. He could shoot for almost fifteen seconds longer than *Gregory* with its primitive Patrol blasters. Or had Ngen had time to upgrade to Sirian specs? No matter either way. In that time, they might be able to at least cripple the big ship.

The targeting computers read mass, acceleration, light

speed, redshift, particle mass and a host of other variables, figuring the trajectory of the blaster bolts and how they would bend and warp at that speed. Fire control refined the targeting comm, aiming the deadly weapons, adjusting to within the angstrom, at points in space which would eventually allow hits on *Gregory*.

"They're targeting us, Captain," Anson called. "They're triangulating from far orbit. Must have eyes out there."

"At our velocity, it's all probability. They've got a mass trip, a vector, and a velocity. It's a long shot that they'd tag us." Still, Ngen had reacted with surprising speed.

Neal let himself imagine the confusion on the bridge as they discovered the speed at which he was diving down on them. There would be frantic confusion as they tried to determine the amount of time it would take to get their weapons functional. They wouldn't believe such a small ship could pose a threat to them.

Time dilated as Neal waited, knowing that to his eyes the activity on their bridge would seem a humanly impossible blur while he wouldn't seem to move from their perspective, relativity being what it was.

The targeting computer closed its calculations and four violet streams shot out, seeming to arc together in a curve as they shot toward *Gregory*. The shields on the big ship dazzled with color. Violet laced the vacuum before them as *Gregory* returned fire.

"We've got hits!" Anson yelled. "We're chewing holes right through his shields!"

"Full power to shields!" Neal ordered, feeling the odd flutter as the grav plates shifted with the acceleration. They seemed to splash through violet, blue, green, yellow, and red as they passed through the beams. Too many beams, Neal realized in sudden confusion. *Gregory*'s entire blaster bank was firing at him. Shooting along his vector.

How? He allowed himself to wonder for a brief instant before his screens flared from overload.

"Full acceleration!" Neal screamed. He felt himself pushed back into the command chair, knowing he'd overridden the blasters and some of the shield's capacity, but the technicolor ceased.

Neal checked the displays as a klaxon wailed angrily. Atmosphere dropped alarmingly in the aft compartments. They'd been hit! How bad? Neal threw a frightened glance at the reactor stats. He froze, swallowing hard. The fields wavered, snapping back and forth. Angrily, he smashed a fist against the control chair. How had the Fathers scrambled so quickly? How had they managed to put together a defense that rapidly? They hadn't had that much time even with the special relativity effect!

"Engineering?" Neal called. "What can you do with that reactor?"

"Pray," came the laconic reply.

Neal did just that, looking curiously up at the effigy of a Spider which had been drawn on the panels overhead.

Neal wet his lips. "Nakai." He sounded far away. "Divert all the power you can to transduction; bleeding that much will help drain the fields. Send everything to the Admiral on scramble. We may not have much time. *Push it!*"

"Yes, sir. Sending now, sir. I'm refining the beam as we send."

Neal waited, trying to drown the frantic calls coming through comm with the grinding of his molars.

The feared call came five minutes later. "Captain, we're losing control of the reaction. You have less than a minute to blow it . . . or we'll make a new star out here."

Feeling his heart stop in his body, Neal Iverson snapped the "dead-man's box" open and looked at the two red breakers. The comm pickup was monitoring, the channel left open, sending everything happening on the bridge. He pulled the first breaker and hesitated. Ahead of them stretched perpetual blackness, the nearest inhabited star some eighty-nine light-years away. The potential for rescue? Nonexistent. If Ngen thought they were worth it, his ships would take an eternity to catch up.

Iverson looked at the second breaker that would save their lives for the moment. On the reaction monitor, the gauge continued climbing past the critical point.

"*Captain!*" came the strained cry from engineering. Neal looked into the ashen faces on his bridge. They wouldn't last two months before they turned to cannibalism—but air would be gone in five weeks. That far out, there wouldn't be enough solar energy to keep the units going.

Neal's fingers were still on the breaker as the ship shivered, the reactor eating its own guts.

The voice filled comm. "*Captain! For the love of God, blow the . . .*"

The reaction decayed. Antimatter and matter annihilated itself beyond containment. In the heart of the ship, the explosion was instantaneous, creating a visible record of blinding light which leaped for the stars, like the ripples left by a pebble tossed into a pond.

On the bridge of *Gregory,* Ngen Van Chow was almost surprised by the flash his sensors picked up forty minutes later. He chuckled with glee. He'd gotten them after all! Only the death of a ship could release so much energy. He settled himself into the command chair, looking down the rows of gun crews who stood, staring blankly at their blasters on the gun deck.

So long as they were rotated every twelve hours, they would stand there, always ready, always alert, minds empty except for what they needed to run the equipment.

Damage control reported six breaches in the hull from the mysterious blasters. They'd made cheese of his shields. Ngen reached for M'Klea's hand, running fingertips down her smooth skin.

"Very exciting!" she breathed, replaying the records of the fight. "Too bad they destroyed themselves. Wouldn't they have made grand entertainment?"

Ngen grunted, thinking about those odd blasters. He called up the spectral analysis, checking for redshift. Impossible. They couldn't have actually exceeded light speed? The bolts didn't exhibit the right signatures. The whole effect could be likened to a particle appearing where a particle was supposed to—from outside space-time.

"What does it mean?" he wondered, chin propped in one hand. Absently, he let the fingers of his other trace a design over the firm flesh of her pelvis, as if outlining the life growing within that warm wet sanctuary.

University Station: Arcturus.

Ten MacGuire walked down the curve of the engineering corridor of University Station, blinking at the gritty feeling in his eyes. A department meeting? At this time of night? Only the Director could have called it. But then, things were no longer normal. The whole Directorate had become an insane place riddled with conflicting stories of stations blown out of space, and planets bombed and Deus rising in Ambrose Sector, spreading into Gulag. The Fathers preached openly—even in University. Already the name of Deus had become commonplace, scrawled on walls along with anti-Directorate graffiti.

At the same time, Spider cult devotees roamed the streets and corridors. Too much had gone topsy-turvy—and now they had faculty meetings in the middle of the night?

Ten entered the main faculty lounge, seeing most of the engineering department, and the professors from physics as well, waiting in the chairs, appearing as owl-eyed as he himself.

"Ten?" Veld Arstong asked, getting to his feet. "What's this all about? We had a message through comm. Emergency, it said. What's—"

"I don't know," Ten cut him off. "I don't know a thing about it."

"But you called us!" Coree Mancamp jumped to his feet, pointing. An eruption of irritated voices filled the room.

Ten waved his arms, quieting the throng as a couple of late arrivals entered, looking as wooden-faced as the rest. "Enough! Hear me out. I *didn't* call this meeting. I just had a message that an emergency existed and assumed it had been routed through comm from the Directors. Now, before we all leap to conclusions, let's wait for a bit and see what happens. If the Directors need us to solve some problem, they'll be patched through soon.

"On the other hand, *think,* people! If it is an emergency, and the Directors need us for some sort of rear cadre, they'd be upset to call us up and find out we'd gone home on the spur of the moment.

"You've got a point," Helmut agreed. "I . . ." He sagged. "Christ! You don't suppose it's the undergraduates again."

"They wouldn't have!" Veld smacked a fist into a palm and looked around. "Well, we ought to be used to pranks by now. If that turns out to be the case, Coree, you think you can ferret out the individual or individuals responsible?"

A new voice called from the back. "That would be nice, gentlemen—but futile."

Ten squinted up the aisle and gaped. The men filing in the doorway carried deadly looking police blasters.

"Hey! What the . . ." He stopped short, staring down the barrel of one of the weapons as a dark-haired young man jumped up beside him. No more than twenty, the skinny man didn't look like a police patrolman. The brightly colored clothing he wore had a use-shiny look to it. Ten couldn't miss the slight odor of sweat from an unwashed body.

"Your questions will be answered in a moment, Doctor MacGuire. For now, we want all of you to get to your feet. Make no efforts to delay us or to escape. I assure you, we'll not hesitate to blow off a foot or a hand. All we need intact are your brains, ladies and gentlemen."

Ten looked past the ugly snout of the blaster and into the man's eyes. No student, this, he had a hard look about him.

"I think we'd better do as he says," Ten said into the suddenly quiet room.

"I think you're right," the man agreed, an oily tone in his voice. "I get paid whether you're in great shape or missing something. Makes no difference to me."

Veld cried out, "The Directors will . . . w—" He stuttered to a halt as a blaster was shoved into his crotch by a skinny blonde girl wearing the severe garb of the Fathers. She smiled wickedly into Veld's bulging eyes.

"Yes? You were saying, Doctor Arstong?"

Veld's jaw worked, no sounds issuing from his O-shaped mouth.

"Move 'em . . . or lose 'em, Doc," the girl giggled, jabbing harder with the blaster.

The brigand laughed sharply. "As I thought. No more comment from Doctor Arstong. All right, esteemed intellectuals, on your feet. Let's go. We've thirty minutes to make it to the spindle. Your boat ride should be waiting."

"My . . . boat ride?" Ten cocked his head, thoughts half on his wife and children sleeping so soundly a couple of floors away.

"Yeah. It's a figure of speech. You guys are drafted." The leader leered happily. "Let's go. We don't have a lot of—"

"I'm not going anywhe—" Coree stumbled as a blaster clunked hollowly on the back of his skull.

The leader grinned into suddenly ashen faces as Coree moaned and collapsed, hands to the back of his head. "Oh, yeah, you're all going—and your families are already on the way. Relax, don't worry, our people are in control at the Spindle, seeing to it they get into the shuttle. Now, come on, let's go."

Rough hands yanked Coree to his feet; he reeled up the aisle as hands pushed him along.

"Let's go, Doc," the blonde added, backing up. "Try and run and I'll see if I can't blow your balls off with this thing. They haven't given me much time to practice, you know? I might get more than your balls."

Veld started uneasily toward the door, walking awkwardly.

He shook his head, struggling with disbelief. "You'll never—"

"—get away with it?" the gang leader finished. He laughed, motioning Ten ahead of him with the blaster as men and women filed out the doors. "Want to make a wager, Doctor? Considering what's about to happen to Arcturus, you'll be lucky to ever be missed."

Aboard *Gabriel* decelerating into the Arcturian system.

"Identify yourselves, and await confirmation!" A stern Patrol woman looked Torkild Alhar in the eye as her image formed in *Gabriel's* bridge monitor.

He studied his ship's position. He and Sira's *Michael* were decelerating, shedding V with full power.

Torkild forced his face to reflect relief as he primed himself for the exchange. The speech he'd worked so hard on, spilled out, made frantic by his nervousness. "We're two unarmed GCIs from Santa del Cielo, I think you can understand why we don't have registration. On board are civilian casualties. We're seeking refuge. This is still the Directorate, isn't it?"

The Patrol woman hesitated. "Explain yourself."

"You haven't seen what we've seen! We want sanctuary! The Fathers are killing Directorate citizens right and left back there. Now, do we get clearance? Or do we go to the Romanans? It is our understanding they'll at least do something about the Fathers." He glared at the woman, tightening his throat muscles. *"We need HELP! Damn it!"*

She hesitated again, a sudden uncertainty in her eyes. She nodded slowly. It had worked! He'd played the part of a frayed, desperate man and they'd bought it!

"*Ganges* allows your approach along your present vector. Do not deviate from your line of approach or you will be destroyed. Follow the buoys in and dock respectively at Admin Docks 357 and 358. Personnel will be present to assist in resettlement and debriefing."

"Thank you, *Ganges*," Torkild said in unfeigned relief.

He took a deep breath to still his singing nerves and sank into the seat. "It's been a long trip. We're overcrowded and short of food and water. We have wounded aboard needing med, too."

"Affirmative, GCI, we'll have med waiting. Be aware that Security will board your vessel at the lock, and your passengers and ship will be screened and inspected."

Torkild nodded respectfully. "We understand and have no objection . . . so long as they're not Fathers."

Torkild shifted his eyes to the other bridge monitor which displayed the lines of Arpeggian blaster crews who sat alongside their guns, laughing, joking, thinking about the raid they were about to pull off. In five hundred years, no one had fired a shot at Arcturus. They were making history.

The Patrol monitor went blank and Torkild could see *Ganges* moving slowly out of their vector. They would pass within thirty or forty kilometers of the big ship. How long? Twenty minutes? Maybe a little more?

"Mikhail! We have one antimatter torpedo aboard. Break it out. Prepare to fire on my signal. Program the targeting computer for *Ganges.* " Torkild laughed. Oh, for the expressions on their faces if they could but see his daring gamble!

"Blaster crews! Anticipate a follow up attack on *Ganges.* They'll try to destroy our torpedo. With luck, we can demoralize them enough to cover the attack."

Torkild swallowed reflexively. He took a risk worthy of the House of Alhar. The Patrol might react so rapidly as to blow him out of space before the torpedo hit. Throat going dry, he calculated the trigonometry as *Ganges* inched out of their path. He'd need ten seconds from release to impact. In that time, he *had* to keep his ship alive.

Torkild felt a grim humor build within him. "Open a line to Sira—voice only—as tightly focused as possible." He waited.

"What?" Sira's gruff voice asked tartly, keeping communication to a minimum.

"Stand by to accelerate on my order. I'll need backup!"

"That's *not* the plan!"

"Do it! You've no choice! Otherwise, we're all dead!" He glared at the speaker.

"Your life may be at stake, Alhar," Sira's voice dripped threat.

"Yeah," Torkild muttered, watching the growing bulk of

Ganges. Behind the white mass of the huge Patrol Line ship, the intertwined strands of Arcturus, the largest city-state in the galaxy, wrapped around its red star like a ring of burning wire. Praise Deus, no imagining of Arcturus could prepare a man for the actual sight. An entire city, orbiting one star!

Torkild's heart rapped painfully against his ribs as he thought of what he was about to try. With one blow, he was going to destroy one of the largest battleships ever built by man on a raid that took him to the very center of civilization. Not since Alaric burned Rome in 410 AD had so audacious a plan come together.

The minutes dragged as Torkild knotted his fists, tendons straining to keep the fear from showing in his trembling hands.

"Damn, that's a big ship," Bruno whispered under his breath as they closed. "If they fire . . ."

Torkild swallowed hard. If they fired? Yes, the big if. How would M'Klea react when she heard her loving brother had died at the hands of the Patrol? How long would she cry in his martyred name?

He watched the seconds counting on the clock. "Five, four, three, two, one, *Fire!*" he shouted. *"Sira! Accelerate!"*

A sense of frantic relief rushed his system as Sira's *Michael* erupted reaction mass to shoot ahead. His own blasters were lacing the side of the huge battleship, cutting through the shields, ripping along the white sides in constant explosion as plating buckled and atmosphere jetted out.

As he had hoped, *Michael,* moving ahead, drew most of the fire. At the same time, his gunners targeted the blaster banks that were giving Sira the hardest time. The flash of the antimatter torpedo's contact with *Ganges* overwhelmed the screens, blanking them white, overloading sensor systems, burning out boards.

"Accelerate!" Torkild ordered, seeing a glaring explosion arcing across the few kilometers that separated them. From the boiling gases and debris blowing out of the battleship, he couldn't estimate the damage he'd done.

"Mikhail, get busy on those burned out sensors. Replace the L panels now! Otherwise, we're blind on that side. Damage control, get me a report on what we suffered. Now, people! We're in the middle of the enemy, by Deus' brooding blood.''

"Sira on the comm," Bruno called.

"We're short of eyes and he wants to tie one up." Torkild slapped the command chair armrest. "Very well, put him on."

"My God!" Sira's face formed on the screen, expression incredulous. "What did you do? How . . . how did you . . ."

Torkild waved it off. "We needed to have our way out clear of any possible interference. Arcturus lies bare before us, Sira. The solution was simple really. No matter how large *Ganges* was, she had a weakness. They were so powerful and we seemed so helpless, we were able to do the unexpected. There's a lesson in that."

The captain looked at him with new respect. "I understand, Torkild Alhar. I think I have learned it. I must compliment you on your cunning. I bow to your wisdom." He inclined his head.

"Enough of bowing," Torkild smiled, feeling a euphoric rush of victory burst in his body. "You make your appointment at University. *Gabriel* will pick and choose, blow up this and that. Come, let us exercise our blasters. Arcturus lies unscathed before us. Perhaps the star will have an oxygen atmosphere when we are through."

"Well met, Torkild!" Sira laughed happily, slapping his leg with a hard hand. "And your audacity and daring will have the Messiah's full ear in my report!"

Like two raptors, they descended. Arcturus sprawled, glowing in the light of the giant red star—simply too gargantuan to destroy all in one raid. They had no idea when the Patrol might show up with something more powerful and strike a vengeful blow against them. Thoughtfully, Torkild sat on the bridge, defining target after target, watching in amazement as his guns blasted and ripped and tore through the huge, spinning tubes that were Arcturus.

Directorate Administration: Directorate Section, Arcturus.

The room around Director Skor Robinson pulsed in eternal luminescent blue. Robinson floated, curled into a tight fetal ball, thin arms and legs tucked tightly against his chest in the zero gravity of his control station. Had anyone been present, they would have seen his face contorting, lips lifted to expose rudimentary teeth. Flickers of anguish tightened his eyes, trembling spasms jerking down flexed limbs to knot the delicate hands in impotent horror. From his rarely used throat issued broken whimperings—those of an animal in searing pain.

Frantic, obsessed with horror, Skor closed decompression doors throughout the huge sprawling city, heedless of the panicked throngs pressing through. Comm conductor strips severed under melting jets of hot plasma as bulkheads ruptured. Blaster bolts raked entire sections of the huge stations, spilling the contents into the vacuum of space where the screams of the dying were cut off in a puff of condensed air and blood as spasming lungs ruptured. He shifted circuits, pasting together a new Gi-net nervous system as he tried to keep the endless maze of corridors closed and power flowing. He could feel the touch of An Roque and Semri Navtov as they directed the evacuation and defense of an infinitely vulnerable city.

"How did this happen to us?"

He cried out, lungs convulsing as violet blaster bolts continued to detonate entire sections of the capital into fiery death and jets of plasma. Arcturus shook and quivered, the huge tube of the main structure buckling, twisting, and breaking loose as blaster fire cut through a half kilometer of graphsteel. Skor shifted as the floor jumped and pulsed around him. He bounced painfully against an iridescent blue wall and screamed in horror as power flickered for a moment, then stabilized.

Physical pain lanced up his side from his bruised arm, knee, and hip.

Panicked, he blinked for a moment before realizing he was still alive. In his head, entire portions of the Gi-net blackened and died, leaving a stygian hollow in his mind. Numb, terror-locked, he wept aloud, tears shimmering the endless blue of his room, blurring his vision. Mucus blocked the back of his nose to discharge from his nostrils. One by one, sections of his mind began to go blank—as if the very neurons in his head flickered and died.

He wailed into the rumbling nightmare of Arcturus' devastation.

Wrapping atrophied hands around his bulbous cranium, he howled, afraid as he'd never been. Trembling, almost spastic from hysteria, he pulled the helmet from his skull.

Gasping for breath, he quivered, the blackness gone—severed with all its mayhem and havoc. He shivered, in stunning isolation, to huddle at the end of his catheters and whimper. Only now, in the absence of the system, he could begin the task of reintegrating his faltering mind.

In the insulation of solitude, he sobbed to himself, choking on the phlegm his lacrimals produced, blinded by the water beading on his eyes. Abject in his dazed misery, he teetered on the verge of giving in to the gibbering demons pulling at his sanity with taloned fingers.

"What's happened? What's happened to me?" he cried out, body throbbing to the thumping detonations felt through the very air.

In desperation, he grabbed at the only fragile link to humanity that came to his shredded mind.

"Prophet? Teach . . . me," he wailed as tears, like jewels, formed on his lashes, tiny clinging globes in the zero g.

"Prophet?" His voice echoed through the empty room, challenged only by the subtly conducted vibrations of death and destruction under the bombardment. "Prophet, what is this madness?"

From his memory, the words formed in Chester's easy voice, *"Life is experience, not a series of puzzles interpreted by your computers. We are on the verge of an age of passion. Passion is emotion channeled . . . as a wall is composed of stacked bricks."*

"Passion? Around me millions are dying irrationally. *Dying,* Prophet."

". . . Death is nothing. It lies on all sides of us, distracted by one cusp, enticed by another."

"And what of death, Prophet? I . . . I may die any second. Death is everywhere around me. Fear is thick in the very air. I am scared, Prophet. Don't irritate me now. Tell me what to do! Tell me . . . tell . . . me . . ." His lungs jumped within, rattling his breath in his throat.

Chester's voice soothed, *"I am a teacher, a teacher is a constant irritation; and the worth of man is God. Death lies on all sides, Director. Accept your humanity. Accept your passion. Passion is the key to knowledge. It is the way of Spider."*

"Spider. You told me I was part of God, Prophet. Part of God. Inside me. In my soul." Skor sniffed, rubbing at the sticky discharge from his nose. He blinked the tears away to float like miniscule crystal planets in the zero g. Trailing his catheters, he swam to his helmet, cuddling it to his belly like a frightened baby.

"Spider sent me a Prophet. A teacher." He drew faith from that, finding a sliver of strength deep within that he'd never experienced before. A hollow bang echoed through the deep security of his comm center. Somewhere beyond his heavy hatch, a man screamed orders.

"Need me," he whispered softly. "They need me." He lifted the huge helmet, placing it carefully over his head so the deep brain electrodes matched, feeling the black spots of dead computer net. Valiantly, despite the pain eating at his fibrillating body, he fought to save the rest of Arcturus, numbing himself to the desperation of billions as they died.

Only the magnitude of the disaster shook him now.

He'd known they were in trouble. The blinding flash that had spelled the death of *Ganges* had caught him completely by surprise. The sensor immediately registered the spectra as an antimatter explosion.

He flinched at the sudden loss of communication with an another entire segment of the huge complex. Desperately, he fought the vertigo of his mind going blank, dead. His atrophied stomach lurched, the nerve triggering a vomit response. He heaved, a nasty taste ejected into his throat. Was this death? Reeling from the horrendous damage, Skor tried to still his staggering mind. Visual showed him thousands of wiggling, kicking bodies being blown out of the ripped station walls. How many?

"Don't think about it. Save all you can. Count the dead later." He bit his tongue, despite the taste of bile, using pain to still his desperation.

Navtov? Roque? Where are you? he inquired time after time, seeking to patch a bridge from one blasted system to another.

"I am alone," he whispered, appalled at the thought. "I've never been alone before. God, how terrible."

"You are God. It is the way of Spider."

"Damn you, Prophet! You've seen this. Damn you!"

The nightmare continued for three hours while Robinson sent out distress call after distress call, relaying pictures of the death of *Ganges* and the destruction wrought at Arcturus. Blocking his mind, blocking his new-found humanity, he willed himself to work, to struggle, to drive himself past exhaustion. He shut down reactors, blocked compartments from decompression, shut off water, dispatched tugs, deployed damage control teams, sweating as he fought to save something of his capital. In his frantic passion, he found strength. To do otherwise would have left him a gibbering hulk, addled at the enormity of the waste and death and ruin of six hundred years of human civilization in space.

Arcturus, the crown jewel of humanity, burned and bled—its precious resources destroyed by the dead chill of space, the gruesome corpses contorting in halos of their own crystallized blood, breath, and urine—all weirdly lit by the rich red light of the giant star.

Skor barely realized when it stopped. The station ceased to jump and buck and creak and rumble. Power remained steady as he waited for a new breach that never came. He floated, totally immobile, vital signs at a low ebb, while atmosphere ceased boiling out of the blackened ruptures and the corpses spun lazily through the hell light and dispersing clouds.

Semri? Assistant Director? Roque?

Silence.

The system had become a void, ominously mute. Not even the survivors jammed the net with screeching calls for relief. For a second, Arcturus reeled, stunned by the stillness.

A ghost in an electronic reality, Skor probed, tracing the living quarters of his counterparts out of the fragmented maze of still functioning comm units. Switching to visual, he accessed the holo in Navtov's zero g room. Skor closed his eyes, a wretchedness sending his thoughts spinning. A different kind of pain lanced his heart. He refined the image to see his fellow Director floating in the air, limbs outstretched, digits twitching, eyes half bulging from his head. The mental activity diminished even as Skor watched. Skimming the med readout at the same time as he reactivated Semri's ruptured system, he found the cause of death. Navtov had just died of a massive cerebral hemorrhage. The stroke had paralyzed him at the height of the attack—just seconds after Skor had abandoned his own helmet.

Roque? An, are you alive? Skor patched into Navtov's system, finally finding a parallel system, cross-looping into an area accessed by Roque's net.

I . . . Alive? I . . .''

Take Navtov's system. I have to see what I can salvage. Count the dead and attempt to find help.

Help? Find help? Find . . .

Skor shifted his visual access, cross patching through a crazy quilt of systems to Roque's curious purple room. The Assistant Director stared vacantly, mouth slack, drool running down his chin to hang like some clear snake in the zero g.

Roque? Answer me, Roque?

The eyes continued staring into infinity.

"Blessed God," Skor whispered. "He's gone completely mad. There's . . . there's only me."

Robinson studied the monitors, isolating Roque from the net. Devastated, reeling, he began organizing rescue parties, coordinating evacuation of the wounded. Directing repair crews to reconnect comm and power. Tugs were dispatched to stabilize entire sections of Arcturus which had been blown in two. He could see external decompressed debris hurling out toward the blackness from angular acceleration. The internally oriented decompression damage had spewed out materials which now settled back, some hanging on the plating, some drifting past, falling outward.

Robinson increased the adrenaline pouring into his bloodstream from the tubes that supplied his liquids and fed his thin body.

"I am alone." He closed his eyes. "Spider, help me, what do I do? How can I Direct this all on my own?"

He had four ships of the Line left: *Uhuru, Kamikazi, Toreon,* and *Amazon.* Three years ago, he'd had a fleet of eleven of those magnificent ships. Now, the Romanans had taken three. The Sirians had destroyed two, the Fathers had captured one, and destroyed another.

Mind-numb, he struggled to balance his options, finding no strategic value in leaving the mighty gun platforms in their respective Sectors. He could find no line to hold when ships could jump outside the real universe from one corner of human space to the other.

"But I have to do . . . I have to . . ." He sniffed at his plugged nose, aware of the tears again. "I have to . . . Prophet? Help me?"

Skor shuffled the preliminary casualty figures. Two hundred and ninety million people had died in that three-hour spree of death and violence. Tugs were scooping up all the debris, material, wreckage, and bodies they could before it drifted out of reach.

Two hundred and ninety million people? And they had all depended on him, on *THE* Director.

He shuttled several emergency calls to the remains of security until they called in an emergency.

Riots broke out in the Arcadia housing domes in the Russian section—once the poorest part of Arcturus. Skor monitored the videos, staring woodenly as frightened people rampaged through the streets, demanding Patrol protection.

"Protection?" he mumbled listlessly to himself. "Protection from where? The Patrol couldn't even save us. Maybe . . . maybe they can't even save themselves."

He focused on a man wrapped in cloth who had been hoisted onto the shoulders of others. "Deus will protect us! The Messiah's right! Satan's loose in the Directorate! Death to the Directors! Bring us peace! Bring us Deus!"

The mob roared in appreciation.

"Bastard!" Skor gritted and began shutting down the life support until they passed out for lack of oxygen. No Director had ever been forced to subdue his own population in such a manner.

Arcturus—the holy grail of Directorate space had been brutalized and raped. His people were ripe for revolt—ripe to accept even the Fathers and their abominations of psyched men. Skor swallowed hard.

A horrible ache filled his wracked chest. Hideous discolorations had formed on the side of his body that had slammed into the wall. One avenue remained open which might save him, Arcturus, and humanity.

He accessed a subspace transduction channel and waited, hoping his terms of surrender would be acceptable and contemplating how lucky Semri Navtov had truly been.

CHAPTER XXVIII

Aboard *Abraham* in GEO orbit over Santa del Cielo.

Winston Zimbuti came to attention as the Messiah's face formed on the monitor.

"Good day, Captain."

"Messiah." Winston lowered himself into the comfort of

the command chair. Around him, his Arpeggian and Cielan officers went silent, attempting to look busy while their ears sharpened for any word.

Ngen cocked his head. "You and I, Winston, we go back a long way."

"To the Sirian docks, Ngen. Yes, indeed. You've surprised me." He raised his black hands. "Look at this. Who would have thought an assassin like Zimbuti would command a warship?"

Ngen smiled thinly. "Who, indeed. But then, I always admired your skill and intelligence."

"And you'd always better."

Ngen stiffened, eyes narrowing. "Yes, I should, shouldn't I? I take it you've received your quota of supplies?"

"Yeah, Ngen. We have. Thanks for seeing to it so quickly, we're looking forward to taking some time. Getting the kinks out. Maybe a good drunk or two, a couple of women with big—"

"You're spacing immediately."

"Hey, man, that wasn't—"

"Did you hear me?" Ngen pointed a slim brown finger, eyes glittering, a deadly expression on his flat face. "You think, Winston. Think hard. Who got you that ship? Me. That's who. I've seen fit to extend the grace of Deus to you. Understand? Never . . . never forget I am the chosen of Deus. To you, I am Messiah. Ngen is no longer. You call me Messiah."

Winston clamped his lip with white teeth, biting off the hot retort. *And where would you have been without me eliminating the opposition? Planting the bombs? You're getting pretty damn high and mighty for a dockside smuggler.* Only the power *was* Ngen's. And Winston Zimbuti hadn't gotten where he was by being stupid.

"Ah," Ngen's oily smiled widened, wicked, knowing. "You see, don't you. I've always read you well, Winston. An early exhibition of my godhead. Yes, you saw it in me even then, didn't you? You knew way back that I was chosen, that I . . . *I,* Ngen Van Chow, would be the Messiah!"

"Yeah, sure . . . Messiah." Winston swallowed the bile that choked the back of his throat. "So where are we spacing for?"

Ngen clapped his hands eagerly. "A special task. One worthy of your skills. While Sira hits Arcturus, I've saved the Romanans' World for you."

Winston nodded slowly to himself. *Thanks, Ngen. You're a real jewel of a man. You stupid fat-headed bastard.*

"Sure, Ngen, we'll knock it—"

"*Messiah!* You *will* call me Messiah!"

Winston stared into those possessed eyes, a sudden flutter in his heart. The man was mad!

"Yes, Messiah."

Bridge of *Spider's Knife* in orbit over Arpeggio.

Her fingers crushed the padding of the command chair, dimpling the heavy upholstery. Tense as spring steel, she watched the *Knife*'s big bridge monitor. On the screen, the slim dart of the AT closed on the gray-shadowed side of the station, centering on the spin axis. The place fit all the criteria for an orbital farm. An elongated rotating cylinder, it stretched a little over a kilometer with a diameter of some 350 meters. Inside would be a fusion power source to run the atmosphere and provide light for low g food plants growing in dirt held in place by angular acceleration. She held her breath as the AT punched its reinforced nose through the plating. Wisps of gases curled out around the torn rent.

"We're through," Corporal Mishima's voice reported over the comm. "We got another farm all right. The marines are deployed." Several seconds passed. "No resistance, Major, just like at Mystery."

Rita relaxed and twisted a red braid around her finger as she settled back in the instrument-studded command chair, letting her eyes play over the hanging monitors, tracing the narrow curve of the arced bridge. The panels needed cleaning again, there were fingerprints on the white graphite. The atmosphere fan hummed in the background. Pulling uneasily on her braid, she waited for the marines to report. Max Wan Ki stared anxiously up from his pilot's couch, tension in the line of his face, fingers rapping a nervous staccato on the comm console. Apprehension, like tendrils of smoke, drifted through the *Knife*'s very air. Neal had made a quick pass by Arpeggio. Evidently he hadn't damaged it much. The system still bustled with activity—unlike the horror they'd left behind on Bazaar.

Rita's people had seen the legacy Susan's blasters had left on Bazaar. Rampant, the specter of starvation and death twined blackly through the dry dusty air. Shrunken skeletons of corpses lined the streets. Bodies lay unheeded where they had fallen, while gaunt, hollow-eyed people steadfastly walked each day to stare at blank monitors, unable to comprehend their place didn't exist anymore. At night they walked home only to return the next day and stare with empty eyes until they, too, fell by their stations—more of the corrupting dead, their decaying flesh adding to the drifting stench.

The entire planet stank of death; flies hovered over sightless eyes as the corpses desiccated in the hot arid winds. To Rita and her crew, it had been like walking through a twisted version of hell. Only the once tame dogs and cats relished the macabre scene as they slunk among the corpses, bellies bloated. Pete Wing Smith had accidentally kicked a swollen corpse, jumping back as a white ball of maggots tumbled from a young woman's burst belly to writhe and wriggle in the dark torrid air.

Only the dead had peace.

Images of the living clawed at a person's sleep, the rustle of their parched flesh scraping around the edges of tortured dreams to leave the haunted sleeper awake in the dark, staring at the ceiling panels, wide-eyed.

When asked, the emaciated survivors raved about their place, stubbornly trying to make their way to blasted factories or deflating, lifeless farms. Others sat in grounded airtrucks awaiting directions to drive among the sand-blasted ruins—oblivious to the empty charges in the batteries. Others dismantled and reassembled engines they had taken apart and assembled the day before, engines for which no fuel remained. But they worked on, bones protruding from their starved bodies. Mindless eyes stared from masks of incipient death, skulls grinning under the sagging skin of their faces.

The eerie silence in so human a place ate at the mind. Only the wind remained, moaning and rustling through the corpses, fluttering dry clothing, exposing withered heatblackened skin shrunk tight over bone. Lightning cracked and boomed, searing the dust-ridden skies, flickering in the sunken eyes of the gaping dead. The living mumbled among themselves—and died in silence. The sound of their shuffling was faintly audible as they still tried to get up and walk to their places.

Rita's tough Romanan crew—veterans of Sirius and hundreds of bloody raids—had recoiled at the horror, vomiting when the stink of death hung cloyingly in the grit-laden air. They stared over their shoulders as they walked broad avenues lined with the sightless dead. Blasters drawn, nerves at fever pitch, they jumped and started at the noises of a dead planet.

And my order left Mystery the same way. Only we'll never go back to see. None of us could stand that. Spider, what have we done? We crushed Mystery as thoroughly as Susan did Bazaar. What legacy is ours?

She'd tried everything to bring the Fathers back to consciousness. Pain, threats, beatings, reasoning, nothing changed their routine, including the psych unit in her hospital. The results had been marginal at best. They could adjust a person's behavior so he didn't go to his "place," but they couldn't reinstall values or survival skills. They couldn't make them *think* again. The Patrol psych units couldn't rebuild an entire personality.

So she and her crew would continue to live the nightmares. She'd left Bazaar to starve itself to oblivion and moved on to Arpeggio. Here, at least, they'd found a functioning hive of human machines.

And here, too, I can look down and see the people I will murder. On Arpeggio, I will create the same version of hell Susan made of Bazaar and I made of Mystery. Spider, help us. What madness do we send to you through all these suffering souls?

"Major!" Max Wan Ki called. "We've got company coming. Two bogeys dropped out of jump, shedding V. They're putting out strong sensor scans."

"Can they pick us out yet?" Rita peered up at the screens, noting the intruder's sensor location. The bastards were coming in from Ambrose Sector if she was any judge.

"Negative, Major," He was shaking his head. "We have maybe six or seven hours before they can obtain a clear enough reading to pick up out in all these stations. That's assuming they know what to look for. I guess that's one advantage of being little for once."

Rita settled back in the command chair. They'd found Arpeggio defenseless, not a sensor scanning for incoming mass or reaction. Unopposed, they had approached in the sensor shadow of a tug and dropped unobserved into the halo of stations surrounding the planet. The only ears they'd picked up were hidden behind the bulk of the planet: a huge shipfitting center in geosynchronous orbit, busy for the moment converting GCIs to military use.

So what were her options? She looked at the intruder vectors Max had refined from Doppler sensors. She had six hours to decide how to handle the situation. Rise and fight? Gamble *Knife*'s agility and four Fujiki blasters against the unknown capabilities of Ngen's ships?

After almost two months of prowling, shooting up planetary systems, and jumping between Ngen's planets, they were low on supplies. Antimatter could always be generated out of anything. Food, on the other hand, needed restocking. Raiding the stations of the Fathers was easy, lucrative, and safe. Mindless farmers tended the fields, letting the Romanans pick what they wanted. They showed no reaction as Romanans took coup from screaming victims, stole their remaining personal items, or committed any kind of atrocity. And for the moment, they needed food.

"Major? Look at this." Ki motioned to one of the monitors. One of the optical scanners had focused on the planet below—a magnification of an open, rocky field. On it, a large body of men and women were advancing in what was obviously a military operation.

"They're perfect!" Rita breathed, watching the waves of soldiers moving as if they were orchestrated by computer.

"That's not all," Ki remained grim. "With the exception of manufacturing and food growing centers, the rest of Arpeggio is the same. Everywhere I look, they're practicing with blasters, demolitions, beach-heading, you name it. The Arpeggians are all playing war down there."

Cold vacuum sucked at her soul. "Not playing, Ki. That's dress rehearsal for the rest of the galaxy. I don't doubt but that somewhere out in the Sectors they have another bunch doing the same in preparation for station warfare."

"I thought Ngen's god would hand him the galaxy." Ki looked skeptical. He ran a stylus back and forth in his fingers, shaking his head.

Rita's twisted smile took him by surprise. "It won't hand him the Sectors *we* control. You think the Admiral's going to let a single Temple be built in our territory? Not in this lifetime. Not only that, we've been out of touch. We don't know what the Admiral has in mind for that anthropologist. I'd wager Ngen isn't putting all his faith in his jihad. Too many places in the Directorate are learning about Bazaar and Mystery and will end up fearing his mindless ghouls."

She glanced anxiously up at the bogeys, Ki's definition of their vector down to a half degree now. What in hell was she going to do about those damn ships? Could she take them? Was it worth the risk? Her inspection then turned to Bud's AT where it stuck in the rotating station.

An idea scratched its way to the surface.

"Bud?" Rita turned to the comm. "I don't care how you do it, but when you get that AT loaded with food, cut us a hole in the side of that tin can. We've got two bogeys coming in. I want to slip this ship inside, understand? Any real people in there?"

Mishima's grim face appeared on the screen. "Just Ngen's monsters, Major. We'll do it. I take it you'd like as little commotion as possible?"

"You take it right, Corporal. We're laying a trap." To Ki: "Move the ship up close. I want us to get out of sight as soon as possible. Keep coordinated with Mishima. I want enough holes ripped in that can so we have eyes and ears. Further, as soon as you can coordinate targeting comm on those bogeys, let me know. I want them monitored all the way in. No surprises."

"Yes, ma'am." Ki bent to the task. He was old-time Patrol to the bone—one of Ree's bad boys, a crack officer.

Rita pulled a cup of coffee and waited.

Mishima's people were the cream of the forces who'd survived Sirius. Powered by the AT's reactors, heavy assault lasers began slicing sections out of the station end, atmosphere boiling away in a puffy haze of crystals. Too bad ag stations had to be so damned humid.

"Targeting is locked," Ki called almost an hour later.

"Keep track of them. You might also give consideration to how we're going to keep our eyes open inside that can."

"I think I can run remotes, Major."

She paused, thoughtful. "I'm curious. You know, Max, Ngen's missed a bet. These people he's psyched," she waved at the stations around them, "aren't the slightest bit interested that a strange ship is hovering out here while our AT cuts up the neighbor's house. No one on the planet's surface has noticed. They're totally oblivious. Now, why would the brilliant Ngen Van Chow allow that to happen?"

Ki considered. "I guess he figures the balance between stability and the security risk is met. It's a compromise he's forced to make."

Rita stared at the station as a final section of the wall

quivered and fell inward under Mishima's skilled guidance. The station lay bare, lights shining from the fusion plant batteries. while a low fog of crystals rose from the decompressed rows of dirt and the long green fields, the plant's vacuum ruptured and freezing in the 3° Kelvin of space.

"There's an exploitable weakness here. But it . . . Hell, the son of a bitch is planning a lightning strike out into the Directorate, Ki. He has to know, but he's minimizing the risks, preparing to move quickly, remove any reliance on Arpeggio as a major base of operations. Damn it, if we just had more time."

He nodded, eyes narrowed.

"We've got to ruin this planet. Hit him as hard as we can. Maybe we can slow him."

Ki filled his lungs, turning to the overhead monitor delineating the vectors of the intruders. "We have to live that long, Major. Hope we get the chance."

The *Knife* slid into the depressurized station as if it had found a perfect sheath.

"If we live that long." She nodded. "Well, for the moment, we're safe. How long until the bogeys are within range?"

"Four days, Major."

"All right, tell everyone to relax and make their peace with Spider. You know what happens if we don't kill those ships? If someone down there *has* been keeping their eyes open?"

Ki swallowed hard. "Yeah, we'll be blown out of this can like feathers out a tube."

Cargo bay aboard the Deus ship *Michael* accelerating for jump from Arcturus.

Veld Arstong stared around the cramped cubicle. The place measured ten meters by ten, the walls and ceiling featureless. A small portable toilet cubicle had been set in one corner. Now a constant line waited anxiously at the flimsy door. The packed room had an average of one person per point seven five square meters.

How in the name of hell had this happened to him? He squatted in a corner, back braced in the angle of the wall. Before him, the press of bodies might have been cattle. A baby cried in the far corner, hugged protectively to its mother's breast. Some slept, others simply stared as he did—lost

in disbelief. Fear reeked from the packed bodies. Nor could
he particularly blame them. For once Veld could honestly be thankful he'd remained a bachelor. Of course, if
Leeta . . . No, long gone and dead on a far star.

True to the gang leader's promise, the families had all
been waiting at the Spindle, summoned from their own sleep
by an order from comm—allegedly from spouses—claiming
they needed to make a quick journey to a facility in the
Directorate section of Arcturus. Only they'd all been queued
up and loaded into a big shuttle despite the hysteria.

The trip had been short. The shuttle linked to a ship and
they were paraded out at blaster point into the vessel where
both gravity and lights flickered as if some incredible power
drain damped the system. Now they waited, the feel of the
ship and the odor of human uncertainty the only reality.

Ten MacGuire picked his way carefully through the press
to squat next to Veld.

For long moments, neither spoke.

"What will you do when we arrive where we're going?"
Ten's voice had lost its usual buoyancy.

Veld scrubbed his hands over the tops of his knees, letting the rough fabric scrape the sweat away. "I'll do what
they say." He cocked his head. "Seriously, Ten, you saw
what that wretched dirty girl did with her blaster back in
the faculty lounge. She was serious. Damn it, I was looking
her right in the eyes. She was waiting to castrate me with
that damn gun, daring me."

"Veld, listen to me. I say we don't work. We cross our
arms and flat out refuse. We . . . we demand that they let
us contact the Director. It has to be some plot to ransom
us. They must be desperate for . . . for credits. They . . .
Veld?"

Arstong shook his head woodenly. "You're one of . . .
no, maybe you are the brightest engineer alive, Ten. Look
around you, man. Look who they have here. Engineering
and physics? What does that suggest to you? Ransom?
Hardly. They want us to build something. The idea that it's
ransom is simply a placebo someone thought up. We're impressed labor."

MacGuire grunted. "I'm still not working. We've got to
have . . . We *need* a consensus, Veld. A firm commitment
from everybody here. If we're united, they can't make us
do what we don't want to. We'll—"

"You're a fool if you really believe that."

MacGuire's facial muscles jerked as he struggled for control. Voice forced, he began, "May I remind you, Doctor, that you're the junior professor here. This is still *my* department, and I'll run it the way I want. You *will* follow my instructions. You *will not* work on any projects these pirates assign you to. Is that understood?"

Veld smiled slightly, a pained sorrow in his chest. "You really believe that, Ten?"

The steely-eyed response couldn't be mistaken.

Veld nodded, lips pursed as he looked out over the packed room. He remembered, they did ship cattle like this from Range. Packed tight to be butchered somewhere. "All right, you believe it." He waved at the crowd. "This still hasn't sunk into your shining mind. What you see here is—"

"Don't try and give me any crap about—"

"Shut the *fuck* up, Ten! That's right. Shut up and listen to me. I'm being realistic. Like maybe we'd all better be, because this isn't just a bad dream we'll wake up from. We're living a new reality here. All right? Understand? I'm not being a jerk off. I want you to listen—and think."

Ten started to stand, shaking his head. Veld clamped a hand in his clothing, twisted it, and hauled MacGuire back down. The room had gone silent, people staring, awed, frightened at the outbreak. MacGuire tried to pull back, nervous, wetting his lips.

"You'll listen, Ten. You'll listen now, because I don't want to suffer for your bullheadedness."

"You—you're crazy, Veld. You have been ever since you got mixed up with that broad Jeffray committed suicide over."

"Uh-huh, maybe I am. Maybe, on the other hand, I started putting some facts together because I knew Leeta. Maybe I paid real good attention to that transduction message she sent on the Romanans. Maybe I got to thinking about her . . . and Jeffray . . . and why he killed himself. Maybe I got to thinking about the old Jeffray . . . and the one Leeta dumped." He cocked his head. "I started reading something besides engineering texts because, all of a sudden, Leeta got blown up in a war, Ten. We weren't really all that close—but I knew her. She went out and got killed saving an entire people from genocide. All that from a lady I used to party with and dated a couple of times. Makes your perspectives change."

"Then, if . . . if she could stand up for what she believed, why won't you?"

"Because I have some idea of what's involved." Veld sighed. "Ten, I just asked you to think. Do it. The way this was handled, it . . . Damn it, Ten, they're too good. Understand? Think about what you're going to do when they take your oldest daughter over there, and put a blaster up to her head. You going to work like they told you?"

MacGuire's eyes widened. "You're not serious! She's just a little girl! What sort of—"

"The same sort that threatened to castrate me. Want me to make it worse? These are the Fathers. Not Romanans. I read everything Leeta and her people broadcast. No, we're a brain cadre for the jihad. There's no rescue coming, Ten. We're on our own."

MacGuire shook his head. "You know, I think you need a trip to the Health Department. If I'd known you were taking such an interest in all these Romanan things, and anthropology, and all, I'd have made a report out to—"

"And had me end up just as dull and mindless as Jeffray?" Veld snorted his laughter. "Jesus, Ten. I don't know who to fear worse. You? Or the Fathers? But that's neither here nor there for the moment. Right now, we have to stay alive. That's all. Just survive—and you think what you're going to do, because if you consider all the angles, our families are the real hostages. Not us. You want your family to live? You'll work."

Ten inched away until he was out of reach and stood, eyes shifting nervously. "You're a sick man, Veld. I had no idea you were so deranged. You work if you want to. But the rest of us . . . we're refusing. You join them . . . and I hope you're real happy with your decision."

Veld closed his eyes as MacGuire began working his way across the room again. Dejected, he dropped his head into his hands and fought the sudden surge of tears.

Aboard *Spider's Knife*: GEO orbit over Arpeggio.

"Major," the voice brought her out of a sound sleep. Rita sat up in her bunk and blinked herself awake. The featureless white walls had become a too familiar reality. The place needed something, life, color.

"Here, Ki. What's up?"

"Those bogeys will be in range within an hour. A drone

ship dropped by the station hatch. We shoveled some cabbages into it so everything would look normal. I doubt the Fathers will notice the decompression bruising.''

"Be right there.'' Rita stood up, stretching, feeling frustrated as she tallied all the days since she'd seen Iron Eyes.

"Too long for a horny old gal like me,'' she decided bitterly. And damn it, he'd hold her everything would work out in the end. Life had purpose when she could talk her troubles over with Iron Eyes. But then the two warships approaching might make all of that moot anyway. Atomic plasma didn't have the same concerns as Rita Sarsa had in her present form. She pulled on her armor, checked the vacuum status and snagged a helmet from the rack on her way into the bridge.

Ki and Mishima bent over their consoles, busy with calculations.

"From the registries, they are Zymer Cheng's *Joseph* and Pietre Raskolnikovski's *Daniel*. From what we hear, they've been raiding Directorate space, tying up the Patrol's ability to respond.''

"How close will they pass to our position?'' Rita asked, eyes on the ships, noting the blaster ports which had been cut into the normally fat GCIs.

"Given their present course, they should pass within eight to nine thousand klicks, Major. That's almost point-blank.'' Ki was grinning. "And they didn't give us more than a passing glance. Figured the mass was about right for a station, I guess. Not only that, everything else ought to look perfectly normal to them.''

Rita began to experience the adrenal rush of combat. Consciously, she looked up at the spider artfully drawn on the ceiling. "Give us these, two, Spider. Then, we'll clean house on these foul abominations.''

She settled into the command chair, feeling it contour to her figure, and began checking status reports.

"They're within range, Major.''

"Combat alert!'' she snapped, slipping her helmet onto her armor and checking comm and life support. "Gun crews, stand ready, targeting will be visual, line of sight. Range sensors, Doppler analysis, and bolt focusing on standby.'' She frowned. "Engineering, be ready to give me one hundred percent. When we cut our way out of this can, it may be touch and go.''

"Acknowledged.''

Rita grinned sourly. She waited, the hype of imminent battle pumping up in her veins. Through all of history, her species had felt this heightening joy. As bowels loosened, breath came quicker and muscles seemed like taut bands of rubber.

"Range twelve thousand meters and closing," Ki called.

Rita watched the bright dots that were her enemy moving against the blanket of stars. "Targeting error?" she asked, fighting the urge to holler: "Shoot!"

"Five percent," Mishima called.

"Eight thousand, five hundred meters!"

Rita could hear herself breathe, the air making a low roar to her ears. "Bud, have numbers one and two take the ship on the left. Three and four have the one on the right. What's your targeting error?"

"Without sensors, four point five percent now, Major." Bud's back had tensed, muscles bunching under his armor.

"Fire!" She could live with four point five percent.

The Fujiki blasters ripped through the thin metal of the station, lining up on the two tiny dots on visual. Rita ran the magnification up and watched her fire control crews dial the deadly bolts directly on target. *Joseph* flared violently, hiding *Daniel* in the flash.

"*Got him!*" Mishima yipped. "Recalibrating three and four to first bogey. Bastard never knew what hit him!"

"Forward, full speed!" Rita ordered. "Targeting Doppler on, sensors on, keep *Daniel* in line until she's dead!"

She watched as *Knife* moved out of the wreck of the station. Seconds clicked by as the targeted ship pitched and yawed, trying to avoid the fire that raked her, gouts of flames and boiling atmosphere marking her wake as the hull ruptured. Rita's remaining guns locked, pouring their fire into the ship. One second, two. . . . *Daniel* disappeared in violent death when its reactor failed.

"Two for Spider!" She slapped a gloved hand on the armrest. "All right, people, Arpeggio is ours! Helm take us to that shipyard. When we're through with that, stations and ground based targets are fair game!"

Ki sent them sliding around the planet, Fujiki-amplified threads of violet rupturing stations like ripe fruits in a shotgun blast.

The action on Arpeggio became a haze, a routine of target definition, triangulation, and a flicker of the lights as the discharge of the Fujiki blasters pulled power from the reactor. To completely prostrate the planet took two days of death showered out of the skies through a haze of blasted, scorched station debris. Below them cities burned—marked by brown smoke palls on the ground.

One of the orbiting antimatter power plants dropped from its destabilized orbit. The crater it left brought the sea boiling into a bay that filled half a continent. The overcast from smoke, steam, and fallout increased to make targeting prohibitive.

"Bogey, Major. It's a big one. Could be *Gregory.*" Ki's voice brought her blinking and upright from where she dozed in the command chair.

"All right," Rita scrambled to pull her wits together. "This thing supposedly has legs, find us the best way to run—and turn on the juice, Max. Let's see what this baby can really do!" She let her eyes shift to incoming mass reading. The Doppler indicated the big ship wasn't shedding V. It might turn out to be a close race.

CHAPTER XXIX

Aboard *Bullet*: GEO orbit over World.

"Damn!" Damen Ree shouted at the top of his lungs. "Dump it, Neal! *Damn you, dump!*"

He stood, jaw out, fists clenched at his sides, veins standing from his neck. His heart pounded, a triphammer. Desperate and helpless to affect actions two hundred light-years away, and on time dilation delay at that, he was panting with the effort, watching the steely look in Iverson's eyes, seeing the terror that clutched each of the strained faces on the bridge. With no warning, the screen simply went blank.

"Oh, hell," the words were torn from Ree's throat. "Why did he let himself go like that?"

"They had V just a hair under light," Maya reminded from where she sat in a command chair. "Damen, what choice did they have? Go quickly or die in a long, suffering agony? We couldn't have gotten to him for months, maybe years. He wouldn't have had the power to transmit or to keep his life support going. How much food do you think he had aboard?''

Ree slumped into his chair. "I know," he mumbled. "He was dead as soon as Ngen breached him. When engineering couldn't stabilize the reaction . . . well, after that, it's just a matter of time. He was just . . . .''

"A special young man," Maya added gently, dropping one of her hands on top of his.

Damen pulled a full breath into his lungs. "That's right. A very special young man—but aren't they all?"

"Honestly, no. Some are better than others. Neal—"

Ree jumped to his feet, pacing the bridge, hands clasped behind him. "You know, he was the real brain and soul of the resistance off Sirius. He sat right there in that chair, developing counteroffensives and defensive strategies." Damen stopped, cocking his head, eyes blank with the memories. "How many times while we were ambushing corridors, hanging in the blackness, did his voice come through comm. Damn it, Maya, he . . . You don't know how much a calm voice can mean out there in the dark and the cold, with death all around. To this day, I don't know how he kept his cool while Ngen's people chopped away at *Bullet* a deck at a time."

"He was . . . Damn it. But let's not forget what he just did for us. He bought us time. Not only that, but he taught us something. Ngen's response was too quick. Neal's tactics were perfect. *Gregory* shouldn't have reacted that fast. I think we've finally got some substantive data to deal with. Neal's telemetry is priceless. Spectrometers can determine if those are Sirian-style blasters—and I'd bet they are. We've got analysis of the Fujiki blaster against his shielding. We've got an idea of his strengths—and maybe we can make a determination of his weakness. All we have to do is figure out how he gets that response time. Brotherhood tricks?"

"Our people have hurt him." Ree nodded, trying to force his mind away from Neal Iverson, away from memories of the eager young cadet he'd taken a shine to. "Susan pasted Bazaar. Rita has struck hard at Mystery, and several of the stations. Last word from her was at Bazaar. I guess we can just about write that one off from her report.''

Think, Damen! But . . . Neal . . . Neal. . . .

"Conversions to meet your specs are coming along," Maya told him. "At the same time, we're getting our Romanan marines. I don't know who's training who to be what.

I have half my crew out wandering around the Bear Mountains and half the Romanans are painting ugly black spiders all over my ships! Just like that.'' She pointed to the spider overhead.

He's dead, damn it! Accept the fact. You knew people would die. A commander sends people into risky situations. You could lose all of them. Rita. Iron Eyes. Susan. Yes, even Maya.

Ree looked up, swallowing hollowly, suffering another, older hurt as he left his eyes caress the fading effigy on his bridge panels.

Spider gives you no guarantees. Like Leeta. Like Neal. Like how many to come?

"That was drawn up there by Leeta Dobra many years ago just before you were going to destroy my ship. Moments later, your blasters killed her. Odd, isn't it? Strange how the web of Spider has pulled us around and wrapped our lives into shapes we'd never have guessed.'' *And killed Neal.*

"Director Skor Robinson on transduction,'' comm announced without ceremony. The melancholy of the moment shattered like crystals under the hammer of galactic reality.

"Put him on,'' Ree said, making a listless move with his hand. *Damn him! Did he have to call now? Couldn't he leave a little time for grief?* Ree forced himself to pull his thoughts together, to think clearly despite the aching loss.

The gargantuan head of the Director formed. Ree straightened immediately. Robinson's eyes glared from red pits in his pinched face. Either his health was failing or some severe trauma had occurred.

"Greetings, Director,'' Ree began cautiously. He squared his shoulders, face hardening, eyes glinting.

"Admiral. I do not have time to bandy words.'' The thin voice wavered. "I am . . . willing to turn over the power of the Directorate to you and your fleet. I can no longer . . . It is distasteful to me, but I believe you and your Romanans may represent the . . . the only salvation of civilization. Just hours ago, forces under the command of Ngen Van Chow killed over two hundred million people . . . and we are completely open to any further attack. Totally defenseless. My people are . . . are rioting in the streets. Social decay is rampant. They plead for protection and I . . . I can give them none. I must rebuild my city, but is there a reason to? What do I do, Admiral? The Patrol is in shambles. Ngen's forces torpedoed *Ganges*. Blew her apart. I am powerless to stop the end of civilization.''

Ree sat stunned while holos of Arcturus started coming in. He and Maya gaped as selected clips of the entire attack from the fiery death of *Ganges* to the last explosion of ruptured seams flashed before them.

Ree nodded, swallowing hard at the enormity of the disaster. The yawning pit widened inside. First Neal, now this? To strike so callously at Arcturus—with such effect—would throw the entire Directorate into anarchy.

Ree staggered, trying to make sense of the implications, realizing how limited his options were. What could he do? How could he get to Arcturus, make a show of Romanan force? If only Chester . . . No, he did have one option. ''I have a fast transport coming in within the day, Director. I'll have as many of my Romanans as possible there within four weeks. You'll have to hold on until then. In the meantime, follow my instructions.''

Ree made it up as he went, drawing from his Romanan experience, from the things Leeta had said, from the anthropology texts he'd read and the lecture Pike had given him. Wracking his brain for ideas, he outlined actions for Skor Robinson's implementation. The Director responded meekly while Ree droned on.

How long? An hour? Two? ''Outside of that, tell them the Romanans are coming and Spider will protect them. There will never be another attack on Arcturus so long as they are under our protection. I promise that.''

Robinson hesitated. ''I would like to know of my . . . our disposition in advance. Assistant Director Semri Natov is dead—killed in the attack. Assistant Director An Roque is . . .'' Skor's voice went hoarse. ''His mind is broken, Admiral. The loss of so much of the Gi-net. The strain . . . Will . . . will you require our imprisonment or executions?''

Skor blinked anxiously into the lengthening silence.

Ree looked like he'd swallowed a rock leech. ''Your deaths? I don't . . . Are you all right, Director?''

''Conquerors usually require such measures upon deposing rulers.'' Skor argued rationally. ''The consolidation of new regimes generally demands—''

''*Damnation!*'' Ree spat, standing up. ''You're not deposed! And . . . and the last thing I'm interested in is taking over Arcturus, by Spider!''

"But the Patrol Colonels were quite adamant on that point! They insisted your goals—"

"*They were jealous!*" Ree thundered, waving his arms. "How did you expect them to react to my supposed defection? Director, you're invaluable in running what's left of our government, but when it comes to human motivation, you've got all the sense of a dead fish!

"You and Roque have been bottled up with your damned Gi-net computers for so long you don't have any idea how men function—outside of what we eat, what we can manufacture and consume, and how to dispose of our organic wastes in the most efficient manner. Chester was right about you." Ree ended up gasping his frustration. "Now, tell your people to behave because if they're not good little boys and girls, my Romanans are going to kick their asses so high they fart out their ears! Understand?"

Ree grinned suddenly, an idea coming to him. Tell them we're sending a Prophet to bring them peace! That ought to quell your riots. You're in Spider's web now, Director."

Robinson nodded. "I am relieved. We have made your announcement. Many have returned to their occupations. Others are still somewhat confused. There are agents, of course, who are stirring up trouble. I assess that we have an eighty-nine point six seven percent probability that they are advance personnel for Ngen Van Chow—although with the current damage, those figures must be accepted as suspect. It would seem that their entire strategy is to ferment social upheaval."

"Tag those," Ree warned. "Have them rounded up and chuck them out a hatch as soon as you can. So long as they're loose—"

"Murder?" Robinson asked, face twitching. "You would have me sanction the murder of—"

"Shit!" Ree slammed a fist into his palm. "You ordered me to burn off the *entire Romanan planet once*, remember? You're not a saint, Robinson; it's just that you've realized you're mortal and your sins are too close for comfort. Don't get pious on me. I won't believe it—and neither will Spider!"

"I . . . I understand. I think we have things under control. May we call you if we have further problems?"

"Sure," Ree nodded, lips pursed. "How far does your cooperation extend. To the Patrol?"

Skor's lips trembled. "I have surrendered unconditionally."

Ree narrowed his eyes, fingering his chin. He shot a sideways glance at Maya. "Have your Patrol ships change vector for World. I'll need . . . let's see . . . six GCIs. Route them to Tygee Station. Wish we had a refitting station here, but we'll make do. We'll need to make some modifications in their design. We've been manufacturing like mad to convert GCIs. I'd just as soon make those changes in Line-class ships; we can do it faster and have a better product.

"At the same time, we'll feed you the data we have on our manufacturing. You're a thousand times more efficient than we are. Currently, Sirius is retooling to do most of our manufacturing and we've made changes in Maya's and Toby's Sectors. If you would be so kind as to coordinate that for us, I would appreciate it."

"What about all the rest of those Patrol Colonels?" Maya asked. "I think the last thing they will want to do is hand themselves over to your control."

"Director?"

"Given their recent statements, they will resist—possibly to the point of mutiny against my authority. You should be well aware of that precedent, having established . . ." Skor stopped short, a panicked look blanching his dwarfed face.

"Yeah, right." Ree came to a decision and nodded. "Very well—Maya, Toby, and I will handle it. They'll be taking on Romanans. It won't be the first time Spider has effected changes for his own purposes. My War Chief and his men can be very persistent in the most insidious of ways. They and their beliefs creep into every nook and cranny of resistance. Spider will take care of any trouble."

"Is that what your pirates did to me?"

Ree winked. "You'll never know, will you, Maya?"

"I have just ordered all Patrol Line ships to World." Robinson sniffed, rubbing a finger under his nose. "I have no more questions. I am preparing a decree of military law under your authority. We are already rounding up Fathers for their radical responses and two have been eliminated through the hatches." Skor looked up as if he was awaiting further instruction, expression puzzled, unsure.

"Director," Ree said gently. "Just do your best for the people. You're not alone. We're here and help's on the way." He paused, as if listening to comm. "Oh, by the way. I have a note here from Chester. He's away from a monitor, but he sends his regards and best wishes. He says he knows you'll do the best you can.''

Skor's mouth quivered, a flutter in his dwarfed blue eyes. ''T . . . Tell the Prophet I . . . Express my appreciation. Have you any other instructions?''

Ree shook his head. ''No. Just keep the place in one piece until my people get there. Call if you've got trouble. We'll work it out together.''

The monitor went blank.

Maya squinted at him, reservation in her eyes. ''You getting uncommonly human in your old age? I'm not sure I like that in an ally.''

Ree steepled his fingers, lips pursed. ''No. I was just thinking of something Chester said about Skor and friendship. Learning my lesson, so to speak. He's a monster, Maya, but it's not all his fault. At the same time, we—all humanity—need him in one piece, sane and thinking, trying to hold it together. He makes the Gi-net—or what's left of it—function. True, I lied when I said Chester sent his regards, but I think Chester will understand and approve. Besides, despite it all, I think the Prophet likes him. No, badgering Skor would have been a mistake. Might have shoved him over the edge. We need all the help we can get right now, and I think this might put him firmly in our camp.''

''But you'll watch him?''

''Damn right.''

''And the Patrol Colonels?''

''They'll have to be replaced, of course. I always have trouble with people who betray me—and they have.''

She filled her lungs disdainfully. ''That was my opinion. How are you going to break them out of their ships? They won't go easily.''

''That's a nut to crack.'' Ree scowled up at the panels overhead. ''And you can put your cunning mind to work on it over the next couple of months until they arrive.''

Maya swiveled in the command chair, nose hidden in steepled hands, lost in thought.

Ree walked to the dispenser, hesitating between coffee and tea before shaking his head. ''Come on, Maya. I've got some magnificent Sirian whiskey left. I need to think about all this. Neal's dead . . . and suddenly I'm the most powerful man in the galaxy. I never asked for any of this. Why me?'' He cocked his head, frowning. ''Damn it, another of my friends is dead!''

''You said it when you talked to the Director,'' Maya grunted. '' I don't know, but I'm starting to convert myself. What did you call it, Spider's web?''

Crew mess aboard *Spider's Revenge* decelerating into the World system.

''Captain? Could I have a moment?''

Susan turned from the dispenser, a freshly filled cup of tea in her hand. The med tech waited, a sober look on her normally grim features. Maybe it came from always dealing with suffering.

''Sure, Corporal.''

The tech looked around the small mess, obviously uncomfortable with the number of people present.

''My quarters?''

The corporal nodded. Susan led the way, stepping over cowl-covered powerlead to palm her hatch. She waited while the tech ducked in and the hatch closed.

''It's Pike,'' the tech explained. ''Captain, he's got cancer.''

Susan settled herself at the little table, sipping the thick Romanan tea. ''I take it that's in the regenerated tissue? The result of stimulation of the gene nodes? How serious is this?''

The tech leaned up against the wall, arms crossed. ''That depends, Captain. We're a week away from World—maybe less according to the scuttlebutt. He's in hardly any danger at all if I can transfer him to *Bullet* first thing. Phil can hook him into one of the big units and we'll pop him out a month from now in better condition than he's been in in his life.''

''But he's out for a month?''

''That's right. Completely out. No interaction, brain activity to a minimum. We'll need to be able to control his entire body all the time. Implant the right thoughts in his mind, monitor his blood, the whole shot.''

Susan chewed at the inside of her cheek as she thought. ''And if we can't afford that kind of time? What's the prognosis?''

The tech shrugged. ''I'm already reducing the stimulation to the growth nodes in the DNA, cutting back on the polymerases. Regeneration will be slowed, but that's where we got in trouble in the first place. As for the tumors, I'm developing a locus specific cytokine battery tailored to Pike's autoimmune system:''

Susan lifted an eyebrow.

"Simply put, we'll initiate a tumor necrosis factor—TNF—coupled with interleukins, monoclonal antibodies, several strains of interferons, and modified angiogenesis to isolate the tumor bodies.''

"That's your area of expertise, Corporal. Do what you need to.''

The corporal hesitated. "Not all that easy, Captain. Nothing comes free. There's a toxic effect involved. Especially with tumor necrosis factor. TNF can damage nerve tissue. It can lead to shock, a number of things. If it gets into Pike's crural nerves, well, the musculo-cutaneous is mostly regenerated while the anterior tibial is complete. It's higher up the nerve where synaptic damage was most severe.''

"You're getting technical again.''

"He may never have full control of his leg. He'll be limping for the rest of his life—or until I can get him into a unit and essentially rewire him.''

Susan hesitated, tapping the tabletop. "Damn. The Colonel's going to want him involved in planning as soon as we're in orbit.''

The tech spread her hands. "That might be. Captain, I won't tell you how it will work out. If . . . and I mean *if*, Pike wanted to, he could will himself past the debilities. But between you and me, I don't think he's got that will. Otherwise, my recommendation will be for full med under Phil's supervision on *Bullet*. Beyond that, the decision—and the responsibility for his health—is yours, Captain.''

Susan nodded, staring at her tea.

The bridge on *Deus* entering the Arpeggian system.

"Damn them!" Ngen Van Chow howled. "I damn their organs to rot within their bodies! Look at what they've done! Every world I turn into a training center, they destroy!" He paced the bridge as the scanners brought him the first images of Arpeggio. Holo upon holo formed. His entire manufacturing and training effort smoldered in ruins. Weather patterns depicted nuclear winter forming over all three of the continents.

Beside him, M'Klea gasped, realization of what she saw creeping into her disbelieving mind. "By Deus," she whispered in a strangled voice. "I will see them *bleed* for what they have done to my planet!"

Ngen bellowed his rage, smashing a crystal decanter on the deck plating as he cursed. The bridge personnel stared uneasily at the monitor, heads bowed at Ngen's rage.

M'Klea continued to stare, shaking her head. "It was so beautiful! The parks, the fields, the cities. Gone? All gone?" She turned her glittering eyes on Ngen. "Kill them! Kill them all! Death! *I want to see them bleed!*"

"Control yourself, dearest love," he soothed, as she stumbled back and focused on him. Ngen's lips parted in a smile. "They shall pay in the end. I promise you. Oh, how I promise you! For every world of mine which has been blasted and burned, so shall they feel my wrath!"

"I've located a ship, sir. They're boosting from orbit. We've got a fifteen-minute delay in telemetry, but they're going hot," the Gulagian who worked the sensors called, knowing enough to keep his eyes on the monitors.

"*Joseph? Daniel?* One of ours?"

"No, sir. They don't answer our code. I assume it's Patrol."

"Let me see it!" Ngen ordered, watching the monitor. Under best magnification, he could see the trim shape of a Patrol supply ship boosting ahead of a bright lance of reaction. "Like the one we destroyed off Tryst," he mused. "Get us within range. Maximum acceleration. *I want that ship!*"

The comm replied with, "Alert. Prepare for maximum acceleration."

Ngen took M'Klea's hand, pulling her away from where she stared angrily at the holos. Arpeggio spun in the silence of space, a muddy tortured ball, the wreckage of stations and decompressed debris a shining ring of destruction.

"Come, my dear. You're not looking well. You need rest."

She complied, shocked, staring ashen-faced back over her shoulder at the holos as he led her past the bridge hatch. She stood silently as they took the lift to their quarters, feeling the gravity change as *Deus* began the pursuit.

"They will bleed," M'Klea whispered finally, eyes focused on the distance. "Bleed . . ."

In his quarters, Ngen saw to M'Klea, easing her into the

grand bed, drawing the curtains as she began weeping for her planet. Burning anger balled around his heart.

He left her, walking out into his gaudy room. Frowning, he accessed comm. "Get me a line to that Patrol ship."

Surprisingly, they answered. A redheaded woman filled the projector screen. She stared at him with cool green eyes, a tightness in the set of her mouth as if she'd been disgusted by something.

"Major Rita Sarsa," he breathed. "Why am I not surprised?"

A twisted smile formed on her lips. "I never knew things could stink across light-minutes of vacuum, Ngen. But there's a first for everything."

"You know you're dead," he said reasonably. "I've got you this time. If you simply surrender, you'll live. I promise you I'll give you the finest of treatment."

She laughed shortly. "Not on your life, Ngen. I saw what you did to Susan. If you think I'm going to purposely let myself within forty parsecs of you, you're as daffy as you're abominably twisted. Nope, I'll bet we live—and that we've got better legs than you think."

"You can't escape." He caressed the rage inside, stroking it, bringing it to a burning passion as he imagined what he'd do to this woman who'd broken his power on Sirius. Ignoring the disgust in her eyes, he forced himself to be reasonable. "There is only death for you."

"The boys and I will take our chances on the other side, Ngen, old buddy!" She tilted her head jauntily. "Besides, you've got to catch me first. If you get that rusty bucket of air close enough to shoot us up, we'll worry about it."

"You've cost me an awful lot, woman." Ngen closed his eyes, relishing the churning vortex within, drawing from the power it bestowed. "I would love to entertain you for a while. I could teach you many things about pleasure. I would love to watch your soul turn within you as you come to despise the very flesh you have cherished all your life!" His voice turned silky as he thought about it. "Yes. Just as I enjoyed your Susan, so shall I enjoy you, Rita. I promise you, you'll be mine, one day."

"Not on your life, asshole. I'm going to keep costing you, bucko-me-boy," Rita laughed, a fiery light animating her eyes. "You keep taking planets, Ngen. With each one you take, I personally promise to leave it nothing more than desolate rubble! I'll see you in hell before I'll see humanity turned into walking dead!''

"Oh," Ngen breathed, "You *are* precious. There are so few women worth as much. You, dear one, would mean more to me than a planet! But you can't stand in the way of a God, Rita, my love. I am the future of all humanity. Your soul—like those of all men—will belong to me. To *me,* you hear?''

"Getting a bit carried away with the god business, aren't you, Ngen?'' She looked down at her fingernails and frowned, pulling a file from her pouch and cleaning under the nails. "Arpeggio was a dirty place after you polluted the atmosphere.'' She wiggled the nail file at him. "A god? You? Not bad for brain-sick dock scum.''

His face worked, the muscles twitching, as he stiffened. "D . . . Don't y-you ever . . . ever c-call me that, *you miserable pustulant bitch!* I . . . I'll . . . .'' Ngen didn't hear the hatch open. M'Klea appeared beside him, face stiff with grief.

"She did it? She ruined my planet?'' M'Klea bent to study the monitor, a curious light in her eyes. Her perfect mouth dropped open as she stared, a nervous white hand clutching the fine white fabric at her breast into a knot.

"Who's that?'' Rita asked, a slight frown on her face. "One who got out of your bed of horrors?''

"Darling, M'Klea, I present Major Sarsa, the woman who cost me Sirius and who has just blasted your beloved Arpeggio into dust.'' Ngen indicated the monitor, a smirk on his face.

"I *want* her, Ngen. When we have you, Romanan bitch, I shall personally enjoy making you wish you'd died five thousand deaths! I'll cut her, Ngen. Make her bleed . . . bleed . . .'' M'Klea moaned like an enraged cat, eyes ice-blue slits.

Ngen stopped her with a lifted hand, easing her away from the monitor.

Rita sipped her coffee, unaffected. "I must say, Ngen,'' her voice was dry, almost tired. "you found a trollop just as maliciously twisted as you are. I never thought there was a match out there in the vast population, but, damn me, you found one. I'm really impressed.''

Sarsa stifled a yawn, goading M'Klea to shriek with rage. Ngen pulled his consort back from where she clawed at the holo and laughed. "You are precious," he repeated, eyes narrowing. "I don't know who would enjoy you more, me or my beloved M'Klea?"

"Anything else worth saying, Ngen?" Rita asked, looking bored.

He shrugged. "Which of your commanders had a ship like yours? I killed one over Tryst. A friend? Your lover Iron Eyes perhaps? Or could it have been Susan?"

Ngen studied her intently, watching the pupils dilate. Ah ha! He'd gotten to her. She'd indeed known and been fond of the dead ship's commander—although she handled herself so very well. The reaction didn't have the impact she'd feel for Iron Eyes or Susan, however. Nevertheless, this Major was a superb example of what a woman could be. The contrast between this iron Amazon and his trembling M'Klea became startlingly obvious. But then, M'Klea was young—untried. And certain allowances had to be made for pregnancy.

"Yes, Major," he whispered intimately, the words used as expertly as a twisting knife. "I killed them all. They thought their blasters a match for my trained crew. They're gone. I'll send you the tape if you wish."

"Spare me the joy." Her face pinched under the steel mask of control "I suppose my blasting Cheng and Raskolnikovski makes us a little even, doesn't it?"

"You don't look as affected as I had hoped," Ngen mused. "Evidently, my beloved Susan escaped along with that foolish dolt she rescued. I almost had his soul, too, Major. Oh, how I'd like to take yours. The ways of Deus are strange—but perhaps in the end, you, too, will be mine."

"Susan's alive and well, Ngen." Rita had straightened. "You won't get us still breathing. You can't damage us without destroying us. There's no chance of me or any of my lads being guests at a soul party of yours, dock rat."

He smothered the flash of white rage as she stung his raw nerves.

Rita chuckled at his reaction and yawned again, kicking a foot up in relaxed effrontery. "Now, have you got anything else to add, or can I get back to my nap? We got bored shooting up those Arpeggian insects you created. Those two converted GCIs didn't even shoot back! You got anybody on your team with initiative?"

M'Klea uttered a strangled noise, face red, the muscles at the corner of her jaws knotting and cramping. Her fingers had tightened on Ngen's arm until the nails drew blood.

"I shall see your atoms flash across infinity, Major," Ngen promised, voice mild. "That, or I shall have you for a guest. Tell that delightful Susan I'm waiting to resume our acquaintance. I still have a special place in my heart for her."

Push her, see if you can get a reaction. Ngen smiled wickedly and reached up as if stroking Rita's image in the holo. "Yes, I broke her, Major. Turned her lovely body against her. Made her pant for me . . . as you shall one day."

Sarsa tensed, expression tightening as her fists knotted and she shifted—not quite a squirm, but controlled revulsion. Superb control, a worthy opponent for his beds and psych machines. Could he break her?

"Don't cream yourself, Ngen. I'll tell her." Her voice betrayed a slight edge. "I know for a fact she has a special feeling for you, too. Unlike yours, it's not very flattering. Said something about having more pleasure with a ten-year-old boy. Say hello to the docks for me. Hugs and kisses to your whore mother. I'd send the same to your father—if we only knew who he was."

Ngen jerked as if slapped, rage flashing.

Rita gestured a flippant farewell. The screen went dead.

"You bitch . . . You . . . I will twist your soul from your body! Leave you screaming for death. You'll be flayed alive. Eat everything I cut from your body. You'll bear my demon child and choke on its raw flesh *as I rip your bloody womanhood from your body!*" He brought his fist down violently, parting the plasteel paneling.

M'Klea stood back, eyes black with hatred. "Get her, my husband. Get her for me if you never do anything else for M'Klea. I will have her scream her agony until she's torn the very chords from her throat! I want her to bleed."

On the bridge of the *Spider's Knife,* Rita Sarsa sagged in the control chair, trying to still her trembling. She began sucking in deep breaths, blowing them out loudly as she fought to still the horror inside. Ki handed her a glass full of whiskey.

"Nice guy," he muttered.

"Did he see me start to crack? Did . . . did I pull it off?

Thought . . . thought I was shaking so badly the *Knife* was jiggling.'' Rita wiped away the sweat which had begun to bead on her pale brow.

"No, Major, you looked like a rock." Mishima patted her shoulder, serious concern on his craggy face. "Was all that true? Could he really do that to you?"

Rita's eyes dulled as she nodded hesitantly. "Yeah, it's all true. He's like that Satan he preaches about. You've seen what he's made of the men he's conquered. He does worse to his special victims."

"Susan survived him?" Ki asked.

Rita's voice was like broken glass. "You don't ever mention a word of that to anyone . . . or I'll kill you myself! You've forgotten you ever heard it. I'm goddamn serious."

Ki nodded soberly. "I can understand what it means to Susan."

Mishima smacked a fist into his gnarled palm. "Spit-licking Sirian filth. I'll get him. I'll—"

"Bud? You hear what I said?" Rita studied him from slitted eyelids.

"I heard, Major. I've got a lot of respect for Susan. If she . . . she was in his hands. Well, ma'am, that she's still coherent makes me proud to know her. Hell, no, I never heard nothing. But I want a chance to kill that maggot choking bastard."

Rita puffed a sigh. "Yeah, you may get it. But if he ever gets me, you take me out. Shoot to kill. I mean it. Death is better than Ngen."

"Got it, Major."

Ki went back to his monitor. Rita sat in the command chair trying to still the violent emotions savaging her.

After several minutes, Ki sang out, "I've got some bad news for you, Major."

She straightened in the chair, breath tight in her chest. "What?"

"You'll have to deal with him next time," Ki kept his face straight. "We're gonna outrun him by a healthy margin. It means a little stress and cooking almost fifty gs, but the *Knife* has it in her if the grav plates don't buckle."

"From what we've seen, squished flat is better than that slime puke." Mishima jabbed a thumb back in Ngen's direction.

"Praise be to Spider!" Rita whispered fervently and

gulped the rest of her whiskey. She winked at the effigy drawn so neatly on the panels overhead.

CHAPTER XXX

Aboard *Spider's Revenge* after establishing GEO orbit over World.

Darwin Pike twisted in the med unit when Susan entered the room. He was groaning, struggling, sweat building on his face and trickling down shiny skin, soaking the fabric under him. The horror of his nightmare reflected in his twitching face.

"Doctor!" Susan grabbed his shoulder and shook him. "Wake up! It's the dream!" She saw his eyes flutter and open, centering on her. As suddenly he recoiled, features glazed with fear as he pushed back.

"Pike! Damn it! It's me! Susan! Get it through your head. I'm *not* your ghoul!"

"Oh, God," he said hoarsely, body relaxing as he panted. 'Does it ever stop?"

She shook her head slowly. "It hasn't for me. I guess I've just been learning to live with it. You wake up, stare at the bulkheads for a while, and finally go back to sleep, afraid you'll live through it again. As time goes by, you have a few more happy dreams mixed in with the rest.

"So, what's the good news." He tried to chuckle, but it came out as a dry hacking.

"We're over World," She settled herself on the edge of the med unit. "We'll be here long enough to pick up a squad of Romanans and space immediately for Arcturus."

"When do I get out of here?"

Susan studied the monitors, fighting to find the right words. "There are complications, Doctor. The regeneration treatment stimulates the DNA to act like it does in a fetus. Sometimes it goes too far. Too much grows. You've got cancerous tumors. That's why you've been down for as long as you have. We've been trying to stabilize it."

He swallowed and looked up. "Okay, so that's a simple

treatment. A little cytokinal manipulation and . . . What's wrong?''

''Pike, Pallas Mikros used that wand on you. Remember?''

He moaned under his breath. ''Yeah, I'm not likely to forget, either. Thought my skull would explode. Nothing could hurt that much.''

''Well, that's just it. The pain came at the expense of your nerves. I don't really understand it, but the corporal was telling me there's a toxic effect to TNF. It affects nerves— and Pallas played hell with yours already.''

''I'm moderately up on med regeneration.''

''Okay, then you know the risks.'' She laced her fingers together, studying the floor. ''I've got a decision to make, Doctor. A gamble, if you will. We've had a change in plans. Your leg, maybe your ability to walk again without a prosthesis, hangs in the balance. Or maybe the cancer can't be controlled.''

''You want to get to the point?''

''Are you willing to put all your mind and body to work against Ngen? Do I risk your health? It's your brain or your body. We're spacing for Arcturus. The corporal wants to put you in med for a solid month on *Bullet*. Ree wants you in the fight for Arcturus—but he left it to my discretion. It's your body, Darwin. What do you want me to do?''

Pike blinked, the implications sinking in. ''Let me see the med reports on the TNF and nerve growth factor.''

She accessed them, letting him read the corporal's analysis of his chances.

For long minutes, Pike closed his eyes, lips sawing between his teeth. ''I . . . Let me think about it for a bit.''

''Sure. If it helps, you'll be in med here a while longer. I talked to Phil. He thinks maybe some therapy coupled with nerve growth factor can lessen the effects. They can put you in a mobile unit as soon as your testicles. . . . What's the matter?''

''My . . . testicles? No! I'm not . . . not . . .'' His jaw worked feebly as the monitors measured his panic in raw figures.

She grabbed his hands, forcing him to meet her eyes. ''You're fine! The corporal regenerated two from the remaining damaged one. There're two new ones in the tank there waiting for implantation. You're not a eunuch! Is that what you wanted to know?''

She watched his hope return, wondering at what a vulnerable creature a man was. Did they all define themselves by that little bit of connective tissue?

"Thank Spider," he whispered, looking away suddenly, shamed and embarrassed that she knew his weakness, knew of the damage to his male organs. Still, she couldn't help but remember the way he'd been mutilated. The image of Pallas cutting him, handing the testicle to Tiara, would live with her for a long time. And Pike had watched—watched his own flesh treated that way.

At the same time, another side of her had gloated over the pain inflicted on that horrible male member. She'd felt a divine justice in that. *My own horror, Pike. The legacy Ngen left me with. Nothing personal, you understand.* She glanced uneasily at him. Uncertain eyes rested on her.

She sighed, feeling deflated. "You know, neither one of us is cured of what Ngen did to us. I suppose we never will be. With . . . with me . . . if it had just been physical rape . . . He . . . he . . . Never mind."

His hand tightened on hers. "I can't talk about it either. Maybe I'm just shy." His grin didn't cover his discomfort.

"Why? Because Ngen conjured up an image of me?"

"I don't know." He couldn't quite tear his eyes away from her. "I guess I'm kind of fond of you. But Ngen made Tiara and you . . . I can't . . . It doesn't seem right when someone you like talks about your private parts. Well, it's just that I . . ." He closed his eyes and muttered, "Oh, hell, I don't know!"

She couldn't help but laugh. He looked so helpless. And somehow he'd touched her. It sobered her.

"Look," she said seriously. "Forget it. I just came by to check on your condition, let you know what was happening. Don't scream at the techs about it. They had their reasons for keeping quiet. They think your mental health is about to crash and burn. Now that I think about it, I remember. Friday was pretty jealous about his balls, too. I guess the corporal thought knowing, well, it might affect your recovery. Maybe she was right."

"Yeah," he said dryly. "I suppose so. It's just that not having them is like not being a whole. . . . It's a symbol of what Ngen did to me."

"The new ones are doing fine. You'll never know the difference."

"I'll know. I'll remember." He avoided her eyes. "Just

like you were different after what Ngen did to you. Maybe . . . maybe it wouldn't have bothered me . . . but coming right after the dream, after seeing y . . . Tiara . . .''

She took a deep breath and cursed.

"What's at Arcturus?" he asked, struggling to change the subject.

"While we were headed in, a couple of Ngen's ships blasted the place. They've got billions dead or so. I guess the casualty figures are still coming in. Anyhow, Skor Robinson surrendered the entire Directorate to us. We're going to take possession and begin our campaign for Spider. We're the new military government. Patan is the high priest. You coordinate the effort and I provide any enforcement we need.'' She crossed her arms, curiously bothered by the change in conversation. His uncomfortable intimacy had appealed to some long felt dormancy inside her.

"Can you send me the tapes of any conversations? I'd like to hear what the Admiral said.''

"Glad to.'' She smiled at him. "I'll let you have the whole thing: all of Ree's orders, the holos of Arcturus, everything.'' She stood up.

"I suppose this means you'll be seeing Giorj?'' His voice sounded forced.

She stopped and looked down. "He's out of the system right now, taking *Victory* on a shakedown cruise.''

"I'm sorry,'' he managed, trying too hard to keep a pleasant face. "I know you miss him.''

Susan felt herself turn empty inside. "Yes. I do. There's no one to watch while I sleep. Just because I can live with it, doesn't mean being alone with the memories is easy.''

"No, it doesn't. *I live in a prison here!*'' It came out unexpectedly. "This damn machine puts me down and I'm stuck with nightmares! Every damn time I sleep! Pallas is there and Reesh dies and Ngen whispers in the back of my mind. And y—Tiara eats . . . Damn Patan anyway! I'd have killed myself but for him!''

She couldn't disagree with him. She herself had been so close. The suffering in his eyes was her own. "Doctor, I'll do what I can. In the meantime, think about the options. We don't have much time.''

She gave him a thumbs up and walked out.

Pike stared at the hatchway she'd just vanished through. He swallowed hard, remembering the carefully couched wording of the text. Damn it, he could die. The cancer could be beaten at the expense of his nerves. It might mean a prosthetic nerve net.

"A billion dead?" He tried to imagine and shook his head. "The Directorate surrendered to the Romanans?" Impossible! Unless Ngen . . .

"Strength comes at a cost, Alaskan." the Santos' words haunted him. *"Do you know how a knife is forged? It is done in fire with a hammer. When the steel is right and glows with spirit, the iron is hammered into shape. Then, while it still burns, it is plunged into cold oil and heated again before the fire is quenched in aged leather to impart spirit. Then the blade is ground and polished and given its final edge. . . . And when the forging is done, the knife is tested."*

Darwin reached for the broken Santos blade, running his thumb along the irregularity of the break.

"Comm," he called softly. "Inform the Captain that I will be traveling with her to Arcturus."

He stared up at the panels overhead. "Ngen, I guess we'll just see if you can beat me in the end. Leg . . . or no leg."

She didn't see Pike again that day. Instead, her time was filled with ATs ferrying marines from World to her small ship. Bales of supplies were unloaded while Sirian and Patrol techs checked from one end of *Spider's Revenge* to the other, refining the inflight refitting she'd undergone and adding new improvements the indefatigable Giorj Hambrei had developed from working with other Patrol ships. As a final touch, two huge spiders were stenciled on either side of the ship's hull, marking her once and for all as part of the Romanan fleet.

Susan managed to keep her concentration during a meeting with Admiral Ree, John Smith Iron Eyes, and Maya ben Ahmad. She noted the way the Colonel and Ree were both paying each other extra attention, speculated on whether they had become lovers, and realized she didn't have time to enjoy the thought.

"I do have a message from Major Sarsa," Ree added grimly after they had finished the regular business. "I haven't made this one part of the record like the others, Susan."

"Is Rita all right?"

"She's fine. Ngen surprised her at Arpeggio. She outran

him but had a little chat in the process. She's on her way back to our territory this very instant.''

"And?'' Susan raised an eyebrow.

"Here's the tape. Review it at your leisure. I'd suggest you do it in private. After that, its disposition is up to you. If you want it made part of the record, fine; if not, we didn't see it.''

"Arcturus is yours,'' Iron Eyes told her. "Your duty is to stabilize it, and ensure it remains ours. We have no idea when Ngen will strike again. As soon as *Miliken* is refitted we'll send her after you. Keep the populace under wraps no matter what. Your command is small, but most are Sirian veterans. Keep in mind, you're a peacekeeping force. *Spider's Revenge* may be called upon to fight off Ngen's ships, but he's suffered setbacks from Rita's kills.''

"We'll handle it.'' Her lips twisted into a wicked smile. "Besides, it won't be the first time a Prophet went to Arcturus. Only this time, they'll remember for a lot longer. We'll have spiders on every wall in Arcturus by the time you arrive, War Chief.''

Then had come the manifest signatures, combat reports, engineering reports, introduction and inspection of her new crew, duty assignments, and finally, all the miscellaneous things which couldn't be delegated. She arrived at her quarters feeling half dead and stopped as she passed the hatch. She suffered a twinge, looking around at the tiny white room.

She considered for a moment before turning, walking down the crowded, bustling corridors. She ducked into the hospital, seeing Pike where he slept in the med unit's control.

Folding out the little chair, she propped herself there. "I didn't get a chance to thank you, Pike. You know, you're a brave man, after all.''

She settled herself to sleep.

Aboard the *Gabriel* in passage of the Samarkand system.

Torkild Alhar studied the monitors as his *Gabriel* lifted away from the blinding flash which eliminated Samarkand. The light dimmed, leaving a twisting serpentine vortex of swirling atmosphere rushing toward the crater. Even from this altitude, the effect could be called nothing less than incredible. The antimatter device had blown a gouge out of the planet that looked like a man had bitten an apple. Samarkand was dead.

Ngen had doubled the price: for each planet of his the Directorate had killed, two of theirs would die. The Messiah had been sending that through space on a transduction signal. Torkild nodded. Arpeggio had deserved better than to become a wasted desert.

Perhaps the Romanan world would be next? Torkild had almost felt snubbed when Winston Zimbuti's *Abraham* had been picked for that job. Zimbuti didn't have half the skill it would take to blow World away. The invincible Damen Ree would be waiting in his famous *Bullet*. Ah, now there lay a challenge truly worthy of Torkild's mettle.

Torkild kept the scanners going to make sure of the effect on Samarkand and accessed his comm for a channel to *Deus*.

He got one of the bridge hands, a new man, possibly Arpeggian from the look of him. "One moment," the man told him. Then he looked back. "The Messiah is temporarily indisposed. Here is the Empress."

Torkild perked up in the seat. He'd heard of this Empress, a woman of allegedly magnificent beauty. He almost groaned at the memory of his beloved M'Klea. At the death of each world, he flushed with revenge achieved for his little sister. It was, therefore, with a reaction akin to shock that he looked into M'Klea's very much alive face!

"Greetings, brother," she told him, a new haughtiness in her voice.

"You . . . *you're dead!*" he cried, drawing glances from his officers who sat at their stations.

"It is I, brother, as I told you it would be so long ago."

He shook his head. "You are dead with mother, father, and the rest."

"I am quite alive, brother." She inclined her head. "I am your Empress. You, of course, will receive special treatment. You see, Torkild, for all those years you spoiled me . . . now I can reciprocate and extend my favor to you."

"Ngen has . . ." He left it hanging unable to finish it.

"I am his wife, brother. In *all* the aspects that word entails." Her eyes held an air of superiority. She stepped back so he could see the slight swell of her belly in the formfitting clothes. "My child is due in six months. His will be the Empire of Deus. He will be as a God!"

"No . . ." he whispered in disbelief. "Did you have

father's approval? You must have left before Arpeggio was attacked! Where was the marriage? When did this . . . Why didn't you inform me? M'Klea, you didn't . . ." He realized his voice had become shrill as his mind reeled at the implications.

She was laughing at him, enjoying his confusion.

Her voice dropped, mocking. "Father would *never* have given me permission! He really didn't like the Messiah. As to you, I didn't want to hear your prattle. Honestly, Torkild, for all your affection for me, you've insisted on being a bore all my life. Well, brother, I took matters into my own hands. Did rather well, don't you think? Instead of marrying some lackey friend of yours, I'm an empress. The 'wedding' took place in Ngen's quarters the night I arrived."

"But honor!" he cried, pounding a fist on the console before him. "I'll beat you to within an inch of your life, M'Klea! That you could so drag our honor through the—"

"Honor? You self-righteous . . ." She straightened, face growing black with rage. Her voice came in a strained hiss. "Honor is dead, Torkild. The Messiah has killed it! May it rot!" Her face twisted. "If you ever address me in that manner again, it will matter not that you are my brother. I will have your head brought dripping to me on a platter of gold. You will *never* take that tone with me again!"

He sat, as if turned to stone, heart pounding, breath forced.

"What means your honor!" she spat venomously at him. "I was a prisoner on Arpeggio! Oh, you had it all, brother! You had friends! You went out every night to party and dance and attend feasts. Where was M'Klea?" Her eyes questioned. "In her room! Starved to be human, waiting for your smug, half-drunken face to appear, flushed with excitement and telling me about the women's gowns and the handsome young men! There is *your disgusting honor!*"

Anger sparked in her blazing eyes. Settling himself into the command chair, it seeped in around the edges of his consciousness that she had changed. This creature couldn't be his sister. He could remember the impetuousness which was hers, the rages, the tantrums, the mood swings which had amused him when she was but his little sister. Now those same emotions—intensified by unlimited power—frightened him. The Messiah had done this to her. The Messiah had changed her, contorted pretty little M'Klea into this . . . this *whore!*

He saw triumph in her eyes. Subtly, her manner changed. "Indeed, brother, you read me well." She bit the end of her finger in a coquettish manner. "You always were my favorite study, Torkild. You—unlike father—always let me get away with anything. A form of self-imposed blinding, don't you think? You, however, took special manipulation. I had to play you like a fish on a string. It took artful molding to get you to do my bidding. It pleases me that you made captain on your own. Still, your relationship with me has privileges, use them wisely."

"But what of . . . honor?" He struggled to understand who this woman was, feeling a horrible loss for the bright-eyed, shining creature his innocent little sister had been.

"I told you, honor is dead, brother," her voice spurned. "Your precious honor and position mean nothing anymore. Only your favor with the Emperor has meaning. Ngen is making a new reality. You are either part of it, or against us. Make your choice, brother!" Her words stung like a lash on sensitive skin.

For her, he had done everything. The death of his love rattled hollowly within. Never again would he experience that moment when her eyes looked in adoration at him. Never again would she clap her hands when he brought her a trinket . . . or told her a story. Ngen Van Chow had killed her, taken and dirtied her with his filth, used her to spawn his disgusting bastard child! They were not even wed!

Blessed Gods, get me away! I can't stand to look at her! That she has come to this . . . the Messiah's prize whore. Only, what now, Torkild? Where is your way now that honor is dead?

"I am reporting the complete destruction of Samarkand," he said stiffly, unable to look her in the eye. "I thought I killed it in revenge for your death, M'Klea." *I just didn't know how dead you really were, sister.*

M'Klea laughed again. "How priceless! I'd been awaiting the right opportunity to inform you of my good fortune. How magnificently wonderful that it should occur in exactly this manner." She clapped her hands gleefully.

M'Klea remained radiantly beautiful despite the foulness of her situation. Yet in the familiar lines of her face, Torkild saw a stranger. *Or did I ever really see her? Perhaps . . . perhaps father's warnings weren't all dusty words after all? Now all that is left is the memory of what she was—and the monster she's become.*

His stomach churned at the thought of Ngen Van Chow's hands caressing her. "My report is finished. I am continuing on to Radian which I will destroy in the name of the Messiah." He closed the channel, knowing he'd cut short her ability to gloat. In that small way he'd make her furious.

She would have been able to see the hatred building. She would have known his pain. A woman without honor would have betrayed his passion to Ngen.

Closing his eyes, he saw her, imagined Van Chow pawing her sacred body, imagined him impregnating her. Torkild stifled the cry of rage which battered to escape his chest.

How could he even the score with the man who had taken his innocent M'Klea and degraded her so? Van Chow had killed the sweet child who had once doted on Torkild, dancing blue eyes looking up in worship. Now, those same eyes stared at him with superior disdain—without honor! Van Chow had changed her, polluted her. For this, Arpeggian pride and duty *demanded* blood!

A flame of pain lanced behind his eyes and his head began to ache. Honor was the reason for life. Ngen knew how much honor meant to Arpeggians. He'd taken the sister of his finest captain and raped her. Torkild Alhar straightened. Such an insult merited death! But how could he get close enough to kill him?

How? The question plagued him as he got to his feet, conscious of the stricken stares of his officers. The blood in their veins had been nurtured on Arpeggio. Arpeggian soil had borne them up to the stars, imparting its strength. Their ancestors had weaned them on the milk of Arpeggian custom and honor. He must act—or lose the respect of his men. With the energy of anger, he paced the deck plates.

Behind his command chair hung the portrait of the Messiah, those smoky black eyes glaring into his, raping his soul with their superior mien.

"Take *that* down!" Torkild ordered, pointing to the profanity. As junior officers sprang to do his bidding, Torkild stared at the star map. He was roughly six weeks ship's time from anywhere in the galaxy. No one would miss him for two months. His crew would remain loyal to him and to the ideals of his people.

"Course for Radian established," Bruno called out, feeding figures into comm.

"Belay that," Torkild ordered. He could see their surprised faces. Slowly, an idea began to gain substance.

"Bruno? Heinar? Tell me. Have I earned the respect of my crew? Have I won the right of command through wisdom, cunning, and victory—as has been our way for almost five hundred years?"

Bruno looked uneasily across the bridge. He nodded before he spoke. "Yes, Captain."

"My sister has been dishonored by the man we serve. She carries the spawn of his rape. He hasn't even deigned to marry her."

Heinar dropped his eyes, cheeks hollowing as he chewed on them.

"I assumed you would understand. Only now, let's take it one step further. We assume the Romanans destroyed our world. Could it be that Ngen did it through his own omission? What loyalty do any of us owe a man who didn't even take the precautions of protecting *our* homes and families? Does such an ill use of our planet merit respect or obedience?"

Bruno stood, snapping out a stiff salute. "I can speak only for myself, Captain. This first officer will follow Alhar. Your enemies are mine. I trust you'll lead us well, provide us with booty and a way to rebuild our world."

Torkild walked forward, clasping the man by the shoulders, hugging him in the age-old Arpeggian token of taking fealty.

"I'm with you, Captain." Heinar stood. "I'll follow where you lead—so long as it's to rebuild our planet, and serve honor."

Torkild's pride brought a tear to his eye as he hugged Heinar and, one by one, the rest of his officers. Ngen would pay. There were many ways to uphold honor.

Captain's quarters aboard *Spider's Revenge* in GEO orbit over World.

Wearily, Susan slapped the lock plate, entering her confined cabin.

Darwin Pike was slumped in one of the small chairs, head back, snoring like an internal combustion motor. From the knee down, his lower right leg was encased in a walker.

She'd struggled up from the dream, haunted, alone, Ngen's smooth voice whispering in her ear. Hollow-eyed, she'd stumbled down to where Pike slept in the hospital.

"You're out today, aren't you?"

''So they say.'' He'd grinned up, sobering as he saw her eyes. ''Dreams?''

She'd thrown her hair back over her shoulders, checking to see that no one remained within earshot. ''If you're willing to risk your reputation and those precious new male testicles, come to my cabin tonight. I . . . I've got two bunks in there. Maybe we can prop each other up for a while.''

And she'd left, too frightened by what she'd said to hear his answer.

So he'd come. As she knew he would. Maneuvering around him, she folded out the second bunk, and suddenly realized what it meant to share quarters with him.

''Darwin, wake up!''

He blinked awake and looked thankfully at the bunk she'd set out. ''I didn't know where you'd want me.'' He said, an innocent smile on his face. ''I didn't want to just rummage through your cabin.''

''Looks like you didn't have any dreams.'' She blinked, deadly tired, wishing he weren't there—knowing his leaving would be worse.

''Couldn't with my neck in that position.'' His face contorted as he rubbed it.

She shifted awkwardly from foot to foot. ''There's a disadvantage to small cabins. Look, I hope you don't blush.''

''I'll look the other way.''

Susan slipped out of her clothes, shut down the lights and sighing, lay back on her bunk.

''I hope I don't scream,'' his voice came, nervous in the darkness.

''Me, too. Please, if you'd rather, you can always go back to the hospital. You're worried, I can tell by the tension in your voice.''

''What will Giorj say?''

Susan laughed. ''What kind of relationship do you think I have with him?''

''Why . . . a normal one,'' he sounded puzzled.

Susan fought a tightness at the base of her throat. ''I can't have a 'normal' relationship with a man. Not after what Ngen did to me. I consider Giorj safe; he's sterile, impotent as a result of a radiation accident.''

''And Friday?''

She smiled wistfully in the dark. ''Friday and I were lovers once. After Ngen's chamber of horrors . . . well, part of the rape was to use psych. When Ngen was pawing me, my mind saw and felt Friday—while the neocortex knew better. After it was all over, after Ngen . . . It didn't matter then that I still loved Friday desperately, needed him so badly I cried. I couldn't bear the thought of a man touching me. I . . . I couldn't have loved him like he wanted. May Spider cherish and nurture his soul, he never demanded it. Never even asked about Giorj and me . . . although it ate away at his mind and made him so incredibly sad.'' She remembered the pain in his face as he laughed and told another outrageous story. "I'll always hate myself for that,'' she whispered miserably.

"What makes me different from Friday?''

Susan stared into the darkness. "At first, you were almost a comic figure. Don't feel bad about it. You just weren't capable of being threatening.''

"Gee, thanks.''

"It was a matter of experience. You hadn't seen the horrors I had.''

"And now?''

"Now, Darwin, you've seen the horrors. You know how fragile it makes you. I don't think you'd hurt me.''

He chuckled in the dark.

"Why is that funny?''

"Susan, you're a trial. I never knew what to do with you. I thought you were the most beautiful, magnificent woman who ever lived. I also thought you were made of steel, efficiency, and anger. I wondered if you went out of your way to make me miserable, yet I couldn't help but be fascinated by your strength. You seemed so competent—almost inhuman—with no vulnerabilities. Nothing that made you real. I called you the 'Iron Lady' and had decided the reason you liked Giorj was because you could turn him inside out whenever you wanted. My portrait of Susan Smith Andojar wasn't very attractive.''

She shifted to stare at him in the dark. "So why did you waste so much time trying to impress me?''

"Because I could see you were hiding something terrible. Then I spied on you one time when you went in to see Friday. I saw you as human.'' His tone turned grim, "And I still thought you were the most viciously attractive woman I'd ever seen. I think I'll drown when I look in your eyes.''

She found that funny. "You sound like a moonstruck boy.''

"I was.'' He hesitated. "I still am. Mostly.''

"Darwin," she said softly. "I can't be your lover. I can't even try. I don't know that I can ever let myself make love to a man again."

The silence stretched.

"I'm not sure I can ever be your lover either." He shifted uncomfortably on the bunk. "It's something deep inside. Tiara, with the blood running down her mouth. Ngen, playing on 'my Romanan lover.' Yes, he conjured you in my mind. Tiara and you merge, shift, in the dreams. That last . . . where Pallas cut me and . . . and . . . Ever since that day, I haven't had an erection."

"Maybe it was the catheter in the med unit."

"In the dream, you become Tiara. It's you who . . . Well, you saw the tape. I . . . I don't know. When I'm awake, I can tell myself that you're you. You're the woman I've been infatuated with since the day I saw you knocking the stuffing out of that combat robot. I'm here to maybe break the dream with the reality of the Susan I fell in love with. Not the ghost Ngen left planted in my mind."

She ordered the lights to stay off as she sat up. "You know, there's more to it. That neural stimulator Pallas used damaged something called the pudic nerve. The corporal thought it might have even affected the brain."

"So, you're safe. Nothing's happening." He flopped uneasily. "Hey, you've got duty in a couple of hours. Get some shut-eye. I don't really want to see you all ragged out like last time. I'll be here if Ngen comes." He sounded so lonely.

She stood up, hand on the light control to keep it off. Heart pounding, she slid into the bunk, feeling her skin, cool against his.

"Susan? What are you—"

"Shhh!" She reached out and pulled him to her. "Let's sleep now, maybe the dreams won't come."

But they did. He woke first, shivering. Then later, when she found herself straining as Ngen's hands moved on her body and his cooing voice twisted her soul, Darwin's strong arms were around her, bringing her back to safety.

Main cargo receiving bay: *Deus* **in GEO orbit over Santa del Cielo.**

"What you will do, people, is study these schematics." Ngen Van Chow, the Messiah of the Fathers, stood before them.

Veld looked around skeptically, noting the uncertainty of his fellows. The large room felt too cool, almost chilly. At one end of the twenty meter long room, Ngen—dressed in bright red, yellow, and black fabrics—stood on the podium, looking at where they crowded together like frightened sheep. Fathers, eyes dull, blasters in hand, lined the featureless white walls. The air carried the rank odor of fear and unwashed bodies as well as a metallic bite that stung the nose. The future had caught up with all of them.

"Some progress has been made," Van Chow continued. "We have the basic concept decoded from the original Brotherhood data. What *you* must do is build the *Fist of God*, the station which will allow me to jump a singularity outside of time-space."

"He's mad," Ten MacGuire whispered.

"No, Master Engineer," Ngen smiled, looking down over the bobbing heads. "I'm not mad at all. I believe the Brotherhood built something very similar to this once. I have begun your work for you. Already, Cobalt Station has been stripped of its population. The engineers I've been able to find have begun installing reactors and preparing the basic remodeling of Cobalt to be the *Fist of God.*"

MacGuire had gone pale. How had the Messiah heard him? Veld shifted his gaze, throat dry, looking for the monitoring equipment, seeing none.

"In the meantime, your wives and families will remain here with me on the *Deus.*" Ngen waved his hands easily. "Progress will be rewarded by visits to your loved ones. Insubordination, a certain lack of enthusiasm, and, well, you've seen some of the Fathers. Rather mindless, don't you think? I'm sure none of you would want to see your lovely wives, husbands, sons, or daughters walking around in so menial an existence."

Ten MacGuire closed his eyes, a dull misery on his haggard face. Veld reached over, placing a bracing hand to keep him from falling. MacGuire felt limp, ready to collapse.

"Steady," Veld muttered out the side of his mouth, nervous the Messiah would hear that, too.

"Your every need will be met, people. You may have all the building supplies you desire. You may eat, drink, and treat yourselves as you believe you deserve so long as you make progress. You may do anything so long as you build for me—and you'll keep your families in similar comfort on my ship. You may not, of course, build a transduction device. I would similarly take a very dim view of your trying to escape. Were you to do so, I'm afraid your families would suffer most horribly."

Somewhere behind Veld, that triple-cursed baby started crying again.

"Very well," Ngen said with a smile. "You are dismissed. You have one final night to enjoy your families. A shuttle will take all engineers and physicists to Cobalt Station at the beginning of first watch. Until then, good evening." Ngen strode easily out of the huge room, billowing robes folding around him.

"How did you know?" Ten asked, staring glumly at Veld while the room erupted into a roar of disbelief.

Veld rubbed the bridge of his nose. "Just simple inductive reasoning. Of course, I never thought he'd psych people into ghouls. A blaster to the head, well, it would be a lot quicker. More merciful in its way. How did . . . Damnation! Whatever spawned a monster like that? You still going to refuse?"

Ten MacGuire looked numbly at him as Therisa, his wife, clung to a sleeve, staring dry-eyed up at her husband. Ten shook his head, running his hand through his wife's golden hair. "And see her psyched? No, he's got me, Veld. I'll build his damnable machine. Just . . . just pray we get through this alive."

"Yeah, sure, if God really exists."

CHAPTER XXXI

Approach to Directorate Section, Arcturus: Main Admin Dock.

Darwin was shocked at the huge segments of ripped steel that thrust incongruously out of the gutted portions of Arc-

turus. Whole sections of the intertwining spaghettilike complex were contorted—blasted in two. Segments had been
tethered in place by cable stretched across the gaps.

"Incredible!" he breathed. Susan stood by his side on
the cramped bridge.

"Prepare for docking. Moshe, take her in easy. If we
bump them, the whole place might collapse."

Spider's Revenge floated easily into what had once been
a Patrol slip. Susan watched comm hook into the system.
"First party, disembark!" An image formed on one of the
monitors. José Grita White Eagle led a group of combat-
armored, blaster-wielding marines trotting down the lock
corridor. Susan was taking no chances although Patan
seemed unconcerned. Not that Patan's concerns mattered
much; what a Prophet thought important and what preoccupied Susan for the moment might be two very different
things.

"Secure, Captain." White Eagle's voice came through.
"Admiral Kimianjui is here with an honor guard of Patrol
marines."

"Thank the Admiral and give him my warmest regards."
She looked around the bridge, motioning. "All right, the
bridgehead looks secure. Let's go, people! Moshe, keep your
power up in case we have to shoot our way out."

"You've got it, Susan." He grinned wickedly. "Let's see
'em try!"

Darwin wore his Santos coup on his belt next to the Randall. A powerful Patrol blaster hung from catches on his
other hip. His wasn't much compared to Susan's impressive
belt. Everyone wore combat armor, just in case. Spider
alone knew what kind of surprises Arcturus might spring.
Assassination?

His prosthetic left him off balance, limping slightly. The
damn thing had all the class of a ball and chain—at about
half the weight. Still, it kept his tissues regenerating, therapy for the nerves. Maybe.

Stepping into the lock, Darwin couldn't help but think of
how his freshly painted Spider effigy shone starkly on the
white of his armor. Where had he lost the man who had left
here not so long ago, headed for an academic adventure?
And more, what or who had he become? A man's hair hung
at his waist. The knife with which he'd killed rested under
his right hand. Where once his head had been filled with

theory and cultural dynamics, now a haunting dream spun from a horrid reality lurking under his thoughts—eternally goaded by Ngen's insidious voice.

The Patrol marines stood lined to either side of the lock, eyes straight ahead, faces grim. Here, before their eyes, passed the final chapter of a long and glorious history. The Patrol was dead and they knew they were seeing the last throes of its demise. The pathos of pride and pain stirred him with the overwhelming power of the moment.

The lock itself opened out into a long, domed waiting area now filled with a sea of faces, all staring, voices a droning buzz. At the end of the line of Patrol, one small black man stood, prim and proper in a blazing white Patrol dress uniform, the triangular neck piece a deep laser blue.

As Darwin stomped forward behind Susan, the Admiral stood alone on his little podium. A final gesture of station. Even so, the effect lost something as Susan came to stand before Kimianjui. In her tall grace, she met him eye to eye.

Kimianjui bowed. "Captain Susan Smith Andojar, I am here to turn over my authority to you as representatives of Admiral Damen Ree's Romanan forces. I assure you that I and all of my people will render you the best of our service. Our offer of cooperation is made in the hope the transition of power will be peaceful and beneficial to all concerned. We wish only to continue to serve humanity in this moment of great trial."

Susan nodded, taking his salute. "Admiral, we come not as conquerors but as allies in a time of need. Martial law is hereby decreed. Orders will be issued by myself, Doctor Darwin Pike, or one of my superiors.

"Existing Patrol companies will remain intact." Eyes turned at her words and she pivoted to meet their reserved stares. "You are some of the finest military personnel in the galaxy. Romanans value the honor of that. Unfortunately, there are too few of even the best.

"Our Romanan system of military authority will seem odd to you at first." She began walking along the ranks, inspecting them like a commander. "Suffice it to say, I'm available at any time. We don't work on protocol like the Patrol. I expect you all to be professionals. Treat yourselves that way and you'll get along fine with your new comrades in arms. There will be one standing order. No knife feuds!"

She looked archly down the white, gleaming ranks.

"Since you don't know about Romanan law, I'll tell you. I declare this war trail. That means Romanans won't scrap with you. Besides, you can get enough of that in joint training sessions. The other things we won't tolerate are slurs against our religion, our Prophets, or our mothers.

"For the present, you're to see to the settling in of the Romanan forces. Get acquainted. I think all of us will benefit from this assignment. Any questions? None?" She smiled. "That's what I thought. Professionals, by Spider."

Susan marched smartly up to Kimianjui and turned on her heel. "Dismissed!"

They looked at her in amazement. The Romanans began filing out of *Revenge*, chattering excitedly as, almost to a man, this was their first time in a station. They pointed and peered, feeling the deck plating, sometimes stomping to see if it quivered under their weight.

"White Eagle," Susan called. "Keep them out of trouble." She waved at the throngs of Romanans tramping through the lock. "The Patrol will show you to your quarters. Sam Smith Iron Eyes, I want you to keep the new recruits from doing anything foolish, like drinking out of the lavatories."

"Admiral?" Susan asked as her lieutenants trotted off, "Could we discuss duty rosters, patrol schedules, areas of specific concern for pacification and access to supplies and comm facilities? We've got a lot to do in the next couple of days. We'd better be at it."

"Most assuredly. This way, if you please." The little man led the way, his honor guard clearing a path most effectively.

"How'd I do?" Susan mumbled out of the side of her mouth.

"Not bad." Pike winked surreptitiously. "Can't think of anyone else I'd ever want to surrender a civilization to."

She filled her lungs, nodding uneasily. "Yeah, right. And it could all blow up at any second. Remember that. We've got five hundred warriors to how many Arcturians?"

Directorate Section: Skor Robinson's control room.

So they'd come. Skor blinked, realizing the shimmering came from tears building in his eyes. He blinked hard, the only way to clear the corneas in zero g.

"The symbol of my final failure. Romanans have arrived." In the holo, he watched Susan Smith Andojar's marines rush out, armed, fearsome looking with human hair hanging on their belts and stuck to their shining white armor. The spiders painted on their armor came in many colors and sizes. Here and there, a Santos cross still adorned an arm or shoulder.

"The barbarians have come to Rome," Skor whispered, blinking again. "And they've come at my bidding. How did this happen? Where did I fail? Everything I did was logical, based on the most rational thoughts . . . yet I led us to this? What . . . what legacy is mine?"

"Oh, poor humanity, I've failed you horribly."

He watched Susan Smith Andojar walk out, a young tigress. Men looked twice at her beauty, but Skor could only stare, a yawning cavity within he'd never before experienced.

"Does no one weep for me?" he wondered. "Does no one care that I hurt inside—and the catheters can't compensate. Chester? By your wretched Spider, I wish I were dead."

Arcturus Moscow Section: Arcadian slums.

The old man waved his arms, pirouetting on the air converter cover. Arcadia stretched along the four-meter-wide street. Little more than a corridor, squalid shops lined either side of the dirt-gray avenue, graffiti-scrawled fronts stretching up to the ceiling four meters overhead. No one in Arcadia ever escaped the feeling of living in a tunnel. The air carried the odor of humans, poverty, and waste. Pervading everything, the sound of the balancing pumps throbbed. Here and there, scars from the recent riots marred graphite walls—occasional scorched places marking the sites of snuffed fires—never cleaned. But then the supervisors never worried about right, or the future, or their chances of starving now that everything had been blasted apart.

A growing circle of people paused, stopping to listen to the dancing scarecrow. Life had used him hard, reflecting the tribulations in the lines around his eyes and mouth. Now he wore dirty gray robes, stained, frayed at the hem. His impassioned gray eyes searched the faces before him as he opened his toothless mouth to speak.

"I tell you, we pay the price of our sins! Deus has wreaked his vengeance upon us for rotting in the foul taloned hands of the Directorate. And now? Now the ultimate blasphemy! Satan's spawn have landed on Holy Arcturus! Satan's demons have come home! My soul hovers on the verge of eternal damnation . . . as do all of our souls!''

A shout of agreement rose as people raised their fists. *"Death! Death! Death!"*

"We are charged with the holy responsibility of driving this scourge of Satan from among us! Too long have we watched our people starve under the Directors! Too long have the lies of the Patrol—the psych of the Health Department, and the corruption of the Romanans been loosed upon us! Arise! Follow me! Arcturus prays for deliverance! Deus is the way! Come with me! Help me cast this abomination of Spider into the abyss!''

"Kill the Romanans!" a woman screamed, climbing half up a pole to hang by one skinny, smudged arm.

"Kill Spider!" bellowed another as the crowd swayed. Someone had obtained a metal bar and now began smashing out the comm terminals.

The rest surged forward, shouting, clogging the street before the ragged old man. Desperate faces lit with a new frenzy of anger.

The old man danced from foot to foot, shouting, "Spider is Satan! This Prophet is an abomination! Satan's filth is upon us! Arise! *Arise! ARISE!''*

Their enthusiasm gained voice as the old man dropped to the street, leading his throng forward. A pavilion crashed down. Windows shattered. The mob boiled after him, screaming, enraged, as they shook fists, and smashed store fronts.

The old man headed straight for the long corridor that led toward the Directorate headquarters. He stopped short, staggering backward into his crowd as a rough hand reached out from around the corner and knotted in his filthy robe.

"You called Spider an abomination?" The man who strode out of the corridor, pushed the old man before him. The milling mob rolled to a stop, staring, hushed whispers flying.

He wore gleaming white armor and two long black braids hung down to either side of his muscular shoulders. A black spider had been drawn on his chest piece and a long gray blaster gleamed where it hung, clipped to a sling.

"Spider? What . . . Yes, yes! An abomination!" the old man howled. "Filth! And this Prophet is Satan's demon come among us. We'll throw these Satan-driven Romanans to their deaths!''

The warrior lifted the old man, physically throwing him back into the arms of his incensed rabble. Feet braced, he crossed his arms, blocking the way to the corridor. ''Very well, old man. Throw me!''

''Throw . . . Throw . . .'' he stuttered, suddenly perplexed.

''Before I count coup and teach you obedience, I am ordered to tell you all to go home like good Directorate sheep. If you don't leave here now—''

''A Romanan!'' someone shouted, seeing the spider clearly reflected in the light.

''Kill him!'' The old man leveled a crooked bony finger. ''Deus commands you!''

They surged forward, reaching with grasping hands, faces shining with anticipation.

Sam Smith Iron Eyes reached for the old man, whirling him around, the long fighting knife glinting in the light as it pinned the old man's throat.

''Very well! You would see the Power of Spider? Step closer, and this piece of Arcturian trash dies!''

The mob swayed uncertainly, awed by the old man's tortured expression as he tried to swallow under the keen blade. Feet pounded in the corridor as more Romanans formed up behind Sam.

''Go home,'' Sam ordered reasonably. ''This filth would stir you to fight against Spider. He would make you a tool of Ngen Van Chow.''

''Let the Father go!'' the skinny woman shrieked from the back. ''The rest of you, Deus commands you to kill the Romanans!''

Sam's arm sawed once, quickly, as he pushed the old man to fall in the space between them. A gagging rasp could be heard as the old man clawed forward, a gush of brilliant crimson staining the dirty tiles underfoot. He flopped once, turning to expose his slit throat, now bubbling in a rush of blood.

Sam's voice carried calmly in the sudden quiet. ''Do *not* call Spider names. Do *not* call our Prophet filth.'' The people began backing away. ''I have seen Bazaar. You people have no idea what filth means until you've seen the ghouls of Deus. You have no idea what suffering means until you've seen what Ngen did to Sirius. Go home. Thank Spider that we've given you your lives.''

''Kill him!'' the skinny woman shrieked where she hung on the lamp pole. *''Romanan filth!* Kill them whe—''

A blaster bolt ripped out and exploded her head. The body jerked and pitched into the stunned crowd.

''Go home!'' Sam Smith Iron Eyes yelled, motioning. ''Get your senses, and think! Is this what you would send to Spider? The memory of a wild rabble? Where is your honor? Where is your pride? Are you sheep or men and women? Are you beasts or human beings?''

The young man with the metal bar charged from the side, swinging his club. Sam sidestepped neatly, the bar clanging against the wall. Sam pivoted and drove his long knife into the man's side, cutting upward and back. One hand in the young man's hair, he carved the coup loose, before kicking the dying youth down next to the corpse of the old man.

''So you see,'' Sam remarked. ''I have taken the first coup on Arcturus. Go home. Act like a people with honor. If you can't behave—I'm sure a Romanan knife is waiting for you somewhere.''

Horror stricken, they stared. Slowly, the ones in front pushed back, eyes riveted on the dangling bloody hair Sam clasped in his fist. Mutterings of disbelief carried in the humid air as individuals flitted away from the mob. Suddenly they broke, the entire body of people melting furtively into the warrens of Arcadia.

Romanan rule had come to Arcturus.

Bullet's bridge: GEO orbit above World.

''Got him!'' Ree muttered, pacing the bridge as the sensors got the fix. ''I want targeting locked. Maya, we're feeding the bogey's vector. Can you match?''

''Affirmative, Damen. *Victory's* never responded like this. Giorj is here on the bridge with me. He's computing the figures now. Uh . . . hang on. Right! Yeah, Damen. We'll be able to match by the time he's three light-hours out.''

Ree turned, checking the system map. Three light-hours? ''That's pretty close, Maya. We'll assume he's going to try and torpedo World. You worry about matching. We'll worry about tagging the torpedo.''

''Acknowledged.''

Damen Ree stared at the dot of light bearing down on

World. Well, Breeze, in *Coup,* had killed two bogeys off Sirius already. Ngen shouldn't have made such a big deal out of the vendetta. Only maybe this time, just maybe, they could get a bogey in one piece. If only *Victory's* increased shielding and Fujiki-amplified blasters were up to the trick. And if *Bullet's* targeting comm could pick up the torpedo.

Sobered, Ree stared down at the planet below. World waited, a serene ball, unaware that death drove down out of the stars at just under the speed of light. If he missed, they'd all die down there. *Bullet* would get no second chance.

Directorate Sector: Arcturus.

Darwin lifted his leg down as the physician checked the readouts.

"Well?"

"Fifty-fifty, I'd say." The woman studied a couple of charts that displayed on the monitor. "Untreated, you'd definitely have to wear the prosthesis. If you had to land anywhere, Arcturus has the best medical therapy facilities in the Directorate."

Pike nodded and sighed. "And the cancer seems under control?"

She nodded. "I think so. The entire syndrome occurred as sequelae from the regeneration process. They pushed too fast."

Pike pursed his lips and nodded. "At least it's better than I thought. Thank you, doctor. I appreciate it. I'll be in touch."

"And you'll be in therapy if you know what's good for that leg."

Pike nodded, glancing at Susan as the physician walked to the door, passed the Romanan guards, and left.

Susan leaned back, rubbing the bridge of her nose with a thumb and forefinger. "I pushed it, Darwin. Blame me." She stood, taking the headset from her brow and twirling the unit by the end. "Good old Susan, all guts and go and no sense. Don't save for later what you can do yesterday."

"Hey. Settle down. I don't blame you." He stood, wincing at the tingling the treatment left in his leg. "Remember how it was, Susan? Bazaar? The ghouls? Remember how I looked? Yeah, I've scanned the tapes. I'm not sure in your shoes that I would have wanted a man lying around thinking about all that. Besides, you needed me. The Admiral's brain boy, remember? Combat decision, wasn't it? Responsibility? A sense of guilt?'' He grinned. ''Besides, I think you actually liked me. Even then.''

She sighed, smiled shyly at him, and pushed a spill of hair over her shoulders. ''You know, Pike, you can still be a pain in the ass at times.''

He grinned, stumping over to look at the readouts. ''How's it going?''

''Moshe and I have set about establishing a headquarters and a logistical network. Parties of Romanans with Patrol escort are making the circuit of unstable portions of Arcturus. A riot erupted almost immediately in Arcadia, but Sam did a pretty good job of tying that down.

''A couple of hours later, a bunch of toughs tried to ambush Sam's patrol. They had a lot of fun. While only five people were killed outright, an entire dome was sacked. Hundreds of terrified Arcadians are in med units growing new hair while their severed guts reknit. Want to hear the cries of outrage? Seems Arcturus isn't keen on rapes and mutilations.'' She shrugged. ''From what I've seen, Arcturus needs the new blood.''

Pike squinted at the growing list of complaints and condemnations. ''So? What are you going to do?''

''Let them rock for a while. Then I'm issuing a proclamation to let them know that next time, there will be no med for rioters. They'll be left to cover their gleaming skulls as best they can.

''Then I've got two Fathers we caught hanging Ngen posters and demanding the formation of a Temple. I'm showing segments of our scout on Bazaar along with lengthy follow-up debate by psych specialists from University. White Eagle ceremoniously threw the Fathers out to breathe vacuum. The next Fathers encountered were ripped to pieces by the Arcturians down in Moscow Section. I think we've turned the tide on social control here.'' She cocked her head. ''And what have you done besides tie up medical expertise?''

''Want to sleep alone at night? No? Okay, I put together a session with some of the philosophy department heads. I'd like to conduct a complete interview while Patan turns on his charm. I think we'll leave the faculty crying for more.''

She nodded. ''I'll get you the air time. We can use the

transduction net—broadcast system wide. The entire Directorate will hear.''

''And that ought to just blow it all wide open.''

She nodded, a frown tightening her brow.

''What?''

She lifted a slim hand, shaking her head. ''Oh, I just keep remembering Sirius. Keep reminding myself that war doesn't go the way it's supposed to . We're setting up billions of people to be murdered.''

He met her eyes.

Kythros: Moscow Sector.

Kythros is a type VII terrestrial planet with Martian attributes. Originally settled in the early Confederate period, Kythros has undergone substantial terraforming by means of artificial stimulation of vulcanism to promote increased utilization of the CO_2 cycle. Continued settlement, the introduction of genetically altered terrestrial plant species, and satellite ozone production have increased the habitability of the planet. Population continues to grow, the majority of the inhabitants living in the major city of Kytheria, the complex still domed for atmospheric protection.

Regis Hyplar crossed his arms, a mark of his negation. His office had the neat look of efficiency. His staff waited, seated or standing around, worried eyes on the monitors. Why had the Fathers come in five ships this time?

''I'm sorry, commander, but we've taken the census of the population. The bungled attempt by your agent to assassinate me cemented popular resistance against your cause. The same with your attack on Arcturus. We can't have anything to do with butchers who murdered a billion people. We've seen the holos recorded by Damen Ree's people. We remain loyal to the Directorate. You have no port here, so I suggest you space for Bazaar or Arpeggio, or wherever you came from.''

''You force my hand,'' Teder Vincente replied with a shrug. ''This is the third time the minions of Deus have come to establish a Temple. We hear your words.'' The holo flickered off.

''Sounds like they'll never learn.''

Regis filled his lungs and exhaled, tuning to look at his Assistant Secretary. ''You think?''

She lifted a shoulder, eyes meeting his. "They haven't so far."

"All right, back to work, people. The fun's—"

"Sir?" Will Weemer called, looking down at his monitor. "We've got shuttles dropping from the Fathers' ships. Six, seven, nine, must be twenty of them."

"Dropping? I told them—"

"We're getting a systemwide broadcast."

Regis turned, looking up at the comm net. Father Teder Vincente looked out grimly. "People of Kythros, you are about to be occupied by a military force under the command of the Messiah. Those who resist will be shot. Those who do not will not be harmed. We are now in control of your planet. Resistance is futile and will only lead to unnecessary violence and suffering. Further instructions will be given as soon as the Temple is completed." Then there was silence.

Regis turned. "Scramble security. I want—"

A concussion rocked the Directorate Administration building. Through the window, Regis could see the billowing arc of smoke and fire. He stared, disbelieving.

"That was the security building," Will whispered. "And here come the shuttles."

In the monitors, the delta-winged craft landed, ramps dropping while scores of armed, armored Fathers tramped out.

"What now?" Regis mumbled. "Where's the Patrol? Where's sanity anymore?"

Teder didn't give him a chance for more questions. A well placed gelatin bomb detonated on the roof. Regis and the others died instantly.

In the streets under the dome, the stunned populace watched as the mindless Fathers paraded in. Here and there a man or woman stood up to shout obscenities at the invaders. Each was methodically shot down, the exploded body left where it had fallen. Deus had come to Kythros.

Directorate Section: Arcturus.

"Are you ready for this?" Pike asked, a hand on Patan's shoulder.

The Prophet looked up, expression softening. "It's already begun, Doctor Pike. But yes, I'm ready and at peace. But I must ask, are you? In many ways, you're too compassionate for your own good."

Darwin frowned. "Am I? I'm not the one who's condemned to face—"

"We're all condemned. That's the way of Spider. But, Doctor, you must not let your feelings, your compassion, prevent you from letting me follow my path. Do you understand?"

Pike began to form a protest.

"No, Doctor. No matter what, you must remember who and what we're fighting. As you see me grow more distant, more mad, fill your mind with images of Bazaar. Yes, you understand now, don't you? What's one man's insanity against that of an entire species?" Patan reached up to grip Pike's shoulder. "I must make my appearance, face the galaxy now. The archbishop has just arrived with some fascinating questions."

One by one, the religious heads asked for audiences. Darwin scheduled them: Moslem ayatollahs, Jewish rabbis, Buddhist monks, Catholic cardinals, Neo-Christian ministers, they all lined up for a crack at Patan Andojar Garcia. The Prophet handled them with ease, agreeing to the sacredness of their religions, explaining that Spider was but another name for the ultimate reality. The fundamentalists he handled by demonstrating their claims to be the same as his—so long as they accepted the souls as God's domain.

Darwin shook his head with envy. Patan made it all sound so plausible, somehow skimming over the obvious problems. And the price had to be paid. Darwin would almost have to carry him as soon as he was off stage.

"It is horribly exhausting," Patan told him. "I have to balance myself, sending part of my mind into the future to see what they will say. Then I have to make an answer, search out the responses they will make, how I will counter, what they will say in turn. When I reach a dead trail, I have to back up and do it all over again. At the same time, I have to appear to be intent on their questions. I have to argue hundreds of problems at once in my head."

"Get some rest, Patan. You're done for the day." Darwin patted him on the shoulder.

In the meantime, Patan's predictions began to tell. He foresaw the failure of a major seam in the American sector which would have killed a hundred thousand. Darwin rejoiced in the shouting mob which greeted Patan as he rode through the sector, literally its king and savior.

After each of the prophecies, however, Patan would with-

draw, refusing to eat, eyes haunted by what he was doing.
His lined face would reflect exhaustion and fear.

"It is always more difficult to get back," Patan whispered
once.

Darwin hesitated, watching the phenomenal change of
spirit which washed through Arcturus. The people had new
life in their faces. The economy was picking up. Spiders
were appearing in places as unlikely as the huge Christian
church in Open Market. The Bishop didn't order it removed.

Patan attended services in every major religious temple,
tabernacle, church, pagoda, and lodge in the huge orbiting
city. Success followed success. The library staggered under
a flood of requests through comm for information. Musical
instruments disappeared from shops, snapped up overnight
after the Prophet stated music was enlightenment for the
soul.

Dress began changing to Romanan styles. Veterans like
José White Eagle said it was Sirius all over again. The Romanan patrols, originally avoided or insulted, now received
gifts of food, offerings of sex, free room and board, trinkets
and so forth. A real Romanan fighting knife became priceless and the spares carried by warriors in their kits brought
fortunes. The barracks were piled with the loot showered
on the occupying troops.

Darwin returned to his quarters after making sure Patan
had eaten a large meal and was securely behind locked doors
with his usual Romanan guard under the jealous eye of José
Grita White Eagle. The place had all the decadence of Soviet Earth. The commissars of Moscow in the twenty-first
century might have lived like this, surrounded by carefully
engraved wood paneling, with thick svee moss carpeting the
floor (only they wouldn't have had svee moss). Gold filigree
intermixed with silver accented the carving. The furniture
looked antique, but hid antigrav plates to support a person's
body weightlessly. Comm terminals had been artfully designed to match the decor. The air always smelled scented,
slightly jasmine.

He was putting the finishing touches on the speech he
would give the next day before the commercial assembly
when Susan entered, face haggard.

"You look beat."

"What's the word on Patan's revival."

"Superb." Darwin pulled his headset off. "Today, the

Christians practically capitulated by saying Spider was but another aspect of the Holy Ghost. Damned if I know how they justified it. Logically, it makes no sense, but the word came *ex cathedra* from the Arcturian Pope himself.''

''Ngen has killed three more planets,'' she said listlessly. ''Another entire Sector has fallen to the Fathers according to Ree's latest report. We have another six FTs crewed from *Victory* and *Miliken*'s ranks at Ngen's rear, harassing his back country. The Fathers tried to bomb Sirius again. Breeze blew them out of space first.''

She raised her hands, eyes anguished. ''It's a matter of time. With all the space they're taking, eventually they'll break through and kill my planet. The worst is, they captured Kythros with a military assault. It was a trial run after the Kytherians tore down the Temple the Fathers were building. The war is escalating, Darwin. It's becoming deadly serious for everyone. Where's it going to end?''

He smiled. ''*Miliken* is spacing for here. You won't have to worry about us being caught with our britches down. Rita is on the way in. She'll be here in a couple of days. At least Arcturus is safe. We've made a lot of progress here.''

She ran cool fingers down either side of his head. ''I'm scared, Darwin. Our first converted GCI spaced for Father country last week. They'll burn off more and more planets. Ngen will retaliate. We're building dead zones. Killing entire Sectors. Independent stations are boosting like mad for uncharted space. Two GCIs were stolen on Earth, loaded with refugees and spaced for who knows where away from the threat of this ghastly war. Entire planets would be abandoned, but the people can't get off. There are riots everywhere, all of humanity is terrified of the Fathers.''

''The tapes have worked.''

''Sure they've worked, but we've broken the people. They don't have anything to believe in. They're even committing mass suicide in Ngen's path.''

''The whole species has gone crazy,'' Darwin whispered. ''Death by psych or death by antimatter. There's never been a war like this.''

''Where will it end?'' Susan whispered. ''Will it end with World blown away? We have the potential to destroy everything, Darwin. Eventually, every major planet could be blasted into nothingness. Only some of the stations will survive. Whole Sectors of space will be lifeless. Oh, God! Where is Spider's purpose in that?''

He shivered suddenly with premonition. Standing, he hugged her, dimming the lights and huddling with her on the bed.

"We're losing the war," Susan whispered, desperate. "We can't stop him!"

CHAPTER XXXII

Victory's Bridge, on the fringes of the World system.

Maya ben Ahmad smiled wickedly into the monitor pickup. "You've got the choice. Surrender or die."

She looked over, watching the converted GCI growing on the screens as *Victory* closed the gap, her modified grav plates compensating for the additional thrust her reactor built. Deep in *Victory*'s guts, Giorj Hambrei monitored his instruments, trimming the last possible performance from the giant ship of the Line.

Winston Zimbuti swallowed hard, dark features paling as yet another salvo of his blaster batteries flared uselessly against *Victory*'s augmented shielding. Frantic eyes kept shifting to his bridge screens.

Maya cocked her head, knowing he watched *Victory* pounding down on him, shields holding firm while the spectrum flashed as his guns fired ineffectually. Fingering her throat while she studied his growing anxiety, she added, "We're real familiar with the design of the GCI. Not only that, but at this range, you're as good as point-blank."

"Ben?" she called over her shoulder. "Put a shot through *Abraham*'s forward refrigeration unit."

"Acknowledged, Colonel."

Maya switched her gaze to the targeting monitor, watching brilliant violet arc into *Abraham,* the shielding buckling to an explosion of light and boiling atmosphere.

In the holo, Zimbuti staggered as his ship shuddered under the impact, bridge klaxons wailing. He grabbed the arms of his command chair, eyes raised to the readouts overhead. His mouth had dropped open, exposing straight white teeth. His breathing seemed labored as he blinked and stared into the transduction pickup.

"Care to try me any further?" Maya prodded.

Zimbuti closed his eyes and shook his head. "No, Colonel. I don't need a monitor to read the writing." From off screen, he took a damage control report inaudible to Maya. Turning back he added, "I still have a choice, Colonel. I can explode my ship rather than suffer capture. And if my torpedo makes it in, you won't have anything to protect anymore, either."

Maya leaned forward. "Sure enough. I'm betting that no matter what, Damen's blasters are going to tag your torpedo just fine. We know the vector you released on. And, as to blowing up your ship? We'd rather not push you to that. We're not demons, Winston—no matter what Ngen might claim."

Zimbuti's mouth worked distastefully, broad black face sweat-shiny in the bridge lights. "But I do have that choice."

"You do. And *Victory* is far enough away you can't take us with you. But, Captain, why die? You're a young man— and you were a successful smuggler. Mendez tried for years to take you. Why throw all that talent and youth away? Give us your targeting program—or detonate the torpedo—and you're off hale and hearty instead of dead. Besides, Winston, you never know about the future."

He leaned forward, eyes hot as he gestured at the pickup. "I'm not about to be psyched, Colonel. Not by the Directorate . . . or your Romanans. So far, I've beaten the odds against the Health Department." He pointed to his head. "This brain is mine! Untampered. And I want it to stay that way. Once I surrender, I lose the right to even take my own life. Understand, Colonel? I've been a big man with Ngen's forces. You mean to tell me that you'll forgive the blown away worlds? You'll let me live after being part of making Ngen's monsters? And what if my torpedo gets through? What if I blow that planet down there to crap? You going to forget that?"

"Oh, we won't forget, Zimbuti. I'll make you a couple of promises. We won't execute you and there will be no psych. It's not free, of course. You're enough of an operator to know that nothing comes free. Consider it a trader's deal. Your life for information. You know a lot about Ngen's organization. What's your pleasure? Live and take a chance? Or die. You're out of time.

"Ben, target *Abraham*'s reactor room."

"Targeted, Colonel."

"Five seconds, Zimbuti. One. Two. Three. Four. Fi—"

"All right!" He raised his hands, palms outward. "We surrender. Your terms." He look around uneasily. "Besides which, Ngen's getting weird. You know what I mean? Like he's taken to believing he's really this Deus." Winston cocked his head, lowering his voice. "I don't know, me and the boys, we'd thought of running a time or two. But, man, where was there to go? The pumpkin heads?"

"And the torpedo?"

"Sorry, Colonel. It's just a stasis field that breaks down on impact to release the antimatter."

"Send us the vector information on your bomb. You'll dump V and follow us in. Any deviations will result in your immediate destruction. Any—"

"What about my crew, Colonel?"

"You're all to be treated as prisoners of war, Captain. That's an antique concept that goes back a long way. It means we won't just blow your heads off. No, instead you'll probably be held on World someplace. It's not a bad life. Shoveling out corrals and hauling manure to gardens beats spending from now until eternity flying through space as radiation, doesn't it?"

Zimbuti lifted his lip in disgust. "Helm," he called over his shoulder. "Dump it. We're through. Follow the course corrections sent in by *Victory.*" He looked back at Maya. "You win, Colonel."

"And you'll send all the targeting data on that antimatter torpedo you launched." Maya leaned her head back. "Damen will probably hit it—but you'd rather not be left on a planet suffering that kind of climatic upheaval."

Zimbuti flared his broad nostrils and slapped his hands futilely on his knees. "Weapons Officer, relay the release data on the torpedo to *Victory.*"

Bullet's Bridge: GEO orbit over World.

Where he watched the bridge screen, Damen Ree nodded. "Tony! Quick, process that data. I want it loaded into a backup system. Make sure it mirrors what we've picked up so far with our sensors."

"Got it, Colonel." Anthony frowned as he processed the information. "Looks good. If there's a glitch in what they sent, it's small."

Ree's jaw muscles ached. "How small does it have to be, Tony? That packet is maybe eight by ten meters, coming at point nine eight C. We've got a Doppler image that's hazy at best. We don't know the exact vector it's on. If there's a guidance system integral to the antimatter cage, it could shift minutely enough to still hit the planet. If we miss by just a hair, World is dead."

Tony said nothing, buried in the computations, coordinating sensor data with weapons and spectrometry.

The minutes ticked by.

"Power up," Major Glick called from his station in the reactor room.

"Come on," Ree whispered, watching the telemetry, every one of *Bullet*'s eyes on the expected path of the lethal missile. "Spider, if I've ever called in a favor, this is it." His knotted fist pounded absently on the back of the command chair. Around him, the spacious bridge gleamed whitely, buzzing with the noise of frantic men and women busy at duty stations.

"Range estimate in ten seconds, sir," Tony called. "Targeting error unknown."

"Fire upon range. Weapons tie to comm. Use your best shot, people—and Spider keep you."

Bullet pulsed as she poured searching fire up toward the stars in violet threads.

Seconds passed as targeting refined. Ree stared at the monitors, fists clenched, awaiting the flash that would indicate a hit. A sheen of sweat beaded on Tony's brow.

Damen stared up, eyes aching as he watched the blaster bolts flickering, changing, tendrils of energy seeking in vain for such a tiny target with so little mass. Where in that vastness did death fall?

"Come on," Ree whispered through gritted teeth. "Spider, *help* us."

Seconds stretched like hours: endless. Violet threads raked the heavens without effect.

"Maximum output, Colonel," Glick's voice intruded. Every erg *Bullet* produced lanced upward to travel forever between the stars, particles interacting to spread the violet beam into eventual nothingness.

And below, World waited, oblivious to the death hurtling down toward it.

"Come on!" Ree rasped, peering nervously at the chro-

nometer. "We've got a minute to impact, Tony. Where *is* that damn thing?"

Tony remained silent, concentrating on his comm, shuffling information to targeting. So many variables. At the velocity the torpedo approached, space had the resistance of air to a bullet. Solar windage, gravity, even scattered hydrogen atoms affected its course.

"We've got a Cerenkov shadow."

"Refine!"

"Refining . . . refining. . . ."

The blaster bolts shifted slightly, violet bands sparkling as atoms flickered in violent death and particles obliterated everything in their paths.

"Cerenkov is clarifying, Colonel. Shifting targeting."

"Damn it, come on!" Ree bounced on his toes, staring at the screen, heart hammering. "Where in hell is it?"

"Thirty seconds to predicted impact," the helmswoman called softly.

Ree paced, fingers working as he glared upward.

"Refining," Tony added, a solitary voice in the tension.

"If Zimbuti lied, so help me . . ."

"Cerenkov threshold passed! Targeting! Six zero zero one one three. *Fire!"*

Ree froze, eyes glued to the screens as the blasters flickered, shifted ever so minutely, and a glaring white streak flashed through the violet strands, spreading across their screens.

"Comm! Shields on full!"

Bullet's blaster fire disappeared into ghostly luminescence as the shields drew power, stabilized, and absorbed the radiation bath.

Ree sagged back in the command chair, gasping for breath. "By Spider," he mumbled. "That was cutting it damn close."

Tony sat up, pulling the headset from his sweaty brow, eyes coming back into focus. "Somebody was riding with us." He winked up at the spider drawn on the overhead panels.

"And Zimbuti's data?"

"Within the parameters of variability. He didn't try and snooker us." Tony looked up from under lowered brows. "I'd say that without that revision of the scopes, we might have missed it."

Ree puffed out his cheeks, shoulders slumping. "You know, I'm getting too old for this."

Confederate Section: Arcturus.

Patan Andojar Garcia raised his hands overhead, eyes gleaming with the power of his personality. "I have come among you to bring you the message of Spider. So many of you are feeling lost, looking at your lives, wondering if your very existence has meaning. You see the Directorate crumbling around you. The Patrol has faltered. And you look to the stars at night, wondering what horror may fall from the unknown heavens. You wonder if all reason has gone from the universe!"

Darwin felt himself tense, waiting for the answer, as if the Prophet's words were for him alone. Before him, the thronged masses of Arcturus waited, breathless. The crowded room had once been a huge open plaza before the attack. Afterward it had turned into a refugee camp. Now, with order mostly restored and reconstruction occupying all hands, it had become Patan's forum.

Overhead, the huge holo projectors sent Patan's image to the battery of transduction disks—then to the stars. Here, in the confines of the largest open space in Arcturus, the vibrant roar of humanity filled the place, echoing across that sea of listeners who waited to hear the Prophet's words. Spider lurked here, waiting, eating into the minds of human beings, touching the tendrils of their wavering souls.

Patan's eyes danced and his face seemed lit by an ethereal glow. "There *is* purpose, my children. You have souls which are ties to Godhead." Patan's voice rose in pitch. "There *is* that spark within you which is God. Hear the message of Spider. Take that spark and nourish it. Cherish and guard it! Go forth into your worlds and stations. See! Feel! Shout with joy! Cry with sorrow! You are placed here to live and learn and savor every moment.

"Fear not death. It's but a passing of the physical body. That everlasting, eternal part of you is God. What will you send back to Deity? Ask yourselves if your lives have been worthy of the trust God has put into your keeping. Ask yourselves what you have tasted of life. What single gem of knowledge would you teach God? It is a quest each of us has which is more noble than the search for the grail, more noble than the vigils of the knights of old, more noble than the martyrdom of the saints . . . *and it lives within each of us!*

"Fear only the darkness which descends upon us, for this foul Ngen Van Chow will take God from us. He would strip our very souls from us and deny us that divine spark! He will deny Spider the choice of free will! To battle this vileness, do I forfeit my own sanity!" Patan's eyes burned and he gestured—as if to pull them to him.

Darwin let his eyes roam the audience, cataloging the Prophet's effect. Like himself, they were hanging on each word. All but the hooded figure who stood off to one side. Darwin studied the silhouetted form. Could it be? No, impossible! Patan reclaimed his attention.

His voice was lower, serious, almost pleading. "I don't have much time to remain with you. I have come to give of my love, to give of my knowledge, to give of myself. That's all I can offer. I would give my soul—but that is eternal, and Spider's."

The keen eyes seemed to pierce Darwin, transfixing him to the spot. "Spider guards free will. Prophets, so many of you have heard, do not meddle with the future. They do not play idly with free will. To do so leads to madness. A trap lies there into which I will fall."

His voice thundered. *"I will let my soul slide into the maze of the future in token of the love I feel for you and for Spider. I will gratefully give of myself to destroy the evil blot, Ngen."* Then, softly. "Can anyone do more? When I go, I go for you."

His eyes searched the mass of humanity which filled the arena before him, a benign smile on his lips. "I see the future. I see Ngen spreading death and destruction. There is fire and death coming to Halifax Sector. Ngen seeks to surround the Quantum Reach mining colonies with two converted GCIs. To the people of the Quantum Reach who would save their souls from Ngen's abomination, I say, your mining tugs can be converted to rams mined with antimatter. Use them against Ngen's ships." Patan wavered on his feet, face contorting, sweat beading on his waxen features.

"The planet Antares V has been spared for the moment. Good people, you have a respite. Ngen will now demand your destruction as a demonstration that I am not all-seeing. As I speak, I see your safety. Place your trust in the young leader Markus. He sees your . . . your salvation." Patan staggered again as his face creased with effort.

A gasp rose from the audience.

Darwin stepped forward only to have Patan wave him back. He raised eyes brimming with agony to the pickups which spread his image through all of Directorate space. "The future . . . beckons me," he said with a sigh. "How delightful it would be to fall into the arms of destiny, to let my spirit float along the branches and paths, watching changes as each of you make your cusps."

Patan pulled himself straight again. "Ngen Van Chow!" he shouted angrily. "Beware your training base in Ambrose Sector. I see the assaults you would launch on Retreat and Apasha. They have defied your Temples and kept the faith in their own religions. Their God *has* heard! They will be waiting. You can no longer surprise them. They hear my voice. They know that Spider watches them, helping them help themselves. Thousands of souls are saved from your ghoulish, mindless abominations!" Patan raised a defiant fist as he shivered and trembled.

A rumble of awe rose from below.

"The future calls," Patan whispered, disoriented. "To allow myself to fall . . . to fall to bliss. Why do I stay on this pillar of pain and anguish?" His face turned eyes lost to a vision beyond Darwin's perceptions.

The silence in the huge expanse seemed deafening.

It took several seconds before Patan pulled himself back to the present. Eyes clearing, he looked out at the now motionless mass of humanity. "Your love, your devotion, draw me back. It is by those of you who hear me, that I return to fight Ngen. With each of you who turns your head away in disgust from this Deus, I experience success. Each of you who vows to learn, to better your lives with experience, makes my coming insanity bearable. My death will not be in vain!" His voice became a column of strength, rallying, swelling with the animated light behind his eyes.

Darwin almost swayed at the power of personality Patan exuded. Infectious, it filled the room, tangible, powerful. The thin Prophet seemed to grow, expanding, becoming one with humanity.

"*I am the power of Spider!*" The Prophet thundered. "*I am the future! You . . . you are the future!*"

The crowd swelled before him, moving like a wave, surging against the EM barriers which kept them back.

"We are the future!" a man shouted from the sea of faces. It was echoed in a tumultuous roar. "*Spider! Spider! Spi-*

der! Spider!'' A passionate, pounding chant built below Patan Andojar Garcia's raised arms.

Pike saw the hooded figure floating through the press, people stepping unconsciously out of its way. He noted how the curious individual appeared to be studying the reactions of the people to the Prophet's words.

"White Eagle?"

"Here." White Eagle's voice formed in Darwin's ear piece.

"See the hooded guy?"

"Acknowledged."

"He was in Ngen's Temple on Bazaar. Or his twin was. See if you can put the grab on him when all this is over. Be quiet about it."

"Acknowledged, Doctor. We're on him."

For long minutes of thundering applause, Patan stood like an unbowed tree, then Darwin pulled himself together enough to lower the lights. As soon as the Prophet was hidden from the crowd, he collapsed into a limp pile. Throat closing in fear, Darwin settled himself, running hands under the sweat-hot body, lifting. Patan swung in his arms, as limp as boneless meat. The Prophet coughed, muttering to himself, voice almost inaudible, eyes rolled back in his head. But for the burning flush of his features, he looked like a man on the verge of death.

Two Andojar clan men ran out, taking the weight. "Quick, get him to his quarters." They placed the oblivious Prophet in an aircar, rushing down deserted white corridors, air streaking past them as the car raced.

Susan entered the Prophet's rooms, headset on, portable monitor in hand, as Darwin laid the scarecrow figure on the bed. With a hand held med scan, he checked the vital signs.

"How bad is he?"

"He needs rest. Let's put him on med watch. If his blood sugars drop too low, we'll have to hook him to the med unit again."

She nodded, hair moving in a silky black wave. The contrast made her fine-boned face appear even more delicate. "How does he do it? Even from the security monitors, he was overpowering."

"Yeah, and it's killing him." Darwin blinked fatigue away as he looked at the frail figure before him. "Each time he influences the future, he's drawn to make further changes.

His energy is spent in fighting that urge. I guess he's like a moth who sees an open fire. Eventually, he has to burn.''

"I always thought I was brave," she whispered, clutching at Darwin's hand. "But he's casting Spider's web throughout the galaxy. He's the spirit and hope of the people. He's giving them direction and will to live.''

Pike put monitors on Patan's sallow flesh and led Susan from the room, seeing White Eagle's men taking over.

"Darwin?" Jose lifted a hand, beckoning him to the side. "That hooded guy. He lowered his eyes. "Weird. He just seemed . . .''

"Go on.''

"Well, to vanish in thin air, you know? I've doubled security. All Warriors will sleep lightly knowing there's an assassin loose around a Prophet.''

"Keep me informed." Darwin slapped him on the shoulder, worried, following Susan.

They walked down the secure corridor to the opulent room they shared. Stripping off his sweaty shirt, Pike draped it over a chair as Susan accessed comm, checking on status, entering some final corrections to duty rosters.

"You look horrible," she added, coming up behind him to massage his shoulders.

"He's giving so much. I . . . I watch him wasting away, day by day, knowing the price he's paying. And . . . and . . . is it doing any good? He's killing himself for . . . for all of them. Do they understand? Do they even care? *Damn it!*'' He slammed a fist into the thick plastic console. "Ngen's out there . . . waiting.''

She bent down and kissed his neck. "Honestly, we don't know what effect he's had yet. Darwin, it's Patan's cusp. Let him take it. Spider's already taken his measure of you.''

"Has he? How do we know? He took Leeta Dobra, Philip Iron Eyes, Friday, Hans. How many more, Susan? You? Me?" Darwin stared absently into the distance. "Patan warned me. I . . . I just didn't know it would hurt this much. Is . . . is anyone out there listening?''

CHAPTER XXXIII

The Quantum Reach: Halifax sub-Sector.

Initial exploration: 2380-2397. Colonization: Confederate period by independent stations drawn to the particularly rich Lagrange points around the system B2 primary known locally as "Bright Boy." Current census information indicates thirty-four thousand people living in a total of twelve different stations at L5. Industry consists of extractive processes involved in the recovery of metals and commercially viable ceramic crystals obtained through asteroid processing. The region's wealth is apparently tied to an abnormally high percentage of octahedrite and ataxite asteroids—many as much as 30 k in diameter. In addition to precious and industrial metals, ^3He, gallium arsenides, silicon carbide fibers, and graphites are staples of production. For all practical purposes, the Quantum Reach is both isolated and self-sufficient, import/export conducted by automated GCIs on three-month rotation AST.

Feng Gosh Wan hooked a pale, skinny leg around the chair—a long, mushroom-shaped knob protruding from the wall that wrapped around the cylindrical beige conference room. Wan looked at his fellow council members who seemed to stud the other walls, hair standing out in the opposite direction from which they had turned their heads last. The screen went dead as the Prophet on far-off Arcturus ended his transmission.

In the silence, the hum of the station's life-pumping machinery seemed extraordinarily loud.

Shocked faces looked around. "The Fathers . . . coming here?" Feeper Dish asked, floating toward the coffee dispenser and poking his zero g bulb into the spigot.

"So it would seem," Feng Gosh Wan said. "The Prophet has given us warning. We can mine the tugs. He said that would save us. We'd better not lose any—"

"Why *here?*" Sing Hamilton's face displayed disbelief. "I do *not* believe this Prophet. He says he sees the future!

No one sees the future. What kind of God is a Spider anyway? Deus is more to my liking. My grandparents came here from Earth. I've heard about YVEH. That's how God's supposed to—''

"What happened to Ambrose Sector?" Wan asked. He looked around at the blank faces. "Come, people. The time is here for us to decide. Like this Prophet says, it's our cusp.''

"The Patrol will—" Teng Fry Bing began.

"The Patrol's gone over to the Spider people." Wan protested, kicking loose and floating to the center of the room. He spun slowing in the zero g, facing each member of the council in turn. "Our galaxy is changing." He implored through gentle movements of his hands. "As the Prophet says, we must choose. We've seen the holos of the battles on other planets. We have seen the holos the Romanans have taken of stations captured by the Fathers. I personally will not be made into a mindless human machine. I can't stand the thought of my right to think being—''

"The Messiah says they are touched by the hand of Deus, that they live in eternal bliss," Hamilton objected. "Why believe the Spiders when the Messiah claims the broadcasts are fakes? Propaganda spread against his truths?''

Wan smiled thinly, reedlike arms making a delicate movement of sympathy. "He comes with warships to bring us into the world of Deus?" He tilted his head. "Must bliss be sold at the end of a blaster? Is it not that he needs the helium-three, the alabandite, carlsbergite, GaAs, gold, and chromium we mine in the Quantum Reach? Our time is limited. Myself, I find a lot of sense in what the Prophet says. Mining tugs with broadcast beacons turned off don't show up on ship's sensors.''

Fry Bing moved her head in agreement. "Antimatter's cheap. I move that we arm our tugs. If we send them out when the Fathers arrive in their warships, we're ready to defend ourselves. If the Fathers don't show up, we've lost nothing but time. And what's that? The schedules are all screwed up because of the war anyway. So we determine if the Romanan Prophet's a farce. If they do show up as he says, we've found a new truth!''

Wan agreed enthusiastically. "If the Directorate is failing, these Romanans may be the new power. If we can establish our independence, we could sell our minerals for more. They have toron to trade and we have raw materials.''

Hamilton looked dubious. "You'd trade for more credits with the Romanans? That's not acting for the common good. That's against the teachings of the Directorate. You'd steal food from someone's mouth to line your pockets? I can't believe you've fallen so low."

"The teaching of the Spider Prophet violates everything the Directorate preached," Wan agreed easily. "At the same time, he transmits to us from Arcturus. Romanans have promised the Directorate protection from the Fathers. They've brought peace to Arcturus. You saw the holos! The Messiah killed billions!"

"Romanans hit his planets first!"

"And you saw the reason why! I want freedom for the Reach. I want—"

"At what price?" Hamilton wondered.

"Let's protect ourselves and not find out," Wan growled with conviction.

The council voted.

The tugs were in position when the GCIs closed, their captains demanding the immediate surrender of the Quantum Reach. It was Wan who triggered the antimatter stasis fields and killed Ngen Van Chow's ships. The next day, Spiders appeared, painted on the white bulkheads of the stations composing the settlement. For the first time in the history of the Reach, the populace ordered books in exchange for their next shipment of valuable metals and ceramics.

Antares V: Ambrose Sector.

Originally colonized during the final days of the World Soviet, Antares V meets many of the Titanian model criteria. A large cold planet, Antares V began as a processing colony extracting organic polymers from the aerosol layers of the Antarean atmosphere. Subsequently, it became an outpost for the exploration of Ambrose Sector. In such condition, it sided with the Brotherhood in the overthrow of the Soviet but had insufficient political clout to influence the Confederacy. While some industry was attracted to Antares V, economic development deeper in Ambrose Sector tended to pass it by. Currently the census is expected to be about 1.2 million terrestrial inhabitants living in the burrows-excavated subsurface after the polymer layers were depleted and deep minerals, toron, and geothermal energy were found to be feasibly exploitable.

On Antares V, Fidor Roch, the Directorate coordinator studied the broadcast of the Prophet's speech with unease. It was, of course, being displayed on every home and public screen all over the planet. People would be terrified. And just what did the Prophet mean, they were spared for the moment?

He stared out the window, looking at the boiling methane, ammonia, and nitrogen composing the atmosphere outside the dome of the ancient governmental center. Sheer foolishness to hang around up here where something could fall through the roof at any time—but the dishes were all here, along with the up-link to the transfer stations, shuttle traffic control, and all the other host of administrative tasks.

And the damn Prophet had to bring up Markus? He winced. Of all the incredibly poor judgments, why did the Prophet have to give *that* young lunatic a forum?

Muttering to himself, he accessed comm.

Markus Vyhar followed the drone into the plush offices Fidor Roch occupied. He glared around the room out of baleful, yellow eyes before centering his gaze on the white-haired man.

"Am I finally here under arrest?"

"You saw the Prophet speak?" Roch asked, his concentration on the mists beyond the dome.

"I did. I wonder how he heard of me?" Markus looked about the room nervously, wondering where the recorders where.

"I almost ordered you psyched last week. You're a disruptive factor in society. You lead the young into claiming recognition. That upsets the balance of society . . . leads to competition, profiteering, and eventually to violence."

"Those who subscribe to my beliefs think it's time for some changes. I mean, hey, man, look around you! This place is a dead end! Some of us want more. We want a chance to make something out of our lives instead of just shooting one bucketload of ore after another out to LEO Station." He raised his arms and let them fall limply. "As for what you're worried about, it would seem the violence is coming upon us anyway. That is, if the Prophet was correct."

Having given himself up for dead anyway, Markus sat on

the nearest couch. Roch rubbed the back of his neck. Silence stretched.

Finally Roch steepled his fingers. "Should the Fathers invade, as the Prophet has said they must, what would you do?"

Markus leaped to his feet, eyes fired by a strange light. "Can you provide a holo of this entire world, one which shows all the tunnels, domes, and stopes?"

It came into existence immediately, hanging in the air. Markus walked around it, squinting, nodding, and muttering to himself. "Better than we thought."

"You and your hooligans have already given this some thought." Roch lifted a lip. "Our intelligence isn't anemic, Markus. Only the disruption from the Fathers and the raid on Arcturus allowed you to keep your freedom till now."

"Yeah, man. And now you need us, huh? Like, we're all in this together when the Fathers show up with psych machines. Okay, pay attention. Here, here, and here," he said, pointing. "We can detonate explosives. That leaves the core of the planet accessible by only two routes. We have nothing to keep the Fathers from establishing control of orbit or landing where they will. If we let them have these outer galleries, they'll believe they control the high ground."

"Believe, my foot. They will!"

"Right. So they relax, huh? Believe it's only a matter of time before we must capitulate," Markus agreed. "We can hold these two corridors for at least a day. Since an air plant will be in their territory, they'll have no fear for their safety. People get careless when they think they've got the situation under control. They quit carrying masks with them. Pain in the ass, right?"

"We have a second air plant down below, too. What are you talking about?" Roch was clearly confused. "I don't see—"

"We mine the surface locks here, here, here, and here." Markus grinned. "If we also blast the two major access ways—and I mean thoroughly seal them for one hundred meters—then blast the surface locks from previously set mines, what happens?"

"My God!" Roch was on his feet. "We'd kill them all! The methane, mixed with the oxygen would burn catastrophically!"

"But it wouldn't explode!" Markus agreed. "There are enough inert and inflammable gases that it'd simply roast the Fathers. Our closed access tunnels would insulate us from the heat. At the same time, I suggest we immediately drive two new tunnels to the surface. They won't be on Directorate schematics. If I could train some of our young people, we could strike them on the surface at the same time we blow their locks. The planet would be ours. No muss, no fuss. But, man, your office here would bite it.''

Roch leaned back. ''I suppose your politics go along with cooperation?''

Markus shook his head. ''Not necessarily. Save the planet first, huh? We discuss that later. I wanna be a live, thinking, breathing man first. I got no desire to be a psyched ghoul for Ngen Van Chow. And besides, you gotta deal with the Prophet, man. It's a new game. Hey, Leeta Dobra set it all off, you know? Lot of us watched Ree off the Spider world. We learned. Things won't be the same again. You with us— or against?''

Roch chuckled to himself. ''I suppose it is a new world. Do as you will, Markus. I, myself, trust this Prophet. The Romanan didn't tell us how much time we had, so begin at once. Tell me what to do and I'll handle your logistics.''

Spider figures began appearing in the Antarean corridors within hours. Markus threw himself into the midst of the frenzied activity, preaching individual freedom at the same time. It took hold. Animated workers—breathing chants to Spider—drove two new tunnels to the surface and sunk explosives into the old locks.

Prepared, Antares V grimly waited for the Fathers.

Tierbault Station: Sol Sector.

Established 2075, Soviet era: Tierbault Station is one of the oldest independent stations in space. Portions of the station date back to one of the first solar stations employed in the Soviet mining of the Jovian L4 Greek Trojans. Subsequently, the station was dismantled and moved farther and farther out, expanding all the time to support a larger population. Transported to Barnard's Star, Tierbault obtained a matter/ antimatter power plant and began drifting on its own in search of micro nebulae and asteroidal accumulations. Current census estimates place the population at 1.6 million. The industrial base has grown with the station over the centuries. Now an extended cylinder of 8.2 k with a diameter of 1.5 k, Tierbault Station produces some of the finest fab-

rics, electronics, insulation, and building components in Directorate space.

Tierbault Station continued to rotate. One of the oldest of the independent stations, it hovered in the dust cloud from which it had drawn its subsistence for five hundred years. The Messiah's GCI hovered at the terminus of the spin axis, as it had for five days.

Pietre Vas Goah watched bitterly as the Fathers went about erecting their Temple. The broadcast by the Romanan Prophet had been declared illegal, of course. Like so many things, a transduction receiver didn't take a lot of skill to build—and since the Dobra broadcast, a lot of receivers had sprouted around the outer wall of Tierbault Station.

So Pietre watched along with most of his friends. He'd felt the power, looking into the Prophet's eyes and seen his pain and sacrifice. Now, he watched the Fathers' workers, dull-eyed, just like the holos of Bazaar. They would do that here?

He looked around at the others who had gathered with him. One man was painting a spider on the wall behind him. The Romanan Prophet said the Fathers stole a man's soul away from God—away from Spider. Was it not then better to die and give Spider the knowledge that life was appreciated?

"I am a man!" Vas Goah asserted to himself. "When I look out there, all I see are beasts. Mindless human wreckage."

"You heard? Kythros resisted and the Messiah sent men with blasters. The last broadcast showed people being marched through the Temples—shot dead if they fought back."

"They have but one guard." Taeler muttered. "If we could take his blaster, we could kill the rest with our bare hands!"

"No one has stood against the Fathers before," another warned. "Only Romanans!"

"Have any ever tried?" Vas Goah demanded. "Will we be made mindless?" He chuckled dryly. "Besides, I heard Romanans said Directorate people were sheep. Sheep, huh? You like being thought of as a sheep?"

"Better than I like being thought of as a ghoul." The young woman, Micah, shook her head. "What's it like to not think? People ought to be half crazy at the idea of having their ability to think . . . just erased like that!''

"There are many in Tierbault Station who truly believe the Messiah was sent to us from Deus!'' a bearded man insisted.

Pietre Vas Goah turned on him. "Deus is not my God! Spider's my God. I'm part of Spider. In this chest, right here, my soul beats along with my heart. Me and God, one and the same. Got that? What's death to a man who knows he has God?'' Vas Goah felt himself glow and knew it was Spider inside him. From his belt he took a short segment of metal. Sharpened to a molecular edge by a laser hone, the tip shimmered, mirror bright. It lay cool and heavy in his hand.

"See them down there?'' Vas Goah asked. "The people, our people, stand around and watch, not knowing they could resist. They say, 'The Fathers have come. We will do as the Fathers say,' and that *is* wrong!'' He couldn't keep the passion from his voice. "We're part of Spider and Spider wouldn't want us to be sheep!''

"I can kill the Father who guards,'' blonde Micah added. "There's no reason why Deus is God. What the Prophet says about Spider makes sense. Spider tells me there's order and purpose. Where's the purpose in Deus? To be mindless?'' She drew a vibrating knife from under her cloak. "No, I'll be a Romanan before I'm a sheep.''

"If you'll kill the guard,'' Vas Goah said, face shining with ambition, "the rest of us will kill the Fathers working on the temple. If they kill us, by my grandfather's beard, they'll kill free men. I'd die to send that back to Spider. That they killed a *free* man.''

She just smiled as she walked down to the guard. Micah remained attractive, despite her years hooking in the taverns. She thrust herself against the guard, posing suggestively as she whispered in his ear. The man leered at her and leaned close, trying to grope her breasts and buttocks. He fell as she slipped the blade through his chest and practically cut him in two.

"For Spider!'' Vas Goah screamed, and with his piece of steel, he pounced on the mindless Fathers. Tierbault Station rocked with riots for five days until Fathers with blasters exterminated the last of the rioters.

In another week the Temple stood, shining, new, giant powerleads routed in from the main generating plant. Those who preached the gospel of Deus marched in with pleasure, heads held high as they thronged to worship their coming savior. The vast numbers of unconverted watched, wondering at the difference in their glassy-eyed fellows as they walked out the side doors, faces blissful—and vacant. The majority stared uneasily at the drawn spiders—and the bloodstains on the walkways.

When the Fathers came again, forcing people into the Temple at blaster point, more and more spiders appeared. Overnight, Tierbault Station convulsed in a nightmare of bloody civil war.

Solakriis Station: Ambrose-Gulag Sector border area.

In the beginning, it was known as Solakriis III Station for the planet it orbits. Constructed in the early Confederate era ca. 2380-2400, the station served as a fuel producer for heavy hydrogen and helium-three—basic staples of most early fusion systems. Its primary, Solakriis, is an RV Tauri type K star of variable luminosity. The station orbits Solakriis III, a Jovian gas giant rich in the ratio of liquid-metallic-hydrogen to the nickel-iron core. As a result, mining slowly improvised methods of extraction powered by the planet's magnetosphere while at the same time employing older gaseous fuels obtained by ram-scoop mining methods. Currently, the census estimates the population to be approaching five hundred thousand.

Solakriis was poised like an antique-style giant hypodermic syringe, the needle forever piercing the cloudy surface of the banded multihued gas giant. In the light of its sun, Solakriis gleamed whitely, the superimposed tori like a stack of tires up the main power cylinder. The top of the plunger might have been the docking facilities, antennae, and transduction dishes.

In the huge open dome in the main cylinder, Ngen Van Chow's face looked out over a vast audience of fluid engineers, electrolysis specialists, carbonyl processors and containment techs. The auditorium arena was completely filled; the giant holo projector covered an entire wall.

"Satan is upon us!" Van Chow's voice curled around the dome. "His foul hand has guided the Directorate and sought to eliminate Deus from the holy!"

The swaying crowd watched, many mesmerized, bodies

jerking in spasms of religious ecstasy. "Gather, my brothers!" the Messiah cried. "Throw out the infamy of Satan! Kill the blot of his foul hand! Death to Spider and his ways!"

The crowd rocked back and forth chanting, "Death! Death! Death!"

"Deus is freedom!" Ngen's voice reigned supreme.

Crack-booom! The holo died abruptly as the projector fragmented into the audience. Where Ngen's face had filled the wall, only ripped plastics smoked and burned. Those in the forefront of the audience screamed, some the recipients of the bomb's shrapnel.

A roar of outrage broke from the crowd. A single man walked out onto the platform and looked at the mass of milling humanity. "God is Spider!" he cried, bringing a hush to the crowd.

An undercurrent of anger rippled among the packed bodies below him as they reeled in shock.

"Mark me," the man cried. "This has gone far enough! If Deus is real, if he brings peace, where is it? I see the Directorate engulfed in war! What does Ngen send us but holos? Where is this peace in the tapes we have seen of Bazaar?"

"Blasphemer!" a woman yelled, rushing forward to point at the lone speaker. "Death to the blasphemer!"

The crowd recovered, surged forward and tore him from the scaffold on which he stood. Thousands of Solakriians, watching on comm, were horrified as the crowd ripped him to pieces, reveling in the blood. The next day, Spiders began to appear on walls and tapes of the Prophet were run in competition with those of the Messiah.

Violence flashed as tempers rose. Solakriis, the beautiful city, rocked, as explosions, death, and destruction spread. The Temple the Fathers had begun was torn down. Within two weeks, each of the Fathers had been pitched into the clouds below. Tattered and scared, the Solakriians looked at each other with new awe and began piecing their lives together again, all too aware of the numbers who'd died in the name of religion.

Respit: Gulag Sector.

Little more than a tortured wind-blown ball of rock, Respit's colonization dates to the Late Soviet period when Yugoslavian miners deported after the strike of 2098 were landed *on the inhospitable planet. Subsequently, the tiny colony at Respit continued to grow. Siding with the Brotherhood in the Confederate revolution, Respit expanded, finding markets more than ready for the jewels and precious metals carved so laboriously from the hard ground. With surface winds in excess of 600 kph in the violent seasonal swings, Respitian civilization developed subsurface in the maze of mining tunnels carved by the heavy lasers. With the gravity of 1.95 gs, Respitians suffered markedly in the first couple of centuries, dying of stroke, heart failure, and associated circulatory and degenerative diseases. Nevertheless, by the F_6 generation, a short, stocky, and durable people had evolved. Always restless under the yoke of the Directorate, Respit hailed the Dobra broadcast with relief and curiosity. Too long had they been at the end of the water chain on their arid planet.*

When the Fathers dropped from the heavens and fortified the underground spaceport, the doughty citizens of Respit looked on with curiosity. When the Fathers marched out, blasters in hand to lead a small group of citizens into their newly constructed Temple, the resulting riot left three hundred Respitians dead.

At that moment Yuri "Tito" Amahghre observed that mining lasers might be deadly when stacked against hand blasters. He and his brawling, hairy-fisted miners literally cut the Fathers to ribbons.

The GCI in orbit immediately leveled the few aerodynamically designed buildings of the city. Respitians spent three days drilling, digging, and placing explosives in the solid gray granite beneath the impregnable spaceport. The retaliatory explosion blew every living Father, their shuttle, and the Temple into atoms. Two months later, five GCIs dropped into orbit and landed thousands of screaming, frenzied Fathers.

In the mining tunnels, warfare raged. Bloody, grinning citizens cheerfully mined holes, cleared passages with lasers, and caved in sections of tunnel to suffocate the Fathers. Days later they would burrow back, collect the weapons, and carry the fight to the surface. Stalemated, they looked out of their holes at the heavens they couldn't control, grinned at each other, and prayed to Spider.

Damen Ree stared out of a fuzzy holo. "Hey! We sorry the image isn't so good, Admiral. But it tough to make a good dish with only a crater and a couple of wires. Not only that. Hyperconductor get a little—uh, shall we say bent— by explosion.''

Ree's fuzzy features wavered as the power fluxed. ''And what would you like me to do, Mr. Amahghre? For the moment, we can't get to you. Ngen's applying pressure all across the board.''

''Hey! You no worry about Respit, huh? We just want you know that Prophet of yours talks to the heart of Respit. Spider keep you, Admiral. Spider keep all you Romanan warriors! You need something, you come here. We treat you right. Bring water and we trade for some damn good jewels and chrome-steel. We hold on here. We just can't get them damn ships up in orbit.''

Ree chuckled. ''When this is all over, we'll send you some water, Mr. Amahghre.''

''Hey! Is just Tito to you and Romanans. That Ngen Van Chow, *HE* call me mister! When you get chance, Admiral, you come blow these filthy Fathers out of our sky. In the meantime, we hold on. We wonder at Spider's purpose and study the new meaning in lives, eh?''

On the bridge of *Bullet* the image—poor to begin with— faded into a grayish-blue haze. Ree shook his head. ''Respit? Is that a place?''

''Yes, sir. Got it here, Admiral. For a planet, it's hell. People have to live like moles in the solid rock. I guess they've done a bit of human adaptation study there. They live in almost 2 gravities. No water but what they can render out of granite and limited manufacturing potential.''

Ree fingered his chin. ''Tito, huh? And he and his people have pasted the Fathers for the time being? Well, Tony, I just guess we'll have to send a ship his way first chance. Folks like that just warm something in the bottom of my heart.''

Anthony raised an eyebrow. ''They're in the middle o Ngen's territory.''

''He said he'd hang on.'' Ree walked over to punch his coffee cup into the dispenser. ''And somehow, I believe him.''

Aphas Station, Sol Sector:

Aphas Station fissioned from Santa Cruz Station in 246 over some disagreement lost to Directorate records. Eco

nomically, Aphas Station is a micro-mining facility, employ-
ing a sophisticated Bussard Ram to power its fusion systems.
Station mobility is provided by a more powerful matter/an-
timatter propulsion unit—although the station does not have
FTL capabilities. Census figures indicated that some seven
hundred thousand people live in Aphas Station at this time.
Currently, the society is structured along two moieties, the
elder heads of each having final jurisdiction in council re-
garding economic relations, station course, etc.

On Aphas Station, Pedro Angustura enjoyed reading. The
magic of the written word was his one great thrill and passion. When the elders petitioned Ngen for a Temple to Deus,
they thought to bring back the sacred legacy of Guadalupe.
Pedro had turned down his father's invitation to go to the
new Temple of the Fathers. When his parents and his little
sister returned, beaming their pleasure and acceptance of
Deus, Pedro became a little curious.

"Why is Deus God and Spider not?" he asked.

"Spider is Satan! Satan is the hand of Evil! You will never
speak that name again in my house!"

Pedro nodded, and went back to his books, and also began studying the holos from the Messiah in contrast with
those from the Prophet in Arcturus. He watched with interest as he compared the holos of Bazaar with the other systems. It finally sank in that the Temple was indeed a
psyching facility. He looked at his father where he reclined,
praying by himself.

"When do you go back to Temple, Father?"

"When I am called by Deus. You, my son, will go tomorrow. I have been given the word from Deus that all must
attend. Most are obedient. It is good to be obedient in Deus,
my son."

"The Temple is not God, Father. They have psyched your
brain." Pedro felt very tired. His father had never been
special to him like so many of his friend's fathers were to
them. Mama, his stepmother, was nice but aloof. There was
no family unity or love. Only the more Pedro thought about
it, what the Fathers had done was wrong.

"You know of Satan only!" Senor Angustura shouted,
rising to slap his son. Pedro ducked the blow and studied
his father from the other side of the room. The words of the
Prophet hovered in the back of his mind, buzzing like flies.

"I will go to Temple tomorrow," he agreed, and the old man nodded and returned to his prayers.

Pedro went, but he never entered the Temple. He watched the people walking in through the huge ornate doors—some uncertain and frightened. Some he saw escorted by men with blasters. They looked scared—like those in the Prophet's broadcasts. Slavery. Get psyched . . . or die. Others smiled happily to themselves, faces reflecting internal bliss—eyes glazed by the mindless rapture of their spirits.

When they came out, they all walked, talked, and smiled alike. None ever came out the same doors by which they entered. Pedro thought about that and went back to his books. His friends and his teachers had always told him what an odd boy he was. Some had suggested to his father that he might want to psych the boy and make him right in the head. Senor Angustura had shrugged. What did he care about his son? Only Pedro had accessed the tech manuals on psyching when it had first been mentioned. And so what if everyone thought him odd? Let them!

Pedro began reading chemistry and physics texts and listened to what Spider really taught. He compared, drew his own conclusions, and began lifting materials from the manufacturing bin where they made subspace transduction devices.

Pedro watched his father sadly and began building his own device.

"What is that thing you are tinkering with? All the other boys are learning to be soldiers and you tinker. Why do you do that?"

"Father, Deus ordered me to make it. In the Temple, he gave me the instructions. It's because I'm a little odd in the head that he chose me to make this." Pedro watched the reaction.

Senor Angustura nodded happily. "Ah, see, you have your place. This time all my family will go."

Pedro nodded, having seen men like the ones in the holo during the last few days. No one seemed to notice them as they walked the streets. It would be as Bazaar had been in the Romanan tapes. The old men had ordered everyone to the Temple. When Pedro met the Fathers in the street, he imitated the glassy-eyed mindless walk. No one stared frankly anymore. They'd all been drawn in—or forced at blaster point. It would be lonely.

Pedro carried his device under his poncho. Easily, he

skipped out of line, ignored by the bored guard with the blaster. Just outside the exit door, Pedro set his device down and inspected the portal. He clipped a wire into a powerlead and another into one of the powerfield units. He drew a spider in the dirt and left.

Thirty minutes later, the explosion rocked the very skeleton of Aphas Station. Pedro shrugged to himself and went back to his books. Were it not for them, it would have been very miserable in the city of the walking dead. Pedro had a long time. He would slowly have to kill all of them, but Spider gave him the perseverance and skill to do so as long as he could access the books.

CHAPTER XXXIV

Ree's quarters aboard *Bullet* in GEO orbit over World.

The lights had been dimmed until only the faintest outline of Ree's personal quarters could be distinguished in the shadows. The white walls reflected grayly while the spider drawing faded into the hand-tanned leather it had been drawn upon. Only the eyes seemed to shine, as if the artist had paid particular attention to that aspect of his creation. On the opposite wall, the Romanan knives and rifles made a mosaic of black forms on white.

The center of attention, however, proved to be the holographic star map projected to hang in the middle of the room. For the moment Damen Ree walked easily through the lights, some flickering yellow to delineate Ngen's territory, others, uncommitted systems in the Directorate, gleamed white, while the Spider-controlled solar systems glowed in blue.

Maya sat, legs crossed, elbows braced on the armrest, the golden circlet of a headset like a shimmering tiara on her brow. Her face reflected fatigue and frustration.

John Smith Iron Eyes made a mental note into his headset while he slowly turned the end of one of his long braids between thick callused fingers. For the last hour he'd studied the star map, seeking some way to exploit it to their advantage. The problem could be likened to that of finding a single raider who swooped down on a people's herds. Self sufficient, where did the quarry disappear to? How could he be brought to bay and crushed along with his minions?

"So, if we assume Santa del Cielo is his home world now, we can make a determined strike." Ree pointed to a yellow dot of light indicating the star system. "We can't guess how much of his fleet we can destroy, but it's a start."

"And if he's not there when we arrive?" Maya spoke from the shadows. "What then? If there's any place Ngen knows we'll eventually show up, it'll be Santa del Cielo. Think he'll be waiting around for us to—"

"We've got to start someplace," Ree replied seriously. "But go ahead, Maya, Tell me where. I'm open for suggestions."

"Don't get haughty, Damen. Damn you, if I had an answer, I'd have spoken before now."

They glared at each other for a moment until Iron Eyes cleared his throat. *We're starting to show the strain. The Patrol ships are coming in. Damen's afraid. Maya's feeling helpless. The balance of power is shifting—and we can't trust it. In the meantime, Ngen takes planets by force now, his converts laying the way, betraying their worlds. And we sit here at World, helpless to fight back. No wonder we're at each other's throats.*

Iron Eyes got to his feet, padding softly between the flickers of light. "He's doing the same thing we are. Biding his time. Building his strength for the showdown." Iron Eyes squinted at the pattern of the lights then waved his arm at the display. "No, tackling Ngen out there isn't going to be simple."

"I'm not sure you understand the realities of space war, War Chief. I—"

"Maya," Ree warned. "If anybody understands the intricacies of space war, Iron Eyes does."

John lifted his muscular shoulders. "I hope your faith is founded, Damen."

"You want to lose, War Chief?"

Iron Eyes stiffened. "I *never* want to lose. I hate the very suggestion of it. It's not in my blood, Damen."

"I rest my case." Ree turned, walking obliviously through the Orion arm of the galaxy to pick up his inevitable coffee cup. "Now, what were you thinking? Bounce it off us, and let's consider it."

Iron Eyes wet his lips, looking at the stars. "The problem

here is all the space. Myself, I agree with Maya. I don't think Ngen's at Santa del Cielo. From what Rita learned at Arpeggio, he's in a position to waste worlds. What's behind doesn't count. No, I think Santa del Cielo has been sucked dry for his immediate purposes. It's a soak off, a trap laid. Otherwise I don't think he'd be making so many broadcasts from there—if he is broadcasting from there. Ngen's moved on with most of his power base. He's too canny. Like a Santos with stolen horses, he'll be moving.''

"Why?'' Maya wondered. "Why not consolidate, build his power structure on Santa del Cielo? That's in character with what he did at Sirius.''

"Not if he learned the lesson we taught him there. Remember, he lost. And Neal's FT punched six breaches through Ngen's hull that we know of from the telemetered transduction. The resolution was poor because of speed and distance and redshift distortion, but we can prove three solid hits. All that despite his augmented shielding. Ngen's no one's fool, he won't want *Deus* where we can get her with Fujiki blasters. We know Zimbuti sent a transduction of the first shots he took at *Victory*. Seeing his Sirian blasters sparkling ineffectually off Maya's shields is going to slow him, make him even more cautious.''

"That's why we've *got* to hit him now!'' Ree smacked a fist into his palm. "We've reached the point here where he's going to pull farther and farther ahead. Sure, *Bullet, Miliken,* and *Victory* could carve his *Deus* to scrap, but what are we going to do six months from now when he's converted another twenty or thirty GCIs? Ganged up, they could manage to overcome our shielding. Blind us enough to get an antimatter torpedo in, and poof, we're so much plasma—just like *Ganges.*''

"Lightning strike?'' Maya wondered, "Run transects across all of his space?''

"And who guards World? Can one of our converted GCIs stand up to *Gregory?*'' Ree shook his head. "The resources we pour into a ship of the Line versus what we put into a converted GCI are two real different things. From inside a cobbled up GCI, you can't sneeze at those Sirian blasters—and he's got a battleship full of them.''

"Breeze has held Sirius against his attacks.''

"Breeze has, *Coup*—Ngen's old *Helk*—too. That ship isn't a quickly converted GCI like the others we've been building. We've had to sacrifice sophistication for efficiency and speed in the later conversions.''

Iron Eyes stared at the stars. ''I've looked at this and looked at it some more. I can't see a pattern—at least, nothing we could exploit to sweep Ngen into a corner somewhere. Space is open to him in infinite directions. There's no way to bottle him up. Given what we have available to us at the moment, the only way you'll get him is by luck. And, of course, we all know the surprises Spider lays for those who would make a deity of luck.''

''That's it?'' Maya snapped, a pinched quality to her voice. ''That's all you've got to offer?''

''Maya!'' Ree cautioned.

Iron Eyes waved it down. ''Easy, Damen. We're all on the wire here. We've been hamstrung for too long.'' He turned to Maya. ''Outside of my observations about the obvious, I've got an idea to try on you.''

Maya inclined her head, eyes glinting in the darkness. ''Go ahead, War Chief.''

''Ngen could be anywhere, at any time, Colonel. No, a Romanan would look at it differently. The problem here isn't how to chase Ngen. We can chase from now until Spider's web crumbles in entropy. The Romanan way is to provide some irresistible lure to get him to a given place at a given time so we can destroy him. If Ngen were a Santos, I'd say we had no problem. Instead of spending the rest of our lives searching the Bear Mountains, canyon by canyon, a herd of prize racehorses would bring him at a run. We can't afford to search star by star, so what would bring Ngen at a run? What prize equivalent of a racehorse can we offer him?''

Ree nodded. ''World? Sirius? He's already let Breeze blow three of his ships to scrap trying to torpedo Sirius. Maybe we've bled him enough over that to make it a matter of honor?''

''How about setting up some kind of diversion in his back country. A massive rebuilding and retraining project on, say, Bazaar. Some sort of slap in the face to his—''

''Arcturus,'' Iron Eyes whispered, eyes narrowed. ''He doesn't *want* Sirius. All he's after there is to teach a lesson. No, he needs something symbolic.''

''But he already blew the piss out of it!'' Maya pointed out. ''Why would he . . . Oh, I think I'm getting the . . .''

''Ah, yes, you see,'' Iron Eyes gave her a saucy wink.

"Sure, he hit Arcturus. That was for effect, strictly a blow to Directorate morale. He needed to destabilize human space. Like all raids, it didn't work perfectly. He did stun the Directorate—but he threw what was left of the power right into our hands when Skor capitulated. A move I'm sure Ngen didn't anticipate. Nevertheless, he shocked the rest of human space into falling either his way or ours, polarizing the battlefield. Had Patan not been ready to sacrifice himself, our situation would be considerably worse. Deus would have roared across space like wildfire. No, he could slap Arcturus, but he wasn't strong enough to *hold* it. That's the key."

"All right, Arcturus is the symbol of human power in space. How do we make it work in our favor? How do we lure him?"

Iron Eyes worked his jaws. "That's the one detail I haven't been able to work out. The fact remains that Ngen has two choices in the end regarding Arcturus. He can take it— or destroy it completely. To do otherwise is to leave a defiant symbol out there reminding all the uncommitted worlds and stations that he's not invincible."

Ree walked over to stare at the red star, looking around in all directions. "It's the most indefensible place in the entire galaxy."

"That's why the Confederates chose it in the first place," Maya reminded.

Iron Eyes bent his head. "Nevertheless, it's the key."

"We *can't* fight a pitched battle there!" Ree spread his arms. "Sure, I'll grant you everything you just said, War Chief. He's got to take it or destroy it. We've got it. Toby's headed there with *Miliken*'s augmented firepower and Rita's on the way with the *Knife*. He can't take it from us. So his only option is to destroy it. Spider's guts, Iron Eyes, we *can't* defend it! That's a couple billion people! If he comes in from all directions running at light, *Arcturus is dead!*"

Iron Eyes crossed his arms. "That's right. What do we do, Damen? Let him have those billions of people, and the symbol as well? Or do we take the chance that we can tag *Deus* and most of his fleet? The whole Directorate is hanging in the balance. What's the capital—and all those billions of lives worth? The future of humanity?"

"Unacceptable," Maya grunted. "I can't be party to mass destruction like we'd let loose there."

"I'll bow to a better idea," Iron Eyes responded soberly.

"Arcturus makes a perfect trap—at considerable risk to the innocent. Do we pay the cost to get Ngen? You see, I'm not sure that in the end this strategy of blowing up each other's worlds and stations isn't a much bloodier business. The end results will be worse the longer this is prolonged."

Ree sighed and shook his head before rubbing the back of his neck. "You know, I'd have never thought of it, John. That's the difference between you and me. For the moment, I agree that using Arcturus for bait is the strongest option we've got. Maya?"

She stood, walking into the holo, a couple of stars from the projection glistening on her cheeks like colorful tears. "I don't have anything better to offer. Pustulant gods! We've just hung fully three or four billion lives in the balance. This isn't a simple academic argument, damn it. We're . . . we're talking about human beings, Damen!"

"I was born there," Ree agreed dumbly. "My family lives there. Two sisters, a brother, and all their kids. Everything I ever . . . Well, never mind." He turned away.

"Whether we win or lose, this'll be on our souls forever." She closed her eyes, fists clenched at her sides.

"If we lose, our responsibility will be even more terrible," Iron Eyes told her. "We'll see the entire species turned into ghouls if we fail."

She gave him a red-eyed stare, saying nothing.

Ngen's wardroom aboard *Deus* accelerating from Pellar system.

"The problem, Messiah, is in quality. We're drowning in manpower, but the number of individuals capable of solving a simple mechanical problem is woefully small. If a minor power flux trips an antique breaker, an entire factory may be shut down for as much as a day until one of the techs can be routed to the plant. Of course, once he's there, it takes all of five seconds to walk to the panel and reset the breaker. Then he's off halfway across the planet to punch a reset button. In the meantime, that much labor is halted, the Fathers all standing at their places, waiting."

Ngen chewed his lip, brow lined. "We've noted that with the military operations, too, Sira. Once an attack is planned, changes in strategy—or tactics once the operation is implemented—prove to be almost impossible. We don't have flexibility. I'm not sure what to do about it. The Gonian engineers have been trying to adjust the psych, but so far they can't seem to push the technology past what we've already developed. The wide field just doesn't allow for finer discrimination. If we had more time . . .''

Sira looked uneasy. "Perhaps instead of psyching all the people, we could leave the converts alone? The loss of loyal brain power to—"

"*Loyal?*" Ngen started half out of the chair. "Loyal? Like my beloved citizens in revolution? Like Sirius? Damn it, Sira, don't talk to *me* of loyal followers! They turn on you! Hear? You don't trust the very people you help! That's the lesson I learned from Sirius! *They betrayed me!*"

Velkner moved uneasily in the holo, licking his lips. "I'm sorry, Messiah. I hadn't meant to—"

"*Betrayed!*" Ngen pounded his armrest vigorously. "Betrayed by the very people I freed. Can you believe it? After all I did for them, they went to the Romanans! Like kicked dogs, they slunk away, tails between their legs! Turned their backs on Ngen Van Chow! The First Citizen of their glorious revolution! After what *I* gave up, for *them!*" Ngen's eyes lit weirdly. "No, Sira, people who are loyal are filth! Trust them like you would trust a hungry rat."

Sira stiffened, thoughts racing, a sudden pallor whitening his swarthy skin. Silence stretched as Ngen lost himself in his own thoughts.

"Messiah?" Sira finally dared to speak. "Messiah? We've got to have some way of utilizing a greater percentage of unpsyched skill. Perhaps something like the way you stole the engineers from—"

"*Yes!*" Ngen leaped lightly to his feet, pacing up and down the bridge, the pickup panning his movements. "That's it! Brilliant, Sira. That's why you've risen to be my second officer. It's your astounding brain. Your dedication to your own cause."

Sira frowned in sudden confusion, mouth half-open as he tried to integrate this sudden shift from anger to excitement.

"*Ha!*" Ngen clapped his hands with a hollow pop. "You notice I don't call you loyal, eh? Precisely! Loyal people turn on you in the end. But you, Sira, you have your own goals to be gained. I can trust that in a man. You work for yourself. So like Pallas. Ah, Pallas, Pallas! Susan, I'll pay you back for that."

He stopped, head tilted, staring thoughtfully at the bridge monitor which displayed Cobalt Station. Huge towers had

risen from the outer circumference of the torus. The exact
outline couldn't be determined since the structures were
draped with a gossamer webbing of silver scaffolding.

"Um, Messiah?" Sira asked nervously.

"Yes?"

"Well, um, what do I do? I mean about the problem of
competence among our workers?"

Ngen tilted his head back. "Yes, brilliant indeed. We'll
keep half the population, Sira. They're predictable, not
loyal, you see? You can trust them to hate us. You know
where you stand. No one to try and cut your throat after
you've done so much for them, given so of yourself and
all your . . . your . . . You need techs? Keep them
unpsyched—but from among our enemies, Sira. They'll do
our work for us—and hate us all the more for making them
part of our success! They'll—"

"From among our enemies? They'd do anything in their
power to damage our prospects. Harm us in any—"

"Exactly! Predictability, Sira. That's what we're after.
The one thing you know about your enemy is that he's predictable! And for that he's weaker."

Sira's dark eyes reflected reservation. "I don't see . . .
Well, I mean . . . I guess I've had a lot of unpredictable
enemies, Messiah."

Ngen's smile mocked. He raised a finger, the brilliant
vermilion of his robes falling back to expose a thin pale-
skinned arm which contrasted with his darker features. "Not
quite, Sira. No enemy ever did anything for your ultimate
benefit. The one thing you can count on from an enemy is
that he'll try and harm you. A loyal follower, however, can
never be counted on. Vermin. That's what they are. Vermin."

Sira remained silent.

"You still doubt?" Ngen chortled gleefully, half-skipping
across the deck plates. "Even after what they did to me at
Sirius, you still find it in you to be a skeptic? Consider,
Sira. Think back to all those eager-eyed chattels flocking
into our Temples. Can you seriously believe they would have
remained that way? We've done them a favor. The psych
removed any chance of their recanting, of their sowing dis-
cord. They came to us needing, yes, NEEDING to be mindless followers. We gave them only what they desired—and
they'll never turn on us now."

"I believe you, Messiah. How do you want me to implement our new policy of . . . of saving our enemies?"

Ngen's eyes twinkled. "I do like you, Sira. Truly, you've never attempted to mislead me. If you ever attempted to fawn, to prove your loyalty, I'd cut your throat, you know. Yes, I see it in your eyes. Good. So long as you're honest with me about your skepticism, I'll do anything I can for you. That kind of honesty deserves its reward.

"Very well, for the moment, concentration camps will work perfectly well for our, shall we say, hostages?"

"I can see to that."

"Good. Since you know you'll be dealing with enemies, I'll leave the details of implementation on the ground to you. You've survived this far, Sira. I'd say you were good at it. Of course, I'm not interested in hearing the details. Use them as you see fit. Make them work for us . . . and hate it. Keeps them predictable. If that's all, you're dismissed."

"Thank you, Messiah." The holo flickered blankly.

Ngen paced to his command chair, a twitch at the corner of his mouth. "Hostages? What can you buy with hostages? Worlds, perhaps? And as for you, Admiral Ree, you're a good solid enemy. A worthy one. Driven by passion and hate—and that's your weakness. That and your idiotic honor. Very well, let's see just how predictable you are. Indeed, we *shall* see. What will you do now that Sira has handed me yet another weapon to use against you? What will *you* do for your *loyal* followers of Spider? Hmm? Shall we see if you'll turn your back on them?

Directorate Section: Admin Docks, Arcturus.

Spider's Knife slipped quietly into the dock beyond the snaking tube of the lock. The monitors showed her, white, gleaming, a slender and deadly shape, the outlines of her two stowed ATs visible beneath. The grapples thudded and bumped through the plating underfoot as communications from both the vessel and the dock control were drowned in the bubbling roar of excited voices. Spectators surged against the EM barriers.

The overhead monitors displayed the lock gantry as it linked its suction mouth to the *Spider's Knife*. Now the hollow banging came rolling down the sinuous tunnel. The sucking hiss of a hatch opening could be heard by all.

Darwin stood in the rear as Susan saluted the grim Romanan veterans who trotted through the lock and into the bright light and noise, fresh coups slung on belts and vests. Darwin glanced up at the comm pickups, strategically placed to show these warriors who had bloodied the Fathers. Everything functioned flawlessly. The Romanans walked out to victory before the whole galaxy.

A cry of "Hurrah" rose from the massed Arcturians Darwin had carefully chosen, orchestrated, and prepped. They waved Spider banners, showering the warriors with flower petals and strips of paper. Some warriors were picked up and sported around the lock on Arcturian shoulders.

The feeling of a festive celebration thrummed in the very air.

Major Rita Sarsa stepped through the lock to the sound of blaring music; the cued crowd went wild. The din of the close-packed crowd rose and swelled, echoing off the curved ceiling tiles overhead. A wary Rita walked up to a stiff Susan Smith Andojar who snapped out a perfect salute.

Rita chopped a salute back and glared around the room. "What the *hell* is this?"

Darwin stepped forward, a professional smile on his lips. "Window dressing, Major," he grunted, keeping his composure as he bowed, back to the monitors. "We'll fill you in later, but I think you'll be pleased with the results."

Rita shot him a skeptical look and shrugged. "Just don't make me into a puppet, Pike."

"Play the part of a conquering hero, Major, and enjoy yourself. That crowd out there is desperate for heroes. They'd never seen live ones until we arrived. We're happy to show them more."

Rita muttered a string of curses. "Aw, what the hell," she concluded and marched over to a packing crate. The crowd screamed a crescendo as Sarsa climbed up to a commanding position.

She waved her arms, trying to still the shrilling whoops. "People . . . people of Arcturus. You fill something in my very soul with joy. The way I feel now, well, it's a bit of happiness I'll cherish until I die—and then I'll send it on to Spider." An explosion of sound erupted as men and women cheered approval. Feet stamped, hands clapped in a cavorting bacchanal.

Sarsa waved them down again. "This welcome, well, it's too much to hope for. Last we heard, Ngen had broken the back of Arcturus. Killed your spirit and will to live.'' In the resulting wash of silence, Sarsa looked around the packed room. ''Well, you don't look broken any more . . . and my boys sure pasted the hell out of the Fathers! *We can lick that bastard yet!''* she hollered, waving a clenched fist over her head.

The milling crowd almost broke into a riot. From where he watched, the effect came off even better than Darwin could have hoped. *Miliken* had dropped out of jump an hour ago. She still might be two and half weeks away, but any ship of Ngen's was farther. Arcturus, at least for the moment, was safe.

The band struck up while, one by one, civic leaders read Darwin's carefully composed speeches. Then, the *coup de grace*, the huge holo that had displayed the arrival of *Spider's Knife* flickered to life.

People murmured to themselves, a hush falling as Skor Robinson's face formed on the holo.

Darwin nodded to Rita and smiled his enjoyment as she paled.

''Major Rita Sarsa,'' the huge-headed Director greeted. Behind Skor's bulbous skull, an endless blue seemed to extend to infinity. Like a circle of daylight, the radiant color contrasted with the white of the wall. ''On behalf of the Directorate, I wish to welcome you to weary Arcturus. Not in three hundred years has Arcturus welcomed heroes. You and your warriors are but the bright beginning to a new tradition. Welcome. Welcome to Arcturus with open arms. We, the people, salute you.''

Rita stepped forward on the podium, every inch the hard-bitten veteran commander. ''Director Robinson, we thank you for your kind welcome. Such enthusiasm and appreciation are more welcome than you can know after the horrors we've seen in Ngen's wake of terror. Indeed, let this mark the first step of a new era of human growth and glory. On behalf of the Romanan people, and the warriors of Spider, we thank and salute you for your warm wishes.'' At that, she stamped her feet and saluted the holo.

People went mad with whistles and yips and shouts of encouragement. From his booth, Pike made sure of the recordings, getting every last bit of the drama, capturing the expressions on the faces of the Arcturian people. Here a little blonde girl rode on the shoulders of a coup-decked Romanan warrior, his smile offsetting the scar down his cheek. There an attractive young woman reached up to kiss a burly warrior in gleaming battle armor. At the lock, Darwin got a shot of a young boy with a marker, drawing a poorly-rendered spider on the white wall. An old man hugged his gray-haired wife, tears of joy streaking his wrinkled, lined face. Most of all, Pike caught the looks of hope, the joy of the occasion, all of which he broadcast, the transduction nets straining to send it all.

Susan walked up in the final moments as people filed out of the crowded dock, singing, arm in arm with Romanan warriors all headed to the huge reception and banquet.

"Well?" she asked, leaning over his shoulder to catch a glimpse of the monitor.

"Victory! If some of those scenes don't melt hearts across space, the species is dead."

"I want to see you both." Rita stood behind them, hands braced on hips. "Now, if this charade is over, we've got a lot of catching up to do. You have someplace we can put together a conference?"

"We don't see the whole picture," Rita said, freckled face frowning at the monitor as she, Darwin, and Susan settled around the table comm in Susan's quarters. Skor's face filled the holo, his sunken eyes and pained mouth showing the strain of the last weeks. "The Admiral and Iron Eyes are making do, but the strategy we're developing is something new. I still don't know how to rate the impact of Patan and your *esprit de corps* campaign, Doctor. Do you have any information, Director?"

Skor's dwarfed mouth barely seemed to move. "Transduction throughout the system is in shambles. No one listens to either our instructions or requests through the net."

"Damn, we're still pretty much in the dark from the standpoint of military intelligence, too." Rita reached for the cup of tea she'd drawn.

Pike spread his arms. "We don't know how Patan is affecting people. I can point to the fact that Arcturus is now solidly behind us. At the same time, comm is flooded with requests for information. Every world and half the stations in space want a Prophet sent to them. On that basis, our sphere of influence is growing tremendously."

Susan rocked back and forth, a knee tucked under her chin as she leaned back from the table. "We get bits and pieces of the effects Patan is having on Ngen's military plans. Every time he makes a new sally, we're ready for him. Not all of Patan's information goes out on the public channels. *Toreon* blew an entire invasion out of existence when Ngen tried to take the Solar System. Earth is safe for a while. Whoever holds it has certain advantages from the standpoint of morale.''

"Why can't Patan tell us where to find Ngen?''

"I don't know," Darwin said reluctantly. "It's as if . . . well, I've asked him a couple of times. All he does is give me that damned smile and say I have my own cusps to deal with.''

"You know, we're still not winning this thing." Rita sipped at her tea, looking from face to face. "Ngen has expanded to the point where we can't stop him. The difference is that he's got an army of millions to drop wherever he wants. Then he psychs the people, pirates their manufacturing, and moves on.''

"Like a human form of virus," Skor noted, eyes narrowing.

"Yeah, I guess you could use that analogy. He has manufacturing hidden away in so many places that even with the information Patan has given us, we can't hit them all with the ships we have ready.''

"How about long-range prognostications?" Susan asked.

Rita waved it away. "If everything remains status quo, we might get him in five years.''

"Five years!" Darwin cried. "Patan won't last that long! He's weaker and weaker every time he makes a choice. After each of his appearances it takes longer and longer to get him on his feet again. It's killing him!''

"Spider guards free will very jealously." Skor's lips worked feebly. "I never really . . . So much . . . so changed." Then his expression changed. "Transduction from Admiral Ree.''

As suddenly, Ree's face formed on the holo. He met them with that serious stare that seemed so much a part of his personality now: half desperation, half exhaustion. "I've just had a communication from Ngen Van Chow," Ree greeted without formality. "The war just got more convoluted. Watch for yourselves.''

The screen split in half and Ngen's hawklike features filled one side. Darwin felt himself tensing and unconsciously sought Susan's clammy hand with his. *Easy. It's only a holo. That's all. Just a holo. He's not here. This is Arcturus. Not*

Bazaar. Susan's here. She's real. Holding my hand. Don't panic, Pike. You've made it through worse. Don't . . . don't panic.

"Your Prophet is most interesting," Ngen's soft tone filled the room. Pike ground his teeth against the soothing voice, feeling it eating like acid into his shivering soul. "So are the raids you have been making on my installations and worlds. The very hand of God is against you, Satan worshipers. I will have you know this, next time you blast one of my planets, you will kill your own loyal followers. Only half of my peoples will be purged of Satan from this moment on. I am making efforts to place at least one colony of your Satan contaminated hordes on each of my converted planets. Similarly, stations will contain captive populations. If you strike as foully as you have in the past, their blood will be on your evil hands."

Ngen waved pleasantly. "I've paid very close attention to your Prophet. I know how you value these souls for Satan's fold. Nevertheless, I'll use Satan's own against him to bring the new order to mankind. I'll wipe Satan from the galaxy eventually. In the meanwhile, each time you murder your loyal followers, I will be more than glad to tell of your hypocrisy. What is victory worth to you? One billion innocent lives? Two? I'll read your desperation in the helpless millions you kill!" Ngen laughed and vanished, the screen shifting to fill with Ree's image.

"Bastard!" Susan grunted.

"From now on," Ree told them, "we have to hold space overhead while we root them out. It makes the process much more painstaking and our military casualties will skyrocket."

"On the other hand," Darwin reminded, "we won't be turning habitable planets into barren wastes. It's difficult to win at that kind of cost. Sort of like cutting the patient's head off to cure a headache."

Ree nodded, "There is that. But it will come at the expense of lots of human lives—ours and theirs." He hesitated. "Since you're all there, we've given Ngen some thought. We're still working on the details, but we might have a way to get at him."

Rita leaned forward. "I'm all ears, go ahead."

Ree swallowed, color draining from his flushed features. "It doesn't come without risks. We'll tell you the extent of it when we can put it all together. But what you should know

now is that we want to use Arcturus as bait. Suffice it to say, we're desperate.''

"Everything has a risk," Susan growled, staring absently at a spot on the thick carpet.

"What does Chester say?" Rita demanded hotly. "I can't imagine him just—"

"Chester says nothing!" Ree banged a hand somewhere out of sight. "He just gives us that damn Prophet smile and hums classical music and whispers about cusps and traveling to the stars. Now, Major, what do you make of that?"

Rita sniffed and puffed her cheeks out. "Yeah, I've been the route with Prophets before. Sorry, Admiral. We've asked Patan, too. He just smiles uneasily and cryptically says, 'Wait.' ''

"Anyhow, that's what the brain tank on World has come up with. Until we can find something a little easier to swallow, we'll lay our plans for Arcturus." Ree shifted his eyes. "Incidentally, Doctor, your fine broadcast of Rita's welcome is the first step. We're touting that as undeniable proof of Ngen's fallibility. How can he call himself liberator when he can't even get a forum on Arcturus?"

"So, I'm the first tool?" Darwin whispered under his breath. The images rose in his mind to haunt him. "Then who's worse, Admiral? Ngen? Or me?"

"What was that, Doctor?"

"Nothing." In shocked silence, Darwin staggered under the rush of his tortured thoughts. Mouth dry, he winced, the image of Patan's fevered face dominating his thoughts, the pain in the Prophet's haggard features shared, a haunting agony. Only when Susan tightened her grip on his hand, did he come back.

"If only there was a way of getting to him." Susan was saying. "If we could just get a team onto that ship of his. One squad of marines would clean house!"

"If you can find him, do it! There's an awful lot of space out there and *Victory* is already on the prowl. I assure you, Maya wants him as badly as anyone. Anything else to report?" Ree raised an eyebrow.

"Nothing beyond what we sent earlier," Rita shook her head. "Tell Iron Eyes I miss him."

Ree nodded absently and the holo went blank.

"One team of Romanans," Susan said. "All we'd need to do is get on board the *Gregory*. We could have him within a day! If we had a Patrol vessel with legs to make sure he didn't escape, we'd really have him!''

An icy premonition clutched at Darwin's queasy guts. "And that would put us in *his* reach again." He stared at Susan, hollow-eyed, Ngen's voice whispering in the depths of his mind.

CHAPTER XXXV

Bullet in GEO orbit over World.

Damen Ree walked the long white corridors of *Bullet*. Alone, he prowled the depths of the ship, living with memories of his youth—and the pain of what he'd have to do to Arcturus.

"Well, old girl, we've begun sending the transmissions. We've got Zimbuti confessing that the Messiah's a madman—goading him. Ngen will have to react now. We're building Arcturus as the final bastion of resistance to Deus. We've hung all those people out to dry. They trusted me and most of them don't even know they're being used for bait.''

He bounced the heel of his fist off the bulkheads as he walked. "So much for trust, huh? Blessed Spider, what have I become?''

He placed a palm on one of the cool graphsteel walls. Beneath his warm flesh, he could feel the pulse of life within *Bullet*'s very guts. As always, the feel of the ship soothed him, lulled the inner distress, reminded him that here, at least, *Bullet* carried him safe within her womb.

"Tell me, old girl, did we do right?''

Around him the soft humming, the subtle vibrations might have been *Bullet*'s *sotto voce* reassurance.

Ree laced his fingers behind his back, walking slowly in the quiet corridor, at peace only with his ship. "Damn it, what other way is there? Pursuit of the greatest good? Why don't I feel heroic? What would Leeta say? What would she advise?''

He walked into one of the observation bubbles to stand, bouncing on his toes as he stared out at the winding foggy spatter of stars. In the patterns, he could picture her face, the image of her blue eyes meeting his, clear and level.

Her voice wound out of the darkness, committed to a course of action. *"So much at stake, my dear Colonel, God knows, it may damn us all. But then, you've got to accept the responsibility, Damen. In your shoes, I'd do the same thing."*

She'd say that.

Beyond the transparent curve of the dome, a streak of reaction flared across the stars. "I know what you'd tell me, Doctor. That sacrifice is a prerequisite for human survival. That's what you would have learned from your moldering prehistoric bones, isn't it? That's what your anthropology would have taught you, the lesson you learned on World."

"Damen?"

Ree turned, seeing Iron Eyes silhouetted in the light from the pressure hatch.

"Here, War Chief." He turned back to look out at the myriad of stars graying the heavens in wisps and sheets. So peaceful out there in the empty cold.

"I've been walking, talking to the ship . . . talking to Leeta."

Iron Eyes lowered himself to one of the spectroscopy seats, propping a muscular leg so he could look out. "It does Leeta's memory honor that you'd talk to her like that. One day, she'll know. Your soul will be returned—like all souls—to Spider. The knowledge will be shared." Iron Eyes smiled wistfully. "Not many humans leave such a legacy."

Ree nodded, catching another hint of reaction mass flickering the black of space. Big ships maneuvered out there, blasting to match orbit. The skies of World had become crowded.

The emptiness inside remained.

Ree waited, enjoying the silence of the moment. Out beyond the blister, he could lose himself. Live the peaceful lie of the stars.

After some time, Iron Eyes spoke gently, "You're still upset about Arcturus?"

Damen nodded. "After seeing so much death and suffering and horror, War Chief, I'm loath to inflict it on the innocent. They trusted me, John. They came to *me* for protection. And what am I doing? I'm trying to prepare myself for afterward. Nightmares of the dead . . . Burned. Decompressed. All those sightless eyes popped from the skulls, staring at me, asking why.'' He lifted his hands, palm up. ''And I don't have an answer for them.''

Iron Eyes ran a hand down the tight fabric on his leg, as if massaging the quadriceps. He gazed out into the eternal peace, eyes somber.

''The answer is Spider's. None of us are innocent, Damen. We're born human—and responsible for our actions or lack of them. We only get in trouble when the idea of justice comes up. For the moment, you're feeling guilty that so many will die when we kill Ngen. Guilt comes from a sense of injustice. You didn't make the universe this way. Spider did. Not only that, you wouldn't like it any other way, given the choice. What's justice? An artificial human construct. A symbolic abstraction for human impotence. Were justice to exist as an ultimate truth, I think it'd be a self-limiting concept. A blending of behaviors that would finally end in uniformity. Injustice—along with pain and suffering—is the fuel of the universe. Without it, nothing changes.''

''All right. So I'm accepting the guilt. It's still my action, *my* decision that's a death warrant for billions. *I* am betraying *their* trust. That's the part that's got my gut roiling. So what? I've gone from being the hero of Sirius to the monster who sold out Arcturus. Yeah, and I know you're right about injustice. At the same time, just because that's the way it is, doesn't mean I have to like it.''

Iron Eyes ran toughened fingers through the coups on his belt. ''So long as we bear the guilt, Damen. So long as we don't like it, we'll try and change it. You can't stop the process. Neither can I. That we suffer for it plays right into Spider's hands. We learn . . . and teach Him about what He's created.''

Ree reached out to spin the spectroscope hood around. ''You know, I keep going back. The sights, the smells, familiar faces. They all come back. Even the dirty scuffed corridors of the lower levels. I keep remembering things I thought I'd forgotten. I hated Arcturus. My folks, well, they had more than their share of trouble. My father got hurt as a kid. Fell on his head, damaged his brain. Mom and he lived together because they couldn't get anybody else. That tells you something about my mother. Not the greatest . . . Well, let her rest in peace.

''No one goes hungry in the Directorate but you live according to your means. We were out on the edge. Arcturus was built that way. Someone was always welding another box on the rim outside. Higher angular acceleration on the outer edge. You could measure a man's social status by where he lived. The people up in the low g sections were well off. We were so far down that under my bedroom floor was two centimeters of shielded graphsteel and then vacuum. Growing up in one point two g made my body strong. Let me get into the Patrol.

"Anyhow, there used to be a little shop four levels up and a couple of complexes spinward. Little old man from a city on Earth owned it. Came from a place called Moratuwa on some island south of India. He used to make the most wonderful drinks from chocolate, frozen milk, and grain malt. I'll always remember that he gave me one free every now and then because I didn't have the tenth credit it took to buy one. It was a long time ago—but if old Chanandras is still there, it's a hell of a payback for the things he did for me. Be nice to a kid. Talk to him. Treat him like a real person for the first time in his life . . . and see what you reap in the end."

Iron Eyes remained quiet.

"Until the day I die, I'll always remember, he told me the only real sin a man could commit was to let a dream die. That when you did, something bright flickered out of existence in the universe." Ree propped his foot on the railing. "Funny how you remember some odd things like that, how it sticks with you all your life. I never forgot. Let it be my motto in university, and then when I came to *Bullet*. I guess in a lot of ways, old Chanandras brought me here, to this, simply because he took the time to impress it on me that day."

Iron Eyes filled his lungs and exhaled. "And how many dreams will die if we don't crush Ngen? Did your friend ever tell you that a dream could die to free another dream? Dreams are like men, Damen. One dies, another is born."

Ree nodded. "I'm not trying to talk myself out of it, John. We don't have any choice. Like Leeta said that day so long ago, 'Nothing left to lose.' If we fail, humanity falls to Ngen. I guess against that future, even a couple of billion Arcturian lives don't mean much. It's only when you get to expanding your consciousness, like Schopenhauer talked about—finding that unity of identification with all people. We are me; I am us. But for an accident of time, it could have been me about to die on the big station."

"Don't you think that's the answer to the problem, Damen? You've put yourself at risk so often, don't you think humanity can take its chance? If you can make that stretch of consciousness to say, 'We are me,' isn't the inverse true? From the standpoint of society, can't you say, 'We are you'? And, since humanity is the prize in all this, the risk isn't just Damen Ree's . . . but everyone else's, too.''

"Logically put, Iron Eyes. But for years and years the Patrol beat it into my head that *I* was here to protect *them.*"

"They're free. Let them take the responsibility for it. Chester told the Director that we're all condemned to be free.''

"If Ngen doesn't destroy that condemnation. He can, you know, he's killing free will.'' Ree spread his hands, peering into the stars. "I don't know, I think maybe some of us are more condemned than others. Myself, I'm tired, John. I've borne the burden for others for a long time. I'm ready to see this thing over. I've spent the last year training young men and women to fly off to the stars and die. Ngen's power grows like some fungus on meat. Spider's word goes out to the stars and we wait, knowing so many will die, and we can't see an end to the violence and horror.''

"Damen, don't assume blame that rightfully belongs to Spider. Such behavior is for saints and Prophets, not soldiers.''

Ree rubbed the back of his head, grunting irritably. "What would you do, John, if we could have a respite from this?''

Iron Eyes pursed thoughtful lips, a distance-probing squint to his eyes. "Raise horses for a while. Train rambunctious colts into sharp sensible mounts. Have Rita close where I could simply love and enjoy her, talk to her, touch her, laugh and joke, hug her when I'm tired.'' He paused. "Maybe raise a child of . . .'' He smiled, suddenly self-conscious.

Finally, Iron Eyes added, "You know, Chester is right. You have to feed your soul. And if you get to feeding it nothing but horror, I'm not sure you stay healthy. I'd like to send Spider a balanced version of existence. Not just the pain, but a little pleasure and bliss, too.''

"Maybe that's my problem.'' Ree straightened, arching his back and wincing. "Maybe I've lost part of me since all this began. I don't know, it seems lately all I do is worry. If I get to feeling too callous, it scares me. Then I get to feeling like this, like I'm responsible for every helpless individual alive. And it scares me that I'm becoming a sobbing, bleeding heart. And there's no time to find a balance, find solid footing in the precarious web." He lifted his hands. "And to be honest, I miss Chester. I wish he was still here to talk to. Even when he never answered my questions, just having him around made me feel good."

"And, of course, you don't know why he wanted on that FT?" Iron Eyes lifted an eyebrow.

"Prophets are your area, War Chief, not mine. Hell, no! Does a Prophet tell anyone anything? What was I supposed to do? Chester wanders in, humming something from Bach, and asks if he can get on the FT. What do I do? Say no? To a Prophet?" Ree made a strangled noise and shook his head. "But it . . . it bothers me. Two of them in Arcturus at once? Both sitting on what's about to be ground zero? And they both just smile in that maddening way of theirs."

A brighter flare of reaction shot out among the stars. "The Colonels are here," Iron Eyes added softly. "That's why I came looking for you. When comm said your headset was off, I got a little nervous. Took a while to locate you. Then I thought maybe I'd better come check. Maybe take a moment to talk, to make sure. You've been pushing for so long now."

"Baby-sitter, eh?" Ree smacked his lips dryly. "So, it's finally time to pay the bill?"

"We're all part of Spider's web, Damen. They've come. Do we stick with the plan?"

Ree closed his eyes, breathing deeply. He nodded, head moving in short jerks. "You know, I envy you, Iron Eyes. If we live through all this, can actually put a stop to it, you've got horses and Rita to look forward to. I've just got my *Bullet*, but maybe she's enough after all."

He started for the door but stopped short, head tilted as he watched Iron Eyes getting up. "No, that's a lie I tell myself. As much as I love *Bullet* something's missing in my life. Sometimes I wonder if it's worth it to keep fighting, trying, and never being sure everything isn't about to come tumbling down."

"Condemned to be free," Iron Eyes reminded, a hardened fist tightening on Ree's shoulder. "That's the way of Spider, Damen. You struggle or your soul rots. You live only to learn, to serve Spider. Really, when you think about what you've done, where you've brought so many, has it been such a bad life? Were you to die tomorrow, you'd have an earful for Spider. Isn't that the greatest contribution any-one could glean from a lifetime?''

Ree met his eyes, a grim smile curving bloodless lips. ''I suppose it hasn't been such a bad life. Only after it's all done, if we lose Arcturus in killing Ngen—like I know we will—I'm leaving. Going somewhere with *Bullet* and finding my own horses—whatever kinds of things they might be.''

Iron Eyes clapped him on the back. ''I think another dream is born, Damen.''

''And now we're off to yet more dirty work.'' Ree shook his head, stepping into the white of the corridor, the peace and quiet of the stars left behind. ''And I take it all the details have been attended to?''

Iron Eyes grinned wickedly. ''I doubt your counterparts have any idea what the coming conference is going to cost them.''

''Let's just hope we know what it's going to cost *us*, War Chief.''

Directorate Administration center: Arcturus.

''The fact remains, we evacuated the entire city. Do you know what that entails? One and a half million people don't just pick up and walk out. Not on Kidian. Transportation is subsurface here. We had people killed in the panic. And for what? A nuclear disaster that didn't happen. Now, I don't know what sort of silly game you're—''

''Did you check the valve? Patan said one of the power-vane valves had a flaw in it.'' Pike gripped the corner of the console, bracing himself as he stared into the pickup that sent his image to Kidian.

The supervisor ran a nervous hand over his fleshy features, ruffling the bush white eyebrows that rose like tufts on his bald pink pate. ''Yeah, the valve got replaced two weeks ago. And yeah, the reason it got replaced was be-cause it had a crack in the main jackshaft that powered the fluid control vanes. But that was two weeks ago. So what's the trick? You guys are playing with fire with Fathers al-ready trying to set up a Temple here. Support for Ngen just doubled on Kidian. How am I supposed to keep the lid on when—''

''Please, I understand, Supervisor. I've seen Bazaar. Did the preliminary recon there, in fact. Help us. What about the valve? How did you find it? What happened? How did it get

changed? Tell me anything you can. Please, we're as confused as you are. Patan's never missed one like this before." *And blessed Spider, why's it happening now?*

The supervisor sighed. "Okay, all I know is the head
tech's wife left him three weeks ago. Said the guy was more
married to his job than he was to her. Anyway, Vik—that's
the tech—buried himself in the power plant. The valves were
overdue for inspection and he was feeling pissed and wanted
to keep busy. He tore down the main section and started to
run a fluoroscopic—"

"But he made a choice, right? He didn't have to do that.
It wasn't part of his routine?"

"Yeah, like I said, his wife . . . Uh, what are you getting
at. Hey, you all right. You sure got white."

Pike closed his eyes, wincing. "The cusp. Patan missed
the cusp."

The Supervisor cocked his head. "Right, well you'd better keep your boy on a leash, Doctor, because you may have
just thrown the entire ten million people on Kidian into
Ngen's arms. He's already got agents rolling around the
streets hollering about the Prophet's failure to—"

"*Damn you!*" Darwin exploded, panic eating at the bottom of his heart. "Don't you understand? He's failing! Falling into the future, changing cusps. He's going mad,
Supervisor. Killing himself, losing his ability to get back to
this reality! He's calling the future from too far away! Losing . . . Oh, damn it, Patan." Pike slumped down onto the
small chair.

The Supervisor shifted nervously, the holo picking up
graphite paneled walls in the background, a holo of a smiling woman and a couple of kids on the man's desk.

"Look, I'm sorry the Prophet's failing. But, Doctor,
there's a lot of people in trouble right now. I'm one. If they
sell this Temple to the people, or if one of their hit men
knocks me off, a lot of ghouls will be made on this planet.
Now, Kidian is pretty miffed at the shortages around here.
Sure, there's a war going on. But empty bellies coupled with
distrust of the pumpkin heads makes Ngen's message sound
real good to a lot of the locals. They don't necessarily believe the Bazaar holos. That's your word against Ngen's.
This planet's wavering. You helped make this mess, bail me
out, okay?"

Feeling gutted, Darwin nodded. "I'll call Admiral Ree.
He's got a GCI boosting from refitting with a Patrol crew

from *Miliken*. I'll see what I can do. Tell your people it's coming to keep Ngen's ghouls away.''

The Supervisor nodded. ''Great, one battleship's worth fifty flimsy Prophets.'' The screen went dead.

Pike sat there, an ache developing back of his eyes. The tech had acted through free will, made the decision to stay at work. He'd passed a cusp—and Patan hadn't seen which future was real. He'd lost his perspective. And it would get worse as Patan got sucked farther and farther away from reality.''

For long moments Pike stared at the dead monitor. With numb fingers, he lifted the headset from the counter, wiping his cold brow before slipping the circlet on.

''Transduction,'' he ordered comm. ''I need Admiral Ree on World.''

Glendivian: Moscow Sector.

Glendivian was initially constructed in the first days of the Directorate. The small colony was established to conduct deuterium, liquid hydrogen, ammonia, methane, ethane, acetylene, and sulfur extraction from the Glendivian slush. As such, the miners live in a station which essentially moves through the slush as a self-contained ''swimming'' unit. Exports are ferried to the gaseous interface, lifted by means of powered skyhook to synchronized LEO transshipment stations, and subsequently ferried by GCI to industrial complexes like Argus, Range, Chouhoutien, and Simon's Planet. Population is currently estimated at 1.2 million.

The Prophet's features faded from the holo in Max Vestilski's offices.

The Supervisor lifted a thick black eyebrow, wrinkling the incised lines in his sloping forehead. He tapped thick fingers on the foamsteel desk and looked around at the advisers seated in the plush chairs around his office.

''Well?'' Seely asked, flipping the thick wealth of her shining blonde hair over a shapely shoulder. ''You've decided to side with the Romanans and the Spider Prophet? Somehow Max, I knew you would. Must be the blood of barbarians in your veins, huh?''

Yeah, you'd think that, you throat-cutting, backstabbing bitch. Well, this makes things a little more difficult, you frigid vampire! Max squinted at the dead holo monitor, jamming a thumb toward it. "That's what that skinny kid on Arcturus says."

Seely cocked her head, a challenge in the deep pools of her blue eyes. "For a man who always prided himself on being 'his own man' some of us are happy to see you have some weak points."

Max resettled himself, seeing the grim reactions around the room. Well, she'd thrown it out in the open now. Sure, he'd thought about siding with the Romanans—throwing the latest batch of Fathers out to freeze in the slush. See if their faith in Deus could keep them alive breathing ethane at forty degrees Kelvin. And the Romanans had appealed to his ruthless personality. Only now Seely would use it against him. She'd been after his seat—his power—for years. And, damn it, she had the brains and the cunning to get it, too. Not to mention she looked like a perfect goddess while his own beetled brows and big-boned face reminded people of a troll.

"Well," Max said, exhaling, "Since you brought me this holo, you've already made your plans?"

She lifted her chin, letting the shining yellow hair roll in waves off the deep blue of her cloak. "I've made the announcement that you've sided with the insect god, yes. Certain stirrings of disappointment are already being heard among the people. This time far Arcturus has handed you to me, Max. By this hour tomorrow, you'll be out of this office and back in product supervision where you belong."

Max twitched his lips, expression sour. "Think so, huh?"

She cocked her head, lifting her eyebrows, the rest of the advisers shifting, shooting uneasy glances back and forth, knowing they teetered on the brink of a new power structure.

"Comm?" Max leaned back, lacing his fingers over his belly.

"Acknowledged."

"Please inform the delegation of Fathers their request to build a Temple is approved. Furthermore, extend my most heartfelt welcome to their embassy and let them know the resources of Glendivian are at their disposal."

"But you can't! Not just like that. The Fathers are the opposite of everything you've ever . . ." Seely's full lips parted, a look of shock on her perfect face. "You wouldn't! You deceiving, no good . . ."

"Next time you drop by, Seely, please, knock first." Max

smiled his satisfaction. "Now, if you'll excuse yourself, the door's over there."

Administrative offices, Directorate Section: Arcturus.

Never thought I'd be happy to have the pumpkin-headed bastard looking over my shoulder! No wonder he and the rest got a little bonkers! This is a double-damn disaster! And it's only Arcturus?

Comm interrupted, "I have a message for the Major."

"Go ahead!" Rita sang out, relieved to be distracted from the dark thoughts ruining her concentration. The piles of forms, approvals, denials, requisitions, and the assorted allied administrative details twisted into a bureaucratic nightmare. And this was only what was left after Skor handled all the mind-boggling parts!

Rita glanced up to the main screen as a young man's face formed. Despite the relative youth of his appearance his expression betokened anything but innocence. Tension pulled the skin tight around his cheeks and the corners of his eyes as he studied Rita. His blond hair looked perfectly combed and he wore a uniform of sorts, almost Arpeggian in cut. The cold blue eyes might be staring at her over a blaster for all the warmth in them. He seemed nervous, as if unsure of himself.

"This is Major Rita Sarsa. I'm the temporary Governor of Arcturus. What can I do for you?"

The man cleared his throat. "What would you give for knowledge of Ngen Van Chow's movements?" He spoke with an accent, his posture stiff, face as expressionless as molded clay.

Susan and Darwin leaned forward from where they worked, attention locked on the screen.

"That depends on who you are." Rita leaned back and picked up a stylus. "And it depends on what you want. We have absolutely no qualms about doing business . . . if the price is right."

"I am Torkild Alhar, captain of the *Gabriel,*" he said with pride. "I'm the first man to raid Arcturus in all of history. I blasted the Patrol vessel *Ganges* from space. I and my crew have killed four worlds. I am the . . . the last of the Arpeggians."

Rita nodded, cool eyes on his as her mind raced. "I take

it you saw what Ngen made of your people? Is that why you want him?"

"Your *Patrol* killed my world." Venomously, he added, "Let's not pretend, Major. For that reason alone, I'll never befriend you. You killed my world in an act of war. Not dishonorable—but unforgivable, nevertheless. But let's get this straight. Because you acted in war and from duty, I'll deal with you. In the end, there can be no peace between us. I don't forget, Governor. Our dealings over Van Chow are strictly to facilitate his destruction. Thereafter, our aggressions toward each other will resume as before. That is the scope of my offer." A fist accented finality as he pounded the desk top before him.

"You blame it on the Patrol, huh?" *Damn fool! What would you have done in . . . No. Wait! He doesn't know! Ngen's kept him in the dark!* Rita chewed on the stylus end. "You think we just went in and executed all those people? Spider's crap, Captain! They were . . . No, you'd never understand. Suppose you let me send you some transmissions of what we shot up on Arpeggio?"

"Tapes can be doctored. Why should I believe you?"

Rita shrugged in annoyance. "Captain Alhar, I really don't care what you believe. It's just that for one of Ngen's men you surprise me. You seem like a real thinking, breathing human being . . . with integrity to boot. You're not like the last Arpeggians I saw. They'd all been put through the psych treatment at the Temple. Look, Captain, I may not deal with you in the end, but at least I can salute you as a man—and respect you while we shoot at each other. Can't say that about the rest of Ngen's abominations."

"Send your tapes. My comm is receiving." A flicker of curiosity glinted in the steely eyes, as if he'd appreciate the chance to disprove her words—expose any sham. And she'd touched a nerve when she mentioned the Temple.

"Arpeggio was known for courage." Rita raised her eyebrows, shaking her head as she pushed back from the comm, stiff-armed. "I don't know how Ngen conned them."

She could see him watching the battle records comm sent on tight band. For long moments she cataloged the changes in his expression from irritated disdain to disbelief to horror.

"These were not . . . These are Arpeggians? They act like robots. Beasts without . . . without . . ."

"Less than that, Captain. We didn't even want to planet

at Arpeggio. We saw enough of Ngen's nightmares on Bazaar. We took the simplest course of action. We neatly,
cleanly sterilized the entire planet. I'll show you what happened on Bazaar. I'm accessing that and sending it along.
Your comm should be receiving. That's the entire record,
Captain. Get yourself a good eyeful. See what Ngen did to
your planet.'' She hesitated, seeing she had him. ''If you
don't mind my asking, how long since Ngen let you see
home with your own eyeballs?''

''Almost two years planet time. Dilation from acceleration, however, lessens . . . I haven't been . . .'' His expression hardened as he thought about just how long it'd
been. ''He's had a lot of time. We were always met en route
to be resupplied. I assumed it to be for reasons of efficiency.''

''Maybe it was. Ngen has a habit of being damned efficient. In fact, the bastard's brilliant. Look, I don't mind a
good stiff fight, but if I'd killed a planet of people—even if
they were my enemies—I'd be sorry, Captain. You know,
you do certain distasteful things as part of your duty. Killing
worlds leaves you with a feeling of regret—or it should if
you have any humanity in your soul. What we did to Arpeggio was a mercy—''

''Why? Why should I believe these tapes?'' Cold blue
eyes settled suspiciously on hers. At the same time, his fingers worked, knotting and unknotting. He sat stiffly, body
rigid. A strand of blond hair had come loose to stick to the
sweat-sheen on his pale brow.

Rita pulled herself up and glared into the screen, waggling the stylus at him. ''I don't much care if you do or
don't, Captain. You just don't look like the kind to be part
of monstrosities like that. If I remember, Alhar was one of
the old families on Arpeggio. I think your father would have
made you remember honor and pride.'' *Good shot! Got a
reaction out of that!* ''Don't take my word though, check it
out. Or does Ngen ever let you see the rear lines? I'll bet
he doesn't. He couldn't keep many good men that way. Of
course, there're always dock rats who can be picked up for
rear echelons. Pallas was one—''

''Maybe I shall investigate,'' Torkild agreed, voice
forced. The tendons stood from the backs of his powerful
hands where they gripped the desk.

Rita's eyes frosted as she slipped the stylus back and forth
through freckled fingers. ''You do that, Captain. Find out

for yourself . . . and tell the rest of your commanders what happened to their families and friends. We didn't kill your people on Arpeggio. They were already dead in mind and spirit. We simply sterilized a cancer.''

He seemed to be trying to read the truth, seeing only her bitter certainty.

''Look, there's nothing I can say that will prove it. You're right, the tapes could be doctored. I'm not going to try and sell you, Captain. I've got better things to do than try and teach you that facts are facts. You wouldn't believe anything I tried to sell you anyway. Just go look for yourself. Then we'll talk. In fact, I'll bet your price goes down.''

Rita killed the connection.

''Why did you let him go?'' Susan cried, jumping to her feet. ''He was invaluable! A line to . . .''

Rita exploded in happy laughter, grinning like a trickster as she whooped. ''Oh, sit *down*, woman! I doubt he'll agonize over that stuff for ten hours. He's hooked, Susan. He wouldn't have called unless he was already fed up with Ngen for some reason. That one's all ego and honor. I slapped him in the face with it. No matter what his decision, he *has* to call back just to save face.'' Rita jumped to her feet, body pumping with energy as she smacked her fist repeatedly into a hard palm.

She waved down Susan's skepticism, enthusiastically continuing, ''Consider this, too: He's Arpeggian and I'm a female commander. Arpeggians are funny about women. Worse than you Romanans because they pedestalize them. So I've got a couple of things going for me. First, he called me to dicker, thinking he held all the cards, and I talked down to him, condescendingly. I played on his ignorance of what happened to his own planet! Dominated the whole conversation. As we speak, he's fuming—and he doesn't even know why. For me to know more than he does, puts him at a disadvantage. He has to prove himself worthy. And he's already made up his mind to betray Ngen. I just gave him more ammunition.''

''So, if you know that much, what motivates him?''

''Something involved with Arpeggian honor. Alhar is an old house. Hell, maybe Ngen slapped his old man or something. Made a jeering remark about his mother? Who knows? They kill each other on Arpeggio for stuff like that.'' Rita raised her hands. ''For a bunch of ex-pirates, they got pretty high and mighty over the years. I don't know, I guess if you haven't got any glorious history, you innovate and make up a bunch of high-handed status behaviors to cover for your crummy past.''

Comm interrupted again. "Doctor Pike? The archbishop is waiting.''

Darwin kicked himself to his feet, the bulge of his prosthetic barely visible under the tailored trousers. "That's my cue. I'll see you ladies later. Three gets you five, Rita, you never hear from him again.''

"Taken!''

He palmed the door latch and left.

Susan's troubled eyes lingered on the door.

Rita lifted a red eyebrow. "Whoa, what's this? Do I detect an undercurrent of interest?''

"No there's . . . I mean . . . It's just . . . Oh, hell, we've been sharing quarters. It makes the dreams go away. His. Mine.'' She looked stubbornly at nothing.

"His? Ngen bent him that badly?''

Susan met her questioning eyes with a shrug. "You remember that tape you ditched of me and Ngen? Well, I ditched one of Ngen and Pike. It wasn't the same. Ngen didn't . . . I mean, the way he raped Pike wasn't . . . In its own way it was worse. If I told you what happened, you'd never believe me.''

"Bear spit! When it comes to Ngen, I'd believe any kind of atrocity you want to think up. Our Pike's not the same starry-eyed golden boy, is he?''

Susan stood and stretched her muscles. "After you've seen hell, Major, you never are.'' She paced slowly back and forth, arms crossed on her chest, head down, face hidden in the tunnel of her spilling hair.

"I worried about you for a long time, Susan. I took a hell of a risk on you.''

Andojar nodded slowly. "Spider knows why. And Rita, the risk was bigger than you'll ever guess. You don't know how close I was to the edge after the Sirian affair. I came real close to falling apart into a million pieces. I . . . I wanted to kill you because you knew. And every day when I get up, Rita, I still live the nightmare. I'm not fixed, not well, just able to deal with it . . . for today.''

"And Pike?''

"Like me, he's a patchwork personality. All it would take would be the wrong word and he'd fragment. And he's sick, Major. He doesn't know it, but he's holding dead even, losing a little, gaining a little. It's fifty-fifty whether he'll live or die. We . . . *I* pushed the regeneration on the way back from Bazaar. His leg nerves are growing back bit by bit, repairing the damage, but the cancer's spreading through his system. If we get time and can put him into a med unit, Pike has a chance to live. Only we don't have time. Like tonight, he'll be with Patan after the interview, making sure the Prophet is all right before he comes home. Then he'll agonize over Patan until he falls asleep. Then the dreams will come a couple of hours later, and he'll be up half the night in cold sweats. Tomorrow morning, charged by the horror of the dreams, he'll be thinking up another strategy to get some other religious leader to fall into Spider's camp and join in the attack against Ngen's ghouls.

"And I'm keeping his health secret—even from him." She clamped her fists at her sides. "We can't take the time to heal him. His brain, the way he cuts Ngen's propaganda apart is priceless. And no one else can cover for Patan—interpret the things he says. You know that Patan hasn't been one hundred percent accurate? Well, we've caught it every time before it's gotten out. And Pike's thought up a permutation to make it look like we're on the money." She ground her teeth. "So I hide the med reports, doctor the record to keep him fit when he's dying on his feet. You know how that makes me feel?"

"Sounds pretty tough. Maybe we should send him back? Pull rank and put him in full med for his own good. Get someone else to . . ."

She shook her head. 'Major, you'll kill him. Like me, he lives to fight Ngen—to pay him back for . . . for . . . Unlike me, he's got someone he can trust because I've been there, too. Take that from him and he'll die. He'll will himself to death just to avoid the dreams."

"You love him?"

Susan stopped short. Straightening, she pulled her long shining hair back, eyes sharp. "I don't have the ability to love, Rita. You damned well ought to know that. Ngen burned it out of me back over Sirius. I'll never love. . . . She bit it off, turning on her heel and slapping the lock plate as she rushed out the door.

Rita exhaled slowly and settled back in the comm chair. A weary burning ached back of her gritty eyes. Idly, she looked up at the star map glittering on the far wall. Would the hell ever end? she wondered, thinking about the blood, death, and violence that awaited her warriors on half a hundred worlds. And Susan was right about needing Pike's genius.

"And I don't have the time to save your man for you, kid. Not even if I could."

CHAPTER XXXVI

Central Administration: Directorate Section, Arcturus.

Skor Robinson hovered weightlessly, redirecting the commerce of his dwindling empire. Some planets and stations stood against Ngen. Others folded, welcoming the horror of the Temples with open arms—refusing to believe the evidence of the Romanan and Patrol reconnaissance.

"Why?" Skor cried out in the silence of his room. "What did we do that they'd believe Ngen instead of us? How has this come to be?"

You have no understanding of the motivations of human beings. Chester's voice echoed out of his memory.

"No, we didn't." Skor stared sightlessly into the distant haze of blue. "Sterile. We were sterile. Only now, all that remains is hurt. And . . . and I have no one to talk to."

In the silence of the room, he looked into the twirling blue distance and suddenly hated it. Confirmation had come through. The younger Directors, the three children in the labs, had suffered as a result of the Fathers' raid. Evidently the power had fluctuated, shutting down the life support systems for a moment. Unable to cool their blood, brain temperature had risen dramatically in the minutes between—coupled with the scare, the brain damage couldn't be corrected.

"So I'm the last of my kind." Skor blinked into the cerulean eternity. "Navtov is dead. Roque is crazy—locked in his own mind. Speech is such a limited means of communication. The last of my kind." He curled into the fetal ball he so often adopted these days, feeling the security of hugging his bird-thin knees to his bony chest.

"Oh, Chester, I'm so alone! Where are you Prophet?

Come and talk to me. Please, come. I can't bear much more of this. I can't bear loneliness!''

Aboard *Deus*, decelerating from jump for Cobalt Station.

Ngen Van Chow watched the comm angrily. A wave of yelling Romanans charged forward, cutting his line of resisting Fathers into ribbons. It wasn't that the Fathers didn't fight, they did—with admirable tenacity. After all, they had been psyched to do exactly that. Romanan vitality made the difference. The spider-painted barbarians seemed to be enjoying themselves! Ngen might be watching a replay of scenes from Sirius. It all looked too familiar.

Rank by rank, he threw his forces at the Romanan bridgehead and rank by rank they were blasted and hacked into oblivion. The Romanans made no mistakes. They stood up to the onslaught, armor spattered with blood, charred and flaking from near misses. They sang, shouted to their Spider god, and fought on, the bloody coups hanging from their armor streaking and smearing the white plating on their legs in crimson designs.

Ngen cursed. If only he could get a ship in before his army was wiped out—but he couldn't. The Romanan vessel in orbit carried those infernal blasters that chewed up his GCIs like fangs in hot butter.

Violet light sent a tornado of destruction racing through the ranks, playing death over the horde of Fathers who rushed for the battle zone. It closed on the comm center and the screen went blank.

Ngen cursed, kicked the bulkhead, and stood, brooding. They'd cut his communications. For all he could tell, the battle was over. He'd lost Angel to the Romanans.

He paced back and forth, chin on his chest, features deeply lined with thought. The Spider religion had pumped new life into the uncommitted worlds and stations, stiffening opposition. At the rate momentum was dissipating from his jihad, it would squeal to a stop before he had half of human space under his control. How did a man fight a Prophet who knew strategy and tactics before they were even dreamed up?

With a fist! He smacked his palm with his knuckles, making a hollow popping sound. Playing with his goatee, Ngen accessed comm.

MacGuire's harried and sweaty face formed in the holo, a headset slightly cocked on his blond-gray scalp as if it had been placed hurriedly over the fleshy features. In the background, Ngen could see the rest of the team bent over their tasks. Monitors flickered in multicolored displays of numbers and diagrams. A bustle filled the very air, as if some underlying tension charged them. He could see the characteristic clutter left by engineers and physicists at work. Coffee stains marked large transparencies. Stacks of flimsies, printouts, and diagrams canted in uneven piles perched on every available space. Comm generated holos overlapped in laser-bright colors. A hush fell on the room as eyes looked uneasily in his direction.

"Messiah?" MacGuire greeted, bowing slightly, his fear evident. And this was the pompous ass who'd threatened to boycott him? Ludicrous!

"Doctor MacGuire, have you made any progress?" Ngen asked.

The man nodded. "Yes, Messiah. We've managed to work out the power flux problem. The gravitational waves we induced were buckling the graphsteel in the station's structural supports. While we've beefed up the skeleton and added more struts, we've had to balance the stresses by counter gravitation. You have to understand, no one's built on this order before. Matter behaves peculiarly at these orders of magnitude. Cobalt Station still needs considerable structural renovation. For the moment, power is being added to the rim. Those are the reactors you see situated at the base of the projection towers. The proper procedure for balancing the gravitational pulse is currently under consideration by my second, Helmut Eng."

"And the Brotherhood mass converter?"

"There is progress, Messiah." His eyes darted miserably to the side.

"But not much, I take it," Ngen's voice was a hiss.

"Messiah, if we understood all the underlying assumptions, it would simply be a matter of technological innovation. We're having to build a whole new physics out of bits and pieces!" His hands stretched out imploringly. "If you could provide the unifying theories from which you want us—"

"*I can't!* You have all the data I got."

"Then surely you can understand the difficulties we—"

"You have not forgotten your liabilities, have you?" Ngen

smiled. "Your daughter is so young, with such pretty hair. I have ways with young girls, engineer. Remember that."

"My . . . She's only twelve!" MacGuire's face turned a pasty white. He mouthed a pleading word, gaze dropping. At last he managed to whisper, "No, Messiah. None of us have forgotten."

"Good," Ngen thundered jovially. "Make it work, MacGuire. Give me a Fist with which to smash the Directorate and this abomination, Spider!"

He cut the connection. For long moments he stared at the gleaming white tiles overhead, trying to put it all into perspective. No, he was still winning, but it had slowed. The command structure had begun to balance out. Enough men, frightened of what they saw happening to others, were willing to save themselves by enlisting eagerly in Ngen's forces. Flexibility was slowly returning to his forces. Perhaps the added adaptability would—

"Messiah?" the comm tech called. "Perhaps you would like to see the latest transmission from Arcturus?"

Ngen gave the man an icy scrutiny. "Is there anything I should be aware of?"

"Yes, sir. Winston Zimbuti is—"

"Run it."

Zimbuti's face filled the monitor. "Ladies and gentlemen," Ngen's former captain began in his soft voice. "I've been allowed the chance to speak . . . to tell you the truth about the man I once served. You know him as the Messiah, Ngen Van Chow. I knew him as the dock rat he was on Sirius. I assure you, in his days as a low criminal on Sirius, I never would have guessed at the range of his insane—"

"No more!"

The holo snapped out. *"This comes from Arcturus?"*

The comm tech nodded, eyes downcast. "Yes, sir. Of course, they could bounce the—"

"They'll PAY!"

He left the bridge, fuming, in his mind seeing Zimbuti's body dismembered piece by piece. Raging, he walked through the silent corridors of his ship. Had the Romanans managed to turn the entire conflict in their favor? Angel wasn't the first world they'd taken back. Yes, the momentum remained, but now Arcturus was rebuilding—and was sending messages from the likes of Zimbuti to undermine him. The holos they sent of the Prophet, of the huge machines

that welded the broken sections of torus together, all spoke
of a renewed power.

They threw Arcturus in his face, using it as a symbol of
his impotence. What would it take? How many antimatter
torpedoes to blow it all away into twisting junk? The attempt would have to be made and soon. Unless some breakthrough came with the Fist. The Fist . . . THE FIST . . .
THE FIST!

With it, he would *be* God!

He wound his way up to his quarters and found M'Klea
lying in the huge bed.

Flowing white waves of some fragile gossamer fabric
floated down over her body, and he enjoyed the look of her
golden hair spread in shimmering waves over the deep blue
bedding. She looked up, her blue eyes deep pools of emotion. Her breasts had begun to grow, pressing against the
fabric, and her once trim belly had swollen now. At the
same time, her complexion had changed, intensifying, holding a glow of health and vitality.

The rage and anger melted, curling away to a smoldering
resentment. Here, at least, no one questioned his power.
He'd planted the proof of that deep within this striking and
magnificent woman. He smiled and settled himself on the
bed, dropping a hand to the firm flesh of her swollen abdomen, feeling the life within move.

"You're worried, husband?"

"We just lost Angel. They took it with one converted
GCI and a thousand Romanans." A bitter taste clung to the
back of his tongue. *Zimbuti called me a dock rat! CALLED
ME A DOCK RAT!* He closed his eyes, anger like a razor-
honed spear within.

"We must expect setbacks, Lord Emperor," she told him,
tracing fingers along the delicate skin of his arm. She shifted
her long legs under the gossamer skirt.

"We've suffered setback after setback! *Damn that
Prophet!* He's countered my every move. We're stalemated!
Each world, every station, every parsec becomes a struggle
of blood! Sira reports pictures of spiders in the compounds
of the hostages! You look at the unpsyched, and you see a
new light in the eyes of the people! They actually fight back
when my Fathers land on their worlds! They lose, of course,
but they resist!" He ground his teeth. *Zimbuti called ME a
dock rat!*

"Their Prophet speaks less and less. He's losing himself

to madness, Ngen. There are rumors in the transduction that he missed several of his predictions. That an accident on Kidian didn't occur. Supposedly a transmission error in the transduction. Maybe he is becoming mad? If you get 'lost' in the future, do you lose accuracy in your predictions?'' She smiled. ''As yet, another hasn't come to take his place. He must succumb soon. He himself says so. They can't see our ultimate victory.''

''No, they can't.'' Ngen agreed easily. ''All the more reason to move on Arcturus next. Destroy it, and I've rid myself of this Prophet. Rid myself of the plague of Arcturus. It's become as much a rallying symbol to the people as Spider. That abomination of a Director has his holo at every function Rita Sarsa supervises. But the Prophet's the final key. Break him, and I've broken Spider. When I finally take the Romanan World, I'll burn the Prophets slowly. I'll hang them over smoldering fires and watch them twist and scream.''

''You're tense,'' she said, running hands up and under his robes and down his chest. ''Your eyes tell M'Klea that you're disturbed. Perhaps you need relaxation?'' She began shedding her garments.

''Yes,'' he grinned, standing suddenly. ''I've been too long from my leisure. But not you, beloved. No, this time, I need to break someone, to hear them scream under my flesh.'' He laughed accessing his personal comm. ''There are many new ones. Will you choose? Which one?''

She drew on a robe and stood, lips pursed as she studied the screen, ungainly body awkward now. One by one, she studied each of the haunted faces, looking for one who might challenge him.

''That redhead from Santa del Cielo. Only this time, Ngen, I'm coming to watch. You know I've always enjoyed your art. I want to enjoy the pleasure as you turn her into a whimpering slut.'' She smiled up at him, running fingers down the side of his face in gentle strokes. ''I want to share your victory. You will make her scream for a long time?''

''But of course,'' he smiled, ''I suppose you'll want to use the whip on her?''

She laughed, wrapping thin arms around him, leaning her head back, throat exposed, white teeth gleaming. ''Dearest love, you have no idea how much that will please me. It will drive you to a fever pitch—and I can show you what

I've learned about torture while you've been so busy with war.''

Arm in arm, they left the cabin, Ngen already anticipating the redhead's screams.

Officer's tactical conference room aboard *Bullet* in GEO orbit over World.

Damen Ree waited in the dim corridor, watching his counterparts as they threaded through the ship. Each had brought a crack squad of marines. Quite a bodyguard. None had wished for this meeting, each balking in his own way, crackling subspace with their hurried transmissions, plots, and strategies.

''Surely you're safe when *Bullet*'s outnumbered three to one,'' Ree had added, the ghost of a smirk on his lips. And they'd come. One flaw in Patrol commanders, they had too damn much pumped-up egotistical pride.

I'm not ready for this. I'm tired of it. No matter what I do, what I say, it will boil down to a show of force. I can't win here—only deepen the roots of hatred. I'm tired. For the first time in my life, I want an easy way out—and I'm not going to get it. Spider? Why are you testing me so? What in hell are you doing to me?

Swallowing, he palmed the lock plate and entered the sparkling white conference room through a rear hatch. He stopped face to face with the remaining power of the Patrol. In their cold expressions he read only condemnation. It would be a hard uphill fight all the way.

''Greetings, everyone. Welcome to World. I hope your—''

''Cut the shit, Damen,'' Tabi leaned forward. ''What's your game. We all came. But we didn't leave ourselves vulnerable. In the event we lose contact with our ships, the orders are to blast *Bullet* and immediately after that, to cook your god-rotted planet of barbarians to slag.''

''Nice to see you, too, Tabi.''

The bodyguards stiffened, fingering blasters, eyes darting around the featureless bulkheads.

Ree turned his attention to Tabi Mikasu. Commander of *Kamikazi*, she stood 1.4 meters tall, hair graying and drawn back in a bun, her dress uniform was immaculate. The broad bones of her face betrayed her Oriental ancestry. Seething black eyes stared back at him from under the heavy epicanthic folds of her eyelids. Her tan skin had begun to wrinkle at the corners of the eyes. She waited straight, haughty, fists clenched at her sides.

Claude Devaulier of *Uhuru* might have been in his fifties, 1.75 meters tall, he looked too thin, almost a walking skeleton. His orthognathous face was thin, even for a Caucasoid. The long narrow nose dominated his features, almost sharp enough to cut with. Even though he was almost bald, his eyebrows looked like gray bushes pasted to his pronounced brow. A clever mind lay behind the facade of those sleepy brown eyes.

On the other hand, Amelia Ngurnguru of *Amazon* practically vibrated, the spare muscles of her tiger body smooth beneath satiny blue-black skin. Her hair had been pulled back over the left ear to hang in a stiff mass of tight ink-black curls. She claimed undiluted Ashanti ancestry from one of the oldest families to have been deported to Kumasi during the Gulag period of the World Soviet. She stood back, studying Ree through her oddly slanted eyes, waiting, deadly. Of the three, she was the smartest, the quickest to see the gains, and for that reason, the most dangerous. At the age of thirty-six, few had made the rank of Colonel quicker.

"Please, sit down. Make yourselves at ease. This looks to have the earmarks of a long session. And by the time we're finished, we'll have to completely remake the command structure."

Ree settled himself at the table, aware that the three Colonels still stood. He slapped the table. "Oh, come on! Damn it, the time for defiance is long past. I know exactly how you feel about the whole situation. Yaisha Mendez even refused the Director's orders. Yet I don't hear any condemnation of her."

Claude Devaulier shook his head. "Damen, it isn't going to be that easy. We, that is, myself, Tabi, and Amelia responded to an order by Skor Robinson. We were *ordered* to World. We're here." He straightened. "To be honest, we thought we were coming to burn *Bullet* out of space and destroy the Romanan menace. Had we known the true intent, we too, would have stayed and fought the Fathers on our own. God alone knows how many more are dead because of our retreat from—"

"*Damn you, Claude!*" Ree clamped his teeth, turning his head away as he fought for control. Rage stifled, he looked up into those faded brown eyes. "Don't you get the picture yet? Ben Mason lost his ship to Ngen. It's called *Deus* now. And what about Peter Petrushka? No one's fool, huh? A silly trick by a converted GCI blew him and *Ganges* to plasma. As to protecting planets and people, we're beyond that. We can't . . . *can't* protect anything! Why? Because you're all that's left! Sure, Yaisha sits in the Solar system, big as life, and, sure, she blasted Ngen's attempt to take Earth. One planet. That's what she's saved. But what about all the others? New Macao? Gone. Bahia? Gone. The Antilles Stations? Gone. Do I keep naming planets that Yaisha's responsible for? Want me to start looking into your own Sectors? Making a tally of the—"

"What's your point, Damen. Let's hear it so we can get back to our ships."

"It's all over." Ree looked up soberly. "That's my point. The centuries of Patrol are gone—outmoded. Our only hope is in a concerted—"

Tabi Mikasu cocked her head. "*Kamikazi* didn't come here to listen to you preach defeat. We're powered up, Damen. On my order, she'll shoot. My ATs are on alert, ready to go. Perhaps you'd better step down from your command now. Without bloodshed. We won't leave here with the Romanans at our backs. We came to finish what you started in the beginning. We'll fulfill the Director's original orders—neutralize the planet—and get back to saving humanity. That much has been decided already. We accepted your invitation to come here in person to appeal to any sense of responsibility you might have left. Simply give us your ship, Damen. We'll leave you on the planet with the rest and see about putting Ngen back in his bottle."

Ree chewed the insides of his cheeks as he considered. "So nothing's changed, has it? Ngen's out there, gobbling up worlds by the handful, and I'm still fighting the Patrol."

Devaulier leaned down over the table, looking sleepier than usual. "No, Damen, nothing's changed accept that renegades like you broke the power of the Patrol. Effectively castrated our ability to do anything about Ngen Van Chow! Now, we're remedying the situation. You first, then Maya and Toby. With the fleet rebuilt and at full power, we'll sweep . . . What? What are you laughing at?"

"Comm," Damen ordered wearily as he stifled his chuckles. "Prepare the battery test on the Romanan moon, Harvester. Proceed when ready." He looked up at his counterparts. "I hope you're still in contact with your ships. You might stress that we're engaged in a demonstration, not an attack. Please have your weapons officers run a special analysis of our firepower. And if you do decide to shoot, our augmented shielding is fully as effective as our blasters. Despite your numerical superiority, *Bullet* can absorb every erg you pour into her."

The holo flickered to life to show Harvester, the terminator stretching across a full third of the pock-marked surface. The Colonels looked up as two deep violet beams lanced the moon.

"Cease fire," Ree ordered. "We don't want to crack it in two. And, yes, we only used two batteries to keep the damage to a minimum. As to the effect of the Fujiki blaster on your ships' shielding, we've already sent copies of Neal Iverson's attack on *Deus*. Ngen thought he'd upgraded his defensive shields—but Neal still raked him pretty good."

He could see them concentrating on their headsets, getting the information about the Fujiki capabilities.

"It's over." Ree sighed, spinning in his chair to punch his battered coffee cup into the dispenser.

"Nothing's over so long as we have our ships, Damen." Tabi crossed her arms defiantly, head back. You've forgotten one thing. We're here, and you're alone. You're under arrest as of this moment, Damen. I don't think you can resist."

"That's just it. I can. If your muscle, there, points a weapon at me, your ships are forfeit. You'll have nothing to return to but orbiting debris. I don't want that. You don't want that. But why force my hand? There's another way." Ree smiled dully. "You don't have your ships. You see, *Bullet* is *the* power in space now. You came to demand that I surrender my command. I now demand it of you. The fact of—"

"*You?*" Devaulier cried, slapping his leg at the inanity of it. "*You* demand of us?" He shook his head. "Damen, maybe you don't think so straight anymore. You're outnumbered, three to one! You're—"

"More than capable of taking all three of your ships. Please, people, the decision is yours. Surrender, or join the fight. As I was about to say, the fact of the matter is that time's run out. For all of us. I can't afford any silly pretensions of Patrol honor, or tradition, or any of the crap we've stuffed our shirts with for years. I'm going to war and I need your ships."

Tabi snorted through her nose. "He's mad. Let's get out of here."

The wall panels lifted silently. Iron Eyes and his Roman-ans crouched behind energy barricades, blasters lifted. The Colonels and their bodyguards stood absolutely still, not even quivering.

"Admiral?" Tony's voice came through comm. "I've got a surrender order from the three Patrol ships of the line. We're to hand over their commanders in thirty seconds or they'll open fire."

Ree waved a hand inoffensively. "I suppose they will, Tony. Stick to the plan. On my order cut the powerlead trunk ahead of the main reactor stanchion. Warn them where our shots will be placed so we can minimize loss of life while we break them down. If they continue to resist, follow Giorj's schematic to minimize structural damage. We don't want to waste too much time putting them back together."

"You're out of your mind!" Tabi cried.

"Admiral, *Kamikazi* is firing."

Ree looked up, seeing the violet threads concentrating on *Bullet's* shielding. He shook his head. "Claude, Amelia, I suggest you hold your fire for the moment. We're keeping your lines of communication open. Look, take some time, see how the shielding holds. Tony? Give them a minute to clear their personnel out, then take out *Kamikazi's* main powerlead."

Two lines of violet encountered *Kamikazi's* shielding. The fields wavered, climbing rapidly through the quanta to buckle and cave in. Atmosphere boiled through the deto-nating plating as the Fujiki blasters clawed into the heart of *Kamikazi*.

"Shoot!" Tabi screamed at her companions. "Damn you, shoot! *He's destroying my ship!*"

One bank of *Kamikazi's* gun deck flickered out. Seconds later, so did another.

"The engineer still has time to damp the system. It gets a little touchier if we cut a couple more main leads."

"You can't bluff us, Damen," Claude insisted.

He searched their faces, pounding the table with a thick hand. *"Damn it, people, I'm trying to save lives here! What does it take? Your broken, bleeding bodies? Can't you see? I'M NOT THE ENEMY!"*

Ree stood, feet apart, arms stiff-braced on the table, jaw out. "Come on! Tabi's launched her ATs and I'm going to be forced to blast them out of space one by one. All those men and women will be dead, you hear? *Dead!* And why? I beg you, *think!* What are we doing to ourselves that it's come to this? Even the Director is on our side against Ngen! *What more do you want?*''

"Tabi." Amelia said softly. "Cease fire. His shields are holding—barely strained. Do you notice even a fluctuation of power in here?"

"He could be routing this room separately. The rest of—''

"Tabi." Amelia planted herself in front of the Colonel, smoky eyes pinning the smaller woman. "The communications channels are open to our ships. If *Bullet* didn't have more than ample power to spare, we'd be cut off."

"Amelia?" Claude's face wore a strained expression, a curious glitter in his usually dull eyes. "What are you—''

"I'm looking to my interests, Claude. I'm siding with Ree. I didn't get where I am by being a fool." She turned back to the smaller woman. "Tabi. Cease your fire before *Bullet* destroys your ATs. Call them off, Tabi. You and Claude can't stand against both *Bullet* and *Amazon.*''

Tabi's face twitched as she closed her eyes, mouth pinching in defeat. Tabi Mikasu settled into one of the chairs, resistance folding. The glare of blaster fire dimmed until *Bullet*'s shields shimmered in the afterimage, dissipating the fearsome radiation.

"ATs are shedding delta V, Admiral." Tony called from the bridge.

Ree lifted a finger, motioning. Iron Eyes and Sammy Andojar Wing stepped forward to disarm the Patrol personnel. Amelia raised a hand, eyes slitted, as they approached her own group. "Is this how you treat me?"

Damen spread his hands. "For the moment, Amelia. Until we see how things shake out. I mean, put yourself in my position. You just backed down because the impossible happened. Saving your own skin? Could be. If the roles were reversed, would you just smile at me and say, 'Come on aboard, Damen. Here's the secret to invincibility! Welcome to the team and no hard feelings that you just tried to cut my throat . . . again.' ''

She cocked her head, a smile of appreciation revealing bright white teeth. "No, I suppose I wouldn't."

"What of us?" Claude demanded. "What happened to communication with our ships? What is this, Ree? A double-cross? My people won't stand for it. You can't just keep us hostage!''

"Care to bet? For now, you stay right where you're at. I need lists of your best officers. Everything you've got. Qualifications, performance abilities, command capabilities, psych profiles, stress resistance—"

"What for?" Amelia lifted an eyebrow, watching him, expression impenetrable.

"I'm stripping your crews for all the potential officers I can get. I've got a fleet of converted GCIs building out there and no one capable of piloting and commanding them. Romanans learn fast, but commanding a warship takes a special something the Patrol has been cultivating in our ranks for a long time."

"And what about our crew positions? You can't seriously believe we can space *Uhuru* with empty bunks! That's ridicul—"

"You'll space Romanans, Claude. And like it! One thing I do have is a pile of trained Romanan techs who can maintain blasters, fix comms, read spectrometers, and double as some of the meanest damn marines you've ever set eyes on."

"Why the rush?" Amelia asked.

Ree turned the coffee cup slowly in his fingers. "Arcturus is being set up as bait for Ngen. He's going to hit it sometime in the next year. When he—"

"*Arcturus! You raving lunatic!* You're condemning all those people to—"

"I'm *damned* aware of that, Claude! Now, shut up and sit down! It's *got* to be Arcturus. He'd have to make a major strike. Withdraw enough of his forces in anticipation to tip his hand. Intelligence will give us enough—"

"If your *Bullet* is so damned powerful, why don't you go blow the *Gregory* into plasma and solve the whole thing?" Tabi demanded. "Or do you only fight from the rear, Damen?"

Iron Eyes stiffened, eyes narrowing as he fingered his knife.

Ree blinked and shrugged. "I'd be glad to. Where's he at, Tabi? Kahn Station? Freeport? Spatzgrad? Or is he someplace else? Ah, you begin to see. Surprise, Tabi; yes, we've actually been racking our brains over the problem for some time. Sure, we could guard Arcturus, sit there, and wait in strength for years while Ngen solidified his control over the rest of human space. Unfortunately, I've been in contact with some of the resistance out there. Just regular people who've stood up to Ngen and said no. And to be honest, Colonel, those few plucky men and women out there are what keep me going. But that's neither here nor there for the moment. Let's get back to Arcturus. So Ngen's power base expands? Then what? He could ignore Arcturus while it starved to death. Only by that time he'll have the entire resources of the Directorate in his hands and we'll be so far outnumbered, defence against his billions of psyched ghouls will be a moot point.''

Amelia raised her eyes. "And he'll hit Arcturus? You're sure of it?''

Ree ran his thumb around the rim of the coffee cup, slouching in his seat. "The one thing we know about Ngen, his one failing, is that he's a vain bastard. Yeah, he'll hit Arcturus. We've been slapping him in the face with it for the last couple of months.''

Amelia crossed her arms, scuffing the floor with a booted toe. "Without access to my comm, I'd say you'll kill at least half the population. We can't get everything he sends in. Considering the number of ships he's capable of dropping into the Arcturian well, plus battle debris, it's too much to track.''

Ree nodded numbly. "Yes, I know. And I accept it. If there were just another way. But we've—''

"I say hunt him down!'' Claude tilted his head back.

"We don't have that kind of time,'' Iron Eyes spoke up. "This war will drag on and on and it will never have an end unless Ngen is stopped. Once and for all.''

"If we can get him,'' Amelia added soberly from the side.

CHAPTER XXXVII

Aboard *Deus* decelerating for Cobalt Station.

Ngen climbed to the observation dome and stared soberly at the stars. His latest conquest had been a disappointment: the woman hadn't had much stamina. Generally, when they began fighting like that, straining at the EM bonds, they had some inner resistance. He'd anticipated taking his time, enjoying a hard fought battle to break her, bit by bit. The greatest enjoyment came from doing it slowly, tearing her psyche in two. The ultimate double bind. Make her hate herself. Instead she'd broken almost immediately, babbling, letting him possess her without even a spark of hatred in her eyes. Not even M'Klea's growing skill with the whip brought a reaction from that dull piece of flesh. He'd strangled her as he reached climax, wringing at least that enjoyment out of her flaccid body.

He searched the vastness expanding before him, glittering fields of fire spread out through blackness—suns upon endless suns. The brighter lights he knew to be unimaginably distant galaxies. What sights did they contain? What forms of life lurked there to be discovered? What vistas would be worthy of his gaze?

Ngen flexed the stringy muscles of his chest and arms in an isometric as his frustration built. The galaxy spread before him—waiting. Greater wealth and glory than any man had ever brought under control. Yet, no matter how he succeeded, he couldn't own it all even if he psyched every man, woman, and child in space. He, Ngen Van Chow, wouldn't live long enough to bring all that vastness under his command! For the first time in his life, the horrible truth of futility wiggled its claws into his thoughts.

"I want it all . . . *all!*" He pounded a fist against the glassy surface of the wall. Stymied by distance, mortality, and human frailty, he couldn't possibly live that long.

And his son?

How many billion light-years across was the universe? How many worlds, species, battles, and dead lay between mankind and ultimate destiny? So very, very many! Too many even for his son to see.

"*I want it ALL!* I will not be stopped by Romanans and their false God! I will *be* God!" He raised his head to the glittering stars. "Do you hear me? I . . . will . . . be . . . God! I am the taker of men's souls! Hear me and bow before me! I am Ngen Van Chow! Lord Master of the universe! *I AM GOD!*"

His voice echoed in the empty confines of the observation room, only it sounded hollow—even to the ears of Ngen Van Chow. He turned, looking up at the now mocking stars.

"Very well," he agreed, reluctantly. "You will have me

as your master—or I will leave you and your Romanans nothing!'' The idea took form in his mind. "Yes, nothing! *You hear me? NOTHING!''*

Turning on his heel, he left the room to the stars and silence.

Damen Ree's personal quarters aboard *Bullet* in GEO orbit over World.

John Smith Iron Eyes padded down the long white corridor. His muscles had lost some of the tone, the spring which he'd always maintained. Where once he'd prided himself on clear thinking, being able to see the potentials and pitfalls, now things had turned into a muddle. His very understanding of the roles of God and man had just been shaken.

Patan, Patan, what happened? Spider, what does it mean when a Prophet can't see what will be? I'm lost for once, What's happened to our People—to our Prophets? What's happened to me? Day by day, I battle problems created by others instead of the enemy. Is this the way you left for me, Spider? Is this the purpose for which you molded me? Bear, am I doing right? Shouldn't I be out there someplace, laying traps for Ngen's ghouls instead of chasing bits of electronic data? Shouldn't I be helping Patan?

He stopped before a plain white hatch, staring down nervously at the pocket comm he carried.

"Damen?" he called out, looking at the pickup.

"Come in.''

Iron Eyes passed through the hatch as the heavy door slid sideways, passing through the main room, barely glancing up at the Spider effigy on the bull hide to walk into Ree's private quarters. Considering the power and influence of Damen Ree, his sleeping quarters didn't consist of much. A holo depicted sunrise on World. Another showed a young Damen Ree at graduation. The largest, the single image that dominated the room, consisted of a real time holo of *Bullet* in orbit. The last thing Ree saw at night, it was the first thing to meet his eyes when he woke.

Other than that, a set of fatigues hung next to a dress uniform. The combat armor waited, within reach, along with a well-used hand blaster and a large shoulder version—both of which were plugged into the chargers. Ree's battered coffee cup sat half-full of cold black viscous liquid on the tiny stand by his spare bed.

Damen, in underwear, sat up in the middle of his bed, eyes red, face puffy with sleep. Catching Iron Eyes' expression, Ree blinked, sitting up straighter. His voice grated like gravel. "What now? Or do I want to know? Ngen's just blown Arcturus out of space? Took more territory? It's trouble with the ship, some malfunction that—"

"Patan's failing. His latest prophecy . . ." Iron Eyes took a deep breath, grinding his teeth. "Damn, I didn't know this would be so hard." He swallowed and grabbed up Ree's cup, dumping the goo into the converter tube before sticking it into the dispenser.

"You know, when you're born Romanan, you come to have a reverence for Prophets. They're perfect in a way ordinary men just can't . . . I guess we never knew what a Prophet really was, Damen. How human they are despite the way Spider has laid for them. Patan . . . Patan's been getting worse—losing himself and missing predictions. He had a spell a couple of days ago. Some meeting with an archbishop on Arcturus where he said the Glendivian miners would repulse an attack by the Fathers. Well, it seems the miners there sided with Ngen. We don't know why, but they did. Van Chow is having a heyday with it."

Looking haggard, Ree took the coffee and sipped. "Star shine! Why? I thought that Prophets . . ." He looked up, meeting John's fear-bright eyes.

"Before I came up to see you, I took an AT down to visit with one of the Old Ones. They've been pretty reclusive, but they agreed to see me. Damen, they're not very happy about what Patan's doing. But at least they explained what's happening to him."

"And?"

"He's going crazy. The deeper he gets into the future, the more he tries to see across the cusps. It's like looking down too many trails at once, you forget where your feet are, or which path you were even following. The human mind, for all its power and intricacy, can't handle that. Patan's bright, sensitive—and he's dying, losing his sanity, falling so deep he doesn't know what's what anymore. Damen, I never thought I'd see this happen. We . . . *we can't trust him.*"

Ree dropped his chin to his chest, rubbing the back of his leathery neck with a thick hand. "Well, to be honest, he's lasted a lot longer than I thought. And we knew he'd goofed before. Just not to this degree."

"Spider guards free will."

"Damn free will! John, I'm tired of choosing. Let Spider do it for once! Why is it always us? Huh? Can't we strike a deal? We choose one day, Spider the next? How come we're the ones who . . . You don't look enthused. Don't think the old boy will go for it?"

"No."

Ree winced. "Well, it was just an attempt at humor. We don't find that much to laugh at anymore."

Iron Eyes nodded, flipping the pocket comm onto the tiny table with a clatter as he settled himself in a small chair. "You sleep any?"

"Tossed a lot. Where's Maya when I need her?" He frowned at that. "Damn, you know, I really miss her."

"We've got other problems, too. I had a bit of trouble with Devaulier. He tried to jump Billy Sanchez White Eagle. Sanchez was a little quicker on the comeback and broke a couple of ribs. The marine guard hauled him off before he carved the Colonel's coup off, but he left a nice cut on Claude's scalp. The Colonel's in med as we speak. Phil's got him under full observation."

Ree's facial expression reminded Iron Eyes of burped bile. "Crap! What am I going to do with them? We haven't exactly got much in the way of cooperation out of *Uhuru* or *Kamikazi*. I can't let Claude or Tabi or Amelia out of my sight. And we need to get the modifications made on those ships before Ngen hits Arcturus. We've just got to. Maybe, just maybe, it'll spell the difference in lives."

Iron Eyes settled himself across from Ree. "You know, it's like letting rock leeches loose in the corridors. You don't know when one's going to be clamping on to your leg, poisoning your blood."

"John? Am I being a sap? If I just jail them, what happens? We'll be fighting their crews for years. Maybe have the ships go pirate after we get Ngen. If I let them go, I can't turn my back on them.

"It's a goddamned trap! We can't whip Ngen unless we rebuild their ships. We rebuild their ships, and they can cut *Bullet* to ribbons to get even. And then there's Amelia. How goddamned far can I trust *her?* She's the trickiest of them all, the brightest, and the meanest. She doesn't do anything unless it has six or seven levels of complicity."

"I suppose now is a good time to tell you that a bunch of marines from *Kamikazi* tried to effect a rescue of Tabi.

Pedro Grita caught on and we got them all. They're in detention down on the planet, disarmed, with a bunch of warriors wandering around their pen, sharpening knives, telling bear stories, daring them to try and escape.''

"Great!"

"So we're trapped no matter what we do." Iron Eyes pulled at his braid again. "It's not a total loss. We've got Romanans aboard all three of the ships and more are on the way. That's worked before, eating away at Patrol morale, undercutting the backstabbing and intrigue."

For long moments, they sat, lost in thought.

"Patan blew it, huh?"

More silence. "You know, a lot can go wrong with the Arcturus operation. One of the Colonels could escape, get to a comm. Ngen might smell a trap. Patan might lose his mind and blurt it all out some night on the subspace net. Who in hell knows."

"You know the alternatives."

"Yeah, endless war. Raid after raid, each side blowing away the other's stations and worlds until nothing is left to fight over but wreckage and corpses. And Ngen's twisted enough to push it that far." Ree rubbed his face, digging fingers into his rheumy eyes. "God, what a way to lose it. Stuck between a madman and nothing."

"Spider isn't nothing."

"No, I didn't mean it that way. I was thinking of the alternatives. If we just ran, John, it would solve so much for us."

"But we can't." Iron Eyes winked reassuringly before he stretched, rippling the muscles of his arms. "You know that, Damen. Deep in your soul, you'd hate yourself forever."

"Arcturus, Arcturus, Arcturus! Star spit, it's all I think about anymore. That and the fact that no matter what, we're losing this."

"Looks pretty grim, doesn't it?"

"Admiral?" Comm interrupted.

"Here."

"Transduction from Major Sarsa on Arcturus."

Ree shot a worried glance at Iron Eyes. "Damn it, what's wrong now?" Then, to comm: "Run it."

Rita's face formed on the wall screen projector. "Admiral?"

"Rita, what's happening?"

She smiled crookedly. "Things that nervous there?" Then her voice dropped, "Hello, John? How are things?"

He grinned and winked. "Remember when you told Leeta you were going to capture *Bullet* way back when?"

"She said I was out of my raving lunatic mind or some such thing as I remember."

"We're getting there. Want some nasty Patrol Colonels?"

"Not on your life." Rita cocked her head. "Of course, if they could be whipped into bureaucrats, I just might after all. If I have to read another administrative report on rivet failure, I'll puke. Skor's taking all the advantage of me he can. I think he considers military occupation a vacation."

"What's the situation, Rita?" Ree returned to the subject.

She turned cool eyes his way. "Colonel? What would you give for a line to Ngen?"

Ree's lips moved, a flicker of hope in his eyes as he straightened on the bed. "You serious?"

Rita sobered. "What's wrong? There's something going on there that I don't know about?"

Iron Eyes nodded hesitantly. "There is. The strategic situation is getting pretty desperate. We know about Patan. How secure is this relay?"

She narrowed her eyes. "About like any from Arcturus. Not very. If you've got something, keep it under your hair. I can't guarantee this end."

"Rita," Ree raised his hands imploringly. "We're interested in any line on Ngen." He swallowed hard, eyes pinning hers. "A lot of lives might depend on it. I'll take any risk. Go for it. Whatever you do, if you can get a finger on Ngen, it's worth it."

She read his desperation. "Any risk, Admiral? I'll see what I can do."

"Rita," Ree added seriously. "Put your best people on this. I can't tell you what's at risk, just in case. But, believe me, I'd sell my soul for this one. Get me Ngen, and I'll pay any price."

"Any price?" She raised an eyebrow.

Directorate Section: Arcturus

"Look, I don't know what's cooking. Something big, and from the sounds of it, something extraordinarily dangerous."

Susan paced the room, oblivious to the thick carpets underfoot, the major export of Mamagonian and costly enough to bankrupt a royal treasury. "And you don't know anything about Alhar?"

Rita shrugged. "He's got an axe to grind with Ngen. I've considered all the options. If it's a plot of some sort, I can't figure the curve in it. Alhar made no conditions on who'd go with him. He just wants Ngen dead. That's all. I remember what you said about getting a small band of marines in. Maybe, just maybe, this is it. If you want, you've got your chance." Rita turned, gripping her by the shoulders, looking her in the eyes. "Susan, the decision is yours, but make damn sure you think it through. Remember the last time you took a small team into enemy territory? Remember what it cost you then? The risk is the same . . . no, greater than anything you faced on Sirius. This time, we've got no guaranteed rescue coming for you."

Susan closed her eyes, avoiding that deadly green stare. *"Pleasure, my dearest Susan. I have come to set you free. Let me show you the joys of your body. You will cry out for me, wish for my touch on your delightful flesh. You can't deny me, Susan. No man has ever filled you the way I have. No man can ever bring you such pleasure . . . pleasure . . . "*

"Damn you, Ngen!" She shivered and broke away from Sarsa's restraining arm. "I'll go, Major. I . . . I have to kill him. One way or another, I'm damned tired of living like this. I want it over, once and for all."

Rita studied her, head cocked, expression reserved. "Uh-huh. You know, it's not just you. You'll be taking Sam and the rest of your team with you. It's not just your life you'll throw away if Ngen—"

Susan whirled on her feet, leaning down to stare face to face with Rita. "Major, I'm goddamned aware of that. I'm not the gibbering, quivering meat Ngen left behind on Sirius. Oh, I don't lie. I'm not one hundred percent when I hear his voice. But I looked the bastard in the eye on Bazaar and blew his fucking face off the holo. No, I want a chance at him. That's all, and—by Spider—you promised me that once.''

''You'll use your head?''

Susan smiled grimly. ''I'll use my head. I paid the price for being stupid and angry and emotional on Sirius. No, I don't want to fall into Ngen's trap again. Maybe I'm more cautious about that because of what he did to me.''

''Okay, you've got it. Go for it.''

''And I want Darwin to go. He's got to. He found the key to Ngen's success last time on Bazaar. Maybe he'll find the key to undoing the Fathers this time.''

''You're taking him away from med, you know.''

Susan swallowed hard. She whispered hoarsely, ''I know. You said the Admiral said any price? I . . . I think Darwin and I . . . we, we're little enough. And if we can stop Ngen, expose a weakness, a vulnerability the Admiral and Iron Eyes can exploit? Well, I think I can speak for both of us when I say we'd pay that price.''

''What about Patan?''

Susan sighed, taking the time to finger the Cutlan scrollwork carved so painstakingly into the walnut cabinet. ''Rita, Patan's not only killing himself, he's killing Pike, too. I mean it. Darwin has some empathy with him. The deeper Patan falls, the more haggard Darwin gets. You've seen, you know. Order him out of here. Find him some fresh task to do that doesn't seem so horribly inevitable. Otherwise, Patan will lose himself—and Darwin will give up. Med or no med. You know the power of the human mind when it comes to a body as sick as his. You can will it either way.''

''And you're safe at night, huh?''

''*Damn you, Rita!* That was a cheap shot!''

''But one I want you to think about.'' Sarsa flipped a wealth of red curls over her shoulder. ''If you're going, I want you going with your eyes open. Sure, I'll sacrifice you and Pike. Damen said any price was worth it, but let's lay all the cards out, shall we? No crap here. When you go, you go knowing all about it—even the things you don't want to admit to yourself.''

''You're a real bitch, you know.''

''So are you. I guess we're even.''

Susan didn't flinch from those hot eyes. Finally, she admitted, ''Yes, I suppose I am.'' She walked across the room, letting the golden light filter down from the filigreed ceiling.

"No rescue this time. Well, if we can kill the bastard, it'll all work out, won't it?"

CHAPTER XXXVIII

Aboard *Gabriel* on the fringes of the Arcturian system.

Torkild Alhar watched the holo critically. The world depicted exploded into a violent flash, the rising mushroom cloud partly hidden from view by the curve of the planet. Currents of atmosphere, like rings on a pond, condensed whitely as they compressed in the shock waves. Then the entire atmosphere convulsed, streaming for the tortured vacuum left at the explosion site as matter and antimatter reacted. The whole planet shivered and rolled, tectonic forces unleashed as the axis, balance, and integrity of the world were rudely violated.

"Magnificent!" Torkild praised. "I must say, your University has excellent technicians."

"Yeah, well, considering what was left after Ngen's people blew up engineering during the raid, you're lucky to get that. I believe you now have a perfect alibi for your lack of communication with Ngen. We've just released the news of Radian's death through our subspace net. Radian, of course, has been apprised of the sham. They're satisfied to remain quiet and hidden so long as Ngen believes them dead. They're as safe that way as they would be with a battleship overhead." Rita's cool gaze rested on him.

In the silence, he studied her. Such an attractive woman, she'd have made a wondrous wife. Intelligent, capable, with such perfect features. Her nose blended into the curve of her brow, the green eyes challenging, proud, and powerful. The line of her jaw accented those wonderful lips, and that red hair sparkled with the light. Of course, she had to be a good ten years older than he, and, undoubtedly, like most Directorate sluts, she'd carelessly wasted her virginity on the first hard prick to come around. Still, she had presence to augment her beauty.

A crooked, humoring smile traced across Sarsa's lips, as if she could read his thoughts.

"I have your ship on scan," Torkild announced, breaking the awkward pause. "I expect rendezvous within ten hours."

"You realize the risks you're taking? Ngen's nobody's fool when it comes to—"

Torkild felt himself bristle. "Major, when a man has no honor, he does not deserve to live. Ngen Van Chow has degraded my sister. He processed my people into mindless pigs! He killed my family and my family's honor! If I die taking him to destruction, I die well." *Take that, you icy beauty! I may be young, but you'll know you deal with an Alhar!*

"You know about his chamber of horrors?" she asked to Torkild's bafflement. "If I know Ngen, he has a room somewhere on that ship full of captive women. You might take the time to find it and see how he might have," she blushed slightly, "amused your sister."

"He wouldn't dare. M'Klea is the . . ." *What? What is she? What kind of plaything did Ngen make of her? And how does this angelic looking Major know of such . . . The Patrol is different. Without morality. M'Klea, M'Klea. . . .* Torkild felt his guts tighten. "I will investigate. I promise you that."

For long moments, he struggled with the thought. M'Klea in Ngen's hands. Well, alas for fantasies, no woman who'd mention such sexual depravities could possibly be worth an Alhar's serious attention. And the Major would have been such a superb mother, wife, and adornment otherwise.

"One last thing." Major Sarsa seemed reluctant to talk. "Yes, Major?"

She looked as if she'd come to a decision. "Be careful with Captain Andojar and Doctor Pike. They both spent time as Ngen's captives before they escaped. I don't know how much they'll tell you about themselves—but that's *their* business. If I could give you a word of advice as one commander to another, don't pressure them. They have enough nightmares about Van Chow as it is."

"After having reviewed the information, I can understand," Torkild bowed slightly, to indicate his respect and ability to honor her wishes. *What secrets are theirs? What do they know of Van Chow? Better yet, how do I find out and use it to my advantage? Oh, I'll honor your advice, Major, but I'll keep my ears open.*

"Major," he asked suddenly. "Why did we have to wait

for that fast transport?'' He'd hoped to catch her off balance.

''The ship carried a special passenger who requested to accompany you. You'll find out who soon enough. Suffice it to say your mission is considerably strenghtened as a result. Among our people, we don't question his kind. They go where they will and do what they want. I think you'll find him interesting.''

''Thank you, Major, for your cooperation and help. I send you the best regards of the House of Alhar. I shall be in touch if I have any other questions.''

''Captain, we all wish you the best of luck. No matter how this turns out, I salute you.''

He sat and pondered the changes in his destiny long after the screen had gone blank. A strange passenger? Straight from World? He turned to comm, computing the acceleration, jump, and deceleration. No, this mysterious passenger couldn't have known. He had to have been in transit long before Torkild had even thought of contacting Sarsa.

''But if this is a trick, my dear Major . . .''

Aboard *Spider's Revenge* matching V with *Gabriel*.

As they neared the Fathers' converted ship, an uneasy feeling grew deep in Darwin's gut. He shot a quick, uncertain glance at Susan. The shape of Torkild's *Gabriel* had expanded from a tiny dot of light to loom out of the star field.

Everything happened so quickly. Rita had sent the order for him to pack and meet the FT. Desperately, he'd taken a final reading on Patan's condition, fearful as he looked down on those fragile features, seeing the Prophet's eyes wiggling in REM sleep. Damn it all, he'd grown so pale, so thin.

And I had to go? Damn, who's going to keep him alive? Don't they understand? Can't they see what he's giving up? No one should have to sacrifice so much when all of humanity remains so callous.

And now the Fathers' ship filled the screens. What madness was this? A wild plot to get close to Ngen? Maybe assassinate him? Of all the crazy . . . And Susan would be placing herself within Ngen's foul grasp again. What if it was a double cross, some insane scheme of Ngen's to . . . No, don't even think it!

Darwin swallowed and moved over next to Susan, letting his eyes range up and down her trim, muscular body. Patan?

Susan? Wasn't there something he could do to save them both? The futility of it rose within him. *Damn, Spider, where's the point to all this? Me? Worthy? Hell, no! I'm only a simple man in the middle of insanity. Just let my people live and do with me what you will!*

But I've got to try, he told himself as he gazed at Susan's perfect face. Like a master sculptor, he absorbed the slight hollow of her flawless cheeks, worshiped the lines of her brow and nose. Suffered the memory of her smooth soft hair in his fingers, dazzled by the richness of it all. Damn it, she was too precious to risk.

"I'm having a change of heart," he said, voice low. "I don't suppose I could talk you into staying with Rita and letting me go on."

She looked at him, surprised. "What are you talking about?"

He shrugged, a little finger of fear tracing his spine. How did he tell her? "Listen, this is going to sound hokey, but I . . . I love you. I'm trying to make my mind understand that you're a soldier—a Romanan warrior. All I see is the woman I love. Look, don't go. Stay here, let me take the risks. If you . . . If anything happened, I . . . I . . ." He felt queasy inside, and fumbling didn't make it any easier.

She started blinking and he realized she fought tears. He pulled her close, hugging her gently to him. Reveling in the familiar warmth of her firm body against his. Damn it, she was so precious, so incredibly precious. Her arms circled around him, her bear hug almost driving the air out of his lungs.

"Thanks." She pulled away and jabbed his ribs. "Is that your male organs talking again?" Her lips smiled a little crookedly.

"I wish," he muttered, thinking of how he had lain next to her, night after night, and hoped, so fervently. There had been moments, but each time he'd felt his body respond, Ngen had whispered in his ear and an unbidden part of his mind showed him the ghoul so remarkably like Susan. Always, at that moment, desire fled, broken, to leave him limp and shivering.

"Have you ever heard Dvorak's *Carnival Overture?*" A soft voice asked at Darwin's shoulder.

He spun, suddenly angry that anyone would dare sneak close while he was having an intimate conversation with Susan. He clamped the harsh words in his throat.

''No, Prophet, I haven't.'' He knew his voice was sharp.

''You should. It is delightful music. There is a vigor in Dvorak that stirs the soul, whips it up, and whirls it around. Magnificent.'' He drew air into his lungs and walked off, humming what Darwin assumed was the music.

Susan convulsed with laughter. By some artful magic, he, too, was suddenly infected with the humor of the situation.

''Such an odd man. You think he did that on purpose?'' She winked at him. ''Be sure of it.''

Darwin released her, grinned at the new spark in her eyes, then started checking his combat armor.

Susan held his gaze for one last moment, a softness shining there he'd never seen before. Then she bent, lacing armor tightly to her muscular legs. She lifted the thick hair hanging loose about her head and shoulders, flying fingers weaving it into a glossy braid.

''Maybe Chester was telling us that our worries are trite compared to what the universe faces. That or he truly believes we should spend more time listening to music.'' She cocked her head, frowning. ''You know, when you get right down to it, I can't think of anything better at the moment than sitting up in the Bear Mountains with a warm fire, listening to music.''

''Uh-huh,'' Darwin grunted.

Then they stood, waiting, as the converted GCI grew in the monitors. The thought that the fresh blisters on the side held Sirian blasters, was sobering. And, of course, those mighty guns were powered up, primed to release their deadly energy on the poorly shielded FT should Alhar see the slightest impropriety.

The FT slid alongside the streaked hull of *Gabriel,* the ship that had blasted the Patrol ship of the Line *Ganges* to plasma.

''Thirty seconds, people,'' Moshe called from the bridge. ''Everything looks right.''

''Form up on me,'' Susan called, taking her place at the hatch.

Darwin's heart hammered as he crouched behind a long blaster. Through his booted feet, he felt the slight tremor as the ships matched and the locks sought each other. Metal clanged and clunked hollowly. Gauges registered and the hatch slid open to a puff of condensing atmosphere.

Two stiff-backed officers stepped through and stopped.

Susan stood and saluted. They returned it, to Darwin's eyes almost dripping with ceremony. He studied them, the first Arpeggians he'd ever seen. They wore finely tailored cobalt blue dress uniforms with golden wire sewn on the stiff shoulder boards and down the long tapered sleeves. One dark skinned, one light, each kept one hand on a holstered blaster, clicking their heels as they waited.

"Compliments of the Captain," one said. "We are your escort."

Susan bowed. "Excuse your welcome, gentlemen. Not that we doubted your word to honor truce, but we have dealt with Ngen Van Chow before."

"The Captain said to expect as much, ma'am. If you will follow us?" He turned smartly on his heel and returned to the Arpeggian ship. Warily, they advanced, Darwin getting a shot of vertigo from conflicting gravity fields. The inside *Gabriel* could have been the inside of *Spider's Treasure* or any other converted GCI. Manufacturing diversity hadn't been a Directorate strong point. One model serves all.

The Arpeggians they passed looked nervous, shifting from foot to foot, hands locked behind them.

Gabriel had a metallic odor mingled with the scent of human sweat. She'd packed a host of human bodies for a long spacing. Nevertheless, she looked tight, clean, maintained to perfection. Throughout, *Gabriel* smacked of a sharp crew and good discipline.

They met Captain Torkild Alhar in what had once been a cargo bay. Now the huge room held tables, carpeting, and crash webbing. It had been turned into an impromptu banquet hall. Alhar, in a gaudy uniform—cobalt blue with white trimming, lots of glittery gold, and jewels sparkling in the lights—stood at attention like a young god, face grave.

"Captain Susan Smith Andojar?"

Susan nodded, sizing him up. "Captain Torkild Alhar. My pleasure."

Alhar stared into her eyes for a long moment, attitude changing imperceptibly. "Indeed, I think not. I do believe the pleasure is all mine, lady." Bending at the waist, he kissed her hand, eyes dancing with sudden interest as he literally drank in her beauty.

Darwin growled under his breath, jaws tightening. He pushed forward. "Darwin Pike, Captain. My pleasure to be aboard." He caught Torkild's hand with his own, matching the steel grip.

The smile he got in return had to be forced past bloodless lips. "My pleasure, Doctor."

Susan interrupted from the side, sensing the tension. "Captain, I'll inform my pilot that everything is according to form. We'll begin off-loading supplies if that meets your approval."

"Most welcome, Captain." He bowed curtly, snapping his heels together.

Pike took the moment to study their new ally. Torkild looked the part of a descendant of the Arpeggian pirates. Perfect features made him coldly handsome, in some ways a dashing figure. From the expression on Alhar's face, Pike couldn't escape the conclusion that Torkild was no stranger to admiration. In the meantime, the war party chiefs crowded up, fighting knives gleaming and clattering on their armor, coups hanging in silky waves from belts or vests, raptorian eyes hard on the Arpeggian Captain.

"Quite a fellow," Darwin said under his breath. "Almost like an anachronism from Earth's past."

Susan slipped him a knowing look. "I take it you don't like him?"

Darwin shrugged, feeling foolish. "We've been shooting at him—remember?"

"Ngen took his sister—remember. There's Arpeggian honor at stake here. The old families are pretty taken with it. I guess it made them feel superior to their origins." Susan looked at him, suggestion in her eyes.

Torkild managed to pull himself away from the warriors by introducing his officers. He bowed slightly. "I hope our warriors will mingle without friction." He locked cold eyes on Susan, stepping close to her side.

"My men have been given orders regarding knife feud. They'll be as polite as they can, Captain." She hesitated. "I understand the concept of Arpeggian honor. At the same time, please keep in mind that my warriors have an honor system all their own. They'll cause no trouble unless pushed."

"Ah," Torkild nodded agreeably. "If you would, Captain, please accompany me to my cabin and we shall discuss our situation." Gallantly, he offered his arm.

Darwin forced himself to breathe easily. *Don't push it. What the hell's the matter with me? Of course he's trying to exclude me. I'm just the dingbat anthropologist. Sure he's turned on by Susan. What man with normal hormones wouldn't be? Susan can take care of herself. He couldn't lay a finger on her without . . . All right! Admit it! You're jealous! And he's a pompous stuck-up martinet son of a bitch!*

To his relief, Susan turned to him. "If you would, Doctor, I think we could use your expertise, too."

Darwin nodded easily. "My pleasure, Captain." The partially hidden disappointment in Torkild's eyes shot gleeful laughter through his thoughts.

The Captain's quarters could be called Spartan at best. Torkild opened a cut crystal decanter of unknown age and incalculable value. "May I offer some Arpeggian brandy? Given the present nature of things, it's probably the last the galaxy will ever see."

"Nice bottle," Darwin noted. "Looks like it might even be Earth manufacture. Possibly Russian, twenty-first century, if I'm any judge."

"Really?" Torkild handed the bottle over.

Darwin lifted it carefully and studied the bottom. "Waterford!" he breathed. "Made in Ireland for the Premier of the Supreme World Soviet!" He lowered it with a sudden reverence, tracing the cut crystal with admiring fingers.

"There were many treasures like that on my world. My father gave it to me years ago." He waved it off, "I'd never studied the markings. They made no sense to me."

Darwin carefully replaced the decanter and sighed. The priceless treasure probably dated to the same period as his Randall. If only glass could talk, what stories could that priceless vessel tell of worlds and blood and death and pirates? What list of prominent men and woman had run their fingers over that scintillating glass?

"Enough of trinkets," Alhar said shortly. "To victory!" He raised his glass and bowed to Susan.

They drank and Darwin had to admit, the brandy was good.

"How do we get close to Ngen?" Susan asked, getting to the point. "Can you land us on *Gregory?*"

Torkild seated himself in one of the gravchairs and leaned back, face suddenly wooden. "I'd blow him out of space myself were this ship powerful enough. My duty is to kill him. Honor demands it. I believe I can get your people and my crew aboard. At that point, you will create a diversion and allow me and my picked men to kill Ngen Van Chow. I'll depend on you to take the ship for me."

Darwin tensed, waiting for Susan to gut Torkild, the grinding of his molars loud in his ears. The man was a bumbling fool! He expected the Romanans to take the ship for him? He wanted Ngen all to himself?

Even more surprising, Susan nodded in agreement. Darwin quickly bent down to study the decanter, hiding his incredulous expression.

"I think we can do that," Susan agreed, undertones in her voice. "My people have a great deal of expertise with Patrol Line ships. *Gregory* won't be the first we've taken."

Darwin caught Torkild's smile of satisfaction. "Excellent! To the Romanans!" he toasted and they tossed down another draft of the last Arpeggian brandy.

"How do you propose to get us to the *Gregory?*"

Torkild waved it away. "My sister believes I'm still a loyal minion of this bastard Ngen. I'll ask to pay my respects, to offer her my brotherly benediction."

"Will she believe you?" Darwin couldn't help but ask.

Suddenly Darwin faced the defiant glare of a dominant male in the presence of a beautiful woman. The thought of it amused him, angered him, and left him annoyed with the pettiness of it all. After Ngen, and the horror in Patan's eyes, and the walking dead on Bazaar, nothing this martinet did could seem threatening.

"She will believe me. I will satisfy her of my responsibility to family." He laughed at the irony, but his eyes remained coldly on Darwin's.

Pike nodded inoffensively, reserving judgment. His jittery nerves grated, getting worse. Torkild might have been smart enough to have killed *Ganges* with that torpedo, but his cloak and dagger ability seemed slight at best. Ngen would smile, as he listened, nodding seriously, as if he hung on every word—and cut Torkild's throat the second he looked away.

Susan smiled wickedly. "Just so we're straight on that, Captain. I would consider it a matter of honor that you did not allow a slip. I've taken responsibility for my people. I promised them coup and loot in return for silence and obedience. I think an Arpeggian could understand my responsibilities."

Torkild's eyes narrowed as he studied her. "You would have done justice as a queen of my people, Captain Andojar."

Darwin forced himself to relax, as those hawklike eyes

begin to appraise Susan again. It became a challenge to control his building dislike.

Comm buzzed. The GCI was not, after all, a Patrol ship. Things like comm remained primitively inadequate.

A thin-faced man formed on the screen. "I think we have a spy, Captain."

"Bring him here," Torkild looked curiously at Susan as the comm snapped off. "A spy, Captain?" He tilted his head. "Less than twenty minutes aboard my ship and I have a spy? Would you care to address that?"

Susan crossed her arms, feet apart, eyes smoldering. "I brought no spies." Her voice held contempt.

Darwin began to tense, he'd already picked his first target on Torkild's body. After days of stomping around on the prosthesis, his leg muscles were fit. The combat reflexes dropped neatly into place. He barely acknowledged the realization that he'd changed. This time there would be no hesitation. He'd kill quickly, efficiently.

The hatch slid open and two burly guards almost carried a medium-sized man into the room. Susan smiled to herself and Darwin shook his head at the incongruous sight. He hoped none of the Romanan warriors had seen it. Of course, there'd be a raging battle in the halls right now if they had.

The Prophet looked up at the grim Arpeggians who held him. When they let go, Chester walked forward and studied the decanter, oblivious to them all. In the silence of the room his slight noises of appreciation seemed loud.

"Who are you?" Torkild asked, seeing the changed expressions and becoming wary.

The Prophet let his fingers run over the glass, feeling the texture of the cut crystal. "So very beautiful." He looked up, a light of enjoyment in his eyes. "Beauty like this must bring you hours of satisfaction. Beauty is such a necessary part of our lives. Without it, our souls would wilt; a part of us would shrivel and darken."

"I asked your name!" Torkild reminded, icy eyes unforgiving.

"Allow me . . ." Susan began only to have Chester raise a thin hand, his loose sleeve dropping to expose the pale skin of his forearm.

"I may be disturbing to you, Susan, but please. I have my own vocal chords and am quite capable of using them." The moonfaced man smiled at her as she lowered her eyes to avoid his gaze. He turned then, inspecting Torkild. "Yes, I see."

"See what?" Torkild demanded, pulling himself to his full height, hand on blaster.

"I have just been wondering about you." The Romanan almost shrugged. "And, yes, I will answer your questions. First, I am Chester Armijo Garcia. I was not spying since, as you will learn, I have no need to spy. I can already tell you that the twenty armed men behind bulkhead seventeen are unnecessary. There will be no violence—and there is no Romanan treachery."

Torkild paled. Darwin started to his feet. Susan's grim look of satisfaction spoke volumes. Oblivious, Chester continued, "I am here because I wish to see the outcome of our venture in person. It is the only way I may be allowed to talk with Ngen Van Chow face to face. Several cusps are pending to allow this, of course. At the same time, you, young man are very much in need of teaching as is your entire crew. The decision is yours. I am not here to deny your free will, but if you choose to learn, I will teach." Chester, smiled, nodded with a bob of his head, and returned his admiring gaze to the decanter.

Torkild, fighting for equilibrium, shot a nervous glance at Susan. "This is the one of whom Major Sarsa spoke?" His darting eyes betrayed a deep-seated confusion at work.

"This, Captain, is one of the infamous Prophets," Darwin said, brimming with satisfaction. "Beware, they have a habit of changing your life."

Chester, humming under his breath, waved Pike's warning away. "Spider brought you into His web all on His own, Doctor. There is nothing to be done against a man's cusps." He smiled. "I am not so courageous as Patan. I am much more simple and, I must admit, unheroic."

"Skor Robinson wouldn't think so," Darwin muttered.

Chester frowned. "He has learned a great deal about life, and himself, Doctor. I do hope the cusps will allow us to talk again one of these days. For the moment, Skor is engaged in a very special fight of his own, learning to live with only himself. When Torkild's attack on Arcturus nearly destroyed the hope of the galaxy, the Director called the Admiral. That was a major cusp. By his action, the Director saved thousands of souls and millions of cusps for the edification of Spider. Now, I wonder what cusps must be filled to keep that edification?'' Chester raised an eyebrow, voice dropping pointedly. "Any ideas, Doctor?"

Darwin swallowed hard, fingers of fear tightening in his guts. "No, Old One, I have no idea about the cusps. Nor do I wish to know." Darwin filled his lungs, all his bravado fled. To rein in his racing fear, he reached for the brandy, pouring his glass full. Damn it, he'd seen too much of the future through Patan's eyes.

Chester looked up at Torkild mildly. "In answer to your next question, Captain, I am not babbling nonsense. I was teaching the good Doctor."

"And I learned, Prophet," Darwin whispered reverently.

Torkild opened his mouth and sputtered.

"No," Chester shook his head, smiling serenely. "I do not read minds."

Torkild's mouth worked, like a fish gasping in air.

"Yes," Chester assured him. "I am purposely answering your questions before you ask. It saves time in the end . . . and your mother's sister married a rice merchant named Fillona." As an afterthought Chester added, "There are three children in her family and they live on Too Far Station at the edge of the Sirian Reaches."

Torkild stood, stock-still, a sheen of sweat on his features, completely undone. Chester smiled at the two Arpeggian guards. "You may see me at your leisure and I would be happy to tell you why I can do this. Your Captain no longer has need of you here. You have time to make the banquet before the 'Dirty Romanans' eat all the food." Chester's eyes twinkled with amusement.

The Arpeggians looked as if they'd swallowed raw fish as they glanced in horror at Torkild. The Captain, still pale, waved them out.

Chester eased himself into one of the chairs and looked up at Darwin. "The Captain has the ability to fool his sister. The key here, is the word 'ability.' He must learn something of himself first. The decision to do so, of course, is his. He must first ask himself the question of motives; however, until he does, he has no knowledge of himself or his potentials. Until then he is like a rubber ball rolling on the deck of a boat, bouncing off this and that as the deck pitches."

Susan shot a nervous glance at the Arpeggian.

Torkild sat down, shaken. "Motives?"

"But of course," Chester agreed, "although you yourself have no idea of the reasons for your actions."

"Honor!"

"Honor?" Chester asked, a warm smile on his face. "What is that exactly? Define it for me and tell me where and how your honor leads you. You need time, Torkild. Currently, you are reacting emotionally. Do not believe that emotion is undesireable. Rather, it is a weapon which—when properly used—can bring you the greatest of achievements. When allowed to flash rampantly, Captain Alhar, you can quite inadvertently cut your own head off with it."

Alhar studied Chester with disbelief. "I could have your head for talking to me that way."

"And have your own private war to the last man," Susan gritted. "This is a *Prophet!*" She thrust a pointing finger, eyes flashing. Darwin braced himself, one hand gripped on the Randall.

Chester slowly raised his hands, drawing everyone's attention to his beaming face. "There is no need for all this. You must all come to understand that hostility, anger, and threats will not bring you to your goal." Chester looked around easily, humming a few bars of John Williams' *Olympic Fanfare*.

Satisfied, he nodded. "You still look at yourselves as enemies. The cusp is yours. Will you be so? All it takes is one negative vote by the people in this room and you will have made a cusp. Another future will be mine to see. If you vote to work together, however, I will have much to teach you."

Susan dropped to her knees, eyes lowered respectfully. "Prophet, I will learn what you have to teach me. I will vote for peace and trust."

Darwin nodded, looking Chester in the eyes. "Ngen is the worst threat." Chester smiled blandly at him. All eyes turned to Torkild.

The Captain ran nervous fingers over his blaster handle. In the end, he raised his hands in supplication. "I'm at a loss. I don't understand you people. What do you do? Play games? Is that it? You're playing with me? Some sort of test?" His blue eyes searched for an answer, driven by his sudden confusion.

Chester motioned impassively. "We do not play, Captain Alhar. At least, not at this moment. A game is a wonderful teaching device for building understanding and knowledge about the way we live. Simply stated, at this moment you must choose your future and the futures of several billion people. Do you choose to remain as you are now, or become someone different? Do you wish the galaxy to be ruled by Ngen Van Chow, your sister, and her children, or by men who desire to rule themselves? You must be willing to question yourself and your motives. Why are you trying so desperately to punish yourself for the destruction of Arpeggio? And why do you feel so guilty over a choice your sister made of her own free will? Why do you fear what you may learn about yourself?''

For a brief moment, a battle raged within Torkild's confused mind. Darwin's fingers tightened on his knife. Susan waited, one leg shifted to allow her to kick suddenly and viciously.

Torkild's eyes never wavered from Chester's. "Have you no fear for your life, Prophet?"

"My life matters not, Torkild Alhar. Depending on the cusps, I might die within seconds, hours, days, months, or years. I can see each of my deaths. Some are pleasant, some are not." He shrugged, "The end result is the same, my soul goes back to Spider."

Torkild smiled unevenly.

Chester sighed. "I see your decision."

Susan relaxed from her spring-steel posture.

Torkild's skeptical voice mocked. "Teach me, Prophet."

CHAPTER XXXIX

Damen Ree's personal quarters aboard *Bullet* in GEO orbit over World.

It had become too much of a commonplace occurrence. Damen Ree heard the comm paging him, banishing the dwindling fragments of his scattered dreams. He fought to open his eyes and shake the groggy fuzz from his mind.

"Yeah," he grumbled, voice echoing his irritation. "What is it?" He sat up in bed, the lights going up as Rita Arsa's worried face formed on the comm. Behind her stretched a lush room, filled with thick carpet, real wood-

paneled walls decorated with carving and ornamentation,
polished brass and expensive antique furniture. The effect
struck a chord of old Earth decadence.

"Admiral," she greeted. "I'm sorry to bother you, but
this is important. It's about—"

"It's *always* important," Ree muttered dryly. Then the
screen widened as resolution refined and Patan Andoja
Garcia's scarecrow body appeared, loosely propped in an
overstuffed grav chair.

Ree winced at the tortured horror in the Prophet's face.
Waxy yellow skin hung from the bones of his cheeks, forehead stretched shiny tight. Below the sagging claylike flesh,
the skull lurked in the sunken remains. Lips pulled taut over
dry teeth. Only the eyes burned, eerie, crazy-bright. The
death's head betrayed itself in the Prophet's ghastly rictus.
Patan's horrified features contorted—as if he struggled to
focus on Ree's face.

The words came with effort, rasping from deep within,
labored. "You must have your warships . . . ringing the Gas
Cloud Colonies within eighty days, Standard," Patan managed, reality fading from his eyes. Facial muscles jerked
spasmodically, uncontrolled. Sweat beaded and trickled
down febrile grainy skin as he fought to retain consciousness. He blinked owlishly, a bright glaze of fear in his eyes.
"Ngen . . . Ngen Van Chow will make a full-scale attempt
to capture the Gas Cloud Colonies' fiber, graphite, and molecular string industries. His fleet . . . they will never be
grouped like this again. It is your last chance . . . to stop
the Fathers."

Patan's eyes wavered as he reached out with trembling
hands of desiccated bone and tendon. Taloned fingers curled
darkly. "H . . . Hear me! The Fist . . . C-Cobalt Station
must . . ." He frowned, losing the thread of his thoughts.
"Must . . . Must be . . . Destroyed. Outright. Outright de-
stroyed. Destroy . . ." He swallowed dryly, lips working.
"As . . . as you begin the operations. First . . . first target.
First . . . Your success . . . success hinges on that. Blast
. . . Blast it immediately upon closing . . . with Ngen's . .
Ngen's . . ."

Patan weaved back and forth, head lolling on his thin
sweat-damp neck, as if the muscles had failed him. "I think
. . . I think you'll . . ."

"Eighty days?" Ree mumbled, heart leaping. "That

arely time to scramble! Barely time to get there! We don't ave all the modifications made to the Patrol line ships yet!''

Suddenly, Patan's eyes cleared; his body stiffened as if he orced backbone into his rubberlike spine. "Listen to me. Earth time will provide a known reference . . . by . . . by which to coordinate your actions. Attack at . . . yes, at exactly 2:30 a.m. The relative date will be June seventh on the Earth calendar. Greenwich time . . . You can . . . can destroy . . . entire fleet. Most of . . . mobile army if . . . Attack . . . eighty days . . . 2:30 Earth time. Blast Cobalt . . the Fist . . . the Fist . . . You have . . .'' Patan's eyes ost focus, going glassy. For several seconds, his mouth worked silently. "You have. . . .'' Lips froze in horror, teeth beginning to chatter as his body trembled and he collapsed, eyes vacant, muscles slack, to the floor.

"Patan!" Rita cried, grabbing him by the shoulders and shaking him. "Wake up! Come out of it.'' She slapped him hard across the cheeks. Frantic, she became more violent.

The eyes had lost their luster.

"Major,'' Ree called softly, a poignant understanding taining his soul. She turned. "I think it's no use. He's gone . . lost in the future.''

"What do I do?''

"Has he ever been this bad before? Gone so thoroughly?''

"I . . . Pike always . . . Let me check the records and run a scan on him.''

Ree rubbed a hand over his face as he waited, watching Rita's frantic efforts.

"Not like this,'' she whispered. "His brain scan's never been anything like this. The med comm can't even analyze it.'' Anxiously, she stared up at him. From where he sat, he could see the pulse racing under the pale skin of her neck. "Damen? I'm scared. This . . . this looks . . .''

Ree filled his lungs, swallowing. "You know what he just did, don't you? He just biased a million cusps. The ramifications . . . He said I'd know when he went.'' Damen winced, a stinging lance of regret twisting in his soul. "A million cusps. He's gone over, Rita. He made me promise. We owe him this much. He may have just saved the galaxy. Kill him. Don't question, just do it.'' Ree's voice had gone toneless.

"Admiral!" Rita protested. "This is a Prophet! I . . .''

Ree thundered. *"Kill him, damn it!"* He met her frightened eyes. *"Think*, Rita! We can keep him alive artificially for another forty years. Do you want him to fall into the future for that long? I gave you a direct order. Kill him, now. Humanely!"￼ Ree rose half out of bed, a knotted fist emphasizing his words.

Rita swallowed and nodded. She gave Patan Andojar Garcia one last look, seeing the lost expression, the gaping jaws with drool beginning to run from the corners of his flaccid lips.

"Dear Spider, forgive me!"

Her punch was perfect.

From where he knelt in his bed, Damen heard the snap of cervical vertebra. He sighed out his anxiety and rubbed the back of his neck, aware of the blinding tension headache building back of his eyes. The Prophet was gone. How long until they could really understand his legacy?

Or had he been gone already? Was the prophecy nothing more than the lunatic ravings of a man who couldn't realize reality anymore?

Rita stared, mouth open, chest heaving.

"Major, what do you . . . Major! Weep later, damn it. When we can afford it. Just now, I need your advice."

She tore her gaze from the pitiful pile of wasted flesh and bone on the floor of her quarters. She glared wildly at Ree, ghost pale, red hair frayed, fists clenched at her sides, balanced to strike out as her nostrils flared with each breath. How long since he'd seen her that frightened, that uncertain? Ree experienced a queasy lightness in his stomach. They were all out of control, on the very edge.

"Admiral?" She blinked, face blanching until the freckles stood out whitely.

"Rita, tell me. You've been around him. What do you think? How many calls has he missed lately? The Glendivian thing? How many more?"

She licked her lips, breathing hard, propping herself against the thickly upholstered divan, a haggard look in her eyes. She shook her head, running anxious fingers through the loose strands of hair. "I don't know. We've quit broadcasting most of the visions. Too . . . Too many, Damen. He's been running about fifty-fifty. Maybe a little less this last week since Pike left. I . . . I don't know, I've been tied up in all the foolish paper trails it takes to run this place."

"Fifty-fifty at best?" Ree clamped his eyes shut, wishing he could lose himself in the peace of dreams.

"Rita?" he gasped. "What do I do? What if I scramble the fleet and Ngen's not in the Gas Clouds? What have I got? The word of a half-mad Prophet? In eighty days . . . Oh, blessed Spider." He sagged, staring at nothing, heart thudding in his chest. "No way to wait to see what Susan and Pike . . . The last chance to stop the Fathers, Patan said." A numbness settled on him. "But Rita, did you hear him? There at the end? Did he sound sane to you? Did that sound like a man with any grasp of reality?"

Pain-dull eyes stared into his. Flushing with guilt she didn't want to admit, she slowly, painfully, shook her head—an anguished betrayal of faith.

"Less than fifty percent." Ree dropped his head into a hardened palm. "Less than . . ."

"Damen?" Rita's red-rimmed eyes bored into his own. "There are no guarantees. Remember Leeta? Philip? Friday? All the rest? We could all end up like that. No guarantees."

He nodded, the hollow place inside expanding. "I . . ."

The last chance to stop the Fathers? And all the machinations of Devaulier, Mikasu, Ngurnguru, and all the rest? And how long do we wait? If . . . IF the Prophet had one last lucid moment, could this save Arcturus? Or would that trap even have worked in the first place? WHAT DO I DO?

"Comm!" Ree ordered, coming to a sudden decision. "Scramble everything we've got that'll space. All ground leave canceled. Emergency condition! Any further technical modifications are to be conducted during transit. Contact Maya and Toby, we'll rendezvous at the Gas Cloud Colonies in exactly eighty days. We'll coordinate on the way."

Ree could hear comm calling *Bullet* to alert. He looked up at Rita's somber eyes, realized he lay completely exposed, and pulled a sheet over himself. She didn't seem to have noticed in her dazed condition.

"Damen, are you sure?"

"I just followed my intuition. I, well, what else was there, Rita? In the end, what else do any of us have? It's the best call I can make. And who knows how the cusps will work. Like you said, no guarantees—not even with a mad Prophet. Spider preserve us."

She gripped the divan, fingers sinking to dimple the fabric as she stared at the lifeless pile of meat at her feet. "Patan . . poor Patan."

"Major," he said easily, "it had to be done. He told me

it would be this way. He said he'd warn me at the last minute, when as many cusps had been decided as possible. Patan knew how close it would be. He just didn't know about the mistakes. How powerfully the future would draw him. I told him I wouldn't let him go on forever in the future. He feared that.''

''Spider's blood, Damen. Let's hope he was right. If he wasn't . . .''

Ree rubbed his hands nervously along his muscled arms, shivering slightly. He hunched on the bed, an awed expression on his face. ''Right, wrong, he did the best he could. Look what he did to himself. Maybe that's why I chose. Because I had to. For him. Spider take him, he was the bravest man I ever knew.''

''I'll send out the news that the Prophet is dead.'' Rita straightened. ''That might stir up some resistance for us. He told them all when he . . . he died, it would be a signal, that people would take freedom in their own hands.''

''Right.'' Ree agreed. ''You might as well meet us at the Gas Cloud Colonies. I guess it's make it or break it. If we lose there, I don't suppose it will make much difference what's protected and what isn't.'' His face was sour. ''Huh! Two hours ago, I'd have killed to keep from having to use Arcturus for bait. Now I'm scared gutless that I've just made the biggest mistake in my whole career.''

''The Gas Cloud Colonies. We'll have our people ready. I'll come roaring in with bells on at 2:30, June 7, Earth time.'' She looked up. ''Damen. What if . . . if . . .'' She stopped, chewing nervously on her lower lip. ''Never mind.''

The comm went dead.

Riballus Station: Moscow Sector.

Like so many major stations, Riballus began as a conglomeration of mining colonies at the edge of the Rockpile, an accumulation of stellar matter pumped out of the highly dissipated Fallen Angel supernova remnants located in various places about Directorate space. Established early in the Confederate era, Riballus for many years was noted for its educational facilities and deep-space structural engineers. Subsequent to the initiation of the Directorate, Riballus faded into obscurity.

Thyakild Mourton, First Speaker of Riballus Station watched the solemn procession as the body of the Prophet was entombed in acres of concrete on far off Arcturus. He sat stunned. The Prophet had died just as he had predicted.

Mourton shook his head. The depth of his words, the messages of hope—that man's soul and God were one—had touched him, spurred him to meet each day with renewed vigor, despite the occupation. So many of the Prophet's predictions had come true—all of them he knew of, in fact. Thyakild ran his tongue over the polished surfaces of his teeth as he walked slowly up from the latrines.

He stopped at the gate and looked out at the occupation force of Fathers who had taken half of his people and locked them away in these lower levels of Riballus Station. From where he stood, he could see a spider roughly sketched on the wall. The Prophet had taught them of Spider.

Mourton walked passed a hatch which no longer operated automatically. He looked up and down the long corridors and continued past the comm spy monitors. No one suspected they had an illegal receiver in the latrines.

In the dormitories, Mourton whispered into Brady Batsich's ear. "The Prophet has died that we be free. He is buried on Arcturus."

Brady looked up, startled. "It's time, then. Spider died that men be free!" he whispered back passionately and leaned to carefully mutter into the ear of the man next to him. Within an hour, people prowled the lower levels, looking around, grabbing bits of tubing, splinters of plasteel, lengths of wire attached to separate handles, sharp spears of heavy gauge wire, anything which might be considered lethal.

Thyakild thought it odd that he had no fear. The Prophet was dead. The end of tyranny could be felt just over the horizon of the future. Spider was calling the forces of justice from among the captives. He reached out, touching the souls he shared with them. The time had come to live free! The message of Spider had had time to spread, his web to set!

Time. The horizon neared.

"Father!" Mourton called to the guard on the other side of the hatch which marked the captives' territory. "Deus is God! You're keeping me from experiencing the ultimate bliss! Let me through! The Temple calls! My life is for nothing here with Satan!" He raised his hands, pleading.

The guard—unpsyched, of course—slid the hatch back, blaster in hand and checked the passageway. "Come through, pilgrim," he muttered. "Just rush to Deus slowly, huh? Real careful like."

Mourton kept his head bowed, mumbling a prayer to Deus under his breath. The guard looked him up one side and down the other, then turned to the intercom. The last molecular cutting shears in the station laid the guard's spine neatly open and he tumbled through the hatch. With the shears, Mourton sliced the control panel in two. An alert siren wailed somewhere as his people came charging through the hatch.

"For Spider! For Freedom! The Prophet is dead! Spider! Spider! Spider!" they screamed, a new light glowing in their eyes.

Mourton had plucked the guard's blaster from his fingers and now led his mob through the almost empty corridors. He blew the monitors out of service as they passed. The next hatch snicked shut and Mourton almost exhausted the charge blowing it open.

"Spider! Spider! Spider! For the Prophet! *For Freedom!*" he screamed as he charged through, a boiling, irresistible human wave behind him. They bolted into the main part of the station. Two guards stood in the corridor and Mourton crisped them both, enjoying a surge of giddy emotion as he watched their hated bodies exploding.

He handed the blasters around, snapping a fresh clip into his failing weapon. More guards appeared, shouting, gesturing, and ordering them to stop.

"For Spider!" Thyakild shouted. "For Freedom!" He reveled in the blaster crackle as the bolt shot through the air. He killed one, then another, before a well-aimed bolt blew his leg into fragments.

He flopped on the floor, watching his life gush hot and bubbling from the numb stub where his knee had been. "Take the blaster!" he screamed as a man rushed past. He felt more than saw it ripped from his hands, gratified that they continued to rush past him. Then they were gone, all two thousand three hundred and ten of them. All who could walk, fight, and die for the Prophet; the last of the free men!

Sounds of receding feet, screams and shouts, the cry of men and women fighting against the odds, racketed back to him. More and more, the place grew quiet, subtle vibrations reaching him through the floor.

Two dead bodies lay to either side of him. Mourton clawed his way to the nearest, leaving a bright red streak of his courage and pain on the floor. The first man may have been Jackson, but the blasted remains of his head left Mourton unsure. The other, Thyakild could see from where he lay, had been pretty Stephanie Guild.

He felt faint, and fell back, head resting on Jackson's still warm hip. The corridor whirled, going gray before his eyes. His stomach wanted to throw up. The pain from the blast began to beat at him, insufferable, as the shock wore off. He winced and looked up, vision hazy. He blinked, sure that a strange hooded man was standing over him, watching pensively.

"I'm free," he croaked up at the shadowy figure. "Free."

He tried to stem the endless flow of blood. No use. He had trouble seeing through the gray now, felt light-headed and floaty.

"Spider," he whispered. "Prophet, we heard. We're people . . . and we're free!" The euphoria built as the world seeped from gray to black. "Free," he whispered as his soul started the long return to Spider and Thyakild Mourton died with pride.

The hooded one straightened after hearing that last dying breath and walked silently in the direction of the fighting.

Apella: Lenin Sector.

Apella, second planet of the Tau Ceti system. Apella had been settled early during the Soviet period, one of the terrestrial type planets. Fortunately, the CO_2 cycle in Apella's greater planetary mass compensated for the lower luminosity of its primary, Tau Ceti. Outside of its highly saline marshes, the planet has been relatively exploitable. Major exports consisted of organically produced textiles including cotton, hemp, wool, and other traditional luxury stuffs from the volcanically fertile soils.

On Apella, the response came spontaneously. The Governor settled himself smugly in front of the comm. The people had grown increasingly sullen over the last months. Of course, he'd never really realized the effects starvation and the horror of the psych produced on a captive populace with a long tradition of liberty.

Among the hostages, anxious as well as unruly faces looked up. Chuckling, he imagined the questions filling their worried minds. More conscripts for Deus' psych machines? Were the Fathers coming again with their blasters? Another slave work detail? Which specialties did the Fathers require this time? People's eyes went furtively to the gates of the compound which enclosed them, leaving them to slowly starve to death.

The Governor smiled at the huddled, miserable masses. "I have the great pleasure to inform you of a glorious victory. This very day, the will of Deus is done. The Romanan Prophet of Satan is dead!"

"The Prophet is dead?" someone shouted. "Once more, his predictions are true!"

"The Prophet foretold that we would be free the day he died!" yelled another voice.

"I'm tired of hunger!" A woman stood, shaking her fist at the monitor. "I won't live in terror. I'll die before one of Deus' goons takes me from here to be a ghoul!"

"Yeah! They can't kill us all!"

A shout went up.

The Governor straightened, startled even behind the safety of comm. "I don't think you heard what I said. The Prophet's dead! He . . ."

"For the Prophet!" The cry went up. The guards at the gates felt secure, most didn't even pull their blasters.

No one knew the names of the ones who died on the electrified wires while others crawled over their insulating bodies and tore the guards apart. Apella freed itself within ten hours although the Fathers killed many of them.

The handful of Apellan survivors, vicious with rage, fell upon the psyched monstrosities with blasters, metal bars, bludgeons, and bare hands. Blood ran for days on end as the orgy of killing went its course. On the outside of the Governor's center, a big red-brown spider was painted with Apellan blood. Weary, the few survivors settled down to begin piecing their lives together as they sent message after message to the universe, proclaiming their freedom in the name of the Prophet.

Three Paw Station: Gulag Sector

Called a station, Three Paw is actually a planetary habitation site built on Three Paw, the first moon of the fourth *gas giant planet of the K1 primary known as Nikita Red Eye. (The several myths concerning origins of the star's name must be considered spurious.) Constructed in the early days of the Confederacy, Three Paw supplied purified sulfur, phosphates, nitrates, and liquid oxygen to developing manufacturing centers in Gulag. Surrounded by an atmosphere of frozen SO_2, ammonia and H_2S, Three Paw is a self-contained environment, shielded from the intense radiation emitted by the planet. At the same time, the station is protected from tidal effects by employing gravitational compensators powered by an electrical discharge as the moon travels through the planet's magnetosphere.*

In Three Paw Station, the news came in the middle of the night. The next morning, technicians, fluid engineers, and those remaining in the Fathers' captivity arose to see the news of the Prophet's death flashing in huge letters across the main chamber.

"Hope is gone," a gray-haired, long-boned tech said, rubbing the stubble on his jaw.

"The Prophet said he'd die. He said it."

"So? Who's gonna fight the Messiah now? The Romanans? You got any idea how long it will take them to get here?"

"Well, what of it?" A woman asked, dull-eyed. "We're not getting out of here." She stared at the guard who leered at her, making a gesture, sliding his index finger in the tunnel he formed of the fingers on his other hand.

She shivered. "And if there's no hope, I've had it. I'm tired of the rape, of the beatings."

"But if we don't stay alive," the gray-headed one reminded, "the complex will fail. You think those goons," he jerked a thumb over his shoulder at the surly guards, "could balance the generators? You know what happens here if the tides aren't balanced. One crack, and it's all gone."

"You know, I wondered why they put that psych machine there at the gate. You think it works?"

The woman looked over at the portal, the powerleads plugged suggestively into the panels. "They took my whole family. Where do you think they sent what was left of my husband?"

"Who knows."

"Let's say it's powered," the gray leader mused. "Suppose we all walked through at once. Psyched ourselves.

Who'd balance the grav fields? Who'd keep the processors going?'' He looked meaningfully at the guards. *"They* couldn't. If I don't check the capacitors in the next five hours, the fields will collapse. They won't know what's wrong until the power goes out.''

"In here, unpowered?'' A third man shivered. "God, that'd be worse than the psych.''

"My family's dead.'' The woman ran a delicate hand through thick waves of hair. "I'm tired of being company whore to those smelly unwashed vermin. And the Prophet's dead. Everything's dead.''

"Let's go.''

Within the next hours, the entire captive populace walked through the psych gate to stand dumbly, vacant-eyed, waiting instructions to go to their places.

"Hey,'' the security chief wondered, "why'd they do that? They knew!''

"Beats me,'' the guard shrugged. "Hell, I can take them smart or dumb.''

"But who'll keep the generators and the pumps and—'' Then the lights went out.

Mytylene Station: Trasvaal Micro-nebula.

Mytylene Station's origins date back to the Confederate revolution. Originally a supply dump and refugee center, Mytylene Station's location in the Transvaal served the purpose of concealment amid the dark dust and gas clouds. Subsequent to the cessation of hostilities and the implementation of the Confederate Council, station habitues determined that a profitable trade could be derived from the surrounding dust. Used for nothing more glorious than lightweight radiation insulation, Mytylene's economy was born.

"Damn it! Look at 'em coming!''

"What the hell?'' The guard scratched the back of his head, seeing the hostages running for the gate. "Shit! They'll fry on the . . . Crap!''

The surging horde overran the gate, bodies crackling and cremating on the huge electrodes. The main capacitors arced, an acrid smoke rising from the heavy canisters.

"Damn Deus' bloody balls! *It's a damn riot!*''

Blaster fire from the guards laced the screaming crowd, exploding the unprotected bodies.

"Hang on." The supervisor ran back to the strong house they'd established overlooking the concentration camp. Mylene, fortunately, had been built to contain. The only way out of the lower levels was via the main ramp.

With quick fingers, the supervisor undid the lock box, obtaining access to the fire control switch. Above his head, machinery whirred as the heavy blaster rolled forward on its track.

"Duck!" he called, triggering the mechanism. Lights dimmed as the big gun sucked power. Violet death raked the corridor. He lost count as the heavy gun pulsed the narrow ramp. In the end, the beam exploded the bulkheads, support structures, and vaporized ceiling panels as they fell.

"Goddamn!" A guard called in the silence created when the supervisor shut the gun down.

Another guard rose, one side of his face a bright red from the UV burn. He swallowed and looked down the wreckage of the hall, awed at the piles of twisted burned corpses. None lived. The entire population lay dead in the debris.

"What got into them?"

"Got me." The supervisor shook his head. "Mentioned their Satan-cursed Prophet died. Got tired of all them spiders they was drawing down there. But what could have got into them? I'll never understand."

Phygold: Ambrose Sector

A Mars-type low gravity planet, Phygold developed as a manufacturing center for refined epitaxic silver germanium superconductors for super lasers. Through their expertise, the colony expanded into micro-lenses, capacitors, vacuum centrifuges, and assorted high-tech industries. At the same time, the domed cities expanded, employing miners, educational specialists, and scientists.

Phygoldians had chafed under Ngen's rule, horrified at the mind theft and zombification of half their population. Restricted to Cee Dome, they'd watched fathers, sons, daughters, and mothers in combat vacuum suits conducting exercises beyond. The whole thing had been incomprehensible to them. When the practice rods were replaced with blasters, and the last of relatives and friends had been lifted to the stars, the Prophet's wide-beam broadcasts began appearing on their receivers.

Now the Spider Prophet had died on shining Arcturus a
he'd said he would. That morning, another order had com
for the people to assemble. At the order to march throug
the Temple, a man shouted the word which would becom
Phygold's motto: *"Never!"*

They not only overran the guards, they captured an or
biting GCI and shuffled the screaming, pleading crew
through the air lock. After painting a spider on the hull
they went hunting Fathers, blasting a swath through space
the thirst for revenge barely satiated as they reviewed holo
of lost relatives who'd marched mindlessly to menial job
and back until they'd been drafted as killers and sent Spide
knew where.

News of the Prophet's death spread through Directorat
space in ripples. Where the web of Spider had touched,
passionate outbreak of one sort or another resulted. Spide
had been loosed in the galaxy. The web was being draw
in, the tendrils affecting every man, woman, and child.

CHAPTER XL

**Bridge aboard *Deus*: accelerating toward jump from
Gulag Sector.**

Ngen Van Chow, exhausted, irritable, and almost shakin
with fatigue, drew another cup of coffee from the dispense
Around him, the pristine white of the bridge cradled hi
ragged thoughts. *Deus* hummed and pulsated. In the arc o
his vision, the techs bent over their various stations, work
ing frantically, with the constant threat of the psych in th
back of their minds.

Ngen ran knotted fingers through thinning black hair
hardly aware of the places the scalp had begun to shin
through, and stared out with reddened eyes from under lov
brows.

Almost fifty percent of his border holdings had rise
in revolt: gone by one means or another. Reaction to th
Prophet's death had caught him completely by surprise. H
remembered the joy, the rush of relief and vindication whe

e'd heard of the Prophet's end. The smile on his lips ghosted with bitter irony. At the time, he'd been so happy. No one could have predicted the effect. It made no sense! Unarmed people—worse, unpsyched men and women who should have had more sense—had run to their deaths before the blasters of the guards, dying to the last person. Others fought until they killed every last one of the occupation soldiers—and then went on a spree, killing the helpless, mindless Fathers.

Those few captives who'd been taken alive had a curious quality of insolence, resolve, and spirit Ngen had never experienced among Directorate citizens. What was it? From whence did they draw that inner strength? Some curious deep-seated conviction drove them on.

Of course! It came to him suddenly; they had that same burning defiance the Romanans had!

Ngen sank nervous teeth into his upper lip, chewing as he thought. He took a deep breath and blew it out. Damn!

He slammed a knotted fist angrily against the arm of the command chair. "I should have thrown everything against World and *Bullet!* No matter the losses, I should have crushed them all, first thing!"

And lost my entire fleet without the ability to strike back when the rest of the Patrol came to its senses, his better judgment told him.

Who would have believed the Prophet could have stirred men's souls to the point they would die rather than accept captivity? Where did they find the motivation? What deeper strength permeated the Romanan religion, that it could fire men with such passion?

Ngen looked up at his star map. The jihad suffered with each defeat, reeling perhaps, but the inevitable stretched before him. "Too little," he whispered gently, "too late. Look at my worlds! Compare the resources. You think you can stop me now? At my command are millions of mindless warriors, millions of inexhaustible workers who'll produce until they drop. And only the capos can turn against me. And for what? Where can they go among their mindless slaves? No, I control the Gonian techs—and with them, the secret of the wide-field psych. Too late, Damen Ree. Too late, Romanans. You—and your Spider god—can't recover now. You've only slowed me for the moment. Behind me, the momentum has massed. I am irresistible."

No single man had ever built an empire as large as Ngen

Van Chow's. With the benefit of psych, it would neve
crumble and fall apart. The independent stations woul
never stray out of his control and into open space. Ngen ha
built to last. Built to dominate!

To what purpose? The thought came unbidden and h
scowled up at the white panels over his head. "To prove i
could be done," he whispered. "To prove to the univers
that I am the Messiah!" A fierce pride welled in his breast

He swiveled the command chair. One by one, he note
the worlds which had broken away in revolt and declare
independence in the name of Spider. This revolt had com
too quickly. If only the engineers would finish the Broth
erhood device!

Laughter rolled up from the pit of his belly. "You fools
Did you think I learned nothing from Sirius? Did you thin
I'd let anyone turn on me again?" His eyes lost focus as h
imagined the antimatter devices buried so deeply on th
border worlds. Sleek silver-gray boxes, the stasis field
charged through the power grids so long as the switche
remained closed. A complex, coded transduction coul
change that, of course, opening the circuits.

"If only I'd had more time. It's only a matter of time
But, for the moment . . ." Angrily, Ngen activated the wid
dishes. *Deus* activated the comm; the sequence was sent
Seven worlds and forty stations died in a sudden burst o
light.

"If I can't have it," Ngen whispered, eyes narrowing
"no one can!" He glared at the star map, a grim feeling i
his gut. They would beat him only to find dust and vacuun
where once women had laughed and children had played
There would be only black emptiness where men ha
dreamed! Ngen laughed sourly.

"I *am* God! *Let no one take what is God's!*"

Observation blister overlooking the rim of Cobalt Station: accelerating for jump from Gulag Sector.

Ten MacGuire stared out the ports at the huge reactor
which had been so laboriously welded to the sides of Cobal
Station. Theory had started to jell—insane but ingenious. *A*
fantasy idea that reality consisted of nothing more than :
shimmering illusion that could be pressed into a differen
illusion beyond the fiction of singularity. He shook his head
watching the streaks of reaction shoot into oblivion as th

station powered for jump. They were following the *Deus*. No one had ever tried moving so much mass through the jump. MacGuire shivered. It took the brilliance and power of the Messiah to attempt it—and his resources!

"Why do I have to ride it?" MacGuire wondered. His thoughts—as always—returned to his wife and daughters. In the distance, he could see the glare of *Deus'* mighty reaction drives. His family rode there, Therisa, his wife, and his four golden-haired daughters, all living in fear that he wouldn't do his job and make Ngen's device work. That's why he rode it. That's why he prayed Cobalt Station could make the jump despite its mass.

"Master Engineer?" Ten turned at the listless voice.

"Yes?" he asked the mindless being standing before him.

"Helmut Eng wishes your presence." The man's eyes never even focused as MacGuire turned and followed him. They went down two levels, finding it difficult to move between the hastily installed grav plates. Cobalt Station had been accelerating at twenty-five gravities for weeks. Whoever supervised the mindless Father work crew had placed the plates too widely. A man got curiously heavy between them. MacGuire didn't like it. He could practically feel the metal fatigue. First the micropulsations from the gravity generation, now this. They'd be lucky if they built a singularity at all. More lucky still if Cobalt Station didn't fold into so much crumpled metal from the compression forces.

It was all a slipshod job! It had been a nightmare to balance those mighty reactors. Ngen had stolen power plants from half a hundred stations, leaving them dark and dead in an effort to generate enough power to thrust Cobalt Station to the jump. They needed that energy to shield it through to the other side and then power the device. That is, if the device could be completed. If it would function. If the station didn't break apart. If it didn't kill them all in the first second. If it didn't blow them all to Ngen's hell in the meantime.

He entered the planning room and found Eng and Veld Arstong bending over a fluctuating color holographic display. The place looked like engineers and physicists worked there round the clock. Papers, coffee cups, and styluses piled around free standing holos where men peered and ran comm generated feasibility tests.

Eng's forehead had pinched itself into a thousand vertical

lines. Veld muttered under his breath, peering at a mathematical model on a monitor.

"What is it, Eng?"

"Where have you been?" Eng didn't lift his eyes from the model. "Comm couldn't find you anywhere. Observation platform again?"

"Where else can a man think? What have you got?"

Eng tore his gaze from the display and looked up with curious tranquillity. "The device is not only feasible, it'll work." Helmut's blunt, red face looked almost ecstatic. "Remember, the Messiah said we'd understand the purpose of the toron arcs? I don't know how he knew the principle, but we can build the device. Check the model." He indicated the monitor.

"Be careful, my friend," he whispered. "Between you and me, it's Ngen's idea. Before others, it was granted to the Messiah by Deus. Remember that, or it could be your mind which goes next."

Helmut nodded, suddenly searching the faces of the other engineers. Who might be a plant? Who might be there to inform on the unfaithful? Veld Arstong caught the scrutiny and shook his head. Of them all, only Arstong seemed to have avoided paranoia. Could he be the plant? The calculating informant?

MacGuire shoved it to the side of his thoughts and bent to study the figures on the monitor. The pieces fell into place. So much energy could be concentrated on a small amount of dense matter that—if properly focused—it could artificially compress the matter beyond the Swartzchild light barrier and hence "outside."

"The ultimate weapon," MacGuire whispered, awed. "With this, Ngen's invincible."

"And the toron arcs provide the shielding and transmit all those trillions of ergs into the electromagnetic containment bottle," Eng agreed. "By manipulating the energy input, we can sling a quantum black hole anywhere in the universe. It's simply a matter of refinement and learning to control it."

"Is this the secret to the *Satan Sword?*" MacGuire wondered.

Eng shrugged. "That was alien technology. From the records, the *Satan Sword* simply made matter disappear. This will create a devastating explosion when the compacted matter is released from our control."

MacGuire sank into his seat. "Seven centuries ago the Hawking effect was predicted. It has never been tested in reality."

Eng's chunky face showed a sour amusement. "Do you think it won't work?"

MacGuire shook his head. "The proofs have been too well defined through the centuries." He paused, expression blank, eyes unfocused "What are we creating for Ngen? What are we allowing him to become?"

"God," Veld said softly. "So long as he holds our souls in his hand—and controls singularity generation—that's what he is."

MacGuire nodded, mind racing. "He's promised we would be magnificently rewarded. Our families will be freed when we make the device operational. My girls . . . Please. Make my little girls be safe."

Eng's eyes were knowing.

"How long to build it?" Veld queried, face tightening in warning.

MacGuire looked at the model on the monitor and thought of the assembly time. "Probably by the time we're out of jump—provided we make jump. We should be ready for trials as we decelerate for the Gas Cloud Colonies."

Eng began nodding, eyes straying absently to the model on the screen. "Truly, Ngen will be invincible."

"We have the ability to stop him," Arstong barely mouthed the words. "Think about it."

MacGuire swallowed hard, a hot flash of guilt at the base of his throat. Immediately, he cast about for eavesdroppers.

"I suppose we do," Eng agreed. "But will we? Could you stand to murder your own family? You'd be killing Ten's little girls. You'd be murdering my wife and my son and my parents. Could you expect me to be part of that?"

Veld sighed and lifted a shoulder. "Ours? Or millions of others?"

"It'd be barbaric!" MacGuire whispered. "I *will* not destroy my family and my happiness." He'd made his decision the first time Ngen had threatened his family—but it haunted him. He could imagine Ngen's fingers curling in his daughters golden hair, the terror in her eyes as he reached down to . . . Firmly, he suppressed the horror rising in his mind.

* * *

Main crew lounge aboard *Gabriel*: Accelerating from Arcturus.

A hundred light-years away, Chester Armijo Garcia sighed as another segment of the future formed in his head. A cusp had been made and he curiously awaited another branch of reality now twining its way toward him. A different version of the future began to spin out now.

Chester looked up as the man entered. He lifted the head-phones from his ears and smiled. "Greetings, Captain. It is a good day to live, don't you think?"

"Good day?" Torkild asked, "Good day where? We are nearing the speed of light, Prophet. When what we see as a day is a week to another, what meaning does time have?"

Chester laughed. "Your point is well made. Does it matter what the length of an hour is? Does it matter what the meaning behind a word is? What is discrete and what is relative? Do any of those words have any real meaning beyond that assigned in your head and mine?"

Torkild craned his head back, staring at the Prophet nervously. "I suppose not. Why, then, is this 'day' any better than any other, Prophet?"

"Because we have it to live, Captain. We have it to pull the air into our lungs, to feel our hearts within us." Chester ran the tips of his fingers along the deck plate. "We have it to touch, to see color, to suffer hunger. We live in all the various permutations of life. Life, dear Captain, is too often taken for granted."

Torkild laughed. "You're a most unusual man."

Chester shrugged, the ever-present smile on his lips. "I have never met a usual man. Tell me what one is like? I would assume that if the unusual exists, so does the usual."

Torkild thought about it then scowled. "You play word games, Prophet!"

Chester nodded easily, almond eyes on Torkild. "If you remember, I told you that games were most illuminating. Many things can be learned through games. A Prophet is a teacher. And you might look within yourself and see if you can discover why such simple little words bothered you so just now. You do not have much time, Torkild. We are but four weeks ship's time from the Gas Cloud Colonies."

Torkild turned white. "How did you know where we were going? That is *my* secret! You've done something to my comm? I myself just learned!" His hands locked in the cloth at the Prophet's neck and lifted Chester's unresisting body while he stared into the serene eyes.

"I do not fear, Torkild." Chester's voice remained unaffected. "Go ahead, strike me. I will not resist it if it will teach you that your anger has no purpose. On the other hand, if you kill me, you will precipitate your own destruction and you will die so rapidly you will learn nothing. Thus my death would serve no purpose. I will have had no impact on what your soul would take back to Spider. But then, that is *your* choice. Your free will."

Torkild trembled and let the Prophet down. "I looked into your soul, Prophet. Do you fear nothing?"

Chester's enigmatic smile grew a little. "To fear is human, Torkild Alhar. I fear many things, but they are beyond the pettiness of my own life. I fear instead for the fate of humanity, for the souls which will have no chance to achieve, learn, or experience. I fear for the abject degradation of God. I fear for the safety of Spider's experiment with men. Like your fear for your life and existence, my fear, too, is meaningless in the end, Captain. Ngen cannot kill Spider. He cannot abrogate ultimate reality. You see, like you, I am being silly."

Torkild squinted. "Why do your words make no sense to me?"

Chester lifted his arms and spread his hands. "We speak on two levels of experience. You have lived the life of a sheltered, pampered, Arpeggian male. In all your life, Torkild, you have never been forced from the safety of what you perceive to be your reality. You are locked too deeply into your concept of who you think you are. You must step out of it and see yourself from a different perspective."

Torkild laughed. "My reality serves me fine."

"Of course, it does. Ignorance allows the belief in perfection. You need never question. At the same time, never to question is one of the few real sins for which your soul can truly be damned. Nevertheless—depending on your cusps—you may better yourself."

"You seem pretty sure of yourself."

"Of course I am. You might say that's one of the benefits of seeing the future." Chester bowed slightly, ignoring the ridicule in the Arpeggian's voice. "I see several different Torkilds. At the moment, you don't really like yourself, Captain. You are very clever and you are motivated by your distaste for your life. Answer me these questions: What is

it that you don't like? Why are you dissatisfied with who
you are? What do you really want to become, and, most of
all *why?*''

Torkild was shaking his head disdainfully.

"Oh? I am easily convinced. I see you in the days to
come, Torkild. All you need to do is answer those last four
questions to *your* satisfaction and I will believe you."

The Arpeggian watched him through piercing blue eyes.
He finally took a deep breath and snorted. "I must inform
the Romanan woman of our rendezvous with Ngen, Prophet.
You will excuse me?"

Only, despite the bluster, it was a very confused Captain
Alhar who left the Prophet.

Chester stood and stretched, letting his mind ramble
through Mozart's *Requiem* and walking slowly down the
companionway. He entered a blaster port and settled himself next to the big man who sat quietly in the dim light,
fingering a short knife.

"Desperation is a very interesting phenomenon, Doctor.
What does it teach you?"

Darwin Pike laughed. "Is the nature of the universe futility and fear, Chester?"

"Partly. Is the visual spectrum made up of yellow? Are
there not other colors as well? Perhaps you have blinded
yourself with goggles which only let yellow light through.

"Susan's lied to me. I . . . I guess I know too much for
my own good. My medical records sort of looked out of
balance. Parts had been edited, others hadn't. I found out
why. I've got artificially induced oncogenetic cancer, Chester. The cells are all through my body by now. Hopefully,
the lymph system's got a line on most, but who knows. She
might have killed me."

"And that really bothers you, Doctor?"

"Hell, yes! Damn it! I love . . . I mean I'd have given
anything for her. Would have given my—"

"Would you have given humanity for her?" Chester
cocked his head, waiting. "Would you like me to save us
both some time, Doctor. Aren't you hoping I'll magically
come up with some circuitously derived rationale whereby
you can blame Susan for doing exactly what you already
know you yourself would have done anyway? Given the
choice, would you really have abandoned Patan? Would you
have allowed Susan to take this risk alone while you stayed
safe in a med unit?"

Pike stared, a wretched anguish in his eyes.

Chester reached out with a warm hand and clasped Pike's arm in a reassuring grip. "No, that's not your problem. You'd like to blame Susan. It's always easier to blame someone than it is to lay the blame on anything so cold and uncaring as Spider or circumstances."

"I suppose. It's just that I . . . I don't have a purpose anymore," Pike said as he raised his hands and let them drop. "Back when I was innocent, there was always purpose in my life. Now, I live for hatred and revenge. And the dreams, the goddamned dreams! Every night, Ngen's voice . . . the ghoul eating. . . . Everything's polluted! Even the love I feel for Susan. I'm afraid to live for anything for fear of what I might lose. Like Susan—and my health."

Chester smiled serenely, eyes thoughtful. "There is a lesson in that, isn't there? Go ahead, Doctor, you are teaching me."

"Huh?"

"I am feeling the same frustrations and fears and I have the answers. I am feeling futility. How would you combat such an emotion when you have no answers?" Chester inclined his head.

"Faith?"

"Ah! A good answer, faith. But let us consider this a little further. Faith is an artificial support for those who do not have a logical framework by which to understand their beliefs. Faith by itself is an assumption. Do you agree? You do? All right, then. Do you, therefore, fight despair and futility with an assumption?"

"That's a trick question, Chester."

"Of course it is. That is the basis of both of our problems, isn't it? We are tricking ourselves. Let's go back to the lesson of the colors. Myself, I am seeing the black side. Somewhere I have forgotten the rainbow ecstasy that was mine when I first heard Beethoven. And you forgot the first time Susan looked into your eyes with love."

"I don't understand," Pike looked uneasy at the mention of Susan.

"We are both staring too deeply into the future, Doctor. We are dwelling too much on what we see. You, in your imagination. I, in one of several realities which has not yet been chosen."

"Maybe I'm dumber than a rock, but don't you have to

look ahead? I mean you only plan ahead if you can imagine.''

"We are little more aware than rocks if we convince ourselves we have determined the future and can no longer change it or our own lives. In that case, we are cheating Spider and not learning from the entire spectrum of our existence, don't you think?''

Darwin chuckled. "I suppose so. There are just times when it remains difficult to keep a light at the end of the tunnel.''

"Doctor,'' Chester said suggestively. "Are you dissatisfied with what you are about to attempt?''

"I'm scared stiff. At night, the dreams are always there. We're walking into the Devil's lair, Chester. I'm scared stiff he'll catch me or Susan again.''

"And if you had a choice between yourself and Susan, who would you hand over to him?''

"Didn't we just go through this? Myself! I wouldn't let that miserable . . .'' Chester's hand stifled the outburst.

"So, in your futility you do have love. Is your life not given purpose by that? And if you and Susan are the price for the rest of humanity, Doctor, what then? You may want to think about that.''

"You see something,'' Darwin whispered, voice unsteady. "My God, Chester, *tell me!*''

The Prophet smiled easily. "Very well, my telling will not affect the cusps. Depending on the way things work out, you may have to choose between yourself, Susan, and humanity. You will not be alone. We all must make choices which will save or break the species. What will you send to Spider in the end?''

Darwin shrugged and looked hauntedly at Chester. "I don't know.''

"Don't look so guilty about it. Of course you don't know. Not even a Prophet knows what he'll do at a given cusp in the future. For the moment, however, I want you to think of something else. I should tell you that Patan Andojar Garcia is dead. He has made his last cusp. He fell into insanity and Rita Sarsa mercifully killed him.''

"My God.'' Darwin shut his eyes, caught by a soul-deep pain.

"Why do you allow yourself to suffer so? For what reason? There is no pain in Patan's passing, that is past. He goes now to Spider, joyous, having learned more in his short life than scores of others will in a multitude of existences. Did not Patan choose his own destiny? Did he not accept his fate of his own free will, seeing his death in advance?''

"I carried him to the med unit when he was starving," Darwin cried, looking down at his arms.

"I watched him on World as he was about to kill himself with his own knife to stop the visions," Chester said amiably. "He would have died at his own hand then. He might have died of starvation later. Ngen might have decided to proceed to Bazaar and he could have killed you all there. Patan had the option of leaving your party at World despite Admiral Ree's suggestions. We all die. He simply chose his moment."

"We never know what we truly have, do we?" Darwin mused.

Chester shook his head. "Rarely. How would you feel if I told you again you're seeing yellow. What if I told you you only had the next five hours to see colors? The next day? The next week? No, that's not future sight, but the point of my lesson."

"I'd say, 'Here I am, wasting this perfectly good day moping in a dark blaster port.' "

"And Susan will be needing you to hold her in about fifteen minutes. Like you, she is fearing the future . . . and Ngen."

"And I might lose her to him," Darwin whispered in terror.

"That will remain a possibility. Go to her now. Hold her. Share your hope and strength." Chester smiled, walking out of the dim light and positioning his headphones to listen to his beloved music.

Officer's detention office: Aboard *Bullet* in GEO orbit over World.

"So the victor returns." Claude greeted, speaking in an aloof nasal voice.

Tabi laughed while Amelia waited, one eyebrow raised.

Ree stopped, hackles rising as he studied Devaulier through slitted eyes. "Colonel. I came down here to offer you your command back. I just ordered a combat alert."

"Ngen?" Amelia asked. Always balanced, she waited to see in which direction to leap.

Claude sprawled loose-limbed at one of the desks. Tabi

sat hunched at a small table to one side of the office. On the holo screens hanging down the top half of the white walls, images of the ships, World, and the bustle of activity could be seen. Leaning against the bulkhead, arms crossed, one knee bent, Amelia missed nothing.

"Our intelligence reports that Ngen's headed for the Gas Cloud Colonies. If we can box him, hit him by surprise, maybe he's dead. If we can destroy his fleet, we can get back to—"

"And my people won't cooperate without me?" Devaulier queried, smirking. "I could have told—"

"Sorry." Ree met his sarcasm deadpan. "You know better than that, Claude. In fact, someone murdered your Major within hours of your apparent detention aboard *Bullet*. Oh, you've got a real loyal crew on *Uhuru*. Half your people met my Romanans with open arms, trying to curry favor. The rest seized the reactor room and were only disarmed when one of them sold the rest out. Makes you real proud inside, doesn't it?"

"And my people?" Tabi cocked her head.

"About the same—not quite so cutthroat as Claude's."

"Then why, Damen, would you give us our commands back?" Amelia pushed off the wall, walking forward in that sulty manner of hers. Lithe, a female panther, she stopped before him, thoughts veiled as always.

He met those smoky eyes, reading the challenge, the curiosity. "Because Ngen is too important. Within the hour, we'll all be boosting to the Gas Clouds. I've just talked to Giorj, modifications to your ships are underway. We can't put Fujiki blasters in—we don't have enough hyperconductor. Still, we can upgrade, modify your existing guns to Sirian specs. At the same time, we've got a few tricks for beefing up the shielding so Ngen can't rake you without concentrated fire."

"That doesn't answer my question."

Ree turned, staring directly at Claude Devaulier. "You're going because I don't have any command grade officers to fill your positions. The best available out of your crews, I already sent off to Tygee Station and Sirius to man GCIs we've converted. Your expertise overbalances your potential to cause trouble."

"I shall accept your kind offer to return to my ship," Devaulier cried with a sharp laugh, springing to his feet.

"But there's a catch isn't there, Damen?" Amelia's eyes never wavered.

Ree nodded. "Yes there's a catch. Do I look like a complete imbecile? I told you, you're spacing with Romanans. Half your techs are going to be my people. And besides, your Patrol marines are already infected. During the time you've been here for . . . consultation, your people have been all over the planet. Some have been in trouble. I assure you, their hair will grow back nicely. As to the command structure, each second in command will be a Romanan War Chief—Sirian veterans with considerable skill in high-tech war."

Claude had cooled. Tabi, somehow diminished since *Bullet* effectively neutralized her ship with two blaster batteries, simply nodded.

On the other hand, Amelia's eyes sparked.

Ree crossed his arms and strolled across the office. "So, no, I'm not letting you have a free hand. With the exception of the actual engagement, course, navigation, and general orders will be sent via transduction from *Bullet*. The Romanans are more than aware of your potential to ruin this entire mission. They'll be watching. Further, they'll kill you rather than risk the raid. You might say, it's in their blood."

Amelia straightened, arching her back, shifting. "Very well, Damen, so we play along. We give you everything you ask. Then what? What do we get out of this. What's our percentage?"

"You get your ships back afterward."

"But we only have your word on that." Claude wet his lips, the implications sinking in.

"That's right. And I'll honor it. Consider the other alternatives. You're sure that because of what passes for morality in the Patrol, I'll double-cross you in the end. You might ask yourselves, what reason would I have? What reason would you give me? Then again, the decision is yours. Take it or leave it."

"I'll take it," Mikasu agreed. "Do I get out now?"

"A Romanan guard will escort you to an AT. Claude?"

"Yes. I'll go for your deal. It beats rotting in here."

"Amelia?"

"I'm thinking, Damen."

Claude and Tabi left, anxious to escape the confines of the office. Ree settled himself on the corner of the desk, swinging his leg back and forth while Amelia prowled the room. Catlike, she whirled. "I want more, Damen."

"I figured you would."

She smiled for the first time, features lighting. "Good. I'll play your game. More than that, I'll be the perfect lieutenant in your fight against Ngen. I'll give everything I've got." Her expression, the very movements of her sensual body, demonstrated the extent of her offer.

Ree's leg stopped swinging. "And?"

"And I want the tech specs for the Fujiki blasters and the quantum augmentation for *Bullet*'s shields. Not only that, but you've done something structurally, something with the grav plates and structural members. I want that, too. I want everything you've got in return for my letter perfect obedience."

Ree nodded slowly. "And if I refuse?"

She lifted her chin, eyelids lowering. "I'm not Claude Devaulier or Tabi Mikasu. You're dealing with Amelia Ngurnguru. Think about that, Damen."

She moved close, the bursting swell of her breasts barely grazing his arm, the curve of her hip hard against him.

"And if I say, 'Maybe'?"

She shook her head, raising a finger to trace the line of his jaw. "I think you're obsessed with killing Ngen. I think that destroying him and his monsters means more to you than anything . . . and I can make the difference. With me, Damen, the balance of power is unalterably tilted in your favor. No one can threaten you again."

Ree experienced a rush of adrenaline, heart beginning to pound as he looked into her eyes, the deep wells almost sucking his very soul into their depths. A prickling fire stirred as her breasts pressed closer, firm, insistent.

Ree forced himself to chuckle to break the sexual tension, reaching out to grab her muscular shoulders, pushing her away as he stood, gathering his defenses, aware of the throb in his loins, aware of her perfect figure, the slim waist, the swell of her hips, that flat belly, the upward thrust of her breasts.

"I'll take your deal, Amelia." He turned on a well-planted heel, observing the glitter of triumph in her eyes. "But let's spell out the details. When it comes to adversaries, I don't intend on trading you for Ngen in the end. Given the choice, I'd rather have you. Ngen's sick, debased, psychologically diseased. You, you're simply power-hungry and damned brilliant at advancing yourself. I can accept unlimited ambition so long as it comes from a balanced brain.''

She moved close again, appreciation in her demeanor. "You're worthy, Damen. I'm impressed by you." Her arms went round his neck. Head on his shoulder, she added, "Together, you and I could be unbeatable. We . . .''

He removed her arms, holding her hands in his. "No. Not that way.''

She cocked her head, thinking. "You want me, Damen. I can see it in your eyes, in the flush of your skin. I can feel your heart, your very pulse. You want me badly enough to burst.''

He nodded soberly, meeting her searching scrutiny. "Yes, I want you a great deal. But it's pure animal lust, Amelia. And I've learned through the years that passionate indulgence can haunt you for years. No, we'll leave it at cooperation in return for technical information. And this way, too, we'll keep that respect—and wariness—between us untangled by emotions and all those other problems.''

She stepped back, head lowered, straight arms ending in fists. "You know, it's been a long long time since a man turned me down. I'm not sure I like it.''

Ree spread his hands. "You're a beautiful woman. I don't think you have to worry about it becoming common practice. I'm just—''

"Smart, Damen. That's what you are. And it's been a long time since I had to deal with a man I could honestly respect. Damn! I really believe you'll keep your word.''

"If you keep yours.''

A slow smile found life in lips and eyes. "Let's go get Ngen.''

"And pray my measures keep Claude and Tabi in line.''

"What of Yaisha?''

Ree shrugged. "Spider alone knows. Let's just pray like we've never prayed before that Ngen doesn't have some surprise waiting for us in the Gas Clouds.'' *Which he will. And as for you, Amelia, you're as trustworthy as a Silurian sand cobra. You'd turn on me quicker than subatomic spin— and in as many directions. Spider take it, what choice do I have?*

CHAPTER XLI

Aboard *Gabriel* in jump.

Torkild Alhar puzzled over the confusion he felt. Talking with the Prophet time and time again led him to wonder just what he had ever held sacred. He'd made it a point—yes, a game—to try and shake up Chester, but he never could seem to get that leverage. Of course, he suffered from the perennial problem of trying to outargue someone who already knew what you were going to say.

Another problem occupied more and more of Torkild's time: the delightfully beautiful Romanan Captain, Susan Smith Andojar. He worried whether he could compete successfully against the anthropologist, Darwin Pike. Just *what* did she see in him?

Insane! How she could have eyes for the anthropologist when Torkild Alhar, heir to a House, brilliant commander and war leader, filled a room with his presence? What woman could resist his superb charms? Was he not handsome and dashing? Had he not proven himself in combat? On Arpeggio, women had swooned in his presence, hidden smiles reserved for him. More than one virgin from a major House had offered herself discreetly into his arms.

And so would Susan Smith Andojar eventually. What a magnificent wife she'd make. A commander in her own right. Fit, athletic, intelligent. Her graceful hips would bear strong sons capable of rebuilding Arpeggio. The House of Alhar wouldn't be the last of Arpeggio. She wasn't married to the anthropologist, had never been married for that matter; therefore she was suitable.

Of course, it pained him that she'd lost her virginity, the one serious mark against her. And serious it was! Indeed, when she finally surrendered to him, how would it feel? Through the years, each time he mounted her, the knowledge would haunt him. Each time he entered those warm tissues, he'd know another had entered before him, lain where he did between her thighs. Each orgasm would be capped by the knowledge that another had spent himself dry there before.

"Only she's so beautiful, so powerfully attractive." He closed his eyes, remembering the way the light caught in that incredible black silken hair as she swirled it over those muscle-firm shoulders. He lavished himself in the memory of her movements, the deep softness of her eyes, the perfect hollow of her cheek, the way her breasts shadowed the lines of her stomach. And that fire in her eyes! To capture that, to harness it to his will, to see it burn for him! What was a little virginity when the prize proved so rare?

He found her in the exercise room. Fresh spiders had been painted on the wall in glossy black paint. They had been cropping up all over his ship—an irritation. An erosion of discipline. At first he'd ordered them removed. There had been a little grumbling by his men. Later, he'd found Chester painting a spider on his First Officer's battle armor. He couldn't very well order Chester, of all people, to remove his own handiwork. Like some creeping pestilence, spiders had claimed his ship.

As he entered, she leaped high in the air, landed, rolled, and came to her feet in a balanced stance. Some sort of Romanan dance? She twisted suddenly, and, with astonishing speed, kicked out, flashing her arms about in a most spectacular manner.

"Very good!" he called out, applauding.

She flipped that wealth of hair over her shoulder and smiled at him, white teeth contrasting with the tones of her skin. "Thank you, Captain," she called, nodding, firm breasts heaving from activity.

Torkild's heart tripped.

He sauntered in and leaned against the grav bar. Cocking his head, he said, "You are a most attractive woman, Captain." He flashed her his winning smile. It had always affected the women on Arpeggio in a most singular fashion. He had even seduced the eldest of the Sattar daughters with it. Thank God, old Elam Sattar had never learned of that!

"Again, thank you," Susan's voice had dropped. Her spirited eyes met his, challenging.

He smiled again, giving her the dimples in his chin, trying to look young and gay, conscious of the way the light would enhance the muscles of his chest. "I have never met a female Captain before. It will always leave me wondering who might have won had we met in battle."

Susan walked toward him and he almost shuddered with anticipation as her hips swayed and those firmly toned thighs led his eyes to that delicate triangle. An enticing combination of curves composed that superb female body.

"I'd have killed you. You're good, Captain Alhar, but you've never truly been tried in combat. I think you've been lucky. You never faced the supreme test of life and death."

The nerve of her!

"I have—if you will recall—destroyed a Patrol ship of the Line. I was Ngen's greatest commander!" He gave her a self-confident look, letting his eyes twinkle as he tightened the smile muscles.

She actually laughed at him! "But you never looked death in the eye. You were lucky. They were fooled. You've never watched your life or your sanity hang by a thread."

He knew he betrayed skepticism. "And this anthropologist has?"

"And then some." Susan's eyes reflected amusement. "He spent a day living in hell—and he's dreamed of it ever since. He's still paying the price for seeing his soul twisted and seared on a spit. What he survived would have broken anyone else I know—except perhaps the Prophets or the War Chief himself."

"I would not break! A gentleman does not break. I am Alhar. The son of thirty-four generations of Arpeggians. I—"

"I guess we'll never find out," Susan replied, voice mellow. "If you'll excuse me."

I can't believe it! She doesn't take me . . . ME seriously? I am Torkild Alhar! Doesn't she realize just who . . . Then the time has come for an impetuous, dashing advance!

"Captain!" She turned questioning eyes on him. "I have told you, you are a very beautiful woman. I would have you know that my heart races when you are near. Perhaps I could win you away from that anthropologist. How many ships has he killed? Where are his battle coups? I only see one on his belt."

Her eyes widened. *A telling impression!* A twitch quivered the side of her mouth as she froze in mid-step. The initial surprise over, her eyes narrowed. His heart began to pound and he stepped closer.

"I . . . I would love you," he murmured. "You need a man."

Her eyes widened in shock. *Good! Off balance! Follow*

up, demonstrate passion and desire! Light the fires within her!

He threw his arms around her and bent her head back to kiss her. She trembled in the power of his embrace, her body tensing against his, straining for the briefest instant and—

The room spun him into blackness.

Wracking pain blurred his thoughts. Torkild tried to blink his eyes again. His breath seemed stuck in his lungs. The face before him shimmered in and out of focus. Finally, he pinned the whirling features—Darwin Pike, the anthropologist!

Groggily, Torkild tried to bring his scattered wits together. His skull seemed to have cracked jaggedly wide open. He heard himself moan.

"There," Pike's voice sounded confident, "that's brought him around."

"Do you suppose we should have warned him?" Chester's voice said.

"Rita told him to be careful around Susan and me. We, uh, monitored the conversation. Well, you know, what Rita doesn't know . . ."

Torkild finally blinked Pike into focus. "Wh . . . What happened?" he croaked from a dry throat.

"You made a pass at Susan."

Did the damned anthropologist have to sound so amused? Down deep, a flicker of anger leaped to life. Then, as he wondered why, it all came back: the feel of her taut, firm body against him. Then the room had whirled and . . . nothing.

"She thought she'd killed you," Pike chuckled. "She was most upset."

"She thought . . . she'd killed me?" Torkild frowned against the splitting pain. "But, she's so delicate. Just a . . . a woman."

"Uh-huh," Pike grunted. "They're the worst kind. Get you every time."

Torkild pulled himself up. He gawked around, surprised to find himself in his quarters. Pike and Chester watched him closely, Pike studying his eyes. "Pupils seem the same size, they aren't badly dilated. I'd still bet he's got a bit of concussion."

''I don't understand.'' Torkild winced, head literally crackling with pain.

''Susan is the combat champion for the Romanan fleet. Of course, the title does switch back and forth depending on whether Major Sarsa gets time enough to keep in practice.''

''Combat?''

''Hand-to-hand stuff. That's what she was practicing in the exercise room. She goes there every day.''

''She was dancing! On Arpeggio that's an open invitation to . . . to . . . For a man to . . .''

Pike began to laugh. The noise of it almost crushed Torkild's head.

''Dancing? What you saw was an extremely advanced form of hand-to-hand combat. That lady is more deadly with her hands than ten men in a small room with blasters.''

Torkild gathered scattered resolve and shot the man a look that would kill. Pike threw him a wicked smile in return as he got to his feet.

''You'll live. I'll go tell the crew. Susan—oddly enough—is concerned, too.'' Pike palmed the lock plate and disappeared with a snicking of the hatch door.

Torkild swallowed, trying to work some feeling into his dry throat. Chester continued to sit, his forever smile beaming from his wide face.

''I think I will die.''

''It is not in your immediate future. I see no cusps which would change that fact for the next two weeks.'' Chester's voice soothed serenely.

''I should kill that Pike!'' Torkild whispered. ''What do they call it? Knife feud?''

Chester's eyes went vacant for a moment then his smile broadened. ''It would not be a very good idea. He would kill you inside of a minute. Are you that ready to take your soul back to Spider?''

''Who *are* these people? I . . . I wanted only to show my love for the woman!''

Chester raised his hands. ''Captain Alhar, they have seen and experienced more than you. Their realities are different. Do not concern yourself. The final decision is yours, but do not let your feelings for Susan Smith Andojar cloud your reason.''

''But she's so beautiful, so talented and poised. She's one of the few capable women I've ever . . . Answer me this,

Prophet. Had she and I fought our ships, who would have won? Can you see that?''

"I need not even look." Chester's smile widened. "It was one of the cusps long past. She would have killed you and your crew."

"But she is just a woman!"

"That is correct. I hardly doubt you could have missed observing the obvious, especially given your recent behavior.''

"I'm tired, Prophet," Torkild shuddered, feeling totally defeated. "Go and let me rest."

"No, Torkild, you are not tired. We both know why you would like me to leave now. And I will. Remember," Chester reminded as he stood at the hatch. "I told you once you needed to examine who and what you were from various perspectives. Now might be an excellent time to begin such an endeavor.''

He was gone before Torkild could find his blaster. Of course, the very crackle of the bolt might have broken his head. The feeling of inadequacy grew, expanding through him—most disquieting.

"He'll live!" Pike greeted, entering the cabin he shared with Susan.

She crouched in the corner of the bunk, legs drawn tightly under her, chin on knees, lost in thought. "I couldn't believe what he was doing!" She shook her head, brow furrowed. "It didn't make any sense."

Pike lowered himself beside her, taking up one of her limp hands. "You never realize how attractive you are. You drive men wild."

"I just reacted instinctively. Did I hurt him badly?"

"Concussion. He'll have a fierce headache for a while. He's got bruises over his ribs and an elbow that's swollen. Nothing like I'd expected. What happened? You slipping in your old age?"

She shrugged. "I couldn't believe what was happening. I just clenched up and flipped him away. I didn't strike. That probably saved his life.''

"He wouldn't have raped you in the middle of the exercise room."

"I didn't take him seriously. Must I always fight men?"

"Not if you were my wife." He swallowed, suddenly unsure of what he'd done. Puzzled by his own sincerity. "I

. . . I . . . I don't know why I . . ." He stared at her, blinking in confusion.

She looked up at him, arms snaking around his neck. "I . . . I'd like that," she whispered. "You'd take me, knowing that I couldn't. . . ."

"Neither one of us is normal." He grinned. "I don't seem to be much of a man in the classical sense. Impotence should bother me more than I let it."

"I thought all men worried about that?"

"If you didn't love me anyway, maybe I would." He bent his head down and kissed her. "Don't ever leave me and I'll never know I'm not perfect!"

To his surprise, she reached up and kissed him. "That's a deal . . . for both of us." Then she sobered. "Darwin. I . . ." She closed her eyes, masking the misery. "I have to tell you something about the med. The regeneration. It's all my fault and I take responsibility for the whole thing. When this is over, you may hate me. I . . . I'll understand if you never—"

"Shhhh!" He placed a finger to her lips. "About the cancer? I know. I know what you did and why. Chester and I have already talked about it. Nothing would have been different, except maybe I couldn't have given as much of myself to Patan—and he deserved everything I had. What's a little cancer compared to what he sacrificed?"

"And the nightmares? How do you stay with me? I mean, knowing that I castrated so many men on Sirius? Knowing I . . . Well, how do you live with me when I'm such a fragmented psychotic bitch? I've done horrible things—"

"Hush." He smiled and winked. "I just love you is all."

Her lip trembled as the tears flowed silver into her eyes. "I love you very much. Don't . . . don't ever leave me. Never, you hear?"

Tactical planning room: Aboard *Bullet* accelerating for jump to the Gas Cloud Colonies.

Ree paused to make sure he had everyone's attention. Each of the holo projectors hanging in a curve from the white ceiling projected a different person, the backgrounds curiously interwoven. His own people looked up from their comms, eyes following his every move.

"By their very nature, the Gas Cloud Colonies are mostly isolated. Subspace transduction, of course, ties them to the rest of humanity, but the cloud itself will keep Ngen from knowing we're there until the last minute. For the most part, his mass detectors won't pick us up until we're within visual range.''

"If the Prophet was right," Tabi Mikasu grunted.

Ree didn't deign to reply. "The first priority of business is to locate Cobalt Station. That's your initial target, ignore everything else. Patan said it was important. And, after Sirius, it'd worry me if Ngen didn't have some horrible surprise.''

"Cobalt Station was in my Sector," Claude reminded. "How would they get it to the Gas Cloud?"

"Maybe it's a different Cobalt Station. I don't know. I only know what Patan reported. At the same time, Ngen has been reacting viciously against the border areas that revolted. He's destroyed several worlds and stations. The others have either been quashed completely or have thrown the Fathers out.''

Claude Devaulier looked up crossly. "In other words, Damen, we're jumping in blind. *All* we have is the word of a Romanan mystic that Ngen and his crew will be at the Gas Cloud Colonies and we can bash him there. You *don't* have any solid intelligence. You *don't* have the slightest idea as to his deployment or strategic situation. We're bloody *blind!*''

Ree drew a breath and fought for control. "Yeah, because Patan said so. Because, personally, I don't want to set Arcturus up for the fall. You know what will happen if we do. Here's a chance, a gamble, sure—but still a chance to get Ngen without buying him with three *billion* human lives!''

"Damen," Tabi waved a reedlike hand. "Not all of us are convinced as to the psychic powers of your Romanans. We've got the savages roaming all over our ships. They have the temerity to draw on the walls, and worse, they convert our marines! There's hardly a single lieutenant who isn't complaining of these spider drawings all over! Discipline has gone to hell!''

"That was part of the bargain," Amelia reminded. She grinned wolfishly. "At the same time, my War Chief is quite efficient . . . in every manner.''

A jab? Had Philip Grita White Eagle filled the position she'd planned for him?

Iron Eyes stood, his huge bulk almost dwarfing the Admiral. "Do not worry about your discipline, Colonel Mikasu. Your War Chief will handle it. If you should really encounter a breach of regulations that would compromise the safety of the ships, any threat of knife feud, or disregard for rank, contact me immediately.

"But I recommend that you let your people mingle with the Romanans. Damen and I saw the results on Sirius. I've already heard through my own lines of communication that your marines and techs are fascinated by the progress made by those of our warriors taking their first trip to space. Admiral Ree and I went to great pains to split up the veterans and lessen cultural stress in the present situation. Trust your officers, commanders. They are fully capable of creating the finest fighting force ever."

"As if we had any choice," Claude was shaking his head, as he glared venomously at Ree. "And you knew all along, didn't you? Not content with killing your own command, you've killed the entire tradition of the—"

"Damn!" Ree shouted, pounding his fist. "Tradition is a flipping crock of crap! We're not fighting for anything so prosaic as the Patrol. We're not fighting for the Directorate, or honor, or duty! Don't you damned well understand? We're fighting for the very survival of our species! Ngen's running full bore through civilization, leaving human ghouls in his wake, and we're all that stands between him and what's left of mankind! Can it, Claude. You had your chance back at World."

Iron Eyes leaned forward, one hand on his fighting knife. "There was a reason why Maya ben Ahmad and Colonel Kuryaken came to us when they did. Side by side, we faced Ngen Van Chow at Sirius. We know what and who we're fighting. New tactics must be employed. We're fighting a new kind of warfare, one which shouldn't even exist by the logic of military sense."

"Got that right," Amelia Ngurnguru nodded, her speculatively predatory gaze on Iron Eyes. Sizing him up for her bunk? She looked around, cataloging her fellows. "Commanders, we have a definite problem. Part of which lies in the fact we're here right now. I don't believe in the Prophets *per se*. At the same time, it sure looks like this Patan provided correct intelligence about Van Chow and his rendezvous from Captain Andojar's report."

She smiled grimly. "I don't know about you, but I have new blasters, more powerful shields, and we're moving, together, in force. Wherever we need to go, we can. *Greg-*

ory can't stand against us. The Spider religion is spreading like wildfire. That gives us the tactical, strategic, and social advantages we need to turn this whole disaster around. I'll stick with the Admiral and the Romanans.''

Claude's head tilted back. "Care to tell us the deal you cut after Tabi and I left?''

Amelia crouched, leaning forward, as if poised to strike. "Claude, I'll take only so much from you. I made my decision based on the greatest good for the greatest number. Considering the threats we made on the way in, considering the strategic errors we made concerning Ngen, I'm willing to admit I was wrong. I can no longer believe the Romanans are the enemy—not with them swarming all over my ship.''

Tabi snorted disgust at the entire situation. "We must all learn new tricks, I suppose. The universe is turned upside down.''

"Very well," Iron Eyes continued. "We won't know how long Ngen has been at the Gas Cloud Colonies. As a result, we'll deploy the ATs at first opportunity. That allows the greatest flexibility in the event he's cooked up any surprises similar to the ones he loosed on us at Sirius.''

"With the ATs deployed," Iron Eyes accessed a holo of the Gas Cloud Colonies, "I will take each of the stations occupied by the Fathers. If they haven't been taken, we'll effect boardings of the Fathers' ships, and, if necessary, *Gregory* herself.''

"While the marines do that," Ree added, "our battleships will surround the area, offering covering fire, destroying anything that runs. I'm taking it for granted that Cobalt Station can be tagged for targeting and destroyed.''

"How about targeting deflection and bounceback inside the cloud?" Tabi asked.

"Good question. We shouldn't have any trouble when we get close. The reason the Colonies settled there in the first place was to milk the Gas Cloud of elements. The dust has all been swept up near the Colony stations. They move as they use up the resources. It should be crystal clear in there.''

Ree looked from face to face, knowing how hard it was on these people. He'd taken them prisoner, stripped their ships of old faces and given them back a diluted command. Who'd cut his throat the quickest? Claude? Tabi? Or sweet, ambitious Amelia—now his strongest chauvinist?

"That should do it then. We're pushing the jump, if

there's nothing else, I call this council adjourned.'' The holos slowly flicked off, leaving the white walls of the room bare.

"I'd rather command a snake pit," Ree muttered. "They hate what I've done to them."

"So did you, once." Iron Eyes had a grim smile. "I remember a time in your quarters. Rita had just taken your ship. Leeta and I were there to negotiate. I'll never forget the look on your face when I slit Major Reary up the middle with that fighting knife. You looked like you'd just swallowed a rock leech."

Ree pondered the memory and laughed. "We've come a long way, haven't we? It doesn't seem so long ago in real time. But, my God, look at the changes wrought on humanity! We're still on the firing lines, War Chief. I wonder if we'll see a final restabilization or not."

Iron Eyes looked vacantly across the table, interlacing scarred fingers, playing with the two missing joints on his left hand—the symbol of Romanan grief. "I suppose it's in the hands of Spider. What will be will be. The cusps will decide, Damen. Our free will is only such a small part of the whole. We're living in the middle of an upheaval. Once a fire is kindled, you can't control the smoke."

"And Spider is loose in the galaxy." Ree sighed and slapped his hands on his thighs. "Come, I still have just a little of that Sirian scotch."

The War Chief nodded and followed the Admiral out, throwing one last glance at the spider which had been drawn on the hatch as it slid shut behind him.

Bridge of *Spider's Knife*: Somewhere in the Gas Cloud.

"Lieutenant, *what the hell do you mean, we're BLIND!*" Major Rita Sarsa thundered across the bridge.

Will Hanson would have cowered if he hadn't been so concerned over their situation. He heaved a sigh and checked his blank monitors. "Major," he muttered, his gut sinking. "We must have overjumped. We came out *in* the Gas Cloud. We're moving right at light speed. I mean, that's a lot of mass out there. The friction burned off everything outside and hull temperature is rising. Shields are gone! We don't have any protection from the—"

"*Full dump!*" Rita cried, realizing the implications. "Put everything we've got into slowing this bucket! Blow a hole in the soup with the reaction!'' The *Knife* swayed and jerked under the pull of deceleration.

Angrily, she glared at the blank monitors. The jump didn't always work the way the book said it was supposed to. Accelerating to light speed, the shields held them in stasis as they boosted past C and ''Outside'' the universe men called rational.

Mass readings allowed navigation and, while in ship's time it took weeks to traverse the Outside, they appeared to have been gone from sublight for only several hundredths of a second. At the very moment Rita was knotting her guts with worry, she knew *Miliken* had dropped out somewhere half a light-month behind her.

''Give me visual!'' Rita sang out, hoping the lenses hadn't melted along with the sensor pickups and shield generators.

She could feel her body being pulled as Moshe Rashid squeezed every bit of reaction he could into the mighty engines that controlled the racy supply ship.

Visual formed, compensated for the way light bent and folded around them, and gave her a picture which reminded her of flying through dark smoke. A bright streak of incoherent light flared, lancing out behind them as volatile gases burned on their hot hull.

''Hanson? Any estimate on how long it will take to repair those sensors? Do you have any idea about how to locate those damned beacons the Colonies use?

''I can't tell about the sensors until we're cool enough and moving slow enough for an EVA inspection, Major. As to the beacons, we should be able to pick them up on visual.''

Rita exploded with a curse and stomped off to her cabin. There wasn't a damn thing she could do until the ship shed the incredible delta V. She looked up at the spider effigy she'd personally drawn on her overhead panels and scowled. ''You better have a damn good reason for this. There are times I'd still like to kick your ass!''

And saying that stirred memories she'd been too busy to entertain. Once, long ago—or so it seemed—that had been a joke between her and Iron Eyes. Now, running blind, shedding V with everything they had, Rita wondered how she was ever supposed to keep that rendezvous with the Admiral. Iron Eyes would be there, leading his marines. And Major Rita Sarsa would be out bumbling around in the Gas Cloud, looking for a fight, her subspace transduction out, with no way to keep track of time or locate the Colonies.

Life proceeded—unpleasantly—on *Spider's Knife* while Rita fumed. The grav plates were strained to their capacity and frantic Patrol techs sought to replace the vital sensors with little luck. The preliminary burn had scorched almost everything and peeled a half inch of Rygellian graphite-steel away like it was soft wax.

Rita cut the deceleration while Hanson bravely made a hull inspection in spite of the banshee wail of gas and dust.

In the med unit, they patched his micro punctures and sent him up to report. "We'll have to manufacture everything from scratch, Major. In essence, we have to build an entire set of ears for the outside and mount them."

"No spares on this crate?"

Engineering told her no. Fast transports always met the big Patrol battleships out in open space. They weren't designed for this sort of work. Rita growled, kicked the deceleration up again and fumed at the time they were losing.

Five days later they found the miner.

"Ship on visual," Moshe sang out.

"Can we catch them?" Rita asked, prepared for any kind of answer at that point.

"It will take a day or two," Moshe decided, studying the craft in his scope. "We'll need to swing a big circle."

Rita thought the hours were dragging horribly as she tried to figure their deceleration and the relative time passed compared to what the date should have been on Earth. The best she could do was determine she might be anywhere within five days of the rendezvous.

The miner filled the screens, dwarfed by the huge FT as they pulled alongside. Rita herself was the first one to pass the hatch. She almost tumbled as she hit the zero g inside the small mining tug. Three long-limbed, fragile-looking crew stared back, their shaved heads almost shining in the bright light. Wide-eyed, they waited, pale, frightened, crowded in rear of the main compartment.

"We peaceful!" one of the men pleaded. "Please we . . ."

"My greetings," Rita bowed, trying to remember as much as she could about Gas Cloud behavior. "I'm Major Rita Sarsa of the Patrol and the Directorate. We're from the Patrol vessel *Spider's Knife*. On entry to the Gas Cloud, our sensors burned off. It is imperative that we proceed to the

Colonies. The Fathers are coming to take your freedom and make you their slaves. We are here to help.''

Their dialect verged on the incomprehensible, Rita scuttled her urge to growl as she listened to them talk to each other.

"We help." One long, skinny fellow agreed, his flesh giving off that full, almost bursting effect common in people who don't know gravity.

"Can you take us to the Gas Cloud Colonies? How long?"

"We take," the man asserted, owlish eyes going from Rita to Moshe, who stood in the hatch. "Not take long. You okay. Spider on uniform. You soul is God. My soul is God.''

Rita wondered about that, trying to figure how long they'd floated around in the dust, trying to figure how to convey Earth time to a Colonist who'd probably never heard of the place. She gave up and smiled graciously. "We thank you.''

"You follow?'' A stringy, eight-foot tall woman asked. "We go now?''

"We follow. Thank you. You need anything we have?''

"You got Prophet?'' One man asked, eyes lighting eagerly.

Rita laughed and shook her head. "No, I'm real sorry we don't because I sure wish we did.''

The miner had lined out, boosting at maximum capacity—zero point three g. Incredible acceleration considering the stresses the Colonists thought were bone wrenching. They'd crumble into dying heaps in one standard g, skeletons crushed, hearts bursting, arteries unable to cope with the load.

Time dragged.

In the meantime, Moshe, Hanson, Sam Yellow Legs, and the rest of her crew labored to manufacture the sensor pickups which would enable them to employ the targeting computers for the fight they hoped they wouldn't be too late for.

"I think I'm going nuts!'' Rita cried at the end of one of her watches.

Moshe looked up, a knowing twinkle in his eye. "So are the rest of us, Major. Begging your pardon, ma'am, but I think we'll get there when we get there.''

She studied him through slitted green eyes. Moshe raised an eyebrow knowingly.

Rita went and practiced combat in the tiny wardroom, the gravity dialed as high as she could get it. Sweat helped.

As close as she could figure, another two excruciating days limped past before they passed the first beacon. Unfamiliar with navigation in the Gas Cloud, she didn't have the slightest idea what it meant. A day later they passed another one.

"How are those sensors coming?"

"About forty percent reliable at the moment, Major," Hanson told her, nervous, awaiting her reaction.

Rita thought about it, ran a finger over the outline of the spider on her armor, and laughed. "I know you boys are doing the best you can. If we miss this, it will be the most important fight in all of history and there's not a damn thing you or Moshe or I can do about it but cuss. Sorry, I've been so jumpy."

Hanson had smiled warmly. "Aw, we understand, Major. What happens if we could turn the final trick and save the day? The Admiral might be counting on us and we're fooling around out here in the fog."

She nodded, punched him playfully in the shoulder and went back to her command chair.

It was really an honest mistake that she'd made. With so much time spent in the Gas Cloud, lost, working double shifts to fix the equipment, who could judge? With the transductor burned out, she couldn't check. The stress of impending combat has a way of making time stretch out almost to the point of being unbearable. The mining tug seemed to creep along slower than phybite crystals in a test tube. As a result, Rita had no idea as they pulled out into the vast empty space of the Gas Cloud Colonies that they were a day too early!

Bridge aboard the *Gabriel*: Gas Cloud Colonies.

Torkild Alhar's curse brought Susan upright. It was the first warning that something might be amiss.

She had been studying the huge station. It was surrounded by gigantic reaction pods leading up to a tiny ball, seemingly stuck on the end of a spike. Five huge metal arches swelled from each of the reaction pods and curved upward to the ball. The whole thing proved rather eye-catching, sort of like a Gothic cathedral of old Earth.

"Cobalt Station," Torkild had said. "I was the one who captured it . . . in the middle of Ambrose Sector! How did they get it here?"

"Must have jumped it using the pods for power. What's it for?"

Torkild shrugged. "When I took it, none of the spires and towers had been built."

It hadn't taken long to find out. Once every three or four hours, the thing vibrated and surges of power registered on the mass detectors. At the same time, mass would instantaneously read out in the cloud, then disappear. Minutes later a flash would register, Dopplering back to the Colonies. Some sort of awesome new weapon.

Susan jerked her eyes away from the scanner.

"You know that ship?" Torkild asked. His eyes still filled with shame every time he dealt with Susan.

"Patrol supply ship. We've got about ten raiding Ngen's back country. That one's been through the mill, no markings, the hull's polished." She stood suddenly, face ashen. "Whose? Ngen's? Ours? Spider take it, they're wide open down there!"

"They must have come in though the cloud and missed the entry beacons," the helmsman responded. "I heard one of Ngen's captains talking about it."

"Can we hail them on tight beam?" Susan demanded. "They're in a trap!"

"Bruno? Get a—"

"Communication coming through from *Deus*, Captain."

Torkild winced. "Run it."

"Capture that ship!" Ngen's order came through. *"Gabriel! Senachal! Uriah! Move! Box him up and cover him!"*

"Go!" Susan agreed, anxious. "Maybe we can take them. There might be some way of turning this to our advantage."

She felt her heart race. Who could it be? It had to be one of the other Colonels' people. None of *Bullet's* ships were in the area.

"What's that?" Torkild asked.

"They're deploying their ATs," Susan told him. "Get me tight beam on the closest one."

Almost immediately a face formed on her comm. "Moshe!" Susan cried. "You're surrounded by Ngen's people. Don't talk back, just surrender. This is the *Gabriel*. We'll figure out something."

"All right," he muttered nervously. "We're coming aboard."

Torkild accessed comm, and with Susan out of sight, reported. "The one AT has surrendered. We are taking it aboard and making its crew captive. These Patrol are nothing, Messiah. I had only to remind them of the death of *Ganges* and they cower to my will."

"Excellent, Captain!" came Ngen's soothing voice.

Susan froze as blaster bolts leaped from the other accelerating AT. It died in fire. The Patrol ship seemed to be floundering. Suddenly its blasters centered on a GCI and laced fire through the ship's shields, missing the hull.

"I don't believe they missed!" Torkild propped himself, shaking his head.

"Whatever polished their hull must have damaged their fire control!" Susan tensed, heart battering her breast. The blasters were correcting, correcting. Violet lanced the silver sides of the FT. She breached in a puff of atmosphere.

Susan waited, breath held in burning lungs. The reactor didn't overload. Two lighters approached cautiously from either side to disgorge a swarm of suited figures. Jetting, they swarmed over the vessel. Under magnification, Susan could see figures being passed through the breaches in the hull. Ngen had captives.

"Blessed Spider, no." She shuddered, feeling faint.

At the same time, the AT closed, docking with *Gabriel*. Susan sprinted for the lock. Moshe Rashid jumped through, somersaulting, blaster at the ready. He saw Susan and grinned in uneasy relief.

"How did you get here? Where's the Major?"

"She stayed on the *Knife*," Rashid looked grim. "You haven't got in to see Ngen yet?"

"He hasn't granted us an audience. We've been sitting here for almost a week. Torkild's pissed enough to breathe vacuum." Susan accessed comm and had the holos enlarged, studying the bodies they were handing through the hatches.

"There!" Susan cried, pointing a finger. "That's her armor. I'd know it anywhere! Oh, Spider, no! Not Rita. Not in Ngen's . . . No!" She bit back the welling tears of frustrated rage.

Darwin had come up from behind, seeing Moshe, suddenly coming wide awake as he realized the captain should have been on far off Arcturus. His eyes took in the monitor and he understood the situation.

"They've got Rita." Susan cried out to Pike. "That means Ngen has her."

Darwin stood dumbly, mouth slightly open.

"That's not all," Moshe told her. "The Admiral's about to fall on this place like a pile of neutron stars—with an entire fleet. If Ngen psychs any of the crew, the whole thing's gonna be out of the bag but quick!"

Darwin had turned ghastly pale. "We've got to go in there. Get them out before he can question them."

Cold fear traced like ice up Susan's spine. Unwanted, the voice came seeping in from the corners of her mind. *Plea-sure, my dearest Susan . . . Let me teach you pleasure. Your body is mine . . . forever . . . forever . . ."*

CHAPTER XLII

Main access lock of the *Gabriel* in the Gas Cloud Colonies.

A jostling riot of bodies packed the AT, crowding more than twice its recommended complement into the craft. Still, they anticipated no fancy maneuvers. The mission: purportedly, the simple transfer of prisoners. In actuality, the armed penetration of Ngen's flagship, *Deus*. Unless some unanticipated flaw exposed them, they would board the ship under the cloak of Spider's deception. Pending no incident, the AT had been routed to land at a regulation docking lock. Unlike most hostile boardings, they didn't have to spear their way through the ship's hull.

In the cramped quarters, marines bumped shoulders with Arpeggian crew. The noisy clatter of armor mixed with shuffling feet, banging locker covers and clicking fasteners. The entire one hundred meters of deadly needle boiled in confusion—a babble of voices shouting over each other as men and women armed themselves. The suddenly stale air carried a metallic odor, hot, sweat-charged with the tension that builds before death is unleashed by human hands. Occasionally, here or there, someone stenciled a spider on clean white armor using gaudy fluorescent colors. Veteran warriors fingered the coups at their belts, seeking a moment of internal silence in the din to center themselves—to touch the mystical spirit power of their visions.

"Ngen is still at Cobalt Station." Torkild bent, strapping on unfamiliar combat armor. "We've got time."

The Messiah had transferred to the station immediately after Rita's capture. Everything in the Gas Clouds seemed to revolve around the huge station and its curious flying buttresses veined with heavy powerlead and capacitors. Since Ngen had shuttled in, Cobalt Station had begun pulsing and vibrating while flashes of light echoed violent mass fluctuations on the sensors.

"Cobalt Station?" Moshe asked, looking up in surprise from where he checked the fit of his Arpeggian "guard's" uniform. "Where did you hear about that?"

"What do you know about it?" Susan stopped where she field-stripped a heavy shoulder blaster. "We've been watching it for days now. What is it? We don't have the foggiest idea of what it does."

"Before the Prophet died, he said Cobalt Station had to be destroyed first thing. He said its destruction was imperative. I don't know why." Moshe glanced nervously from face to face, dark eyes flashing.

Susan took a deep breath, slapping the thick charge pack into the magazine before flipping the charge gate closed with a solid click. "You said the Admiral's hitting this place on June 7, Earth time, right? Moshe, we haven't got the haziest idea what the date is on Earth. If we send a subspace transduction out of here, Ngen will want to know the reason why."

"Ree could come stumbling in here at any time," Darwin added thoughtfully. "That thing," he motioned in the direction of Cobalt Station, "seems to be a mass thrower. On transmissions they talk about it as the 'Fist of Deus.' "

Susan paused for a moment, checking the back sling on Torkild's armor before clipping the heavy blaster to it. Brow creased, she shook her head. "No, we get Rita out first." She pulled her helmet up and checked it. "Ready?"

Moshe opened his mouth to protest, saw the look in her eyes, and nodded unhappily, snaps clicking as he hung his heavy blaster in its shoulder sling.

"All right, let's go."

Torkild gave Susan one last look, unable to articulate his feelings in this final moment. Silently, he went forward occasionally clapping a shoulder or sharing a joke with the nervous Arpeggians.

Moshe, who would pilot the AT, gave Susan a wink. "Spider keep you, Captain."

"You, too, Moshe."

"Hold the lock a moment." A voice came over comm.

"What the hell . . ." Susan began. Who'd be late for this?

Then: "We're clear!"

Torkild shrugged, passing the hatch to look around. The craft surprised him. Of course, everyone had heard of ATs. The Sirian fighting had been full of holos and descriptions. The bridge, for all its diminutive size, packed an incredible array of comm equipment and monitors. The command chair sat to the rear, capable of swiveling to any of the several consoles. Forward to the right, the pilot sat; to the left, the weapons officer with his targeting comm. Moshe had settled himself into the pilot's chair, pointing toward the command chair, misgivings in his eyes.

Torkild settled himself, working out the curious system of straps and buckles, feeling the chair contract around him. Taking a deep breath, he ordered a channel open to *Gregory*.

As he'd somehow known it would, M'Klea's face formed in one of the monitors before him.

"Greetings, brother." She inclined her head, not quite hiding a smirk. "I had hoped to receive you in grand style. Still, the blundering arrival of the Patrol provides a certain flare, does it not?"

He felt his anger rising. Though he chafed with irritation, she was still his sister. His eyes searched her face, looking for any trace of the yellow-haired girl who had once looked up at him with worship. Chester's words suddenly filled his mind. Questions about the nature of duty, of true honor and responsibility poked into his thoughts, confusing him. Through it all an insistent, irritating voice demanded, *What do you really owe her?*

"I . . . I'm bringing the prisoners, M'Klea." A conflicting spear of yearning rose deep within as he tried to sort it all out. Should he warn her? *She is my sister!* Give her the chance to remove herself from harm's way? His duty . . .

"Torkild?" she lifted a silver-gold eyebrow, sensing his hesitation, that look of unease growing.

Damn! She'll know something is wrong! She always could . . . No. Don't panic! THINK! She can read you like a book! Everything will fall apart. Fool! You'll give it all away!

A smiling Chester pushed his way onto the bridge, out of M'Klea's sight. Torkild's fluster began to fade, leaving a feeling of loss and sorrow to replace it.

"No." He smiled at her wistfully. "I'm fine, M'Klea. It's you . . . Well, sister, use your head. Why would I feel this way? Could you possibly guess?"

She stiffened, eyes narrowing. "Don't, brother. I'll take very little of your supercilious righteousness. You don't realize the power I—"

"Oh, but I do, sister." He shifted to one side, braced on an elbow, heart racing. *Careful, Torkild. This could kill you. Keep your wits . . . keep your control.* "But . . . but tell me. How did father take it? Mother? How did they react to your—"

"Father was his usual boorish self. Mother, however, beamed like morning sunlight, joyous. She was so proud, Torkild. In the end, with so much power in sight, even father wished me well. Oh, I miss them. If only the Satanic demons of the Patrol . . ." She averted her eyes, mouth tight.

Liar! You vile, mind-twisted liar, M'Klea! I see it now. Father, no matter the gain, would never have compromised his honor. No, sister, you've given me more proof than all the tapes Sarsa could have provided. You live the lie, sister. Everything between us is dead—dead as my parents' minds long before Major Sarsa burned the planet.

Stone-faced, he added, "We'll arrive at Dock 9 within five minutes. My men have the Patrol rabble under guard. You needn't burden yourself with heavy security. My people are doubly armed and hoping for an incident. I believe you will find the prisoners, shall we say, pliant enough?"

"Pride, Torkild? You never change, do you? You know, pride is a curious thing. I myself have a great deal of pride—especially in you. None of the other captains in my husband's fleet are so dashing. Tell me, brother, have you found many females to take captive? Ah! But then the noble House of Alhar would never descend to such activities, would it?" Her expression held an odd hostility he was unused to. Now that he looked, he could see thin lines at the corners of her eyes.

"No, M'Klea," he almost whispered. She could see the pain in his eyes, misreading it, reveling in it. "Not pride. I'm just doing what I have to." He slipped a glance at Chester, seeing the understanding in those knowing brown eyes.

Half to M'Klea, he added, "It seems I've been slapped in the face with reality lately. You and the Messiah. What the Patrol did to my home. I can't help but wonder who I was . . . and who I will become. You might say, I've found my soul empty."

Her face twisted to a victorious pout. "I don't think I like this new person you've become, brother. You've lost a certain, shall we say, spirit? You used to be horribly righteous. Where is that brashness now? Are you no longer convinced of your immortal perfection? Do me a favor, brother. Don't take your wounded soul to the Temple. I, well, wouldn't like the results." Her eyebrows lifted, but she couldn't hold the expression without laughing sourly.

The Temple? The pus-rotted Temple? The same that stole our world? And now you joke? Knowing, as you do, what sort of horror you and Ngen perpetrated? You despicable piece of human vermin!

He paused, considering his words. "M'Klea, I don't think you'd understand. It took me until now to see clearly. There is more to life than pettiness. You and I have fooled ourselves."

"Brother!" She squealed with delight. "How wonderful! I can hardly wait for you to bore me with this new concept. I have a smashing idea. We'll discuss it while we play with the electronic whip. Have you ever seen one? It's a delightful device. Produces pain, Torkild. I can't wait to use it on the Romanans. We'll psych a few to see them suffer first. I've seen the tapes. They die in a most revolting manner. What? No reaction?"

He started at her, stomach churning.

"I had thought you'd be on your feet, Torkild. You know, bellowing, shaking your fist, giving me some shocked and outraged lecture on morality or honor. Or doesn't your honorable stomach accept such doings?"

Empty now, emotionally exhausted, he simply stared, soul-sodden.

She cocked her head, quizzical. "Indeed, you have changed. Accepted the inevitability of my power? Is that it? Do you now see me as I really am? Your superior? Your Empress? Good. I still love you, you know. I'll make everything better for you. And, brother, don't ever forget what *I* can do for you. We *will* have a delightful time."

"Delightful . . . I'm sure." He swallowed and nodded. "I look forward to seeing you." He killed the transmission.

For several timeless seconds, Torkild Alhar, of the old Arpeggian family, closed his eyes, fighting against the burning throb behind his nose. He sniffed to keep the treasonous wetness of frustrated tears from exposing his wounded soul.

He knew Chester had placed a hand on his shoulder, although he couldn't feel it through the battle armor.

To salvage something of his dignity, he talked, a curious release in the vulnerability of his confession. "There at the beginning, I was feeling horribly bad about betraying her. The old ways, the traditional teachings, all those lessons my father beat into me still so strong. The memories of who I always thought I . . . But then you know, don't you. You understand. Then she lied. She knew what Ngen did to Arpeggio." He knotted a fist, the tears, like acid, eating through his defenses. *"Damn her! She knew!* My parents . . . all sold for power. All sold to become the Messiah's whore. She . . . she'd watch you die such a ghastly death. Prophet, in warfare there's a need to win—no matter what the cost. Horror and terror are weapons. Anything to break the will of the survivors. People—men, women, and children—are expected to die in ghastly ways, expected to suffer. That doesn't include going to the extremes of eliciting pain and agony simply for the sake of *doing* it!''

"Warfare is always waged for control of the mind—one way or another. Nevertheless, cruelty for its own sake is different: a disease of mind and soul. Often the roots of the illness lie in gross psychological insecurity. To inflict pain is proof of power—at least over a single subject. Too often it is exhibited in times like these.''

"Wait a second. Why are *you* here?'' Torkild demanded, suddenly realizing Chester was supposed to have stayed in the GCI.

"I saw you would need me.'' His warm smile lifted something gravid, gray, stupefied, and strangled from Torkild's soul. "Like you, I, too, have my duty. I will go my own way as soon as we dock. It is a cusp.''

"No! We can't risk you. The danger . . . I . . .'' He stared into those powerful eyes—like looking into God's eternity. "Spider go with you, Chester.''

The Prophet smiled, patting his shoulder reassuringly. "I thank you for your concern, Captain. By that extension of 'self,' your soul is enriched. We are all in Spider's web, my friend.''

"Docking in two minutes.''

At Moshe's voice, Torkild lifted his eyes to the monitor.
The Prophet smiled to himself, humming under his breath
as he walked from the bridge.

Dully, Torkild stared at the monitors, seeing the giant
mass of *Deus* drawing ever closer. Moshe, proficiency evident, eased the AT into the dock. Metal clanged as the grapples settled them into place.

Susan's voice came over the comm. "Let's go!"

Torkild sprinted for the lock, forcing his way through the
pressing throng of bodies. He took his place in the front,
wolfish Romanans and Patrol marines lining out behind, that
knowing undercurrent vibrant in their voices. Energy, like
a thing alive, stirred with the very air. Weapons clicked
against each other as feet shifted and whispered on the deck.

"Let's make this look good! Guards, look like you mean
it. Prisoners, look humbled, mad, uneasy. Remember,
you're captives. I've been in touch with my . . . the Empress. You're to be tortured."

An uneasy silence fell. Torkild met the sea of eyes, seeing
some demon loosed in Darwin's tight expression. For some
reason the big anthropologist's presence gave him strength.
"I'll bluff my way as far as I can. Maybe . . . maybe there
will be, how do you call it? Coup?"

To his surprise, the Romanans howled gleefully, the
ruckus deafening as they clapped hands and whooped. A
bright sliver of courage warmed his fear-cold guts despite
the tight, stuffy air.

"When it falls apart," Susan called, "take as much of
the ship as you can. Coups for everyone. Remember, you've
got a guard partner. Stick with him! Each guard carries two
blasters. When the time comes, take the weapon you're
handed—and Spider take the hindmost!"

A shout of anticipation exploded from tense lungs while
Susan waved for silence.

Torkild—heart juddering against his ribs—palmed the
hatch. On adrenaline-light feet, he marched out, haughty,
scared stiff, enjoying it for the futility of the gesture. But
when he looked back at the grim faces of the Romanans
under the guns of his Arpeggian escort, he could see no
defeat in their eyes. Damn them, the Romanans were
primed, unconcerned about the odds they faced. If the sham
went sour before the blasters could be handed off, all they
had were the long knives dangling down their backs beneath
their armor—and indomitable courage!

"And that comes from Spider?" Torkild mused.

He saluted the guard at the hatch, heart sinking like neutronium. They were outnumbered almost two to one.

"This way," a gruff voice called and Torkild let himself follow the broad back. He looked around, noting the dull eyes of the guards—each and every one of them psyched. His own people must have looked like that before the Patrol burned Arpeggio. A slow flood of anger roiled in his breast, folding in with the fear.

For this he had blasted planets, destroyed stations, and helped to enslave almost a quarter of the Directorate? He looked at the mindless guards and thought of the tapes of Bazaar and his own beloved home. He stared, face to face with the legacy of Deus—and his soul shivered.

True to plan, they marched toward the very guts of the ship. Inside a huge holding room, Torkild put his hand on the guard's shoulder. "Get me my sister. I need to talk to M'Klea. I have a special prisoner for the Messiah." He could see Susan's face go gray, a panic behind her eyes. Darwin—dressed in his Arpeggian uniform—had almost stopped breathing.

"I hear you," M'Klea's disembodied voice came through a speaker. "Which prisoner?"

"This one, sister," He pushed Susan forward hard enough so she fell to the deck. She'd begun to shiver, fear bright in her wildly darting eyes. Sick? No, petrified with terror. Unnerved, his own gut knotted. he forced the quaver out of his voice. "She escaped the Messiah on Sirius. I believe he would like her back. Call her a present from his most loyal captain."

"Ah! Of course, Susan Andojar. I shall look forward to watching him break her. He is most adroit, Torkild. Maybe I'll let you view the tapes in the end. Ngen's a true artist in the finest sense. Follow the drone, brother."

Turning to Moshe, Torkild added coldly. "I'm leaving you in charge of the Romanan prisoners. Until I return, you'll make sure these mindless maggots don't let any escape—or suicide."

Thank Spider, no counter order came from M'Klea. They'd worried about that, about being separated at the last minute.

"Yes, sir!" Moshe snapped out a salute. He promptly began issuing orders, spreading the guards out, surrounding the knot of Romanans, getting those extra blasters within easy reach.

A small light appeared and led them off through the corridors. Torkild put Susan in the lead, unable to help noticing how she trembled, muscular control shot, reactions almost jelly. He shot a quick glance at Darwin Pike, observing the same near verge to panic.

"Buck up!" Torkild hissed.

His own muscles trembled at the tension. Damn it, so much could go so wrong. The little light continued to lead them down featureless white corridors. A bead of sweat tickled down his neck.

They stopped before a hatch guarded by two blaster-bearing clear-eyed men, alert, unpsyched. The drone snapped off.

"Pass them!" M'Klea's sharp voice ordered.

One of the guards stepped aside, eyeing Susan eagerly, a leer on his blocky face. "Someday soon, sweet," he whispered.

Susan's knees buckled, Torkild and Darwin catching her, rushing her forward as the hatch opened.

"He's dead," Pike promised under his breath, supporting Susan's trembling body.

Torkild stopped as the hatch whispered shut behind him. Mouth falling open, he gaped, amazed. Along either wall row upon row of bunks abutted, some occupied by naked, trembling women. Susan went limp in his arms, murmuring mewling noises to herself.

"Strip her!" M'Klea's voice ordered. "Bind her with EM restraints and put her on one of the beds. What? Frozen in your tracks? You can do that—strip a woman—can't you, my precious, righteous brother?"

Torkild barely heard, his disbelieving eyes on the monitors running over some of the captives. He recognized Ngen's naked body moving on the women. The victims watched with dull, horror-filled eyes as they screamed and moaned on the screens.

"I don't . . . This . . . What . . . M'Klea?" The urge to vomit tightened at the base of his throat. "What . . . *is* this place?"

"Ngen's chamber of horrors." Darwin gritted, under the cover of M'Klea's piping laughter. "Help me get Susan back to her wits." Darwin bent down, lips close to his belt comm, he whispered "Go!"

Torkild, dazed, stumbled down the beds, revolted, searching for Sarsa. He found her. Three beds down, naked, clamped spread-eagle by EM restraints. Her gaze was locked on the monitor overhead—glazed with fear and desperation. He barely noticed as his stomach lurched and heaved. Through it all, M'Klea's laughter echoed over the comm.

Ngen's private quarters aboard *Deus*.

The dreams stirred jaggedly, battering images of concussion, visions of acrid fire circling into erupting flame, twisting deck plate away, searing, dripping and exploding outward with decompression as Ngen's blasters cut her ship to ribbons.

Something mighty slammed her. Impact. Then nothing.

Now, after the fire, the scorching heat, her flesh was cool. Her backside rested on something firm, support under the entire length of her body. A low murmur of sound drifted with the air moving over her skin, heavy air, with a cloying scent. She tried to move and experienced lances of pain. She swallowed, tongue dry in her mouth. Something restrained her wrists and ankles. Restrained? The knowledge settled in her woozy mind.

"Welcome back, Major Sarsa," the warm, intimate voice of nightmares caressed Rita's consciousness.

She tensed, despite the sudden ache of tender muscles. *No! Spider, no! It couldn't be. Not . . .* She won the struggle to get her eyes open. Blinking the hazy film away, she looked up into Ngen Van Chow's leering features. Hollow sickness, like a wounded snake, curled in the pit of her belly.

A blonde woman, her features somehow familiar, stood to one side, her bulbous abdomen swollen with child.

"So this is hell," Rita whispered, closing her eyes tight. Supple, warm fingers gripped her chin, turning her head, causing her to look up into Ngen's intense eyes.

"No, dear, beautiful Rita. This is paradise." The lilting voice carried its own conviction. A conviction that had haunted her dreams since she'd first heard it on the tapes so long ago over Sirius.

Come on, girl. You gotta brass this one out. Just like in Big Man's village. Just like the reactor room on Bullet. *Just like all the times in the past. Remember Sarsa? The rebel broad with the big mouth and all the guts? You gotta dig her up. You gotta be tough, Rita, 'cause if you can't take it, he's gonna break you, tear you down, and leave you quivering wreckage.*

Under her breath, she whispered, "Damn you, Spider, I want to kick your ass!"

"What was that?"

"I said, who's the fat bitch?" Rita asked, trying to ignore the clammy fingers of terror tightening around her intestines. Could she sting him to such anger that he'd kill her?

"You will *bleed*," the blonde promised. From behind her back came a long wand. Rita couldn't quite suppress the shudder. She'd seen it before on captured tapes of Ngen's rape of Susan: the electronic whip.

"So you know?" Ngen laughed as M'Klea played the darting tip over Rita's toes. White pain burned, causing her leg to cramp against the EM restraints. She'd screamed at the first touch. She couldn't stop as agony—a white-hot metal rod—impaled the length of her body. Inside, fat and blood seared, dripped and charred on the bone. M'Klea kept at it, a horrid smile creeping over her features.

"That's but a touch," Ngen said, raising a hand. The whip lifted to hang, poised with promise over her quivering flesh. Ngen dropped congenially to the bed. "I do promise there's more coming. You insulted me last time we met, Major. Do you remember what you said? You gave me a most revolting message from Susan Andojar."

She clamped her jaws together, slitting her vision against the echoes of pain, knowing if she looked down, instead of blasted tatters of flesh, she'd find herself looking whole, flush and pink.

Damn! I thought I was tough. I'm not. How long can I take that? How long? Not even a second and I'll give in. Give him anything! She swallowed. *C'mon, Sarsa, fight back.*

"You Sirian dock rats get the funniest ideas."

His eyes looked pained as he stiffened. "I assure you, I will make you revise your opinion of me. I shall make your body sail on clouds of rapture! Oh, to be sure, your mind will hate it. But, dear Rita, I warn you now, there's nothing you can do to prevent me. I'll break you . . . and you'll know it as each fiber of resistance parts. In such a short time, I'll be your complete master. And all through the pleasure of the flesh." His voice invaded, an intimate, passionate whisper.

She looked up at the ecstasy in his eyes and began to shiver. *C'mon! Guts, woman! Is this the bitch who challenged the Directorate? Where's the hot redhead who defied the galaxy?* But she cringed, remembering the horror of Sirius, remembering the trials and the pain. Then she remembered the insanity in Susan's eyes.

"Come!" Ngen cried, clapping his hands and getting to his feet. "You look sad, Major! I suppose right now you're regretting the anguish you caused me on Sirius. Please," he smiled forgivingly, "this is a time for us to make up. A time for deep ecstasy and pleasure. Don't fret over past mistakes! We shall become very close. Very, very close." He leaned over and placed warm lips on her left breast as she tried to squirm away.

"Go to hell . . . BASTARD!"

M'Klea laughed with amusement. "Oh, she will be excellent, Ngen! Look at the fight and spirit in her eyes. I'll wager you can't break her in three days!"

"Taken, dearest!" Ngen cried. "You said that about the last redhead."

Think! What will goad him? Fight back, damn it! Her gut worked, twisting inside as he gracefully stepped out of his robe, letting it drift lightly to the floor. He filled his lungs, expanding his skinny chest, stretching up on his toes, thin strips of muscle tightening on his body.

"First," he explained, bending over her, "I'll soften some of your resistance, Rita. Not too much, just enough."

"Didn't your whore mother ever—" Pain blew it away. She jerked and arched against the restraints as the whip bounced supplely in Ngen's hands. Shattered fragments of sear-blinded mind heard the scream as pain arched blue-white along the insides of her calves and thighs.

The feeling might be akin to euphoric when the agony dissipated to mere tingles in her flesh. She could feel the cool air rushing into her lungs, her spasming heart pounding a staccato against her ribs, blood rushing in her ears.

She blinked, trying to swallow, throat raw—and froze at the sight of him. His engorged flesh pulsed before her as if ready to burst. A crystal drop of fluid formed.

"Pleasure, my dear Rita." The gentle tones of his voice crept insidiously into her mind. "This time it will be me alone who possesses you. But next time? Ah, you see, I know you're not Romanan. The psych will help relax you. While I lead you to pleasure, you'll experience your lover

Iron Eyes, to the greatest delight. And slowly, bit by bit, we'll wean you from the psych and you'll know the fullness of my abilities. Then, Rita, you'll cry for the bliss I can give you.''

"Think so? Didn't I hear Susan once say a five-year-old boy had more finesse than you? Even dock scum like you . . . Ahhh!'' He slapped the whip across her breasts.

Trying to recover ripped and scattered thoughts, she felt him lower himself beside her. Panicking, she threw herself against the restraints, jerking, bucking with all the strength of her fear-charged body. His skin slid against hers, cool, dry, as practiced fingers moved over her sweat-flushed body. She bit off a scream as his warm mouth moved on her fevered flesh.

She barely heard M'Klea's voice from somewhere in the fog of panic. Choking down tears, eyes clamped shut, she felt him shift, tightening every muscle inside against his entry. *All right, Sarsa. You can beat him. Fight back. He wants you panicked. C'mon, you're the feisty broad, it's just rape. You'll get the chance to kill him.*

Only he didn't move to cover her.

She could feel him stand. *Wha-What, Ngen? Another trick? Some subtle torture to wear me down? You vile bit of human pollution, what are you going to do? How . . . how long until he breaks me? Leaves me a gibbering idiot like the rest?* She swallowed hard, trying to still the spasming of her diaphragm as it pulled at the knot constricting the base of her throat.

Desperate, she shivered unconsciously and looked up through slitted eyes. M'Klea had handed him a comm. He stood for a moment, nodding, sighing, and finally taking the headset from his brow.

"I'm so sorry, Major," Ngen whispered sorrowfully. "I've just been called to Cobalt Station. They've learned to control the singularity device I call 'The Fist of Deus.' Imagine, I can throw a tiny singularity anywhere in the Directorate. Rita, my beloved, I really am God now. With the Fist, I shall destroy Damen Ree, the Patrol . . . and yes, even your Romanans.''

He traced his fingers across her shivering breasts and down the muscular sweep of her belly to twirl in her hair . . and lower. She tensed against the exploration of his fingers. Ngen smiled a wicked promise, delighted by her revulsion.

"I take it all back, Ngen. Everything I ever said abou
you."

He raised an eyebrow.

"I don't think it's your mother's fault. I think she aborted
your fetus into the mold down under the dock. Raised by
green slime, you didn't get any social skills to—" She
grunted as he prodded her hard, reaching a fist back to hi
her.

"Easy." M'Klea grabbed his arm. "That's what she
wants, husband. If she can goad you into losing your tem
per, you'll make a mistake."

Ngen nodded, the anger draining from his fevered eyes
"Yes, I'll enjoy breaking her."

"Too bad your silly Arpeggian bitch isn't enough for you
dock rat." Rita shifted her glance. "That bother a sill
whore like you? That he has to go to . . ." Ngen's hard sla
across her face stopped the rest. Rita worked her mouth
tasting blood.

"You will bleed," M'Klea swore through clenched teeth
He leaned down and sucked the side of her neck. He
stomach pumped suddenly and she vomited.

Ngen had pulled himself artfully away and shook his fin
ger at her. "Not very nice, dear Rita. You must learn t
treat God better—considering the gift of physical delight I'
about to bestow on you. Think of pleasure, my sweetes
Rita. True bursting bliss. Let me teach you . . . let me brin
your body to its fullest fruit . . . yearning for me, deare
love."

"I doubt I'll ever get excited by dock slime, Ngen," Rit
half-choked on her bile.

He smiled warmly at Rita, a tic in his cheek. "Indeed,
really hate to be rude at a time when you're warm and s
ready for bliss. Being an Emperor, however, entails certai
sacrifices. But I'll return. And maybe let you watch while
destroy *Bullet*, Damen Ree, Arcturus, and the Romanans!
He smiled happily, sighed, and took M'Klea's arm, the hatc
sliding shut behind them.

"Blessed Spider, this can't be. This is . . . is a drean
It's not real. I'll wake up in a bunk. Hear me? I'm going
wake up in a bunk on the *Knife*." But *Knife* had been blow
in two. They'd barely contained the reaction as it was.

Minutes later, a man entered, slid a cleaning unit out
the wall, and sopped up her mess, cleaning her body as
she were no more than a piece of equipment. She tried i

sulting him, getting no reaction from those dead eyes. Cold fingers on her flesh made her twist with disgust.

After he left, the holo formed over her flat prison and she looked up, shocked to see herself. She closed her eyes and tried to ignore the screams and the cackling laughter of M'Klea Alhar. That creature had been Torkild's sister!

The holo ran over and over and over again. Rita found herself drawn to watch just like the wretches on the beds around her. Some, she'd noted, stared with hollow, crazed eyes, others with rapt attention, caressing themselves.

"Not me," Rita promised. "Not . . . not like them."

How will it be, she wondered, when Ngen has time to complete a cycle of pain and pleasure? How will I react when I have to look up and watch him—and my too-willing body? How long can I last against my own self-revulsion? And it works, damn it. The deep brain can be trained no matter what the conscious mind does. And he's a master at it. But what will John . . . *No, never, never even think it!* She burst out in tears, sobbing hysterically for the first time since her former husband had died so long ago.

"Admiral!" she whispered passionately through the snot clogging her nose. "Get here quick! Get here and kill this ship!"

Only the holo continued to spin above her.

CHAPTER XLIII

Ngen's personal quarters aboard the *Deus*.

She was close to jelly when the others arrived. But when she saw Susan—saw her collapse—Rita bit off a sob. How could Spider have delivered Susan back to this demon? Could she do something? Distract Susan's guards? Give her a chance to kill them quickly—and perhaps rescue Rita, too? The ragged shreds of her mind began working again.

She was getting ready to scream when she recognized Darwin Pike bending over the limp girl. The other, of course, was Torkild. She bit her lip. Torkild? That foul M'Klea's brother? Hesitantly, she turned her wild stare to the holo, mind rattled and reeling. Call out? Or had something gone terribly wrong?

"Are you all right?"

She looked over, seeing Torkild wiping at his wet mouth, propped unsteadily against her platform. He bent down, checking the EM restraints at her wrists and ankles.

"I . . . I don't . . . k-know," Rita shuddered. The alert klaxon bellowed beyond the bulkhead. In the background, comm began blaring orders.

Then Susan—ghostly white, grim-faced and shaken— loomed over her, unlocking the EM restraints. Rita found herself looking into those frightened, dark eyes she'd become so used to. They shared a communion of terror now.

"You gonna make it?"

Rita felt herself nodding, unsure. "He didn't . . . get everything done. I . . . I'd kill myself otherwise."

Susan's strong hands took hers, pulling her to her feet. "No, you wouldn't," she muttered angrily in an attempt to cover her own fear and hysteria. "I didn't. You wouldn't." The words came out in a snap, brittle.

"You're stronger than me."

"Put these on." Pike returned from rummaging through a locker. "They might fit. Careful of the chafe on your wrists and ankles."

She noticed how bunched his jaw muscles were under that pale sweaty skin. At each sound, Pike jumped, jittery, a nervous finger on his blaster as he searched for danger. Damn, the man teetered on the brink.

"You two are awfully brave," she whispered. "Coming in here . . . here where . . ." She caught Torkild—his eye glued to the monitor. He was watching M'Klea play the electronic whip over Rita's feet. He stared, shocked, mouth open, face slackly listless, slowly shaking his head. Through the replay of Rita's screams, a whimpering noise came from deep in his chest.

"What about him?" She jerked a thumb at the Arpeggian.

"*Torkild! Damn you!*" The voice cracked sharply over the comm. "What . . . *What have you done?*" M'Klea screamed as her face formed on comm.

He spun and looked up at her, hatred mingled with disbelief as he blinked tears from his anguished red face. "This *can't* be you!" Hysterical, he pointed at the holo. "*You tortured this woman!*" He swallowed hard, revulsion twist-

ing his mouth. "My sister! My beloved M'Klea, you are a
. . a *monster!*" Tear trails glistened, jagged in the light,
as his face worked. "I believed in you! You were so beautiful. So precious, a thing to be loved and cherished!"

"Torkild!" she snapped, voice haughty. "The Romanans are
loose. I *order* you to lock up the women and take your men in
hand. Put down this revolt against the Messiah and me!"

Torkild Alhar's *"Never!"* cut clear and ringing. "I'm a
free man, M'Klea. I hereby declare your Messiah a fraud.
Deus *is* Satan, sister, *and you are his WHORE!!*"

She recoiled, eyes flashing. "You'll pay, you filthy over-
bearing bastard! You weaseling foul braggart! You miserable—"

He lifted his blaster and blew the comm off the wall.
"Come on!" Torkild led the way to the hatch as Rita pulled
the too large tunic over her head, taking the spare blaster
Torkild handed her.

Darwin palmed the hatch. Nothing.

"Locked!" he gritted, frantically pounding his hand on
the latch.

"This used to be the officer's wardroom. Stand back!"
Rita motioned them away from the wall and easily blew a
panel out. "That's one of the thinnest bulkheads in the
ship." She swallowed hard and jumped through the gap.

Fear rushed in every cell of Darwin's body. His bowels
had gone loose and runny. The specter of Ngen Van Chow
loomed, looking over his shoulder every step of the way.
As he followed Rita through the door, he pitched headlong
into the middle of a group of Fathers trotting down the corridor, blasters drawn.

The panel Rita had shot out had fallen on some. The
Major exploded in the middle of them, striking, chopping,
and kicking in a combat frenzy, the blaster in her fist lacing
death into their midst. Pressed in among the bodies, Darwin
pulled the old Randall from his belt, cutting, slashing, and
ripping as Susan had taught him for close quarters. The
Fathers were mindless, fearless, without care for their
well-being. They turned, practically diving onto Darwin's
knife. Susan appeared beside him, her combat-armored foot
catching a man's throat, snapping the neck before lashing
out at another.

Fear—so long bottled—broke loose in a howl of rage as
he bowled into a group of Fathers seeking to bring blasters

to bear. A berserker, his weight bore them all to the floor
kicking, screaming, and yelling. Darwin thrust with hi
knife, kicking a rising blaster away, and twisted to slash
man's throat. Hot blood shot everywhere.

Darwin rolled out of the press, tripping as he careene
to his feet. He staggered against the wall—a blaster bol
barely missing him—and slipped on blood, sprawling fac
first. The blaster skittered from his jarred grip. The dec
plates next to his head exploded, splattering hot metal o
his skin as another bolt sought him. Crabbing frantically
Darwin got his feet under him, crouched, ready—and sa
his death.

The Father braced himself in a marksman's stance, linin
the blaster on Pike's chest. Darwin—in a last-ditch effort—
rushed, Randall held low to thrust into the man's bowels
Too late, too far away. Darwin howled his rage; anger at
fever pitch.

A half-second before he triggered the weapon, the Fa
ther's head exploded, showering Pike with blood and brain:
The corpse flopped, clattering to the floor.

A sudden silence filled the gruesome corridor. Confuse
Darwin spun on his heel to find Torkild standing there,
line of smoke traced to his blaster. Pike sucked cool breat
into his laboring lungs as he met the Arpeggian's eyes. Gri
acknowledgment passed between them.

Susan and Rita rose from among the dead, blasters i
hand as they checked the charges. Darwin found his blaste
then quickly took coup, tying the grisly trophies on his be
to drip blood down his armored leg.

"We've got to get out of here," Torkild gasped, pushir
out from the blasted bulkheads. Exploded graphsteel, lik
the petals of deadly roses curled out behind him. A slee
trace of smoke hung in the hall, the air reeking of charre
flesh and pungent with the tang of bright blood.

"We've got to destroy something called the Fist," Ri
growled, fighting for breath. "With that mass weapon, Nge
thinks he can destroy the Admiral. Maybe the whole fleet!

"The Fist? Cobalt Station!"

Rita blanched. "Shit! Patan said Damen had to destroy
first thing. Damn! If we only knew what day it was o
Earth!"

"Earth? How in hell could we—"

"Let's go," Darwin grinned in a rictus. "Ngen's ther
I want that bastard!"

"Not *half* so much as I," Susan hissed, bending down, ripping a sonic grenade from a dead Father's belt. Setting the fuse, she tossed it back into the chamber of horrors. Then another and another, and then they bolted at a run back the way they'd come.

"Why did you do that?" Torkild cried, pounding along beside her.

The explosion tore the ship around them, buckling the walls, slapping the deck underfoot up and down. Concussion pelted them with heat and compressed air.

Ducking, Susan shot him a grim-eyed look, jaws clamped. "They don't want to live, Captain. I just did them a favor."

"But all those women? Maybe with psych they could. . . ." he stopped talking, stunned by his words. "Oh my God!"

"Yeah, maybe with psych? I *lived* through that nightmare back there. Damn it, Torkild, lived it, you hear? It isn't easy. Every night I live it again. I'da been lucky if I'd died long ago."

The bitter, cutting edge in her voice silenced him. Lost in thought, he followed, panting as they sprinted, retracing the corridors under Rita's lead.

The sounds of combat, distant at first, raged louder ahead of them. They passed small contortions of bodies: Fathers, coups taken, skulls spattered with blood where the tissue had been ripped loose.

Rita led them expertly to Dock 9. Rita and Susan dropped, sliding on their knees, weapons raised as Fathers started forward. In tandem, marksmanship deadly, they blasted the guards apart and sprinted for the AT. Rita slapped the lock closed on the way and collapsed, panting for all she was worth.

"Piss-poor security. Couldn't have got away with that on a Patrol ship." They rested a moment, gasping, staring hollow-eyed at each other while sweat dampened hair and raced patterns down hot cheeks.

"Let's get out of here," Pike puffed and pushed himself up.

Rita jerked her head in a nod, pulling damp red hair back as she shoved off the metal and staggered forward.

Susan grinned, reaching up to kiss Darwin and hug him tightly. "Made it so far," she said between breaths. "Lot of coup in that."

He grinned, dragging her close to kiss her soundly and

slap-her on the bottom. "I'll get us some hotter firepower. You go drive this thing."

Her smile was ravishing as she pushed away, white teeth bright against the glow of her skin.

"How about me?" Torkild asked.

Pike shrugged, pushing forward.

Susan dropped easily into the fire control station. "Darwin! Rita needs combat armor! You and Torkild strap into the crash webbing. We're going into Cobalt the hard way."

"What about the warriors? We can't—"

"They're on their own!" Rita shook her head furiously, bringing the system to life with flying fingers, slipping the headset over her wild red curls. "With the Fist, Ngen can kill the entire fleet! So what if we all die? Damn it, that's what it's worth!" A pause. "Susan! Turn the guns on those damn grapples!"

The AT shuddered under Darwin's feet, almost pitching him into the locker he was fishing through. He found Rita's size and ran for the bridge. Grateful green eyes met his as Rita shucked the oversized coveralls and began strapping the armor on.

"Glad we got there in time."

"You wouldn't have been," Rita muttered callously. "He got called away. As it was, I was shaken enough. Damn, don't know how Susan did it." Rita's eyes smoldered with emotion. "How can she stand it, Pike?"

He swallowed, noting her confusion, seeing how close she had come to breaking. "I guess she didn't know in advance, Major. You had lots of time to dream about it. Ever since that tape you reviewed. She went in cold. Spider might hate it, but there're times when ignorance can help."

Rita dropped her eyes and nodded, her spirit suddenly drained. "Yeah, I suppose. Thanks, Doctor. I needed that. You might have just given me back a little self-respect."

"Well Major, for what it's worth, there are damn few people I respect more. I'll serve on your team any time." He winked.

She stopped, fumbling for words, a wetness in the rim of her eyes.

He took a moment to hug her, gave her a slap on the back, and turned to go as she slid in next to Torkild and motioned him away. Following the Arpeggian, Darwin called over his shoulder. "Hey, you two remember how precious the cargo is back here, okay?"

The lights dimmed as Susan triggered the big guns. The clap of the exploding grapples jarred the AT, power whining in the thrusters as Rita broke them away from *Deus*.

Torkild was already strapping into the crash webbing, face colorless, eyes haunted. Darwin snapped himself in and sagged gratefully in the cushiony elastic. He took a deep breath and blew it out past his teeth, realizing how bloody and gruesome he looked.

Torkild still stared off into space, listless.

"You all right?"

"What happened to her? What happened to make her . . . How could my sweet M'Klea . . . ?" He turned his head, hanging limply in the webbing.

"I didn't know her before. I can't really say."

"She was my little sister who . . ." Torkild stumbled confused. "I have to . . . to kill her now. Duty . . . My honor . . . Oh, precious God! *What's happened to me?*"

"Torkild? Why not let her go? It's her life, let her live with it. She made her choices. You can't change them and you can't blame yourself for what she's become. That's Spider's responsibility. Free will. Nothing, not love, not honor or duty can change it."

"I wonder." With one free hand, Torkild Alhar drew a crude Spider on the front of his armor. "There is always responsibility, Doctor Pike. There are choices men have to make regarding good and evil and right and wrong. How foolish of me to have ever thought otherwise. How foolish that I once thought life was easy, patterned to fit into a silly code." He paused and laughed to himself. "I have so much to learn yet, Doctor."

"We all do, Captain. Thanks for that timely shot back there. Maybe I can repay you sometime."

Torkild nodded, weaving his free arm back into the webbing. "You know, I didn't like you when I first met you. I didn't understand who or what you were. I blame my limited experience for that."

"Yeah, well, I guess we're even. I thought you were a pompous, self-centered bastard. I was wrong. I didn't think you had change in you."

"Spider wants us to live and learn," Torkild reminded. "I only wish my people hadn't suffered that I might see."

Pike shifted, checking his position. "The way of Spider, I suppose. Who are we to question the purposes of God? Damn, when my soul gets back to the old boy, I'm sure gonna give that numinous, spit-sucking son of a bitch a piece of my mind.''

"You . . . you'd say *that* about God?''

Pike chuckled grimly. "That's what we're here for, Torkild. I used to question. Used to wonder if God even existed. Then I got a good dose of reality among the Romanans. Yeah, Spider expects exactly that out of us. Honesty, not fear. Experience, not mindless worship. I only wonder what Spider's going to make of Ngen's soul when He gets it. Might set a precedent for self-amputation of spiritual essence!''

Torkild shook his head, nervous at his proximity to such blasphemy.

Pike sighed, understanding the man's complete bewilderment. In the space of hours, everything he'd held sacred to the root of his soul had been cast loose to the interstellar winds. Torkild had come eyeball to eyeball with complete sociocultural dysfunction.

The AT rocked and shuddered, lights dimming as Susan played the blasters against some unseen enemy. Rita had begun evasive maneuvers. Pike and Torkild bounced pitched back and forth—weird bugs in Spider's web—while the craft gyrated under Rita's skilled hand.

Torkild swallowed, eyes darting to the hull around them as if aware of just how thin it was.

"We're all caught in Spider's web, Captain.'' Darwin motioned to the crash webbing they hung in. "I've come to the conclusion you just take your lumps and do the best you can.''

He paused, wetting his lips. "And Torkild? Listen. if I don't make it through this, take good care of Susan.''

"Susan? Doctor? I—''

"Hang on!'' Rita bellowed through comm.

Aboard *Bullet* decelerating into the Gas Clouds.

Worry continued to chew a little hole in Damen Ree's stomach. Around him, *Bullet* hummed, decelerating at thirty five gravities in order to keep schedule with *Uhuru* and *Kamikazi*. Maya and Toby, of course, had improved gravity compensation, but the slowest dictated the pace. And Spider knew, they'd be pushing it to make Patan's figure.

The huge curve of the bridge glistened whitely, practically vibrating with energy as comm, weapons, engineer

ng, and assault teams shuttled data back and forth. The
overhead monitors flickered in laser-bright color, feeding
information to techs who analyzed and corrected and rein-
putted. The pilot reclined in his chair, eyes closed as he
maintained the navigational comm. Other techs stared dry-
eyed at screens, monitoring the space around them, *Bullet*'s
ears searching passively for any evidence of Ngen's presence or vessels. Overhead, Leeta Dobra's ragged spider
hung, waiting.

Comm noted no less than eleven different routes into the
Gas Cloud. In technical terms, the cloud consisted of a black
globule which Directorate astrophysicists had determined
would be a star within another hundred thousand years.

The navigational routes—laboriously mined out and periodically swept free of dust and gas by ram jets—allowed
interstellar transport to decelerate without being abraded.
Of course, any ship could come in shielded until slowed
sufficiently to avoid damage. Ree heard his stomach gurgle
as he hoped his four other battleships had hit their holes.
The GCIs, with less sophisticated navigational abilities,
would follow behind, unable to shed V as quickly. In the
end, they'd be the reserves—hopefully unneeded with their
reduced shielding. At the last, however, their Fujiki guns
might make the difference.

With nothing left to do but dive in, Ree watched the first
buoy flash by as the stars dimmed behind *Bullet*. Sensors
had picked up the next buoy and were correcting course.

"That's it," Ree admitted, raising his arms. "We're
committed. Tony, drop the first beacon for the GCIs, string
them out at two AU as we decided."

"Acknowledged, Admiral." One of the monitors displayed a flare of light as *Bullet* laid a trail for the following
GCIs.

"No word from Rita or Colonel Kuryaken?" Iron Eyes
asked, hard eyes somber, muscled arms crossed over his
thick chest. "They have the most difficult coordination."

"No. And to be honest, I didn't expect any. They
couldn't have tried to coordinate with us. They're on the
other side of the cloud. Too much chance of Ngen picking
up the directional subspace. From the rega bounce, he'd
deduce it was close. Even if he couldn't break the code,
he'd have his ears out. Be warned. Let's hope we've caught
him completely unprepared."

Iron Eyes nodded, a deeper worry in his eyes. Hell, a

man had a right to worry about his wife, didn't he? "How long now?"

Ree glanced at the comm monitor. "Figuring relative to standard, five days from our perspective."

As the days dragged slowly past, the clouds of gas grew thicker, warmer, as they compressed, gravity overcoming molecular resistance. The pitch black had lightened in the visible spectrum, reddening slightly as longer wavelength light penetrated the dust.

And the Colonists liked living where they couldn't see stars? Whatever sort of folks they were, they made the finest molecular strings and the toughest graphite fiber in the universe. Back in the old days—so the records said—entire ships had been constructed of graphite. Just another example of lost Brotherhood technology.

Ree eyeballed the charts displayed by holo. Halfway there. The chronometer displaying Earth time continued slowing, correcting for relativity. Like a speed gauge, he could read their deceleration.

Damen Ree fretted and paced, spending long hours at the battle comm, trying to anticipate, perfecting roll maneuvers to shift gun decks should one lose power. The new people, the young Romanans on their first spacing, became proficient in damage control drill, loss of gravity under acceleration, vacuum conditions, and evacuation.

Iron Eyes watched impassively, constantly communicating with comm, calculating weaknesses among his people. In drill after drill, his Romanans and marines worked until they could barely stand up. They practiced assault techniques, constantly in zero g, the wardrooms simulating the atmosphere of the stations—or in vacuum.

One day to rendezvous. A tension had settled, drawing tight like a fine heat-shrunk plastic about the entire ship. Jokes became short, laughter forced, Ngen lay there, just beyond the reddening gas they approached. Hull temperature rose from the increased infrared as gases compressed around them. The shielding glowed now, a streak of yellow light flaring behind them as more of the countless beacons glared blue-white and marked the path for the GCIs.

The first inkling Ree had of trouble came with a fluctuation of the mass detectors—the reading slight, coming from a long way off.

"What the hell?" He looked up from where he'd been frowning over an imaginary problem of Ngen reversing

rollover to fire torpedoes. Coffee cup in hand, he glowered
at the monitor. "If that's a glitch, I want it fixed. *Now,*
people."

Techs immediately began crawling over the equipment,
making sure they didn't have a sensor malfunction. Desperately, Ree wished he could talk to S. Montaldo—the Directorate planetologist directing World's toron exploitation.
What could cause that much disturbance to the mass detectors? Four hours later, the monitors jumped again. None of
the meters had turned flippy, making quirks in the reading,
so it must be something in the clouds.

"Admiral." The somber technical lieutenant looked up
from the guts of the sensor, her eyes hardened. "If I was
to guess, I'd call that a micro singularity. But, well, sir, we
know they didn't exist within a couple of seconds after the
Big Bang."

Ree frowned, staring anxiously up at monitors, *Bullet* occasionally punching through wisps of weirdly lit gases. Like
flying through a fog bank, he thought. You never knew
where the mountains were. The Gas Clouds hid more than
light. What else had been brewing inside the hot glowing
gases? Ree's stomach tightened; the little thing that ate at
him sank razor-white teeth into the soft tissues of his gastric
system.

Nothing improved as *Bullet* neared the Colonies.

"Admiral? We've got that gravity flux again," the lieutenant called. "This time, sir, we've got a fingerprint, too.
Compression wave along with a pretty powerful gamma ray
source. The mass fluctuations have increased in frequency."

"And?" Ree chewed his nails to nubs as the lieutenant
ran simulation after simulation, strain lines engraved in her
brow and the lines around her eyes. In the end, she kept
coming up with one consistent explanation.

"Hawking effect."

"You're sure?"

The lieutenant's sigh expressed it all, but she added,
"Admiral, to be honest, I really and truly don't know. The
presence of quantum black holes in the Gas Clouds would
have been well known. Too many people have been mining
here for too long. Worse, the figures I'm getting are too
small for Big Bang residuals. It's just, well, figure a proton-
sized hole with, say, a radius of 10^{-13} centimeter and a mass
of maybe a billion tons. You can compute the erosion of the
hole through the amount of Hawking radiation. Mass di-

vided by erosion leaves the average lifespan of roughly ten billion years. Holes that big should have blown up four billion years ago. So we're dealing with larger holes at this point in the universe's history—only the readings we're getting off these explosions are magnitudes too small. Parallax on gamma rays estimates the distance of the particles across an arc of 20 AU. Well, sir, from the predicted size of the eroding primordial holes, we should be experiencing an explosion on the order of ten to twenty million megatons. And we're not.''

Ree exhaled through his teeth, staring absently down into his coffee. ''Best guess, lieutenant?''

''Tiny eroding black holes. Perhaps we're only dealing with mass on the order of pounds. Compress that far enough, you get the singularity effect. Hot, radiating like a bastard, and incredibly unstable. Instant primordial black hole with a life expectancy of something like 10^{-36} second.''

''But we've got a spread of these things. Why?''

The lieutenant scratched her head. ''Uh, I don't know I . . . What the hell, with that kind of power, maybe they can sling them around.''

''God, no!'' Ree stiffened. ''That Brotherhood data Ngen stole. It has to be.''

The lieutenant swallowed, turning pale.

''War Chief?'' Ree turned. ''You get all this?''

Iron Eyes nodded. ''I think so. Ngen's surprise? Just like off Sirius?''

''Lieutenant, I don't want this information all over the gun room. Your speculations are top secret. Understand? Good.'' Ree rubbed at the tightness around his eyes. ''John, my quarters. We'd better take a solid look at this. Consider the options.''

They walked in silence, the humming life of *Bullet* around them. A sanctuary? Against what sort of weapon?

Ree palmed his lock plate, eyes playing over the wall where his Romanan weapons hung on display as they entered. Had it really been in this lifetime that he'd recovered those? From there, his eyes went to the empty scotch bottle. Too bad. A lot of memories were tied up in that bottle—and right now he desperately wished it were full.

The hatch hissed as Iron Eyes walked through. He noticed the scowl on Ree's face and dropped into a chair.

''Well, what does it mean? Are we heading in to be butchered again? Is this another Sirian debacle? What ca quantum phenomena do to us? Zip right through the shields?'' The expression on Iron Eyes' face was uncertain. ''And wouldn't that much energy released, even at the levels the lieutenant was talking about, destroy us?''

''You've learned something.''

Iron Eyes smiled a crooked smile. ''Lots of time in sleep stim. Lots of time talking to techs and learning about what makes ships run. Quantum physics defy me, at least the mathematics and practical applications do. But, yes, I've managed to keep up with my studies despite the war. Having Rita gone for so long helps. It's easier to fall asleep under stim and learn things like astrophysics than to long for her.'' He spread his fingers wide, looking at his hands. ''And I promised Leeta once, a long time ago, that I would learn to read. That knowledge is like a good horse, it takes you to so many wonderful places you never dreamed of finding. But the math? Well, that's another story.''

''She'd be proud, you know.''

Iron Eyes rubbed a callused hand over his face, changing the subject. ''You were saying about generated mass?''

''Right, but unlike the big singularities, these have a very brief existence. I think they have something which compresses matter so violently that its mass slips ''outside.'' When it reappears, the internal stresses of the mass exceed the gravitational force which is trying to hold it together. Boom!''

''How do they do that?'' Iron Eyes asked as he fingered his fighting knife and frowned.

''I have no idea. The technology is so far beyond ours that it's like blasters against stone clubs. Theoretically possible, of course, but the implementation is impossible given our understanding of materials and stress limits for matter.''

''So are Prophets.''

''Don't remind me. I'm scared enough as it is.''

''Then we have to leave our trust in Spider.'' Iron Eyes reminded. ''The one thing we have which Ngen doesn't, is surprise. That, in the end, may win the entire battle.''

''And if we don't, it'll be over in seconds—assuming he can aim that thing. And the GCIs coming in won't stand a chance.''

''Then we'd better do this right. If we don't get the ATs off, target Cobalt Station—which we can assume is the mass compactor—and blast Ngen's battleship, our souls will be on the way back to Spider post haste.''

* * *

The closer *Bullet* got to the rendezvous, the more significant the mass anomalies became, to the point where even
light could be detected in the compressing clouds.

"We just passed the last buoy," the helmsman called.
"Time?"

"It is 2:25 a.m., GMT Earth at this moment, Admiral."

Ree nodded at the comm. "Deploy your ATs, Iron Eyes.
Good luck! You should break into the Colonies in exactly
five minutes. We'll bottle this hole and give you whatever
cover we can."

At 2:30, Ree opened the channels and yelled, "Let's hit
them for Spider!" *Bullet* emerged from the pall of dust and
gas, blasters seeking anything that looked like converted
GCIs. That day, Admiral Ree got only one bit of good news.
The surprise was a complete success. His Patrol forces ren-
dezvoused perfectly except for *Kamikazi*.

Then the Fist unleashed.

CHAPTER XLIV

Aboard AT22 in the Gas Cloud Colonies.

A loud crack split the air deafeningly. Darwin surged against
the crash webbing. The AT had been stopped dead as he
and Torkild jiggled like puppets in the webbing.

Susan jumped lightly through the lock, pulling a shoulder
blaster from the locker. Darwin unsnapped and dropped to
take one from her. He gave her a quick smile as Torkild
took one of the big guns and began strapping charges around
his waist. Sack by sack, Susan handed out grenades.

"Take all you can carry. We leave the AT, we're on our
own."

Rita motioned them into the hatch. "Vacuum conditions.
Helmets up." Her nimble fingers helped Torkild. "Comm
check?"

One by one, they sent and received.

"Okay. Let's go. Careful out there now. We can't care
for wounded. You're hit . . . you're left."

Rita thumbed the hatch open a crack. She tossed a greıade out and ducked back. The blast ruptured bulkheads in ₊very direction, swirling the debris in a whirlwind that ushed in a whistling howl for the rupture the AT had torn n the hull behind them.

Decompression alerts bellowed someplace, growing faint ₊s the air whooshed out.

"I'd say the best bet is to hit the power units first." Susan uggested, jumping to push forward against the decompres-ion. "If we can destroy one, the station should be crippled. ¯he more we get the better."

Torkild jumped out behind her. "What do you think the ₊dds are that we four will cripple such a huge place?"

"Better than no odds at all."

"Spider's will," Rita grunted. "Let's go. They ought to ₊ave a hatch we can blow somewhere."

Pike trotted forward, climbing over waist-high black rolls ₊f number five powerlead, lots of the big spools canted and ħoved into piles by the impact of the sharp-nosed AT. The ↔oreroom they'd invaded had a deformed look, the walls ₊pped loose and canted by the intrusion of their craft. Only ₊wo of the ceiling lights still worked. From the gravity, he ₊upposed they'd landed on the side of the rim instead of ₊oming up through the floors.

"Here." Rita waved, placing explosives on a wall. She ₊ucked down to the side. Flash-bam! and she was through ₊ıe rent, atmosphere whistling through the jagged hole she'd ₊rn.

None of the door lock plates worked, overridden by se-₊urity or decompression alert. They marked progress by ₊ulkheads blasted and rooms decompressed, occasionally ₊assing a gasping, suffocating Father, prostrated as air ₊ushed along the path they'd blown, whirling along flimsies, ₊apers, and plastic wrappers. Each wall took a sonic gre-₊ade, blasting out dying men and swirling debris.

"Look out!" Darwin saved them. From the corner of his ₊ye, he caught movement coming up from behind. Sighting ₊ıe heavy blaster, he blew the first of the Fathers in two and ₊harged to the rear as another wall fell before Rita's demo-₊ion.

Darwin scuttled around the edge of a sagging structural ₊ıember and crouched in the semidarkness, heart pounding. ₊wo more Fathers jumped an overturned desk and crouched ₊own, out of sight. More were crawling through the wreck-₊ge of overturned grav chairs, dead monitors, and spilled

comm cards. Two rooms away, Darwin knew another wall
had been blown. As the Fathers advanced, Pike steadied his
weapon and blew them apart. They died horribly, bodies
decompressing, while their fluids boiled and puddled on
carpeted flooring.

Darwin advanced, getting farther and farther from Susan.
Another squad could be seen, pushing their way forward,
the advance perfectly executed. Pike settled the big gun and
waited. The first wave trotted across the empty room. Darwin blew them away.

"Pike?"

"I'm holding the rear. Keep going! I'm doing fine."

"Darwin?" Susan's voice. "Don't do anything heroic.
Stay alive."

He winced at the pleading hidden in her words.

Blaster bolts sought him from the covered positions of
the second wave. Debris and hot metal peppered his armor.
Darwin tossed a sonic grenade—horrified as it curved in,
possibly against a wall. Coriolis effect! The wall disintegrated, scattering the attack and Darwin wreaked havoc on
them, blaster bolts brilliant in the dim light.

Just like trapping arctic hares! Trap? the thought came to
him. Taping a sonic grenade to the wall, he ran a wire—
pulled from a piece of shattered equipment—from the grenade trigger and strung it across the doorway. Picking up
his blaster, he scuttled back, stopping only long enough to
booby-trap each of the gaping holes. Would the mindless
Fathers ever think of checking?

Seconds later, he felt the concussion coming from behind. How eerie to walk through the silent, dark rooms,
feeling the floor tremble beneath his feet. Lights worked in
some of the disheveled rooms, litter was strewn everywhere, the constant breeze of decompression pushing against
him. He almost missed the hot spot. It was only after he
looked up from setting the grenade that he noticed the wall
beginning to glow red, then white. The metal turned molten
and sagged out, bursting with a hiss. A long telescoping
tube shot out under compression.

Darwin stepped over his trip wire and inspected it. Portable lock! Flanking maneuver.

"Susan? Rita?" No answer.

Cut off? Dead? No time to think about it. Gotta go! He
stepped to one side as the hatch opened a crack. When the
grenade came through, he batted it back in. Ducking, he

jerked under the impact of the shrapnel in his armor where it peppered the lock walls.

Now what? On impulse, he opened the lock, stepping in over the dying and dismembered. The Fathers on the other side cycled it. The wounded underfoot, he dispatched with his hand blaster. How many? Eight? On the other side, they wouldn't expect him to pop out shooting. *Too damned insane. No idiot would do that! Suicide!*

He swallowed hard. And if Susan and Rita had . . . Act, don't think. Keep moving. Buy time. Pray Susan's alive. That's it. She's just out of comm reach. Too many walls in the way. That's it. Make a diversion. Take the pressure off.

The lock began to fill, his combat armor crackling with the change in pressure. His last sonic grenade, set on short fuse, rested heavily in his hand. The lock opened, Darwin smiled into the dull eyes of the Father, and tossed the grenade out. He slammed the door while the outside rocked. Flinging the portal wide open, he laced fire into the wiggling forms on the floor. Then he was through, shooting, screaming, and killing.

He plucked grenades from one of the dead and ducked behind stacked bodies as blaster fire sought him. Pulling off his helmet, he almost gagged on the stink of charred flesh. Foul smelling liquid ran from a punctured gut cavity to pool green-brown and acrid under his nose. The severed intestine sputtered just above his ear.

He choked, trying to keep from vomiting. "Gotta get out of here." The corpses jerked from blaster fire.

"Squads three and four, move right. Get around his position. Attack sequence three. Move . . . *now!*"

Pike tried not to breathe and chewed his lip. Fathers couldn't fight without direction and someone out there wasn't psyched. The smart ones—officers—had to be on the way.

"Gotta move—or I'm cooked."

He set the timer and flipped a grenade over the body pile. Coriolis got him again as the grenade clanged off the doorway and exploded, fragmenting the Fathers with slivers of steel. Pike charged, half slipping in the gut juice that had smeared his front.

He didn't quite get them all. A bolt clipped the edge of his armor, numbing his elbow. Fighting to keep the blaster up, Darwin sprayed the room and sprinted through another doorway and into a corridor.

"Section two, double back, he's . . ." The man looked up, eyes going wide, mouth falling open as Darwin charged down on him. His shot took the man square in the chest, blowing the rib cage open to spatter light pink lung and thick heart muscle fragments around.

He leaped the corpse, hearing the cackle of comm behind him. Someone else hollered orders, regrouping the Fathers. Pounding down the corridor, he ducked into a companionway and climbed to the next level.

Panting, Darwin stopped in the empty hallway, wincing as he worked his elbow. The command structure would recover real quick, reorganize the Fathers, and be after him.

"But they aren't combat veterans," he grunted. "Crap! Neither am I!"

Somehow, he had to get to one of those reactor pods.

A squad of Fathers clattered on the stairs behind. Pike ran, belting his way down the corridor. One of the officers burst around a corner, stopped, and began shouting orders into a pickup. Behind him, his command of ghouls surged forward. Pike dropped to one knee, snapping his shot, nicking the side of the officer's head, exploding scalp and skull.

The Fathers positioned themselves, firing bursts, the violet bolts taking out sections of wall as they charged. Pike crabbed sideways to avoid shots coming from behind.

"No goddamned way out," he grunted. Desperate, he noted the grillwork. He kicked in the ventilation shaft and tumbled through. Blaster fire continued, the bolts increasing, louder. Around him, the very guts of the station trembled from the concussions as he hunkered in the restricted space. Somewhere a shriek of pain wailed.

"Stupid asses," Pike whispered to himself. "They're out there shooting at each other. Good riddance."

Only another officer would show up soon to coordinate. So long as he could keep moving, keep from being pinned down, and kill their officers first, he had a chance. On hands and knees he scrambled to the main vent, an oval shaft maybe two meters in diameter. He poked his head out cautiously, finding the tube dimly lit by a fluorescent panel on each floor. There—praise the name of Spider—a rung ladder went up.

Darwin looked down to the gray-floored bottom, one level below. Powerlead—big stuff, like 150—ran along the thick station skin. Shrugging, he blew it in two, puncturing the station wall in the process, and clipped a new charge into his blaster. Grimly, he looked up; lights dwindled into pin-points—wrong way to go. Or was it? Diversion? Get higher and split their forces? Take the pressure off Susan?

Wrapping a hand around a rung, he started to climb, thankful for the lower gravity of the station. He'd made four stories, realizing his muscles had lost some strength. He'd begun to pant again, sweat drenched, chest chafed by armor as his lungs worked. His healing leg acted stupid. Damage in the prosthesis?

"Just a bit of the fatigues. That's it." *And not the can-cer—not the damaged nerves that are fraying now that the adrenaline's wearing off. Face it, you're dying. No med for almost two months now. How many little tumors are growing like mushrooms? How many hundreds of oncogenes gone crazy from regeneration? That's why you're slowing down.*

He ground his teeth, forcing himself up the rungs, faster, proving to himself it wasn't true.

He missed the first subtle vibrations, aware only as the sound grew in the very air, increasing, louder as the steel bar he held to shivered at high frequency. The whole station shuddered suddenly, a low frequency hum building to a crescendo. Darwin tightened his grip, eyes closed as his mind staggered. Totally disoriented, he blinked, suffering vertigo as gravitational fields interlaced and pulled against each other—then a split second of silence.

The "Fist of Deus" from the inside, he decided, snorting to clear his ears. His sinuses smarted, feeling stuffed and pressured. Teeth clenched, Darwin continued to climb.

Dripping sweat, he hauled himself upward. Forever he climbed, muscles trembling, aching, the ragged edge of fa-tigue eating at his stamina. He refused to quit, to crawl out on one of the floors, driven by the fear of the cancer. His weight had dropped with the decrease of angular accelera-tion from the station's spin. Blinking, he looked over his shoulder, staring down, dizzy at the height.

"Diversion. Get up there and shoot some more. Hurt 'em. Keep them busy. Buy time." He'd climbed high enough to sail along two rungs at a time as he got farther and farther from the rim. He climbed out into a huge room in almost zero g. Giant filters filled one wall leading out into high-intensity UV sterilization tubes before pumping air into the shaft. He paused, cooled by the breeze on his hot wet skin. Clever. Pumps pushed the air up the vents to be filtered, and angular acceleration pulled it back down again.

Using zero g skills, Darwin sailed to a hatch and palmed the lock plate. Cautiously, he stepped out and closed the portal behind him. Artificial gravity hugged him down. Bright light—almost blinding after the darkness of the shaft—showed him a typical white station corridor.

"Which way?" He chose right. Advancing cautiously, feeling uneasy until he recognized the sensation—like on *Spider's Revenge* when they'd been repatching the grav plates. Gravity pulled unevenly, leaving a queerness in the stomach. A comm unit studded one wall. Pike looked it over and realized he had no idea how to access the station status.

Sprinting down the corridors, he pulled to a stop, blaster raised, only to be passed by a dull-eyed man and woman walking obliviously past. They ignored him.

"Bad planning, Ngen, old buddy! First your troops shoot each other because they can't distinguish friend from foe. Now, here I am and your ghouls don't recognize threats! Tough for security."

From the very air, the hum built again, like tiny insect wings in the ear, louder, louder. He stopped, clapping hands to his ears, head bent down. The station began to shiver, then shake, and finally quake as the mass generator built and released. Pike staggered, the gravity flux ringing in his ears, leaving him physically sick: the sensation that of his guts and blood and brains all being pulled every which way at once. Somehow it seemed balanced. Of course, he'd almost made it to the center of the station.

With a grunt, he headed up again, seeking the axis. Somewhere he'd find the base to that spire the ball rested on. Perhaps there would be powerleads there? Big ones that could be destroyed—sever the flexor tendons on Deus' Fist?

Hurrying now, he had to limp on his bad leg. A raw burning had started in the calf muscles and foot. Cramps irritated his sapped muscles. So tired.

He stopped at a hatch, slapping the lock plate. The thick panel slid silently in its tracks. He charged through and almost killed himself. Gravity disappeared beneath him and he slammed, tumbling helplessly, into the far wall, shivering the panels, rebounding in the zero g. Pain shot up his back as he collected himself, pushing along.

He passed more ghouls—station born, long-limbed, fragile looking, reminding Darwin of the fish that lived deep in the oceans of Earth. Human speciation at work; adaptation to an environment lacking gravity.

He sailed along to a round-walled room. A corridor bent around, the tight curve indicating the center of the station. So? Had he found the right level? He located a hatch and palmed it. No reaction. Locked! Excellent. Ngen had something to be protected on the inside.

Darwin pulled his hand blaster and looked around, seeing the companionway vacant. The violet bolt blew the latch open with a sputtering of sparks and smoke. Darwin wedged the tip of the Randall into the door and levered it open.

Bracing fingernails and foot, he heaved against the weight until he could wiggle through. Blood-spattered, smelling of ruptured intestines, he straightened warily, coups in disarray. Before him, a group of men hunched over, intent on the monitors before them. The throb of power began to build again. The room shook as the walls almost seemed to thunder.

Darwin blinked, shaking his head to clear his sight. After the power release, Pike called, "What's the status of the fighting in the rim?"

A harried, pale-looking man with thinning silver-blond hair started and looked up, standing hesitantly.

"Who are you?" he demanded. "What are . . . ." It took a while for Darwin's slaughterhouse appearance to soak in. The man swallowed hard, a hand straying idly to a desk top.

"Don't touch that!" Pike warned, swinging his heavy blaster around. "Tell me the status . . . and who you are."

"I'm Ten MacGuire. The fighting's bottled up between power pods four and five." His eyes had gone round as they stared at the gun's ugly belled muzzle. Somehow, Pike didn't think the image of the wild looking man behind it helped either.

"Ten MacGuire? Used to be Department head in Engineering at University?"

"That's right. Just who *are* you?"

"You came to rescue us?" Another man stood up from one side. "That's a spider on your armor. You're—"

"Shut up, Veld!" MacGuire barked. "He's one of the Messiah's men. Who else would know who we were! You want to kill us all?"

"Never goddamned mind who I am. Real carefully, tell me the exact time on Earth." Pike moved to the side quickly, realizing he'd already been picked up by every security comm on the station. Outside he could hear an alert blaring.

"Where on Earth? It's a planet. You could mean any—"

"Hell, I don't know! Um, what's the most likely? The date line? What?"

"Generally they use Greenwich." Helmut Eng accessed comm as Darwin's heart raced. "It's almost three a.m., June 7, 2789, AD," the man said, swallowing.

"So the attack's begun," Pike whispered, sagging back against a comm bank that rose behind him. He could feel a faint vibration in the heavy unit.

"It has," MacGuire replied. "We've already destroyed two of the Patrol battleships."

Darwin cursed, seeing movement from the corner of his eye. He spun on one heel, lifting the blaster, cleanly shooting the Father's head off. He waited, heart thudding dully in his chest. Would more charge through? He stepped out into the room, ready, eyes glued to the hatch. He was caught by surprise when a man landed on his back, driving him into the arms of Ten MacGuire.

Bullet's bridge: Gas Cloud Colonies.

"Find Cobalt Station!" Ree thundered.

He didn't have long to wait. The targeting comm tagged something which looked like the holo Claude had sent him. An odd pentagon-shaped series of arches—like flying buttresses—met at a little ball on the end of a tapered spindle rising from the axis of the huge wheel. As Ree studied the thing, he could see it tremble. When it ceased, the mass indicators went wild and *Uhuru* vanished from existence in a blinding flash.

"Blessed Spider," Ree mumbled dully, then: *"Kill it! NOW! All batteries, FIRE!"*

Fire control centered and blaster bolts laced space around the station. "They shielded it! They have the damn thing shielded! *Hit it!"*

The Fujiki blasters flared brilliantly against the resistance, shields beginning to buckle and waver.

"Shoot! Shoot! *Shoot!"* Ree pounded the heel of his knobby fist into his hard palm.

A GCI moved between, taking most of the beating, absorbing their fire.

"Get that thing out of the way!" Ree growled, pacing. The GCI finally disappeared in a haze of radiating plasma, under the combined blasters. Bits of debris spiraled out—then a blinding flash as the reactor failed, discharging antimatter.

Sweat beaded on Ree's brow. Cobalt Station had shifted, throbbing again. *Miliken* died then.

"Toby! Oh, God, Toby! Kill that damn station!"

Screaming in rage and hurt, Ree glared at the screens as the shields around Cobalt Station flashed and wavered. Another GCI came sliding into place, shields flaring, buckling, blocking his shot.

"Damn them!" Ree raged, bundled energy charging his springy muscles as he paced back and forth, jaws clamped. "Full speed forward. Maybe if we get close enough, they can't shoot without destroying themselves in the backlash."

The ATs, like a thousand cast darts, spread out over the Colonies, weaving, corkscrewing, as blasters sought them. Some miscalculated—or were finally targeted by the Fathers. They died as flickers of light as Ngen's converted GCIs moved against the backdrop of glowing multihued pastel gases.

For some reason *Gregory* only offered sporadic fire at the closing Patrol ships. Ree frowned. For the moment, he'd take any advantage without complaining.

Channels open, he looked up, meeting Tabi's and Maya's frightened eyes. "We have this one opportunity to kill that thing!" Ree wiped at his hot face. "If we don't, nothing in the universe can stand before Ngen Van Chow. Ram it if you have to. No holds barred on this. Here we live or die." Damen Ree swallowed with difficulty and looked at the station which was now filling his monitors as the GCI before it exploded under his Fujiki guns.

Ngen Van Chow's yacht in the Gas Clouds.

Ngen Van Chow reclined in the command chair of his private yacht, tapping a rhythm on the comm console with happy fingers. They'd found the key, made it work.

"I AM God!" He laughed, made slightly silly by the thought of all that power. Nothing could stand against him! Not as long as he controlled Cobalt Station. Of course, he'd have to move his command. Now that he'd proved it could space, the vaguest thought of letting that power out of his sight seemed ludicrous!

He caught the incoming message, shifting it to comm. M'Klea's blanched face formed on his comm. "The Romanans have broken loose in the ship!"

Ngen stared, unable, for a second, to comprehend.

"The Romanans have . . . Get them under control. Use any means necessary. Don't you understand? After what they did to me . . . After Sirius . . . Call in all the squads. I'll transfer as many as I can from duty in the Colonies. We've barely begun to establish psych gates here. The Colonists can wait; they'll go nowhere."

He sent the appropriate orders and leaned back, mind racing. Had Rita Sarsa been a feint to draw him out? If so, it had been poorly done. Her ship had been disabled by the dust and gases. No, he'd learned in the past that overestimating Romanans bore just as many dangers as underestimating them.

But who cares! The Fist is working! MacGuire has learned to control it. The ultimate weapon is now MINE! Thank Deus for the Brotherhood. Their computer banks gave it to me! Thank Deus, indeed! I am God!

"Ngen!" M'Klea face formed again. She stared out in panic, mouth working nervously as her hands knotted the fabric at her belly. "Sarsa has escaped. Torkild has betrayed us to the Romanans. They're stealing an AT. What do I do? Kill them, Ngen! Stop them before—"

"Now, dearest," Ngen smiled. "Where can they go? How can they escape? Anywhere they go, our destroyers will blast them. That AT cannot pose a serious threat. Which dock?"

She looked at monitors. "Nine."

He switched his receivers, dialing in the dish and refining the image. As the AT broke away from his ship, the GCIs began shooting.

Ngen leaned back, talking to himself, euphoric with the new high of his power. "Come, Rita, do the audacious thing and run for it. Entertain me. Let's see how much we get from this game. Oh, I love you, Major! How I'll miss individual spunk and courage. From now on, I'll simply crush the opposition from a distance. A pity." He swallowed, laughing, as the pilot—Sarsa, of course—dodged with great skill. The AT's fire control laced death out at two of his closing ships. Ngen grimaced as one of his fleet veered off, atmosphere boiling from rents Sarsa's blasters ripped in the hull. Decompression shot fire and debris from the gray sides of the converted cargo vessel.

The AT flipped, rolling away from seeking bolts of blaster fire, darting between two vessels, and looping around a baffled CGI's targeting dishes. In a gyrating corkscrew, the AT lined out, flares of reaction bright lances against the red and blue of the clouds.

Ngen noted the direction. "No, she *couldn't!*" He pulled himself upright. Euphoric joy vanished in a sudden torment of fear.

"Kill that AT!" Ngen raged into his comm. "Get them! Cobalt Station! Alert! You are about to be boarded by Romanans. Have all security teams respond to the breach!"

Ngen cursed and bucked violently up and down in his command chair, driven by anxiety. Damn her, what could Sarsa do against an entire station? Sirius played like a sick dream in his head. Sarsa, and her Romanan filth—

"Ngen!" M'Klea's voice shivered in sheer terror. His troubled eyes darted to the comm. M'Klea had gone deathly white, eyes widening. Sweat formed a glaze on her upper lip. Her breathing caught in strained rasping breaths.

"What?" He pulled half out of his chair, fists clenched, veins standing out along his neck. "Have the Romanans—"

"It's the baby!" she gasped. "Your son is coming!"

"Not *now!* Damn you, M'Klea, of all the poor timing. Oh, hell, get to med!"

She seemed to wilt, her attention turned inward, mind on other matters than him. She added listlessly, "The Romanans have it. I'm going to my quarters. Ngen, this hurts, Ngen. This . . . so strange . . ."

"Well, go! I don't have time to worry about you or the rat right now anyway." On the other screen he saw the AT rip through the side of Cobalt Station. To that comm he ordered, "Cobalt, you are breached near number four reaction pod. Repel the boarders at all costs! Scramble every available fighter to the rim."

"We hear and obey, Messiah!" At least they weren't caught napping. "Security is scrambled. We've got teams moving toward the breach. Unit commanders are forming up, attempting to determine defensive strategies and implement containment procedures."

"Keep me constantly informed. Channel all comm into the flagship." Ngen wiped thick perspiration from his face.

Damn it all! M'Klea picked *this* moment to whelp the brat; he'd hoped to take his pleasure from Sarsa; Romanans charged around loose in his battleship; other Romanans had landed in Cobalt Station and might damage the Fist! What else could go wrong?

Fuming, he settled his yacht into the lock, dropping down until *Deus*' grapples could lock in. On a hunch—that old wary inner voice crying out—he left the power stabilized.

His honor guard met him at the hatch as Ngen rushed for the bridge, clamping a headset onto his brow.

"Cobalt! Report!"

"We have the invaders contained between pods four and five. They can no longer advance. We're massing to wipe them out. Evidently, a sally to flank our forces has been contained on level two. We've taken severe casualties in restricting the advance. Enemy casualty numbers will be provided as soon as we search the wreckage and identify the body parts. Level two has suffered severe damage as a result. That report should be processed soon, sir."

Another voice cut into the comm. "Unidentified craft approaching the Colonies."

"What craft?" Ngen stepped into the lift and set it for the bridge. When he stepped out and passed the hatch a fear-fist tightened in his guts.

"Damn! No!" On the monitors, Patrol Line ships emerged, ghostly specters appearing out of the swirling dust and eerily glowing gases. The huge obovoid shapes glared whitely, reaction flaring brilliantly from their gimballed drives as they broke out into the Colonies.

"Damn them! A damned diversion all along! General alert! Call to Quarters! All commanders, prepare to defend the complex." He ran to stare at a pickup to Cobalt, screaming, "MacGuire! MacGuire! Concentrate your fire on the Patrol ships. Do you understand me, MacGuire? Kill them. *Kill THEM!*"

"I understand, Messiah. We're shifting attitude, adjusting for range, and concentrating on the closest. Fields are building up again. The station intruders are stopped on the rim. We're in no danger." MacGuire's fleshy face lined in concentration. He didn't even look up. "Just keep us blocked. We have the shields up and they are far enough away so I think we can get them all."

Ngen watched desperately, disbelieving eyes on the Patrol battleships as they oriented. Waves of ATs scattered like minnows. Ngen scrambled his own to intercept—half-manned since his marines battled Romanans in *Deus'* guts. The Fist pulsed. One of the Patrol ships vanished in a blue-white vortex. Radiation monitors on the bridge flickered under the onslaught.

One down.

"Ship's status?"

"We have the Romanans blocked off on Decks 15 through 22 and contained in D through I Sections, Messiah." A dull-eyed guard reported. "We are attacking with force. Praise be to Deus. Praise be to the Messiah!"

"Good work. Keep me informed. Kill them at any cost! Kill them, you hear? Kill them all. No matter what."

"I hear." The Father turned. "Kill them. No matter what the cost. All units are ordered by the Messiah to attack." Faint concussions of blaster fire sounded through the pickup.

Ngen fought to control himself. He'd come close to raving. What had happened to his control? But Romanans? Here? How had they known? Who could have possibly . . . Torkild! The thought clamped an icy steel band around his heart. The bastard had betrayed him.

Curse it! He paid, now, for Alhar's foolish idiocy concerning his honor—too glaring a weakness to overcome. Damn! M'Klea had warned him, told him flat out that Torkild should be quietly killed.

"Bastard Arpeggian! When I get my hands on you I'll . . . I'll . . ." Ngen smashed a fist into his chair arm, springing to his feet to pace the curve of the bridge, staring into the monitors as his officers struggled frantically, feeding figures into fire control, shuffling tactical information, directing the fighting with the intruders.

"Messiah?" MacGuire, looked up, desperation in his eyes. "Could you pull some of this blaster fire off of us?"

Ngen checked status to see those brilliant blaster bolts flaring on the shields of Cobalt. Frantically, he ordered a GCI to take up the burden. Calming himself, he began moving his ships, placing each to protect the Fist. One by one, the GCIs died as they took the brunt of the firing. Then another Patrol ship flashed in death as the Fist of Deus shivered and released its compressed energy.

Two down.

"I can win this. It's coming around. Three to go, that's all. Just three to go!" He hunched over the monitor, licking his lips, his heart racing. "Cobalt has Sarsa stopped. Yes.

She never thought she'd have so many martyrs to tackle. I'm killing the Romanans aboard—and destroying the Patrol. Three more shots, and then the ATs. Just three more shots!"

"Ngen!" M'Klea cried.

He accessed comm to form a holo of her. She lay in bed, her voluminous skirts pulled up and crumpled under her chin, exposing the bulge of her white belly. A widening wet spot darkened the bedding where her water had broken.

Her eyes glazed, begging for him. "Am I dying?"

For a second he stared, fascinated by the expressions as her face twisted and contorted with pain and fear. Something flared in the corner of his eye, bringing his attention back to the bridge.

"I don't have time! Leave me alone!"

"*Ngen!*" she screamed. "*I'm scared!* Come help me!" She reached up, pleading with him. The skin worked tightly at her neck as she swallowed. The bulbous bulk of her pale belly moved, the child pushing inside. "I'm so frightened!"

"*Shut up!*" Savagely, he cut the channel, killing her access. The baby was her problem.

The ship shuddered under him. Ngen flipped channels, finding one in the after section that still worked. As if to leap through his very monitor, Romanans—grisly coups tied at their waists—charged forward, rushing the pickup. So, they'd broken out of the starboard and were headed for the reactor room. And if they got it? He was chewing his lip frantically. He winced at the hurt, and, testing it with a finger, saw blood.

A group of his Fathers came trotting down the corridor. Through the pickup, Ngen heard, "The Messiah said to kill them all."

The Fathers set up—only to be cut to ribbons by a hoard of screaming, yelling Romanans. Then came the hated sight of Romanans carving the scalps off half a dozen of the casualties and pouring on, unstoppable.

The ship shuddered again, breached by heavy blaster fire from outside. Ngen studied his fire control and settled then to shooting back at the big Patrol ships.

What had happened to the Fist? MacGuire didn't need that long to reestablish the fields. Why had no more Patrol battleships died?

"*MacGuire?*" Ngen thundered, running to the right monitor. The control room on Cobalt Station looked like bedlam—a scene of riotous disorder. A man staggered up out of a rolling pile of arms and limbs, intestines streaming from a gaping belly wound. Driven by unbridled terror, he pawed at his spilling insides, futilely trying to hold the bloody dripping mess inside. He slumped on the console, dying eyes staring horror-locked into Ngen's.

A dull shock growing in his mind, Ngen looked at the monitor following the Romanans on *Deus*. An Arpeggian stood in the front of their ranks—and calmly blew a Father's head off. They bolted down the corridor, headed for the reactor.

Arpeggians with the Romanan rabble? That meant they'd be able to understand and exploit the reactor system. His hold on the ship was eroding. Hate-slitted eyes shifted to the monitor on Cobalt. The dead man continued to fill it, staring sightlessly into *Deus'* bridge, blocking all other views.

Run! Now! Get out! Don't be a fool. Save your skin! Fight another day! Run! Run! RUN, NGEN, RUN!

"No, they don't have the Fist yet." He calmed himself, ignoring the intuitive voice.

So long as he controlled Cobalt Station, he would bring this all together.

He took one last look around, seeing the techs and officers frantically trying to defend the vessel. Carefully, quietly, he turned, walked through the hatch, and palmed the lock plate. He entered the lift, dialing it for the dock where his yacht waited.

RUN! NOW! GET OUT! the voice insisted.

CHAPTER XLV

Ngen's personal quarters aboard *Deus*.

M'Klea cried out fearfully. What was happening to her? Why did she feel this terror? The wrenching pain shot up from her hips and dilating cervix to crush and grind the fragments of thought in her brain. Her womb continued to pulsate with life demanding that its time had come. She contracted again, strangled whimpers breaking from her throat.

"Do not fight it. You shall not die in childbirth." The voice soothed her whirling fears and she felt a warm, soft hand on her head. She looked up gratefully—only to gasp with horror *into a Romanan face!*

"Oh, God!" She whimpered, fear almost gagging her. *"Ngen!"*

"Do not fight," the warm voice reminded. His eyes seemed timeless. She tried to lift herself as another contraction destroyed her concentration and flopped her prostrate.

"I can't . . . stand pain." Her eyes felt distended. "No! What are you doing? What are . . . What . . ."

The Romanan, a satisfied grin on his face, climbed up on the bed, trapping her when she tried to flee. Hands grabbed her knees, forcing her to spread her legs. As another contraction seized her, she couldn't find strength to resist.

"No . . . no . . . no . . ." She tried to cry as yet another contraction constricted painfully. The barbarian was going to rape her even as the child came! But instead of his weight upon hers, he knelt, head cocked, hands resting softly on her. She sobbed, hysterical, as his long knife came out of his belt. Cloth ripped—fear and pain banished conscious thought.

Hurting and wrenched, M'Klea heard herself moan from far away. She tried to work her tongue in her mouth, but it stuck to the roof, dry, like a piece of thick cloth. She rolled her head to one side.

"There," came the soothing voice. "It's over." She tried to sit up, but his hand restrained her. "No, it is not time for that yet."

"Who . . . who are you?" she asked weakly, wringing with sweat. Looking up, she froze, the memory coming back. The Romanan warrior stood there, smiling down at her. "You have cut my hair off?"

"I have not taken coup." He smiled serenely. "I have come to see you—to wonder why you have turned to Ngen when your brother loved you so. What are your motivations? Why did you do that? What were you thinking?"

"I will have you killed!"

"Is that your only response to questions concerning the very conduct of your life? Ngen has fled the ship. He has left you here. Do you still wish only to kill? Your brother would forgive you. I have seen him do this."

"Torkild would . . . No. *Never!* He's a traitor. He sold

me to the Romanans. I told Ngen to kill him. I told Ngen
that his stupid honor was going to bring ruin upon us all. I
told him!'' She gasped at the ache within, hatred in her
eyes.

''Do you not want to find another reality? Do you not
want to change your soul, to send—''

''Oh, no. Not me, you don't. I've heard of your kind.
Well, you'll not take me off and . . . and make me your
whore on World. You'll never take the Empress from *her*
throne. When Ngen comes, I'll see you psyched—psyched
slowly so you die a most horrible death! I'll see you suffer
like . . . like the dirty animal you are!''

''That is your decision,'' the Romanan nodded, a sad cast
to his face. ''You would take hatred to Spider? When so
many wonderful—''

''I would see you *dead, bastard Romanan!*'' The venom
in her voice burned like acid. ''You probably raped me while
I was unconscious! You filth! You vile . . . vile . . .''

The Romanan flinched at her fury. ''You have not even
asked about your child.'' A deep sadness hung thickly in
his gentle voice.

''You didn't kill it? You . . . you must have pulled it out
so you could rape me. Yes, that's what you did. I know it
now, a woman knows. Foul beast, I'll . . . I'll roast your
testicles from your very body!'' Her voice had gone shrill.
''Ngen will come for me, you'll see!''

The Romanan stood, shoulders bowed. Taking off his tattered hide shirt, he carefully wrapped the little gurgling in-
fant in the leather, smiling happily, eyes beaming as he did
so.

With the child still needing cleaning, he sat back on the
bed, heedless of the woman's raving hatred. He stared at
the comm and finally it came on.

The Romanan bowed as Ngen's face formed. ''Greetings,
Ngen Van Chow.''

''Where is my wife?'' Ngen demanded. ''Who are you?''

''I am Chester Armijo Garcia. Some men call me
Prophet.'' Chester inclined his head, smile serene as he
laced his fingers over his naked stomach.

''You have killed my wife?''

''She lives,'' Chester said, voice dispirited. ''She has
reached a cusp. Her future is decided.''

''You would ransom her?'' Ngen asked, cunning eyes

shifting to where M'Klea pulled herself painfully up, hope sparking in her pleading eyes.

"Would you take ransom? You still have time to change your mind. Your cusp is not yet complete. You could order your men to cease their fighting. There is yet that within you which might make a contribution to Spider . . . that is, beyond what you have already made through the miseries in the lives of others. Can you think of a greater purpose in life?"

Ngen laughed crisply. "You're amusing, little man. There is no Spider. There is only Deus and I am He! The Fist of Deus is *mine,* Prophet. With it, I'll blast you and your people out of existence. From here in the Gas Clouds, I can kill any planet or station within the galaxy. When I dispose of the Patrol, I'll blow the ship you're in to hot plasma. Kill you and—"

"You would kill this child which lies here beside me? This is your blood, Ngen Van Chow."

"What is a child, Prophet?" Ngen spat. "M'Klea amused me. The child was a test to see what she would give for me. Many women will fawn for a God!" He laughed while M'Klea's breath chattered in her lungs.

"No . . . no. You'll come for me," she whispered. "You'll . . . come . . . for me!"

"Seriously, M'Klea, I expected more from you. Come for you? And your bastard brat? Do you really think I'd risk having to brave Patrol fire to rescue some squalling imp? *I am Deus, woman!"* Ngen leveled glittering eyes on her, mocking triumph in the set of his hard lips, the lines around his smug mouth. "See me! I am the master of humanity . . . of the galaxy itself! What matters one son? Women shall bear me an army of sons! My genes shall eventually compose all of mankind! *I am GOD!"*

Chester smiled wistfully. "You are presumptuous to send such a legacy to Spider. I am sure your soul will provide Him amusement, Ngen. Spider will learn so very much from you. All of it tarnished and filthy."

"You will address me as *Messiah!"* Ngen ordered, eyes flashing. "I am unstoppable, Prophet. I shall smash the Patrol from the sky, and kill your World . . . Arcturus . . . Earth . . . anyone who stands before me!"

Chester ignored the woman who crawled across the bed behind him. He studied the room, detached, deciding he looked out of place in the lavishly decorated quarters.

"Ngen *is* God!" M'Klea shouted, eyes passionately fired. "*I* am his Empress!" Her eyes flickered, lit by a new madness. "Ngen, blast this Romanan dog where he sits! Psych his mind with your magnificence! Kill him!" She giggled half hysterically. "Kill his soul like you have done with so many." She raised a blaster she'd produced from somewhere and held it to the side of Chester's head. "Kill him, husband!"

Chester's smile remained benign, unconcerned. "Make your final choice, Ngen. You turn down this child?" Chester cocked his head, oblivious to the hard nozzle pressed to his skull.

"Keep it, Romanan. Nourish it from the damned blood that runs in your veins. You won't live long. Take your own soul to this Spider of yours. You are Satan, Prophet. My Fist will smash you!"

"Smash him!" M'Klea cried gleefully. "Smash him! Smash him! Show him your glory, husband! Show the galaxy your power!" M'Klea cried out, raising both hands to the monitor, imploring, heedless of the blaster.

Ngen shook his head slowly, almost sorrowfully. "You were almost as much fun as my other women, M'Klea. You amused me . . . kept me company. You were so very easy. Tell me, was your time as my Empress worth your brother's love? Was it worth the pain of childbirth? Did you truly enjoy the belief that you would be mine forever?" He leaned forward, anxiously studying her for a reaction, lips parted in anticipation. "Was it worth your soul to sell your people and your precious honor, M'Klea?" Ngen laughed. "Oh, how I enjoyed you!"

"I am . . . Empress! I am . . ." She shook her head, suddenly unsure. "I have borne your . . . your son!"

"*I am Deus!*" Ngen roared back. "What means one son, M'Klea? I shall be the Father of a race!" He laughed maniacally. "And you are mine forever! No man will have had you but me, M'Klea. I was your first . . . and I will have been your only man. You'll die now, M'Klea. I, Deus, so order. Your soul is mine, spoiled little golden girl. I've destroyed you and it was worth every moment!"

"*No!*" she screamed, the import of his words finally sinking in. "No!" She shook her head. A low, wailing moan broke from her lips. Her eyes strayed from the screen to stare at the Prophet in shocked disbelief. "I am . . . Empress," she whispered to herself.

Chester sighed. "You are nothing but Spider's receptacle. That is enough for anyone."

"Liar!" She spat and raised the blaster. "Now, you die! Die at the hand of M'Klea. Die at . . ." A croak caught in her throat. Face horror-locked, blanching colorless, she looked down, lips moving silently.

Chester's hand had barely moved. The handle of the Romanan fighting knife protruded from under her milk-heavy breasts, the tip of the long blade stretching the skin beneath her shoulder blade. The shock of it paralyzed her for a moment. Her delicate white fingers traced the smooth wood of the handle as she looked up at Ngen.

"I am Empress," she whispered in disbelief. "You will make me live?" Her blue eyes beseeched Ngen Van Chow.

"You are a slut!" Van Chow chortled as M'Klea began to slump onto the bed, a spreading pool of scarlet seeping into the rich Arcturian fabrics. She coughed, bright red froth rising to her lips, spilling down alabaster cheeks and throat, tracing curves around her heavy breasts. With Ngen's words still echoing in the room, she stiffened feebly, and died, eyes staring into nothingness.

Chester shook his head sadly. "Her soul is gone to Spider. It was her cusp. When a soul will learn nothing more, it serves no purpose in this sphere of existence." Chester pulled the knife, wiped it clean of gore on a pearly-white thigh. With careful strokes, he cut the long golden-haired coup from the girl's skull.

"Enjoy your prattle, Prophet. That was a delightful end for her. I had originally planned to kill her myself. I, too, would have stuck her with something as she died." He laughed, leering at the body. "I suppose you splitting her with your weapon is as deadly as being split with mine."

Chester picked up the fragile child. "I must find this one food. He will be hungry soon. I would not have him suck of the hatred in his mother's dead breast."

"Do as you will. You'll be dead soon. Have you any questions to ask of your Deus? I will grant one question, Prophet. Then, of course, I shall kill you."

Chester looked up. "Indeed, I have come here to do just that. What purpose does your evil serve, Ngen? That is my question. Where is your purpose? What do you do? What would you make of mankind?"

"I said one question, Prophet!"

"Those are one, Ngen. Truly, you cannot answer one

without answering them all. I am a teacher, yet I would be taught. Teach me, Ngen. I listen. You see, I ask because you and I are one. Can you understand that? I would know you, for you are me in another dimension, another phase change of existence.'' Chester's smile was back in place as he stroked the golden hair and looked at the child.

''My purpose is to remake the universe in my image. Mankind will become Ngen. I shall have the finest geneticists control my cloning. There is, you know, a fine balance between the male and female genetic structure. By removing the Y chromosome and adding a second X, I can grow my female opposite. She shall be my queen, Prophet.

''Mankind will be Ngen. It will think the thoughts of Ngen, for I am Deus. That is my purpose, Prophet. You see, life is struggle. By succeeding, I have proved myself the ultimate human. I will propagate my perfection!''

Chester smiled. ''Spider will find the examination of your soul most interesting. I wonder if He will think in the end that your soul is worth the loss of data from all those whose free will you psyched away?''

''I am tired of talking, Prophet!'' Ngen glared. ''You have your answer. Enjoy my child since you have very little time left.''

Chester smiled. ''Indeed, I shall enjoy your child, Ngen.'' He cocked his head again. ''Although I doubt you would find its life very rewarding.''

The comm had gone blank. Chester sighed and smiled at the little being who struggled to move its arms.

''Spider works in mysterious ways,'' Chester said with a happy grin. He patted the long flowing hair of silver-gold that now hung from his waist and began humming a Liszt tune as he left.

In Cobalt Station: Level 1.

Susan Smith Andojar fired a blast at the Fathers streaming into the gash blown through the wall. In the dim light of the blasted room, the violet bolts seared the eye, ripping the Fathers, their bodies jerking spasmodically as they exploded, pieces of flesh cartwheeling.

''I can't hold them!'' Her last grenade arched into the mass, blowing limbs from bodies and sending boiling blood foaming lightly to the floor.

"Pull out, Susan!" Rita's voice called. "I can't raise Pike. I think he's either gone or out of comm range."

Darwin? G-Gone? Like H-Hans? and Friday? Spider, no! Don't do this to me. Not to me. I've suffered enough. I don't deserve to lose him, too. I . . . I . . . NOT LIKE HANS!

Susan clamped her jaws, blinking back panicked tears. She wasn't going to think of that. Not now—not while there was still time to fool herself. Desperate, dazed, she forced herself to think, to escape the growing horror that Pike, too, was dead.

"Blow that section of the rim, Major. Let's try circling around. Maybe there's handholds or something on the outside."

There, action. That helped. Anything but thinking about Pike, imagining his corpse, lifeless, blasted, and torn.

Susan pinned a group of Fathers with her blaster as she threw herself through another breach. An explosion shivered the wall as a grenade went off in the room she'd just vacated. Damn! Didn't they ever run out of Fathers?

The floor under her feet jumped, batting her into the rapidly thinning air, sending her sprawling.

"What the. . ."

"We're through!" Rita's voice sang out.

Susan cradled her blaster and met the Fathers who tried to rush through the hole in the wall with a violet lance of death. "See anything?"

"Yeah!" Rita's voice sounded cheerful. "Blaster fire is making this place a technicolor wonderland. I think the Admiral's here. He's trying desperately to blow this station—and us, by the way—into tiny bits!"

"Great!" Susan breathed. "What now, Major? I've got two charges left for this weapon!"

"They're pushing me back!" Torkild's voice came through. "I can't hold them."

"Outside is our only chance!" Rita's voice sang out. "I've got a way we might just make it up the side."

Susan emptied her charge into the Fathers rushing her position. They disappeared in a shower of boiling blood, chunks of spiraling meat and bone, and amputated limbs. She slapped another charge into the weapon. Fear pumped energy into throbbing muscles as she ran.

Darwin's back there . . . somewhere . . . on the other side of that horde. Damn it, he wasn't even a warrior. Just

*a bumbling, kind, caring man. The kind she should have to
hold her. To . . .*

She'd escaped death by well-honed reflexes too many
times now. Darwin, bless his heart, didn't have her training.
He didn't have that little sixth sense she'd picked up on
Sirius.

"Don't think about it, Susan," she whispered, knowing
that vulnerable empty spot waited just below consciousness.
"If he's dead, you can't fall apart now."

She sprinted the last hundred meters, dodging through
gaping, punctured walls, leaping wreckage, to reach the hole
Rita was pulling herself through. Blaster bolts made a sieve
out of the opposite wall, blasted slivers of hot metal clattering around. Torkild dived through, ducking the hail of
shrapnel that splattered from the walls.

He was shaking, trembling all over, crouched over his
weapon, staring back the way he'd come. Susan grabbed his
hand and pulled him close. "You all right?"

"Yeah," he breathed, "Damn, we're trapped! By this
Spider of yours, we're dead, aren't we? It's only a matter of
time."

"Maybe. We were in a tighter spot on Sirius, once, or
maybe twice." A blaster bolt laced the space over her head
and Susan flopped, bringing her weapon to bear, blowing
the Father's head off as it looked through a hole in the wall.

"Go!" Susan yelled, physically kicking the Arpeggian
through the space Rita had just vacated.

She fired another burst at the ruptured wall, switched her
fire to the doorway in time to stop a sally there, and, with
a gulp, clipped her blaster to her back and dropped through
the hole. Below her, endless nothingness waited.

Torkild hung there, looking out at the dazzling light show
under his feet with awe-widened eyes, mouth open, nostrils
flared. The combined firepower of the Patrol flared into the
shields, blocked periodically by something out of sight. Un-
imaginable magnitudes of death whirled in a twisting vortex.

"Move it!" Susan called through her helmet comm.

"I . . . I . . ." Torkild's voice cracked, fear-locked in his
lungs.

They were hanging by their hands from the twisted metal,
feet dangling over eternity and the hellfires of blaster and
wavering shield. Hell, another half hour out here and the
radiation would kill them all anyway. Susan noted how Rita

had made her way. She'd shot a length of line that had grappled to an antenna. Tied off from a rip in the metal, she'd gone hand over hand to the hanging structure.

The effect could be likened to flies hanging from the bottom of a huge, spinning wheel. The gray wall stretched endlessly overhead. Susan fought to swallow, lacing fingers on the cord, gripping the thin line. Below fell away into nothingness shredded by blaster fire. Fear lent her strength. Looking up, she could see blaster bolts crisscrossing the darkness. There was no going back!

Susan grabbed Torkild with her legs. "Let go!"

She jerked her body, forcing his grip loose, and heard him scream. Terrified, she swung out over endless space, reaching for another handhold. Rita's line seemed to cut right through her armored fingers. Her breath came in short gasps.

"He wounded?" Rita called, concerned.

"No . . . just scared." A pause. "He's not alone either." She gasped, feeling her fingers cramping.

"Oh, God!" Torkild moaned.

"I can't make it," Susan grunted through gritted teeth, feeling the trembling of her muscles. A brilliant flare of light shot up below them as a blaster sought to buckle the shields. "I'm losing my grip!"

"Damn, kid!" Rita cursed sharply. "Hang on! I'm coming to get you!"

"No!" Susan shouted. "The extra weight might break the line!"

"Susan!" Torkild's strained voice filled the helmet. "I'm crawling up. Let me loose."

She gratefully released the scissors hold she had on him, her forearms burning with strain as he put his arms around her shoulders and pulled himself up. They bucked and tossed on the line, her feet swinging free. One of Susan's hands came loose as Torkild reached up and caught the line.

She was panting, sweat running down her face as his arm circled her shoulders and pulled her up. Together they worked their way to the antenna. For a moment, Susan let her gaze drop. The lights of death flickered into eternity below them.

Rita reached out a hand and pulled Susan's heaving body onto the sensor mount. Torkild scrambled up next to her. Rita did something and the line came loose. She cast the end up around another of the endless projections.

"Major," Susan managed through heaving lungs. "You're out of your mind!"

"Why? We're dead anyway. Ree's gonna break this egg eventually and when that happens, we're cinders. You okay, Alhar?"

"After that I can do anything. I died back there. My heart stopped dead in my chest. From now on, anything else is borrowed."

"Good," Rita said, pulling on the line. " 'Cause in another fifteen minutes, we're out of air anyway." She swung out over the vast emptiness, dangling under the huge weight of the wheel.

Not like flies. No, they were spiders, crawling along on one thin filament of web. Susan had caught her breath. Torkild motioned her ahead and she swung out, knowing one little slip would send her falling right into fires hotter than hell's. Her fingers cramped, the muscles of her forearms burning, as she fought her way across, grimacing as each swing brought her closer to that infernal sensor mount where Rita busied herself even now, tying off for another cast.

Hot sweat dripped blindingly into her eyes as she struggled, shoulder muscles trembling. The sockets of her arms stretched and knotted, hurting. The cooling unit for her armor labored, overloading. At this rate, she'd cook alive before radiation—or Ree's blasters—got her. Hanging by a thread over eternity, Susan grunted and fought, wondering how long she had before her arms gave out. Looking down, she shuddered and forced herself to move.

CHAPTER XLVI

Cobalt Station: Gas Cloud Colonies.

Darwin reacted immediately. His big blaster was trapped between him and MacGuire, the grip ripped out of his hand. Grasping fingers sought the Randall. With it, he struck out viciously at the man on his back, hearing a horrid intake of breath behind his ear. But others were piling on top of him now, driving him to the floor. Pike roared in anger and desperation, feeling his blade biting into warm flesh. Fear-charged, he laid about him.

The melee became a press of confusion. A man screamed as Pike plunged the knife into his gut and twisted. The fellow shrieked and staggered back, horror in his eyes as he tried to hold his spilling intestines in.

Pike cut his way loose, slashing a throat and scrambling back as the crimson stream blew over the milling mass. The man tried to scream through his severed trachea, expelled air making an odd whistle and blowing foaming blood about the room. Pike backed up and pulled out his hand blaster.

To one side, the man called Veld backed away, the heavy blaster in his hands. "Don't shoot!" he called. "I'll watch the hatch. They'll be back." And Veld pointed the heavy weapon at the battered hatch!

"Get up!" Pike screamed, backing away, eyes on Veld and the heavy shoulder blaster. "Get up . . . or I'll kill you all!" A dead man lay on one of the comm pickups. *"Get up!"* Pike screamed again, half-hysterical with fear.

"You heard him," Veld grunted. "Quit being sheep and do it."

"Wait!" MacGuire cried, hands lifted where he knelt, gasping. "For God's sake, don't kill us!" He stumbled to his feet, feeling his way along the wall. The others followed, forming a knot behind MacGuire.

Pike shot a quick glance at Arstong, trying to decide whether to kill him or take a chance. "What's your angle? Whose side are you on—and why?"

"I'm Veld Arstong." He didn't take his eyes from the hatch. "Um, you might say I have an interest in Romanans. A woman I . . . Well, you ever hear of Leeta Dobra? The anthropologist who—"

"Forget the background. What about her?"

"Long ago, before she went to World, I used to date her. Learned a lot from her. Admired her. Read all I could on Romanans. Then Ngen kidnapped us all out of University to build his weapon. I've been hanging on. Waiting. Now, you're here and I have my chance to strike back. I'll do anything to stop Ngen now that I've got a chance. The mindless abominations he's been breeding, this device we've built . . . He's got to be stopped. What do you want me to do?"

Pike weighed it. "Why? Why should I trust you?"

"Damn it, I . . ."

A Father's head popped up in the hatch. Unused to the weapon, Veld's shot went high, but the Father disappeared anyway.

"God!" MacGuire quivered. "Don't hurt us. We just did what the Messiah—"

"Shut up." Pike glared, in no mood for pleading. "Veld, how do I put this place out of business?"

"Eng. Tell him."

"We'll shut the reactors down." Helmut Eng said, expression shocked as he looked at the blood sprayed all over. His hands started to shake and he swallowed reflexively.

"Get to it!" Pike growled. "This thing's killing people. Shut it down!" He waved with the blaster and Eng stumbled to his feet. With MacGuire's help, he began powering the reactor pods down.

"Veld, move over a bit. See if you can get a better angle on that hatch. How long until this thing's harmless?"

"It is now," MacGuire's breathing caught heavily. "It an only operate at full power."

The station shivered slightly. Eng pulled up an image on one of the monitors. "We're still under attack. If we lower the shields, we'll die from the Patrol blasters."

"That might not be so bad. How long does it take to power this thing up from where you're holding power?"

"Fifteen minutes."

"Keep it there. The shields will keep the Patrol away until they get Ngen off their backs. If you can get me a line out of here, we can surrender."

Veld shot again from where he crouched. "Damn! I got one! I got one of the damn mindless bastards! How about that, Leeta? *I got one!*"

"Careful, Veld." Pike propped himself against a monitor where he could see everything and keep his back safe. Still wondering if he could trust Arstong, he frowned and fingered his blaster. Oh, for a drink of water! The smell of his sweat rolled out of the combat armor.

"So why'd you build this thing?"

"Ngen will kill our families!" MacGuire turned a different shade of white. "Oh my God! He'll kill my daughters, my Therisa! You've got to let us get out of here. Let us . . . Oh my God! It's too late . . . too late to—"

"Shut up! Veld hissed from the side. "Damn it, MacGuire, your family's nothing, you hear? Nothing! Not compared with what this thing can do. Remember, Ten, we just

destroyed two of the biggest battleships the Patrol's got.
And you damn well know what we could do to any planet
in the Directorate from here. Damn you, think of more than
yourself for once!''

MacGuire turned on his heel, shaking. "Damn you, yourself, Veld. You've . . . you've been against us from the beginning! And now you side with this murderous madman
who—''

"Who's here to stop Ngen's weapon. Damn right I am,
Ten. And I'll help him do it if I have to shoot you in the
process.''

"Your families? Where are they?'' Pike asked.

"Ngen's battleship,'' Eng breathed, eyes wide with disbelief as he stared in horrified fascination at the two corpses.
Other men huddled across the control room, swabbing at
bleeding cuts, unnerved by the sight of their own blood.

"Guess they're in Spider's hands.'' Pike licked dry lips
with a thirst-slimy tongue. "You're in mine. You gonna get
me that line outta here?''

"Message coming in,'' Eng swallowed nervously. "It's
the Messiah, what do I do?''

"Ignore it!''

"They'll psych our families!'' MacGuire pleaded. "My little
girl. She's . . . You can't let that happen to my little . . .''

Darwin lifted his lip, glaring at the sweating man. "Look!
There're Romanan warriors roaming all over that ship. Your
families are probably safe or dead. I told you, the only God
that has that ship is Spider!'' He smiled wickedly, pointing
at the effigy drawn on his battle armor.

"Spider,'' Veld muttered, triggering the blaster again.
"Got another one. I think I'm getting the hang of this thing.
By Spider, if Leeta could see me now. Say, uh, what's your
name, warrior?''

"Darwin Pike.''

Veld tore his glance from the hatch for the first time.
"Out of Anthropology?''

"The same.''

"I'll be damned. That's how you knew who we were?''

"Uh-huh.'' Pike laughed sourly, shifting his hard gaze to
the engineers. "Listen. I'm no different from you. I'm an
anthropologist, a professor from University. I'm caught up
in this like the rest of you. We're not enemies. It's Ngen
who's the damned abomination! Do you really believe in his

Deus business?'' He searched their guilty faces, seeing lowering eyes.

"Yeah,'' he grunted. "That's what I thought. You've seen the zombies he's psyched and got walking around.''

"The what?'' MacGuire asked.

"Sorry, it's an old Earth term for walking dead.'' Pike spit his contempt. "They may still be metabolizing—but they're every bit as dead.''

"Deader if I can get another one,'' Veld growled. "God, I've waited for this moment. Damn it, at least I took some with me.''

"I believed at first,'' Eng said, looking up. "He was going to unify humanity. That was laudable with the Directorate falling apart and civilization about to fall prey to the Romanan barbar . . .'' He looked like he'd swallowed a grenade.

Pike bit his lip as Eng began to shake. The physicist closed his eyes and began to mutter a prayer.

"Forget it, Doctor. I'm not going to kill you so long as we keep Ngen's secret weapon inoperable. When it goes back on line it's at my orders, Admiral Ree's . . . or because we're all dead. Isn't that equitable?''

Silence stretched.

Veld shot again. "Missed.''

"What's the status of that fight on the rim?''

Eng looked at the monitors. They're outside now. I see three of them. It looks like they're trying to climb the sides of the station.''

Three! Blessed Spider, Susan was alive! Praise be the . . .

'Any way of calling off your dogs?''

"They're under direct control of the Messiah.'' MacGuire shook his head.

"What about that line to the Admiral?'' Pike reminded, shifting his bloody knife suggestively.

MacGuire nodded, taking a deep breath. "Do you know the frequency?''

"Nope,'' Pike hitched himself onto a console and narrowed his eyes in warning at a man who was backing behind the other techs. The man froze.

"Let me try.'' MacGuire shivered, and pushed the gutted man off the pickup. "Open channel to Admiral . . . What's his name?''

"Ree, Damen Ree.''

"Open channel to Admiral Damen Ree,'' MacGuire

enunciated unevenly, as if something heavy were about to fall at each syllable.

"Go ahead, this is *Bullet.*" A crisp voice came through.

"No good," MacGuire shook his head. "I just lost the signal. Something began jamming."

"Very good, Doctor MacGuire." Ngen Van Chow's smooth voice filtered through the comm. Darwin jumped, heart leaping at the honeyed tones of nightmare.

"You will now take the power up to maximum and proceed to blast the remaining Patrol ships. This stalemate has continued long enough. The time has come to destroy the Patrol and all their filthy rabble. I am—"

"No!" Pike felt his soul twisting as the voice woke his memories. "No way, Ngen! You're gone, bastard. I'm in here with a shoulder blaster and a pistol. You make these guys touch a control panel and I blow the whole shooting match. *Do you understand me, you murdering piece of human filth?*"

"And who . . . Wait, it's coming to me. Some old friend. Who . . ." Ngen's subtle voice mused.

Pike shivered, sucking in air, phantoms wiggling through his mind, shadow thoughts of knives, of chewing ghouls, and Pallas' sweaty face shimmering in his mind. Suddenly terrified, he lifted the blaster and pointed it at the console where MacGuire stood frozen, trying helplessly to swallow.

"Doctor Pike!" Ngen actually sounded pleased. "How delightful to speak to you again. I'd thought you almost a broken man after we parted last time. You even sound rational."

"Put me on comm," Darwin gritted. Ngen's smiling features formed. A second monitor displayed his yacht setting down at the axis hatch. A cold sweat began building in the small of Pike's back. He shivered as it spread over the rest of his body.

"There you are?" Ngen looked surprised. "Dear Doctor, do be careful with that blaster, I can see the safety is off. You realize of course that if you destroy those panels you'll destabilize the reactors." He looked almost paternal.

Pike nodded nervously, sweat trickling on his face. "Y-Yes I do, Ngen, you damned abomination!"

"Come, Doctor, I'm the Messiah!" Van Chow's eyes gleamed. "I am Deus! Your soul is mine . . . just like it was on Bazaar. Remember the knife in Pallas' hand?" He arched his eyebrows. "We can avoid that this time. Just get

p and walk out of the control room. It will all be finished.
'ou can go! Find your sweet Susan and enjoy her.''

"Don't do it," Veld's low voice called.

Pike swallowed hard and looked down at the spider on
is armor. He took a deep breath, tracing the lines of the
ffigy. Something settled in place deep inside, his heart
lowing, his breathing easing. "Ngen," he said steadily.
'Go to hell!"

"Damn right." Veld grunted from where he crouched
ver the heavy blaster. The weapon's rip of discharge filled
he room for a second. Veld smacked his lips. "Broke that
harge all to hell. Thing sure makes a mess when it hits
omeone."

"Forget it," Pike rasped. "You can still surrender, Ngen.
.ee's out there . . . I'm in here. Seems to me, you're stuck
etween the proverbial rock and hard place."

"My," Ngen cocked his head, looking disappointed.
'This is a most disagreeable meeting. *Think!* Take your
ut, Doctor. You don't want to deal with me. Remember
ast time? Was it really worth it? Why do you defy me,
)arwin? Is the pain and anguish you're causing humanity
vorth it? Walk out, Darwin. Find your Susan and live hap-
ily. I have no need to bother you. You could die in that
oom."

"No." Pike shook his head, uncontrollable spasms pull-
ng at his muscles. "Get out of that ship of yours, bastard.
'ome in here and sit with me for a couple of hours." Dar-
vin lifted the knife. "Let's play association. What do you
1ink I'll do to you?"

"Your sanity is crumbling, Doctor. I'm not your enemy;
:t me heal you. A little psych, maybe?"

An image twirled out of the depths of his mind—the
quare boxy unit descending, blocking out Spider and the
:st of the universe. The ghoul watched from the side, jaws
vorking, bloody lips moving to the . . .

"Damn you! Come on, Ngen. Get your butt in here and
:t's see how godlike you are after I've gone a couple of
)unds with you." Pike sneered his hatred at the screen.
'Come on! *Show me your God powers, you filthy bastard!"*

Pike's breath caught in his throat, a choked sob. The chat-
:r of his teeth wore at him. Every muscle tensed and trem-
ling, he stood, shivering in fear.

"Easy, Pike," Veld murmured. "He's trying to get under
our skin. Hang in there."

Ngen looked pained. "Excuse me, Doctor. I'll get back to you. I do have other business to attend to." The monitor went blank.

"*Coward!*" Darwin roared at the blank comm. "Talk to me! Damn you, Ngen! *You stinking, filthy worm! You pus licking, foul—*"

"Hey, easy, Darwin. Cool down," Veld called from the side. "Maybe that's what he wants. Frenzy, emotion, no sense and rational reactions."

"Yeah . . . yeah . . . Veld. You . . . you're right. Cool down. Right." Pike shivered uncontrollably. The scientists watched him owl-eyed, faces white. Muscles twitched, cold sweat beaded on his clammy flesh. Ngen's voice cooed in his mind, easing its way through his resistance.

"Wh–which of you d–draws?" Pike wiped at the sweat on his face. They didn't move. "You!" Pike pointed at a tech. "Get a marker. Stand on that table and draw a spider on the ceiling. Draw it big, you hear?"

The man nodded, fingers so unsteady as to almost drop the thick pen. He climbed onto the table, peering sideways at the blaster, and began. The rendition wouldn't have won awards, but it looked right on the gleaming panels.

Darwin smiled grimly. "That's better! Now, MacGuire, break that jamming signal he's put on us."

Minutes passed as Pike felt his nerves begin to jangle. What did Ngen plan? Was he outside the blasted hatch even now, waiting with an army of ghouls to come jumping in?

"Careful, Veld. He's planning something. Keep your wits. Don't let him trick you. Take your time and shoot carefully. Don't rush."

Arstong chuckled grimly. "You know, Pike, I already have myself written off as dead. I've got nothing to lose."

"Get me Ngen again!" Pike ordered, feeling jittery and irritable. He teetered on the edge. His hands were shaking and the techs watched, seeing him come apart, terrified. He knew what a picture he made, eyes wild, expression that of a man possessed.

"Comm says he won't talk to you now," MacGuire shrugged, eyes centered on the barrel of the blaster.

"You tell him that he either will or I'm flattening that console you're leaning against." Pike lifted the blaster.

"He says he's answering some foolish question your Prophet asked," MacGuire pleaded, voice breaking.

"He has one minute!" Pike growled, watching the chronometer. MacGuire began inching away from the console.

"Doctor Pike!" Ngen called sharply, obviously excited. "You will now surrender my control room. I have just talked to Satan. This Prophet called Chester is ready to die. MacGuire, run the power up to full and blast the *Deus!* The time has come to show our true strength! In the name of *Deus, I order you!*" Ngen raised his fist.

"Touch one control, MacGuire, and you're in pieces. Just take a look at your buddy there with the slit gullet and remember: I mean what I say."

"*Pike!*" Ngen screamed. "Did you hear me? I ordered you? *I am God, Pike!*"

Darwin looked up at the spider drawn overhead. An image of Chester's serene face formed, banishing the memories of Pallas, the psych machine, the ghoul. "No, Ngen, you're nothing!" Darwin spat, not even upset by the sight of Ngen's face. Chester had done something to unbalance him. "You're a sick, revolting travesty, Van Chow. A lunatic. Know what that means? It means you're sick in the head. The sort of person psych was invented for."

"Pike, I will have Susan eat you alive!" Ngen screamed, face stretched into a horrid mask of anger. "You'll die a horrible death! *Your soul is mine . . . MINE!*"

"Nope. I'm Spider's, Ngen. And I'm already dying. You couldn't make it any worse." And tranquillity settled like a mantle in his soul. *I won. I won!*

From one side, a speaker erupted in a familiar voice. Some antenna had caught the War Chief's transmission. Pike motioned to Eng. The Engineer got a holo of the AT as it was blasting away at the rim.

"Open a line. The War Chief's gonna want Ngen real bad." No matter what, it all ended here.

Command bridge: AT11 in the Gas Cloud Colonies.

John Smith Iron Eyes grimaced as the AT bucked through the shields of Cobalt Station. The craft juddered, pitched, and spun, the pilot fighting like crazy to keep attitude and yaw control. Plasma from deflected blaster fire scored the ablative sides of the lethal lander. Then they were through, the pilot shedding V as he stabilized the craft, racing for the big station.

"I hate that," Iron Eyes mumbled to himself, throat dry.

Sheepishly, he looked down to where his fingers had du
deep dimples into the armrests. The old familiar beat of fea
began to drain from his heart.

Blaster fire flared behind them as they passed. So fa
they'd stayed alive by dumb luck, spinning through the bat
tle, raking GCIs, supervising boarding attacks. As his force
were caught up in individual actions, Iron Eyes turned hi
attention to Cobalt. The War Chief smiled grimly. Luc
wasn't dumb. Such a curious expression.

"There's an AT already inside, sir!" the weapons office
shouted, flashing an image on one of the monitors.

"AT22," Iron Eyes noted, a knot clumping at the bas
of his throat. *So she's already here? Engaged? For Spider
sake, be safe, Rita.* "That's Rita's ship. Pull us down close
Fire control, start picking at those pods. Break them open
Comm, open all channels on hailing."

"Go!" comm intoned.

"Attention Spider warriors, this is the War Chief. We se
your AT. Where can we be of assistance? Rita? Can yo
hear me? Anyone?" He waited, heart thumping inside hi
chest, He rubbed the ugly scar he'd received so long ago-
the scar left after Leeta had saved him from a Santos bullet

The voice came through, faint, familiar, pulling at hi
heart. "About damn time, Iron Eyes! We're trying to . .
climb the side of . . . this thing. It's a no go . . . and we'r
about . . . out of air. Maybe five minutes left. We see yo
. . . coming in at three o'clock. Can you . . . pick us up?'

A flood of relief sent a tingle through his tense muscles

"You sound out of breath. So it took Ngen to finally ge
some work out of you?"

"You get your . . . gawddamned . . . fat ass . . . dow
here . . . and try climbing this."

Iron Eyes laughed and scanned the outside of the whee
as the AT's blasters blew one of the reactor pods apart.
burst, the reactor spinning away to flare blindingly in th
shields.

"There." He pointed to the monitor. "Swing down an
pull them aboard."

"Blaster fire from that breach in the rim, War Chief,
fire control called. "It's just small arms stuff."

"Silence it," Iron Eyes growled, watching the violet bolt
begin ripping back the skin of the station, bodies spillin
out as the floor beneath them peeled away at the 0.7 g ac
celeration. Fathers fell, tumbling toward the flaring shield

below. The reactor pod behind them drew the remaining fire. Antimatter flared, rocking the big wheel as it cracked, structural members rending, plating whirling away in the volcanic explosion of decompressing atmosphere, liquids, and debris.

"Damn!" Rita bawled into her comm. "We're falling, Iron Eyes. How'd you expect us to stick through that? I'll kick your ass for that!"

"Still got them?" he asked quickly, eyes on the monitor, appalled at the violence of the destruction as the station—out of balance—continued to twist itself apart, chunks pulling loose to spill out of the ruptured side. Showers of wreckage spiraled away amid the trailing streamers of condensed gases and crystallizing water.

"We'll snag them up, sir." The pilot nodded confidently, eyes closed as he concentrated into the headset, correcting, sending them in close. One monitor refined on three tumbling bodies lashed together by a safety line.

"Looks like Cobalt's about gone. Maybe we'd better get a line to Damen before he cooks us all."

"Line through."

"Admiral, this is Iron Eyes, the shields are going down and we're inside. Hold your fire!"

"Acknowledged, John. If you've killed that thing, we'll be turning to Ngen's fleet. Should be short work." Ree's craggy face formed—all smiles for the first time in an eternity.

"Give 'em hell, Admiral. We're closing on Rita at the moment. We'll pick her up and finish ripping this thing apart."

Iron Eyes watched as the AT neatly matched with the three tumbling bodies. A vacuum rescue grapple shot out, the sticky end plastering itself around a leg. Cleanly and neatly, the three were reeled in to where willing hands pulled them into the assault lock.

"All right, people," Iron Eyes exhaled in relief, "let's take this station apart."

The weapons officer bowed over his console, blasters ripping huge gaps in the station side.

"War Chief?" An uncertain voice called through the system. "This is Doctor Darwin Pike. There's a small personal cruiser getting ready to leave the hub. Ngen's in it. You might want to get him. In the meantime, we're scrambling to keep this thing from going up like a new sun. If you could desist, we'd appreciate it . . . or you'll kill us all.''

"Cease fire." He turned to the monitor. "Very well, Doctor. We're after Ngen now." Iron Eyes felt the AT heel over and dart for the spindle. The big station was wheeling out of round, a giant hole where the antimatter had exploded. Puffs of decompression spouted along the ragged rip where steel and structural members separated. Two of the huge spanning arches tore loose from the axis needle, slinging outward violently to flop end over end, convulsing the entire station. Bodies, vapor clouds, furnishings, and wreckage continued to spew along the rent, drifting out in a long spiral. Here and there, brief flickers of fire leaped in the atmosphere blasting through the rending hull. The surface shimmered, buckling in places, other sections compressed, smashing together as the gray metal crumpled like tissue. Out of balance, an entire section wrenched loose and flung away.

"Fire Control, target that craft." Iron Eyes ordered as the AT crested the spindle axis to see a long mean yacht rising from the dock. Ngen maneuvered, moving out from the station.

"Fire at will! Tag him quick before he can get our vector. Giorj says he's got Sirian blasters in there."

Four violet bolts lashed at the craft, licking at its shields. The lights drained as Iron Eyes poured more energy into the guns. The shields wavered and the target quivered as her hull breached. The yacht broke in two, one half exploding, tossing the spinning nose section out at speed.

"There goes Ngen!" Iron Eyes laughed, slapping his knee. "Helm, follow him. He's not getting away this time. By Spider, *we have him!*"

With a full power turn, they chased after the cartwheeling section of ship.

Rita—smudged, sweat drying on her face—pulled her way onto the bridge. She looked around, gave Iron Eyes a wink and a ravishing smile. "My hero!" She grinned, bending to kiss him.

Susan followed to hang in the hatch, a somberness in her eyes. "What's that?" She pointed at the tumbling ships's cabin filling the monitors.

"That's your friend Ngen—or what's left of him. No telling what happened when his reaction went."

She nodded slowly, eyes closing to smoldering slits. "So

maybe we've got him after all. It's pretty late to be repaying old debts, but I request the boarding party, War Chief. It's knife feud. Spider's justice.''

He looked into her smoky eyes, reading the obsession so barely masked. Justice? Indeed, a warrior's justice. She'd earned it with Ngen—as he had with Big Man so long ago. Knife feud. "Very well."

"I'm going, too," Rita whispered. "I owe that bastard." Susan's brown eyes welled wetly, pools of pain and intro-spection, as Rita's arm went around her shoulders. Together they disappeared past the hatch.

"He killed my people," Torkild reminded, face stiff and white. He braced in the hatch, weary and smelling of sweat, the lines around his mouth grim. "I want him as a matter of honor."

"Half the galaxy wants him," Susan whispered. "Wher-ever there's pain, Ngen seems to be at the bottom of it."

She studied him, remembering his fright on the outside of the wheel. Remembering the heart-stopping fear in his voice as he climbed over her and then actually carried her up the side of the wheel, knowing his air was going, know-ing they'd die no matter what the effort.

"You can come, Torkild." The dull ache beat suddenly in the pit of her stomach as she looked up at Cobalt Station where it filled the monitor. She glanced up in time to see another section tearing loose, spilling its contents into space. They'd never find Pike's body in the wreckage. Like a blunt-edged dull knife in the guts, the pain twisted.

Grapples caught the twirling chunk of wreckage, stopping the tumbling, drawing it tight, matching as willing hands extended a flexible tubing to Ngen's lock.

Susan led her armored party down the pressurized tube, wary, ready for anything. She blasted the hatch loose and jumped inside, followed by Rita, Torkild, and a half dozen Romanans.

CHAPTER XLVII

Control room: Cobalt Station.

Darwin Pike heard the rending of metal. A monitor showed the two huge arches as they broke loose. The tower snapped back like a spring. Then the station reached up to smash him. Pike slammed to the floor, bounced almost to the ceiling and smashed onto the floor again. Dazed, he lay there, gasping for breath.

"Spider . . ." Coughing, he pulled himself upright and looked around. The floor under him shivered violently and a low rumble pervaded everything. Pike stumbled to the central comm table, bracing himself, shocked to see MacGuire, Eng, and the rest jumbled into a pile. One man's back had been bent into an inconceivable posture, his eyes stared vacantly. Eng's face dripped, a bloody mess. Someone moaned.

Veld pulled himself from under a cabinet, a long ragged cut spilling scarlet down his cheek. He blinked, fingers still gripping the shoulder blaster.

Pike swayed and felt his bruises. The tough Patrol combat armor had saved him. Every panel on the board was lit up, flashing red. That any of it still worked astonished him. The station heaved again and almost threw Pike headfirst through a console. On the monitor, he could see Ngen's ship flaming, breaking apart.

Pike screamed his joy at the holo, swinging a fist over his head. "Get him, Iron Eyes! Get him for me!"

The station quaked and bucked again. Darwin was pitched off his feet and into the pile of dying scientists. Veld slammed violently against the console, agony flashing in his eyes.

Veld groaned. "Think . . . that's about it. Whole place . . . coming apart. Fields are all going."

Pike pushed himself up. "Yeah, let's get out of here."

Veld wet his lips, pain mirrored in his eyes. "I . . . That last time, think I broke my leg."

Pike pulled him up, seeing the truth of it. "Thigh and ankle both."

"Station born," Veld added, a sickly smile on his bloodless lips. "Didn't have the bone mass. Leeta understood. Get out of here, Pike. Get out while you can. This place is going to crumble in on itself any minute."

"Come on. Here take my arm and—"

"No . . . I've had it. No suit like yours. Hear that low roar? Atmosphere's going. Ngen pulled out the emergency suit lockers long ago. Didn't want people trying to sneak out. Good prison, vacuum. I—"

"Come on. We'll find something to . . . What's wrong?"

Veld grinned sickly up at him. "Hey. I got my share. That's all. I did that, Pike. Little, inoffensive Veld who everyone thought was a coward. Well, maybe everyone but Leeta."

The floor shook, the roar louder. "Get out, Pike. Leave me here, huh." He gestured weakly to the spider drawn on the ceiling. "Besides, I need a bit of time to get my soul in order. Compose what I want to say to Spider when I get there."

Pike shifted, looking around frantically. "I'll be back. Find a suit somewhere."

He grabbed up his weapons only to find the door jammed. With the big blaster, he blew it open. The corridors bent and buckled, a jumbled mess. Smoke—billowing from a wall unit—hung heavy. He could smell acrid odors and metal crackled, rending with a high scream in the distance. Somewhere a man continued shrieking his agony.

The station pitched again and Darwin, despite the lack of gravity, was flung into a wall. Half-stunned, he blinked to clear his vision—and saw the hooded figure floating down the hall.

He shook his head and blinked again. It was the figure from Bazaar, from the crowd at Arcturus. The image reminded him of the old medieval drawings of death, except the being carried no scythe in a bony hand.

Darwin crouched, aiming his blaster, aware the atmosphere was draining away around him. "Hold it!" Pike roared. "Stop where you are!"

The figure stopped dead, doing nothing in the process, and Pike's hair rose. He swallowed. It had indeed done *nothing* to kill its velocity. It hadn't braked on the walls, it had simply stopped dead in the air, touching nothing. The effect was as if the thing had no inertia.

The sound of his heart in his chest thudded like a booming drum. "Who are you?"

"Darwin Pike. Is it not?" the spectral figure asked in well-modulated tones.

"That's right," he croaked through a dry mouth, his finger tightening on the blaster trigger.

"You're scared, Doctor Pike. Relax."

"Damn right, I'm scared. What . . . what sort of horror are you? What kind of abomination did Ngen cook up when he made you?"

Laughter rolled out in a deep baritone. "I'm *not* Ngen's creation." A thick brown sleeve rose and the hood was peeled back. The head exposed beneath sprouted light blond hair. The face was perfectly human, eyes alight and intelligent.

Pike nodded. "So maybe you're human. You're not like the rest of us. I've seen you in too many places, doing too many things. You're just floating there. You didn't have to stop. It was like . . . like you didn't have inertia."

"I thought you might break in the control room," the cultured voice said, artfully changing the subject. "You handled Ngen very well, considering what he did to you. You seem to have killed your fear."

"Let's say I was fulfilling an old debt to a bear and a Santos warrior. Wait a minute. How'd *you* know?"

"We were watching, Doctor Pike." The voice remained noncommittal. "We've had our eyes on a lot of things. Ngen took us by surprise, tripping our warning devices on the old Brotherhood comms on Arcturus, and then again on Frontier. We hadn't figured he'd move so incredibly fast . . . or that he'd use our information to such purposes as this." A muscular hand indicated the station around them. "But then, according to the treaty, we gave a Master's oath never to interfere in Directorate events again. It disappoints us, however, that we underestimated Ngen. Perhaps we should have destroyed the information in the beginning, but knowledge, and its dissemination, has always been one of our weaknesses."

The station lurched again and Pike scrambled to keep his blaster on the floating figure. "Who's we?"

The man stared at him, expressionless, thoughtful.

"Come on! Don't you think humanity has had enough

spooks for a while? Damn it, leave us alone! Let us be human!"

Darwin's finger tightened on the trigger, the fear-flush spreading as another terrified cry echoed down the smoky hall. Eerie, the image reminded him of hell.

The floating figure pulled the heavy robe open, exposing a very human chest. "Go ahead, Doctor. Shoot me. Either that or help me save what is left of this station. My people have the three remaining reactors in stasis. We need to make time and warn Admiral Ree to evacuate the Gas Clouds."

Pike frowned, lips twitching. He squinted in confusion at the man and lowered the blaster. "I'm one hell of a sucker sometimes," he muttered. "I don't have any idea why I believe you."

"Sure you do, Doctor." The hooded figure moved past him, floating with no visible means of support. "You can call the Admiral from the control room. That circuit is still open."

Pike pushed off the wall, pulling himself behind the too real apparition. He couldn't see any method of propulsion— but there *had* to be. No one could defy physics that way!

The wrecked control room looked a shambles. Panels cracked and squealed, ripping apart under the strain of the destructing station.

Veld Arstong lay to one side, head propped at an awkward angle where he'd slid helplessly into a cabinet and snapped his neck. His leg flopped horribly. Darwin winced, adding another to the growing number of sorrows eating into him.

"What do you mean, evacuate the Gas Clouds?" Pike asked, reaching down to check Veld's pulse. "Damn, Veld. You were a hero."

The floating man had a comm access on his head. Lights were changing status from red to yellow. "Ngen has unwittingly unleashed powers for which he wasn't prepared. This entire Sector of space is threatened. Within ten hours, Doctor, this area will be the focus of a major gravitational flux. Where you stand right now will be the center of a star. If you help, we can evacuate all those people out there."

"Spider!" Pike whispered, unsure about the physics. Nevertheless, the trembling station lent the idea conviction. Besides, what the hell did he know about black holes and quantum phenomena? Singularities lay well outside the scope of anthropology.

"We've got to get the hell out of here!" Pike cried, realizing the implications.

"We? If we go, I can't hold off the reaction. This station needs two people to man it. Will you live while all these people die?"

Pike studied him uneasily. Why did he have to sound so much like that damn Santos . . . like the bear? A wisp of conversation he'd shared with Chester in a dark blaster blister haunted him now. "What am I willing to give for humanity?" Pike whispered absently. "What's my life worth? Damn you, Chester!" *And there's the cancer. You know that's slowing you down, sapping your strength. Perhaps the time for lying to yourself is over. Pay up, Pike. This is what you've pushed for. Ngen's stopped. Threat, the psych—at least for the moment—has been neutralized. And what's left? Slow, miserable death? A couple of months of wasting, of living in a damn med unit? Am I worthy?*

Pike looked into the pale blue eyes. "I'm dying anyway. I'd need . . . No. Guess there's not much chance a med unit could control all the tumors growing in me by now. Since you put it that way, maybe Spider needs the information, huh?" He felt relaxed now that he'd passed his death warrant. His fingers stroked the short hilt of the Santos' knife where it lay in his pouch.

He put on a headset, turned to the comm, frowned, and tried to access Damen Ree. To his surprise, he got him.

"Admiral? This is Doctor Darwin Pike. I'm in the control room for the mass generator. Listen, you've got ten hours to get everyone out of here. I'm serious. Ngen started a bunch of high powered gravitational fluxes that I frankly don't understand. According to the fellows in the know, the Gas Cloud is going to be a star real quick!"

"Ten hours? Pike, are you . . . Okay, okay, I know desperation in a man's eyes when I see it. Not only that, we've been getting weird readings on the meters that don't match what reality ought to be." Ree scrunched his face, rubbing his blocky chin. "Ten hours? That's cutting it close."

"That's why I suggest you get to work." Pike added dryly.

"We'll have an AT evacuate you, Doctor."

Pike saw the blond man's questioning eyes on his. "Forget it, Admiral. If I leave these controls, the whole place goes now. I estimate ten hours with me at the helm. Maybe can hold it a bit longer.'' Pike's voice changed pitch. ''Get these people out of here!''

Ree's expression tightened. ''Very well, Doctor. Do you need additional help? I might scratch up a volunteer or two.''

''No.'' Pike could see the blond man shaking his head slowly. ''I've got it under control.''

''Anything else, Doctor?'' Ree's eyes pleaded, heart demanding what his head couldn't order.

''Yes . . . yes, there is.'' Pike smiled wistfully. ''When you get back to World, find a nice fat cow somewhere and have it where a bear can get at it. Um, and Admiral, you might keep quiet about my situation here. Susan's had enough trouble—given enough of herself in the past. She's just impetuous enough to . . . I think you can understand. And Rita thinks she owes me a rescue none of us can afford now.'' He hesitated. ''And Susan . . . Tell her how much I love her. She'll . . . she'll know what I mean when I tell her this is probably for the best. She knows why. I'd rather have her remember me like this.

Darwin cut the input before Ree could reply and pulled the headset off. *Susan? Oh, Susan. Damn, why does it have to hurt so much. Go, girl. The monster's dead. You'll sleep now.* He blinked at a stubborn tear that hung in the corner of his eye.

The sprawled mass of dead scientists caught in his shimmering vision. He wondered if their families had made it. He moved over, bending down to straighten Arstong's leg and neck. He looked up after carefully closing Veld's eyes. *They called him a coward. I wouldn't have made it this far if he hadn't covered for me. I guess it's a good day for heroes.''*

''Doctor, would you be so kind as to watch that monitor? If the red line approaches the danger level, please call me.''

''Speaking of calling you, what do I call you? Hey, look?''

''I am James Thompson.''

''My pleasure, James Thompson. Now, tell me who you are and where you came from and how you managed to float through the air and be in all the hot spots at once.''

Thompson looked at him skeptically and smiled. ''Why should I?''

''If we're gonna be the center of a star, what could it possibly hurt?'' Pike asked dryly.

Thompson nodded, amusement in his eyes. "You've heard
of the Brotherhood? It all started about three thousand years
ago. . . ."

Aboard AT11, on the perimeters of the Gas Cloud Colonies.

"Attention all personnel!" comm rapped out.

Iron Eyes turned, eyes on the comm holo.

Ree's face had formed. "We're evacuating the Colonies
immediately. All Patrol vessels will evacuate all Colonists
and personnel. Ladies and gentlemen, we have less than ten
hours. Before that time, you'll all reassemble at your ships.
We have to be on our way out of the system within that
time. Anyone left behind will be on their own. The mass
generator on Cobalt Station is out of control. The Gas
Clouds will be uninhabitable within ten hours."

"Comm, send an acknowledgment and get a tracer on all
of our parties. Let's move, people."

"Acknowledged, War Chief." The bridge began to bustle.

"Rita, are you receiving?" Iron Eyes accessed the system. "Rita! We have an emergency out here. Return to the
AT as soon as possible. Bring Ngen with you, but get out
of there!"

He paced back and forth, watching the monitors. "Rita!
Did you hear me?"

"We heard, John." Her voice sounded grim. "Ngen
won't be coming with us. I guess . . . I guess he's not as
tough as we were."

When the Romanan warriors crawled out and cycled the
hatch, Iron Eyes met them, question in his eyes. The Party
Chief with thirty Sirian coups hanging on his belt gave him
a grim shrug and lowered his eyes. None of the other men
looked up, walking off, ashen faced, expressions grim.

Torkild cycled through next, a bit of red wet flesh and
hair hanging from his belt. The Arpeggian walked listlessly
back and hunkered down on a bench. Rita came through,
looked at Iron Eyes, ghosted a smile, and made her way to
the lavatory.

Susan came last, face strained, pale. Like Rita and Torkild, she had coup hanging on her belt. She sniffed and drew
a full breath, standing tall before the War Chief. "Let's go

he hell out of here,'' she whispered, fighting for compo-
ure, the edges of her mouth twitching.

Iron Eyes nodded and made his way to the bridge. They
oosted for *Bullet* to join in the rescue effort.

To Susan, the trip took forever. She sank onto the assault
ench next to Torkild. Dropping her head into her hands,
he shuddered.

Torkild put his hand on her shoulder and squeezed it.
'It's over, Captain. The nightmare is gone.''

She sniffed again, fighting tears. ''It's never over. God,
hat was horrible!'' She ran her fingers through her gummy,
atty hair. ''Damn, why do I feel so miserable?''

She glanced down at the blood that streaked her armor.
he undid her gloves and worked her tired fingers back and
orth, comparing her tanned flesh with her armor. Where
er skin pulsed dark, warm, and living, the armor lay cold
nd white, streaked with smoke and blood. She wiped her
inger along a red streak Ngen had left when his pleading,
loody hands had grasped in supplication.

''So that's how a god dies,'' Torkild muttered to himself.
'What do I do with M'Klea? How do I treat her? What do
do with Ngen's child?''

''I'd bash its head in,'' Susan whispered, fighting an urge
o shiver uncontrollably. She stared absently at the blood on
er finger.

''She's dead,'' Rita said, dropping next to them. ''I just
hecked with comm. When *Kamikazi* took over *Gregory*,
ey found her. One of the warriors got her. She was knifed
nd coup was taken. Chester has been walking around with
neonate, singing Beethoven and refusing to let anyone
ear it. Draw your own conclusions.''

''You gave the records of what we did to the War Chief?''
usan asked.

Rita nodded her head. ''He reviewed a couple of minutes
nd left the rest. I don't think it will even be made part of
e record.''

''Did we do right?'' Torkild asked, haunted eyes glancing
om face to face.

Susan took a deep breath, feeling like a dry husk. ''An
bomination is . . . Yes, we did right. But why do I still
urt? What does Spider want from me? Pike's dead! Friday
dead! Hans is dead! Anyone I love is taken!'' Her fists
notted in the long pause that followed.

''By damn, I'm tired.'' Susan swallowed hard, looking

around at the familiar guts of the AT, the crash webbing
hanging over the bulkheads, the midship swells on either
side where the reactors and weapons rested. Here and there
a scuff mark on the floor. Overhead, the light panels glowed
brightly—failing to overcome the shadows in her soul.

She sank into the hollow under Torkild's arm and closed
her eyes, tears finally tracing down her smudged cheeks.
"Darwin? Damn it, Darwin. Why did it have to be you?"
I'm alone again. So alone.

Iron Eyes' personal quarters aboard *Bullet* accelerating from the Gas Cloud Colonies.

"Well, I guess we've done it."

She looked up into his black eyes, sinking against his
chest as the hatch slipped shut behind them. "I . . . Oh
Spider, I've missed you, John."

Iron Eyes wrapped his arms around her, feeling the frantic strength in her as she hugged him tightly. "And I've
almost gone mad for worry about you." He ran fingers
through her red hair, cupping her head in his hands to stare
down, tracing the familiar lines of her face, feeling her real
firm in his embrace. .

Her lips met his, the green eyes dancing. "You know
I've been having the most incredible dreams." She ran light
fingers down his combat armor, flicking the snaps loose.

"The last of the Colonists are aboard. *Bullet's* boosting
for World. There's nothing you or I could do. Why don't
we talk about these dreams?" He lifted a teasing eyebrow.

"Talk? Hell!" She giggled and bit his neck lightly, clinging to him.

He picked her up and whirled her around the confines of
his cabin. "And I have you all to myself. Comm! No,
repeat, *NO* interruptions on the War Chief's orders."

"Acknowledged."

She peeled the armor off his muscular body, fingers flying.

Moments later he lowered her to the bunk, lost in the
depths of her eyes. "I swear, we're taking time off together,
you and me." He kissed her, softly, passionately. "Just the
two of us in a small ship, seeing the sights. Whatever you
want, A . . . a honeymoon."

She sighed, closing her eyes to savor the gentle touch of

is fingers on her breasts, reaching down to revel in the
amiliar feeling of his warm flesh.

"Um," she purred. "Delightful." She ran her hands over
is skin, enjoying the feel of his powerful body. Kissing
im fiercely, she locked her muscular legs around his, draw-
ng him to her.

She sighed from the bottom of her soul, opening herself
o him. "Forever, Iron Eyes. That's what we've got. For-
ver."

Together they lost themselves in the dance.

Bullet's bridge accelerating from the Gas Clouds.

Every deck and corridor full of wide-eyed Colonists—
most grav protected against the 1.5 g pull—*Bullet* blasted
ut of the Gas Clouds, the last of the ships to evacuate, her
ugmented grav plates making the difference.

On the bridge, Ree slouched in his command chair, elbow
ropped on the armrest, square chin cupped by his callused
alm. Around him, the familiar curve of instruments and
monitors glowed with status displays. Officers bent to their
uties, the pilot reclined to one side, eyes flickering as he
d data into the headset. The air pulsed with the feel of the
ip as *Bullet* blasted her fierce reaction into the hot glowing
atter rushing down upon her in technicolor displays, the
ields glaring as hot gases and dust burned in a long streak
mark their passing. In the overhead holo, Giorj blinked
xpressionlessly.

"No idea?"

Giorj lifted thin hands, his lifeless eyes deadpan. "Ad-
iral, I can't explain it. For all the mass Cobalt Station
roduced that we can account for, this gravitational flux
mply doesn't make sense. Further, the extent of the fields
emselves defy explanation. Even if you compressed all of
obalt Station, you couldn't create a flux like this. The en-
re Gas Clouds are accelerating toward the Colonies, rush-
g in at a five gravity acceleration. I don't care how you
anipulate the figures, Cobalt couldn't have generated
at."

Ree sawed his jaw from side to side, an uneasy grumble
ep in his gut. "Well, if it can't be happening, why is it?"

Giorj cocked his head, fish eyes narrowing. "I believe,
dmiral, that a great many people will spend a great deal
time in the future trying to determine exactly that. For

that reason, I'm taking as many observations as I can coax out of comm.''

"But no guesses?''

Giorj opened his mouth, hesitated, and swallowed "Nothing I'd care to speculate on.''

Ree sighed. "Very well. Let me know if you get anything substantive.''

The holo flickered off.

"Why don't I like the feel of . . .''

"Admiral? Transduction from Arcturus. Director Skor Robinson.''

"Put him on." Ree looked up. "Good day, Director.''

The huge balloon head filled the holo. Skor blinked his bright blue eyes, so dwarfed by the swell of his cranium. '' have called to offer congratulations. Once again you have persevered.''

"We all have, Skor. You kept the logistics flowing. The victory belongs to all of us. It's been hard fought.''

Skor's mouth twitched. "I didn't think we would win.''

Ree winced. "You know, we wouldn't have. Patan did it He called the right move at the right moment. If I'd ambushed Arcturus like I wanted, Ngen would have crushed us all with his mass thrower. If Patan isn't in everyone's prayers, they're either fools or heartless bastards. He bought us our chance. We can't ever forget that.''

"No. We can't. I've already taken steps in that regard.'' Skor lifted a fragile hand, touching light fingers to his cheek "What now, Admiral? What do I do? You control the power what do you order?''

Ree leaned back, rubbing thick fingers over the stiff muscles of his face. "Good question, Skor. I think Ngen's holdings will collapse now. The resistance will be sporadic at best. As to the Fathers? God, I don't know. Maybe we can figure out something. Listen, put together the best brains you can find. Call it an interim council with you at the head. They'll give you advice. Take what's good and throw the rest back. There's so much to do. So much to rebuild. It scary.''

"What about yourself?''

Ree chuckled dryly. "Oh, no. Not me. I'm not a governor, Skor. Not in my training. First thing, there's a bunch of miners on a planet called Respit. Seems some of Ngen's ships are bothering them and . . . well, folks like that can be ignored. Then I'll go back to World.''

"But for the long term, you control the power! Don't you—"

"Nope! I didn't want it. I don't want it. I'd be lousy at it."

"Then who . . ."

"You . . . and anyone who can be of benefit. What would Chester tell you?"

Skor stopped, eyes widening. "He'd . . . I can hear his voice in my mind, telling me to take responsibility for my usps. To nourish my soul." Skor hesitated. "Only, Admiral, once I knew what to do. Now, I no longer have that faith in my own actions. What if I'm wrong? If I make a mistake . . ."

Ree looked into the frantic blue eyes and gently said, "Welcome to humanity, Skor. You've just fallen into the web of Spider."

Skor nodded, a faint smile tracing its unfamiliar way across his lips. "And you, Admiral? What will you do on World?"

"Spend time with Maya. Maybe hold her hand as I walk down the beach." He smiled. "And once I'm there I think I'm going to spend a while out in the back country . . . with some horses."

CHAPTER XLVIII

The rocky littoral of World.

The blackness consisted of complete, all encompassing void. Against the stygian dark a faint graying appeared, swirled, and rushed toward a deeper black at the center of the phenomenon.

Susan closed her eyes to see it better.

The light shifted slowly through the spectrum from a dull red as the gases compacted to an orange, yellow, green, blue, and finally a searing violet-white; the whole resembling a blaster bolt that swirled and sucked in upon itself. Then the darkness retreated as white light began glowing, contracting still more as the days passed and a B1 star was born.

Darwin, damn you. Why did you stay? Why did you let me go on by myself? Why, my love, did you leave me to this? How could you leave? How could you condemn me to loneliness? I live in blackness while you died in brilliant light.

Susan could feel the vibration, the power, as the surf pounded against the jagged dark rocks where she sat. The sound of the dashing waves filled her senses. She took a deep breath and looked out over the aqua-colored water, spattered white with twirling patches of foam. The salt-damp breeze clung like perfume to her nostrils. High overhead, an AT dumped V, sailing down from orbit to land at the Settlements.

Pike's Star, they called it. *"And Susan . . . Tell her how much I love her. She'll . . . she'll know what I mean when I tell her this is probably for the best. She knows why. I'd rather have her remember me like this."*

"Damn you, Darwin Pike," she whispered through the tears. She clamped her eyes shut against the burning behind her nose. There had been too many tears. Giorj had listened, and held her—lost in his preoccupation with the origin of the Gas Cloud gravity—but she'd outgrown the solace he could provide. Torkild, so far away, directed the resettlement of Arpeggio, Bazaar, Mystery, and the rest of the planets and stations. The Fathers—baffling the best minds in psych—remained human automatons. They'd been put to work rebuilding—a grim reminder of the horror that was Deus.

Maya and Ree were actually married. Rita was pregnant Chester had disappeared with the little baby. Skor Robinson and his cronies were picking up the pieces of civilization coordinating the economic needs of a staggered species Spider had caught humanity in the folds of His web. No les than eighty new universities had been established on sta tions and worlds.

The surf crashed violently below her, shooting a burst c white water high overhead. A wraith of mist settled like tin diamonds in the spilled net of her hair, glistening jewels i the light.

"A happy ending," she whispered, hearing the echoin pain in her voice. She'd been alone for a year now—haunte by Darwin Pike's laugh, feeling the ghostly memories of h arms around her in the night.

The dreams still came, wailing up from the depths of h

mind, Ngen's cooing voice sapping her will to resist. The terror of his body would be thrusting against hers. She'd wake, trembling with fear, and press the button that ran the holo, pirated from the record Rita had made.

Ngen's suited body would turn, the helmeted head looking up at her as she came through the lock. He'd squirm frantically, one leg crushed between smashed equipment, fingers clawing desperately for the blaster just beyond his reach.

And her first words, as she stared down at him: "Hello, Ngen. Greetings. I . . . I've come to teach you pleasure."

She'd stopped then, enjoying the desperation in his fear-bright eyes. He'd raised his hands, pleading, mouth working, kicking frantically, blubbering in disbelief.

In fury, the surf beat below her. Salty mist caressed her face. She ran her tongue along full lips, tasting the salt, enjoying the cool sea breeze that played across her hot skin. Susan took a deep breath as she remembered the sensations, the sights, the sounds.

She'd pulled her knife then and walked up to him, slitting his suit as the last warrior pulled the hatch shut. While the air plant struggled to replenish the atmosphere, Susan had started with her blade, stripping his legs as he'd done with Pike, laying the dripping meat on the console by his glazing eyes. His shrieking screams had broken into whimpers, as they used a medical laser to cauterize the spurting arteries.

Then she'd had pulled his helmet off and gone to work on his face, cutting the eyelids off bit by bit, levering the teeth from his head with the knife point as he gurgled and thrashed, blood dripping from the shredded remnants of his chin.

And before they blinded him, Susan had laughed as she cut his manhood from his body and dangled it before his wrecked face. Ngen's eyes had bugged and he howled like a frightened animal as she popped the testicles from the scrotum and dropped them to the deck. He'd stared, unable to close his lidless eyes.

She'd looked into his eyes as she stomped the bloody tissue, grinding her heel to flatten it. As a final measure, she'd crammed both flattened orbs down his throat, ramming the flesh down with the handle of her knife.

Then Torkild had slit the skin of his belly, reaching inside, pulling the yards of intestine from Ngen's shivering body, splitting the sternum and watching Ngen's black heart beating its fear while he bled to death.

While Rita and the warriors watched with crossed arms and hard visages, it continued, minute by bloody minute, as they took Ngen Van Chow apart piece by piece until even Spider would have been hard pressed to put him back together again.

So the dreams were countered by vengeance. When Ngen's ghost haunted her sleep, she killed him over and over again, rerunning the tape.

"And for what?"

Susan dropped her head limply into her arms. Where was the justice? Why would the dreams never leave her in peace? For what reason had Spider chosen her to suffer?

"What could I have done differently?" she asked the booming surf, watching the spray leap into the crystal sunlight only to spatter on the rough rocks around her. The roiled water cascaded in rivulets back to the green sea only to rise and smash futilely against the rock again.

"Who will put me together, piece by piece?" Her voice drowned in the roar of the surf.

Her heart beat as one with the waves, crashing against an unyielding reality. Behind her, Skyboy, her black stallion, pulled persistently against the reins. He'd no doubt cropped the salty grasses within reach and desired the greener pastures beyond.

Susan worked her lips as she remembered the sight of a star being formed. "From darkness . . . he brought light," she whispered over and over, her soul crying to make sense of it all. "Spider . . . I'm so lonely."

The surf smashed its frustration against the black rock.

She drew deeply of the rich, fragrant air and forced herself to stand, a tall, supple young woman, face into the wind. She flexed perfectly toned muscles, filling her lungs as she raised her arms to the sky, wind whipping her long black hair in trailing streamers.

She would take her tattered heart and pack the *Revenge* with supplies and Romanans seeking the stars and the coup that came of new explorations out beyond the known routes of men.

She looked up at the blue-green sky and sighed, the emptiness yawning. Out there, beyond . . . lay wonders she would be the first to see. The Brotherhood had gone there

. . . somewhere. Spider had given her the stars—if only the price had not been so high.

EPILOGUE

Deep within the Bear Mountain, eight years later.

The soft-strains of Nikita Navaisha's *Martian Symphony* mingled with the evening light as the tall boy climbed the rocks to the cave. Below him, a bear lifted its questing tentacles as the lengthening shadows tinged the canyon with a deep blue that blended into lavender.

"Chester!" the boy called. "I actually rode the bear!"

The older man smiled, fingers tracing the patterns of the music in the air. "And what did you learn from that?"

The young boy frowned. "I felt a kind of unity, Chester."

"Ah! A unity? What does that teach?" The Prophet raised an eyebrow, cocking his round head so one long braid hung free.

"Uh . . . me and the bear are the same?" He looked up, confused, as the night breeze tousled his long blond hair.

"But you and the bear have different numbers of legs. You have no tails . . . and hands instead of suction disks. You cook your meat; the bear digests his in his mouth. Your blood is red; the bear's is black." Chester looked his dismay, lines of anticipation and question in the broad features of his face.

The boy continued to frown, picking up a slender spear of polewood to poke absently at the fire. "But there *was* something there. I felt a similarity."

"Ah! The mystery deepens! A unity? Or a similarity? Words are tricky things. Which do you mean?"

"Unity. A oneness."

"Ah, good, we've clarified that then. Unity and oneness. If it is not your body which is one, what could it be?"

"Living beings are made of body, mind, and soul, Chester. At least, that's what you've taught. Perhaps it's mind."

"What did the bear think?" Chester asked easily, slipping Bach into the comm. The fugue filled the air with soft strains.

"I don't know what the bear thought," the boy admitted, looking perplexed and jabbing the fire harder. "It wasn't thoughts like thoughts, but like . . . like . . ."

"So what is left?"

"Soul," the boy nodded, thinking to himself. "I think I understand. Body touches, mind thinks, and soul feels?"

"Something like that, only you'll find each overlaps." Chester smiled happily and studied the web that was being spun in the corner where the rocks had split in two. The spider amazed him, a truly beautiful creature, brightly colored. The web the little beast produced had become a symmetrical work of art. No wonder his ancestors had equated Spider with God. In the morning, the web glistened like the stars in the sky. Chester had ordered the little beast from Earth, the first live spider he'd ever seen, and—joy of all joys—it actually caught and ate the flies that always hovered around the cave mouth.

"Chester?" The boy looked up from where he poked knifebush root into the coals to roast.

"Hmm?" Chester lifted his chin, looking down his nose at the boy.

The question came with difficulty. "Do . . . do I have a name? There were some Santos who rode up the canyon this morning and asked me what my name was. I couldn't tell them. They . . . they laughed at me and said I was the Prophet's boy. Is that my name?"

"What name would you like?"

"I don't know. That's one of the harder questions you've ever asked me. What should a name be? Can I be Chester?"

The Prophet shrugged. "Would that please you?"

"I don't have any clan either," the boy declared, looking up. "Your father's clan was Armijo. Your mother's clan was Garcia. What are my clans?" The deep blue eyes sought his, demanding.

Chester squatted down next to the fire and studied the flames. For long moments, he thought, turning his words through all the permutations of the future. Finally he spoke. "Spider gave you to me. It was my cusp to take you . . . or let you die. It is the irony of Spider that every good must balance every evil. There is no inherent good or bad to the universe—or to Spider. Despite the horrors committed by your parents, I have foreseen that you, child, may be a great good. That is, you might if such is your free will.''

"I will be a Prophet?" The young eyes gleamed with hope.

Chester grinned, broad face beaming happily. "No, boy. You will never be a Prophet. My good friend Marty Bruk sees inside heads. He tells me Prophets have brains which are different from other men's. Your brain is not a Prophet's.''

He caught the falling of pained young eyes. "Do not feel sorrow. A Prophet's soul is no more valuable than yours. And the ability to see the future is painful at best, a hideous torture at worst.''

"My soul is valuable?" The boy's eyes widened, slightly awed by the admission.

Chester shrugged easily. "That is up to you. What would you fill it with to take back to Spider?''

"What would Spider want?"

"He would want you to live and to experience. To see and do as much as you can crowd into your years. Most of all, he would want you to learn, to think, to use your free will.''

"I will do that!" the boy cried, face bright with anticipation.

"He would want you to not only learn, experience, and feel, but he would want you to bring those same qualities to other minds." Chester stood, unable to keep his gaze off the spider's web. Like a little boy, he could stare for hours, fascinated by it.

"There is coup in that?"

"There is wonderful coup in that," Chester agreed, seeing the web glisten in the flickers of firelight. "Your lessons are excellent. You are reading well. Your studies of history are beyond those of other boys your age. You use weapons and comm as well as most warriors and better than other men. I have done all I can for you now that bear has taught you his lesson about souls.''

The boy was frowning as Chester turned reluctantly from his spider web. "You are sending me away?"

"Perhaps you will yet be a Prophet? You seem to see the future," Chester mocked, face serene.

"I don't want to leave you, Chester." The boy flew into his arms, hugging him tightly, sniffing back tears.

"This sorrow is unusual. What purpose does it serve?"

He tilted the young head back and looked into the pained blue eyes.

"What if I never see you again?"

"That would be your cusp. What is your free will, child? Do you stay here with a dreaming, doting Prophet? Or do you wish to be of use to Spider? I can teach you facts, boy. I cannot teach you of life. Will you waste yourself . . . and your soul?"

"I don't know," the boy whispered, sinking down next to the fire. "I'm frightened, Chester."

He rumpled the unruly hair with a brown hand and nodded. "Fear is part of life. I, Chester Armijo Garcia, will give you an unfair advantage. I will tell you of the future. You will not die soon. You will find a different sort of happiness. Your curiosity will find an outlet and you will see sights never seen before. And out there, beyond the stars, you will fill your heart with love and beauty and a sharing of souls. Pain lies ahead of you . . . and possibly bliss."

"Where are you sending me?"

Chester pointed out, past the second moon where the stars shone dimly. "Once, your father wished you to inherit all those stars. You will go to your inheritance if you choose to serve Spider."

"You won't come with me?"

"I will go elsewhere. I go to teach humanity about their souls. You, I hope, will go and show humanity new realities, new worlds and challenges." Chester smiled. "Nothing is ever free, boy. Out there are horrors worse than Ngen. There, too, are glories more wonderful than bliss. They will be encountered no matter what your decision. What will you do? This is your cusp, decide."

Chester leaned back, eyes closed, a segment of future falling into place as the boy made up his mind. Finally, he nodded his head. From a pouch, he took a coup of tanned leather. The boy gasped as the shimmering, golden hair tumbled in the firelight.

"Coup!" the boy gasped breathlessly.

"I killed your mother, boy. The day I took you, I sent her to Spider . . . and with this knife," he tapped his belt, "cut this from her head. Take it. I give it to you. A reminder of the evil you could fall into." He handed the trophy to the boy.

The boy's hands accepted, unsteady as he hefted the prize. He looked at the Prophet, mouth open, awed. Chester unbuckled the belt with the heavy fighting knife and laid it on the ground before the lad.

"You killed my mother?"

"You will have to live with the knowledge that your friends killed both of your parents. An important lesson lies in that knowledge. Can you learn it?"

"I . . . I don't know. I . . . Yes, I'll learn it." A pause. "Where will you send me?"

"We will ride for the Settlements in the morning."

At that moment a bright streak of light shot across the evening sky.

"AT!" the boy cried, pointing.

"That is from your ship. It has just arrived from a survey. It has been gone for over five years." Chester nodded. "You will be on it when it leaves the next time. You have much to learn, boy, and the ship will take you to a place called University. Then, later, it will take you on a survey . . . out there, beyond the stars."

"I will learn, Chester. I promise."

"It is also your cusp to heal." He followed the trajectory of the fading light. "Your teacher will be Susan Smith Andojar. She is a great warrior, the Captain of a survey ship. She is very lonely, boy. You will go to her and the evil of the past—which is your legacy—will be molded into something else, something very different."

"Evil is my legacy?"

"And it might be your future. What is your free will? There are tapes on any of the ships. Your father was Ngen Van Chow. Your mother was called M'Klea Alhar. Study them and what they did. When you reach each of your cusps, look at your mother's coup and ponder your actions. Learn from your parents. Learn from Susan—who killed your father—as you have learned from me, who killed your mother.

"Remember, always, what you owe Spider. Remember, always, that your life, boy, is your own. You have free will to be what you will, to experience what you will, to make your life complete."

The boy pulled the heavy knife from its scabbard and watched it gleam in the firelight. "I should have a name," he reminded. "I don't want to be called Van Chow Alhar."

"Ah, I will send you forth with the names of heroes. Susan will tell you about them, who they were, and what they did. You shall be known as Friday Hans Pike. That is a good name. It is a name which heals."

The boy tried it on his tongue, a broad grin stretching his features.

A second AT streaked yellow across the sky as he slid the big knife back into the scabbard. Somewhere a bear squealed in the darkness and Chester settled on his heels, smiling while his fingers traced the last movements of Bach, eyes straying to the spider web that hung silver and beautiful in the firelight.